TOTALLY HEROTICA

Books by Susie Bright

The Best American Erotica 1993 (editor)

The Best American Erotica 1994 (editor)

Herotica (editor)

Herotica 2 (coeditor, with Joani Blank)

Herotica 3 (editor)

Susie Sexpert's Lesbian Sex World

Susie Bright's Sexual Reality: A Virtual Sex World Reader

TOTALLY HEROTICA

A Collection of Women's Erotic Fiction

EDITED BY SUSIE BRIGHT
AND JOANI BLANK

Quality Paperback Book Club
New York

HEROTICA

Table of Contents

Acknowledgments

My admiration, gratitude and thanks to Joani Blank, Honey Lee Cottrell, and Debi Sundahl for their insight, support, and particular genius which helped me edit and introduce this anthology. Invaluable editorial assistance was provided by Deborah Sachs, Leigh Dickerson Davidson, Elinore Fox and Elena Chieffo.

Introduction

What comes to mind when she shuts her eyes and thinks about sex? What appeals to the female erotic imagination?

Before we can courageously reveal the correct answer to this question, we have to admit it's a tough one. Women's sexual expression has been Top Secret for as long as we've been wondering. It's such a taboo that women themselves don't share with each other what turns them on. Oh sure, you'll get game show confidences that masquerade as women's desires ("Bachelorette Number One, what color eyes really turn you on?"), but to reveal a woman's lust is to admit a sexual power that not everyone is prepared to bite into.

I began my pursuit of women's erotica looking underneath my girlfriends' beds. Stashed away, but within arm's reach, I discovered back issues of "men's" magazines, Victorian-era ribald short stories, trashy novels with certain pages dog-eared, plain brown wrapper stroke books that seemed to have had a previous owner, classics like *The Story of O* or *Emmanuelle*, and even serious critiques of pornography that were paper-clipped to fall open to the "good parts."

Women build their erotica collections in a dedicated but haphazard manner. One friend raided her brother's bedroom in the early 1960s for pulp novels with lesbian themes. Another holds onto a ragged copy of *Valley of the Dolls* because it was the first risque literature she had ever come across. I can remember when all my junior high girlfriends passed around an excerpt from *The Godfather* (the famous pp. 27-28), describing a woman with a large and insatiable vagina who finally meets her match. One plain brown wrapper in my collection came courtesy of a hitchhiker who left his coat in a friend's car with a copy of *Doris and the Dick* in the front pocket. While many women would never walk into a liquor store to purchase a brand new copy of *Penthouse*, there are always garage sales, wastebaskets and back issues from male friends who never notice that the May 1978 issue has disappeared forever from their stacks.

Feminism opened new opportunities for the female pornographic library. On the blatant side were the feminist erotic pioneers, who proudly issued the first volumes of women's sexual points of view. Nancy Friday's successful fantasy revelations (*My Secret Garden, Forbidden Flowers*), Betty Dodson's call to self-orgasm (*Liberating Masturbation*), Tee Corinne's explicit *Cunt Coloring Book*, and Anais Nin's erotic short stories (*Delta of Venus*) appeared. Women finally had a handful of literature that could turn us on. Moreover, we could enthusiastically embrace each author as one of our own.

Another side of the feminist movement in publishing revealed a more devious method for women to discover their prurient interest. If it hadn't been for Kate Millet tearing apart Henry Miller's sexist prose in *Sexual Politics*, a lot of us might never have been initiated into one-handed reading. As anti-porn theoreticians made their case, they cited examples as shocking and outrageous as they could find, apparently disregarding that their audience could be just as easily aroused as offended, and probably both.

Since the late 1970s, both mainstream and underground women's erotica have grown in fits and spurts. On the plus side we have an explosion in X-rated home videos, a whopping 60 percent of which are rented by women. Virtually all these movies are man made, and of moderately to extremely poor quality. Women are exasperated but well-practiced in "taking what I can get and making the best of it." This has been the theme song of women's sexual repression. Subverting men's fantasies and using them for our own arousal is the foundation of every woman's under-the-bed bookshelf.

When women have taken a hand in the production of erotica, the results have been underpublicized and thwarted in distribution, but tremendously rewarding. For the first time, we have women producing diverse, contemporary clit's point-of-view erotica. Note the success of sexual fiction anthologies like *Pleasures, Erotic Interludes* and *Ladies Own Erotica,* of a magazine like the lesbian *On Our Backs,* or women's erotic videos like those of Candida Royalles' Femme Productions and the lesbian video companies Fatale and Tigress.

There's still a lot of confusion about what the label "women's erotica" means. At its worst, it's a commercial term for vapid femininity, a Harlequin romance with a G-string. The very word "erotic" implies superior value, fine art, an aesthetic which elevates the mind and incidentally stimulates the body. "Women's pornography," on the other hand, is a contradiction in terms for many people, so convinced are they that pornography represents the darker, gutter side of lust. We are enmeshed in a semantic struggle for which words will describe our sexual creativity. What turns women on? And why have we been silent on the subject for so long? As we begin to reveal, in detail, the complexity and scope of our sexual desires, the appropriate language will evolve.

I recently saw a bumper sticker that said in plain blue letters: HONOR LUSTFUL WOMEN, and I thought, "Now here's someone who might understand the concept of an earthy woman's erotica or an elegant female pornography."

At least we can get one thing straight before we wander down the path of feminine hedonism: some women want the stars, some the sleaze. Some desire the nostalgia of the ordinary, some the punch of the kinky. And some want all of it. Our sexual minds travel everywhere, and embrace every emotion. Our sexual fiction is not so different from men's in terms of physical content. Its uniqueness lies in the detail of our physical description, our vulnerability and the often confessional quality of our speech in this new territory. Above all, because we have had so little of women's sexual fiction, there is absolutely no formula to follow.

Men's sexual literature has been commercialized and compartmentalized into little catalogs of unvarying formulas. In the same way that women have had to "make do" with men's porn to satisfy their sexual curiosity, men have had to fit the diversity of their experience into the same pair of tight shoes over and over again. The result is some very stubborn callouses. Men have had the Faustian bargain that if they agree to keep their erotic interests out of their family life, and out of the public eye, they can enjoy the privilege of varied and no holds barred voyeurism. But that variety and access only go so far. The embarrassment, shame and double standard that surround men's license to pornography are stifling, and breed cynicism.

Women's sexual fiction is new, it reflects up our skirts (and jeans) like a patent leather shoe, and it squeaks and pinches, drawing out mysteries and unexpected sighs of pleasure.

How can we tell if it's the real thing? Is there any foundation to women's erotica that will define the new breed?

The most obvious feature of women's erotic writing is the nature of the woman's arousal. Her path to orgasm, her anticipation, are front and center in each story. Even if her climax is not part of the scene, it is her sexual banquet that is being served, whether she is the initiator, the recipient, the reciprocator, the voyeur, or the exhibitionist. There are even times when the female reader is drawn to identify with a male character, but it is in the spirit of vicarious interest.

Women's erotica objectifies all the sexual possibilities, which is a more precise way of describing "foreplay." It doesn't matter whether it's describing a lover's body for her own pleasure, or a titillating meal for her consumption. Wake up, class, it's time to redefine "objectification." We're not talking about being chased around the boardroom or accosted in the street. In sexual literature and art, the process of objectification is a very natural and sensitive one. The reader integrates the words and pictures into her own sexual imagination in order to create heat; this means manipulating images for her own pleasure.

Women have not had the chance to do this before, because men were always exposing themselves to us before we had a chance to give them the once over. They had the permission to look, read, and suit themselves — we were told to wait, refrain, and submit to the inevitable.

Women's contribution to erotic objectification has been to ex-
pand the territory of compelling sexual possibilities; not only to
romanticize, but to virtually fetishize erotic environments. I
used to laugh at traditional women's supermarket novels where
every chapter is filled with minute details of what the heroine
is going to wear next. Now I realize this was a repressed goody-
girl version of sexual objectification. Bad girls, as they say, go
everywhere, and costuming is just the tip of the iceberg.

So far, women writing erotica have been ambivalent about
the responsibility of sexual portrayal. Danger and physical risks
are often a part of sexual fantasy, and each female author seems
to have a different take on how much reassurance they should
give to the reader that this is, after all, fiction. There's a rebellion
brewing among female sex writers, because they're desperate to
explore sex for sex's sake, not as a health issue. Often they're the
same people who have been on the front lines of birth control
counseling, or safe sex education. Women writers have been far
more prolific about the consequences of irresponsible or harm-
ful sexual behavior than they have been describing either their
erotic identities or the brutal consequences of sexual repression:
on our health, independence and self-esteem as women.

For *Herotica*, we chose stories which range from fantasy to
autobiographical, nostalgic to pressing, quick and dirty to
philosophical and maddening. We wanted to reflect the gender
blending and role switching that has not been previously ac-
knowledged, but that is certainly a part of most women's fantasy lives. It's often lamented that the categories of straight-
gay-bisexual don't do justice to our erotic identities. I believe
this collection takes a first step at revealing the multiple dimensions of our sexual character.

What's hot and what's not for the female audience is going to
continue to be controversial and late breaking news. We are
pioneers not only in putting women's sexuality into overt public
consciousness, but also in giving respect and diversity to erotic
literacy. With any luck, this anthology will find its place not only
under the bed but on a few coffee tables and in a few libraries
as well.

Susie Bright, San Francisco, March 1988

Pickup

Cheryl Cline

He was one cute guy, that guy with the pickup. He had come into Sil's bar, Vickie's favorite weekend hangout, a couple three times before Vickie ever got up the nerve to push herself in his direction. This guy was, as her roommate Joan would say, "A fox." Blond hair, black vest, white T-shirt, blue jeans, black boots — *heavy* black boots. Plus a black leather belt and chains that didn't look like they were *for* anything, and a big blue-handled comb sticking up out of his back pocket. You could see each and every tooth on that comb.

He would come in by himself, standing in the doorway a little uncertainly, looking for his bar-buddy, Steve. If he got there before Steve, he'd go back outside and hang around his truck until Steve got there, and then they'd both swagger in, stomp up to the bar and yell "Bud!" If Sherry was tending bar that night, Steve would always and without fail lean over the bar and leer. "You got something I want, babe," he'd say.

"It'll cost ya," Sherry'd throw back at him, clunking down a heavy beer glass and filling it expertly just to the top, never spilling any over the sides. Sherry always gave the guy with the pick-

7

up a wink as she slid his beer over the counter, because she liked
the way he'd duck his head and give her this shy sort of grin.
That thick blond hair of his would fall down into his eyes, and
didn't she just want to smooth it back for him.

Beers in hand, he and Steve would head for the jukebox, Steve
looking the place over for likely Friday-night girlfriends. The
guy with the pickup mainly looked at the floor.

But tonight his eyes flashed towards Vickie as he walked past.
They dropped just as quickly, but a second later he looked up
again as if to convince himself, hey, she's looking at *me*. The wist-
ful look in his eyes sent a warm hollow feeling right through
Vickie. She peered thoughtfully into her glass. Uh-oh.

At the jukebox, the two friends dug deep into their pockets
for the first of the night's quarters and argued about what to
play. They decided on something loud — they always did.
Screaming, driving, noisy stuff, heavy metal, headbanger music
that slammed right into the pit of your stomach. The ritual of the
jukebox over, they took their beers to a table and sprawled all
over a couple of chairs. In a few minutes they were off into some
energetic talking, with lots of table-pounding, back-thumping
and frequent trips to the bar. Vickie couldn't hear over the blast
of the jukebox what they talked about, but it was spiked with
"Awww, *man!*" and "Awwwright!" and every few minutes
Steve would move into a screaming air-guitar solo.

Once in a while, the guy with the pickup would look over
ever-so-casually at Vickie. Whenever he met her eyes, he'd suddenly turn to Steve with some quick joke and punch or kick him
or something. Gradually Vickie realized he was trying to catch
her attention.

"That guy's looking at you," said Joan matter-of-factly. Joan
was looking out for Vickie's interest. The night before at home,
Vickie had chopped a big hunk of roast into stew meat while
Joan read the personal ads from the *Bay Guardian*.

"Listen here: 'SWM, rock-hard but sensitive, will share membership in posh fitness center with agile woman who likes to get
down and get sweaty.' Chi-rist. Oh, here's one: 'SWM desires
company of bright woman, 18-25, non-smoking vegetarian,
willing to engage in joyous exploration of the overworld as well
as the ecstasy of the purely physical.'"

Vickie pushed the meat into a pile and leaned against the sink.
"Is there one in there," she said, "that says, 'White guy, Van

Halen fan, works, eats and sleeps in Coors trucker hat, wants cute chick for meaningful relationship in the back of a 1972 Chevy four-wheel drive pickup with overlarge tires and a Harley-Davidson sticker in the back window.'?"

"Oh, yeah, sure." Joan snorted and slapped the edge of the table with the paper. Wistfully contemplating a large bowl of carrots, she said, "Those guys never advertise."

Maybe not, Vickie thought, watching the guy with the pickup. But tonight she was going to answer that ad.

"Do you know who he is?" she asked.

Joan blew smoke through her nose. "Nope. But I *do* know a little bit about the guy he's with. He's a jerk." She gave the men at the table her famous once-over and jerked her thumb at the jukebox. "Couple of rivet-heads."

"I can hear that," said Vickie. "But the blond is kinda cute, don't you think?"

"Oh, sure, he's cute. Loves his mother, probably. Look at those brown doe eyes." She sighed, and rested her chin on her hand. "Probably one of those psychotic killers you hear about."

Vickie laughed. "But his eyes *are* nice."

"Just proves my point — there, now look at him!"

The guy with the pickup had just donned a pair of evil-looking black wraparound sunglasses and was admiring himself in a Schlitz mirror.

"Uh-oh," said Vickie. "Someone's coming." Steve had noticed the women's attention, but mistaking its object, had pushed back his chair and was aiming himself unsteadily in their direction. He prodded the guy with the pickup, but his friend merely smiled and held on to his beer glass like it was going to save him from something.

"Look," Joan stage-whispered. "Leave the beast to me. Here's your chance to swoop down on his friend."

With what she was sure was a fatuous expression, Vickie rose and swerved past Steve just as he reached the bar. He spun halfway round.

"Hey!"

"Hey yourself," she heard Joan say firmly, behind her. Now it was too late to back down. The guy with the pickup had seen her and was looking real casual, tapping the wraparounds on the table, shifting his heavy boots.

Vickie sank down in Steve's vacated chair and on a nervous impulse scooped up the wraparounds and put them on.

"How do I look?" she asked, turning her face this way and that, modeling. The guy with the pickup was silent and Vickie's heart fell. She lowered the sunglasses to the tip of her nose, peered over them, and grinned in relief when she saw him smiling a little lopsidedly and blushing clear to the neck of his white, white T-shirt. He jerked his thumb upwards in approval.

"Awwright!"

Hoo-boy, Vickie thought.

He fell silent, searching for something to say.

"What's your name?" she asked brightly.

"Phil."

Vickie put out her hand. "Pleased to meet you, Phil." He shook her hand solemnly. The two of them made their way awkwardly through a couple of rounds of beer and the usual small talk: What do you do, do you have sisters, where do you live, is the rent high there, mind if I smoke, have you been over to Hobie's yet?

It wasn't too hard to get him to talk, really, though at first he answered questions in monosyllables and kept looking over at Steve as if for help. Vickie was very tactful, careful to act as much the lady as was possible in a place like Sil's, sensing that if she made any too-sudden moves, he'd run to the men's room and not come out. The jukebox screeched to silence and Vickie smiled as Joan beat Steve across the room by a length. Before he could argue, she'd fed in her quarters and punched her buttons, and a few seconds later, the Shirelles took over.

Phil became more animated, and, Vickie was surprised to find, more serious as he talked. He talked about himself, of course — beer will do that — but not the way most of the guys at Sil's talked. He didn't brag, or preen himself. He just told her things if she asked, and if she asked the right things, he turned on like a light. Vickie leaned her chin on her hands and looked up at him with absolutely genuine interest as he talked about...bugs. He really knew a *lot* about insects, and not just insects but birds, and deer, and snakes, and wind caves.

He volunteered out at Black Oak Park some weekends, showing people around and telling kids about the deer and the quail, the praying mantises and the poison oak. That's what he wanted to do, he said, work in the park service. He was right in the middle of an entertaining descripion of the mating habits of yellow-jackets, when he suddenly broke off, embarrassed to be talking so much, telling a girl in a bar about *bees*, but Vickie said, "No, no, go on, I'm really interested."

They were gabbing happily, heads together, when Vickie glanced up to see how Joan was getting along. She was feeling a little guilty, since Joan was getting the bad end of this deal. To her horror, Steve was trying to steer Joan over to their table. She had to act fast.

She fought down a sudden hollow feeling and tapped Phil on the wrist, where one of his ubiquitous chains lay, dull silver against the light gold hair of his arm.

"Hey Phil," she said lightly. "Let's go for a ride in that truck of yours." Knowing he was truck-proud, she was careful to include it in the wording of her invitation.

Phil looked surprised, Steve slid off the barstool, Joan threw up her hands, and Vickie's heart sank.

But Phil came through. He collected himself, grinned at her and gave her a feather-light punch on the shoulder. "Aw-wright!" They left a protesting Steve in the bar — Joan giving a thumbs-up behind his back — and walked out into the night air, holding hands.

"The motor vehicle you are about to enter," said Phil, doing a very bad Rod Serling imitation as he handed her into the truck, "is a mostly blue '56 GMC half-ton with an improved V-8 engine and a hunnert fourteen-inch bed." He slammed the door, saluted and skipped around the front of the cab. He climbed into the driver's seat and continued his rundown of specifications. "Three whitewalls, two-forty air conditioning, no AM-FM radio, and the gas gauge don't work. But," he said proudly, "Got a real nice tape deck." Which he demonstrated by filling the cab with "Whole Lotta Rosie."

"Aha, yeah, so I see," said Vickie.

"What?" yelled Phil.

Vickie leaned over and turned the music down.

Phil smiled, nodded, and turned the ignition. The improved V-8 engine drowned out the music.

Phil was in his element. He deftly steered the truck out of the parking lot, hit the street at a cool 40 MPH, screeched to the intersection and slammed the truck to a dead stop amidst squealing tires and the black smell of burning rubber.

"Where you wanna go?"

Vickie glanced out the window at the sidewalk. It seemed so much safer out there on the street. "Oh, just anywhere, I guess. As long as you get me there in one piece."

"I'll get you there in one piece, don't worry," he promised, making a solemn cross over his heart.

Vickie smiled at a bag lady standing precariously on the curb. *Am I making a big mistake?* She looked sideways at her driver, sitting easily on his specially made lambskin seatcover, with his left arm resting on the car door, his right stretched out over the steering wheel, and his head tilted forward so that his soft blond hair just touched the shoulders of his black leather vest. She snuggled back into her side of the lambskin. *Nah....*

So it was that Vickie Kirk found herself barreling out Marsh Creek Road in the cool of a summer's night in a '56 GMC half-ton with an improved V-8 and a good tape deck, driven by a metal fan who liked bugs.

From Marsh Creek Road they turned off onto a dirt road, and from the dirt road, into what Vickie could only believe was a creekbed; finally, they came to a roaring stop under an ancient live oak. Dust from the wheels wafted away, and through the branches of the oak tree you could see the stars, if you looked hard enough. Pretty good for the outskirts of a California suburb.

The truck grumbled into silence, but not the tape deck, which could keep running even when the pickup wasn't. Phil was just sitting there, tongue-tied, probably wondering if he'd made a mistake and this wasn't what she'd had in mind at all. Vickie considered conversational gambits: *Well, here we are. Sure is pretty out here at night.* Maybe, *I hope you're not one of those sexual lunatics who lures women out to secluded places in the middle of the night and forces them into performing loud — I mean lewd — and unnecessary acts.*

"Do you come here often?" she said aloud. Well, she thought she should know. She watched him mentally run through about eight different replies.

"Only in the daytime, usually," he said, glancing at her. "With bunches of little kids."

"Oh."

Vickie looked up at the tree. Phil studied the dashboard. The conversation went into suspended animation.

They lunged at each other at the same time.

Well, maybe lunged isn't exactly the right word. The slight, shy movements they made toward each other wouldn't have been taken by many people as anything but casual, but it got them where they both wanted to be: crushed together with their tongues down each other's throats.

"I'm bad! I'm nationwide!" ZZ Top screamed from the dashboard.

"Mrmpf mrmpf," said Vickie, pushing desperately at Phil. "Wait! Stop! Ygnaah!"

"What?"

"Aah, nothing. I just, you know, need some air...."

"Well, if it's *air* you want, babe," Phil laughed, "come on!" He reached over her and opened her door. "G'wan! Out!" He pushed at her until she tumbled out of the truck, and hopped out after her.

"What? What?" Vickie was a little taken aback by his sudden assertiveness. He took her hand and promenaded her to the back of the truck.

"Just step right up here," he said grandly and helped her step up to the bumper and over the tailgate.

"Wait a minute." He was back in the cab, rummaging around under the seat. "I hope it's not too dirty," he said as he vaulted expertly over the tailgate. He shook out a blanket and examined it critically.

"It'll do, I guess."

"Oh," said Vickie somewhat breathlessly, "it'll do fine."

They spread the blanket in the bed of the truck. Vickie spread herself over the blanket and Phil spread himself over Vickie. Oh my, she thought as she ran her hands under his vest, feeling the curves and hollows of his chest. Oh my.

The warm, slightly beery smell of his breath mingled with the tang coming from the leather, and Vickie just wanted to drink it all in. Phil was amenable to that. He ran his lips over her mouth and then kissed her hard, while he ever-so-gently tugged at the buttons of her shirt until he got them all undone.

"Aww, man," he said as his disappointed hands encountered a peach-colored "near-bare" designer tank top. Vickie giggled and pulled at a heavy chain hooked to his vest.

"What's this for?"

For an answer he kissed her, running his thumb over a nip-

ple through her tank top. She wriggled under his touch, but
stuck to her guns.

"No, what's it *for*?"

Phil gave her a poke. "It's not for nothing, chick. Hush up."

"Don't call me chick!" But Vickie was laughing as she struggled up off the truck bed and pulled at his hair. Her mock attack
only gave him the advantage; he slid an arm around her back
and yanked the tank top out of her jeans. His hands, rough, cool,
calloused, cupped her bare breasts and Vickie let go of his hair
and hugged him close, curling up her toes as he buried his head
between her breasts.

"Mmmm...." He brought his face up to hers and licked the tip
of her nose happily. Vickie smiled up at him and pulled the front
of his T-shirt out of his jeans and pushed it up over his chest.
They lay down, their bare skin pressed together like a secret between them.

"Uh-uhn," he said suddenly, and pushed her hands away.
"You first." The words didn't quite come out with the bravado
he intended and even through the darkness Vickie could tell he
was blushing to his toes.

Wasn't going to stop him, though. Vickie was more than content to let him undress her, which he did with more gentleness
than she would have expected from a guy wearing boots that
heavy. This man liked to take his time. He didn't just pull her
out of her jeans. No, he carefully unbuckled her belt, then
removed her shoes, one at a time, tapping her head with the toe
of one red high heel, making her wrinkle up her nose. Then he
unzipped her jeans and peeled them off, a little clumsily — these
things never go quite as smoothly as they do in the movies —
and then he went after her stockings. All the time he was touching and kissing her, licking, biting, caressing her, nibbling at
each part of her body as he uncovered it.

Finally he got down to her panties, twirled them around a
finger and laughingly stuck them in his pocket. He left her the
tank top, which Vickie thought was very generous of him, even
though he pushed it up to get at her breasts with his hands and
mouth, sending little sparks of pleasure straight up her spine
and back, zzzzzzt, making a warm tingling between her thighs
turn to a deep urgent desire that needed satisfying.

Vickie hadn't been this excited since she let her first date feel
her up when she was fifteen. Phil grinned his lopsided grin and

moved up onto her and she wrapped her legs around him, reveling in the coarse feel of his jeans rubbing against her crotch, the smooth leather against her breasts, the feel of his cock hard under the denim.

"Look at the stars," he said, and kissed her neck, her breasts,, her stomach, not missing any of her if he could help it. Vickie didn't think the stars were all that interesting. She opened her eyes and watched his blond head going down on her. His tongue slid right down there and Vickie came to her senses and sat bolt upright. She startled her new lover halfway out the back end of the truck.

"Phil!" she wailed. "What if somebody *comes?*"

"*Nobody's* gonna fucking come if you keep jumping around like that."

"I mean what if somebody comes *here?*"

"Nobody's gonna come up here," Phil declared. He jerked his thumb at his chest. "I own the place."

"Oh, you do not."

"Sure I do. I claim squatter's rights." He gave her a little shove. "Chick, you worry too much. Are you gonna lay back and take it or am I gonna hafta *tie* you to this truck?"

"Oh...." Vickie sank back down on the blanket.

Pleased at his successful domination of a willing woman, Phil took right up where he'd left off. His head went down between her legs and he reached up and spread his hands over both her breasts.

Vickie closed her eyes and was floating above them; she could see them like that, she naked and spread in the back end of an old truck, Phil in his jeans and boots and leather...her pleasure took a sharp turn and she was going 'round the bend at ninety miles an hour, and then she was all but climbing out of the truck bed. Phil was getting a bumpy ride.

She rolled over on her stomach and buried her face in her arm, embarrassed as she always was after coming like that. Phil clambered up and rolled her on her back again. She squinted up at him with one eye.

"Have we met?"

Phil kissed her. "Silly chick."

He shrugged off his vest and pulled his shirt over his head.

Vickie reached out as he unbuckled his belt. "Lemme help."

"Aw, you're in no shape to help anyone." But he slid his hip over close to her upturned face and gave her a smug, wicked little smile as he pulled the zipper down and wiggled free of his jeans. He was wearing yellow bikini jockey shorts.

Vickie was delighted: "Aren't you afraid to go out in public with those on? I mean you might get in an accident and have to go to the hospital!"

Phil dropped a boot on the metal truck bed, making an alarming clunk. He threw a sock at her.

"Yecch." Holding the sock gingerly by thumb and forefinger, she flung it over the side of the truck.

Divested of all his masculine finery, Phil became shy. He seemed so much more vulnerable now, and of course, he was, since Vickie made a grab for his cock as soon as she realized he was lapsing into one of his awkward silences. He looked so pale and smooth in the moonlight, like a teenager, his chest hairless and glowing white. His muscular shoulders and arms made her sigh, and his behind was soft and covered with tiny hairs that delighted her fingers as she guided him to her.

Not that he needed any guidance. After his initial attack of shyness he was all over her and, furthermore, rather pushy.

"Wait," she panted. "Wait."

He looked down at her in disbelief. "What do you *mean*, wait, chick?"

"Don't call me a — whoops! Aha...yikes, there you go."

"Wait...hell...."

He started out slow, leaning over her so that his hair tickled her nose, but now Vickie was getting pretty pushy herself. She ran her hands down his back and pulled him down on her, arching her back to meet him halfway as he thrust faster and deeper and harder, buried her face in his shoulder moaning, desperate, clawing, crying out; she was going down that hill at ninety miles an hour and Phil had the throttle all the way out.

"Oh, God, I'm gonna come!"

"Do...multiplication tables," she panted. "It's supposed...to help."

He gave her one astonished look, then clapped his hand over her mouth to stifle any more advice. She felt him go all rigid and then he was thrusting again, but slower now and without rhythm, and then all the air seemed to go out of him in a whoosh and he slumped on top of her.

"Mrmpf mrmpf." She got her mouth open wide enough to bite one of his fingers.

"Oh, sorry." He rolled off, but snuggled up against her, and for a long time they lay listening to each other breathe. Vickie was thinking: "I hope he has a box of Kleenex or something." Gradually the world came back into focus: the gnarled old oak tree, the sound of nightbirds, the stars, the slender half-moon, the hard bed of the truck under her tailbone, the radio.

"Iddly iddly iddly!" screamed something up front in the cab. "Keerrang keerrang keerraaaannng!"

Phil ran a finger lightly along her throat. "Look at the stars," he said softly. Vickie tilted her head back and he put his mouth on the base of her throat and blew a loud razzberry.

That must have been what started them off again. You can never tell about some people.

The stars had started to flicker out when, all cleaned up and dressed, they piled back into the front of the truck. Phil changed the tape to something loud, and drowned it out by starting the engine. They bumped and bounced back to civilization. When they reached the edge of Marsh Creek Road, Phil slowed the truck with unusual gentleness and sat for a minute with both arms stretched over the steering wheel, looking at something beyond the windshield.

"You know, Vickie...." He hesitated.

She waited. Not chick. Vickie.

He turned and smiled a little lopsidedly and punched her lightly on the shoulder. "I like you."

Then he hit the gas and the truck careened onto the asphalt, kicking up a mess of dust and one hell of a noise.

Vickie laughed and leaned out the window to catch the night wind on her face. "Awwwright!"

Shaman's Eyes

Nancy Blackett

The drums would not begin until just before sunset, but I woke with my heart pounding like twenty drums. Before I opened my eyes I knew today was the day of the maiden's dance, and in my mind, I pictured the boy of my choice. He was slim, with that wiry strength that seems to come as much from nerve as from muscle. I had noticed him at hunts and dances, and we had often talked. He had a warrior's courage combined with the inward-seeing eyes of a shaman, a mixture I had never seen before, yet he did not seem at war with himself; only guarded, though we talked easily together once we started. It was not his guardedness I loved, but what it protected.

Did he love me? I did not know. But in the maiden's dance, it was the girls who chose, and those choices, more often than not, led to marriage. My real worry today was not whether he loved me, for if I entered his hut, we would lie together, however he felt. My fear was that some other girl wanted him also and that the dance would carry her to his hut before me. My chances were good though, for many girls would not want a stranger. He was not from our village, or even of our people. His own village had been destroyed by white men, and he had come to live with us a few summers before. But he was not strange to me. He had learned our ways, and we could talk together about little things.

I heard my mother moving about the teepee and put away my fears. I had much to do. My teepee was ready, made of eleven buffalo skins that my father had hunted. I went over my dress once more to make sure every bead and fringe was in place and securely sewn. As I was washing my hair, a new worry entered my mind. What if I entered the wrong hut by mistake? I had never heard of it happening, but what if...? When my hair was dry, I ran to look at the huts again. Of course I would know his. I had watched him build it, knew every stick of it.

Mother called me to eat, though I had no desire for food. The day stretched on forever. Then, suddenly, the drums began. I took my place in the line, taking the hands of the girls on either side of me. They were from my village; I had touched their hands countless times as we played and worked together, yet now I felt a tingle of fear at their touch. It was as if they were strangers, though we would be friends again when this night was over as surely as the sun would rise in the morning.

We danced the pattern we had learned, and as the beat changed, we danced toward the circle of huts and began to go around it. My eyes sought his hut — ah! The door covering was not dropped, and I was coming closer, closer, and no one broke the line. Now I was in front of it, and I released the hands of my dear friends, and stooped to enter the hut.

He sat, wrapped in a buffalo robe, looking like a chief but too young, his face more guarded than I had ever seen it. My heart sank. He had hoped for another, and he was trying not to show his disappointment. I said his name in my mind, "Ladan, Ladan!" for neither of us would speak aloud that night. I prayed that lying with him, I could change his mind. It sometimes happened; I had heard women speak of it. I brushed his cheek with my hand. He was so soft and young. Perhaps it was only that. Brave warriors were not always fearless with women. I opened his robe slowly, looked at his naked body and gasped.

Where something should be, there was nothing. For the briefest moment, I wondered if he had met with some horrible mishap in the hunt, or in war, or in the raid that had killed his people. In the next instant, I realized that nothing was missing, everything was there. But Ladan was a girl. And afraid. It was this secret she guarded. The boys in her village must have known, and her strength and courage would have won their silence. No one in my village knew, or had said.

And what now? I had desired Ladan so long, and here we were, and I felt only confusion. She reached out and laid her palm not on my breast, but on my breastbone. I felt the bone melt and open under her hand. She was a shaman. I laid my palm on her breastbone, felt the rapid beat of her heart, and felt desire blossom in me like fire, like running water. The fear left her face, and the bravery as well, and the strength, and the inward look, and all I saw was softness. I knew that it was desire and that she saw the same in me. We smiled and her hand moved to my breast. My hand moved at the same moment, in a dance no one had taught us. She spread out her robe and I took off my dress and we lay together on the robe, touching, stroking, watching the happiness in each other's faces until it grew too dark to see. The hut smelled of earth and leaves, of the wild, not of the village. We only became aware of the drumming when it stopped.

We did not speak, but her fingers were counting mine, were drawing an outline of my body, telling me how smooth and round my buttocks were, singing to me of the softness and strength between my legs. It felt so good to me that I had to touch her too, and tell her in the same way how intricate her ears were, how many times I could stroke her belly without ever tiring of it, and how her shaman's eyes had haunted all my days and dreams. When her pleasure grew so intense that she must cry out of it, she began to weep, and I know that she did not weep from disappointment, but from relief that her loneliness was over.

Nor was I ever disappointed in her, for she was as good a hunter as any man in the village, and, later, there were enough children left motherless from the white man's raids that I never did miss birthing one of my own.

Just a Bad Day

Lisa Wright

Sara stabbed her key into the lock and jiggled it around. "This is all I need," she muttered under her breath. "Damn key never works right. What a lousy day."

First there had been the coffee she spilled on her new skirt, then came the fight with her boss. To top it all off, some jerk from Vermont, of all places, had parked his van in her space. She had had to park two blocks away and run home through a drenching rain.

Sara hooked her dripping hair behind her ear and struggled more vigorously with the key. Finally, it clicked into place. Visions of a hot shower and a warm bed soothed her until she stepped inside. An unfamiliar suitcase sat on the floor by her roommate's door. "Kathy?" Sara called. "I thought you were working tonight."

"She is," a male voice answered from the kitchen. Sara grabbed for the doorknob, ready to bolt.

A man emerged, drying his hands on a dish towel. *He has to be Kathy's brother,* Sara realized. *He looks just like her.*

"You must be Sara," he said, smiling. "I'd know you

anywhere. Kathy talks about you all the time." He extended his hand. "I'm Matt, Kathy's brother."

Matt, she thought. He's the potter from Vermont. Vermont! That's got to be his van. What the hell is he doing here?

Sara hadn't moved since she first heard his voice. Her hand still held the doorknob and a puddle was forming on the rug beneath her. She glared at this intruder half in anger, half in amazement.

Matt dropped his hand back to his side, and shifted his weight from one foot to the other. "Look," he said, "I'm sorry to intrude with no notice. I got a call last night that a space had opened up in the craft show here this weekend. I've been trying to get into this show for years, and I couldn't pass it up."

Come on, Sara, she told herself, straighten up! This is Kathy's brother, not Jack the Ripper. She let go of the doorknob and forced herself to smile. "I'm sorry," she said. "Of course you're welcome to stay."

He looked relieved.

"You'll have to forgive me. I've had a bad day."

"I can see that!" he laughed.

"Make yourself at home while I get out of these wet clothes."

The hot water poured over her body, melting the tension in her shoulders, rounding the sharp edges of her annoyance. He really is rather attractive, Sara decided. The square jaw and wide mouth looked much better on Matt than on Kathy. She remembered a photo that Kathy had shown her of Matt, shirtless. Very nice, she decided. Very nice.

Sara began lathering herself absentmindedly. No one could be as wonderful as Kathy says Matt is, she told herself. Warm, sensitive, thoughtful. Yeah, but taking my parking space was not exactly thoughtful. Still, there is something about him.

The smooth, slippery movements of her hands felt luscious on her belly, her thighs. She made lazy circles around her breasts, squeezing the nipples gently between her fingers. One soapy hand glided down to her pubes. Her fingers slid over and between her labia. A tingling warmth spread into her abdomen and her inner thighs.

Sara reached up and removed the hand-held shower head from the wall. She switched the setting from spray to a pulsating jet and aimed it at her groin.

A blast of icy cold water hit her clitoris. "Shit!" she screamed, and slammed off the water, gasping for breath.

There was a timid knock at the door. "Are you okay?" Matt asked.

"I ran out of hot water rather suddenly," Sara growled.

"I guess that was my fault," he admitted through the door. "I turned the dishwasher on and forgot you were in the shower. Sorry!"

Sara shook her head and sighed. "This is not my day." She turned the water back on just long enough to finish rinsing off.

Half an hour later, Sara emerged from her room, dry and dressed in jeans and her favorite sweater. A delicious aroma hung in the air. Her mouth began to water as she crossed the living room. "Something sure smells good," she called.

She rounded the corner into the kitchen and gasped. Matt looked up from where he was kneeling in front of the oven and grinned. "I thought you could use a nice dinner," he said.

"Nice? I think I'm in love!"

The table was covered with a clean tablecloth. A salad, a bottle of white wine and two wine glasses were set out.

"Pour yourself some wine," said Matt, closing the oven door. "Dinner will be ready in a few minutes."

He finished setting the table while Sara sipped her wine. He seemed totally at ease. She had never known a man who was so at home in the kitchen.

"Not all men are helpless," Matt said, reading her mind. "I've lived alone for six years. It was either learn how to cook and clean or live in a pigsty and eat Burger King. It didn't take me long to decide."

Sara laughed. The wine felt warm inside her. She felt a familiar tingle of excitement in the nape of her neck. "I've been a real bitch ever since I came home," she said. "Do you think we could start all over again?"

"Sounds good to me," Matt agreed. He walked the short distance to Sara's chair and extended his hand. "Hello," he said. "You must be Sara. I'm Matt, Kathy's brother."

They shook hands.

Dinner was superb. Chicken stuffed with peaches and mushrooms was accompanied by tender, young asparagus and hot, crusty bread.

"I wish I could cook like that," Sara said as she pushed aside her empty plate.

"You could if you wanted to," said Matt. "Kathy tells me you're pretty talented too."

"Talented? Me? What do you mean?"

"Kathy showed me the sweater you made for her. It's beautiful."

Sara blushed. "No, it was just...."

"Just beautiful," he insisted. His eyes never left her face. She blushed as she felt his gaze. "Did you knit the one you're wearing?" Sara nodded, feeling him drink her in. She couldn't take her eyes off him. It was hard to breathe. This is crazy, she thought, I hardly know this man.

Matt reached over and ran his hand along her sleeve. "Cotton, isn't it?"

Again she nodded. She watched him caress her arm. His touch was electric. Her gaze moved from his hand to his face. He was looking at her.

"I feel like I know so much about you already," he said softly.

Sara didn't trust her voice. An ache of longing filled her lap.

"The dishes," she said, her voice cracking. She cleared her throat and tried again,

"I'd better do the dishes now."

Matt let go of her arm, reluctantly, and smiled. "I'll dry."

Sara snatched up the plates and carried them to the sink. This is moving much too fast, she thought. I've got to get hold of myself.

The sink filled with hot, soapy water. She plunged her hands in and tried to concentrate on the dishes. Almost immediately her hair fell into her eyes. "Damn it," she said, blowing at the hair. She tried flipping it back with a toss of her head, but it was no use.

"Here, let me help," Matt said. He came up close behind her. Gently, he gathered her hair together and drew it back, letting his hands glide against her face. "Your hair is so soft," he whispered into her neck.

Sara's knees went weak. She was breathing in short gasps. Every inch of her body tingled.

He kissed her delicately behind her ear lobe. "Sara...," he said. Her body was alive with his touch. He kissed her again, moving down her neck to the curve of her shoulder. He held her hair and encircled her waist, drawing her body against his. She gripped the sink with soapy hands. Matt reached for a dish towel and gently wiped her hands dry.

His mouth opened on the curve of her neck, licking, sucking. She pressed back against his body, feeling his hardness against her ass. Sara reached back with one hand and stroked his leg, kneading his thigh with her finger. "Oh God....," she whimpered, "I want you." Her cunt ached, soaking her jeans.

Matt turned her around. His eyes searched hers. Then their mouths were together, wet and hungry. His hands slid up under her sweater, over her back, running down her side, grazing the edge of her breasts. His touch sent shocks through her body. His hands found her breasts, fondling them, teasing the hard nipples. One hand slipped down inside her pants as Sara fumbled with his belt, his button, his zipper. His cock flew out as she tugged his jeans down. It was hard and smooth. She lowered herself to her knees and took his cock in both hands. She licked a pearly drop of cum off the tip and then slid the smooth stalk into her mouth...once, twice.

"Wait, wait," he moaned. He slipped out of her mouth and kneeled down, facing her. His hand slid down through her pubic hair and inside. Her cunt exploded. He drew out his fingers and smeared the cum on her breasts, licking it off as his hand returned to her vagina.

They struggled out of their jeans, kicking them aside. "Come inside me. Please, now!" Sara begged. Matt moved between her thighs and rubbed his cock against her clit until she came again. Then he stretched deep inside as her cunt contracted. She gripped his arms, and he plunged deeper and deeper inside her.

Hello!" Kathy's voice called from the living room. "I'm home. Is anyone here?"

Rapid Transit

Mickey Warnock

The subway train rolled out of the Lafayette station about eight thirty on Sunday night. Linda and I were alone in the last car, on our way home from dinner at her mother's house.

I looked across at Linda, who stared out the window next to her. She was going to get it when we got home. All day long she had teased me sexually when her mother wasn't watching. She had a habit of doing that to me in public, confessing that she enjoyed it, because she knew I'd ravage her when we got home.

Halfway to the Orinda station, the train screeched to a halt. I sighed deeply, leaning back. Just what I needed, a delay.

"Shit, what is it this time?" I groaned, when after five minutes the train hadn't budged.

"Hang tight, babe, it's probably another train ahead of us," said Linda.

"ATTENTION PASSENGERS. DUE TO MECHANICAL DIFFICULTIES OF THE TRAIN AHEAD OF US, WE WILL BE DELAYED UNTIL FURTHER NOTICE. WE APOLOGIZE FOR THIS INCONVENIENCE."

"Damn," I muttered, and lit a cigarette.

"Wanna play cards, Mick?"

"Very funny, Lin. I just want to get home!"

"What's the hurry, we don't have to work tomorrow," she said, reaching over to pat my leg.

"I know, but you were pretty bad today when your mom wasn't looking." I took a drag of my cigarette.

"Oh, poor thing, is Mickey all hot and bothered?"

I closed my eyes and pretended to ignore her. At that moment, Linda jumped up, straddling my lap. I didn't move. She took my head in her hands, breathing warmly in my ear. I shuddered.

"Mickey, I want you...now," she whispered.

I opened my eyes, realizing what she had just said.

"On a subway train?"

"Why not?" she said, lightly kissing me.

"What if someone...." I tried to say, but Linda's lips covered mine.

She started to unbutton my shirt, and I fumbled with hers. We pulled them open in unison, embracing, our warm bare breasts pressed together. Linda's lips left mine. Her tongue slid down my neck to my bare shoulder, which she lightly nibbled. Just then, the train began to move.

"Watch out," I laughed, grabbing onto Linda, who almost fell backwards. She began to do up her shirt when I grabbed her hands. "Not so fast. I want you to fuck me before we get back to Oakland!" I was quite serious. I couldn't wait any longer, not after this.

Shaking her head, Linda undid my fly, and I hers. I gave a low moan as her hand slid between my legs, slipping a couple of fingers inside me. I eased my right hand down her pants. We stroked each other as the train rolled into Orinda. I slightly opened my eyes over Linda's shoulder when the doors parted, expecting some poor soul to walk in. No one did.

Linda curled over me so that I could slip another finger inside her, and my free hand grabbed her dangling breast. The train roared through the tunnels. Linda shoved all her fingers in, and I winced. She was fucking me quickly, roughly. Her teeth dug into my neck, and the rest of my hand squeezed into her cunt.

"Oh, Jesus!" I cried out at Rockridge station, coming in a flood into Linda's hand.

Her hand slowed, but mine moved quicker. She pumped it,

racing, panting in my ear, "I'm coming, I'm coming," releasing me as she gave a long, low moan.

We held each other quietly, catching our breath.

"Better get dressed, babe, we're almost home," I whispered. We limped out of our empty car at the Oakland station...and two other dykes walked on.

Visit to The Mighoren

Emily Alward

What have I gotten myself into? Angelica thought. A wave
of panic jolted her.

The Moonmist was crowded. Hundreds of candlepoints flickered in chandeliers, soft light reflecting off crackleglass windows and the women's dresses. Subdued conversation swirled
around her. A single strand of melody, the pure notes of a lyre,
threaded beneath the babble. The scene resembled one of the
elegant bistros in Angelica's hometown, the ancient city of
Toronto.

Except...the men were all exraordinarily attractive. She'd
noted it before, the predominance of male good looks on this
planet. Her new colleague Rihanna had just smiled and said, "Of
course, Angie, selection pressures."

She shot a worried look at Rihanna now. The Cobalean
woman was surveying the room with an anticipatory air.

"What do I do?" Angelica whispered.

"Well, just pick one you like and go talk to him," her friend
said. Apparently Rihanna herself was engrossed in the first part
of this process. Her gaze darted between a nearby archway and

a table across the room. A dark man with a gaze of smoulder-
ing intensity sat at one end, a cheerfully insouciant blond at the
other.

My god, I have all these choices too, Angelica realized. She
began to tingle inside, a wholly unexpected feeling. Still, she was
scared. "But what if the man doesn't like...." she protested.

"Silly girl! Just go on, don't waste our money."

Rihanna gave her a gentle shove. Angelica stumbled away
from the entrance foyer. She walked slowly between rows of
tables, a glaze of unreality fogging her mind. This couldn't be
happening to her, a well-brought-up young Terran woman
who'd come here to study antique texts.

"Good evening, *nemelyya*."

She looked into eyes as blue as the Cobalean clouds.

"Good evening," she managed to murmur. She pulled out a
chair and sank into it. She had serious doubt that her feet — or
her courage — would carry her any farther. "My name is Angelica," she added shakily, unable to think of any brighter way
to open a conversation.

"Damik mir Nymet," he replied. "Would you like some wine
while you look around?"

"Yes, please. Some for yourself, too," she added, remembering good manners. She stared discreetly at her new acquaintance
while he signaled a server. Those incredible azure eyes were set
in an equally glorious face. It reminded her of those on the
prehistoric Greek statues, or some character — was it Redford?
Voight? — in the old 2-D dramas. He was somewhat taller than
herself, nicely muscled — she searched her memory for the
Cobalean word. *Gherique* — yes, that was it. Would he be *zacuir*
too? She blushed furiously as the question invaded her
thoughts. Her mentors had urged rapid acculturation. She was
sure they didn't have this in mind. Her cheeks continued to
sting, and she looked down in confusion. The outer robe Rihanna had loaned her had come unfastened. She didn't know what
etiquette required here, so she left it open.

Damik held out a goblet of bubbly pink wine to her. He raised
his own in salutation. "To the *nemelyya's* health."

Angelica gave a gracious nod. Talk to him, Rihanna had told
her. Whatever could she say? She'd never known it was possible
to feel at the same time so awkward and so aroused. She stole
another glance across the table. He sat there with one sturdy

hand cupped around the goblet, regarding her. Confidence was written all over his face. Somehow she'd have felt calmer if he'd shown some hint of uncertainty too.

"Mir Nymet. Isn't that an archonial name?" she finally asked.
"*Hai*, it is."

He was polite, even courtly, but was obviously waiting for her to take the conversational initiative. Am I expected to take the initiative in other things too?, she wondered. Panic touched her again.

"But...you're from one of the sixty families." The sixty archonial families formed the pinnacle of Cobalean social structure. "However did you end up in a place like this?"

"Oh." He laughed, but looked shocked, too, at her question. "You're not from this planet at all, are you?"

Angelica shook her head. She was relieved to find herself capable of conversation, but in all fairness she should tell him the rest. "I'm from off- planet. A visiting student at the Institute. So if you don't want anything to do with me, it's all right — "

"*Nyai*. You're a very alluring woman, off-planet or no. I'd be delighted to service you, but if you choose someone else, I won't be offended."

Angelica squirmed. An anticipatory quiver shot through her labia at the overt suggestion. Damn, he was attractive. Luckily this place was not as she had pictured it, with the men half-clothed. She would be attacking him, making a complete fool of herself....

"Mind if we just talk for a little while?" She struggled to sound collected. Reaching for her social scientist facade, she said, "I'd like to ask you some questions."

"Go ahead." He was still looking at her, steadily and appreciatively. Did she imagine a hint of amusement at her discomfort?

"Why are you — I mean, have you fallen into disgrace or anything? I thought the archonial families were very proud."

"So we are." Yes, he definitely sounded amused. "No, I'm not in disgrace, merely waiting for a suitable marriage to be arranged."

"And they let you work here in the meantime?" None of her ideas about the *mighoren* were proving true. She'd supposed it would be staffed by desperate men in some sort of indentured status, like geishas in the old Japanese tales. Instead, this Damik claimed to belong to the ruling class of the planet. He wore the self-assurance shown by aristocrats anywhere in the galaxy. She studied him openly this time, and began to tingle again. Suddenly she wanted very much to try him.

"Do I get a reference in your report as a source?" he asked.

Surprise warred with desire in Angelica. So he was familiar with the apparatus of scholarship, too. An entirely suitable man. Would she be brave enough to carry this through? "If you wish," she murmured. "Please tell me how it works."

"*Hai,* I come here once a week. It provides pocket cash, enjoyable female company, and..." he shrugged, "recommendations from a good *mighoren* increase one's value as a potential husband."

"Oh." She would never understand Cobalean society; it was too strange. The whole planet was floating in sensuality. That didn't matter, though, at this moment. She felt a part of it; she wanted to feel his arms around her, to welcome him into her body. Angelica reached out her hand to Damik. "I'm not looking any further."

The sense of unreality hit her again. How had she ever gotten into this situation? A collage of recent happenings swirled through her head. It had all started a week ago, with another glass of wine....

Shards from a goblet fell at Angelica's feet. The pink wine ebbed around the shattered pieces.

"Dammit," she muttered, fortunately in her native Terran dialect. The spill was an incredible gaffe for a representative of Empire culture to make.

"Your pardon, *nemelyya,*" she said quickly in her shaky Cobalean.

"Never worry, my dear. A server will clean it up," the other replied kindly. "You were saying, about the ancient books?"

"*Hai.*" Angelica fell into the alien language's forms. "I agree with your philosophers' conclusions that they originated off-planet. How they came to be on Cobale is a puzzle."

The woman asked more questions, which Angelica answered as best she could. She was quite nervous now. The official was all graciousness, but she kept staring speculatively at Angelica, almost as if the young Terran scholar had some pitiable condition evident to everyone but herself.

Later, as the reception began to break up, her new colleagues came by, and offered to walk her back to the Institute dormitory.

Angelica was relieved and grateful at the gesture. She'd only known Rihanna and Josinne a few short weeks, but they were the only friends she had on the whole planet. Both were merry and easy to talk to. Perhaps they could tell her if she'd made some irreparable social blunder.

Once out in the capital's narrow streets, the cool air revived her. She listened idly to Josinne's chatter about various men she'd talked to at the party. Just like a teen-ager on any world, Angelica reflected. Well, not quite. Josinne's talk was peppered with terms that weren't in Angelica's hastily-acquired Cobalean vocabulary. I will have to look them up, she thought. What does *zacuir* mean? What is *gherique*?

"And did you have a good time, Angelica?" Rihanna asked.

"Um, mostly. Except for my stupidity in breaking that goblet."

Rihanna patted her shoulder sympathetically. "I'm sure everyone understands."

"I'm not so sure," Angelica muttered. "That official kept staring at me like I was a freak."

"Not a freak, Angie. It's perfectly obvious that you're in need."

"In need of what?" Angelica blurted out. She wasn't sure she understood the implication. Insofar as she did, it was highly insulting, at least to a woman of Terran origin. She reminded herself about cultural relativity. "It's just culture shock," she said aloud.

"Culture shock?" In the two moons' glow, she could see the incredulous look the Cobalean women exchanged. Then they burst out laughing.

"Tell me, friend. Is it Terran custom to spill wine on a high official of state?" Rihanna teased.

"Of course not." Angelica sulked. The conversation was taking an uncomfortable turn.

"How long is it since you've had a lover?" Rihanna asked. Her voice was very soft, and without malice.

"Eight months," Angelica said through clenched teeth. Actually, it had been a year and eight months. These women had no right to ask, of course. Personal relationships were just that — personal — and one didn't enter them without a deep commitment. Geoffrey's commitment had suddenly dissolved when she had decided to study xenolinguistics. The memory still hurt.

"Poor girl," Rihanna said. Angelica snapped out of her reverie. The massive gates of the Institute grounds loomed ahead. She was eager to run up to her room and escape into her studies. She politely thanked Rihanna and Josinne for their concern. Despite the gaps in understanding, she would after all be working with them for the next few months.

"That's all right," Josinne said. She added lightly, "Now we know what we'll give you for your birthday next week."

The days spun by. Angelica immersed herself in research. Books from the Institute library piled up in her room. She sat now, warmed by a beam of the blue smoky sunlight, punching inquiries into her keyboard. She was trying to identify the terms Josinne had used a few evenings ago.

ZAQUIR? she queried.

ZAQUIR appeared on the screen, followed immediately by NETE, which meant "no exact Terran equivalent"; a common notation in alien language study.

The definition appeared. ZAQUIR: 2310 AD: STRONG, VIRILE. Okay, clear enough.

Then another notation jumped up. ZACUIR: 2339 AD: CAPABLE OF EXCELLENT PROLONGED THRUSTING; CAPABLE OF BRINGING A WOMAN TO A CONTINUOUS ORGASMIC PLATEAU.

Wow, Angelica thought, her neochristian upbringing surfacing for a moment. What a hell of a thing for a young girl like Josinne to be talking about openly.

Then her professional curiosity took over. Here was an interesting insight into Cobalean culture. Societies developed terms for those distinctions important to them. She'd vaguely suspected that women's sexual enjoyment was rated higher on Cobale than in the worlds of the Terran Empire. Here was proof. Terran Standard had dozens of scientific and vulgar words for sex. But none of them precisely defined anything about a man's talents for bringing pleasure to a woman.

She punched in another word. GHERIQUE? Again, NETE. Then, GHERIQUE: WELL- FORMED; OF GOOD PHYSIQUE. And, TERM INDICATES A MALE BODY WHICH IS WELL-TONED BUT NOT MUSCLE-BOUND. MILD MESOMORPH TYPE; FIRM ARMS AND BUTTOCKS; ADEQUATELY LARGE PENIS.

Angelica wondered, do these women think of men only as sex objects? She tried a third word.

AGIDAL? AGIDAL: COURTEOUS; WELL-MANNERED. COMPETENT.

Then another note flickered in, preceded by the "!" which indi-
cated disagreement with previous definitions. AGIDAL IS IMPOS-
SIBLE TO DEFINE SIMPLY. IT IS THE MALE COROLLARY TO THE PRIME
VIRTUE WHICH ARCHONIAL FEMALES ARE EXPECTED TO EX-
EMPLIFY. INCLUDES CONNOTATIONS OF GOOD BREEDING,
COURAGE, INTELLIGENCE, PHYSICAL PROWESS, CONFIDENCE, CON-
GENIALITY, COMPASSION. OFTEN USED WITH ALIREL (C.F. AP-
PRECIATIVE AFFECTION AND LOYALTY TOWARD ONE'S LADY) TO
DESCRIBE THE IDEAL MAN. Enough of this, Angelica told herself.
She should be coding the crumbling texts she had been sent here
to study, not brooding over Cobalean sexuality.

The doorchimes jangled. Angelica leapt up guiltily to answer.
Rihanna and Josinne stood in the entrance. Both of them beamed
at her.

"We have a surprise for you," Rihanna said happily.

Josinne leaned over and placed a light kiss on Angelica's
cheek. "Happy birthday, Angelica. Enjoy your gift." She shifted
her books and hurried down the hall, obviously on her way to
some seminar.

Rihanna followed Angelica back into the room. The Cobalean
woman's eyes danced with delight.

"So what's the big surprise?" Angelica asked.

"Oh, Angie, I do hope you like it," Rihanna said. "You are
going to the *mighoren* tonight, and I am going with you."

Angelica was quiet for a moment, trying to identify the unfamiliar term. She knew the root word. *Mighir* was the estrus
period Cobalean females experienced once a month. From the
shimmer surrounding her, Rihanna appeared to be well into
mighir now.

"Excuse me a minute," Angelica said. She walked over and
keyed the new word into her computer. The definition leapt
onto the screen. She frowned.

"Let's make sure I understand you," Angelica said. Shock bat-
tled with concern over her friend's feelings. She phrased her
question carefully.

"Are you saying you're taking me...to...a place...where I pay
for...men...to have sex with me?"

"Why yes, I suppose that's the Terran interpretation," Rihanna said matter-of-factly. "Except that you don't have to pay
tonight, Angie. Josinne and I are treating you."

Angelica sighed. It was completely unthinkable, of course.

Yet Rihanna stood there wriggling with enthusiasm, awaiting her thanks. She'd have to explain her refusal diplomatically. Then a twinge of mischievous curiosity hit her, asking, why *not* just agree and see what it's like? She pushed the thought away.

"Look, Rihanna, it's very kind of you, but I just can't accept. I'd find it too...degrading."

"There's nothing degrading about it!" The other woman flared. "The Moonmist has only high-class men. Josinne goes there every month; she's from one of the most distinguished families on Cobale, and her mother includes *mighoren*-fees in her allowance so she won't go into delirium. Or do something disgraceful. Besides, I went to all the trouble to get reservations, and even the synthetic *mighir*-cream for you — that's almost contraband...." Rihanna sank into a chair and started crying.

Angelica had never expected tears. She was as unnerved as when she'd read the definition. Her pre-embarkation briefing continually emphasized the dangers culture gaps posed to the naive, and the responsibility of the visiting scholar to bridge them. She fidgeted uncertainly. Finally she gathered her composure and reached over to clasp Rihanna's hand, as she'd seen Cobalean women do so often for reassurance. "I'd go, if I could be sure I wouldn't be too uncomfortable," she said.

Rihanna wiped the tears away.

"You won't be. Once you're there, you'll be so excited."

Angelica looked at her dubiously.

"Think about it this way," Rihanna said. She'd resumed her normal rational tone. "If I were a guest scholar on Terra, you'd want to entertain me, wouldn't you? Maybe take me to a 'nightclub' or a concert? Well, this is no different. Except it's more necessary — and more fun." A blissful smile touched her face.

"All right," Angelica conceded. "Just tell me what I need to know and do."

"Nature will take care of that," Rihanna giggled.

"But what do I wear? What if the man can't perform on demand?"

"Wear whatever you like." Rihanna apparently thought the second question too ridiculous to answer. "I'll come by for you at sunfall. All right?"

"All right," Angelica said uneasily.

Shaking free from her memories, Angelica examined the room Damik had led her to. There was no bed, Angelica noticed instantly. One corner held a *conneghe,* the plush-covered area with varying slopes she had seen defined as a "conversation-pit." Now she doubted such a definition. She imagined herself spread out against it, Damik thrusting into her — if she ever figured out how to get to that stage. Angelica was no innocent, but she'd never been in a situation where she'd been expected to take the lead. Certainly not one in which her own wishes took precedence. Just how did one proceed?

Her face felt flushed again. An independent will seized her hands. They wanted to reach out, caress his arms and shoulders, trace slowly down his chest. No. What they really wanted was to tear off his clothes and reach for his penis, tantalizing him, then guiding it slowly, blissfully, into her.

She wasn't sure it could happen, with the difference in biological programming. She glanced down at her arms. The cream had not worn off. Her skin glittered in the lamplight, and she caught a whiff of the unfamiliar musky scent. Rihanna had assured her that the cream worked as well as the real pheromones. She hoped so. It would be unbearable, to be so in need — worse, to have it show, and then find the man unwilling or unable to meet her expectations.

Damik walked to a door opposite and drew some curtains back. "There's a grotto garden and pool. We can have a swim first, or order dinner, if you prefer. Most women don't," he added in an offhand tone.

Angelica took a deep breath. Silhouetted against the amethyst night sky, the planes of his face and body stunned her. He was even more delicious than she'd thought. She had to do something.

"No, we can swim later," she said. "What do I do?"

"It's customary to remove the *medora* first. In fact, it's essential." He smiled gently. Amusement twinkled in his blue eyes, but it was benign. *He's enjoying this more than I am,* she realized with surprise.

He peeled off his robe. She was trembling.

"*Hai?*" She whispered the all-purpose Cobalean word that could mean "well..." or "maybe..." or "yes."

Suddenly Damik was beside her, turning her around and pulling her against him. Their lips met in one lingering kiss, then the clothes came off. Angelica wasn't quite sure of the sequence, her own body's urgent seeking was too intense, but she knew she was flinging aside his jacket, shirt and trousers with unseemly speed. She nestled against him, her nipples erect and brushing over his magnificent chest. Somehow they ended up in the *conneghe*. A slightly-slanting surface met her back. She felt its soft, resilient support and they paused for a half-moment, savoring their shared desire.

His hands cupped each side of her body just below her waist. The touch aroused her beyond all belief. She pushed up to him. For a torturous moment she sought in vain. She would be suspended forever, she feared, his phallus beckoning like a lodestar. Then he was within her. She moaned with pleasure, and heard Damik murmuring the Cobalean love-word, *"Ticara, ticara...."*

They made love for a long, long time. Angelica had never been so satisfactorily pleasured before. She rode through waves of ecstasy, each crest taking her a little higher, till perception shattered in a storm of stars.

In the tranquil afterwash, her fingers wandered tenderly over his body and she reached for an endearment too. *"Tiru...."*

But that was not the end. Much to Angelica's surprise, when she roused herself to thank and dismiss him, Damik demurred. There was no time limit, he said, and didn't she want to enjoy some of the other features of the *mighoren*?

They swam in the grotto garden's pool, lit by opalescent nightmist. They ordered a small supper. Her tension dissipated by what they'd shared, Angelica discovered normal conversational skills returning. Or more than normal. She found the stories he told genuinely interesting, and not only for their insights into Cobalean culture. For his part, Damik asked question after question about her past life, and beamed approval when she explained how hard she'd worked for the chance to go off-planet.

Angelica recalled, seemingly at random, that the Cobalean word for marriage applied only to certain formal arrangements within the upper class. For all other attachments, the word "bond" was used. A comfortable rapport flowed between her and this man now, a sharing she'd never forget. Well, she thought, we've created some sort of a bond, however tenuous.

"Damik," she said. She hesitated, munching on a succulent river clam while summoning her next sentence. "You're a really good person. I don't know what I expected when I came here, but — nothing as wonderful as this."

"*Hai*, it's the same with me. I don't say that as part of my routine," he added, humor and embarrassment blending in his voice.

"I suppose I should ask now about seeing you again?" she said. She was startled by her own boldness.

"Um, I'm here almost every fourth day. You wouldn't have to pay either, except...management insists."

Angelica fell silent, thinking about the future. It would be even better next time, since she wouldn't be so scared. Already an impulse to caress him danced through her hands. Damik was an incomparable lover; she wanted to do it again with him....

On the other hand, there were all those other intriguing men out there whom she could try....

Luckily, her research was going to require staying on this planet for many, many months.

Big Ed

Isadora Alman

I had a new man in my life. Ed was a huge and hairy Mountain Man, a drawler and a brawler from Chickamauga, Tennessee. We were still somewhat new to each other, but we seemed to be going by the book. First the history: home town, education, work, interests, and now we were getting down to the cast of characters in the novels of our lives. I was telling him about my friendship/love affair with Dick, and was getting to a good part, the exciting three-way with Erik at the Russian River a year ago. He took the genuine corncob pipe on which he was chewing out of his mouth and said, "You mean the two fellers got it on too?"

"Well, each of us did with each of us eventually. That's one of the things that was so wonderful," I tried to explain.

"Sugar, you and that crowd of yours, you've been hanging around with too many fairy boys," he said, putting aside his pipe and pulling me against him. I sighed. What an expression! But what could you expect from a Good Old Southern Boy (I have prejudices of my own)?

I began, I thought gently, to broaden his world view. "Ed, if

40

a man appreciates the body of another man...." He toppled me onto my back and lifted my legs over his mammoth shoulders, lowering his head, something I guarantee will interrupt the most impassioned of monologues.

"C'mere, sugar, and let me appreciate your body." His voice was...shall we say, muffled, and I was glad that some of the other California practices were not unknown in the back woods of Tennessee.

Later, when I was cuddled against his matted chest I tried again. "You know, Ed, bisexual sensibilities don't make one less of a man or less of a woman. I rather think they make one more of what one is. Do you find me womanly?"

One of his huge hands was fondling my breast, hefting the weight of it in his palm. "Oh, sugar, how can you ask that?"

"Would you think me less so if I told you that when we're joined together I sometimes fantasize that I'm the one with the penis, that I'm fucking you, taking you with all the strength and sureness that is traditionally male?" As I talked, his left hand moved along my body, found another place it liked, and lingered. With his right hand he began stroking himself.

I became aware of a soft deep rumble of words, so I stopped talking to listen. "What a big cock, what a good strong cock," he was whispering. I closed my eyes and felt his fingers more intensely as they rubbed me to hardness, and realized that his soft words were underscoring the fantasy that I had been weaving — that big hand moving up and down, the heat and intensity gathering in my groin as the words of praise filled my head. "What a big hard cock you have," he was telling me. "I love feeling your cock grow hard."

We climaxed at the same time and it was better than Fourth of July fireworks. "Oh, Ed," I gasped. "I never...I...that was so...."

"Hush, sugar, I know. I know about the man and the woman in all of us. I truly do. Rest now. I've got some thinkin' to do."

I lay quietly beside him enjoying the calm, the huge hairy maleness of his bulk, the smell of his man's sweat and juices that filled the bed. "I'm goin' to take a shower, Jane," he said shortly.

"Can't I join you?"

"No. You go on into the other room. I'll join you in a while."

Well, some people are funny after sex. They feel sad or need to commune with higher powers or something. Maybe I touched some secret chord with our talk or our play, and he needed time to absorb it. I sat on the back porch, listening to some funky blues on the radio, and thought my own thoughts. Time passed, what seemed like a lot of time. I hadn't heard the sound of running water in a while.

"Ed?" I called.

"In a minute, Jane." And then in a few more minutes, "Jane?"

"I'm on the porch."

"Close your eyes!" His voice, usually so deep and rumbly, sounded different somehow, like sexy whispers in bed, softer and more Southern. "I want you to meet Edna."

I opened my mouth to ask questions — where? who?, or to be sociable if I had to, even though I was in my bathrobe. Then, as I opened my eyes, my mouth fell wide open too. I wasn't the only one wearing one of my bathrobes. Actually, Ed had on one of my hostess gowns — a long flowing pink silk affair that tied on one shoulder and was split along the opposite side to reveal the leg. The leg it revealed, I was relieved to see, remained unshaven. So was his chest, and the thick beard I admired was still in place. (My shower drain would have been in big trouble if it were otherwise.) Such an extremely hairy man, and so much of him.

His longish hair was swept to the side and held with a barrette. His blue eyes were made bluer by the same shade of eye shadow and lash darkener. What there was to be seen of his cheeks above his beard glowed with a high pink blush. His mouth was lipsticked. A long strand of my pearls encircled his thick neck tightly like a choker. The nails on his hands were bright red, and from the way that he held them away from his body, apparently still wet with polish. The pantyhose in my dresser, purchased to fit me, a much shorter person, did not reach to his waist. This was revealed by the line low down on his groin which showed through the straining seams of the pink silk.

"Edna?" I understood, of course, that Edna was a part of Ed, like a spiritual twin sister sharing his body. I thought, too, of the part in the movie *Cabaret* where Joel Grey sings a love song to a gorilla dressed in a net tutu. It was a funny scene, immensely touching. I still hadn't said a word and realized that it was up to me to do so.

"Edna?" A nod of response. "Come and let me look at you!"

The huge stockinged feet padded out onto the porch. Well, what were a few splinters on such a momentous occasion. But the height difference. How could I deal with a Romeo and Juliet balcony scene? I took the hand held daintily away from the body and, mindful of the possibly wet polish, gently led the way back into the house and onto the couch. With Edna seated and me standing, the scene would play more appropriately. I poured some wine into a glass and held it out. We both sipped in silence. The glasses were then set aside. I leaned down and placed a gentle kiss on the wet and sweetly sticky lips. My hand rested on the exposed shoulder momentarily and then caressed its way beneath the folds of the pink silk bodice. I took a deep breath and my voice came out in a husky whisper. "What lovely smooth breasts you have, how soft and silky and firm."

The response was a satisfied sigh, "Ah, yes, sugar."

Shades of Grey

Jennifer Pruden

She is sitting on the steps of my apartment building when I get home from work. She cradles her black helmet between thighs clad in black wool. One broad yellow band in an otherwise black shirt clings to her breasts. The biking gloves I bought for her rest inside the helmet. Her blonde hair is pulled back in two barrettes from her wide cheekbones and brown eyes.

I shift the Filene's bag from one hand to the other in search of my house keys. I have three separate key rings: for work, for my car, for my apartment. At last I find them and insert the key into the lock, wriggling it as it makes uncertain progress. Sometimes it takes five minutes before I can get the door open. Today it is cooperative.

She stands waiting beside me, her helmet caught by its straps over her arm, her bicycle balanced beside her, waiting to be carried the three flights to my apartment. It is dry out today so there will be no mud streaks on the stairwell walls to be wiped down. She is breathing hard as I look at her, smiling, the point of my tongue just parting my lips.

I hold the door as she hoists the bike through and starts up the stairs. I watch her ass as she walks up the stairs, her cleats tapping. I watch the muscles move in the backs of her thighs, rippling black fabric.

"I brought you a present," I tell her back. She turns to look at me, smiles. I grin.

"Well," she says, "You're up to no good."

"Brat." I reach out, slip my hand between her thighs to caress her. "Is she hungry?"

"Mmm, you know she is...." She quickens her pace, then stands aside to let me unlock the door to my apartment. The door unlocks easily but I stand, waiting, with the key in the lock. I set the Filene's bag down and start to unbutton my blouse. She hisses at me until I pick up the bag and unlock the door.

"You have to have a bath first," I tell her.

"Oh, do I?" she answers.

"Yes!" I try to put a stern look on my face, but she leans over to kiss me. "That's enough of that right now," I say. She puts her bicycle in the hall and I take her helmet and gloves. I set them on the table by the door.

"Will I have the pleasure of your company in my bath?" she asks me.

"Not this time," I tell her. "Get yourself a towel."

I can hear her moving around in my bedroom as I go to draw her bath. I listen as she undresses. My breathing gets heavier as I imagine watching her. I love the curve where her thigh meets her belly, the shape of the muscle there, the softness of her inner elbow, the line of breast to armpit. I pour a packet of bath salts under the tap and watch the steam rise from the surface of the water, watch as the water is obliterated by a carpet of bubbles.

She tries not to make any noise as she walks into the bathroom, but the hairs on the back of my neck whisper of her movements.

I rise and turn to take the towel from her. I kiss her, her lips, her eyes, her neck. I take one earlobe into my mouth, then move to the other. "I'll be back shortly," I tell her. "Wait until I come back before getting into the bath." She rewraps herself in the towel.

I walk into my room. Her cycling clothes are neatly folded at the foot of my bed. The cedar of the chest lightly scents the air. I undress slowly, take my time hanging my clothes in the closet.

I pick up the few clothes that are lying around. I pull on my robe and belt it loosely.

She is leaning, wrapped in the towel, against the wall. "Okay, lady," I say. "Give me your towel." She unwraps herself. She takes her time. I hang the towel on the hook on the back of the door. "You can get in now," I tell her.

I take a washcloth from the closet and drape it over the edge of the tub, roll up the sleeves of my robe and dip the cloth in the water. I unwrap a new bar of soap and lather up the washcloth. I take one of her hands in mine and wash her arm. I soap her back. I wash her breasts, her thighs, her feet. I rinse her off leisurely. I wash her face for her. I rinse it off, and kiss the water from her eyelids. "Stand up," I tell her. I take the towel from the hook and begin to pat her dry.

"What is the surprise?" she asks me. "Was it in the bag you had?"

"Yes," I tell her. "Yes. Follow me." I bow and gesture toward the door.

"May I have the towel?" she asks. I have returned it to the hook.

"No. Just come with me."

"Any time," she whispers.

Smiling, I follow her into my room. The Filene's bag sits in the middle of my bed. She looks at me, then at the bag. She stands on the rug beside my bed. Her feet sink into the plush so I can see only the tops of them. I open the bag and reach in while I watch her. She looks at the bag, then at me. Our breasts rise and fall in unison.

I pull out four boxes and place them in a row on the bed. "I am going to open them for you," I tell her. I take the small flat box, and sit on the edge of the bed in front of her. I take the lid off and slowly unfold the layers of tissue. They rustle beneath my fingers. From this box I draw a pair of light grey stockings. They are silk, seamed. They wrap themselves around my fingers. She says nothing, just looks at them, at me.

"Give me your foot," I tell her. She places one foot in my out-stretched hand. I rest it on my knee as I roll up one stocking. I smooth it up her leg, adjusting the seam. I place her foot back on the floor, roll up the other stocking, and hold out my hand to receive warm, unclad skin. I bend down and brush her arch with my lips, breathing warmth against her skin. I lick and nibble at her arch until she leans over, places her hands on my shoulders, and moans. Only then do I slide the stocking over her foot, calf, knee, up her thigh. I place her foot back on the rug. She looks at me, eyes slightly glazed. I know that mine are the same.

I take the second box. My fingers search through tissue as I continue to watch her. I pull out a garter belt. It too is grey, but deep charcoal, almost black. I hold it out. No words are needed. She steps into it and I pull it up to her waist, fasten the stockings and trace the lines of the belt, the straps, with my fingers, then with my lips. I moan as her fingers travel my hairline, root through my hair, tangling, seeking. She begins to push me back on the bed but I stop her as I feel the corner of a box cut into my back, a reminder that I have not finished. I place my hand against her cheek, and she stands, swaying.

The third box contains a pair of shoes. They are soft suede, charcoal, high heeled. She gives me her foot. I place it in the shoe and set it down. She grasps my shoulder for balance as she picks up her other foot. The spike heels sink into the carpet.

She stands in front of me. She sways a little, trying to keep her balance. I run one finger around the top of her stocking, then up the inside of the thigh. I trace her lips with my finger. I slip it inside her, probing, then bring it to my lips to taste her sweetness. "One last box," I tell her as her body involuntarily follows my finger's retreat. "One. Last. Box." I can barely speak. Her nearness threatens to rob me of any thought that is not of her. I reach behind me. This is the largest box. I lift the lid and again unfold layers of paper, this time in haste. I hold up a robe for her. More grey silk. This time, an in-between shade. I stand and move behind her. I slip the robe up to her shoulders and leave it untied.

"Turn around," I tell her. I draw my breath in with a hiss, almost a gasp. "Go look in the mirror," I say, barely able to get the words out. "Do you like it?" She answers by coming to stand in front of me. Our bodies sway toward each other. She guides one of my hands between her legs. Her wetness is all the answer I need.

I remove the boxes from the bed, no longer concerned with neatness. Tissue hisses against itself as I sweep the boxes to the floor. I pull her on top of me as I lie back on the bed. Both our robes are open, breasts rub against breasts as we kiss. My hand creeps across her buttocks and down between her legs. She moans into my mouth as I enter her, first one finger, then a second and a third. Her thigh presses against my clitoris. She raises herself up, her knees at my waist, the garters straining as she moves across my belly. I reach up underneath her robe with my other hand to caress her nipples, rolling them between thumb and forefinger.

"May I go down on you?" I ask. I always ask her when we make love if I may eat her.

"Oh, please," she moans to me, already changing positions. My fingers do not lose their place within her. We are two fish sliding against each other in shallow water. I lean down between her legs to taste her, my fingers continuing their progress, making smooth sucking noises.

I love the taste of her. I rub my face against her lips as they open beneath me, blooming. I moan into her as her foot finds its way between my legs. I tighten my thighs around her ankle and my hips find the rhythm of hers. My arms slide under her legs to pull her against my mouth. I can no longer tell the difference between the noises we make: which are hers and which are mine?

Her clit moves beneath my tongue. As she begins to come, I follow. The surface of my skin has expanded and each touch of silk, of skin, of suede, sends me further out until I am too far to call back. We finish with a passion that will leave bruises.

I crawl up her body to lie on top of her. We kiss, and she licks herself from my face. We kiss again and I bury my face in her shoulder. We float off into sated sleep with small noises of contentment.

Later we wake briefly. She places the shoes on the floor, and we crawl beneath the blankets, skin warming skin. We curl around each other, two small animals curved body to body, breast to back. We sleep again.

Work and Play in the New Age

Marcy Sheiner

A few years ago, I was working for New Age Enterprises, a company that operated a mail order catalog of consumer goods for the "hip" generation — everything from camping gear to vitamins. The whole idea had been conceived and executed by one Jason Banks, a guy who had dropped out in the late '60s but had returned to the corporate world with all his business sense intact. I was Jason's secretary, or, to put it more accurately, his office wife.

Jason fascinated me from the start. Despite his soft, gentle manner, he exuded authority and, without much effort, got people to do what he wanted. For instance, although the pay scale at New Age was scandalously low, Jason managed to inspire his staff to put in incredibly long hours through a combination of wit, charm, and sophisticated double talk. Because he himself was such a workaholic, Jason's employees felt guilty if they didn't work more than eight hours a day.

No one was ever paid for overtime, but no one seemed to

mind; the highlight of the week came, in fact, when Jason would put down his pen late at night, lean back in his chair, and begin speaking in his soft, melodious voice. Slowly the workers, most of whom were bright, attractive women, would stop whatever they were doing and gather around Jason's chair. The subject could be almost anything, from the operation of the company to the results of the latest local election; it didn't matter what Jason spoke about, he commanded instant attention.

Although I spent my first few months on the job trying to observe all this with objectivity, I was not immune to Jason's charms. He wasn't exactly good-looking, but his sea-green eyes held my attention. His lean, hard, and energetic body rarely suggested sexual overtures; rather, it seemed that the manner in which Jason assumed control was what excited women most.

As the months progressed, I became less and less analytical about Jason, and more and more responsive to his needs. I would find myself anticipating his wishes: pulling a file before he asked for it, ordering his lunch without his suggesting it, bringing him little gifts of fruit and home-baked cookies. He was always extremely appreciative, and he constantly praised my work, which spurred me on to do more for him. I would happily work until after midnight, even if it meant cancelling a date. I learned to adjust my schedule to adapt to Jason's. I wanted only to give to this man who worked so hard and for whom I had so much respect.

Gradually my sexual desires entered the picture. Jason would be dictating a letter, and I'd lose a whole sentence, imagining his hands on my breasts. Or he'd sit next to me to show me something, and the hair on my arms would become electrified by his nearness. Or we'd be walking down the hall, Jason hurrying along as always, me running after him, and I'd suddenly be seized with the urge to run my hands along his hips, an urge so powerful I thought I'd faint with the effort to restrain myself.

When I wasn't working for Jason I was dreaming of him, sweet warm dreams in which we slept naked beside each other. Or I was masturbating, fantasizing about him fucking me on the office couch, my desk, standing behind a closed door. I knew it could be a total disaster to fuck the boss. I weighed the arguments pro and con day and night. I stopped seeing other men, girlfriends, my family. I never went anywhere except to work. I no longer had any other interests in life: Jason Banks had become my obsession.

One night he and I were working late. Everyone else had miraculously gone home.

"Let me see the layout of page twelve," Jason ordered from across the room.

I fetched the copy and brought it to him, noticing that his shoulders were hunched with tension. Without thinking about it, I followed my instinct and began massaging his neck and shoulders. He moaned softly as I rubbed and kneaded his stiff muscles. After a few minutes I realized that I was touching Jason in more than a friendly manner. I knew that I should stop, but I couldn't. I loved him, and felt so devoted to him, that I wanted nothing more in all the world than to serve him, to ease all his troubles and pain.

I let my hands move down along his arms, sighing as I ran them over his biceps, then rubbed my fingers along his spine, massaging each vertebra. Love poured through my body and flowed out through my hands. I could have massaged Jason all night without ever tiring. He turned and put his arms around me. My breasts were level with his mouth, and he unhesitatingly opened my blouse to suck on them.

He led me to the couch across the room, lay me down and undressed me. I spread my legs and plunged my fingers into my steaming cunt, watching Jason's response. He unzipped his pants and pulled them off. I'd often wondered what Jason would look like naked. Because he was skinny, I'd feared he'd have a small prick. I needn't have worried. Jason's cock was big and hard, and now it throbbed and pulsated inches from my face. He remained standing, holding his penis with one hand while I lapped at it like a hungry little puppy. But I could see how hard it was for Jason to relax, so I sat up and pushed him gently onto the couch, forcing him to lie back while I attended to him.

A workaholic to the end, Jason couldn't just lie back and allow himself to be pleasured. He kept touching my clit, my tits, almost as if he felt an obligation to do so.

"Jason," I said, jumping up. "Stay right here. Don't move. I'll be back in a minute." I dashed down the hall to the supply closet, found a long piece of rope and ran back to him.

"What are you doing?" he asked, only half protesting, as I began tying his hands together.

"I'm going to force you to allow me to give you pleasure. Without your lifting so much as a finger."

His lips crinkled at the corners in a half-smile. I finished tying his hands, then bound his ankles together. Finally, I picked up my silk scarf and rammed it into his astonished mouth. I stood back for a moment to survey my handiwork: there on the couch lay my boss, completely helpless, completely at my mercy. For once, Jason Banks was powerless.

I resumed my ministrations to his cock, which had grown at least an inch as a result of his captivity. I luxuriated in the opportunity to take my time, and licked his prick over and over from shaft to head before actually taking it into my mouth and sucking. When I finally did, I pushed it as far down my throat as it would go. As I sucked, I ground my hips and clit against Jason's leg, getting hotter and wetter until, as I sensed he was about to spill his hot cum into my mouth, I came. I needed to have him inside my cunt, and hurriedly sat on top of him, shoving his cock in to the hilt. He groaned, a low throaty animal sound muffled by the scarf. His eyes, the only outlet for his feelings, bulged, as his cock shot load after load of cum, bathing my cunt with its thick sweet juices.

I moaned as a second orgasm overtook me. My tits ached to be squeezed; since Jason's hands were tied, I had to do it myself. The sight of me coming, squeezing my own stiff nipples, must have driven him wild, because he immediately became erect again and, struggling within the confines of his bindings, thrust his pelvis vigorously up and down until he came once more, shooting into my welcoming belly. Finally I collapsed on top of him and, raining tender kisses upon his face, removed the scarf from his mouth. He used his new freedom to kiss me in appreciation and whispered, "Next time I'll tie you up."

I didn't care who tied up whom, just that there be a next time. And so there was. The next morning, Jason circulated a memo saying that since the company couldn't afford to pay overtime, he was instituting a policy that everyone leave at five sharp. Thereafter we fucked every night, in every possible location: on the desk, in the swivel chairs, on the floor, standing up in his closet, or behind the toilet stall. He tied me to the chair; I chained him to the desk.

Meanwhile, the staff, losing interest in the company without Jason's midnight talks, began to find better-paying jobs elsewhere. To cut costs, Jason and I moved in together and began running the business from home. Eventually we expanded our catalog to include a full line of sexual toys, every one of which is personally pretested by the President and Vice-President of New Age Enterprises.

Love Object

A. Gayle Birk

I have been told about and read about the one I must find and make mine. She has been described as electrifying, pulsating, and totally undemanding. I continued trying to convince myself that to be with her would fill the empty spaces in my life. To be touched by one such as her could mean an end to lonely, endless weekends without touch or conversation. I should find someone to bring me into life as I imagined I wanted to be, to turn to, to give to, take from, and be accepted by for myself. Long ago I resigned from the world. I simply could not relate to those who made demands.

My fantasy sustains me. The thought of meeting the one so deliciously described to me, one I am assured will come to me if I just make it happen, is almost more than I can stand. My vagina becomes wet and warm, my skin feels soft, touchable, and my eyes look brighter as I smile at my mirror reflection. Looking at my body is not an overwhelming event, but I explore it sometimes and even let go enough to stroke my breasts, my pubic hair, my buttocks. The sensation pleases me, but I never thought I could give myself pleasure; there has to be another, perhaps the one described to me by my two friends — my only friends.

When they first told me about this beauty I blushed. They laughed. They said to be touched by one so giving could at first be an embarrassment, but that would be short-lived when it became apparent that my passion would not possess me, and would not have to be called upon unless I so desired it. This lovely, my friends assured me, was the kind that we falsely convince ourselves could never make us happy. One who gives only when asked, who makes no demands and who brings ecstasy and delight as you rise to the height of tidal-wave orgasm.

"God," I thought, "I must experience this." But first I had to put aside my guilt for dreaming of fulfillment. My mother told me that sexual desires were sinful, that women were created to please men and would probably never be pleased themselves. I believed her for a long time.

In my quest to get a better education than my forebears, I realized I had lost my desire to communicate. I was tired. I could not cope with demands, so turned off my valves — sexual and social — to work, to study, to be alone and fashion my future. At twenty-six, I am loved by no one, really, except my lonely mother and my two friends who jarred the cogs of my mind regarding the delights of loving without commitment.

My two friends are lesbians, as I believe myself to be. My lifestyle chose me because I knew as it was, my life was a lie. For a long time I have had deep feelings for women, but have never been gently touched. I am afraid and my friends continue to help me find myself. I experience moments of desiring sexual encounters, and those moments are usually in a half-awake, half-asleep state when I realize I am touching myself, caressing myself. The thought of having another's hands on me makes me cringe. Hands want something and I have convinced myself I don't have what might make them happy.

When I shared my feelings with my two friends, they assured me that one day I must meet the one who could help alter such feelings. They told me where to find such a lovely. They assured me that I will be in control — like flicking a switch. I can have her or not have her at my will and she will give to me until I am done. These thoughts have swirled around in my head for many weeks. I finally told them I would seriously consider their suggestion.

I did. I went out just last evening to the place where they said I would find her. And, God, they spoke the truth. She was just a few feet away. I worked myself toward her hoping no one noticed the effect she was having on me. Wouldn't my friends be pleased. Then I was standing so close to her, I could touch her if I chose. But I tried to appear impervious as I stole glances when I knew no one was looking. The place was about to close so few people remained. Boldly I reached out and touched her. Did she smile?

When I walked out of the store she was with me. I had done it! I had asserted myself for something I was convinced would make me happy. I have what I deserve — Vi my new lover; Vi my vibrator.

I snuggled her against my side, my firm grip assuring her safety. As I drove home anxiety replaced my excitement. Could I do what I had in mind to do? Could I risk vulnerability? I reasoned that Vi would not be capable of capturing me; I would control her just as my friends had promised. How could an inanimate object become the aggressor? No way, I assured myself. Nothing and no one could ever do that to me. I was strong. I had practiced being strong so no one, no thing, nothing, could turn me into a puppet.

When I arrived home, I grasped the package lying beside me and pressed it against my breast. My palms grew moist. Why was I so nervous, so frightened? She couldn't talk, she couldn't implore that I give her something I did not have to give.

I tightened my grip even more as I slid the key into the door lock. Still holding Vi, I latched and locked the door and went into my bedroom. I laid her on my bed and slowly and carefully removed her from the box. She had attachments. One for scalp, one for muscles, and one concave rubber attachment for fleshy parts of one's body. That was the one I wanted, I thought. Jesus, was it? My friends forgot that part of their seductive description of Vi. I knew who was who in American history and English literature, but when it came to my own body, I knew little more than location and functions of its parts.

Vi had two speeds. I would start with the low one. One must crawl before one walks. I screwed in the attachment I had assigned as the correct one, then carefully lay Vi on the bed and plugged in her cord. I stared at her as I unzipped my jeans and let them fall around my ankles. I stopped. Did I want to do this?

Again, moisture covered my palms. I must. I stepped out of my jeans and kicked them aside. I moved Vi over and lay beside her. I took her in my right hand, flicked her switch to low and gently placed her against my abdomen. Then millimeter by millimeter, I moved her toward the place I feared would expose vulnerability.

When the rubber concavity touched my clitoris, I gasped and drew her away from me. Then, gently I replaced her, applying no pressure for a few seconds to allow the vibration to play around and occasionally touch my swelling clitoris. My toes flexed, my legs jerked involuntarily. Vi was teasing me. Damn it, she was calling the shots!

No way. I controlled me, my feelings, my responses. I pressed the concavity onto my clitoris. My legs became rigid, my throat constricted. My intellect told me to stop, my human needs ignored the pleas.

My entire body went into a rigor. I relaxed. I dropped Vi. She hummed beside me. I rolled over on my back. Muscles relaxed, I felt a smile form on my lips. Oh, lord. Relaxed. No one talking, not even me. Minutes or perhaps hours passed. I grasped Vi and again she gave me pleasure. Again. Again.

When I glanced at the clock just before falling asleep I noted the time. Midnight. Machine again had won over "man" — woman. Maybe someday a real woman instead of Vi, a real woman instead of my fantasy lover.

Read Me A Story

Kathy Dobbs

Over and over, my concentration wandered from my lover's lips as the noise outside continued. Damn those kids, I thought, as my tongue instinctively answered Sheila's warm mouth. At the same time she was getting heated up, I was getting close to the end of my rope.

"Could we put some music on?" I asked quietly, trying not to break the mood she was swimming in. It took a second for the words to register; it wasn't always easy to jump from sex mode to reality on such short notice. Suddenly she nodded, and got up off the bed. I took the opportunity to use the bathroom and get a drink of water. For some reason, I just couldn't let myself go tonight. I needed, and indeed wanted, to immerse myself in the mood, the sensuality she and I had together, but I was having trouble even getting my feet wet. Sheila noticed my distraction when I came back into the room.

"Is something wrong?" I was almost afraid to say anything, not wanting to disappoint her. Lovemaking was always beautiful between us. But I knew I couldn't escape her inquisitive eyes.

"Well, I just can't...those damn kids out there...I don't

know...." I stumbled over myself, sitting down next to her beautiful outstretched body. I idly laid my hand on her breast, liking the way the soft flesh felt under my palm.

"Why don't we have a drink?" she suggested.

A few moments later we were naked on the couch, wine glasses in hand. The cool pink liquid warmed my throat. I liked this room of our apartment best. Done in deep blues and browns, it was always the darkest room in the house. Now it was lit with candles and soft-light lamps; the smell of burning jasmine incense was pleasant but not overwhelming. I allowed myself to relax, trying to forget all the things running through my head — what we needed to pick up at the store, bills we needed to mail, things left unfinished. My mind was on the verge of blankness when I spotted the book on the coffee table.

As a couple, Sheila and I were perfectly matched — we both had a passion for the new and exciting, and erotica was no exception. We indulged in new toys, vibrators, creams, even racy comic books. Now I picked up the small freebie paperback that had come with the last shipment from our favorite mail-order sex catalogue. I hadn't even bothered to look at this one, having been sorely disappointed with the last book, which had an equally corny title. These books were written by men, whose views of sex, and of women's sexuality in particular, never ceased to amaze me. My opinion of their ideas might have been biased because I am a lesbian; but I had slept with men, and had found it ridiculous how many of the important details of lovemaking these writers left out.

My lover was at the other end of the couch, reading some magazine. I opened the book. She glanced over at me and smiled. The book's title was *Stud On The Loose*, and the front cover showed a young girl with everything spilling out of her T-shirt. As I began to read, I found that the main character didn't waste any time getting laid.

So, do you want to get fucked? asked Mr. Stud of one of his many lovers. I thought it rather silly of him to ask, seeing that he had her tied spread-eagled on the bed with a gag in her mouth. He didn't wait for an answer as he took his place and plunged into her. Though it was difficult to be sure of her opinion, he obviously thought she was enjoying herself, and continued to thrust into her.

Yes...yes don't stop. Oh, he feels so good inside me. I can feel his cock head against my tight muscles as he pulls himself all the way out then plunges in again...ummmm. Deeper, yes, deeper. Hard, hard, pump me pump me pump that hard cock of yours into my pussy, baby....

He stopped. With his cock still buried deep inside her, he stopped. Reaching over, he untied her legs one at a time. He gave her a quick slap on the thigh and turned her over, her ass in the air, on her knees.

Something inside me stirred, deep. I felt the girl's anticipation deep inside my own body. I knew what he would do, and I knew how it would feel, and I wanted it.

He reached around to her breasts, taking them in his hands, his stiff penis pushing against her ass cheeks. His fingers took hold of her nipples, rubbing and squeezing, and she moaned deeply.

I could feel it. I could feel the stabs of pleasure running through her body, exploding in her clit. Waves of sweet honey ran through her, through me. It wasn't until my free hand brushed against the book that I noticed it was my own fingers rubbing my nipples, sending warm stirrings to my own womanhood. I continued reading, and rubbing....

Yes, you like that, don't you? I bet your pussy is so hot for my prick. Can you feel it? Can you feel my cock against you? Oh, but you want it inside you, don't ya, baby. You on your knees with your cute ass up in the air, your pussy just dripping wet and wanting it. Yes, yes...

Yes, yes please...his hands on my ass, kneading my cheeks with his strong hands...something warm and wet on my ass, licking, yes his tongue...oh, ooh.

He licked her ass, paying special attention to the tight flesh of her asshole, feeling her tense up as he plunged the tip of his tongue into her, then loosen. She moaned as he worked it in circles, in and out. He knew how wet her pussy would be once he entered her. And when his cock wouldn't let him hold off any longer, he plunged.... You like it slow? So you can feel all nine inches of me enter you? Or fast? Fast and deep...oh, listen to her moan....

He put his hands on her waist and pulled her back onto his hard cock again and again, fast...then slow, letting her juices overflow onto his pubic hair as he was deep inside her. And he kept on pumping....

No, don't stop...each thrust sweeter and sweeter...getting stronger...it's getting so close...I'm going to come with him fucking me like this, so hard and so fast....

And they came. In one big flourish, that climactic moment when the blood pounds in your ears and your body starts to tingle. It starts at your toes, and climbs, and explodes through you. Wave after wave of delight, your body tensing and relaxing, rising and falling. That point beyond reality, beyond consciousness, when the world disappears and all that matters is the supreme intensity of the orgasm overtaking your body, your mind....

I wanted to feel those waves. I wanted to crash against the shore of an orgasm and let it take me.

As the plot of the book simmered down, and Mr. Stud was on his way to finding another girl to lay, I realized I had been nearly holding my breath during their lovemaking, and I let out a sigh. Sheila looked over at me, smiled, then noticed my hand still on my breast, gently massaging it.

"Was it good?" she asked quietly, nearly whispering. Her smile told me of her amusement, but her eyes registered passion. I felt slightly foolish, and blushed. Her eyes were growing intense. I smiled quickly and went back to my book. There were times, such as this, when the intensity of her stare was too much even for me.

So once again I joined Mr. Stud on his hunt. But he barely had his new conquest undressed when I felt Sheila's hand on my leg. Every one of her five fingers sent its own message to my body. Each place her hand touched tingled. I was amazed and excited, and I looked up at her. She was still reading her magazine, a mood of nonchalance about her. It seemed she had no idea what her touch was doing to me. Yet she felt my eyes on her, and smiled.

"Go on, keep reading." She said it quietly, sweetly, but with an edge of control. It was an order, and I turned my eyes back to the page in front of me.

As Mr. Stud buried his face between his new girl's legs, she moaned for him to lick her sweet, swollen clit. Her breathing quickly turned to panting, her moans grew more insistent. I was beginning to pant a little myself as the action continued, for behind the black and white of the page were my lover's fingers, edging up my legs, closer and closer to that ache between them. My fingers moved from one nipple to the other, painting circles on my erect points with my fingertips. The sensations became overwhelming, and I closed my eyes, letting out a soft moan to show my pleasure. Sheila's voice startled me.

"Keep reading. Out loud." I opened my eyes in surprise. Surely she was joking. But her face showed no amusement. There was not even the hint of a smile on her lips, and her eyes were demanding. I realized that she was serious.

"I can't...I mean, you're not really..." I stopped in mid-sentence, my mouth hanging open. As stupid as I must've looked, she didn't smile. Her eyes grew even colder, and her hand on my inner thigh began to tighten.

"Do it," she replied quietly, adding a quick pinch to her grip. I wasted no time in beginning my recitation. I knew from experience that she wouldn't hesitate to spank me, bringing her hand down hard on my exposed ass. So I read....

His tongue flicked over her clit, back and forth. He could taste her juices, sweet and warm, and worked his tongue in and out of her entrance. She moaned, squirming on the couch. Suddenly he put his hands underneath her thighs and lifted her up so that his tongue was now in her ass. She cried out, but as his tongue continued to push into her, her cries became moans of pleasure. Her fingertips brushed her clit, and she began stroking her aching need....

I had to stop, if for nothing else but to catch my breath. As I read, Sheila had spread my legs wide, and now her fingers were inside my wetness, rubbing circles on my own hard clitoris. The sensations were so strong I had to close my eyes and give in to them. But when she noticed the interruption she stopped her movement. I looked up into her angry eyes. One again I turned to the page.

He reached down and began unzipping his jeans, releasing his huge, stiff cock. Watching her get herself off had made him as horny as ever, and he could barely wait to put his dick inside her. She looked startled as she caught the first glance of his organ. He was proud of his nine inches, and the way he knew how to use them.

He positioned himself between her legs, taking his cock in his hand and moving it along her wet slit, rubbing her clit with the purple swollen head. She was moaning for him to enter her, and he suddenly obliged, thrusting his full length into her with one quick motion. She very nearly screamed....

I could no longer go on; for as Mr. Stud entered his teenage prey, my lover had plunged three fingers into my very wet and aching pussy. She pumped in and out hard, deep, and I dropped the book onto the floor. This time she didn't make me continue. She knew I was too far gone with her fucking me. My hips began rising in rhythm with her thrusts, pushing her even deeper.

"You want more, don't ya, babe?" she asked between my cries.

"Y-yes, pl-please...." I stuttered, not really wanting her to stop, but knowing that what she had in mind would be even better. She took my hand and laid it between my legs, urging me to rub my clit as she slipped into the bedroom. When she returned, I opened my eyes to see her holding one of our dildos, a nice eight inches glistening with lubricant. I sighed in anticipation, and she sat down between my legs and began rubbing the head along my lips.

She very slowly entered me, letting me feel all eight inches, until she reached my cervix. I had temporarily stopped playing with myself to enjoy the intense sensations as she again, very slowly, pulled it out. Her beat got faster, and my fingers helped build me to a frenzy. I could feel the waves of pleasure getting stronger and stronger.

Just as I felt right on the edge of my orgasm, she stopped. "I know you want it, baby. Turn over," she commanded softly. I obeyed, moving to my knees. The scene from the book flashed in my mind — the girl getting fucked doggy-style by Mr. Stud. The pictures in my head turned me on even more, as I anticipated the dildo entering me from behind.

I didn't have long to wait as Sheila got into position and thrust inside me. Her free fingers reached around to rub my clitoris, and I thought I would faint.

"Yes, baby, that's it. I want you to come for me. I want you to let it take you, sweetie," she said as she pumped faster. "Doesn't this nice hard cock feel good inside you? Yes, you like to get fucked from behind, don't you? Feels so good, so strong...."

It was coming closer. I could feel it. To me, it was like nearing the edge of a cliff, step by sweet step, until finally you reach it...and fall. I was falling. My body was shaking. There was always that moment of fear, the fear of forever falling, and she was always there to catch me. To hold me tight until the spasms stopped shaking me, to tell me she loved me and soothe my refreshed, dream-dazed body.

Wet Silk

Edna MacBrayne

The bronze doorbell was cast in the shape of a human breast. That small touch of wit calmed some of my apprehension, but to tell the truth, I was pretty much of a corporate-urban wreck. My colleagues saw my malaise long before I did, and must have dropped a hint or two close to the seat of power. The arrangements to bring me here were made quickly and with discretion. I was given no choice. "Just go," they said, "and you'll come back a new person."

The front door was open, letting in a warm breeze. I walked into the entry hall, and though not surprised at the elegance, found it reassuring. A magnificent Lachaise nude dominated the hall. It was the one of a figure with her arm raised, beckoning. It looked as light as milkweed and as perfect as an egg.

I heard the click of heels on the stone floor and saw an attractive woman come toward me. "Good morning," she said. "We're so glad to have you here." Her manner was that of someone who thoroughly enjoys entertaining. She gestured for me to follow her through an atrium filled with flowering plants and a small fountain. After leading me through a series of pleasantly disorienting corridors, she opened a door and ushered me into a room. "This is where you can change and relax. You'll find robes in the closet and we'll bring you some refreshments." As she was going out the door, she added, "Take as much time as you want, and when you're ready, go outside and follow the path." Then she took my hand in hers, and said, with a smile that would melt rock, "I hope you enjoy your stay here," and left.

The room was comfortable, furnished with restraint and care as elsewhere in the building. But I was still feeling awkward and nervous. It seemed a bit foolish to be all alone in the midst of this luxury. I was looking out through the wall of sliding glass when a nice looking fellow came into the room with a tray. "If you want anything more, please ring," he said, pointing to a bell, then disappeared before I could thank him.

Getting out of my clothes improved my attitude. I reached into the closet and pulled out a finely batiked kimono. It was as light as a breath. When I put it on it felt like nothing, except that the soothing silk against my skin made me shiver.

I sat down at the table and looked at the tray of food the young man had left me. A soft cheese oozed from its rind. There was paté, crusty bread, and a dish of black olives, as well as a small crystal vase holding pink anthuriums. I poured myself some champagne and felt myself beginning to lounge instead of sit. A grin formed in my toes and wiggled its way up to my face. I cut a chunk of the butter-smooth paté, spread it on some of the bread and bit into it.

With the glass of wine in hand, I walked over to the window to take a look outside. It was impossible to see the extent of the grounds, because of the profuse plantings of shrubs and flowers; however, I could make out two figures, one resting on the grass and the other diving into a natural pool. The scene was idyllic — and a little unnerving. I wondered if I would be able to trust them. I gulped some more wine and realized I was back to my old habits, so I sat down at the table again and nibbled a bit of cheese. I was careful to sip the champagne.

Life was better already. I was much more relaxed, but still the idea of taking a casual stroll outside wearing nothing but a thin robe, and then getting closely involved with two people I'd never met — well, that seemed more than a little alien to me. On the other hand, maybe it was time for me to loosen up, to let my life just happen. Besides, I was curious — and it had been paid for in advance.

This train of thought got me outside the glass doors and into the garden. It smelled wonderful. With only the silk brushing my skin, I was weightless and smooth as I walked to the garden pool.

The two of them were still as I had seen them from the window; one lounging on the grass and the other in the water. Neither wore any clothes.

"Come in for a swim," they invited me.

"How warm is it?" I asked, dreading the thought of cold water.

"It's perfect. If you don't believe it, test it with your toe."

I stuck my foot in. It was perfect. I let the kimono slide to the ground and waded in, surprised to find a sandy bottom. "Is it always this warm?" I asked, surrendering my body to the buoyancy.

"Winter and summer. It's fed by thermal jets. Like it?"

"It's heaven."

The one on the grass let out a sigh. "It's better than heaven because there's no harp music, but I'm confronted by the terrible decision of whether to stay here and roast or immerse myself in the cooling waters. Life is a burden."

"Why don't you be sociable? We have a guest," said the one in the water.

With that, the third body splashed into the pool. It wasn't a large pool. I expected there would be some tentative physical contact, but the light touches I felt were obviously inadvertent. I was pleased by this. It gave all three of us a chance for verbal play and a way to get to know each other. I was beginning to trust them already.

I felt my shoulders loosen and my foot spring with delight as it passed over one of the jets feeding water from the bottom. My progressive relaxation must have been obvious, because my playmates suggested that they give me a massage. That sounded inviting, so we got out of the pool, dried off, and then they led me to a padded ledge built out from the hillside. I hopped on and lay down on my stomach with the sun warming my back. I felt a trickle of liquid down my spine.

"We're using pure mineral oil for a very good reason. You'll find out later."

They rubbed oil into my skin from neck to feet and then began to search for knots of tension. It was a strange sensation. One of them started with my hands and the other with my feet; their intention being, I suppose, to meet somewhere in the middle. As they rubbed and kneaded I felt like a poorly mixed batch of bread dough, full of lumps. "Am I a basket case?" I mumbled.

"Your body is about as relaxed as a steel girder, but let's not talk now. We'll fix it."

They were gentle, but as they got rid of one group of lumps they'd go deeper and find more clusters of tight knots to annihilate with their persevering fingers. I lost track of time. I no longer felt like a giant loaf of bread. Now I was a dipper full of hot fudge sauce being poured on warm cake. I couldn't see what they were doing, but I could feel them moving around me, sometimes accidentally brushing my body with a forearm as they changed positions. There was an occasional swirl of hair against my skin and their touch became lighter, less probing.

Nothing mattered. I was boneless, weightless, and completely under their power.

Their shift in emphasis did not disturb me in the slightest as their playful hands explored my body. They pulled on my fingers and toes to test for any residual tension, and when they found none they began to tease me with their fingers. These were not caresses. There was still strength behind their touch, but the signal was not therapeutic anymore. One rubbed my shoulders while the other rubbed my calves. They acquainted me with bunches of nerve endings I never knew existed in my elbows and knees. Their touch was as delicate as a bubble. Mentally, I purred. I felt the onset of desire.

Thumbs glided down either side of my spine and went back up again. The palms of soft hands stroked the insides of my thighs, never going up as far as I hoped they would, but traveling all the way to my heels and toying with my ankles.

It went on forever. Time was lost, and space became small pockets of my flesh that kept melting.

When they resorted to using only their fingertips, I was fully aroused. I wanted them to climb all over me and cover my body with theirs. I needed their lips and tongues on me in a silky ooze of oil and saliva. My hand reached out to beg them for more, but in an unbroken, lingering stroke four hands coursed down my body. One of them said, "That's enough for now. We want you to join us in a light meal."

A soft moan escaped me. The last thing in the world I wanted was a light meal. I was in the mood for a royal feast of arms and legs and hips. I wanted tongues and lips and fingers, not cheese and crackers. The second one patted me on the rear end and said, "Come on. It'll be more fun than you think. Besides, we're thirsty."

I could hardly argue with that, so I pulled myself up and followed them to a linen tablecloth that had been spread on the grass. In the center of the cloth was a large lazy susan filled with bowls of food and bottles of drink. There were no plates, forks, spoons, or glasses.

"How are we supposed to eat?" I asked.

"Any way you like," they answered.

Each of them tipped bottles of mineral water into their mouths as I sank down on the tablecloth. I wanted to eat quickly and get back to where we had left off. Without much enthusiasm I picked up a spear of asparagus and chewed on it. Most of the food looked as though you would at least need a spoon to eat it.

"Here, try some chicken salad." A hand bearing what looked like a bunch of noodles appeared in front of my nose. "Open your mouth. You'll like it." I tilted my head back and tried to get most of it into my mouth. Inevitably, a few strands of noodles escaped and slithered down my chin. As I sucked them up I began to taste the wonderful combination of ginger, soy, garlic and bean thread. There were even a few morsels of chicken.

"It's delicious," I sputtered through a full mouth, "can I have a napkin?"

"There aren't any," came the reply.

Like a kid, I wiped my mouth and chin with the back of my hand and then rubbed it down my thigh. They both laughed and offered me some wine.

I was trying not to glug down the wine too rapidly when one of them said, "Hold out your hand." I did, and immediately found it garnished with a thick dollop of whipped cream. On top of that went a plump blackberry.

"Thank you," I said, and raised my arm to eat it off my hand. My palm had no sooner reached my mouth when I felt something touch my right nipple. It was a bit of mayonnaise. "Glue,"

I was informed. With this ingenious adhesive a small shrimp and a piece of parsley created a miniature still life on my chest. Still holding my handful of whipped cream, I heard one of them declare, "It's a genuine work of art."

"I agree," said the other one, "but it's asymmetrical. We should do the other side."

And so I was made symmetrical with additional mayonnaise, shrimp, and parsley. The designer said, "You know, that looks good enough to eat," and with lips and tongue, gobbled it off me.

"Aw, now you've ruined it," said the other one, plastering more glue on me and restoring the artful theft. Most of the shrimp was used up this way as I sat contentedly licking whipped cream off my hand while the two of them discussed the merits of my right and left nipples as flavoring agents for seafood or armatures for sculpture.

"The right one has a piquant taste and surprising firmness," proclaimed gourmand number one.

"The left one has a musky flavor and a superior spongy texture," argued art critic number two.

In an effort to settle the dispute they decided to test other areas of my body and requested that I lie down so they could continue their experiment. I was not opposed to this idea, so with a towel for my pillow, I spread myself full length on the tablecloth with another handful of cream and some fresh, ripe strawberries.

I was completely unaware that my body held the marvels now being discovered. My companions had begun to cooperate with each other by this time. They reminded me of shoppers comparing the quality of caviar or fine cheese.

"Have you tried stuffed mushrooms in crook of elbow?"

"No, I'm still testing meatballs in hollowed out shoulder." The mushroom one then sucked wine from my navel while the meatball aficionado spread pork in peanut sauce on my thigh. They took their time with every bite of food, prolonging the act of removing it from my skin with their lips and tongues.

"Now do you see why we insist on using mineral oil?"

"Whoever invented plates and cutlery was a cold, unfeeling wretch," commented the other.

I just lay there with a scrutable grin on my face, shuddering with pleasure as they did remarkable things to my knees with egg and olive salad. To be this passive while being amused and aroused all at the same time was something I never thought possible for myself. But here I was, a human platter watching two amiable and creative people nibble on me. I had a difficult time remaining still, especially when they began dessert.

Slowly they spooned the rest of the whipped cream onto the triangle between my legs. This they studded with fruit. They began to eat, delicately at first, making comments on the freshness of the fruit and the sweetness of the cream. It was all very correct. From the conversation, one almost would have thought we were at a formal dinner party.

Once the fruit was gone and there was nothing left but dripping cream rapidly losing its air content, they started to suck and slurp and use their fingers. I seemed to have hands and mouths all over me, charging my body with a special urgency. That fundamental rhythm, my heartbeat, grew stronger and quickened as if I were running. I clutched for a companion and one of them came to me in an embrace, kissing me with a passion that spoke of mutual arousal. We clung together and I squirmed with delight at feeling the completeness of a whole body next to me.

The fingers and tongues never stopped. They explored creases and crevices, hollows and bulges. They skittered across some areas and lingered, probing in others, inserting wands of pleasure unexpectedly. My body, the former serving platter, had been turned into a musical instrument being played by two accomplished artists.

I throbbed and tingled from the tender friction of their legs, fingers and lips. The groin of one pressed against mine with a solid beat. The tip of a tongue searched inside my nostril for a more sensitive membrane. Each of my hands held its fill of warm soft flesh that I ached to suck, but squeezed gently instead.

We had adopted a single rhythm, moving together. Our breath came faster as we ground our bodies furiously into each other's, rubbing, squeezing, licking, twisting this way and that to find the end solace for our need. Inhibitions abandoned and faces skewed in ecstasy, we pulsed our way past the plateau and rushed to leap into the liquid. Like three pieces of wet silk slithering together in a circle, we were one large organ bursting with a single melody. It roared through us, a cataclysm, about to drench us in release.

At last there was no holding back. We exploded into rich

spasms of flood-like orgasm, making us buck, tremble, and moan as the tension broke through our forms. We held on to the beauty we had created until we began to float, glide, and hover in a state of benign sanctity. Naked, simple, and free, we touched each other with reverence.

Our communion continued in quiet; our bodies now on the grass, dappled in shadows of leaves as the sun tracked its way across the sky. We curled into one another with small, reassuring pats, like children sleeping on the back porch in summer. None of us wanted to get up. The luxury of skin touching skin was still with us, not easily abandoned. With lazy pleading we finally persuaded the one closest to the beverages to reach for a bottle of water that we shared. Drinking necessitated sitting up and from there it was a quick step to dipping some towels into the pool so we could clean each other off. We agreed to a swim. While in the pool I realized that the day was far from over.

"What are we going to do after we get out of the pool?" I asked.

"Oh, we'll think of something," one replied knowingly.

"Yes," said the other, "but first we must have some tea."

The Sensuous Housewife

Bonnie Stonewall

I'm camping atop a cliff. The lawn chair I'm holding down with my butt is the only one around to remain upright during this latest weather tantrum folks here call the Santa Ana wind. Nature seems to go into a daily snit for a few hours in the afternoon. Perhaps in protest of humanity's crass disregard of the blessings of this earth, the Santa Ana sees to it that anything that isn't rooted to the ground is swept away into the abyss. The rugged beauty of this spot is, unfortunately, a last vestige of natural splendor in an area that has been raped by weekend "naturalists." Pavement, motorboat launches, and waterslides have managed to supplant deer trails, the lone canoe, and the thundering waterfall. The land is pockmarked with tents and RVs — the Los Angeles of public campgrounds. As I sit here alone in my summer vacation estrangement, I wonder what a sensualist is to do but retreat into fantasy?

It's become a silly game I play while my husband and children are off fishing or swimming or hiking — trying to decide which of the three T-shirts I've brought on this retreat will make me — a bisexual housewife and mother — most identifiable to the others at the campground. I hope they'll perceive me as I perceive them — the honeymoon couple, the pretty blonde in white shorts brushing her teeth at the water pump, the fiery brunette with the scarlet talons at the cash register in the convenience store, the two lady cops outside the police station. They're all hot for it! I know it, I know it! The wheel of fortune in my mind plays a never-ending game of "Dial-a-Dyke."

There are two women camped nearby. They look to be in their early thirties; wholesome-looking tanned, athletic types. They probably love tennis, eat sushi, and wear white cotton underwear. They drive a blue Honda. I have not seen them away from each other once since they arrived here yesterday morning. They walk together discreetly but closely, they sit in front of their tent in matching lawn chairs listening to their tape deck, they disappear into their tent together as the moon becomes bright and full. I like to suppose that they are on their honeymoon. What if one quiet night I followed the deer path down the hill that separates my campsite from theirs and discovered that they like to leave their tent flap unzipped so they can gaze out at the stars? Brazenly, I'd push the flap all the way back and scurry over to straddle a nearby rock and wait.

Their lithe bodies are backlit by a single lantern. I know they cannot see me hiding in the darkness of the woods outside their tent, but I scrunch down on the rock anyway, trying to make myself smaller. My hardening clit makes contact with a delightful ridge in the smooth saddle-like rock as I lean forward to see and hear what's going on. The maidenly quilted bathrobes and flannel P.J.'s they'd worn to the ladies' room a while ago are now lying in a heap just inside the tent door. My eyes widen like an owl, as I watch. The younger woman straddles her lover's body, positioning her sweet, dripping pussy over the older woman's mouth. I see a long, muscular tongue dart up and down, in and around it, like a hypnotized pink snake. I get a good view of the unfolding lips of the other one's lovenest as her lover leans forward to taste it. She slides both hands under her lover's butt as she pushes the tasty morsel to her searching tongue. At first, their "69" is a lazy exercise in mutual pleasuring. Soon enough, though, the bucking and the moaning begin. They roll convulsively onto their sides, their mouths still magnetized to each other's pussies. First one side of the tent and then the other bulges with the outline of their bodies. Lantern light traces eerie, writhing shadows along the wall. Their flushed bodies are wet with sweat. I find that the rock as well as my jeans are soaked. The aroma of three pussies mingles in the chill night air. They turn out the lantern.

I reluctantly dismount my rock, return to my tent and masturbate myself to sleep.

The next morning, I decide to go for a walk along the lakeshore, in spite of a sky filled with charcoal-colored clouds threatening an imminent downpour. I am halfway around the lake from our tent when the rain starts. Instantly, I am drenched. It is only about 6:00 or 7:00 A.M., and there is no sign of life except for the smell of hot coffee from the convenience store. I have no money, but maybe if they see how wet and bedraggled I am, they'll take pity on me and give me a free cup. I'm so cold; it's worth a try.

The only other person in the store is the cashier. Her dark eyes quickly survey my poor, waterlogged body. As I feel her eyes rivet onto my wet blouse, I notice her emotion change from indifference to, shall we say, compassionate lust. She urges me into the back room so that I can remove my soggy clothing. To allow me greater privacy, she says, she'll lock the front door and put the CLOSED sign in the window for a while. She is almost businesslike as she encases my nakedness in a stadium blanket and efficiently whisks my wet clothes over to the laundromat next door to dry. I surmise from the number of keys she's carrying that she is the person in charge. For all I know, she owns the place.

I'm hopping about on bare feet, clutching the blanket tightly around me with one hand, while I hold the very welcome cup of steaming coffee with the other. I feel her amusedly watching my efforts to get warm. I try to act dumb, but I'm too horny to play games for any length of time. When she finally parts the folds in front of my blanket to slide those warm hands around my waist, I offer no resistance.

Her scarlet fingernails are about an inch long, and she draws them firmly but lightly along my spine, my butt and the backs of my thighs. I shiver from more than the cold. We are about equal in height, but because she has shoes on, at least for now, she's taller than I. She holds my chin in one hand and tips my head back. I feel both my breasts being fondled and squeezed.

She rubs and tugs on my nipples expertly, reawakening them to their attentive state of the night before.

She spreads the blanket on the concrete floor, and we lie down. My belly, inner thighs and clit feel so engorged, I instinctively part my legs. My beautiful hostess decides to breakfast on my tongue. She tastes it and sucks it, running her own tongue round and round it and slurping at it like an ice cream cone. I take matters into my own hands (or legs, in this case) and force her skirt up with my right knee. We fit together like a jigsaw puzzle. It doesn't take me very long to find out she isn't wearing panties. Her clit is as hard as mine as we ride each other's legs. My body is dry enough by now for me to know that the stripe of wetness I leave on her thigh has nothing to do with the rain.

I feel something hard just inside her cunt. I realize she's wearing a tampon, and its string is wedged tightly between her body and my leg. With every movement, friction forces it to move back and forth in her hot, hot pussy. She is crying in Spanish now, "Ai, Dios! Ai, Dios!" over and over. We lie there humping and moaning all tangled up in the checkered blanket for what seems like forever.

We've just started in again for maybe the fourth or fifth time, when we hear someone tapping with a key on the glass front door. My lover jumps up reluctantly to rearrange herself to face her second customer of the morning, but not before she ceremoniously kisses each of my nipples farewell.

I sit there, dazed, sipping the now tepid coffee. I'm listening to her waiting on one customer after another. Then she leaves the store for a few minutes, and soon she's pitching my warm, dry clothes at me along with a blown kiss. It's time to go. Adios, baby.

Fatigue seems to soak into every pore of my being until I feel like I'm made of paper towelling. I practically crawl back to my own tent. Half asleep, I notice a new family has moved into the campsite next to ours. It looks like they're all set up already, and the mom has sent the thunderous herd off for a day of fishing. Some mom! She has prematurely grey hair in a French braid down the middle of her back, she is oh so tan, and she's round in all the right places in her khaki safari shorts and matching midriff shirt.

She's taking a few moments for herself while the dish water

boils, sitting at the picnic table leafing through the stack of vacation books and periodicals. She dreamily sucks her index finger
while she gets engrossed in a magazine. Can it be?! It's a
woman's erotic magazine! Yes!

I mentally rub my hands together in anticipation. I stick my
head and upper body out of the tent flap just far enough so she
can see me and wave. "Hi, neighbor!" She looks up with lovely
sapphire eyes and focuses on what is not left to the imagination
inside my carelessly half-buttoned blouse.

Our families are going to be encouraged to go on a lot of fishing trips this week — and swimming and boating — I can tell.

Jane's Train

Lisa LaBia

Coming from the Loop, the Howard was jammed. Jane was lucky to get a seat, even luckier one next to a window. It was one of the old L's, with green and white stickers outlined in red that said *Do Not Stick Head Or Arms Out Of Window*, and who would in late November unless they loved the stench of the underground? The conductor's voice distorted, crackled and clipped off the last syllable of the last word. The train lurched. People fell forward. The lights blinked on, off, then came back on to stay. What would happen if the lights ever stayed out, Jane wondered. Would people get stabbed? Robbed? Maybe raped?

Above ground she rode backwards, watching the street sink below her. Her head against the window, she saw the same things she always saw. Faded Latin Kings graffiti. Ugly turquoise Nova still in the same spot in the junkyard. Back porches peeling grey, loaded down with old refrigerators, kids' bikes, yellowed newspaper, broken glass. The L tracks came so close to the buildings. She imagined what might happen if a train suddenly derailed and smashed right into one of them. Her kitchen window faced west over the tracks and every time a train rolled past the whole building would shake.

"FULLERTON. CHANGE FOR THE RAVENSWOOD. CHANGE FOR THE B TRA —." Jane watched everyone escape. Asian students heading over to De Paul with backpacks and 501s. Wrinkled women wearing babushkas, lugging shopping bags from Jewel. A couple of black guys wearing those white plastic shower caps. Warm mist from everyone's nostrils. Punk rockers in love in matching leather jackets, wasn't that cute? His was falling apart, hers was new just like her messy blonde hair. Red lips, pale face, tons of jewelry on top of black everything and didn't Madonna do that a long time ago? Jane smirked. They smiled. He put his arm around that Blonde waist and squeezed. Perfect lips formed perfect words. The doors slammed. "NO SMOKING OR RADIO PLAYI —." In a frozen second, he saw her dark hair pressed against the glass, those Egyptian eyes. People fell forward. The lights went off.

She opened the door to her apartment, threw her coat on a chair, and lit a cigarette. Usually Jane's random thoughts on the way home from work slipped away as quickly as they came. Not this time. She knew where they were going. To his crummy little place on Walton. To fuck. She loved the thought of it. She had resisted an incredibly childish urge to stick her head and arms out of the train window and scream "FUCK HIM! I DID!" She breathed in the last piece of smoke and put out her cigarette in the tacky ashtray her mother had given her. She watched the glow of the ashes die right on the red heart between I and Chicago.

She flipped on the TV and stretched out on the couch. Her dark hair cut straight across her forehead and then dropped to her shoulders. Eyes outlined in deep blue points did sort of make her look like Cleopatra and she knew it. Queen of Egypt. Satisfied one hundred lovers a night, or so they say. Concentrating on the TV was impossible. The sounds seemed farther and farther away as she slid her hand under her tight red skirt.

They were almost in silhouette, in the kitchen. A red sun melting down the bricks, the glass, dripping onto the tracks outside. Jane could see the shapes of their tongues moving in and out of each other's mouths. The perfect exchange. She liked to start everybody off that way. He circled the Blonde's nipples with his tongue, squeezed them, rubbed them. Jane's hand went to her own breast, under her sweater. Her nipples crinkled up when they got hard.

Fuck the slow removal of clothing, she thought. Go down on the Blonde. Jane wanted to see it. To hear the sounds of licking and sucking and breathing increase. To watch her spread her legs while his tongue drove her crazy. Don't let her come. Tease her. The Blonde pulled him up by the hair to kiss him, to kiss herself. With smooth consistency, she was all over her own mouth, her cheeks. Delicious.

A warm pink flush spread lightly over her chest. The couch was uncomfortable. She got on her knees and made the Blonde do the same. Go ahead. Suck his cock. He brushed the hair away from her face so he could watch. Only traces of red on those lips now, forming perfect O's, again and again, until all of him disappeared. Tell her how beautiful she looks. Tell her how good it feels.

Her fingers had no sensation of their own anymore. They just kept moving faster, soaking wet in tiny circles. All her favorite images repeated themselves. Flashing like a slide show. The words, the things she made them say, she whispered to herself. That familiar sound in the distance wanting her to come. She made them change position until she found one she liked. She wanted them all to come together.

The Blonde felt the cold linoleum on her back, him inside, thumb on her clit. She traced the way the muscles in his arms tensed up. Watching his face and his long hair swing back and forth, imitating their rhythm. Come on. Jane could hear it getting louder now. The vibration spreading out across the floor, up through her body. Fire. The building started to shake. So loud it drowned out all the sound. When the Blonde came. When he came. When the train came. Lasting seconds. Lasting forever.

When she opened her eyes, it was dark. Noise oozing from the idiot box dragged her back to reality. She got up, turned it off, and walked in to the kitchen to get something to eat. The building began to shake, again, but Jane hardly noticed.

Police Protection

Moxie Light

I'd like to be able to say I can smell a hard-on, like hookers and crooks can smell a plainclothesman. But this one was a dead giveaway: macho, from the tip of his curled mustache, down his lean, coiled body to the huge motorcycle buckle on his belt, proclaiming him a "Rider for Justice" on the streets. He was cocky, standing there, proud of his uniform and proud of his badge. As he leaned into the yellow shag of my carpet, thumbs crooked into his belt, inches away from the polished walnut of his gun handle, his fingers unobtrusively caressed the bulging length in his serge.

"What seems to be the problem?" he asked.

I went into my tirade. Child support weeks overdue, robbed, junkies shooting up in the halls, burned-out hulks of cars smoldering on the back streets. Unlike my neighbors, I would never adjust to life in East Boston.

He walked through my living room into the kitchen and opened my refrigerator to see if I was telling the truth. One lonely quart of milk gave witness. The others had been there the night before when I'd reported the robbery. The solid Irish sorts had come that morning, perfunctorily brushing for fingerprints. When this one had come bounding up the stairs, I'd opened the door without a whimper. He introduced himself by his first name — Michael.

"Have you tried welfare?" he asked, with a worried look on his face.

"I don't qualify," I said. My husband was just being spiteful about child support, pressing for a divorce that he'd wanted for years. My five-year-old spent half a day in kindergarten and kept me busy the rest of the time.

"Is there anything I can do for you?"

"My car," I answered. "Please, just don't tow it. I don't have the money to pay for any parking tickets." I didn't really need a car; I never went anywhere. But as soon as I was divorced, I planned to get out of here.

"Here's five dollars," he said. "And my phone number, if you ever need a friend."

I've always hated cops. Sometimes I think I hate cops even more than I hate crooks. I don't like anyone who uses their power for personal advantage. That five dollars made me feel I was selling my soul to the Devil. "I don't want this," I said. "The coffee shop across the street will sport me for breakfast until I can get a loan."

The fiver flew back and forth between us like a feather, until it landed next to a silver-framed picture of a special friend of mine.

"Who's this?" he asked.

Five minutes in my place and this man was delving into my personal life. I didn't like it.

"Please, would you take back the five dollars?" It was humiliating to be this broke.

"Forget it," he said. "I've paid more than that to have someone put their hand on it."

"Out! Out...you wolf in cop's clothing. And if that man..." I pointed to the picture and sputtered, "ever heard you talking to me like that...you...you'd be dead!"

After he left, I worried for weeks about a pervert on the loose. About that sign on me that said I needed a man. The landlord found out I was having trouble paying the rent, and made me the superintendent of the building. After the next robbery, when the next set of cops came, I couldn't keep from asking. "Do you know a Michael? Tall, thin? Vice or narcotics."

"Michael?" They laughed to each other. "You mean, Old Undersheets?"

They were getting to know me at Precinct 7, this hysterical woman on the other end of the phone: seven burglaries, one drunk falling through a first floor window, one overdose and an accidental death, a woman who bled to death while her husband watched television in the next room. Half my tenants were clients at the methadone clinic up the street. As the landlord evicted them, one by one, they blamed me.

I lived in terror, awakened at night by the phone ringing at two, three, and four A.M. with someone who liked to hear my fear-filled voice. My lawyer said that if I moved again before we went to court, the judge would call my home life "unstable," and I would lose custody of my son. I installed a police lock on my door. It had a long iron bar that went into a plate bolted onto the floor, and made a loud grating noise whenever it was used. At six o'clock at night, with all of the locks clunking in my building, it sounded like a lock-up at Alcatraz. Another contraption, of solid steel, was installed in my car, but that didn't keep them from slashing the tires and the convertible top.

Finally, I felt brave enough to press charges for the phone calls. When I walked into the police station, Michael was the cop on the front desk.

"The detectives just went out," he said. "How are things going?" Seeing him made my adrenalin surge.

I began venting my wrath on the zombies at the telephone company who refused to do anything about my late night calls. Michael, with his handlebar mustache, looked like Omar Sharif.

"Do you still have that car with the Florida plates? Do you know you're supposed to re-register after thirty days in this state?"

I gave him a blank look, though I know a veiled threat when I hear one. There had to be a way I could stay on top.

"I'll be over in half an hour," he said. "And we'll see what we can do to make this jungle easier for you."

I went back to my apartment and spent a few minutes putting away my son's playthings. I went into the bathroom to freshen up and run a comb through my damaged hair. My hands trembled as I applied a little makeup and strategic dots of cologne, giving myself a devious wink in the mirror. The victory would be short and sweet. What Michael wanted and what he would get were two different things. For extra bravado, I brought my vibrator out from its hiding place and gave myself a few orgasms, leaning against the bathroom sink.

Michael arrived, and sat on my living room couch, balancing on his knee the cup of coffee that I had ready for him. With his free hand, he patted the couch beside him. His police radio crackled on the coffee table in front of us. "I have to leave it on," he said, apologetically, "in case I get a call."

"All I want to do is survive," I began. "What the hell is going on? Don't you cops ever arrest anybody? One of my tenants, just last week, took off with a refrigerator and stove. The junkie downstairs comes in every night with a different stereo."

"You don't know what it's doing to me," he said, wearily. "When they call us in for the school riots, I have to pop ten Valiums so that some kid doesn't get it between the eyes. The Red Cross even gives us coffee and donuts. Jesus! It was easier overseas."

"Valium?" I hooted. "Even the cops have habits around here. Let me see your arms."

Michael put down his coffee cup and rolled up his sleeves, revealing a thick leather watch band, blue-blooded veins winding snakily up his arm, and several tattoos: Mary, Ann, and Dominique. "I wouldn't know a track if I fell over it," I admitted. "But you sure are one kinky cop with all those tattoos. Are you into S&M?"

"What's that?" he asked, with interest.

"You know, you phony. Whips, chains...."

Michael smiled. "Those tattoos are my sisters' names," he said. "And I can be very gentle. Do you want to try me?" As he rolled down his sleeves, he leaned forward and kissed the bodice of my pinafore. I could feel my nipples straining against the denim.

"Don't you have to be going?" I said, remembering how soft to the touch I had once been. "There are criminals out there on those streets."

"Tell me you don't want me," he said, getting up to draw the drapes. The police radio crackled its garbled jargon. His fingers were at his belt buckle, unzipping his fly. I almost laughed when I saw how ready he was.

"I'm being followed by private detectives," I said, heart pounding, in a last-ditch line of defense.

"All the better," said Michael, as if he knew me better than I did myself. His lips fell soft as rain on mine. His deft fingers rolled my socks down, bringing goose bumps to my knees and tears to my eyes. He was, after all, a public servant and I, when it came down to it, was hungry for affection, if not love. With his foot, Michael pushed the coffee table out of the way. "Tell me you don't want me," he said, enfolding me in his big, strong arms.

"I don't," I whimpered into the hollow of his neck. Then he was kneeling in front of me, with his face in my crotch, blowing short, hot puffs through the silk of my underwear. My hands were on his shoulders, half-pushing him away. One of his fingers inched its way past the elastic on my inner thigh, parting my resistance; his thumb pressed on the tiny, swollen lie.

Tears were pouring down my face as I hid my embarrassment. "I hate you. I hate you," came my muffled cries. Michael pulled me from the couch as if I were a rag doll, all my resistance gone. In one quick motion, he peeled off my underpants and put them on the coffee table next to his revolver. Then he spread my legs and covered me with his body, still fully dressed, kissing my tears and whispering passionately in my ears.

All the while he pressed himself rhythmically into the gnawing ache of my groin. Soon, a wonderful warm wave began radiating through my whole body. An involuntary moan came from my throat as all the pent-up pressures and loneliness began to recede. My hands fell limp by my sides and Michael undressed me.

It was as if I were hypnotized. His fingertips tracing the curves of my body...his touch both electric and sensual...my hips rolling in an unforgettable motion of their own...my breath coming hard and fast as he bent his head to my quivering thighs, licking, licking, with soft little animal sounds, bringing me to a peak of sensation. It was more than I could handle. My mind felt as if it were unhinging, reeling into a starless void.

"Please, please...." I was afraid and the pleasure had turned to pain. I struggled to free myself from his grip, suddenly sitting up, hands flying, not knowing what to cover first.

"Shhh!" said Michael, kissing my eyelids, one at a time. "Let me. You don't have to do anything but enjoy."

"It hurts," I said, not being able to explain, not even under-standing myself how this whole thing had come about. I had never made love to a stranger before.

"You're dry," said Michael, reaching for his handcuffs. "You're shy and I have just the cure." Firmly, with his other hand, he pushed me down, at the same time running the tip of his tongue around one of my nipples, sucking so gently that it made me weak with desire. I shut my eyes as Michael un-dressed. The air was thick with the smell of lust. He cuffed my wrists to the couch.

This time, instead of the tip of his tongue, Michael used his hands, kneading me between the legs, his knowing fingers bringing me to a passion I'd never known, not all my married life. I could feel the faint prick of his whiskers on my swollen lips as he lifted my buttocks to his mouth; heard the sound of his full tongue, over and over, as I became wet. Then he did something with his nightstick which drove me absolutely crazy, moving it in and out, flicking the tip of my clit with his tongue, massaging my breasts, my buttocks, everywhere at once, it seemed, until I begged him to stop. As I struggled against my bonds and squirmed against the long, hard strokes, my whole body broke out in a sweat, so that I could feel the spray flying as I tossed my head from side to side, fighting the powerful force.

"Do you want me yet?" asked Michael, smiling from the heights.

"Untie me, you sadist," I managed to gasp, just before he did exactly that. And with a great deal of thrashing, sweaty-limbed and all, forgetting all propriety, I climbed over Michael and rode him on waves of ecstasy, over and over, up and down, slowing down every time I felt him ready to explode, then starting up again.

"Mercy," cried Michael, reaching to pull me down to him and entwine our tongues. Now it was me, stretched out full length on him, reaching for his toes with my own, circling his penis with a tightening grip, rotating slowly, coaxing him to come. Michael's fingers pulled on my hair, signalling me, as if we'd been partners for years, until a final, surrealistic shudder passed through our bodies. The feeling lingered for a few joyful seconds. I was flooded with a sense of power.

Sex Education

Jesse Linnell

I pulled up to the driveway, turned off the engine and sat, reluctant to move. Except for the porch light and a light upstairs, the house at the end of the drive was dark. I was glad no one had waited up for me.

The house belonged to Rob and Jenna, a couple I knew only slightly. My old friend Beth had talked me into coming down here for the weekend, promising a great time at the beach. A few days ago, I had broken up with my lover of two years, and though I was glad of the decision, the loss of Everett made me want to retreat into myself. For a moment, I was tempted to turn around and head home. They would never know I'd been here. I could call tomorrow with some excuse.

However, I never did such things, so I got my bag out of the trunk and walked up to the house.

The key was under a flower pot, as Jenna had said it would be, along with a note from Beth telling me my bedroom was the first at the top of the stairs. She'd added at the botom: "Glad you made it. It'll be a good weekend." I smiled at the reassuring words.

I opened the door and walked quietly across the dimly lit living room, past Beth and her lover, Kevin, who were asleep on a fold-out couch. Their sleeping faces sent a pang through me. It was hard to look at lovers.

My bedroom was warm and close from the heat of the day. From across the hall came the faint thumping bass of a rock song. Someone was awake, but I didn't feel like investigating. I changed into pajamas and opened the window wide. Below me was the back yard. A high fence sheltered a small patio, a strip of lawn and a swimming pool. I stared at an odd, black lump at the side of the pool, and decided it was an inner tube. I hadn't seen an inner tube in ten years, I thought. There was a tap at the door, and it swung open.

"Is the radio too loud?"

I looked up at a slightly built, barefoot young man, wearing a T-shirt and jeans. I guessed he was around seventeen.

"No, it's okay," I said.

We introduced ourselves.

He was Chris, Jenna's cousin. He'd been spending the summer with Rob and Jenna while working at the Marine Center. He wanted to be an oceanographer. This fall he was starting college in California. "Ever been out there?" he asked.

I shook my head.

"The coast is incredible. Want to see some pictures I took last year?"

"Sure." We moved to his room.

We sat on his bed and he handed me photos of hulking brown sea lions, draped across rocks in the sun; a brown blur he said was a pelican; the sheer side of a cliff, where he pointed out the remains of cormorants' nests. His voice was high-pitched with eagerness. I thought of Everett, who dismissed so many books, places and people as "a goddamn waste of time." Chris' curly hair was deep brown, almost black, and his skin a light golden-brown. His fingers brushed mine as he handed me the pictures. For a moment I was aware of my breasts under the thin pajamas, but I quickly flicked the thought away. Sexual feelings and men his age were in separate corners of my mind.

We talked about California and animals and then about college. He was surprised to hear that I was an instructor at the university, and he asked about the classes I taught, and what I thought of my students. At two o'clock, we said good night, and I walked back to my room, smiling. What a nice kid, I thought.

The next morning, the whole household packed into Jenna's car and drove off to the beach. We trudged over sand dunes with bags of food, a cooler, blankets and towels, and came upon a perfect beach scene: bright umbrellas, motionless sunbathers glistening with sweat and lotions, radios blaring against the sound of the blue-green water lapping at the shore. We unfurled towels and pulled off T-shirts and shoes. I plopped down on a blanket with my detective novel.

A few feet away, Chris was climbing out of his jeans. His legs were tapered like a colt's. His chest was broad. A few dark hairs curled up his belly from the waistband of his suit. I looked down quickly at my book.

"Aren't you coming in?" Chris asked.

"I don't like swimming in the ocean," I said apologetically. "I'm always wondering what's down in the water that I can't see."

He hesitated. "Well, I guess I'll go in without you, then."

He ran down to the water with long, easy strides. He ran through the waves and, as a curl of water surged to meet him, he dived under it. I watched the water, looking for him. At last he bobbed up between waves, and began to swim in smooth strokes.

I turned back to my book. The detective couldn't decide what time the murder had taken place.

Chris was floating on his back just beyond where the waves were breaking, the ocean slowly rocking him.

The heat made me feel listless. I lay back and closed my eyes, half listening to the sound of the waves and a barking dog. A panting sound came closer and closer. It was Chris, running in from the water. He reached our spread of blankets, grabbed a towel, and began rubbing his face. His chest was heaving, dripping; his dark brown nipples taut and wet. I could see the bulge of his penis under his wet suit. A hot flush spread across my chest.

"Water's nice and warm," he gasped. "You should try it."

"No thanks," I said.

He lay down on his towel, his smooth brown back moving slightly as his breathing calmed. Drops of water, iridescent in the sun, hung on his curls. I wanted to scatter them with my hand. Instead, I jerked myself upright.

"I'm going for a walk," I said. "See you later."

I walked off down the beach, my blood pounding. The year I had first lived with a man, this Chris was probably learning to ride a tricycle. I had never been excited by a man this young. And I couldn't imagine him being excited by me. When I was his age, I had never desired anyone older. I decided that neither Chris nor anyone else would learn of my attraction.

But all afternoon, my body told me of his presence. He sat next to me on the trip home. The shoulder that touched his, the arm and thigh and knee that were next to him knew his every move. At dinner, I watched his full lips as he talked, and my own parted expectantly. As I rose to go to bed, I felt a wetness between my legs.

Chris caught up with me on my way up the stairs. "Want to go for a drive or something?" he said.

He looked so friendly and open — and so young. I felt so deceitful and messy, with my hidden thoughts and sticky crotch. I couldn't believe he was offering what my body wanted.

"I don't think so, Chris," I said. "I'm pretty tired."

"Guess it is kind of late," he said. "See you tomorrrow."

"Good night."

I closed the door to my room and felt like crying. I got into bed with my detective novel. I didn't want to think about Chris, or anything else.

I read, wishing the story would speed up. The detective still hadn't figured out when the damn murder had taken place. I kept squirming under the sheet, my body warm and restless. Finally, I sighed, turned out the light and began stroking a familiar path between my thighs. I let my fingers drift upward across my stomach and up my chest. My fingertips teased my nipples, caressing them to stiffness.

I opened my eyes to see the light from his room framing my door. Then I shut them and let my hand begin to comb through a tangle of pubic hair. My mind roamed swiftly through a catalog of fantasies, selecting The Ravishment.

The fingers became a probing tongue. Hot breath surrounded it, sending a fire through my thicket of hair. A hand reached from behind me to play endlessly with my breasts. Another greedy tongue stroked and sucked and pushed my own. The image of Chris's face intruded, his lashes blackly wet, as he bent over a towel. A penis rubbed against my ass, throbbing at the feel of my skin. A woman's nipples, teasingly erect, nuzzled mine. The tongue at my vulva probed one side of my clit. I imagined Chris at the doorway, watching my ravishment hungrily, his jeans bulging with an enormous erection.

A satiny penis glided inside me and began moving up and down. A hard clit pressed against my thigh, leaving a wet trail. The tongue played with my clit relentlessly; nothing would stop it. My thoughts called out silently: *I want you, Chris. Want you.* The penis slid faster in and out.

I started to come.

"Ah."

My head moved from side to side. My clit and vagina were joined in one burning path. *Want you, Chris. Please.*

"Ahhh."

I didn't care if he heard me. *Fuck me, Chris!*

"AHHHHH!"

My body jerked and my vagina clutched my finger in spasms. I wound down, moving my finger until I was quiet inside. Around me, the house was silent. The light under his door had gone out. I lay in stillness, wondering if he'd heard me. I hoped he had. I wanted him to know.

I drifted off with the image of his full lips hovering close to mine.

Sunday morning, everyone gathered for breakfast. It was assumed we would spend another day at the beach, but I said I wanted to laze around the pool. Beth looked at me sympathetically, probably assuming I wanted some time alone to mourn the loss of Everett. But I was thinking of Chris. I didn't want to spend another day at the beach helplessly staring at him. I hoped crazily that he would stay behind, too. I felt idiotic, passively waiting for a sign from him. But I was unsteady on this new ground, afraid to pursue him openly as I would an older man.

Chris announced he'd skip the beach. He had some things to do around the house. I wondered what they were.

After the others had left, I put on my suit, got my towel and detective novel, and walked out to the lawn. The sun reflected off the pool, turning the water bright turquoise and making me squint. I settled down in the stretch of shade along the fence. The lawn was covered with tiny green flowerettes that had fallen from the trees overhead.

I began reading, and found that the detective had finally pinpointed the time of the murder. Well, that was something. I looked up at Chris's window, wondering if he was still in his room. I decided that if I didn't see him soon, I'd go inside and start a conversation. I had no idea what I'd say.

The screen door banged and Chris walked out in his swimsuit, towel in hand.

"Thought I'd give you some company," he said. He wasn't looking at me.

"Be my guest," I said.

He unrolled his towel and lay down next to me. "Nice out here," he said.

"Yeah." It was an effort to speak. The long slope from the rise of his shoulder to the small of his back was so beautifully curved, so softly golden-brown it made my throat ache.

He noticed my book, where a sprinkling of flowerettes had settled. "These things get all over the place," he said. He leaned over and brushed them off the page.

He wants to touch me, I thought. But I lay as if frozen. For a brief, horrid moment, I imagined him saying to friends: "This older woman came on to me. It was weird." I drove the image away. I couldn't face going back home tomorrow, never knowing if he wanted me at all. I had to try.

"You've got some on you already," I said. I brushed a few flowerettes from his shoulders. Then my hand stroked slowly down his back.

He lay unmoving for a moment. Then, in one quick movement, his arm circled my back and drew me to him. In a huge release, I pressed my mouth to his.

He wanted me. I was light-headed, delighted. Our kissing and hugging became so prolonged that I realized this might be all he expected from our coming together. But his desire had made me bold. I took off the top of my suit and was instantly gratified as his mouth and hands traveled over my breasts as if he couldn't touch them, taste them enough. I felt voluptuous, irresistible. I pulled at his suit; he yanked it down over his legs and kicked it away. I wanted to look at him but his chest was across mine.

I felt the intensity fading from his arms and lips. I knew what had happened even before he said, "It's gone soft."

I kissed him on the mouth. "That doesn't matter," I said. "It feels good just to touch."

I pulled off my swimsuit bottom as he watched, and lay alongside him. I caressed his neck and shoulders, and cupped my hand over the slight swell of his belly, which was downy on the surface and taut within. I played my fingers under the soft bundle of balls and penis, loving the roundness and weight of them.

He pulled me tight to him and our kisses became faster. A movement against my belly — his penis jerking as it swelled erect — made me gasp.

I pushed one leg over his thigh. "Touch me with it," I whispered.

"Like this?" The mushroom head pressed against my clit.

"Like this." I rubbed lightly against him.

He took over. The friction was unbearably sweet. I imagined the cleft of his penis head as it moved against my stiff, rosy clit. Then the tip of his penis was just inside me. *Yes.* I pushed forward onto it. He rolled on top of me, and thrust deep inside, plunging and pumping. I held on to his shoulders. A pulsing started in my vagina, ran through my body, then outside me, becoming rhythmic cries. Chris stopped mid-plunge, groaned, and sank on top of me.

We held each other, stroking and kissing. He faced me then, smiling. He was loose and warm and exhilarated.

"Was this your first time?" I asked.

"First time it was any good," he said, laughing. "Let's go in."

"Inside?"

"In the *water*. Come on."

The cool water was a delightful shock. I hadn't been swimming without a suit in years and was surprised all over again how light and free my body felt. I churned through the water, huffing, in a determined effort at a crawl. Chris skimmed by me underwater, a slim sea creature. The light dappled over him. He reached the end of the pool, flipped into a smooth somersault and shot out toward me. All at once he rose up beneath me, his chest under mine, his arms loosely around me.

"Turn over," he said.

I turned over on my back and he pulled me gently up his

chest. My head was on his shoulder, his hand beneath my breasts. I stiffened, and strained to hold my head well out of the water.

"Just float," he said. "I'll hold you up."

He pulled me along effortlessly, hardly stirring the water. Finally, I relaxed into the rhythmic surge of his body. I let myself go limp; my legs trailed behind me.

We reached the shallow water, where he lifted me into the half-inflated inner tube and kissed me.

"Show me what you were doing last night," he said.

I stared up at him. He'd heard.

"Show me. I want to do it to you."

I hesitated, then opened my legs over the swell of the inner tube, and began to stroke the side of my clit. My face became quickly hot. I was self-conscious but excited. I'd never shown this to anyone.

He leaned close to watch, bringing up dripping fingers to tease my nipples. Then he gently pushed my hand away and began to finger my clit. His mouth bent to mine. His wet lips looked almost red. I sucked his tongue. His black curls glistened. His mouth, hot, wet, traveled my neck, my shoulder, and fastened on my nipple, kissing, sucking, making it melt.

I closed my eyes. The heat beat down on us. The inner tube, cradling my steaming body, bobbed slightly up and down. Chris pushed down on the front of the tube, and water lapped up, just covering my pubic hair. His fingers parted my labia, his mouth dipped into the water, and he blew a torrent of bubbles which tickled over my vulva. Then, his mouth still underwater, he lapped his tongue at my clit. I began to whimper and pant. I wanted him inside me. "Let's get out," I said, my voice thick with urgency.

We scrambled out of the pool and raced to our towels. His penis, erect in a glorious curve, bounced stiffly as he ran. We fell onto the towels and I rolled on top and sat astride his thighs. I grasped his swollen penis and put it just inside me so he could feel how wet I was, how much I wanted him. His eyes were closed; he looked sweetly asleep, except that his lips were parted in a way that made my blood beat hot in my vulva. I eased myself slowly onto his engorged penis. I reached behind and clutched his balls. He moaned.

I began to move up and down. He rose into me, his breath

coming hard. The sensation was sweet, sweeter. My insides, so thick and tight with desire, uncurled. I came in long shudders. Chris went rigid and a cry came from deep within him. I lay down on him and held him fast.

We lay there, wet from sweat and sex and water from the pool. I was lazily content, my face buried in his warm curls. But Chris was energized. He wanted to go in again.

He pulled me upright and led me across the grass to the edge of the pool. The concrete burned pleasantly at our feet. He turned to me with an excited grin.

"Climb on my back," he said. "We'll dive in together."

"Oh, no, Chris." I drew back. All at once I felt brittle and old.

"It's okay," he said. "I won't let you fall." His eyes were dancing. His warm fingers tightened on mine.

"You're crazy," I said, half laughing.

He could tell I'd softened. "You get on my shoulders," he said, "and I'll stand up. Then you stand up and we'll dive in."

He squatted down and I sat on his shoulders, my wet pubic hair against his neck. He gripped my hands, and slowly rose.

"Now stand up," he said.

Awkwardly, I brought one foot up on his shoulder. The glittery concrete looked far away. "Jesus, Chris, I don't know," I said.

"It's okay, I've got you."

I brought my other foot to his shoulder as I hoisted myself jerkily upright. I stood, my bent knees wobbling, my hands clamped to his. His body held me firm.

"Now!" he said.

He lunged forward. I pushed off his shoulders. The sheet of blue rushed toward me. The impact and splash, the surge of water and bubbles thrilled me. I bobbed up to the surface, laughing and hiccuping. I had done it.

My young lover surfaced, smiling as he saw my face. We swam to the side and kissed. He ran his hand up the side of my neck, under my hair.

"Tonight I'll take you swimming in the ocean," he said. "You'll love it."

I believed him.

Workout

Khasti Cadell

No one could have been more bushed than I was. The tension in my muscles seemed to have worked its way into my bones. All week long I had been working hard, and now my body needed to relax.

I called Zora, my buddy who belongs to a trendy health club in Flatbush. The locker room there is a study hall for the appreciation of the body. This is more than your ordinary sweat club.

Zora was trying to get herself into a health club regimen, and she had asked me several times to join her at the club for swimming, sauna, steam room, and massage. She was delighted that I agreed to go with her this afternoon.

I packed my big blue towel, my bathing suit and some skin creams into a small duffle bag and rushed out to the subway so I could meet her by four o'clock.

When I arrived, only a few women were in the club. It was a little early for the after-work crowd. Just as well, for it gave me a chance to have some privacy with Zora.

I love Zora's body. Although we're buddies, not lovers, we

had made love a few times when one of us needed the other. You could say we are friends in love. Besides, she has the most beautifully soft, smooth chocolate skin.

I stripped off my clothes in front of the lockers in the ell off the main area. Zora stood there already naked, her beautiful brown breasts inviting me to kiss them. I pulled her to me and took her nipple in my mouth, feeling it grow as hard and round as a pearl as I sucked it gently.

"Hey, Khasti, I thought you came here for a little relaxation, baby," Zora said, grinning. But she didn't pull away. She stroked my shoulders and my back as she nuzzled my hair.

"I did. But I thought I should give the hostess appropriate thanks." I concentrated on her other nipple, holding her tit from underneath, lifting it to my mouth.

We leaned up against the lockers. Zora touched my cunt lightly with her fingertips, teasing her hand between my thighs and back toward my asshole. I groaned softly. She knew what I liked. I felt fingers entering my cunt, two, then three. I like to feel full in there. She pressed my clit with her thumb.

"How're you feeling now, Khasti, huh? Are you relaxing yet?"

"I'm starting to, uh, unwind...." I kissed her deeply in her mouth. Her tongue played with mine. "Let's move over to where we can be more comfortable, okay?"

We took my big blue towel and laid it on the floor next to the side of the bank of lockers. Zora nuzzled my ear and neck and stroked my thigh.

I couldn't help it. My legs opened to her stroke, and she put her fingers back into my cunt, which was by now dripping and swollen. But I wanted something else as well.

"Zora, I've got to eat you. Open up." I shifted her legs apart, and she bent her knees. I knelt between her legs and she lay back. Her clit was hard and already straining out of the hood. I sucked it gently first, then harder. I fingered her while I sucked. I knew that she loved that, to feel me inside her cunt and sucking her clit hard. Her sweet juice began to flow over my lips, my chin.

"Turn," she whispered. "Turn. Let me have you too."

I positioned my cunt right over her mouth. I felt her straining to reach me and heard her sigh with contentment when she could bite my clit. Her tongue was running all over my pussy, and she stuck it into me as deep as she could. Her mouth returned and she sucked my clit hard, biting with her teeth and shoving her fingers deep inside me. Zora always knew exactly what I wanted as if it were second nature. Her other hand busied herself on my nipple, squeezing hard, rolling it around between her fingers.

I felt the explosion begin. There is always a moment when you know there is no return. You can't stop it by concentrating on your partner's pleasure, you can't stop it by thinking of baseball scores or her tits or her legs wrapped around you lovingly. All you can think of is coming yourself. Zora was getting me there, and she insisted on triumph.

I came, showering her face with my juice. Her cunt was straining toward me, and I sucked it until she came in my mouth, soaking my face and my fingers.

"Are you feeling better now?" she asked.

We sat up against the lockers again, our arms around each other. We both felt good, and finally ready to join the rest of the world.

"Hey, you dykes finished?"

We looked up. The locker room attendant was standing over us. She was about 5'11" and must have weighed 275. She wore a light blue shirt and dark blue slacks. I opened my eyes a little wider.

"You know, this happens to be a public place. We can't have people sucking and fucking wherever they want. Zora, you're a member here, and you should know better. You better come with me, both a'you."

"Don't worry," Zora whispered to me. "Ruth just wants a piece of the action. She probably saw your ass and wants to fuck it."

I smiled to myself, and felt my asshole begin to react with pleasure.

Ruth escorted us to her office, a small room with a desk and a chair and a shade on the door's window.

"There's nothing I hate more than a coupla dykes tryin' to take advantage of the hospitality here at the club." The message was tough, but she had a strange softness in her voice. "I'm gonna have to teach ya a lesson. Now you, Zora, you know better, so I can only think that this bitch here forced you to forget the rules. Is that it?"

"Yes, ma'am," answered Zora meekly.

"Well, bitch, you don't want to be able to come back here, is that it?"

"No, ma'am," I said, taking my cue from Zora.

"Well, then, I can see you're gonna need to be punished for disobeying the rules. And Ruth is gonna do the punishing."

"Yes, ma'am."

She looked beyond me to the window with the shade pulled almost all the way down. "I always leave the shade up a little so if any of the other girls get the same idea you dykes had, they can see what happens."

She unzipped her pants. "Now turn over on that desk. I don't wanna hear a peep from you. Zora, you just stand and watch me fuck your little girl friend here. Don't you move."

Ruth pushed me down so that I was leaning over, with my face resting on the cool wood of the desk. She searched through a desk drawer to collect what she needed. Suddenly she was behind me, fingering my cunt.

"Nice and wet in there." She moved her hand to my ass, kneading and massaging her way toward my asshole. She started to touch me lightly around the edge. My muscles tightened and my ass lifted in anticipation.

"Oh, this ain't nuthin' new to you, is it? I'll bet you like a little ass fucking now and then, don't you?"

"Yes, ma'am," I said softly.

She stopped, and I heard her pants drop to the floor. I waited a moment. "Turn around, bitch. I want you to suck this thing, bitch, and I want you to suck it good."

Kneeling in front of her, I opened my mouth to take in her dildo. She shoved it deep into my mouth. I felt my cunt get wetter, hotter. I put my hands around her ass to pull her closer. Suddenly she pulled out.

"Back up on the desk, bitch. I wanna fuck that ass of yours."

I turned around and assumed the position she had originally placed me in.

"You better be ready, bitch," I heard her mutter, and I felt something cold and creamy being rubbed onto my asshole. I felt the big dildo at the entrance to my ass. She began to push it in. I smiled. This is what I had been waiting for, this is what I loved. I felt her fill up my ass with it, pushing in and pulling out with a hard rhythm. Ruth moved her fingers onto my clit and pulled me closer to her. I wished she would fuck me forever. Suddenly I felt the familiar beginnings of an orgasmic explosion. I began to breathe louder.

"Shut up. I don't wanna hear you come, bitch. I just wanna feel it."

I closed my eyes, quieted my still deep and ragged breath, and rocked to the rhythm. I started to sweat. Everything broke apart, and I never wanted to leave the heaven I was in.

"Had enough?"

"Yes, ma'am." She pulled the dildo out of my ass slowly. Then she shoved it back in, deep and hard.

"Just remember this when you decide to go public in my locker room again." She turned to Zora, who had been watching with her fingers up her cunt and was now leaning against the wall. "And listen, missy, next time you bring a guest to the club, remind her of the rules. Otherwise...." Ruth mock-glared at Zora, who was standing with her head coquettishly bowed.

She turned back to me. "Bitch, you got a name?"

"Yes, ma'am." I looked her in the eye and smiled. "Khasti."

"Well, Khasti, you keep acting cute like that, and I'll have to come down hard on you whenever you're here. You want that?"

"Yes, ma'am."

Ruth smiled. "Well, good. Then we have an understanding, don't we? You and Ruth know exactly where we stand, don't we?"

"Yes, ma'am. I know *exactly* where to stand. And how, too."

"You dykes are dismissed."

Zora and I walked out and closed the door behind us. We looked up, and we saw three or four other women standing nearby smiling at us. They'd watched Ruth fuck me!

"Yo, how was it?" "Did you like it?" "Isn't she great?" They clapped me on the back, slapped me on my ass. "Ruth must have liked you!"

Affairs

Charmaine Parsons

Doris reached for the meat on the top rack and caught her reflection in the freezer's metal plating. As her blouse rode up it revealed the roll of loose flesh at her hips. She quickly stuck the package in her shopping cart and pulled her top over the flaw. There was a smudge on the hem of her blouse. The day was hot and she could feel her hair straggling from the ponytail and clinging limply around her face. Her makeup felt greasy. A young man reached past her for a package of hamburger. He smiled and she drew herself up and smiled back. She finished her grocery shopping in a better frame of mind.

The check-out boy was short but muscular. He was confident and aware of his physical magnetism. He moved with the fluid grace of the young and the good looking. Doris stole appraising glances as her purchases were tallied. She flushed slightly when he picked up the box of douche preparation, but he tucked it into the bag as casually as if it were a loaf of bread.

She fumbled her change paying for her purchases. He scooped up the quarter and handed it back to her. He didn't smile or even look at her. But she was sure his hand hovered a

little longer than necessary; there was a lingering contact between their flesh. She tingled pleasantly, then told herself it was
just her imagination.

After the cool of the store, the hot afternoon air hit like a blast
furnace. Doris began to wilt. She led the boy with her groceries
to the car. Unconsciously she put an extra wiggle into her hips.

The young man loaded the groceries quickly and shut the
trunk lid with a bang.

"There you go," he announced in a bored monotone.

She held out a quarter tip and as he took it, their eyes met. An
electric charge passed between them. She caught her breath but
could tell he had felt the same. He took the quarter and his
eyelids lowered sleepily.

"I get off in ten minutes," he whispered. "I have a car — a van
— in the back lot." He gathered up a few loose carts and then
looked over his shoulder. "Meet me."

She opened her mouth to protest, but he was already halfway
back to the store. She climbed into her car slowly. She couldn't
meet him. She was a married woman. She started up the car and
drove off toward the back of the store.

Doris traced his bare chest with her forefinger. "I have to be
going soon," she said softly.

He nodded and took another drag on the cigarette. She
watched his handsome young face in profile. Probably some
Latin blood someplace, she decided.

"I shouldn't have done this," she said.

This time he turned his head to look at her. "A woman like
you shouldn't belong to just one man."

"I won't be able to see you again."

He merely nodded and looked away....

It was over. It had been good but now it was over. She got up
and began to dress.

She put the bag of groceries on the kitchen table and peered
into the living room. Her husband was slumped in the easy
chair, stocking feet on the hassock and a can of beer in one hand.
There was a ball game blaring and the room had the aroma of
malt liquor and stale feet.

"I'm home," Doris called.

Bert didn't look up from the ball game. She shrugged and

began putting away the groceries. She hadn't expected a response.

Bert shuffled into the kitchen as she was preparing dinner. She heard fast jangling music from the TV and a voice proclaiming the good movie to come so she knew the game was over.

Bert lifted the lid from one of the bubbling pots and squinted at the contents. "What's for dinner?" he asked.

Doris began setting the table. "Pork chops, potatoes, bread, peas...."

Bert bobbed his head, which was as close as he ever came to expressing approval. "I'm starved."

"Be ready in a minute. Go wash up." She looked him over. "Why don't you change shirts?"

He peered down in puzzlement and plucked at the shirt he was wearing. "What's wrong with this?"

She shook her head sadly. "It's full of holes. And you need a shave."

He chuckled and leaned over to rub his coarse cheek against her neck. "My shirt's fine and you love me rough and rugged."

She pushed him away playfully and coyly lowered her head. "Go on now. Get washed up."

Bert ate dinner with gusto, leaning back at the conclusion and punctuating it with a large belch.

"Bert!" Doris admonished.

"Got that job to do tomorrow," Bert said. "Guess I'd better hit the sack." He paused suggestively. "You coming?"

It was his standard invitation to sex. Doris nodded. "Let me get a few things cleaned up and I'll be in. I have to see Dr. Cheeves tomorrow, so I'll shower in the morning."

Doris ruffled through her magazine with a definite lack of interest. She felt small beads of perspiration on her upper lip and licked at them nervously. She wondered if any woman ever felt comfortable going to a gynecologist.

When it was her turn the nurse weighed her, charted and assessed her complaints and then filed her away in a small cubicle with instructions to go to Room Two when she was "ready."

She undressed quickly, folding her clothes neatly on the little bench with her underwear and bra concealed. The paper gown was flimsy protection. She slipped into it carefully so it wouldn't tear. She slid back the door, peered out and scurried to the designated area. Only when she had shut the door and draped the cloth sheet over her lap was she able to relax.

The doctor shuffled in slowly. There were tired purple circles under his eyes, but he greeted Doris warmly.

"Got that infection again, huh?" he asked, scanning her chart. She nodded miserably.

"Weight's up a few pounds," he admonished. "Better get it off. The older you are the harder it gets."

She made a false promise to do something about it.

He had her lie back and put her feet in the stirrups. She flinched as he pulled up the sheet to expose her and clicked on the hot bright lamp. He settled himself below her field of vision. He confirmed his suspicions and withdrew his instrument. The back of his hand brushed against the inside of her thigh and it seemed to her he prolonged that contact.

He rose and did a quick physical exam. "I'll write you a prescription," he said. She still lay with her feet in the stirrups, too shy to put her legs together until told.

"You can get dressed now," he said, moving toward the door.

She closed her eyes and heaved a sigh of relief that the ordeal was over. She began to move from her awkward position when suddenly the doctor was back at her feet.

"What's the matter?" she asked, raising herself from the table, too stunned to realize her legs were still in the spread position.

He leaned over her, pressing the length of his body between her legs and forcing her shoulders back on the table.

"Doris, please," he whispered hoarsely, "I know this is all wrong. I know I shouldn't behave this way with a patient, and I pray to God you won't turn me in, but, Doris...." His voice caught in his throat and he pushed himself back to a standing position. "You are so special, and I've wanted you for so long." He lifted the sheet and looked down at her with moist eyes. "You're so beautiful." He raised his eyes to her face. "Please let me make love to you," he begged.

She knew it was wrong, but the raw lust in his eyes was more than she could bear. She held out her arms to him. "Yes...Jim. It's all right."

And because he was a doctor and knew all of a woman's secret places, it was wonderful — absolutely wonderful.

While she waited for Bert to come home, Doris started dinner cooking and scrubbed the bathroom. She refrained from gagging as she cleaned Bert's hair from the bathtub drain. The man was a gorilla.

"What did the doctor tell you?" Bert asked that night around a mouthful of steak.

She lifted her shoulders with a shrug. "Got that infection again," she said sadly.

"Jesus!" Bert snorted. "Does that mean I have to take those crappy pills again to keep from passing it back?" She nodded. "Jesus," he muttered again.

Bert began raving about "the stupid way women are put together" but she concentrated on her dinner and tuned him out.

They spent the rest of the day as they did every Wednesday evening. They watched a new crime drama featuring the old combination of two young radical cops. There was the predictable blond who was like a brother to his equally adorable brown-haired male friend. They were rude without being abrasive, good looking, tanned, with wide shoulders and tight little backsides. Doris would never admit it, but she enjoyed the show as much as Bert, but for a different reason.

Tonight, though, she was bored and restless. Halfway through the show she decided to leave the two detectives, Stan and Jim, arguing over police procedure. She had just lowered herself into the bathtub and begun to relax when the door opened. Stan, the blond cop, shut the door behind him and eyed her body hungrily through the murky bath water.

"Jim couldn't make it tonight," he said, "but we both have a real treat for you next week."

He began to undress. Doris resettled in the tub and smiled happily.

Our Friends Fran and Jan

Susan St. Aubin

When I tell people about Fran and Jan, they think I'm talking about two women, or that Jan is the man and Fran is the woman. Actually, their names are Francis and Janine, and they've been together for twenty-three years, ever since they ran away to New Orleans to get married when they were seventeen. They were Ed's friends first. He used to be a free-lance paralegal until Fran hired him part-time and encouraged him to start law school. That was two years ago, when Ed and I began living together. I even worked in Fran's law office for a while as a receptionist, but I couldn't stand it. Now I work with computers for a bank, which I like better because I don't have to talk to anyone.

Fran and Jan have this great old house he inherited, along with a lot of money, when his mother's aunt died ten years ago. It's three stories, with three bedrooms on the third floor, a library and a sitting room on the second floor, and a kitchen and dining room on the ground floor. There's also an attic with two guest rooms that have the best views in the house.

Jan was born in New Orleans and likes to say she's a mulatto though she's no darker than I am, with straight brown hair and a small pointed nose. Fran met her in Dallas where they both went to high school. He was born in San Francisco, but his father was a city planner who moved all over the country. Jan was a model for a while in New York, and made enough money to put Fran through school, which was a good thing, because for the first few years they were married his family wouldn't give him a cent.

Jan always looks like she's posing in front of lights and a camera, even though she doesn't model any more, except for an occasional department store ad for the Sunday paper, where she's always identified as "Jan Rose, wife of well-known defense lawyer Francis Rose, photographed in the library of their Victorian home."

One warm Friday night a couple of months ago, Ed and I and Roger and John, two of Jan's friends from Hollywood, were sitting around the oak table in the Roses' dining room after dinner. We were talking about the history of the house. Jan sat with her best profile to us, looking off in the distance beyond Fran's head. She took a sip of wine and licked her bottom lip.

"It was built before the Civil War," she said. "The original owners used to hide runaway slaves in the basement."

"By the time they got here they didn't need to hide," said Fran. "They could work in the gold mines like everyone else. But that's irrelevant because this house was built in the 1890s, long after the Civil War. I've seen the records — you can look up the complete history of your house, when it was built, when it was sold."

Jan picked up her wine glass, curling her little finger around the stem. "An architect told me it must have been built around 1848."

"He didn't have the facts," said Fran. "1890."

"Facts," said Jan, "aren't everything." She smiled at me as if we were conspirators, or could be. I was confused; usually, she ignored me.

While Fran glowered at his empty plate, Ed patted Jan on the head and murmured, "Don't worry, I believe you no matter what Fran's facts are." Then he asked Fran, "Have you ever explored your basement? My uncle found a box of old campaign buttons in his basement in Berkeley. 'Win with Wilkie,' that kind of thing."

"There's nothing there," Fran answered. "And no light to see it by. No windows, either. My Aunt Ginnie used to stand at the top of the stairs and pitch stuff she didn't want down there — dresses, empty boxes, old magazines. It's a trash pit."

"But Ed's right," said Jan. "We should have a look around." She held Ed's hand in her lap.

To tell the truth, I was always uncomfortable at Fran and Jan's house. I knew Ed had had an affair with Jan before he moved in with me, and I knew they were still seeing each other. I couldn't put my suspicion into words, not even to myself, and Ed didn't talk about it. There was a lot unspoken between us.

I didn't like the way Fran corrected everything Jan said, either, or the way he glared at her from behind his bushy beard. But then he always seemed to glare; his heavy black eyebrows knit together in a frown even when he laughed. Now he scowled at Ed, saying, "We should preserve the basement as it is." He filled his glass from the carafe on the table and raised it. "To the unknown forces at the bottom," he said with his frowning laugh.

"And to exploration," Jan added in her funny accent that had no region to it.

John and Roger laughed with their heads together. Jan had known Roger for years; I'd met him once or twice before at her house. She said John was his lover, but Roger looked at her across the table as if he were playing the usual small part he had in movies, the ex-husband or the jilted boyfriend. With one hand on John's shoulder, he watched Jan and Ed try to twine their arms together while they raised their glasses.

I felt as though I were at a party I hadn't been invited to. I imagined Ed and Jan in Jan's brass bed with its velvet patchwork quilt. Ed leans to her as she whispers in his ear, then sucks his earlobe and licks his cheek and chin like a cat. She's slender and quick, so unlike bulky Fran with his dark beard and heavy tread. I couldn't picture those two in bed together, but it was easy to see Jan and Ed, their thin, long arms and legs wrapped around each other, Jan dark and Ed blond.

I spilled my wine. Jan jumped up to get a sponge, and wiped the table carefully while I dabbed at the placemat with my napkin.

"We could go down there tonight," Ed suggested. "Let's gather up all the candles and flashlights in the house and make an expedition of it."

"It's unknown territory," Fran warned. "No maps."

"Terrific." John stretched like a colt ready to race. He looked about nineteen. I couldn't imagine what Roger saw in someone twenty years younger. Ed's eight years older than I am, which sometimes seems like a lot. I tried unsuccessfully to picture John and Roger in bed. "Count me out. I'm afraid of the dark." I shivered.

"What?" Fran laughed. "Only five year olds are afraid of the dark, Anna."

"But what could be down there anyway? It's a waste of time."

"There might be gold," said Roger. "People did that during the gold rush, brought back lumps of gold and hid them in their basements."

"The bones of escaped slaves," said John. His pale blue eyes were wide. "Or the ghosts of slaves."

"1890." Fran frowned. "Keep that in mind. No gold. No slaves. Just a family house."

"Oh, you're no fun." John lifted the candelabra from the center of the table. It was a huge brass thing that held a dozen candles. "Onward!" he shouted.

Fran stood up. " All right, I give up. I'll get some flashlights."

Ed took my hand and pulled me up. "Please come, Anna," he said.

"Well, maybe." I could always slip back when no one was looking, I thought, and go upstairs to the library and read until they came back.

Fran returned with enough flashlights for everyone. "Put that thing back on the table," he said to John. "You'll burn the house down. Follow me."

He led us into the kitchen, and stopped in front of a low door behind the butcher block table.

Jan did a sort of dance, waving her flashlight in an arc across the ceiling.

"Let's take the plunge," said Fran as he opened the door and shone his flashlight down the stairs. The damp basement air crept around our legs.

"Don't worry, Anna." Fran ducked through the door. "You can stand up straight once you're on the stairs. They used to keep milk and vegetables in the cellar before there was refrigeration. It's just one big icebox."

Ed followed Fran, then came Jan. Roger and John held hands behind her. When I looked through the door, I could see nothing but the pinpoints of five flashlights below. Jan gasped and Fran laughed.

"Cobwebs!" she shouted. "My God, I thought some ghost had its fingers 'round my neck." Then she called to me, "Where are you, Anna?"

I turned off my flashlight. "I changed my mind. I'm not coming."

"Leave the door open," Fran shouted, "so we can see the light."

I left the flashlight on the kitchen table and walked through the deserted dining room and up the stairs to the second floor. At the top of the stairs was a framed black-and-white photograph of Fran and Jan's wedding, not when they got married in New Orleans, but the wedding they had in San Francisco when they were twenty-three and Fran's family realized they weren't just rebellious kids anymore. They stand arm in arm on the beach, Fran in a white tuxedo and Jan in a flowery lavender dress with long sleeves, the sort of thing women wore in 1966. Fran's beard blends into Jan's hair so that it's impossible to tell which is beard and which is hair.

Below the wedding photo was an enlargement of a picture I'd looked at a lot because Ed has a smaller print. It's of him and Fran and Jan sitting around a table with a red sun umbrella on it and a beach in the background, not the wedding beach but a tropical beach with white sand. They're drinking beer with labels in Spanish on the bottles, and Jan and Ed have their heads thrown back, laughing, while Fran's brows are pulled together. I know he's probably laughing too, but if you didn't know him, you couldn't tell from the picture. It was taken in Mexico just before I met Ed; he told me the three of them spent a week together in Mazatlan and planned to stay longer, but changed their minds. When I asked why, he shrugged.

I went down the hall to the library, a room with four walls packed with books, top to bottom. Two couches faced each other across a coffee table in the center. There were, of course, all the latest novels, as well as the modern poetry books Jan likes. Ed borrowed these all the time, slender volumes with paper covers written by people I'd never heard of, and inside each cover, in Fran's bold slash of ink, was written: *Fran and Jan Rose.* Even Fran's heavy law books had the same inscription that was in the novels and the books on travel and cooking: *Fran and Jan,* as though they were the same person.

"Looking for something?" Roger spoke directly into my left ear, and laughed when I jumped.

"I thought everyone was in the basement," I said when I could breathe again.

"It was too boring. You can't see a thing even with flash-lights." He squatted beside me. "They're all giggling about ghosts while Fran tries to be serious about history and beam structure. Here. The best books are on the bottom shelf."

He handed me a book of photographs. "This might interest you," he said with a smile.

The pictures all seemed to be of the same two women kissing and caressing each other, sometimes joined by a tall slender man with dark curly hair who looked something like Roger might have before his hairline started to recede. He turned the page to a close-up of one of the women with her head thrown back and her tongue licking her bottom lip. It was Jan, looking as if she'd just taken a sip of wine. I turned back to the picture of the man, and looked at Roger.

"Our first modeling job together," he said. "That's how I met her."

I turned to the inside cover, where Fran had written: *Fran and Jan Rose.* "It must have been interesting."

"Very boring," said Roger. "And freezing cold. It was in some warehouse in New Jersey in March. I thought I'd die. It took them a week, six hours a day, to shoot this. Of course, they only used a quarter of the pictures. It's all an illusion, you know. Nothing really happened."

I paged through the books to more photos of the women, alone and with Roger, and then to a series of Jan and Roger alone together, Jan with his cock in her mouth, Roger licking her but-tocks, and the two of them on a Persian rug, limbs acrobatically entwined.

I felt my face grow hot. When I bent over to put the book back, I noticed the other titles on the bottom shelf: *Women who Prey on Boys, The Story of O, Delta of Venus* — books I'd heard of and books I hadn't, but none I'd ever read. I pulled out *Intimate Sex Lives of Famous People* and opened it to Fran's signature. "Has he marked every book in the place?" I asked. "I'd hate it if Ed did that."

Roger laughed. "How well do you know our friends Fran and Jan?"

"Not very," I admitted. "They're mostly Ed's friends."

"It doesn't matter whose name is on the books." Roger put his arm around my shoulders. "Jan's the one in charge here."

I tried to shrug his arm off.

"Have you seen the view from the attic rooms?" he persisted. "Or are you as frightened of attics as you are of basements?" He dropped his arm, put his hands in his pockets, and smiled at me.

I wasn't quite sure what he had in mind, with John in the basement, not to mention his old friend Jan. I cleared my throat and said, "I've seen it."

The space between us grew, as though I were receding into a tunnel, an experience I'd had many times before while talking to a man who seemed to want something I didn't quite understand. To tell the truth, I didn't always like sex. I mean, it was the person who was important. Sex with a man like Roger who already had a lover just didn't appeal to me. Besides, he'd probably been Jan's lover, and maybe still was. In my mind I traced AIDS from Roger to Jan to Ed. Sex and death. I wasn't interested. I had made Ed promise to use rubbers except when he was with me, but I wasn't sure he did. I wasn't sure of anything.

"What do you want with me?" I asked. I laughed, and so did he as he went out into the hall shaking his head. I heard the stairs creak as he climbed. Maybe he did just want to look at the view.

When he'd gone, I went up to the third floor. At the front of the house was Jan's bedroom with the brass bedstead against the wall between two windows. Fran and Jan had their own rooms, though Fran's was more like a study, with a single bed made up to look like a couch. The third bedroom was almost entirely filled by a king sized waterbed which Jan said she couldn't sleep in because it made her feel seasick. I didn't know what they used that room for, since their guests always stayed in the attic rooms. I ran my hand over Jan's quilt, patches of velvet sewn together.

I thought that Ed and Jan had probably made love on her bed. I kicked off my shoes and fell onto the quilt backwards. The velvet tickled the backs of my arms when I moved them up and down. I pretended I was Jan, Ed's lover, nude on the velvet spread. The walls glowed soft pink from the ceiling light. I shut my eyes and felt like I was on a beach, on the sand, waiting for

Ed, my lover. My fantasies about sex were better than the real thing. Here I was alone and practically panting pretending to be Jan, but when Ed and I were together, something was missing.

It was awful to be thirty years old and know all about orgasms without being quite sure whether I'd ever had one. I think I was afraid to know I hadn't. What I felt during sex was more like a warm cocoon than a hot explosion. Ed was patient with his tireless fingers and tongue, but it was never more than nice, though I would have described myself as perfectly satisfied. If his climax seemed more like an ocean wave bursting through a dam, perhaps that was just another difference between women and men.

On Jan's bed I could almost hear waves, tap-whoosh-tap against the sand. But it was footsteps. Jan stood in the open door of the bedroom and asked, "Are you all right?"

I sat up. "Is the expedition over?"

"No," she said as she came over to the bed and sat beside me. "You don't have to get up, I just want to sit here a minute. Roger came upstairs, I think, but Fran and Ed and John are still poking around down there. Fran was right, there's nothing to see, but once I talk him into something, he won't quit. It's odd, he really doesn't like to admit I'm wrong." She laughed.

I turned over on my stomach and she stroked my back. I suppose I was still feeling the wine from dinner. Whatever the reason, I didn't move. Everything seemed unimportant except Jan's hand on my back.

She lay down beside me, rubbing my back, my rump, and then between my legs. Even through my pantyhose her fingers felt like they carried an electric charge. She stroked the seam of the pantyhose, pressing it between my legs, until there seemed to be a sort of electrical exchange, as if a spark shot from her fingers and went through my crotch and all up inside me. I gasped and immediately the word "orgasm" appeared in my mind like a word on a computer screen: clear points of light in darkness. That was it, so simple and so fast. The word disappeared, leaving a blank screen on which anything could be written. I was sweating all over, like Ed did when he came, and then I was chilled. Jan wrapped the velvet comforter around us. Another word flashed on my mind's screen: lesbian. I pushed the quilt away and sat up.

"I don't like women," I said. "I mean, I like women, but

they've never turned me on sexually. I never felt anything like that before."

"I thought not," said Jan with a smile.

"But I'm not gay, I know I'm not," I said.

"Of course not," she answered. "It doesn't matter whose finger it is, as long as it's moving right. It could be the same with a man, or by yourself. Anna, don't be angry, but Ed talks about you a lot and I've tried to tell him what to do, but explaining without showing him how is as futile as bumping around in a dark basement without lights."

I slid off the bed and put my shoes back on. "You do this all the time, huh? Seduce boys, girls, whoever you can get. And all the while pretending you're doing it for our sake."

She laughed, which made me even madder. "Oh, Anna, don't look so worried. Yes, I do care about people: Fran and Ed and you, too." She sat up and pulled me back down on the bed beside her.

"You and Ed," I said, "you've been lovers for years, haven't you?"

She slipped my shoes off again and pulled off my pantyhose.

"You all went to Mexico together, didn't you, you and Fran and Ed?"

She sighed. "That turned out to be a mistake," she said. "I thought maybe Fran and Ed and I could make love together, we were all such good friends."

"Fran knows about you and Ed?" I felt hypnotized by the fluttering movements of her hands along my arms and thighs.

"Oh, yes," she said. "We both have lovers. But Fran — well, as you saw tonight, Fran is reluctant to explore, and just as reluctant to admit it when an exploration turns up nothing. In Mexico it was deadly, Fran forcing himself to be with Ed and me. He and Ed were such good friends, yet they were beginning to hate each other."

They were as distant to me as three figures in a comic film, laughing around the umbrella'd table. I wished Jan would be quiet.

"I took Fran to Paris," she went on. "We left Ed with a note and a ticket home. He understood, eventually, but I don't think Fran ever has. Oh, Anna." She pushed her nose against my arm, laughing. "Can you imagine making love with two men? It was great. I wish they could have loved each other."

"There's too much I don't know," I wailed as her fingers moved faster along my thighs. "Stop talking."

"I'm sorry," Jan whispered.

I heard a buzzing noise and looked down to see her holding a beige and orange striped tube with a round ball at one end which she rested on her hand while she twirled her fingers between my thighs and up into my wet vagina.

"What's that?" I gasped.

"A massager," she said. I felt its vibrations go through me from her hand while I hung, timeless, until thousands of pinpoints of light danced across my crotch.

"Anna," Jan murmured in my ear, "there's so much I could show Ed about you if we were all together." Her words seemed to drift in the air without meaning.

"Ed?" I asked.

"The three of us," she said.

I couldn't imagine what he'd do except watch, which made me a bit uneasy.

"I did suggest it to him once," she went on, "and he said no, he was afraid you'd never agree. Of course, that was after our Mexico fiasco, when you two had just started living together. But if he saw us now, how could he refuse?"

I heard thumping in the distance, and a door banged.

"Make him lie down," I heard John shout from downstairs. "Get ice."

"Someone's hurt." Jan sat up. "Thank God John's here. He used to be an LVN."

"A what?" I asked.

"A licensed vocational nurse," she answered. "Come on." She jumped off the bed and tossed me my pantyhose.

When we got to the kitchen, John was crouched on the floor with a towel full of ice saying, "Hold it to your nose."

"It's Ed," Jan whispered. He lay on the floor at John's feet.

"More ice," said John. Jan went to the freezer.

"I didn't know it was you," Fran said. "I thought you'd gone upstairs. I heard someone behind me and I didn't know who it was, so I punched him. Jesus, I'm sorry." He rubbed his hands together like he was washing them.

"Can you sit up?" John asked Ed. "Sit up and tilt your head back. Hold the ice under your nose, like this."

Jan knelt beside John.

"I think it's stopping," said John. "Ed? How do you feel?"

"I don't know." Ed sounded like he had a head cold. "My nose hurts. And my head."

"We should call a doctor," John said. "If you were unconscious we should have you checked." His youth must have been an act; there were lines around his eyes. He seemed much older than nineteen now. "He was able to walk upstairs, kind of leaning on Fran," he said to me. "But he wasn't real coherent at first, and Fran said he was out cold. Fran was terrified."

"Fran didn't knock me out." Ed sat up, then slowly stood, leaning on a kitchen chair. "I'm O.K."

John felt his nose. "Well, I'd call a doctor, but if you don't want to, that's your business."

"Anna and I will take him upstairs," Jan said. "Fran, help us. We can carry him. You take his shoulders and we'll take his feet."

"No," said Ed, "I can walk," but Fran had him by the shoulders.

"Just relax," Fran said. "Lean on me. Let Jan have your feet."

Jan and I each took one of Ed's legs and lifted him from the floor.

"To the stairs," said Fran, and we carried him through the dining room and out into the hall, Fran in the lead walking backwards.

"Be careful," warned John, who followed behind.

Fran paused at the top of the stairs. We were all panting except Ed, who had his eyes closed and looked slightly gray.

"Where do you want him?" Fran asked. "My study?"

"No," said Jan. "On the waterbed. The door's open."

Fran backed into the room.

Ed groaned. We laid him gently down, and Jan covered him with a white fur rug.

"Where's Roger?" asked John.

"He went up to the attic hours ago," I told him. "Maybe he went to bed."

John left the room and started up the stairs. Fran stood in the doorway. "Do you want me to stay?" he asked.

"Not unless you want to," Jan replied. "We can take care of him."

Fran vanished, shutting the door behind him.

Jan sat down on the bed, and unbuttoned Ed's shirt.

"You look very pale," I said. "Are you sure you're all right?"

"I'll be fine," he told me, and to Jan he said, "Fran's finally paid me back for Mexico."

"I'm sure it was an accident," she said.

"Don't make too many waves on this bed," Ed groaned. "I'm still a bit dizzy." He closed his eyes.

Jan carefully massaged his arms, then said to him, "Sit up and take off your shirt so we can rub your back."

He sat up and slid his shirt off, then pulled his undershirt over his head.

When he lay back down, Jan rolled him over on his stomach. "Come here, Anna," she said.

I crawled slowly onto the bed and sat on the other side of him. We each took one side of his back and kneaded his flesh in synchronization, up and down his spine and across his shoulder blades, where I felt the knots Jan told me were tension spots, and learned to press them firmly with my fingers until they disappeared.

"Lower," Ed whispered, and loosened his pants so that our hands could knead and rub his ass. He began to move up and down until waves rippled out to the edge of the bed.

"You seem fine, you fraud," I heard Jan whisper in his ear.

"I'm much better now," he agreed.

When Jan slid his pants off and rolled him over, his penis sprung erect. His eyes were shut, but he had much more color in his face now. She unbuttoned her dress and tugged it over her head. I hesitated, then did the same.

Ed opened his eyes to watch us strip. The bed rocked like a boat on the ocean. "I see two women," he said. "I hope this doesn't mean I'm seeing double." He smiled at me. "Anna, I never thought you would."

"Oh, you hardly know Anna at all." Jan opened a drawer in the base of the waterbed and reached in.

"You don't, you know," I agreed.

She took out a small plastic packet and tore it with her teeth, sucking something into her mouth, then took Ed's penis in her mouth. I watched as though I were a spy. I couldn't believe I was in the same room with them. While Jan's jaws worked up and down on his cock, Ed writhed and moaned beneath her. Suddenly she sat up, removing the pink rubber sheath from his penis with her teeth. His fluid burst from him in a white foam that shot higher than I ever imagined it could, landing in a puddle between his thighs. Jan pulled a brown velvet cloth out from under Ed's legs, rolled it up, and dropped it over the side of the bed. Then she leaned over to kiss me. She tasted like a rubber nipple.

Ed was still breathing heavily. He sat up and leaned against the wall at the head of the bed while Jan pushed me back so that I lay beside him. She began to feel between my legs with her quick fingers until I almost felt a flash, then she stopped and, taking Ed's hand, guided his fingers to me. The two of them bent over me.

"Take your hand like this, across," she told him. "Gentler. This is how she likes it, she's different from me. Like this."

When I moaned and moved my hips, waves splashed beneath me. Slowly the ocean grew until it foamed up inside me. I heard myself scream far away.

"God," said Ed. "I've never seen her do that before."

Jan laughed. They lay on either side of me. We heard footsteps in the hall and then Fran opened the door and stood holding the door knob.

"It's late," he said. "Are you going to spend the night?"

"They'll stay," said Jan. "Ed needs to rest. We should leave them alone. She got off the bed and covered us with the fur. "Come," she said to Fran. She took his hand and led him away, shutting the door behind her.

"Well," I started to say, but Ed interrupted me with a kiss. Though I'd known him for years, I realized I'd never known him very well.

"Let's get under the covers," he said, pulling down the blue paisley spread. The sheets had a pattern of blue and green waves; it was like crawling into warm, smooth surf. He took another packet from the waterbed and sheathed his erect cock in glimmering pink.

"We've never done it with a rubber," he said. "Jan likes them a lot. She says men feel harder when they wear them, and smoother. What do you think?"

I didn't feel like admitting I'd never used one, since he'd probably assumed all along I'd been having other affairs; after all, that's what we agreed to do when we started living together. I took his plastic penis in my hand, feeling it with my fingers. It was like an alien being, a little Martian I wanted to suck up into the space inside me. I guided it in and as it slid up and down, I realized Jan was right: I'd never felt anything quite so hard or so slick. Back and forth, around and around, went the pink alien, while Ed's newly educated fingers danced across me and the waves of the bed threatened to drown us both.

"Blast off!" I cried, and the heat of a rocket rose inside me as we came.

When we woke, sunlight glowed through light curtains, revealing dust motes in the air. I sat up, but Ed drew me back under the covers and caressed me in the ways Jan had taught him until I separated and dissolved, my own molecules like motes of dust, every atom of me blown apart and recombined.

I fell asleep and when I woke again, Ed was gone. I dressed and tiptoed down the hall holding my shoes. The door to Jan's bedroom was open, the rumpled velvet comforter just as we'd left it when we ran downstairs last night. I put on my shoes and went downstairs. It was two in the afternoon by the clock in the hall, and not a soul to be seen. I found Ed in the kitchen drinking a cup of coffee.

"Where is everyone?" I asked.

"They left us coffee," he answered, waving a sheet of paper. "It seems that Fran and Jan are up to their usual tricks."

I heard footsteps coming down the stairs.

"Hello? Signs of life in the universe?" Roger called. "There you are at last, you've found my coffee." He refilled the cup he carried. "John isn't awake yet. You should try one of the attic rooms next time. When you leave the curtains open it's like fucking under the stars on a mountain top. I've been up since ten and I'm getting lonely. What do you think of our friends Fran and Jan taking off like that?"

I grabbed the note out of Ed's hands and looked at Jan's small, neat printing, which I'd seen so many times on invitations. "Fran needs to get away," she wrote, "so we've run to Brazil for a while. Special apologies to Ed from Fran. He trusts you to manage things at the office. There shouldn't be anything that can't be handled without him. Cancel what you can and and postpone the rest. Roger, stay as long as you want, and lock up when you go. We'll be back after Christmas. Love to all," and then Fran's handwriting scrawled across the bottom of the page as it did across their books: *Fran and Jan*.

"Just what they did to me in Mexico," Ed laughed. "When

you have their money, you can do what you want and hang everyone. At least this time they didn't leave me alone."

Roger laughed too, shaking his head. "They left me in London years ago, long before they were rich. Not only that, I had to ship their bags home while they hitched around Sweden together. I think I made Fran nervous. He's never known what to think of Jan and me. We both enjoy the illusion of romance, but the problem with Fran is, he thinks everything's real."

The day after Christmas, Ed and I received a postcard from Jan. "Brazil has done its work," she wrote. "We'll be home for New Year's Eve. Please come to our party and stay the night." It was signed as usual in Fran's bold slash.

"This time let's see if we can send Fran to Shanghai," I told Ed. I was finally beginning to know a few things.

Night Travelers

Angela Fairweather

Joanna eased her body onto the thick carpet of grass, adjusting her contours to the soft turf. Although the air was now comfortably cool, she could still feel the heat radiating upward from the ground, reaching into her bones. She took in a deep breath, then released it forcefully, allowing herself to be enveloped by the earth. For the first time in hours she relaxed.

She lay there breathing slowly and fully, letting go of the afternoon and all its problems. The children had bickered at the dinner table, a combination of heat and no naps. Her husband, red-faced and exhausted as he downed two icy gin and tonics, had complained about the stock market and how the subway always stalled under the bridge when the temperature rose above 80°. He had rebuffed her when she had playfully attempted to seduce him after his shower, pulling the towel from his waist and rubbing her body up against him. She both understood and resented his exhaustion. It *was* Friday, and hot after all. Maybe he wouldn't work tomorrow and would go swimming with the kids instead. Maybe they'd cook outside and sit in the dark together after the children went to bed. Maybe they'd make love.

Maybe.

Another deep breath. Her body became heavy, soft, pliant, receptive. The wonderful floating feelings returned. These were sensations she had discovered a year ago while lying in her darkened bedroom one afternoon during the children's nap time. She had not known what was occurring that first time as her body lay heavily on the bed. She had watched in detached wonder as she felt herself become lighter, bouyant, almost dizzy, and the air carried her until she saw herself lying below on the bed, her consciousness above it all. She had observed the softness of her breath, the eyes fluttering slightly, a half-smile on her delicate mouth. And then she had been back inside herself again, on the bed, looking at the ceiling, wondering what had happened.

She had tried several times to repeat the experience, but she had been unable to call it back. Then one night after calming a child held captive by a nightmare, she lay in bed wide awake, waiting for sleep to return. She felt her body becoming lighter and lighter, the sensation of twirling, of lifting, and again she was floating, only now over houses in the neighborhood, floating out toward the reservoir, over the deep black pines filled with the sounds of night. Slowly she circled the reservoir, then glided back toward town, toward her home, her bed, her body. She rolled over and looked at the clock. The entire event had taken less than five minutes.

In bed the following evening she had waited until her husband's breathing became slow and even. She had eased herself up, feet to the floor, gathered up her robe, and slipped quietly down the hall and up the stairs to her office. Settling into the old overstuffed chair, the light from the floor lamp flooding the pages, she had begun to read the books on the metaphysical that she had bought that afternoon. She had explored the mysteries of out-of-body travel: the realm of the occult, the mystical teachings of the ancients and of those more recently expressed. Her curiosity had been insatiable. She had guarded this time as she would a tryst with a secret lover. It was the only adventure she could claim completely as her own. She had decided to tell no one of her attempts to unravel her mysterious travelling. Her husband, she knew, wouldn't understand, or worse, would be concerned about her sanity.

Some nights when her thinking would become so complex

that it held sleep at a distance, she would force herself to concentrate on her body by sliding her fingers down her soft, rounded belly to her slightly parted lips. Slipping her fingers inside, she would pleasure herself until her back arched and muted cries caught sharply in her throat. Then her body relaxed and sleep returned once again.

As the winter passed and warmer weather returned, Joanna had spent many of her evenings in her garden. She would occasionally read there by flashlight, until the night she was caught by her husband, who had woken up and come down to the kitchen for a snack. He had called to her, first from the window, and then from the edge of the garden, his voice patronizing and bewildered. She had answered him jokingly, saying she had been reading a steamy novel one of her students had carelessly dropped. She had slipped the book between some papers she had been grading, then followed him into the house.

Later, in bed, she had rubbed her thinly satined body against his, teasing the edges of her gown lightly against his back. He had informed her gently but firmly that he had a breakfast meeting at seven and he needed his sleep. As an afterthought, he had mentioned that she should perhaps leave sexy novels to the young, who would benefit from them more than a middle-aged mother of two and a noted professor of history. Her body had stiffened and she had turned away. Perhaps *he* might benefit from some sexy novels to remind himself that middle age and a middle-class lifestyle were not deterrents to eroticism.

She had lain awake for a long time, wondering why they had married in the first place, why people chose those so different from themselves. She had known then that she absolutely would not share her new knowledge with him. The old feeling of resignation that she had experienced so many times in the last ten years had returned as well. A mild depression had settled over her and remained with her through the summer months like the pull of an old scar.

Now, lying under the August sky, Joanna began her travelling exercises. She imagined herself surrounded by protective light, a bright luminescence that would help keep her silver cord — the binding between her body and her spirit — intact. In this way she could travel outside her body without much fear of being cut off from it, unable to return to the material world. She evened her breathing, and visualized herself breaking free of the earth's pull, slipping up and out and into the netherworld of the astral plane. She travelled rapidly, whirling through space, losing all sense of time or direction.

She was on the edge of a meadow, lit only by the nearly full moon rising in the east and the thick mantle of stars overhead. The air was clean, heavily scented with pine and cedar. Somewhere in the distance an owl called; otherwise it was silent.

For a few moments she sat completely still, adjusting to the changes around her. Suddenly she realized where she was. She let out a soft cry of delight as she recognized the meadow of her childhood. Between this rich meadow and the rise above it, she and her family had spent their summers high in the eastern range of the Sierra Nevada. She sat in the meadow smiling, memories spilling over her: playing hide and seek with her brother and sister, fishing in the cold deep pools, reading novels, daydreaming, experiencing her first romance.

She chuckled. It had been a long while since she had thought of Shep. For years she had fantasized about him, wondering how it would have been if they hadn't drifted apart. Tall, blond-haired and brown-eyed, he had a powerful build and the easy gait of a young man at home in his body. He had been a junior in college, studing forestry, when they first met, and Joanna had adored him from the moment they were introduced at the rodeo dance on the Fourth of July.

They had seen each other every day after that. On the days he worked, she wrote long accounts of the night before in her diary, and dreamily looked after her younger brother and sister, waiting for evening, when he would be free to court her.

She remembered the first night they kissed, down by the creek where they had watched beavers building a dam. Although they were both inexperienced, when his lips first grazed hers, the sensation had been pure magic. Their first innocent, light kisses gradually gained intensity and passion. By the summer's end, they had begun a tentative exploration. Shep had touched her breasts through her blouse, then slid his hand inside, and finally removed her blouse to feel her full, yielding breasts, their small nipples dancing with excitement.

Two nights before she was to return to her family's home, their passion had overcome them. Shep slipped his fingers inside her panties as her body shook with excitement and fear. He took her hand and placed it against his swollen penis. She had felt the heat and tautness of him, the ridge of his glans pushing against the constraints of his clothes. He unzipped his fly and guided her hand inside, against the hot, delicate skin. The ache between her legs was incredible and she had wanted desperately to feel him enter her, to ease the strange pain she had never experienced before. But as he eased his body on top of hers, rubbing himself against the thin nylon of her panties, she had panicked and pushed him away.

Afterwards, they felt both disappointed and relieved; neither of them was quite ready to make that jump to adulthood. She cried from the tension, and from her fear of leaving him for home and school. He had comforted her, kissed her tenderly and told her he would marry her and take her home to the family farm in Tennessee as soon as he finished school. He gave her a gold locket, and she returned to her last year of high school starry-eyed and in love. They corresponded for a while, but slowly the summer became only a sparkle of a memory. The next spring her father sold the cabin and she never returned to the meadow.

The sharp snap of a stick startled Joanna back to the present. The hair on her arms and neck rose; her breathing became shallow. She sensed she was being watched, but she couldn't determine the position of the watcher. Very slowly she scanned the thick undergrowth. Nothing.

Then she saw the dark form of a man leaning against the trunk of a pine, as though biding his time, making certain she was alone. Terror swept over her. She fought to control her rising panic, to remain calm. She sat totally still, forcing her breath in and out as slowly as possible, trying to quiet the racing of her heart. She silently repeated a mantra over and over, on her guard as she watched the shadowy form. He remained still.

Joanna cursed herself for not having gained more control over entering and leaving her body. She remembered the books' warnings of the dangers of astral travel, of being endangered by unsettled and angry spirits, of breaking the silver cord and not being able to return to the body again. Desperately she tried to think of a plan of escape. She rose to her knees, then to her feet, keeping her body low to the ground. Then the man spoke.

"Please don't...don't leave. I won't harm you." His voice had a pleading quality, almost like that of a child.

She steadied herself. "Who are you? Why are you here?" she demanded. She needed to determine whether he was an illusion, part of the astral world.

He approached her with sinuous, light movements like those of a large cat, emerging fluidly from the undergrowth. Joanna was motionless, frozen in place, all of her senses alert, but powerless to do more than watch as he approached her. It wasn't until he was within a few feet of her that the moon emerged from the edge of the forest, creating enough light to let her see his face. Her body shuddered involuntarily as she gasped, "Shep! Why are you here?"

He didn't respond, but instead looked at her in an intense, half-starved manner, as if he could gain sustenance from her presence. The air crackled with tension. Finally he spoke, so slowly and quietly that she strained to hear his voice.

"I was killed in Vietnam in 1970. But I wasn't ready to die. Now I'm caught here, hanging in limbo; can't move on, can't let go. I've looked for you so many times, come back here, watched for you. Now you've come." He reached out to her, and caught her arms just as her knees buckled. He eased her down into the long damp grass, and steadied her with his broad hands, his arm across her back.

Joanna slowly tried to absorb what he had said. A more detached part of her wondered at the fact that his body felt as real and material as hers.

"Shep, I can't believe this is happening." She turned to face him. "You must have been so frightened, so incredibly alone."

He exhaled sharply. "My tour was almost up. I'd been injured once, shot in the shoulder. When I was dying I felt so angry. I guess I couldn't deal with letting go so young. I still go back to the farm and check on my Mom. My death was hard on her, it nearly killed her when they sent me back in a box. I went to see her a couple of times. She used not to believe I was there, but now she does. She seems grateful when I go to her."

Shep looked away. "And I've come here. I never completely let go of you, Joanna. I always figured we'd run into each other somehow, fall in love again. It's crazy, I know. But I've been waiting for you...."

Joanna sat still for a moment more before shifting her weight so that she faced him again. "I don't know how I got here tonight. I've travelled before, but I can't control where I go. I'm still part of the material world." She spoke as if to reassure herself that this was indeed true.

Shep said nothing. He extended his hand and gently traced his forefinger along her hairline, over her finely planed cheekbone to her delicate mouth. She smiled up at him.

"You look so young," she said. "I mean, older than when I last saw you, but still so young."

"I was only twenty-three when I died," he answered. "Just a kid. It's odd. I feel infinitely old but I'm still in this kid body." He shrugged his shoulders and grinned at her.

"You haven't changed much," he said. "If anything, you're more beautiful now. Your face has softened." He paused for a moment. "It appears that life has been gentle to you, Joanna. Tell me about yourself."

Joanna laughed softly, "Well, I went to college. In fact, I teach at a university now. I got married when I was twenty-five. My husband's a financial analyst, and we both worked for quite a while before we had our two kids, a boy and a girl. Oh, and we have a great old house that we've remodelled, and we live in a small town. You know, it sounds so perfect, looks so perfect on the surface. I feel guilty for even saying this, but I often feel lonely, and cut off, bored...no, maybe restless is a better word. You know, I have no idea how long I can remain here, and I really want to be here with you, to touch you and kiss you." She could feel her face redden at her boldness. He was looking at her, a smile playing across his lips.

"For years I thought about making love with you here in this meadow, how it would feel, how good it would be." She paused for a moment, took his hands in hers, and continued. "We may never have this chance again. It's what's most missing in my life. Intimacy. Deep, loving feelings and physical contact. My husband just isn't there for me and he never will be. I just...." She felt confused now, on the brink of tears.

Shep leaned forwards and kissed her tenderly on her forehead, the edges of her cheeks, the tip of her nose. "Joanna, how many times have I thought of loving you. I don't know how anyone could *not* want to love you over and over."

He encircled her in his arms, embracing her until they fell back gently into the grass, kissing long and deeply. He pressed his body against hers; she slowly rubbed her breasts against his chest, her hips undulating slightly, pulsing her pelvis as he began to swell. His fingers loosened the ties of her thin peasant blouse. It draped loosely, exposing her soft, round breasts, the nipples dark and hard, begging to be sucked. Shep's mouth grabbed one of them, his hand cupping her breast to his mouth, and he sucked long and hard with the urgency of an infant.

He moved back and forth between her breasts, first sucking one, then the other. Her fingers searched for the buttons of his shirt, working them open. They embraced again, hungrily searching out each other's lips, their breath coming in short gasps. She released the buttons of his jeans, with some difficulty because his erection was so great. She worked the pants over the prominent bones of his pelvis, over his rounded hips, muscular legs, ankles. Then she looked at him.

His cock was thick, thicker than any she had known, almost the size of her slender wrist. The glans was prominent, the ridge developed so that his penis appeared like an enormous, perfectly shaped forest mushroom. His hair was like blond silk, so different from her own, which was dark, tightly curled, and wiry. She dropped to her hands and knees, nuzzled her face against his cock, then caught it in her mouth, warm and wet against the smooth dry skin, the droplet of lubrication emanating from the tip. She pulled it deeply into her mouth, forming her lips over it, dragging them slightly to create friction. He moaned and thrust his pelvis forward, feeding her hungry mouth. Her hand caught up his balls, nails scratching slightly, then carefully massaging them, first one, then the other, then both together with the flat of her hand.

"Joanna, oh God, Joanna." His head was thrown back, his muscular chest barely covered with soft golden hair, the muscles of his belly in tight ridges as she sucked and stroked him.

When he could stand it no longer, he lifted her up by her arms and laid her back down on the grass, both hands caressing her breasts, down the curve of her waist, the flare of her hips, to the thin stretch of silk and lace that covered her.

He ran his tongue over the silk, smelling and tasting her delicate scents, the blending of her musk with an exotic Oriental perfume. She was already wet, so that her panties were soaked within moments of his attention. He lifted the sides of the lace, forcing the silk between the lips of her vagina. He worked the silk back and forth. Then he slid the panties loose and over her hips. She watched him, her blue eyes glazed. He kneeled over her, admiring her slender body, the soft fullness of her belly, the deep thatch between her legs. He lowered his mouth to her cunt, parted the lips with his fingers, and allowed his tongue to slip in between the lips, travelling through the folds and crevices he had imagined so many times.

Her body was bucking now, thrashing wildly under him, ragged cries coming from her throat. Her body was overtaken by great wrenching spasms, her breath a series of hoarse gasps. She pulled at him urgently, begging him to enter her, to fuck her hard and deep. He held his cock in his hand as he eased it in. He could feel the strain in her cunt as it slowly yielded to his fullness.

Joanna, eyes tightly squeezed shut, cried over and over, turning her head from one side to the other, begging for relief. Slowly, slowly he worked himself into her until he was fully embraced. Then he thrust forward several times, as the air between them crackled with electricity. "Shep, fuck me, please!" Her legs encircled his back, lifted up toward his shoulders, forcing him in deeper and deeper. She held her hands to her heels, pushing hard against them to create greater tension. Her breasts bounced wildly, not quite touching his chest. She could feel his body tightening, his cock stretching to its limits, then a great explosion as he came hard into her, again, and again, and again.

He collapsed onto her. Her arms holding him tightly, she kissed his neck, his face, his mouth. He released his hold and gently eased his body down next to hers, his arm draped across her ribs. They lay together quietly, breathing softly, his face nuzzled against her neck, resting against the perfumed tangle of her long hair.

Eventually they turned to each other, and talked softly. Her hand found his chest and began working itself over him inch by inch until it dropped down to his half-hardened cock. They began again, this time more slowly and completely until a waterfall of orgasms spilled over them.

"I think I can break free now, Joanna. I think I can go on."

She delayed her response, holding him to her breasts a little longer. "I think you can too," she said finally. "I've been freed as well. Oh, Shep, I'm so grateful for this night, for travelling with you."

"I'll be waiting for you on the other side, Joanna," he replied. "In our next life we can dance together more fully."

They dressed each other, and lay down once more, their arms encircling each other in a tight embrace. Together they drifted silently through the sky.

Joanna became aware of her body, stiff with cold, lying in the grass in the pre-dawn chill. Slowly she rose to her feet, feeling numb and dazed, coming out of a dream so close yet not quite remembered. Returning to the house, she noticed the tenderness of her nipples. As she stood in the darkened bedroom, silently removing her clothes, she was suddenly filled with a great feeling of warmth as the evening returned. Slowly, quietly, she eased into bed, stretching out beside the sleeping form of her husband, his body emanating a welcome heat. She placed her arm around him, pressed up against his hips and back, and relaxed. She wondered if her experience had been only a dream. Then as she slipped into the space between wakefulness and dreaming she was vaguely aware of a rush of wetness between her legs....

Among My Souvenirs

Marcy Sheiner

Five years is a relatively short period of time, and yet so much has changed with regard to sexual behavior in the last five years, that I find myself looking back with nostalgia at a bygone era. With AIDS running amok, the days of following one's desires of the moment are gone, at least for me and most of my friends. My boyfriend Jackson and I are staying pretty much monogamous these days. When we started using pornography to achieve the variety we had always maintained in our sex life, I remembered the journals I used to keep of our experiences, and dug them out to use as turn-ons. I found this story among my souvenirs.

Part of Jackson's attraction to me is that I'm bisexual. Even though we engaged in a threesome with another woman only once, he knows my desire for other women is always there. Like many straight men, he's turned on by the idea of lesbian sex, but he has little interest in male homosexuality.

Jackson is black, muscular, virile-looking. Women flock to him at parties and bars, and, although he says he's just being friendly, he is definitely a flirt.

Despite being clearly heterosexual, Jackson is intrigued not only by lesbian sex, but by the whole gay subculture and life-style. He's always wanting us to go to gay bars, male or female — something I don't feel altogether comfortable doing, since I don't want lesbians to feel like we're hitting on them. Also, I see gay men looking at Jackson as if they could eat him up with a spoon. And they look at me like they wish I'd get out of their way!

Jackson thinks that men are attracted to him because of his style. He always wears a sharp three-piece suit, or a spiffy shirt and sweater with impeccably creased pants. I think the attraction is his delicious ass. I'm convinced these guys are just dying to squeeze and fuck his firm round buns. I myself have stuck my fingers into his asshole while he's fucking me, and know the ecstasy of being inside him: the incomparable sensation of squeezing him from both ends, my cunt sucking the come from his prick while my finger gently circles his hole.

One Saturday night Jackson asked me to go to a popular gay disco. I'd been to the place with my lesbian friends, and knew that although the crowd was mixed, mostly gay men hung out there. I didn't want to go, but Jackson kept after me, implying that I was uptight. I began to question myself: why did I feel so threatened? After all, he'd slept with other women over the years, including once in my presence, and our relationship was still intact. He'd made it apparent that he had no interest in sleeping with men. And as far as lesbians thinking we were out cruising, I just wouldn't do that. We'd go to the disco, dance, and have a good time.

The disco was part of a complex that included a huge bar, dance hall, motel, and restaurant. The place is well-known in three states as a gay haven, although unsuspecting straights wander in from time to time. I've seen Frank, one of the bar-tenders, bring straight couples their check with the first drink, and then ignore them so they'd leave. Fortunately, he knows me, so Jackson and I didn't receive this kind of treatment. If fact, he probably assumed, as did most gays in the place, that I was a lesbian, and that therefore Jackson must also be gay. One aspect of being bisexual is that people on both sides of the fence assume I'm one of them.

At any rate, the bartender was friendlier than usual, making small talk while surreptitiously eyeing the delicious number I'd hauled into his bar. Jackson, in his usual naive fashion, joined the conversation, oblivious to the fact that a dozen pairs of eyes were riveted to his body; that men up and down the bar were mentally undressing him.

Feeling completely invisible, I decided to go upstairs where the dancing was, and leave Jackson to handle himself. Picking up my Bloody Mary, I slid off my barstool, unsurprised that no one, not even Jackson, who was deep in conversation with the bartender, noticed my departure.

Upstairs, men and women — mostly men — danced under strobe lights to the sound of Donna Summer. I sat at a corner table and watched the dancers, most of whom were moving in their own separate spaces, some consciously trying to attract attention. One man, wearing jeans and a purple sleeveless T-shirt so tight his nipples bulged through, was making erotic movements to his own image in the mirror. He held his arms over his head and undulated; he rubbed his crotch and moaned softly to himself.

In a corner of the room a group of women danced in a circle. They were dressed flamboyantly in purple and orange flowing skirts, their long earrings dangling. Recognizing one of them, I made my way across the room and joined the circle.

Dancing to the strong disco beat, with the lights flashing across the colors of the women's outfits, I forgot about Jackson and lost myself to sensation. I must have been dancing for about fifteen minutes when I noticed him in the middle of the dance floor with a man who looked vaguely familiar. He was doing his usual dance step, digging the music and the scene, but his partner was focused on one thing only: my man.

Should I be mature and keep on dancing, or should I go over and assert my rights? Convincing myself that Jackson might want to be rescued, I left the circle of women. As I walked across the dance floor, I suddenly realized his partner was Tony, a bisexual man with whom I had once had an affair.

Tony and I had never been in love, or anything remotely like it. We'd met several years ago in a small town where small minds were stifling both of us. We were so relieved to find each other in that wasteland, that we immediately began acting out our fantasies: everything from dressing in costumes to visiting the nearby city's sex clubs on weekends. Tony introduced me to the intriguing world of swingers, and told me all about the gay male scene. We shared our erotic writings with one another and felt a strong kinship as bisexuals. I never would have made it through that year without Tony.

Now here he was, my brother, my twin. When he spotted me, his face lit up like a light bulb. He left Jackson without a word and rushed over to embrace me. We kissed and hugged and stroked each other's faces. The music was too loud to talk, so Tony motioned for us to go downstairs. I hesitated, looking at Jackson.

"It's okay," Tony shouted in my ear. "He's just a number I picked up at the bar."

"Tony," I shouted back. "He's my boyfriend."

Tony's thick bushy eyebrows arched magnificently. "In that case," he said, a mischievous smile dimpling his cheek, "I suppose we should ask him to join us."

Down in the bar, Tony ordered champagne to celebrate our reunion. We sat in a booth drinking one bottle after another, and Tony regaled us with stories of his latest adventures, most of which held strong sexual overtones. He let it be known that he had a room at the hotel, and more than once touched Jackson's elegant hand while making eye contact with him.

I was amused. I'd seen Tony in action before. More than being merely amused, though, I was getting hot. I imagined Tony's prick in Jackson's asshole, his hand on Jackson's cock.

Dazed by the champagne, I barely noticed as Tony urged us into his room. My fantasy was coming true.

I sat down and lazily smoked a cigarette, wanting to be merely an observer. I knew Jackson was in the hands of a master. Whether with a man or a woman, Tony devoted the same degree of attentiveness and artistry to the object of his desire. I knew he had a fondness, as do I, for brown skin, and for muscular men. And here stood Jackson, my prize, a glorious man if ever there was one, with his well-developed biceps, flat belly, rock hard thighs, and an uncircumcised prick that was six inches at rest. As Tony removed Jackson's clothing piece by piece, I felt as if he were unwrapping a present I had personally delivered.

Tony was so different physically from Jackson that it was hard to remember they belonged to the same gender. A mere 5'5", he was thin and lithe, almost delicate by comparison. But what turned me on most about Tony was his face: huge brown eyes, full sensuous lips, big bushy eyebrows, and a thick mop of dark curls. He was smaller than Jackson in all ways but one — his prick when erect stood out a good eight inches. Now it bulged beneath his black bikini underwear as he finished undressing Jackson, who was casting questioning looks my way. I knew he wanted me to join them, but I signalled him to relax and let Tony take over.

Once he had Jackson naked, Tony began. As if wanting to familiarize himself with the territory before abandoning himself to it, he ran his hands over Jackson's silken skin, first kneading the shoulders, slowly circling Jackson's bulging biceps with his palms, then running his hands lightly down the chest. Jackson shuddered with pleasure as his nipples were gently stimulated, and visibly relaxed.

Tony sank to his knees and caressed Jackson's velvet prick with the tips of his fingers. He lingered a long time before letting his mouth venture anywhere near, while Jackson's breath grew more shallow. My cunt throbbed insistently. I removed my panties so I could play with myself and watch at the same time. By now the men were too involved with each other to notice me. My fingers rubbed my dripping pussy as I watched my man being taken by another.

Tony had all of Jackson's cock in his mouth and was greedily sucking, while Jackson stood, his arms folded across his chest. I could almost feel his cock gliding down my own throat, and I loved the sight of Tony on his knees for Jackson's pleasure. Just as Jackson's face began to soften, a sure sign that he would come, Tony removed Jackson's cock from his mouth and crawled around to face his ass. Jackson leaned his hands against the wall, and Tony licked and slurped, alternating between Jackson's huge balls and wide open asshole. His hand moved up and down Jackson's cock. They were both in heaven.

As Jackson began to come against the wall, Tony stood and forced his own cock into Jackson's asshole. Both men grunted and groaned, and my cunt exploded, aching to have one of them inside me. I was jealous, yet incredibly excited by their involvement with each other and their exclusion of me.

It didn't last long. Before I knew it, their hands were upon me, and I was being carried to the bed, where my hot pussy was licked by two extremely skilled tongues. I kept my eyes shut, so I never knew who was doing what, only that I came again. This time not only was a juicy cock inside me, but another was all the way down my throat as well. Thick come spurted into my mouth at the same moment it shot deep into my cunt.

Exhausted, we drifted off to sleep. In my dreams there appeared endless combinations of lovemaking between the three of us. Later, Jackson and I talked excitedly about the possibilities. For the first time in his life he was eager to make love with a man.

But Tony, always unpredictable, left for Key West. I keep trying to get Jackson to return to the gay bar and try someone else, but he's not interested. I think he's really hung up on Tony and doesn't want to spoil the experience by being with another man.

The next time we saw Tony, the AIDS scare had just begun in the gay community, and he was a changed man. He spoke with Jackson and me at length about AIDS, but since it had yet to hit the straight world, we thought he was exaggerating. Now we know he was warning us.

We look back on our one night with Tony with a feeling of nostalgia, and a sense of sadness for what might have developed had the fates allowed. We still find variety, though, by reading through my old journals, or watching videos, or reading porn. Of course, none of that quite matches the real thing, but it will have to do for now. We keep the home fires burning, hoping, like everyone else, that this too shall pass.

The Art Gallery

Jane Longaway

Perhaps the best thing to begin with is the pursuit. I had never been followed like that before and it had the effect of making me feel both frightened and excited at the same time. He was a big man in his mid-thirties with heavy dark Sicilian good looks and anxious eyes. His large shoulders drooped, giving him a sexy drug dealer look. I was looking at Alice's paintings which were so bad that all I could do was stand in front of each one for an agonized moment and then make my way slowly towards the next.

The man was following as I self-consciously went along the gallery wall from painting to painting as though making the Stations of the Cross. He was so close to me that I felt his energy like a dark hot river behind me. His body towered over me and leaned into me. I found it hard to keep staring at the paintings. Did I feel panic because he might be interested in me or because he might not be? I became confused and stupid counting backward from one hundred to keep a meditative look on my face. The paint had been laid thinly on the canvas, and I couldn't help but think that if only Alice had used more paint I might at least

be able to study texture. The stranger put a hand out and gently placed it on my shoulder. It surprised me because it was a
small fine hand with delicate fingers.

"Let's get some wine," he said in a deep, confident voice.

Too embarrassed to look at his face, I turned and stared at his
black leather jacket. I was grateful for the diversion and for the
chance to drink, so I followed him to the wine bar. I noticed that
his feet, which were in blue boat shoes, were also quite small
compared to the size of his body, and I found both his feet and
hands very attractive.

We took our wine out on a little balcony and sat down on a
plastic bench. I was careful not to sit too close to him, putting
my purse between us and looking demurely at his feet. I was
aware that the costume I wore was ridiculous and artsy, black
cotton leggings with holes in the knees and a low cut white
sweater cinched at the waist by a wide red belt. I had tarted
myself up on purpose that evening to get my husband to notice
me, which he did not. The man said his name was Philip, and
he waited with his eyes on the little patch of white flesh on my
knee for me to tell my name.

"I'm Nina," I lied. Ann seemed so dull.

"I like that name," he said in his low voice. "It suits you."

"Thank you." I looked up at his face and saw him studying
me with a sort of rapture that made him even more attractive.

"I am an artist," he said, softly leaning his head close to mine.
"I'd like to show you my work sometime soon."

"Oh," I said.

"I'd also like to fuck you," he added.

I held the glass to my lips and did not answer. I could feel the
blood rushing to my face.

"I do watercolors," he added, and he started to roll a cigarette
with his thin fingers. I stood up to leave, filled with a sort of terror at what he was suggesting.

"I'm here with a friend."

"Don't go," he said.

"I have to."

He sighed quite loudly and looked frankly at me. It was the
look a hungry person might give a juicy steak. I enjoyed it. I
looked briefly at his thighs which were straining his pants and
imagined what they would be like to touch.

I shook my head.

He followed me back into the gallery where I attached myself to Virginia and Alice. Virginia, reeling with drink, was telling Alice what a genius she was. Alice just stood there pale and drained with a sad little smile on her face. When I turned around Philip was right behind me, standing back but close enough to touch. I grabbed Virginia's hand and squeezed it, asking her to leave with me, but she ignored me with a hazy smile and started in again telling Alice how brilliant she was and Alice stood there rooted to the spot, letting the words bounce off her.

I left the two of them and went to the entrance to get my coat. Philip followed right behind me.

"My studio is real close," he said.

I smiled but shook my head. He was looking at me with such frank sexual interest that I buttoned my coat all the way up to my neck.

He came so close I could see the gold flecks in his eyes. He pinned me to the wall with his arms.

"Why not?"

Was his desire contagious? I felt myself get warm, felt a temptation to ignore the gold band on my finger and pay attention to the intemperate stirrings of my nature. But torn between the possibility of pleasure and my duty I merely trembled in my heavy black coat. I couldn't look him in the face. I broke away without speaking and quickly got out the door and walked fast down the block. It was a cold drizzly foggy San Francisco night. It dawned on me suddenly that I hadn't brought my car but had come with Virginia, only now I was afraid to turn back. I was near Grant Street and could hear the buzz of Chinatown and see the lights through the haze. I walked toward it.

"Where are you going?"

I turned around and there he was. "Home," I called out over my shoulder.

"You live *here*? You live in Chinatown?"

I kept walking. I rushed into the first open shop I saw and hid myself among all the gewgaws and colorful junk. The store smelled of sandalwood and the damp. I looked at myself in one of the small plastic mirrors for sale and saw that all the makeup I had put on that evening was still there. My kohl-rimmed eyes looked pale and sleepy but the lashes were jet black and brittle, my mouth was wonderfully red and moist.

He came up silently behind me. I felt his breath on my ear.

"Let's go," he said. I turned and he was smiling wistfully. His delicate hands were hidden in his pockets.

"Oh...." I wanted to say so much but only "Oh" came out. I wanted to say that I didn't do that sort of thing, that I was not the pick-up type of woman, when it dawned on me that while Ann didn't go off with strange men it was just the thing that Nina might get into.

We walked out of the shop together. In the street he put his arm around me and held me close. He was so much taller than I. My face touched the leather of his jacket and my hair was below his chin. We walked like this without speaking. Once he pulled me into a dark doorway and held my face up and kissed me, sticking his tongue deep into my mouth and licking it slowly. We continued our walk to his place, silently vibrating with expectation.

His studio was small and poorly furnished, but there were paintings everywhere so that when he turned on the light I was startled. The watercolors were all of nude women, very large and realistic. The colors were brilliant and overlaid in a way that made the flesh seem to glow. All the nudes were postured so that their sex was pushed forward and each wore a whimsical little hat.

Philip took my coat and hung it up. He came back with a black straw hat for me to wear.

"Put it on," he said.

The hat fit tight to my skull and had three red feathers that curled down my neck and under my chin. Philip put his arms around me and kissed me, reaching behind to lift the sweater up, squeezing my ass with his hand. He moved his hand under my tights and ran his finger down the crack of my ass. I was sucking on his tongue and letting my mouth go slack and wet. He pushed his tongue to the back of my throat, then pulled away and told me to take off my clothes. I removed the hat first and put it on a table while he dimmed the lights and took off his jacket and shoes. There was a large futon on the floor with thick green and cream pillows. Next to the futon was a large brass church candle holder with a fat yellow candle. He lit the candle and the room was filled with a soft smoky light. In this light his eyes seemed black and as shiny as olives.

I took off my sweater and my bra, then pulled off the cotton tights and fluffed up my pubic hair with my fingers. "Come here," he said from the middle of the room. Hat in hand, I padded over the worn carpet in my bare feet. He took the hat and placed it again on my head, taking care to turn the feathers correctly under my chin.

"The hat is perfect on you with your black hair and pale eyes, it makes your skin like opal and your lips like blood."

He took a pot of red gloss and rubbed it on my nipples until they stood hard and erect. Then he put some of the gloss between my legs. I was already wet but his cool fingers with the sticky, sweet-smelling color made me all the wetter. Slowly, he licked his fingers, then put them in my mouth.

He was still wearing a soft cotton shirt and loose white pants. The shirt felt good next to my skin. As I kissed his mouth, my hands fumbled to unbutton it but he pushed me down with both hands until I was on my knees in front of him. He unzipped his pants and took out his thick short cock, nestled in a mass of brown curls and already swollen.

"Suck me," he said. He kept one hand on my shoulder while he guided his cock into my mouth with the other.

I knelt in front of him and with my eyes closed licked and sucked, making his cock grow thicker and bigger. It tasted like him, with a strong musky scent. I was getting hot. I took his cock out of my mouth for a moment and caressed my breasts with it. Philip was breathing heavily. He placed his cock in my mouth again, grabbing the back of my head and pushing his cock deep into my mouth. I gagged and tears came to my eyes. He pulled his pants down completely. His thighs were magnificent, huge, golden tan and as hard as stone. I ran my hands over them and kissed them in turn and then kissed the broad tip of his cock and his balls.

I sucked him some more. This time he let me do it in my own fashion, holding one hand on his member and licking the head and stem, then closing my mouth over the whole thing, taking in five inches, letting my spit make it smooth and wet so that it pushed into my mouth easily and sweetly.

Philip was moaning.

I relished his cock. While I was sucking on it I took his balls gently in my hand and played with them, resting my cheek against his hard thigh.

"Oh now, baby, we must," he said thickly. "We must lie

down, baby, or I'll shoot it right now into your pretty mouth...oh."

I let his cock out of my warm mouth and it stuck straight up, brown curls now moist around it. On the red flower of his prick was a drop of clear liquid that stood there like a tear.

Outside I could hear a soft rain begin to fall. It hit the windows, making the sound of fingernails tapping glass.

He helped me to my feet and gazed into my face as he adjusted the little hat, his fingers grazing my cheek as he arranged the feathers. I looked at his face but now it was closed to me, his eyes half shut, the full lips partly open in a rather cruel way. When he pulled me to him I could feel his prick prod against my navel. I wanted to say something special, but all that came out were little mewing noises.

"You really want it, don't you?" he said with great satisfaction. "I can tell by the way you sucked me that you want it."

Even saying "yes" to this would have broken the spell, so I continued making tiny soft noises that seemed to come up from my belly. My hands moved on his hard large body which I found so beautiful. I licked one of his brown nipples.

He led me over to the bed. Above the low futon was a picture that dazzled me. It was a large nude about four feet long, and the reclining woman looked a little like me. I touched one of my breasts and almost reached out to touch one of hers. Philip noticed my gesture but did not comment on the picture. He seemed to enjoy watching me look at it. Indeed, the woman who was lying on her side had grey blue eyes shaped similarly to mine with heavy lids. Her mouth looked quite like mine; however, her nose was much longer and narrower and the hair, partly covered by a veiled riding cap, was strawberry blonde.

Philip reached from behind and put his arms around me, caressing me as I looked at the picture. There was an expression in the woman's eyes that made me long for a mirror to see if my eyes were capable of such lascivious abandon. Suddenly I was lowered onto the futon. Philip crouched down beside me whispering, "Nina." The name itself excited me. I could smell him and could still taste him in my mouth. Now he was spreading my legs open on the bed and kissing my thighs. His tongue was thick and wet; when he started licking my pussy I felt for my own breasts and squeezed them. Although modest by nature, I found myself opening my legs wider and thrusting my cunt into his face. His tongue lingered on my clit and he licked at it until it felt so swollen and hot that I pulled him on top of me. He moved up my body, licking my navel and my nipple, then plunged his tongue into my mouth where I could taste myself.

I pulled on his curly dark hair and kissed his face and neck all over while he began to fuck me, placing just the stubby tip of his cock inside, and then taking it out. My pussy widened to receive it. As my hips moved to meet his, he rammed hard into me. The little hat fell off my head and rolled beside the bed.

He came inside me. My pussy felt every cataclysmic move. He stayed inside while I convulsed and creamed and clawed at his broad tan back. Together we lay on the bed, not speaking. I was looking at all the pictures in the room, dreamily expecting the women to step down from their frames and stand around the low bed, all smiles and warm flesh, rosy with pleasure.

"Nina, let me take your picture."

I was astounded. He did not say "draw," he said "take"; this disappointed me.

He jumped up and got a Polaroid which he aimed at me as I lay there. After a few shots, he asked me to stand and put the hat on. I looked at the hat and said that I would only put it on if he'd let me keep it.

Philip looked stunned and lowered the camera to his groin.

"In memory?" he asked.

Actually it was because I couldn't bear to think of another woman wearing it, but I nodded. He put the hat on my head and took his pictures. I posed for him, realizing now why all his models thrust their cunts out like that. His cock was hard again.

This time, with the prints spread around us, he took me from behind, cupping my tits with his hands and biting hard into my neck. On the floor were the color shots of me. He was so big that he covered me entirely. I placed one of his hands between my legs and he massaged my clit until I came; then, taking his cock out of my pussy he put it into my mouth and I took his pleasure into me, caressing his hard balls until he groaned and shot the thickest, most salty juice down my throat.

It was late when I got home, and I was surprised to find Jon waiting up for me in the living room. He looked me over carefully, taking in the little hat that I wore proudly on my head.

"How was that show, Annie?"

"Wonderful," I answered as I looked at my reflection in the hall mirror. My makeup was for the most part gone but my face was glowing and my eyes looked more intense, like they had the shadow of secrets in them.

Jon put his book down and drummed his fingers together. "Where did you get that hat?"

"It's a long story," I said. I took it carefully off and admired it in my hand.

About The Authors

Isadora Alman, M.A., "Big Ed," writes a regular column on sex and relationships for the *San Francisco Bay Guardian* and has a regular radio show. She appears frequently on TV and lectures on general communication skills. She has a private counseling practice in San Francisco and is the author of *Aural Sex & Verbal Intercourse,* a fictionalized account of her experiences with the San Francisco Sex Information Switchboard.

Emily Alward, "Visit to the Mighoren," is an academic librarian, the mother of two daughters, and owner of two dogs. In her free hours she reads and writes science fiction. "Visit to the Mighoren" is her first venture into writing erotica. Born in Lafayette, Indiana, she has also lived in Maryland, New Zealand and Kentucky.

A. Gayle Birk, "Love Object," a raving liberal Scorpio, is currently working as a freelance writer but has been employed as soda jerk, file clerk, secretary, and "even a writer." She was assistant editor of an insurance company magazine prior to receiving a research grant at the University of Texas.

Nancy Blackett, "Shaman's Eyes," is the pen name of a San

145

Francisco Bay Area writer and performer. She wrote her first erotic story, "Omelette" (published in *On Our Backs*), at age 50. "Shaman's Eyes" was inspired by a dream she experienced after attending a workshop on erotic writing.

Khasti Cadell, "Workout," lives in New York City, where her life is ordinary but far from dull. Her habits include chocolate, ogling teenage boys and smiling secretly. A devoted creator of erotic literature, she wrote this fantasy as a gift to Lorna and Joan.

Cheryl Cline, "Pickup," grew up in a family full of dudes and pickups. Her dream car is a cherry-red '57 Chevy half-ton stepside, and her favorite heavy metal band is AC/DC. She lives in Concord, California with her husband Lynn and their white Jimmy Sierra S-15.

Kathy Dobbs, "Read Me A Story," makes her home in Houston and works in animal care, one of her passions. She states, "Erotica being yet another of my passions, I enjoy being both reader and author." Her story is dedicated to Ginger, her inspiration and soulmate.

Angela Fairweather, "Night Travelers," has been writing since she was child, and professionally for sixteen years, chiefly about education, health and food. She is married to "a very sexual man who enjoys erotica and enticed me into writing it for him." She has "a beautiful 15 year old daughter who still thinks sex is a little odd — an indulgence for adults who haven't anything better to do with their time."

Lisa LaBia, "Jane's Train," edits *Magnet School*, the first sexographic magazine. She defines sexographic as using a wide variety of non-sexist, non-violent sexually arousing words and images pleasing to both men and women to incorporate the tender and romantic elements of eros.

Moxie Light, "Police Protection," writes for several journals and periodicals and has written a feminist screenplay in search of a producer. She is the first woman to have taken a psychiatrist to court in Massachusetts and win.

Jesse Linnell, "Sex Education," first encountered erotic writing when she was seventeen, with a book called *Satan in Silk*. "Though the story intrigued me, I found its detail skimpy and its adjectives stale with repetition." Since then, she has strived to keep her details engorged and her adjectives throbbing with anticipation.

Jane Longaway, "Art Gallery," is a writer, printer, voluptuary, and mother of one fine son. She's been known to go fishing when things get weird.

Edna MacBrayne, "Wet Silk," lives in a beach town in Southern California where she is currently working on a series of children's fairy tales. She is also the author of *Alida: An Erotic Novel.*

Charmaine Parsons, "Affairs," usually writes horror and mystery stories. Although this is her first venture into erotica, she plans to continue in this much neglected area. She is married, with three children.

Jennifer Pruden, "Shades of Grey," is a newspaper reporter/photographer. She likes parasailing, marinated artichoke hearts, and cats. She owns a ferret named Hedge and has been published in several magazines and journals, including *On Our Backs* and *Outrageous Women.*

Susan St. Aubin, "Our Friends Fran and Jan," is a writer with the usual alternatives necessary for money: teacher, file clerk, technical writer, secretary. "I'm overeducated, married, no children; I like cats, and I prefer to live as far away from cities as I can financially and logistically afford to."

Marcy Sheiner, "Among My Souvenirs" and "Work and Play in the New Age," is a poet, novelist and journalist whose work has appeared in a wide variety of publications. She sees the merging of the creative and sexual impulses in erotica as a primal form of self-expression. She has recently moved to San Francisco.

Bonnie Stonewall, "The Sensuous Housewife," is the pseudonym of a woman-for-all seasons whose home base is a beautiful suburban tree-lined closet. A devoted wife, mother, grandmother, daughter, lover, friend and sex maniac, she is also a bisexual activist. Currently writing a semi-autobiographical book about women's bisexuality, she's determined to "make a difference."

Mickey Warnock, "Rapid Transit," a self-described lesberado from Hayward, California, spends her free time pencilling drawings of woman images, watching soaps and girls, rock concert hopping and writing—when she isn't working or riding the last car of Bay Area Rapid Transit (BART) trains.

Lisa Wright, "Just a Bad Day," lives in upstate New York with her husband and two cats. "My past experiences as a potter and weaver often find their way into my stories." She writes non-sexist fantasies for children as well as erotic short stories for adults.

Susie Bright, Editor, specializes in erotica and sexual politics. She has worked since 1982 with Joani Blank, publisher of Down There Press and founder of Good Vibrations, popularizing sex toys and sex information especially for women. She is the author of *Susie Sexpert's Lesbian Sex World* and *Susie Bright's Sexual Reality* (both Cleis Press) and co-editor (with Joani Blank) of *Herotica 2* (Plume/NAL). She is the former editor of *On Our Backs* and was the erotic film columnist for *Forum*.

Selected Bibliography

Magazines

Libido, Marianna Beck/Jeff Hafferkamp, editors (P.O. Box 146721, Chicago IL 60614), short erotic fiction, reviews, artwork, word games, sexual trivia, news and humor; quarterly

Yellow Silk, Lily Pond, editor (P.O. Box 6374, Albany CA 94706), poetry, short fiction, reviews, artwork, half women contributors; quarterly

On Our Backs, Debi Sundahl, editor (526 Castro Street, San Francisco CA 94114), short fiction, features, reviews, pictorials, lesbian; bi-monthly

Books

Alida: An Erotic Novel, Edna MacBrayne (Parkhurst Press, P.O. Box 143, Laguna Beach CA 92652), heterosexual

Bushfire, Karen Barber, editor (Lace/Alyson), lesbian stories

Coming to Power, SAMOIS members, editors (Alyson Publications), lesbian fiction anthology and commentary on lesbian power exchange

Deep Down, Laura Chester, editor (Faber & Faber), anthology of literary erotica

Delta of Venus, Anaïs Nin (Bantam), short stories

Dreams of the Woman Who Loved Sex, Tee Corinne (Banned Books, P.O. Box 33280, Austin TX 78764), lesbian short stories, poetry

Erotic Interludes, Lonnie Barbach (Harper & Row), short story anthology

Erotica, Margaret Reynolds, editor (Fawcett Columbine), erotic writings of women throughout history

Field Guide to Outdoor Erotica, Rob Moore, editor (Solstice, P.O. Box 9223, Moscow ID), environmentally aware stories and poems that describe adventures in the great outdoors.

Forbidden Flowers, Nancy Friday (Pocket), fantasies

Herotica 2: A Collection of Women's Erotic Fiction, Susie Bright and Joani Blank, editors (Plume/NAL), lesbian, bi, heterosexual

Ladies Own Erotica, Kensington Ladies Erotica Society (Pocket), short story anthology

Little Birds, Anaïs Nin (Bantam), short stories

Look Homeward Erotica, Kensington Ladies Erotica Society (Ten Speed Press), short story anthology

Macho Sluts, Pat Califia (Alyson), short stories about lesbian S/M

My Secret Garden, Nancy Friday (Pocket), fantasies

Pleasures, Lonnie Barbach (Harper & Row), anthology of short stories based on real-life experiences

Riding Desire and *Intricate Passions*, Tee Corinne, editor (Banned Books), lesbian short stories

Serious Pleasure and *More Serious Pleasure*, The Sheba Collective (Cleis Press), lesbian short story and poetry anthology

Sex for One: The Joy of Selfloving, Betty Dodson (Harmony/Crown), discussion of masturbation for women and men

The *Sleeping Beauty* series, Anne Rice writing as A.N. Roquelaure (Plume/NAL), an S/M trilogy

The Throne Trilogy, Artemis Oakgrove (Lace/Alyson), lesbian fantasy fiction

Expanded bibliography prepared March, 1992

HEROTICA 2

Needless to say, this book is for Lisa.   S. B.

This book is for A. W., who will appreciate it someday.   J. B.

Thank you to Leigh Davidson, managing editor of Down There Press, for her support, patience and persistence.

CONTENTS

viii   *Contents*

INTRODUCTION

When I first started teaching women's erotic writing classes in 1989, I didn't know who would show up. After all, who hasn't written—either in her diary or on the back of a matchbook—at least a few sweaty words, a love poem, or a passionate letter?

But teaching a class to women writers on the art of sensual penmanship indicated that something more was afloat than the inalienable right to serenade one's lover. Women's erotica, as it has come to be called, is a new genre of literature; it is fiction that illustrates the very real changes that have occurred in women's sexual interests and desires.

Women are thirsty, no, let's say ravenous, for sexual knowledge and erotic inspiration. They are offended by notions of romance that exclude or play innocent of sexual satisfaction; indeed, it's no surprise when a woman sings a hit song called "What's Love Got To Do With It?" We have a new understanding about our bodies' sexual responses. We experience sex in and out of all the traditions of love, commitment, marriage, and during and after child rearing. We make love with men and women, sometimes in fantasy, sometimes in real life. Sometimes we are a man in our sexual imaginations. We take the sexual signs of our times, be it X-rated home video, AIDS awareness, G-spot ejaculations, condoms, marriage burn-out, date rape, single motherhood, lesbian visibility, vibrator availability—we take the reality of sex in our era and we insist, indeed, we delight in including these slices of real life in our erotica.

I like to play a game in my erotica classroom. I ask everyone to write an initial erotic sentence, something easy like, "She touched her clit."

"Now keep on going," I say, "and do it in the style of a plain brown wrapper novel, the kind of book you'd find in the back of the sleaziest store in town."

Two minutes later I tell them to stop. "Now switch," I say, "and start writing as if this were a free-verse uninhibited love poem that you wrote on the cliffs of Big Sur." Then I have them switch again, two minutes later, to a supermarket bodice-ripper style: "Me Rhett, you Scarlett." Switch again, to a 1950s beatnik ultra-hip cigarette-after-the-screw style. No matter how unsophisticated the writer, each student has had some glancing experience with each of the styles I ask them to imitate.

Finally, I ask them to end their stories in one last genre. "Finish your story in a 'women's erotica' style," I tell them. And they jump right in. No one asks me anymore, "What are you talking about?" Despite the continual handwringing in the media that no one knows what women want, apparently women do have a collective sense of what they expect out of a sexy story, and it's so well known that I can even ask my students to give me a quick stereotype of it.

I used to have one impeccable standard for what made an erotic story female-centric: the woman comes. This single concept is so rare in traditional erotica that it overwhelms every other feminine consideration. Of course we've all read stories where a woman is overwhelmed with the size of her lover's penis—she screams his name and clutches his breast—but how many times do you actually get a her-point-of-view orgasm? We read about how he sees her responding to him, but we don't see inside her explosion.

I still believe a woman's climax makes a good bottom line for women's erotica. But now I have other angles to consider. There are other aspects of a woman's literary libido that show their colors just as brilliantly as any hot pink orgasm.

Femmchismo

I call the primary signal of the burgeoning women's erotica movement "femmchismo." Femmchismo is exactly what it sounds like: the aggressive, seductive and very hungry sexual ego of a woman. Like machismo, it embodies an erotic arrogance; for women it's clear this is a long-overdue case of conceit. Femmchismo has been a well-kept secret. Women have always talked among themselves in classic pajama-party bravado about their awareness of their sexual power and talent. Sometimes this boasting takes the form of dubious self-effacement. When sexual heroine Claudia "complains" in Catherine Tavel's "Claudia's Cheeks" about her enormous sticks-in-the-air bottom, she is only kvetching insofar as she lets us know that her posterior is the center of sexual attention wherever she goes. A woman would not typically brag openly about having a big ass the way a man might boast of his big cock, but she gets her message across by talking about the trials of being an object of such enormous desire.

Femmchismo draws on both a woman's desirability—the excitement a woman creates simply by being there—and also her sexual talents to influence and make love to her intended subject.

Certainly the stereotype of the female predator is not new; the spider, the manipulator, the schemer. The sex-negative caricature of woman's sexual aggression is that she is evil and that she seeks destruction and castration, not an orgasm. Her scheme of sexual wiles is to procure something *other* than sex. What's new in women's erotica is that when women describe their sexual courage and pride, their erotic satisfaction *is* their explicit goal.

To be sexually adventurous *for her own sake*, to not only feel her desire but also to direct it for ultimate satisfaction. Yes, this is femmchismo, and don't be surprised if its hard little clit comes rubbing up against your leg—purring, of course.

Femmchismo is emphatically not about falling in love or about "the very first time." It's about the value of a unique sexual experience, desire empowered by action.

Daily Details

Women's erotic writing proves once and for all that women are actually less romantic than men. How else can we explain that their modern erotic stories are filled with pertinent yet terribly unromantic details of daily life? In fact, in most women's erotica the traditional duties of women's housekeeping and caretaking are often juxtaposed with a fanciful or daring sexual adventure. In Maggie Top's "No Balance," Shelley is taking her mother for a drive in the foothills, but her daughterly duties are blissfully intercut with a sexual fantasy that conceivably would eject her mother right out of the passenger seat if she could read her child's mind.

Women's concerns for practicality and routine are satirically counterposed to their lust in many of these stories. In Jane Longaway's "My Pussy is Dead," Dido rebuffs the nudist colony director who wants her to be more comfortable: "It had taken an hour to put those white shorts on and for her money they could stay there." In "The Company Man" by Moxie Light, our heroine not only bathes and perfumes herself for a big evening, she also stuffs all her kitchen clutter into the oven and swishes out the toilet bowl before her date arrives.

Women writers are less hesitant, and are even enthusiastic, to integrate the limitations and risks that enter their erotic adventures. In "The Trojan Woman" by Angela Fairweather, a schoolteacher involves her lover in her pursuit of condom research. In "Wheelchair Romance" by Margo Woods, the author describes in detail what her lover's disability means in and out of bed.

Language—The Shape of the Feeling

When feminists and writers first started discussing the future of women's erotica, there was a call for a new women-centric language, a modern vocabulary to discuss women's sexual feelings. As an editor, I find that the language is there at the tip of our tongues. What is harder than imagining the words is saying them out loud. Street vocabulary is easily possessed by women who find no embarrassment in the shape of erotic women's language.

Street slang is just as your mother taught you: absolutely unladylike. But how many "ladies" under sixty haven't said "fuck" by now, in either anger or passion? What women have to cope with in employing four-letter words is not that they aren't suited to us; they suit us just fine. What we have to handle is being shushed by some double-standard.

Obscene words are powerful and forceful—that's why they are deemed unsuitable for "ladies," who are weak and delicate. When we have indelicate sexual feelings we get a little choked up because there don't seem to be ladylike words for lustful emotions. Ladies don't lust. Real women do, however, and it's perfectly appropriate for us to use strong language when the situation calls for it.

Most disputes over erotic language center on trying to find a perfect alternative to words. Is "vagina" too medical or too clinical? Is "cunt" too mean? I think we're wrongly splitting hairs over such quests for the ideal synonym. What's really missing in our erotic language are descriptions of women's arousal, from the first flush of desire and wetness, to the climactic loss of control, to the multiple sensations after orgasm.

In "The Shape of the Feeling," Daphne Slade explores some fifty ways she feels about her orgasms, and each one is a delight to contemplate: "My final orgasm always feels like an afterthought because I never know when to quit. I think the phrase 'you should know when to quit' was started by someone who knew exactly which orgasm to stop on."

When Women Look at Women

Lesbian erotica has been the fastest changing and most controversial aspect of the bloom in women's erotica. Lesbian sex stories have been around forever, but they typically were not written by or for lesbians. They were stories about breaking a taboo, about the sexual possibilities of manlessness. They were more about the men who were not there than they were about the women present.

When lesbians began to speak for themselves erotically, it was often in the context of a coming-out story, a woman discovering she likes women. Self-discovery is the key to the sexual excitement in a coming-out scenario; yet for women of any lesbian experience, one's first sexual encounter with another woman, though an important event, is unlikely to be the most satisfying and revealing experience she'll ever have.

With this in mind, *Herotica 2* introduces lesbian characters who are grownups—women who not only desire and love other women but also have the same sophisticated and diverse sexual tastes as any typical heterosexual female. So often, lesbian protagonists are ingenues, whether they're fifteen or forty, questioning their sexuality, yearning for the security of knowing themselves. Not so in "Seductions," where a middle-aged gay divorced single mom takes her first leap into lust on the rebound. She's nobody's fool; her lesbianism is a matter of course. Like any woman coming out of a long-term relationship, she has emotional reservations competing with a trigger-happy sexual appetite.

Sometimes the history of coming out plays a sweet second-fiddle to a mature love story. Pat Williams's "Ellen, From Chicago" makes poignant reference to the difference gay liberation has made in lesbian lives when two African-American women teachers traveling in the South find themselves boarding at a sixty-year-old woman's home. Their hostess treasures her photos of "her very best friend," an early aviatrix. Her generation lived a love that dared not speak its name, but the post-Stonewall lovers in this story hide nothing from each other.

So much of contemporary women's fiction is considered outrageous simply for being non-stereotypical. While daytime talk shows may regale us with the spectacle of "Black Lesbians" or "Lesbian Moms Who Like Porn," the new lesbian erotic literature is an understated command to *get over it*. Not only is there a lesbian under every bed, but she comes in every color, lifestyle, and political opinion.

The first revolution in lesbian erotic literature was writing from the lesbian point of view. That seems overdue and obvious enough to understand immediately.

But the second revolution in lesbian erotica is not really about lesbianism per se at all. It's about gender-bending and the vicarious experience of erotically placing yourself in another's shoes. In "The Journal," a lesbian novelist sets her hand to gay male porn, while in "There's More of You," one woman lover reads to another from a heterosexual bodice-ripper.

These examples are a complete departure from the closely held myth that lesbians are utterly divorced from any kind of vicarious masculine appreciation. Lesbian purity has been like the last white dress anybody could find to cover up the fact that sexual imaginations wander everywhere. Just because a woman has no interest in a relationship with a man doesn't mean that she might not fantasize about sex with a man, or perhaps imagine being a man. Our fantasies, like our nightly dreams, are not compromised in the least by who we live and love with in the real world.

More than any other group of writers, lesbian erotica writers have grabbed gender-bending by the genitals, taken the whole spectrum of masculine/feminine eroticism by storm. Radical lesbian sex writers took one of porn's most common questions and turned it upside down: why do so many men like to watch lesbian sex? The hip lesbian answer is, "because everybody can and does fantasize about anybody and anything they please." Lesbians can appreciate masculinity whether it's in the traditional form of admiring a woman's unusual strength and perseverance, such as the student/teacher infatuation in Karen Marie Christa Minns's "Amazon," or the "kinkier" aspects of cross-dressing and gender-mixing.

As lesbian sexual themes become less predictable, the uniqueness of a strictly woman-to-woman experience can become more specific, even startling. In Serena Moloch's "I Visit the Doctor," a young woman is growing up in a fascist future much like that of *The Handmaid's Tale*. She seeks out a woman doctor to alleviate her severe menstrual pain. Only women understand this kind of pain and its link to both our erotic and reproductive capacity. A lesbian relationship in this context is intimately explosive.

When a Woman Feels Like a Man

When an ostensibly heterosexual woman writes of her desire for a man, she can also defy traditional roles. It's not unusual at all to find a story where the woman dominates her male lover or the man services her. This fantasy has been seen many times, mainly because it's such a popular turn-on for men.

The rare female twist to this role-reversal is where the woman not only takes control, but she also takes on a man's feelings and prerogatives—which have less to do with domination and more to do with the masculine world. In "Taking Him on a Sunday Afternoon," Magenta Michaels describes turning the tables on her husband.

> He clamps up to prevent me from rubbing him there, but aggression has risen in me and I press on, massaging a moistened finger at his entrance. It's slick there and I can imagine the smell, which excites me; I know that he's concerned about the smell, too—how I'll find him—and this excites me even more.

It's the phrase "how I'll find him" which epitomizes the role-reversal. Traditionally, it is women who "get found," ladies who worry about what they smell like, and men who relish this vulnerability.

Sometimes women subvert male sexual excitement by making their own submission almost, but not quite, impossible. They thrive on exuding as well as seeking masculine energy. It's like a Valkyrie demanding her due. In Susan St. Aubin's "This Isn't About Love," we are introduced to Ilka, a virtual woman warrior, a commando self-defense instructor who revels in her ability to reduce any man to a pulp at the same time as she dreams of a man who could break through her defenses. One dream involves a gun:

> "I was having an orgasm when I woke up," she says. "It was as though the gun that woke me started the orgasm. He finally gave me what I wanted."
>
> "Death?" I ask. My fingers are clenched under the table. "How can you think you're in love with someone who shoots you?"
>
> "But it was like being shot to life." Ilka looks at me and sighs. "He shot his power into me. I can't explain it, there are not words in any language I know. I'm not talking about love, Chris."

The language Ilka seeks is not about love, at least not the Valentine's-Day-card love that women have long believed was the greatest literary expectation our passion could reach. Women are approaching a new lover's language today, a tongue that relishes abandon and adventure, a roar that comes straight out of our undulating bellies.

Women's fertility is no secret, but our fertile erotic imagination has been locked up as if by an iron chastity belt for too long. Shoot it off, shout it out—here's women's erotic language for you, shot right out of a cannon.

SUSIE BRIGHT
San Francisco,
June 1991

Maggie Top

❦❦

No Balance

These wheels were not right. Four tires, purchased, examined, and static-balanced only two short hours ago, were as lopsided as her ex's tits, and now it was too late to do anything about it. Shelley had picked up her mom and left civilization three hours ago, leaving a balmy day in San Francisco for a baking hot dirty day in the Sierra Nevada. The steering wheel shook like a vibrating drill.

"Hold up the map for me," she said to her mother. Twenty more miles to Grass Valley. Twenty more miles of her mom squeaking, "Oh, Shelley, it's so hot!" After thirty years of driving her own 1967 VW Bug all over the country, Mom had decided she couldn't use a stick shift anymore, didn't feel capable of driving at all. Wasn't that a nice surprise. Fine then; she'd sit tight in the passenger seat and make temperature reports every three minutes.

Shelley decided that in twenty more miles she was going to pull up to the first gas station she saw and call the tire man back in the city. She'd ask him what the hell he thought he was doing sending an innocent girl on a 200-mile mountain road trip with wobbly wheels.

She wondered how consumer-indignant she could act with such

a handsome tire man. *"Un jeune homme hyper-mignon."* How could someone that sexy not have a secret passion pit somewhere back behind the tire stacks? She saw herself posing against the yellow Cougar in the garage yard, watching him work. She could see the outline of his cock through his denim coveralls. She imagined pressing her bare belly against it, feeling the wetness seep through to her lips, and wondered if he could smell her.

Fifteen more miles. Her mom was talking about Mr. Harding, who was building his own bed-and-breakfast place, by himself, out of the old Wells Fargo bank building. "Such a masculine man," her mother insisted.

Shelley thought about the tire man again; he would make a beautiful girl if he wasn't already such a beautiful boy. He had excessively curly long hair, made for wrapping round her fingers. She let her hands slide down his smooth chest; he wrapped his arms around her like a vise.

His wet mouth searched for the hollow of her neck. She'd never felt so soft. He wanted to taste her. She didn't know if she could watch. She pulled his face into her pussy, rocking her long legs around his broad shoulders. Lick me. His steady tongue made her clit as hard as a berry. She panted. It was too hot. He was too hot. Her head was bursting and that awful ache opened up in her cunt like someone howling. She needed him inside her Right This Minute.

She switched hands on the steering wheel and wiped the sweat off her palm. Her nipples hurt. Five more miles. Would her mother notice hard nipples on such a hot sticky day? Shelley squinted at the junction ahead and saw the tire man bending her over at the waist across a set of steel-belted donuts. He rubbed himself up against her ass. The coveralls disappeared. His hard-on pressed her cheeks apart and her legs started to tremble. Oh please, Mr. Tire Man, please don't stop. His cock head slid into her. Jesus Christ.

"Shelley, what are you doing!" Her mom jolted forward and grabbed the dashboard.

"Sorry, sorry, I thought I was hitting the clutch."

Mr. Tire Man stirred inside her like a heavy spoon. He pulled out almost all the way and her cunt lips begged him back. Fuck me. She whimpered. He pushed in again, so deep, to the tip of her womb. She flinched. If he hurt her again like that she would scream. If he hurt her again like that she would come. She squeezed her legs together and he pushed into her ass. She cried out and pressed her clit hard against the rubber rims. He held her fast, moving in and out of her sugar walls. She crumbled and clutched at him in spasms.

She hit a bump in the road. It was Grass Valley. A Union 76 on the right.

"Honey, that phone booth looks out of order, are you sure you don't want to just keep going on to Mary's?" Her mom didn't like this gas station. Every time her mom smelled urine in a public place she thought something was out of order.

"No, Momma, just stay here for a second and try to run the air-conditioning."

She dialed the number she had on the business card wadded up in her pocket. "For a Good Time, Call Seaside Tire." Okay, Mr. Tire Man, these wheels are as loose as marbles and I want your cock between my lips right this second. She tasted his cum— so sweet—and kissed him hard on the mouth.

"Hi, this is the girl with the MR2, you saw me a couple of hours ago. . . . The wheels still aren't balanced. Isn't it a little dangerous to be driving like this?"

It was very, very dangerous to be driving with an aching pussy, hard nipples, soaking wet pants, and a front-wheel drive shaking as badly as her thighs.

Shelley yelled over to her mom. "He says, 'don't worry. . . .' He says to bring it back when we get home."

She hung up. "I've gotta get a Coke." She unglued her legs. She was going to stand outside this piss-smell gas station just a minute or two longer and cool off.

Winn Gilmore

Boca Chica

Waves slid up Amara's legs, gently licking, kissing, then swiftly pulling their succulent lips away from her crotch like the ceaseless tease of a "find them, fuck them, flee them" lover. Still beggar at an empty throne, Amara spread her legs, dug her ass deeper into the yielding sand and moaned, waiting for the next ephemeral kiss of the salty ocean. Yemaya lapped up her long—and now very dark—legs. Here on this nearly deserted beach in the Dominican Republic, Yemaya, goddess of ocean and life, was truly Boca Chica, the Girl's Mouth.

Amara sighed and crossed her arms beneath her head. Her hair, hot-combed only three days ago, had taken a vacation of its own: it had gone all the way home. Once again, it was a thick bush sucking up the demanding Caribbean sun and golden sand. She smiled, white teeth greeting the snow-white sun, imploring it to drop down into the gap between her two front teeth and rest its heat along her thick tongue. She'd savor it before letting it slip down between her salmon-pink tonsils. Finally, she'd swallow it and stick her satisfied tongue between the gap as the sun, still pulsating and radiating, slid warm and wet into her stomach. Her mouth watered. She wondered what her lover, Yasmin, was doing back in California.

* * *

"Baby, I can't come with you," Yasmin had whined on their last night together. Wrapping her juice-soaked thighs around Amara, Yasmin had whispered in her ear, "But I'll be waiting when you get back." She turned Amara over, sliding like a well-greased seal down the pole of Amara's back, inhaling the strong sex scent. She pulled back from her lover to behold Amara's quivering ass. She lifted her own fingers to her mouth and moistened them, then spread Amara's shuddering cheeks.

Her anus was like a tiny whirlpool on a heaving ocean, the deep brown ridges twirling inward, daring Yasmin to come closer, closer still, to spin ever down and into a place without time, to the place before the beginning. "Lover," Yasmin whispered into Amara's anus, squeezing a cheek in each hand, "I've got"—and her tongue slid between the crack she'd opened—"too many clients this week." She moaned, catching the tiniest trickle from Amara's anus before it dropped, blessed, onto her clit. "I can't pull myself away," she purred into her lover's damp hole. "We need the money."

Before Amara could protest that *she* would be paying for the vacation, Yasmin jammed her tongue between the buttocks tightened against her entry. Like a swimmer breaking the surface of cold waters and emerging in unexpected warmth, Yasmin's tongue burst free. The back of her tongue constricted as the front lunged into her lover. Probing, stretching out as her mouth watered into Amara's pussy, Yasmin sighed, "Girl, I'll wait for you." She stretched her long arms beneath Amara and squeezed one ripe breast in each hand. She pinched the nipples between her fingers and Amara moaned, her mind slipping past the sadness of the upcoming vacation without Yasmin. She was lost to all but the gathering waves roiling deep inside her.

Amara screamed as the first wave of cum shot from her over-burdened pussy onto her lover's face. She trembled as Yasmin's fingers, like a rock thrown across the water's surface, skipped over her clit, slip-slide, slip-slide, then sank into her heaving ocean. Her body convulsed and she bit her lip, clutching a pillow to her soaked chest. She called Yasmin's name, wishing her girl, and her girl's mouth, were with her on the beach called Boca Chica.

The memory splashed over Amara's sand-caked body like a wave, and she shuddered as she rolled belly-over onto the sand. "That woman's priorities are definitely off," she said to herself. "So what if she had a week jammed full of relaxers, haircuts, tints, and such shit. Cancel them, I say," Amara mumbled as she stood, pulling her bikini top over her hardened nipples.

A merengue band approached, lightning fast da-ta-ta as she ran into the ocean that was barely cooler than the air. The gitarras and guiros cascaded over her, chasing her into the shallow ocean's warm embrace.

Her arms shot out before her, parting the water like a lover's legs. Amara darted forth, gliding past the tiny school of black-and-yellow-striped fish. Then she floated. She propelled herself by fanning out her arms then pulling them back against her waist. Fingers opened; she spread and caressed her curvaceous thighs. She flipped her head to the left, inhaling a bit of sweet salt water as she sun glittered yellow and green against her goggles. Amara stretched out one graceful arm and flipped onto her back, offering her tight, black belly to the ocean's surface and the sun's kiss.

Squinting against the sun, Amara exhaled and slipped her left hand beneath her bikini top. She massaged her right nipple, gasping in water and air at her delectable touch. Yemaya lulled her, gently rocking her in her powerful arms.

She squeezed her eyes shut, imagining Yasmin's long, strong fingers rooting soapily through some client's locks, massaging the scalp as she murmured, "Just let your head go. I've got you, sugar." Amara could see the suds lapping up her arms, Yasmin's eyes closed and mouth slightly parted as her eyes rolled back deliciously in her head. She remembered the first time she, Amara, was beneath those supplicating hands, the fingers digging into her skull like a sea farmer shoveling her fingers into the wet, black earth at the ocean's shore to test its impregnability: could it yield sweet clams and luscious oysters this season?

Amara stroked her pussy lips, then squeezed them together

rhythmically with each rolling wave. She dipped her head back
into her ocean-lover's lap, and stroked her clit. She shot the salty-
sweet water from her mouth as she came, fingers working furiously as her black body lifted above the otherwise smooth surface
of the water.

Red, green, and iridescent blue blasted across her closed lids.
The strolling musicians' merengue bolted across the water and
pounced upon her, and she thrashed from side to side, moaning
deep in her throat. Amara went limp, arms and legs stretched
over the water.

Exhausted, she swam languidly for shore.

Back on her stretch of sand, Amara lay facedown as yet another merengue washed over her still-throbbing body. Her pussy
pulsated staccato from her fingers' and the ocean's gentle lapping. She ran her tongue over her wet, saline lips and sank her
torso deeper into the hot sand.

"¿Ostiones, señorita?"

Amara was nearly dozing when the cracking, melodic voice
broke through to her.

"¿O quizás caracol? Son bastante frescas, se lo juro."

There was something familiar in the young boy's tone; something too knowing, too assuming. Amara tugged her revealing
bathing trunks higher over her firm ass, then relaxed again.

"Si, hombre," she said slowly, hoping to summon more of her
halting Spanish. If only Yasmin were here, she thought angrily.
Count on her not being here when I need her. Her Spanish is
perfect. "Umm, me gusto una docena ostiones, por favor."

Only when she heard the blunt-edged knife prying into the
shell did Amara turn over. Lazily, she looked out to sea.

Finally, the knife slid through the small oyster's shell. It
popped open with a satisfying pthlop! and Amara watched, enthralled, as a bit of its juice trailed over the young man's deep
pink palm. Unhurriedly, he chuckled and lifted his hand majes-
tically to his lips.

Amara's eyes followed the motion, and shielded her unaccustomed eyes against the glaring sun's brightness. Her eyes trailed
the strong arm up, then stopped, puzzled, at his midriff. It wasn't
a man after all, because the oyster-shucker was wearing a wom-

an's one-piece spandex bathing suit beneath men's swim trunks. She's seen a suit like that before . . . in the apartment she'd shared with Yasmin the past four years. Too much cerveza, she thought, eyes sliding back to the ocean before her.

"Perhaps you would also try this tiny clam," the shucker asked in stammering English. Amara's gaze was arrested by the hand squeezing clear liquid from a tiny lemoncito onto the oyster, splayed like a raucous lover before her.

The shucker's hand delved into the battered bucket and pulled out, almost reluctantly, a small, white clam. Expertly this time, the knife found the creature's muscle, popped it open, and the shucker held it out to her.

Amara slid back onto the sand as the shucker moved the still-live clam closer, its muscle standing up like a tiny clit. Her eyes followed the gentle, strong curve of the arm up to the offerer's shoulder, and, astonished, Amara called out, "You bitch! How could you do this to me?"

The shucker crumpled to the ground beside her and flashed a brilliant smile to Amara. "My love, mi vida," she crooned, "did you really think I'd let you come here alone? Let your fine, black self come to some Caribbean island with a beach called The Girl's Mouth? Get serious!"

"Yasmin," Amara said, shaking her head and smiling, "give me that clam."

Aurora Light

❦❦

Bus Stop

My bus pulled away from the bus stop just as I rounded the corner. "Darn," I muttered to myself. Well, at least there was a bench, and it was still warm in the September twilight. A man was sitting at the far end, his face hidden behind the *Wall Street Journal*. I sat at the opposite end and crossed my ankles primly.

People and cars passed occasionally. I checked the time on my watch. The next bus wasn't due for twenty minutes. I wasn't in any particular hurry, but I sighed, already bored.

The newspaper rustled from the other end of the bench. I looked casually at what I could see of its reader. The top of his head was just visible, the hair dark brown and wavy. His clothes were definitely Brooks Brothers: a glen plaid suit; charcoal gray with a subtle deep red pencil stripe, dark gray socks and cordovan wing tip shoes.

I looked away, checking the time once more. At least fifteen more minutes. My eyes were drawn again to the stranger on the bench. I wished he would put down his paper so I could see his face. "Don't be ridiculous," I told myself. "Why should I care what his face looks like?"

Legs crossed, his thighs looked muscular. He shifted his paper again, but didn't put it down. He seemed totally oblivious of my presence, which for some unaccountable reason bothered me. I wondered if he had seen me when I'd walked up and sat down on the bench. And if he had, did he find me attractive?

I took out my compact and looked critically at my reflection in the mirror. I saw naturally arched brows under dark hair, blue eyes flecked with green, a short straight nose, and full-lipped mouth. Then, feeling self-conscious, I hastily put the compact back in my purse.

I coughed softly, and the paper rattled but did not lower. I wasn't used to being ignored. I looked at the hands holding the newspaper. They were well cared for, rather large and deeply tanned. Large hands, large cock. Was that it? Or was it large feet, large cock? Was I thinking about cocks because I hadn't had any for a week?

I checked the time; ten more minutes. I wondered how old the mystery man was. There was no gray in his hair. I shifted restlessly, crossing my long legs and unobtrusively inching my skirt well above my knees. Suddenly, he lowered the paper and looked directly at me. The eyes that met mine were dark and unreadable in the dusk. It was not a handsome face, but rugged, with a sensuous mouth. For a melting moment I fantasized his mouth on mine, our tongues touching. He couldn't have been more than forty. For an intense instant I held my breath, then he turned the page of the paper, and his face disappeared behind it again. My breathing resumed, slightly faster than before.

How rude he was, I thought. He didn't even smile, but then neither had I. For that second I had felt riveted by his penetrating eyes. Penetrating. Why use that word to describe his look? As I said it to myself, I felt warmth between my crossed legs. I was definitely aroused. What was it about this silent, unfriendly man that turned me on?

It was rapidly getting dark and the streetlights had come on. I wondered how he was able to read in the gloom. Perhaps he had not been reading at all. Maybe he used the newspaper as an excuse to avoid talking to me. Or maybe he was thinking about me, wondering what I looked like under my red silk dress. My cunt twitched with that thought.

I allowed myself to imagine him aroused, his cock beautifully large and hard. The thought made me squirm on the bench and uncross my legs. There were fewer people walking past now, and practically no cars on the street. I decided to give in to one of my favorite pleasures: secretly masturbating in a public place. I shifted my large purse, putting it flat across my lap. I pressed my hand cautiously between my thighs. I barely suppressed a sigh.

I increased the pressure of my fingers, never taking my eyes from the newspaper. When the paper rustled I jerked my hand back, my face hot. I had an insane desire to laugh at my reckless behavior. Once more all was silent at the other end of the bench. I squeezed my thighs together. An almost audible "oh!" escaped my lips.

I inched the full skirt of my dress up, keeping my hand under my purse. I slid a finger under the band of my bikini pants, imagining the stranger's cock rubbing over my slippery cunt, caressing my swollen clitoris, finding its way into my pink pussy. I clamped my lips tightly to stifle a groan.

My entire hand was now in my panties, two fingers deep inside my dripping cunt. I stretched my legs out and leaned back on the bench. Two men were walking down the block on the other side of the street. I pictured their cocks, one long, the other short and thick. But it was still the man behind the paper that I wanted to see, feel, suck, and fuck, his cock ramming in, pulling out, in, out. My fingers quickened their thrusting. Just one more minute and I would come. As my orgasm crept up my shaking legs I chanted silently, "Fuck, fuck, fuck!" I closed my eyes at the intensity of my climax.

When I opened my eyes I saw my bus less than half a block away. The object of my fantasy was looking at me, a slight smile curling the corners of his lips. I felt my face flush. I jumped up from the bench as the bus stopped and opened its door, letting me escape into its anonymous depth. I paid my fare with trembling fingers and took a seat next to the window. The bus started up and I looked out to see my inspiration, raising his hand goodbye.

Carol A. Queen

At Doctor d'Amour's Party

Of course I had seen you before at other parties: your wiry intensity, your black cat's grace. I had seen the way you moved through the crowds and it seemed to me you lived in a realm of sexual intelligence. I had felt your hands on me before, too briefly, and so I was pleased that, like me, you arrived early at Doctor d'Amour's party; that I would have a chance to know you without the distractions of a party in full swing, a dozen hands on me, two dozen pairs of eyes. I was pleased to finally know your name. I knew nothing more about you, but if Doctor d'Amour thought you were smart and sexy (and he does), that was enough for me.

We could never have talked about art at a big party. We would probably not have talked about sex either, even though sex was our reason for attending those parties: to watch it, to learn more about it, to have it. Doctor d'Amour's party was no different, but we were early, so there the three of us sat talking about sex and art all afternoon, as easily as if this were a coffee date. We shared a joint, making our talk thoughtful and hazily intimate.

When it neared the time for other guests to arrive we decided to get into our party costumes. I changed in another room so I could make an entrance. I come to these parties prepared to give it all up, to become a sacred harlot, a temple priestess, and the one thing I like to keep to myself is the transformation. It changes my sense of the party space and my sense of purpose when I return garbed in my chosen outfit. The room, the minutes passing, all of us are then ritualized. While I was gone, Aphrodite passed into me.

So I returned, dressed in black leather boots with pointed toes; black net stockings held by garters to leave my thighs, creamy, naked, exposed above them; black silk brassiere and french-cut panties, already trying to work themselves like a G-string between the peach-halves of my ass; and a black leather collar. A peep-show Venus, a slut of the sacred.

You and Doctor d'Amour were next to leave street-clad, then emerge transformed. The Doctor returned as an erotic clown, not an unusual persona for him. In your costume you might have been my consort. Tight black pants of shiny fabric clung to your body like a second skin. That was all: delicate pale feet below, smooth-skinned torso above, lean and muscled, nipples little rosettes that anyone would want to put a tongue to. Face all intelligence and dignity, so sexy. I noticed everything about you as if for the first time. You too were beginning your change, your habitation of ritual space, priest of love.

If we let it, the erotic unfolds for us gradually, like the petals of a flower opening to the touch of the sun. Well, here was another layer of that process. We had begun as strangers, our view of each other internal, subjective; the act of looking almost masturbatory until it was time to reach and touch. Then the diffused erotic in an afternoon of conversation. Now black cloth clung tightly to places we began to want our hands to go; I was dressed for you, and you for me. Noticing gathered purpose, as your black Lycra displayed your cock to me, my black silk invited you to run your fingertips along the length of my vulva.

The doorbell began to ring at last: other guests arriving at Doctor d'Amour's party. A half dozen of us joined in a circular embrace to welcome each other, and with that little ritual the party truly began. You and I were left in the center of the room in one anothers' arms, all that was left of the circle. We swayed, and the unfamiliarity of our bodies touching began to ebb into the realm of the not-remembered.

Body-knowledge established, touch gave way to feline rubbing. We were sex-cats retreating into another world, alone there though guests continued to arrive and the party surrounded us, a parallel universe to which neither of us gave much attention. We were too absorbed in the rising tide of pleasure, of desire. How well we fit together, leg between legs, hands on each other's asses, pulling our hips tight, your cock hard against me, my clit begging for its pressure. So we danced, and before long we began to talk to each other; ohhh, mmmmmmmh, low purrings and throaty moans. When at last we kissed, our hands full of each other's hair, the last vestige of our being strangers fell away and it seemed we knew each other profoundly, bodies already electric before our mouths met.

I was vibrating with our sexual energy, gasping, trembling, clinging to you. I was too aroused to be responsible for my sense of balance, so I slid us both to the floor. We drank the sweat from each other's bodies, and I unhooked my brassiere so the silken cups would be no impediment to your lips. The feel of your mouth on my nipples made me catch my breath: it was like your tongue was already licking my pussy up and down, teasing me into heat. The pressure of your knee, then your thigh, then your cock on my clit made it sing as we rolled and writhed, as I thrust into you as if we were fucking. My hands grasping your ass felt the muscles go tight as you worked against me. Those who scoff at frottage have never ridden a sexual swell the way we did that day, hovering on the curl of energy like surfers on a sea. You orgasmed like a waverider tumbling in to shore. I felt it in my cunt, your orgasm, sharing the energy as if we were old lovers.

We rolled on the floor like kittens, practically mewing from pleasure. Other party guests who lay near us began to feel their own tides. Our eyes met, moving us in an instant from infant's delight to deep, wordless speech. Only then did wonder intrude. Who are we, whom have we become, to meet and mingle this way? And the moment our arms tightened around each other the sexual surge had us again. I moved into you, felt your response, welcomed it with, "Ohhhh, yes," and kept murmuring "yes, yes" in your ear as your arms went tighter. As you lowered your head and your teeth began grazing my nipples, your hand also moved south, cupping my vulva and pressing tight. I knew you could feel its silk-clad wetness, the labial cleavage, the erect and humming clit. I rocked my hips forward for the pleasure of the feeling, my cunt in your hand. Then you began a rhythmic tugging on the silk panties, bringing the fabric up tight between my lips, pulling harder and harder. Your mouth and free hand teased my nipples, and I felt my body curling into the arc of a brewing orgasm.

But my cunt ached, empty. I wanted you to fill me and I gasped: "Oh, fuck me, please!" Your fingers slid easily in. I was the center of the universe then, and my cunt the epicenter, my conscious self near extinguished to the body's pleasure. I rode it as long as I could, trusting you to take me closer and still closer, until I couldn't bear the wait and reached for my clit, a few fast hard circles sending me over the cliff's edge, coming, riding waves in the air. And when we didn't slow our rhythm, my hand on my clit and yours deep inside me, the ebbing of one climax led to the first surges of the next.

On and on. Your fingers almost leaving me, then sinking deeply in. Full circle of energy from hand to cunt, from my eyes to yours, so absorbing that for some time I forgot that we were with others in a room, forgot the day and the year and every extraneous thing. I knew only you and the sexual free-float, my store of knowledge pulsing cellularly, nerve-endings lit like neon, orgasms whirling like high, dispersing winds through my consciousness.

When my awareness reemerged it was into my nipples, which were glowing like points of fire. You were pulling on them, the sensation of such intensity that it bordered on pain: you took me to another erotic level, testing how far I'd stay with you. I was amazed that you would test me then and I felt the wonder more in my cunt than in my mind. How far into the stratosphere was it possible to follow you? In a surge of desire I tasted your power and my own remarkable power to respond. And let it all be consumed by the physical fire, the writhing and response in which even you were all but gone and I became the breath that dwells within intensity. Going high and higher, breathing fast and faster, until you let go and released me into body and then mind again: it was a wholly different kind of orgasm. I wondered whether my nipples burned you where they touched your chest as our bodies were once again pressed tightly together.

I felt you for days.

More sex, more play as we came down from those heights. But we'd peaked, and it was finally time to join the revelry, sip some wine, see who else was scattered around Doctor d'Amour's apartment like Cupid's pick-up sticks. One woman was tying her partner up, another strapping on a dildo, someone else was jacking off, still another watching. The Doctor himself was kissing a man to whom he was bound at wrist and ankle. "Well!" said someone, welcoming us back. "Are you finally going to stop playing Monopoly?"

I sat on the floor at your feet, leaning back into the angle of your open legs, my neck resting on your half-hard cock which stirred sometimes like a sleepy animal. The Doctor's party was a big erotic experiment it seemed; everyone trying something or someone new. Costumes were half on and half off, and laughs, squeals, and sighs filled the room. An unusual place to spend afterglow perhaps, but ours had not been a usual connection. Your hands stayed on me. Tendrils of energy licked from you to me, me to you. The bound man looked as big as Gulliver spread-eagled on the floor, and we watched his companion suck his cock. A pair of people fucking found their way into my lap, his head on my thigh, she atop him riding the rhythm, and still I was as aware of your presence behind me as I was of them. When I reached to cup her breasts your hands covered mine, and I answered your pressure on my nipples by squeezing hers, felt her heart beating in my hand.

The scene shifted again and I watched as you began to play with Doctor d'Amour's cock, a very responsive toy. The Doctor's hands skimmed your body and he growled, a low flute-song of pleasure from your fingering. Your expression of rapt concentration, your fine hands on his hard, pretty cock pleased me utterly. For a minute I wanted all the rest of the party to vanish, all its delights and distractions, so you and the Doctor could absorb yourselves with each other and I with both of you. But too soon the ebb and flow of the party separated you. I wandered into the kitchen, to a table filled with fruit and flowers and luscious melting Brie. I was beginning to think about leaving, and already dreaming about seeing you again.

Doctor d'Amour's party wound down gracefully as we all chatted, licked Brie off our fingers, and shared a big bottle of eau minerale. Gulliver was untied; someone had changed back into street clothes, and by ones and twos everyone joined us around the table. For the first time all evening I glanced at the clock; it was nearing eleven.

You followed me out of the room when I left to change. Words seemed a little banal now, after all we had said wordlessly: "That was so wonderful!"—"Yes, I'm so glad we had a chance to connect."—"Can I get your phone number?"—"Of course." But our eyes were still full of shared heat, our embrace warm and intimate. As I shed my damp black silk and lace stockings, as I transformed myself back into an imposter of the ordinary ready to step out into the night streets in a guise that would draw no attention, I still held your gaze. I knew we would come together again soon, hot to explore this sweet lust that cut right to the heart of things.

"And we don't even know one another yet," you murmured. I shook my head, held you in tight farewell, felt the pulse of our bodies say, *Oh, sex-cat, but when we do . . .*

Taking Him on a Sunday Afternoon

I'm lying on the Sunday couch, dozing between snatches of the television's drone, the newspaper spread around me. My lover crosses my line of half-mast vision to get to the *TV Guide,* naked except for the white Jockeys. My eyes focus on his thighs and crotch, and, not really interested in sex at all, I murmur to him from a half-sleep, "Bring that up here and put it in my face." Startled and smiling, he does. He straddles my head, one foot on the floor, one knee beside my ear, supporting his weight on the arm of the sofa.

I arch up, nuzzling my face into the dampness of the white cotton, snuffling him, inhaling him deeply, smelling both his man-scent and the cleanliness of his shorts. I mouth his hardening front, breathing on it, gumming it with lips drawn tight over teeth. I nip the insides of his thighs, biting hard enough to make him groan, and lap at the skin to disperse the pain.

I stretch the elastic waistband far down, freeing him. I circle his tip with a pointed tongue, stabbing at it, bouncing it, flicking at its underside, and finally drawing its heaviness into my mouth. He is salty, smelling of soap, and I rotate my head as I press my hand hard against his buttocks, forcing him against the back of my throat. He groans low, sucking in air through clenched teeth.

I slip my hands inside the shorts and trace circles on his muscular cheeks, letting my thumb dip down to the space between his balls and buttocks, then sliding a finger up to explore the puckered mouth of his bum. He clamps up to prevent me from rubbing here, but aggression has risen in me and I press on, massaging a moistened finger at the entrance. It's slick there, and I can imagine the smell, which excites me; I know that he's concerned about the smell, too—how I'll find him—and this excites me more.

The thought pops into my mind that if I had a dick, right now if I had a dick, I would wear him out. I would stay in that puckered, slippery, sex-smelling ass as often as I could. I would dominate him, kneeling over him to rub my pubic curls against his lips as I wanted to, and not when he wanted to taste or smell me. I would be the aggressor, and he could not ask sex of me: only I would be allowed to initiate. And when I did, it would be with aching lust and probing fingers and bursting genitals. I would fuck him from behind, his cock gripped in my fist—a gleaming trophy peeking out between my lacquered fingertips—the completion of his pleasure at my bidding alone. I would ride him, standing in a half crouch, my dick slipping in and out wetly, making that squishing noise. And when I was about to come, I would jerk him very fast, his eyes closed, throat exposed, head back against me, allowing me to do with him as I chose. And then I would come, violently, with cramping muscles and teeth bared and curses under my breath, all the while jerking him off, and he would spatter his seed, shooting out a foot from his body.

I would roll the head of his cock gently between my fingers, rubbing his cum into his balls, weighing them in my hand, my own dick still curved hard within him. And then I would let him go. My dick would dissolve, my aggression would fade, and I would become feminine and docile again. And only he and I would know who we were, who we had been, in the privacy of our room.

Lisa Palac

Love Lies

The sheets soaked in sweat and liquid sex, heavy summer hung like a velvet curtain around the city. They were exhausted. At 11:32 P.M., the mercury was stuck at 82 degrees. Her hair separated into tiny strands on her forehead, a matted clump in the back: a screwball, a friend once called it. She brought her hands to her face, loving the way her fingers smelled covered in fuck. It was reckless incense that opened the memory box.

Sometimes she liked to bury her face in his armpit and breathe him in.

"Smell good?" Alex asked, amused at her weird habit.

"Mmmm . . . I love it."

It smelled like potato chips eaten on the beach.

Certain smells triggered instant Polaroid memories for Emily. Anyone with bad breath made her think of Joseph Kazinski in third grade. He was always breathing on her and exposing bits of salami and Wonder bread stuck in his orthodontic jungle. He never brushed his teeth after he got braces.

Then there was the death smell. People look out for the face of death but it's really the smell that gets to you. When Emily was a kid, Mrs. Lindenhart the landlady had been dead upstairs for a week and nobody knew. A horrible odor had wafted down into their apartment and her mother had cleaned out every closet looking for dead mice. This city smelled of dead things. There were probably thousands of lifeless old ladies trapped with hundreds of cats in sixth-floor walk-ups.

Maybe she had been a dog in a past life, or an aardvark or just watched too many *Planet of the Apes* movies where Roddy McDowell constantly flexes his nostrils, but her olfactory factory suffered from oversensitivity. This sixth sense of hypersniff was a real pain in the ass sometimes. She had to sniff everything before she tasted it, including her lovers.

Pheromones made The Chemistry. Sometimes the mix was a dud. Other times it was like drinking orange juice after brushing your teeth. Incongruous chemical reaction. But the intrinsic odor offenders were the worst. These types could take a shower and still smell like an alley in Chinatown. The only way to discover this, however, was to be in an intimate situation. At that point, escape routes are limited.

Emily got into a mess like that with an eighteen-year-old disaster from Detroit who immortalized William Burroughs and had tattooed a flaming cross in the middle of his chest. Posing fashionably as one of the discontented, he asked Emily to buy him a beer.

"What did you spend your fortune on? Performance rights for *Drugstore Cowboy?*" Emily said with a smirk.

But the bar was crowded and the idea of almost jailbait was extremely appealing. Finally, in a deliberately careless way, she let him put his tongue in her mouth as they walked through the door of her place.

His skin was white and smooth, except for the raised pink scar that ran around the edges of his torched crucifix. Immediately, Emily scanned her brain for the best consummate icon adoration position. He could be up on his arms fucking her and the cross would dive right into her eyes, then pull back again with each of his thrusts, like a sacrilegious yo-yo. Maybe she should straddle the symbol, rub her clit against the fleshy imperfection and revel in the vision of divine tattoo fornication. No! Wait! He could be reciting the Act of Contrition while she whipped his ass with a giant rosary! She suppressed her laugh and passed it off as a cough.

None of her plans were put into action because the tattoo disappeared over the edge of the bed and only his face was visible between her legs. Ah, those sweet young lips, so eager to please, so desperate to find the right rhythm. Kneeling on the hardwood floor wasn't too comfortable and he tried to change his position a few times, but she took a fistful of his hair and made him stay like a bad dog. She wasn't about to sacrifice her upcoming orgasm for a game of Twister.

When she was satisfied, he sprawled out next to her and reached for her hand, encouraging her to perform. Suddenly she realized that the foul smell she thought was last week's eggs over easy still sitting in her kitchen sink was, in fact, the throbbing teenager who now lay beside her. All those Marlboros must have covered up this nasty surprise when she kissed him in the bar.

The rude fragrance became so overpowering she could barely concentrate on reciprocating the pleasure. He was waiting for his turn. Emily could feel him squirming around, trying to bring her lips closer to his, rubbing her hand over his crotch, moaning and whispering the revolting phrase, "C'mon, baby."

Possible excuses: lack of expertise, peniphobia, fatigue, insanity.

"I don't feel too well," she said, "I think I had too much to drink. Let me rest for a second."

A second became twenty minutes. She woke up again when he slammed the door on his way out.

Then there was Alex. With Alex, it was a salty wave. Emily tugged at the little hairs under his arm with her teeth.

"Ouch! Don't bite me there!"

"I'm not biting, I'm just playing."

"Well, don't play like that."

"I'm just doing it so I can kiss it, like this, after it hurts."

Alex was thin with barely brown skin and hair that was feeding itself into dreadlocks. She followed the orange tip of his cigarette as it passed back and forth through the full moonlight, to the ashtray balanced on his chest. She'd never acquired the habit, but she loved watching others suck and blow.

"Where's the fan?" he asked. "I'll put it in the window."

"On the floor. By my dresser."

Alex got up to move the fan and she watched the shape of his body stand, stretch, bend over. She loved the curve of his ass, especially just where the cheeks began to divide. She slunk to the edge of the bed and put her tongue on that favorite spot. His hips swung forward involuntarily, almost hurling the fan down four stories.

"This city is so fucking hot, you turn on the fan and it feels like a hair dryer," he said.

She started licking the cheeks of his ass, spreading them, trying to get her tongue right on his asshole. He spread his legs for her.

"What do you say, huh?" she said, playing tough.

"Lick my ass . . . my asshole."

It was so hard for him to say the word "asshole," aside from calling somebody an asshole. But when she found out he was crazy about getting licked "down there," she demanded he voice his request. Every time. The word was a Pavlovian bell that sent shock waves into her cunt.

He bent over completely, so she could see her fingers fucking his ass. The visual was unparalleled; his submission so rare.

She made him stroke his own cock.

"Imagine it's two women fucking you," she said.

The sexual repetition was endlessly fascinating. The way he held his breath and let it out in gasps as he got closer to coming. She wanted to crawl inside his mind and watch the fantasy loops.

The artificial breeze blew droplets of sweet salty juice mixed with sticky dark air all over the place. It was like sand from the Sandman, and the darkness of dreams closed in.

Too bright sunlight hurt her eyes, creating a watery mess in the middle of an urban drought. Emily hated wearing sunglasses because they slid down her nose and gave her tiny pimples on her cheeks, but she liked the disguise. The cleats on her cowboy boots clicked against the pavement and each click brought her closer to the place where she spent 1,920 hours a year.

Every morning she bought a newspaper from Murray's Cafe. The neon sign once read TRY MURRAY'S COCKTAILS! but some of

the letters had burned out and now it read TRY MURRAY'S COCK.
The best part about Murray's was the big glass case under the
cash register filled with all sorts of ancient candy like Black Jack
gum, Mary Janes, and those wax pop bottles with colored goo
inside. Murray was a million years old, but he was always fresh
enough to comment on Emily's outfit.

"You look nice today," he wheezed. Emily was wearing Homage to June Cleaver: a sleeveless yellow-and-white-striped cotton
button-up with a Peter Pan collar and a full skirt cut to half its
original length. Her red hair looked like a palm tree sprouting
from the top of her head, and thick strands of fake gold and
rhinestones dangled from her earlobes.

"Thanks, Murray," she replied. "Hey, when are you gonna get
your sign fixed?"

"As soon as somebody takes me up on the offer!" He started to
laugh, then broke into a raspy coughing fit. She could hear him
hawking the phlegm out of his lungs as she waved good-bye. The
sound made her sick. What happens to your sex life when your
body starts to fall apart and taking a healthy crap is the high
point of your day?

Cool air blasted out when the doors of the bus flew open.
Emily sat in the back on the long, horizontal stretch of blue
vinyl. Nobody could see her eyes wander behind her black lenses,
surveying the crowd. Next to her was a young blonde wearing a
beige Evan Picone suit, textured hose and silly tennis shoes. On
her lap was a leather briefcase, carrying, oh most definitely, her
schedule for "doing lunch" and *People* magazine. Emily's protected eyes rolled. Okay, give her a break. Maybe she reads By-
ron and gets turned on by the models in the Victoria's Secret
catalog. Careful clods jammed the aisle and through their polite
distances she glimpsed the other side. Fatso with a bad complexion and buck teeth, Baldy with a vacant stare. God, was she a
bitch this morning!

Emily opened the paper to Jeanne Dixon, hoping for some
insight into her vile Scorpio mood, when a stifling scent floated
past. It was perfumy and sweet, kind of like the aerosol Glade
in floral scent that infiltrated every American bathroom in the
seventies. Spraying it was a dead giveaway that a horrendous

turd had just been dropped. It never actually got rid of the smell, it simply transformed it into a fragrant Rosepoo. Where did the term "poo" come from anyway? And why did it get tacked on to "sham" to create something you wash your hair with? Shampoo . . . shampoo, the word lolled around Emily's conscious like a psychotic's mantra. After days of persistent pleading, Emily's mother finally took her to see *Shampoo* and they left after the first five minutes. It began with Warren Beatty fucking someone. It was a bad thing to watch people fucking. Yet everyone on the bus existed because of people fucking.

Emily looked around for the stinkbomb and zeroed in on an older woman with a jet black hair-sprayed do and bright orange lipstick that went far beyond the natural outline of her lips. Perspiration mixed with powder as she patted her damp face with a hanky. She was wearing a sleeveless dress patterned with darts that accentuated her huge breasts. Wrinkled skin hung from her heavy arms. Both of her hands clutched a shiny lime-green vinyl purse that matched her sandals. With a chunky heel and wide straps fastened too tightly by a green daisy buckle, the shoes caused her feet to swell. Her thick toenails were painted frosted pink.

Emily closed her eyes and tried to picture what this woman looked like when she had an orgasm. She saw the pink toenails go up in the air while a tongue lapped and slurped all around between her legs. Her soft, flabby belly jiggled in excitement and she begged under her breath for her old man to put his calloused hands on her tits. Her fingernails dug in to the chenille bedspread as she squealed, "Oooh, yes, oooohhhh yes," softly at first then louder and . . .

"Oooooowee! Fuckin' hot today!" The sudden intrusion made everyone look up.

His belch echoed loud and drunk and Emily could see the yellow stains of perspiration on his grimy white T-shirt as he gripped the bar above her head. His teeth were gray and there was dirt caked in every crevice of his rancid skin. This polluted menace set off everyone's internal fear siren. Emily folded the paper and slipped out of her seat, just in time to avoid the string of drool from the drunk's mouth about to land on her thigh. Across the aisle, the lime sandals shifted uneasily and the woman sighed disgustedly. Yet the thing that may have truly alarmed her went completely unnoticed.

Another stagnant day became a lifeless night. The air turned to Jell-O. Everywhere, everything moved slowly, submerged in the humidity. Beastly hot. Hot as hell.

Emily lounged on the couch in her bra, sucking on ice cubes, then spitting them back into her glass of iced tea. The tenacious heat made her fucking irritable. All day long, everyone bitched and fought and spat and you could feel the pressure build in the cooker. Millions of people swarming around like voracious ants, all cutting each other's throats. Alex was smoking and the smell was suffocating. The ashes: he wasn't tidy about his ashes and she felt like she was being buried under them. Every pore was gasping for air.

Alex sat in the window, watching the action on the street, looking for the breeze of salvation. Alex in his Ziggy Marley T-shirt.

Ziggy, she thought. Ziggy Stardust. Ziggy the Elephant at the Brookfield Zoo who killed his trainer and had a broken tusk. Ziggy the nauseating cartoon. Ziggy, Iggy, Twiggy. Whatever happened to Twiggy?

"Come sit with me," Alex said. He broke the train.

"I can't move."

Alex walked over, peeled her off the plastic couch and led her to the window. She set the iced tea down on the window ledge. He started stroking her hair and she moved her head away.

"It's too hot," she whined. But he persisted. He reached over to kiss her, but she pushed off the advance. He reached for the glass and the ice cubes clinked together when he swallowed. Emily resisted another kiss, but he grabbed her head and made her open her mouth when the cold fluid went running down her neck.

"I'll chill your ass, you little fuck."

He pulled down one cup of her bra. His cold lips circled her nipples and his teeth came down hard. She tried to push him away but he wedged her against the frame of the window.

His fingers chased the cubes around the glass and finally pulled two out. He ran the ice over her tits, on the outside of her bra, then stuck one in each cup. Then he squeezed her tits, pressing the frozen bits against her precious points. She gasped and swore while he held both of her wrists in one of his hands.

His free hand fished out another ice cube, this time sending the glass crashing to the floor. He slowly ran the cube up along the inside of her thigh, teasing her pink. His words were sharp whispers without punctuation.

"Spread your legs baby spread those legs and beg me to cool you off."

She was silent.

"Beg me beg me you whore."

He pulled her down and lay her over the windowsill like a seesaw; half her body dangling out, her feet barely touching the floor inside. Emily was dizzy from the height and her breath was ragged. Thick night steam poured into her head like cement and rivulets of melted ice mixed with her sweat and streamed up her neck, flooding her eyes. The acrid scent of rotting garbage burned her nostrils. Somewhere a radio blared the Commodores' "Brickhouse" and someone was pounding metal against metal, dull clinks that chimed with the dirty talk spilling off her lover's lips.

This lover is the one who lets her bad girl dreams rip. He's got a twelve-inch dick and an eternal erection. He is the whore's only Daddy. He fills every nasty hole you can think of and he is the only thing you can fuck in Hell.

His cock is ice cold and as thick as a baseball bat. Her cunt swallows it all. She wants to pull her legs together but he holds them apart. His tongue is long, so long it's like a whip that darts out and lashes her nipples with an arctic sting. His eyes are gleaming white and bloodshot as he pumps his frosty pole into her, keeping in sync with the pounding drone.

"That's a good bitch." His voice is distant thunder. She writhes and smiles and gets ready to be his sacrifice. His cum is a blast from a flamethrower.

She screams and shakes. She licks the fire and sticks her tongue out for more. Her body explodes then settles down like volcanic ash. The heat slowly subsides, leaving watery streaks down her legs. And Alex slowly and gently draws all five fingers out of her cunt.

The floor felt cool against Emily's feverish skin. Alex stroked the small of her back, where the ledge had left its mark.

"I hope the neighbors don't freak out when they hear you scream like that," he said laughing. "It sounds like you're possessed!"

"I was," she murmured.

But he would never know the Devil had a frozen dick.

Roberta Stone

The Journal

P-town without a partner. I look out at the bay through the window of the dark apartment. I have spent so many summers here that they all somehow blur into one another. Two weeks with Marilyn at the Beach Grass, a wild weekend with Jane at the Ship's Mast, many seasons with many lovers at the Lighthouse. One summer, when I had finally booked early enough to get back to the red room at Island House with Chris, the two male innkeepers ran beaming up to me with their file box. "Why, Joan and Chris, welcome back! We've been holding onto this for you since 1979." With that, they proffered a thin silver bracelet lost in the throes of a wicked night involving candles and bedposts. I had to explain to Chris II about Chris I.

Now I am here alone. Not quite alone, I'm sharing the flat with a friend. Both of us without lovers, comfortable together in the way that friends can be; no arguments about dinner, dancing, or the beach. Comfortable to go our separate ways. Vicki is leafing through the P-town *Advocate* looking for who is playing where, which spots are hot, the usual stuff.

"I think I'll bike down to the Express for a capuccino. Want to come?" asks Vicki.

"Now? On a Sunday morning?" I groan.

"Sure. The Unitarians will just be getting out of church. They've got that great dyke minister there. Best cruising spot in town."

"You go," I say. "I'll cruise the Sunday *Times.*"

Vicki throws on a shapeless lavender top and a pair of gym shorts and leaves the apartment. Vicki looks great in shapeless clothes, long and languid. The same styles always make me look . . . shapeless.

After an hour of unrewarding reading my mind begins to wander to the life outside. I wish I had the energy to cruise. I can just picture what I'd be doing if I were a gay man. I pull out my journal and start to write . . .

Peter left the standing-room-only crowd feeling healthy, happy and hot. The Reverend Kate Crandall-Howard had just given another of her famous sermons, "Community Togetherness and Orgasmic Response." Peter joined a group of regulars on the steps outside of church. He disdained the tourists who packed the church during the summer months, wide-eyed lesbians, creaming their pants for a look at the Reverend Kate.

"I loved your story in the Advocate, *Peter," said Helen, a regular summer habitué.*

"Why, thank you, Helen, though most people wouldn't agree that hairiness is an indicator of gay political radicalism."

"No, no," said Helen. "I mean the P-town Advocate. *The one about zoning in the West End and the prohibition of chintz curtains."*

Peter eyed the crowd as they chatted up the local news. In fact, all of them were skilled in this game of rhetoric and dish while simultaneously cruising the scene. Peter caught the eye of a tall, handsome man who was leaving the church. His hair was almost jet black, as were his thick beard and eyebrows. Peter quickly assessed the coloring, looking from eyebrows to beard. "A natural," he thought. As his eyes moved down the man's body, Peter could see a black tuft pushing its way out of the man's open collar. Further down, black fuzz trailed out of his sleeve around a black leather wristband. Peter quickly looked away. Although an outspo-

*ken gay politico, he had an innate shyness that most people
did not notice.*

"Nice sermon."

*Peter looked up, meeting the eyes of the man with the
black beard. "Yes," he said. "I particularly identified with
the part about 'self-love equals safe love.'"*

"Tea Dance at 5:00," said the man. "I'll be there."

*Peter turned back to the conversation on the church steps.
More talk about the abysmal crowds, the trash problem at
Herring Cove, and who was shtupping whom. "What will
I wear?" thought Peter.*

Vicki glides into the room.

"How was it?" I ask.

"The coffee was great but the cruising sucked. Writing in your
journal? My journal has turned into a goddamn novel since I
broke up with Melanie."

"It's not quite a journal. More like a fantasy."

"About sex?" Vicki grins.

"Sort of. But from a gay man's point of view. After all, it
couldn't be as boring as the last five months of my life."

"Or mine," Vicki agrees as she lies down on the couch.

"Everyone's here," she says. "Rita and Linda are at the Lighthouse. Rita was Fed Ex-ing memos to D.C. from the Express.
John and Bill are at the Seaside. John was cruising every boy in
leather on the street and Bill was carrying a telephone in his
backpack."

"In his backpack?" I repeat, astounded.

"He says the Gay Center is battling the city over water problems and he has to be in constant contact."

"I hope my apartment floods while I'm here," I sigh.

"And I get fired from my job and never have to go back," says
Vicki, finishing the thought. We laugh easily.

"Who else did you see?"

"Marina, Jill and Debby are all in town—"

"Oy," I groan.

"Marina and Jill are staying with Bill and John. And John says
he can't get any sleep, what with the fighting. Debby's been

prowling around but she's not allowed to call so Marina runs out to use the phone every now and then. Marina and Debby can see each other every other day but not on weekends. Jill's—"

"Stop, stop," I plead. "Is anyone having a relaxing vacation?"

"Jessica is in from New York. She wants us to come to the bar with her tonight. Girl's Leather Night. It's a fund-raiser for the Women's Health Network."

"Great," I respond. "I brought my leather jacket. Did you?"

"I don't think mine qualifies. It's brown."

"Well, I think it looks great on you. The girls will be at your feet."

I pick up my pad again and bring it and a beach towel down to the garden. I start to write . . .

Peter spent the rest of the day in quiet pursuits: reading, "desk work," as he liked to call it, and long, rambling telephone conversations with a few intimate friends in L.A., New York, New Zealand, San Francisco, Fire Island, Washington, D.C., and Paramus, New Jersey. At 4 o'clock he went up to his room to pick out his wardrobe for the evening. He stood before the open closet thinking, "A body shirt would be very becoming." He imagined the effect of his furry shoulders and back. "Too benign," he decided. "I haven't worn my state trooper's uniform in a long time," he thought, eyeing the starched brown shirt wistfully. "But hats are definitely too queeny at Tea." Then he remembered the leather waistband on the tall, dark stranger. "Yes," he thought. "I'll call his bluff." It was going to be a cool night anyway.

Peter emptied his closet of all the leather that he owned, and placed the items ritualistically across the bed. There were the leather chaps, the leather briefs, the leather body harness, the leather collar, the leather hat, the leather vest, the leather arm bands, the leather jacket, the leather cock ring, and finally, at the foot of the bed, the leather boots. So much black leather was there that Peter had to open the shades, for the room had suddenly darkened. "What to wear," he pondered. This was not L.A. where you could walk into a bar in full regalia and be relatively unnoticed. Besides, if he were to wear everything, he would weigh an

*extra fifty pounds, and he was already struggling at the gym
to lose the five extra he had gained this summer at Franco's.*

*Peter donned a pair of old blue jeans as a base. "This is
P-town," he thought, and quickly slipped on the black cock
ring. He buttoned his fly but left the third button undone.
He then zipped into his black leather chaps, carefully arranging his basket in a most fetching way. Next, the vest,
showing his hairy torso and pecs to their full advantage. The
harness was too much, he decided. "One shouldn't overdress
at a summer resort." Besides, if they came back to his place
it would be at hand. Peter discarded the arm bands, but put
on both wristbands. The cap went back in the closet as well;
his brown curls were at their peak. Peter finished the en-
semble with the engineer's boots he had bought at the yard
sale of a retired Hell's Angel in L.A. They were a steal
and would last forever. Who knew where they had already
been? He quickly threw the rest of the things back into the
closet, lingering over the collar. "A bare neck is so sexy in
summer," he thought, and the collar followed, tossed with
abandon.*

*As he stood before the mirror, Peter was taken with the
image before him. His cock started to come alive and he
could feel the cock ring cradling his semi-hard, cut hunk of
meat. He got the same feeling when he stood before the
mirror prepared for a fund-raiser, dressed in a well-cut tuxedo. He was ready.*

"I'm ready," shouts Vicki.

"You look great," I say as Vicki ambles out into the living
room. She is wearing her brown leather jacket over a black silk
shirt and pants. Vicki bends down to fix her laces and I focus on
the silk folds that drape her ass and thighs. God, I never noticed
what a great ass she has. I'm dressed in black with my black
leather jacket. It goes well with my streaked hair. As I look at
myself in the mirror, shaking my hair into place, I notice Vicki
behind me staring at my back. What a funny look she has. Is it
confusion? Sadness? Longing!

I zip around without looking at her. "Let's go, sweets. We'll
make an entrance."

Vicki and I walk into the bar together. Surveying the room we start getting into the mood of leather and lust. Women are all over the place in varying states of dress and attitude.

"We won't meet anyone like this," I say, and give Vicki a subtle salute, as I walk down to the other end of the bar. The room is hot. Women are moving close together, fingers entwined in hair, leather thongs connecting necks to waists. Two women are "dancing" together slowly, their bodies melting into one another, hands down each other's pants, mouths connected. I am being cruised by a baby dyke in a new leather jacket. Cute enough, but could I stand to wake up with her? I know I couldn't. Several older women sit in the corner wearing no particular costume, laughing among themselves.

"Drink?"

The voice belongs to a beautiful but cold-looking woman wearing nothing under her leather vest. I can't help staring into her cleavage as I mumble, "Yes, yes, a drink." The woman pulls a tray off the counter and I realize I am not being cruised. "Poland Springs, please," I say and throw some change onto the tray.

Across the room I watch the back of a woman who is dancing with my friend Jessica. Jessica is wearing white linen and getting everyone's attention. Beautiful, thin, long hair tossing wildly, Jessica looks like she's coming when she dances. As usual, she has already picked someone up. Her partner is dressed in flowing black and is shaking her ass like mad to the wild music. As I follow the woman's movements with my eyes, I feel my cunt throb. The woman's clothes are sticking to her back with sweat and I can see her luscious pear shape. Jessica is bumping her hips into the woman's cunt and I can feel the heat every time the woman's ass juts out. Suddenly they both turn with the beat. Jessica and Vicki are smiling into my eyes.

Peter stood at the window holding his Ramlösa in a butch attitude. Scanning the dance floor, he noted sweating, horny men of every description: thin, fat, muscled, soft. Balding and hairy, young and old. There was a smattering of lesbians. They always touched when they danced. Peter closed his eyes and inhaled deeply. The smell of men's sweat ex-

*cited him, and he became aware again of his cock ring.
When he opened his eyes his dream man was across the room
at the edge of the dance floor. He was striking in his leather
pants and leather vest. His black chest hair was thick and
curly as he stood at the rail. Peter noticed a line of bare skin
below his armpit, where the hair from front and back had
agreed upon a DMZ. Peter's cock was getting hard at the
thought of this white spot, and it was pushing handsomely
out of his chaps. The man looked taller than he had that
morning at church, and Peter realized that he, too, must be
wearing heavy black boots.*

*They walked toward each other and met at the entrance
to the dance floor. "My name is Jim," said the handsome
leather man. "Dance?"*

*They stepped down onto the dance floor, eye to eye, mov-
ing slowly and smiling imperceptibly. Leather men always
danced slowly; no wild waving of arms, no flailing feet. The
boots weighed about five pounds each. "I'm Peter," he said,
leaning forward. They danced through two dances before
they spoke again. At the start of the third song, a Whitney
Houston which precipitated much screaming from the crowd
around them, Jim leaned close and said in a husky voice, "I
have a room close by with some very interesting features."
Peter nodded knowingly, and the two tall men in leather
left the dance floor. Their space was filled immediately by
two men in bicycle shorts and hats.*

"I think I'm going to leave," I say as Vicki and Jessica come
up to me.

"Don't go," replies Vicki. "We haven't danced yet." She grabs
my hand and pulls me onto the dance floor. "That Jessica," she
says in a conspiratorial voice. "She's such a flirt. She even flirts
with me!"

"What's so strange about that, Vicki? You're beautiful, you're
intelligent and you're single."

"Well, I'm intelligent and single," she says, her brown curls
bouncing down into her eyes. "She really wants to sleep with
you, you know."

And I want to sleep with you, I think. I watch Vicki dance
with obvious delight. Her eyes are closed and she shakes her long

slim body in bursts of movement. I drink in her every curve and can't resist putting my hands on Vicki's hips. Eyes still closed, Vicki dances closer and closer to me. I can feel the hot flesh beneath the wet silk. Vicki is moaning into me now and I can smell the sweet musk of her sweat and see it glistening along the top of her smooth breasts.

All at once Vicki stops moving and just stares into my eyes. We breathe together, just staring. I feel that I'm melting into an incredible softness and realize I'm kneading Vicki's ass with both hands.

"Let's go home," Vicki says. "Let's go home together."

As they walked down Commercial Street, Peter was struck by the man's height and his hard body. "Almost my height," he thought.

Jim was talking to him now about his room. "I rented it through an ad in Drummer. *It came fully equipped," he said. "It has some handy built-ins which I hope to take full advantage of tonight."*

Peter wondered if it was the same place he stayed in three summers ago, the one with the brass rings above the bed and the post in the middle of the room slyly disguised as a ship's mast. That was a wonderful summer. He had devised a signal system for Helen and his other friends: a black leather triangle in the window meant DO NOT DISTURB.

Jim stopped at the gate of an old, weather-beaten cottage. "This is it," he said.

It was a different house! P-town was full of surprises. Peter noticed that Jim's hands were trembling slightly as he worked the key into the lock.

We walk along silently toward the East End. Everyone seems to be going in the other direction. I am mortified. I can't believe this is happening. How could I not have known? Vicki is quiet, seemingly unfrazzled by this turn of events. "What are you thinking?" I ask, fearing I have blown not only our vacation but also ten years of friendship.

"Uh, it's a cool night. Good thing we're wearing our jackets."

"What do you think about what just happened?" I ask.

"At the bar?" Vicki asks. "It was fine. It was okay. I mean, it was great."

"Aren't you upset with me? I mean, this is P-town, you're supposed to be meeting new women, getting laid, not going home with your roommate."

Vicki stops and turns toward me. "But I want to be going home with you. I've been waiting for this to happen. Is that okay?"

"It's more than okay," I reply. "It's fabulous."

We come to the door of our inn and one of the cats jumps out of the shadows. Vicki starts to sneeze. We both begin to laugh and wait outside the door as if it will open by magic.

"You took the key, didn't you?"

"No, you had it."

"No. I distinctly remember giving it to you."

Once inside, the two men looked each other over slowly, receiving the full effect of the powerfully built, leather-clad bodies. Jim reached for Peter's hands and brought them up to his nipples, coaxing Peter's fingers to squeeze the already hard buttons.

Peter's breath hissed between his teeth as he pinched the dark protrusions. "I love a man who likes pain," he said, his face close to Jim's. "How much can you take?"

"Only time will tell," Jim answered, as he backed away toward the bed.

Peter could see that his partner's cock was hard in his leather pants. He released one nipple and slowly moved his hand down the other's body, fingering the black curls as he went. Jim's head dropped back, his chest heaving as he breathed through his open mouth. Peter could feel the washboard muscles rippling under his hand as he continued down to the man's pants. Jim brought his hands together at his zipper to help him along. Peter pushed his hands away roughly. "I'll call the shots," he said. They looked into each other's eyes evenly. There was a palpable tension in the room as the two powerful men measured each other.

"You can do what you want with me tonight," Jim said. "I can take it."

"You will take it," Peter commanded in his deepest voice,

*pushing the other down to his knees in front of him. "Un-
button me and take out my cock," he boomed. The black
bearded man was on the level of Peter's crotch. He ran his
hands up the inside of Peter's chaps and carefully unbuttoned his fly. Peter's ten inches was almost fully hard and it
sprang from its constraints. "Handle it!" commanded Peter,
pushing his hips out.*

*The black bearded man deftly grasped and squeezed Pe-
ter's meat, scooping in every now and then to squeeze his
balls. "It's . . . it's beautiful," he mumbled as he worked the
cock, his mouth watering.*

*Peter's cock throbbed in its cock ring and he pulled the
man's head back by the hair. "Don't be so hopeful. You're
drooling," he said, looking down at him.*

We enter the apartment, take off our jackets and sit down at
the table. We sit in the same places as in the morning but everything has changed. Vicki picks up the pad that I have been using
for my story.

"You've written so much. Can I read it?"

"It's just trash. Just a fantasy. Real life doesn't happen that
way."

"How does real life happen?" Vicki asks.

I rise from my chair and take Vicki's hand. I lead her into the
bedroom and we lie down on the bed.

Vicki starts to unbutton my blouse quickly. "I want to see your
breasts," she says.

We silently undress each other, rolling around on the bed.
Vicki gasps at the sight of my full breasts. She arches her body
over to get them into her mouth. Moans and sighs are all that I
can manage as my friend sucks on one tender nipple. I look at
Vicki's back, rounded as she bends to suck. My hands move down
along her spine and balloon out at her hips. In that instant I
think of porcelain or some fine ivory sculpture. But Vicki's actions belie the fragile feeling of her skin as now she pushes me
back into the bed.

My cunt is throbbing and my skin is pink with excitement and
apprehension. Will this be a bust? Will we wake up tomorrow

and have breakfast together, never mentioning what went before? God, will our friendship be ruined?

"Is this really happening?" Vicki asks, breaking into my thoughts.

"It must be," I say. "I'm too wet for this to be a dream."

With that, I tumble Vicki over onto her back and kiss my way down her body. Kissing and licking, I linger on her smooth belly and settle in to enjoy the shape and feel of the small roundness. All thoughts of our curious situation leave my mind as I become more and more involved with Vicki's silky flesh. I lick and nibble every inch of Vicki's skin, roaming from belly to ribs to hips to breasts, back and forth, rolling her over as I go. She groans and giggles, sighs and gasps, feeling my tongue and lips and teeth.

My passion is growing as I lick and bite at her ass and thighs. "You are so beautiful," I moan into the warm flesh. "I just want to devour you." I lift her to her knees so that her ass is up in the air. And, spreading her legs, I lick down and into her open cunt.

"Oh, baby," moans Vicki. "This is what I want. Yes, this is what I want."

Peter pulled Jim up from his knees and instructed him, "Now that you know what I expect from you, you can show me your toys. I'll decide which ones I want to use on you."

Jim turned and went to the head of the bed. He pulled back the curtains, exposing two leather straps with brass rings at the ends. They were fastened to the wall with brass studs. Then he pointed to the other end of the bed. Fastened to the floor on either side were its mates. Jim squatted and pulled out a drawer from beneath the bed. The contents were carelessly scattered around: leather restraints, cock rings, nipple clips, two tubes of K-Y, condoms, butt plugs and dildos.

Peter was overjoyed at his good fortune, but his face belied nothing. "Those will do," he said calmly. As Jim rose, Peter pushed him face down on the bed, falling on top of him. He humped Jim's ass with delight, his hard cock sliding against the leather. Peter reveled in the subservient posture of his partner. He especially liked to top a hunky guy.

On his knees now, Peter turned Jim over between his legs. Reaching behind him, he grabbed the nipple clips out of the drawer. "I'm going to see how hard you can take it before you beg me to stop." He clipped the hard rocks of Jim's nipples, rubbing and squeezing the man's strong pecs as he did so. Jim let out a deep breath, and Peter could feel Jim's cock growing beneath him, under his leather pants. Peter groped for more toys, and pulled out the soft restraints. He grabbed Jim's hands and tied him to the rings on the wall, looking proudly at his handiwork.

"My ankles. Tie my ankles," whispered the man.

SLAP! Peter's hands stung, but Jim had asked for it. "You don't make the rules here, fella," he said in his most masterly voice. "Put your knees up so I can have a view of your ass!"

As Jim planted his boots on the bed, Peter reached over and unzipped the leather pants all the way down, exposing a brown hairy butt hole, aching to be entered. His hand behind him again, Peter searched for the butt plug, found it, then tossed it away. "I'm going to fuck you like you've never been fucked," he hissed between clenched teeth, as he pulled out the big black rubber dildo. He started to tease Jim's ass and balls with the rubber cock when a wave of caution overtook him. "Better be safe," he thought, and grabbed a condom, ripping open the package with his teeth. Jim was writhing and moaning on the bed as Peter worked the fine, ribbed rubber over the dildo. "Now I'm going to shove my cock into your ass, all ten inches of it," he said, as he prepared the way with a generous spurt of K-Y.

"I want it, I want it," screamed the bearded man, defenseless on the bed. "Oohh, yes."

The head was in, as Peter twisted and turned the rubber cock, screwing it into Jim's tight ass. "Take it, take it," Peter said gruffly as he pumped away. "My cock . . . is in you . . . cock . . . in you . . . yes . . . take it." His own rod was engorged.

"Fuck me, fuck me! Hard, hard!" Jim screamed, as white drops began to ooze in rhythm from his stiff column.

Peter now took his penis in his hand and pumped away, faster and faster. One hand on the dildo, one hand on his own cock; they were the same, hard, stiff and rubbery.

"I'm coming," cried Jim. "I'm coming." And with a jolt that felt like a bolt of lightning, the two men came together, Jim's semen spurting wildly over his hairy chest and beard, while Peter aimed his arrow at the matte black pants.

* * *

Vicki is on her knees and I am behind her and between her legs, nibbling and licking and sucking her wet cunt. The sensations are so intense, the position so intimate, I know that she feels vulnerable and lightheaded. She can't stay that way much longer, balanced on her knees with only the thick damp air holding her up. But she stays and stays, taking it in. My tongue, my mouth sucking and sucking, she hangs on the tip of an explosive orgasm. I reach around and find her breasts. My other hand moves down to her clit. Her body shudders, then falls, her muscles giving way. Over she goes, across the bed, pulling me down beside her.

"I want to give you more, do you want more?" I ask as we lie together.

"I want to fuck you," Vicki mouths into my ear. "I've wanted to fuck you for so long. You'd like that, wouldn't you?"

"Yes," I say, gasping.

"You want it?"

"Yes . . ."

"You want it?"

"Yes, yes."

"Can I? Can I fuck you?"

"Yes, yes. Fuck me, baby."

Vicki covers my body with her own and kisses me deeply, a long wet sucking of my lips and tongue. "Oh, baby, so many girls, so many girls have enjoyed you. Enjoyed your luscious breasts, your belly and your wet, juicy cunt," Vicki whispers as she licks my ear. "So many girls. And now me."

I breathe shallowly waiting for it to happen. My eyes are open and I watch Vicki's head as it moves down my body. I feel the soft lips and hot breath as they move from neck to breasts to belly to cunt.

"Come inside me, Vicki," I plead as I feel the hot damp breaths on my mound and clit. "Come on, honey," I moan.

She lingers there, breathing hard into my cunt. Breathing and licking, blowing and kissing. "You taste so sweet," she says, looking up at my face against the pillows. "You taste so sweet and so juicy."

"Do me, honey. Take me," I breathe.

"I'm going to tease you first. After all, you've waited this long, haven't you?"

My thighs relax as I expel a long breath. It is out of my control now. My lover, friend, will do whatever she desires. "Oh," I gasp as Vicki's tongue pushes deep into my cunt. Hands play on my thighs, pinching and pulling the cheeks of my ass. Her tongue is thrusting and licking, hands playing and taunting.

"Please, baby, please give it to me," I groan.

Faster and faster, Vicki's hands and mouth take what they want. Pulling and coaxing, thrusting and nipping. And I can no longer tell what is mouth and what is cunt, what is fingers and what is tongue. And she is inside me, three fingers in and deep inside. Moaning and rocking, I'm so wide open, swallowing her up, drinking her in. And she is thrusting, in and in, her fingers reaching deeper, her whole hand moving and rocking, rocking and rocking as her tongue and her lips play over my clit.

"Oh, God. Oh, God. Yes, yes," I scream. My cunt balloons and Vicki can feel me taking her in and holding her in.

Peter fell forward over his prone companion, sweating and exhausted. Jim panted, semi-conscious and wet with cum. They lay there like that, bellies heaving against each other, hair wet and curling between them, for what seemed like a very long time. Then Peter reached down and slowly began to remove the dildo from Jim's sweaty butt hole. Jim shuddered. "Easy does it," he said. "Easy does it."

Vicki and I lie entwined, sweat mingling under the covers. Vicki strokes my face and belly and breasts, holding me close and kissing my face. I breathe more slowly now, but the vein in my neck still pulses with the quickness of an electric current.

"Are we still friends?" Vicki asks, looking slyly at me as I lie in her arms.

"I think we're more than that now," I answer.

"After all these years it finally happened," muses Vicki.

I look back at her, tired and pleased. "It was so easy, baby. So easy."

Magenta Michaels

Rubenesque

It was nearly noon when "The Mountain," as she was known to her slimmer and catty co-workers, left the confines of her eighth-floor accounting office, hailed a cab, and within ten minutes alighted at the entrance of the grand and formidable Clift Hotel.

Actually, Evie Satterwhite wasn't really a mountain anymore; these days she more resembled a sweetly sloping knoll, resulting from many months of diminished intake and nearly 5,000 miles on her stationary bike. And while many women still dismissed her as heavy and in need of a good diet, many men looked at Evie and figuratively licked their lips, finding her rounded good looks toothsome and much preferable to the brittle edges of her slimmer sisters. Evie was not unaware of her effect on such men and helped it along. No drab power suits with skinny neckties for her but rather glossed red lips, high-heeled sandals showing off gorgeously arched feet, and softly glowing hair—colored Titian Red—that she fluffed with perfectly manicured fingertips. Men dropped like flies.

And so, in small celebration of her growing self-confidence and her diminishing heft, she came each month for lunch at this fabulous hotel where, for the price of many lunches at Alex's Deli next door to her office, she joined society ladies and literary buffs who assembled to hear the authors of famous and infamous best-sellers discuss their work. And, for the price of the same ticket, have an exquisitely catered, designer lunch.

Once in the lobby, she found her way to The Redwood Room, a draped and muraled splendor heavy with tapestries and chandeliers. She was the first to arrive and the room was empty, though each of the fifty tables in the hall was wonderfully appointed with heavy pink table linen and flowers at every place, silverware and wineglasses gleaming under the lights of the chandeliers. Evie stood in the doorway for a long time deciding where she would sit, and it was then that she saw the two workmen tacking down a portion of the richly patterned carpet. They looked up when she stepped through the polished double doors, and one of them—small and trim with Mediterranean good looks—immediately smiled at her and sat back on his heels, his eyes gobbling up the bounce of her hips as she passed him. She chose one of the smaller tables with two upholstered chairs and a loveseat, set against a side wall. And while the table was not near the lectern, from there she could see everyone who entered without having to turn around to look. She settled herself, checked her watch and was immediately distracted by the arrival of a noisy group of fashionably dressed matrons; fur coats, reptile skins, and expensive perfume ruffled the air around her as they passed. Slowly the room filled, and at 12:45 jacketed waiters began to serve. Her plate was set before her: a gorgeous, spa-inspired creation of poached salmon resting on a technicolor bed of various perfect greens and raw vegetables. Freshly baked bread lay steaming in a cloth basket, and even before she could think to ask, her wine was being poured by her silent but attentive waiter.

From the corner of her eye she saw, still on his knees and very near her table, the carpet man gathering his things to go. Then, with mounting disbelief, she watched him gaze intently at her, look carefully around him, lift the corner of her tablecloth, and quickly disappear, crawling beneath its skirts. Riveted, she stared wide-eyed at her wineglass, its amber contents trembling and then sloshing with the movements of the table as the man settled himself underneath it. Glancing at her neighbors to see who might have witnessed this phenomenon, she found herself unobserved. Not knowing what else to do, she fumbled in the bread basket for the miniature loaf, broke off a tiny piece and nervously began to butter it. Somehow feeling this was not the appropriate thing to do, she lay the bread down and picked up the heavy silver fork, fluffing the salad greens on her plate. The man beneath her table had not moved.

Of course she fully expected him to come crawling out at any moment, confused, flushed, and apologetic, and she, in her excited mind's eye, would smile sympathetically and nod him away, glancing around the room at the other diners who by now would all be staring. They would shrug their shoulders ("These things *do* happen") and then turn their interests back to their exquisitely detailed lunches or the brilliant wit of the speaker who was about to take the lectern. So she waited, gleaming fork poised above the burst of colors on her plate.

But he didn't come out and he didn't move, continuing to kneel there, his breath an intermittent warming to her knees. Through the haze of her growing excitement the oddest array of thoughts possessed her: could he *see* under there? Suppose the waiter spies the tablecloth moving and drags the man out by the scruff of his neck and then calls the police? Suppose the speaker at the lectern sees his feet sticking out, stops in mid-sentence, and points, as all of the diners turn around and stare at her? Suppose . . .

And then he touched her, his hands encircling the shoe of her crossed leg, causing her to start with such violence that her fork clattered heavily to the plate, scattering bits of salmon and vegetables onto the pink tablecloth between the porcelain cups and half-filled, beveled wineglasses. Dazed, she collected bits of food and placed them on the corner of her plate. Broad, warm fingers stroked the leather of her heeled sandal and the nylon at the top of her foot, the tiny rough places on the surface of his hands catching at the silken finish of her sheer stocking. He held her foot motionless for the longest time, and when she did not move or protest, he carefully removed her shoe, slipping it off with one hand and enclosing her foot immediately with the other hand as though he wished to make certain that she remained warm and secure. Then slowly, slowly, he began to knead the arch of her foot, moving his fingers up to the ball and then to the toes. And when still she did not respond, he began to pull gently at each toe, separating and finally rubbing into the crevices between them as much as the nylon stocking would allow. Above the table, the waiter took her plate, Evie gazing at him through dreamy, unseeing eyes.

She could feel the tiny tremors of his cramped position as his mouth bent to the inside of her arch. Caressing more with teeth and tongue than with lips, he moved along the whole inside of her foot, moving his attentions slowly up to her toes, nibbling at her longer, second toe before sucking its tip deeply into his mouth. With bites and tiny caressing sucks, he made a warm, wet trail up the length of her leg from ankle to inner knee.

A rising panic made her feel that she must move her body, that if she did not she would be unable to breathe or that she might fling herself wildly from the table. To calm herself, she carefully drew her foot from his hand, uncrossing her leg and changing her position on the loveseat until she was comfortable again. He, unsure of her movements, waited until she was still again before resting his forehead against her knees. Then he wriggled his head from side to side to part her legs. She could feel the roughness of his stubble, the prominent outline of nose and cheekbones as he burrowed his face against her. She allowed his head to part her as in slow motion she watched her waiter pour more coffee, the speaker at the lectern animated but voiceless for her. "Adventure," she thought dumbly. "This is what they call an adventure," as he nuzzled his way up and up with tiny bites and little licks done with the inside of his lips, alternating between her thighs, nudging her legs farther apart. As he approached her mid-thigh, she knew that he could smell her—that the smell of saliva-stroked skin, wet nylons, and her perfume mingled with the beckoning steam from between her legs, and that it rose to his nostrils as surely as the steam from her coffee floated to her own.

Abruptly the warmth of his mouth withdrew, startling her and leaving the spots where his mouth had been feeling cold and somehow desolate. During this long instant when she felt nothing from him, she began to be afraid. Then, with the purpose and familiarity of a longtime lover, he lifted his hands from her ankles and slid them, in one smooth movement, up the outer sides of her legs, pausing only at the hem of her skirt to gauge its tightness, then swept them underneath to her hips, one warm palm on each fleshy pad. He tugged at her pantyhose and she found herself helping him, shifting her weight from one buttock to the other. He slid her skirt up and up until it was bunched up around her hips, barely hidden from view by tablecloth, napkin, jacket, and the arms of the little loveseat. When he'd finally stripped the nylon from her legs, she sighed almost audibly as though some great weight had been lifted from her body. For a moment he did not touch her, and she knew that he was looking at her, inspecting her, admiring her. It added to her excitement that he could not watch the play of emotions on her face, or that she could not control him or guide him or wiggle or thrust herself up to his lips. She was at once helpless and in total control, able to take all that he was offering without guilt or reciprocation but at the same time unable to move toward him. This last thought made her smile, because should her covering table be somehow snatched away, there she would be, skirt to her waist, legs agape, a strange man with a bag of carpet tools by his side having his way with her.

When he could get no further because of her seated position, he guided her bare right foot to the seat of one of the upholstered chairs tucked under the table, spreading her legs further to allow him room. He pressed his nose against the swatch of silk that covered her crotch, rubbing up and down on either side of the distended kernel that pressed against her panties. He put his mouth to it, breathing on it, blowing at it, and finally pressing it, circling it through her panties with the tip of his tongue. She had all but stopped breathing, the room forgotten, the speaker's voice a senseless drone. Then, with one finger, he hooked the edge of her panties and drew them to one side, and dragged his tongue in one long velvet stroke from the base of her asshole to the top of her swollen clitoris.

"More coffee, madam?" The waiter bent to her ear. She looked up at him, unable to answer as the man beneath the table worked away, massaging her outer lips between his teeth, curling his tongue in her hair, pressing, blowing, sucking time and again the little kernel of flesh. Release rose up in her, washing over her limbs like smoke, and he held her stiffened legs pressed against his sides as she covered her face with the linen napkin, pressing it to her eyes to cover her grimace. Everyone in the room was clapping, the sound coming through to her consciousness like the volume on a TV crowd scene being quickly turned up and then down. Were they applauding her? Him? The speaker?

She opened her eyes to diners, rising to go. The luncheon was over. Crumpled and exhausted she sat at her table until the room was nearly empty. He had knelt back, no longer touching her, and she knew it was time for her to decide what to do. Awkwardly, she lowered her skirts, arranging her jacket and removing her foot from the chair. Feeling with one foot, she found her shoe and swung her legs to the side to slip into it. She pushed the table back slightly and rose to go, her legs wobbly, her head light. As she stepped across the doorway, she looked back at the table, its cluttered surface and pink skirts looking for all the world like the fifty others in the room. It looked as though nothing had happened here except a lecture and a luncheon and she was tempted to go back, to raise the tablecloth to see if he indeed was still crouched underneath.

No, she would not go back. She would not look under, or wait for him to come out and approach her. Maybe it was a dream. But as she stepped toward the main lobby a woman in a fur coat whispered loudly to her companion, "I thought bare legs were only acceptable on thin French mannequins!" And Evie, looking down at her stockingless legs, smiled as she remembered her rumpled pair of damp nylons lying under the table. Queen size.

Cassandra Brent

Strangers on a Train

Alyssa stood on the platform at Osaka's Umeda station and congratulated herself for having left the university early. Maybe she'd even get a seat on the train this time. Yawning, she ran her hand over her close-cropped Afro and kneaded the nape of her neck. She scanned the group of waiting passengers and noticed the white-gloved "pushers" who stood ready to firmly but politely shove as many commuters as possible onto the waiting trains. But they weren't needed now. Not yet.

Out of the corner of her eye she saw a stumbling, drunken Japanese man lurching and reeling down the length of the platform. Two Japanese women stood directly between Alyssa and the drunk. They were speaking softly, occasionally touching each other with the intimacy of close friends. Their conversation was rudely interrupted when the drunk lunged forward and grabbed the breast of the woman closest to him. He hung on as if trying to steady himself, then moved on to her companion and assaulted her in the same way. Both women hung their heads in shame.

Alyssa was livid. The drunk moved toward her, his hands out, ready to grab her. She set her backpack down, put one hand on her hip, and motioned to the man with the other. In a loud voice she said, "Come here, I've got something for you."

215

The man stopped. He opened his eyes a little wider and stared in shock at the angry black woman in front of him. Slowly, he lowered his hands. He glanced nervously up and down the platform, took one last look at her and stumbled on his way.

Alyssa closed her eyes and exhaled forcibly. Before she reopened them, a spasm shot straight from the hand on her hip to her crotch. She shuddered, gasped, and then smiled. When she opened her eyes her train was pulling into the station.

She boarded the train, her legs a bit shaky. The first thing she noticed was that all the seats were taken. Two high school girls were tittering in the seat next to the door about the *"Gaijin"* with *"borondo heiya."* The second thing she noticed was the object of their conversation: a man in a gray suit standing next to the door on the opposite side of the car. His eyes were closed and his blond hair was mussed, falling across his face. His lips were slightly parted, and he breathed with the slow, deep rhythm of sleep. Alyssa stood on the other side of the door and inspected him.

His eyelids, with their long dark lashes, fluttered rapidly back and forth. His collar was open, tie loosened, and Alyssa could see wisps of wiry blond hair peeking out at the base of his neck. He had a wonderful erection. Alyssa blinked and looked away, focusing instead on the black leather briefcase at his feet.

The train stopped at the next station. More people got on than got off; the area by the doors was starting to fill up. Alyssa grabbed the handrail above her head and moved a little closer to the man to keep her view of him unobstructed.

She glanced at his face again; his eyes were still closed. Feeling safe, she let her gaze travel back down his body to his crotch. She would have sworn she could see every detail of his cock, outlined against the smooth fabric of his trousers.

He's perfected the art of sleeping standing up, she thought, smiling to herself, complete with erotic dreams.

Almost as if he had heard her, his cock twitched and strained against his zipper. Alyssa glanced up at his face and was startled to see his green eyes wide open and a crooked grin on his face. He seemed delighted to find her watching him.

Alyssa gasped and spun around, turning her back to him. She

was intensely conscious of her long, full skirt swirling against her legs.

"Caught ya," he murmured. It wasn't an accusation, but an invitation.

"English. . . ." Alyssa couldn't remember being more happy to hear her native tongue. She couldn't return his gaze, but she could feel his eyes on her. She glanced over her shoulder; the crooked grin was still there. He chuckled softly.

The train pulled into the next station and Alyssa watched to see if he would get off. He didn't budge. Alyssa allowed the crowd to move her closer to him. He was right behind her now, and she could feel his breath on her neck.

"I loved the feeling of your eyes on me," he whispered over her shoulder. "It woke me up."

I wonder how he'd like the feeling of my hands, my mouth, or my cunt on him? Alyssa thought to herself.

The train went into a tunnel and they were plunged into darkness. She took a deep breath and said to herself, "I'm gonna do it." She reached behind her and grabbed his cock. She gave it a quick squeeze, then started to withdraw her hand. He grabbed her wrist.

"Aw, don't go away," he begged, placing her palm against his erection and slowly curling her fingers around it. She squeezed it again and he inhaled with a hiss.

The train lurched and Alyssa was thrown against him. He grabbed her hips and held her there. She ground her ass against his crotch. His head slumped to her shoulder and he nibbled on her neck.

The train emerged from the tunnel and they both froze. The man exhaled slowly. Alyssa scanned the car. In her high heels she was taller than almost everyone on the train, so mostly what she saw was the tops of people's heads.

They pulled into another station and more people crowded on. This time the "pushers" were called upon to pack them in tightly. The train pulled out of the station and began to sway gently.

"No one's looking," she said. She held her breath in anticipation.

She felt him grab two handfuls of her skirt and slowly begin to raise it. She put her hands on top of his and stopped him.

"It wraps around; just part the folds."

The first contact of his hands on her skin sent a flash of panic through Alyssa. She strained to see if anyone was watching them. But they were packed tight and all facing the other door. Alyssa closed her eyes and concentrated on the tingle on her skin as his hands slid her panties down. Keeping his elbows between them so as not to jostle other passengers, he caressed the insides of her thighs. Alyssa pulled up onto her tiptoes and arched her back.

"Oh my goodness," he moaned as he encountered her stickiness. He eagerly coated his fingers. "I have to get in there!" he whimpered. Alyssa nodded rapidly in assent.

"Release me."

Alyssa paused for a moment before she realized what he meant. Then she groped behind her and unzipped his pants, leaving the waistband buttoned. She pulled his cock out and gripped it tightly, making him growl deep in his throat.

The train conveniently entered another tunnel and slowed to a crawl. He pressed his hips forward and Alyssa felt his cock between her legs. It wasn't inside her, but against her. It was wet by the juices running down her thighs. She could feel his pubic hair on her ass.

"May I?" he whispered.

"You'd better."

He pulled back so that the head of his cock was just at her opening. She tilted her pelvis back to greet him. His fingers parted the lips of her cunt and he thrust forward, embedding his cock fully inside her. Alyssa's knees buckled; he wrapped his arms around her waist and began to make small movements in and out. Alyssa rocked with him.

Suddenly, the train pitched forward into the lights of the next station. The man started to withdraw his cock, but Alyssa followed his backward movement and kept him inside her. She began to clench her muscles around his cock as if she were sucking him with her cunt.

The doors opened and a few passengers fought their way out.

The pushers peered into the car, assessing the dismal scene, and barred any other passengers from entering.

The man made a little mewing noise in his throat and started mumbling, "You're gonna do it," over and over.

"Shh," Alyssa cautioned.

He slumped forward again and bit her shoulder to keep from crying out. Alyssa held her body stiffly, her fists balled at her sides and her cunt muscles clenching and clenching. A tear rolled down her cheek. She felt the man go rigid behind her, and then his orgasm started, his cock twitching and pumping inside her. She thought he'd bite a hole in her shoulder. Then her own orgasm hit and she tensed against it, her head twitching from side to side. The commuter next to her shifted position and she let her body go limp.

The train entered another tunnel. Swiftly the man extracted his cock from her body. Alyssa felt a pang of remorse; she clutched her thighs together. The man placed his hands on her shoulders and squeezed. Tentatively, Alyssa sent her hands to join his. He kissed her fingertips, then slid his hands out from under hers. That was when Alyssa felt the business card.

"Call me. Please. Call me."

The train came out of the tunnel and pulled into the next station. The man left her. Alyssa sensed him making his way to the door, but she couldn't bear to watch his departure. She leaned against the other door and squeezed her thighs together even tighter.

When the train reached her stop, she stumbled to the exit. She walked the blocks to her apartment in a daze, her body still tingling. She unlocked her door, removed her shoes, and padded across the tatami mats to the ornate mirror in her bedroom. She stripped off her clothes and stared at herself. Clutching the business card in one hand, she ran her fingers over the teeth marks on her shoulder and trembled with the memory. She glanced at the business card, grinned, and reached for the phone.

Kate Robinson

Silver, Gold, Red, Black

Cass and Dru are fighting again, in the blindly bloody fashion of obsessed lovers. "Typical dykes," I say to no one. I recross my legs and light another cigarette.

As their voices subside into teary mumbles, I read the headline for the fourth time. Earth passes through meteor shower tonight, it announces. Good. All the crabby insomniacs created by two weeks of unaccustomed heat should have something to comment on besides my ass.

Now it's silent behind my roommates' door. Seven minutes, I predict to the sofa, checking my watch. Right again. I recognize the first moan as Dru's; long, dark, full, loud. Cass isn't far behind: fluent, young, round, undisciplined. This won't go on for long; after a fight, they're always quick and dirty.

I don't care what anyone says. Sharing a house with a couple is the best way to remember why I'm single.

I calmly finish the paper, rolling my eyes at their crescendos. That Catherine Deneuve look-alike from work crosses my mind once: I see her looking up at me mischievously from between my legs. OK. Out to the kitchen for a beer. I take my time. Cut myself a couple of slices of cheese, take little bites.

When I walk out onto the porch, Cass and Dru are coiled

together on the glider, all arms and legs and red and black hair. I lean on a post and face them, smugly single. I nurse my beer and blow cigarette smoke out the side of my mouth, poised for their disapproval. The sun sets behind me with a radioactive-orange glow.

Dru pushes back her heavy mat of black hair and says, "I wanna go to the lake." Cass and I latch onto the idea and we fan out into the house, hunting for swimsuits, zoris, and towels.

Pressed together in the front seat of Cass's Datsun, the three of us are finally headed in a single direction. Catherine Deneuve drifts up into the air and blows away.

The feeble parking-lot light doesn't reach far into the thick darkness under the trees beside the lake. There are people around us, on land and in the water, but they are as indefinite as minor characters in dreams. There is splashing in the lake. Teenage girls squeal, teased by teenage boys, but nobody plays loud music, nobody is rough or raucous.

Dru and Cass look almost comical in profile. They hold hands. Cass is short and lush; she rubs her bushy red hair on Dru's shoulder. Dru is taller, dark, and solid. I'm the tallest. I walk a little behind.

I stop when I reach the water. The meteors look like stars playing tag. I want to reach up and brush the black velvet and running mercury of their game with the blunt tips of my fingers. If I glance away, I fear I won't be able to burn this night into my memory.

Meanwhile, Cass and Dru give themselves to the water. Dru plunks herself in whole, the sooner the better. Cass submerges inch by inch, savoring each sensation. I'm stalled in the shallows.

Finally, I take giant steps, wading in. The lake is warm, womblike, from the day's heat. When the water reaches the Y at the top of my legs, I pause. Warm wavelets lap at my groin. I shudder, then take two more steps and I am rib deep. I plunge in, scissor-kicking underwater.

Amorphous shapes float around, yellowish-gray, large or small, moving toward or away from me. Some Northern-climate part of me suggests they might be frightening, but I am in far too deep to heed it.

When I surface, Dru and Cass have blended in with all the other splashing thicknesses in the dark water. I am completely surrounded and completely alone. I float on my back, watching. Meteors tumble and burst over my head. I can't help feeling loved and welcomed, suspended in the warm palm of a gentle hand.

As I float farther from shore, I hear the voices of boys on the diving platform. I have a sudden, urgent wish to throw myself up through the warm air and descend to penetrate the lake's surface. I begin to backstroke evenly toward the platform, watching the show above me. I can't look at everything: the sky blurs.

The abrupt closeness of a male voice startles me. I jackknife my body and twirl around. The platform is a dark wall in front of me. Light seeps dimly from beneath me. My daylight self pushes small points of fear into my belly; I appease it by swimming around to the ladder on the other side of the platform.

The light in the water is stronger here, more lunar. The cold should be more noticeable in this deeper area. Instead, there is a warm current flowing up my legs. The current seems to be directed at my cunt. I am disturbed and fascinated.

Far below me, something sparkles. A fish? But I know the only fish in this lake are small, planted trout. I duck my head under the water to look at the shape. It grows larger, moving sinuously, taking on form. It is lighter, less yellow and more silver/gold than the other shapes I saw around me. It is definitely human— torso, head, legs, and arms—but otherwise unrecognizable. The hair is short and the same color as the body. I see neither clothing nor indications of gender.

It is beautiful. The heat and light seem to emanate from it. It moves like the current from beneath the platform.

I am acutely aware of my surroundings—the water and waves, moon and meteors, shore and, distantly, voices—but I am exclusively involved now with the shape. My cunt swells and opens to the rhythms of the current. My breathing is as complex and reactive as the tiny patterns of ripples on the water's surface.

The shape swims up swiftly beneath me. I feel its presence on my skin before it touches me. Its hands, hot and almost dry, slide up my legs, greedily testing and comprehending each muscle and swelling of flesh. My extreme arousal seems to make me float more lightly; the howl between my legs arches my back, makes me reckless. The lake laps impudently at my nipples.

The shape's fingers explore my ass, my belly, the groove between inner thigh and pubis, before it rips away tight fabric to find my own heat. Its hands are clean and smooth and ruthless.

Its head floats near my waist—I stroke its temples, then grip them tightly. That contact releases a flood of sensation. Meteors shoot and burst on my throat, in the small of my back, across my breasts, deep in my belly, behind my knees.

The shape's hands are on my pubis now. Its fingers trail between my inner lips, invade my vagina. One hand balls up and thrusts into me, the other grips my ass.

Its fist smacks rudely upward inside me, the knuckles kneading my walls, which roll and squeeze against them. A stand-up-bass thrum descends from my uterus to my vagina.

With each thrust its arm seems to plunge deeper into me. I seem to grow to eagerly take it in. I let go of the shape's head, unable to tense any muscles unconnected with my cunt. Larger and larger, I'm hungrier and hungrier. The night is scorched by my breath. The shape's warmth and bulk fill me and burst.

My flesh is overwhelmed, I'm lost, I can't see myself. It's happening too much, too long, too hard to see. I think of a woman giving birth but in the other direction; I take it in, in, in. Short time, long time, all time disappears. Maybe one meteor streaks across the sky and flashes; maybe it's almost dawn and the lake has emptied of revelers. The sounds I make are shameless, inseparable from the ripples on the lake's surface.

When it's over, young male voices still sound above me, dark yellowish shapes still move around me. The earth is passing out of the shower now. Individual bursts are easy to distinguish.

I find myself gripping the lower rung of the platform's ladder. I am stripped and hot and glowing gold. I cannot see the shape, cannot feel it banging into me.

I check my belly. I'm surprised that it is still flat. The shape is there; I sense it radiating from me. I expect to blast the ladder and everything else around me into shadows with its brilliance. My brilliance.

Arias tempt my tuneless voice. My bowed legs itch for a foot-race. I want to catch a barn swallow and feel its quickness throb in my hand. Instead, I swing my legs up onto the step, climb onto the platform in a surge of water and muscle, and stride across the platform.

The boys fade into the darkness. They see I am more virile than they. My path is clear.

I walk out on the short diving board. Feeling perfect and ready, I bend my knees, bounce up, come down once again, then rise high over the lake. I fly. I return to earth only because I choose to, insinuating my fingers, shoulders, ribs, pelvis, knees, and heels into the lake's open mouth.

Armadas of bubbles slide up my body, silver and perfect, male and female. The warm sap of my arousal charges the lake, flows outward from me with water and bubbles.

I surface beside Cass and Dru. They are floating together quietly, on their backs and occasionally touching—rafted. I roll over and join them.

When I touch Dru, she hums. I pick it up, then touch Cass and she starts her low sound. We are in unison, we make chords and dischords, passing the sound between us. For long minutes, we are a humming raft suspended between warm water and the silver-black maze of lights. When the song dies, we float silently for a moment longer, then turn to swim toward shore.

Dru and Cass do not touch on the way to the car but they are utterly entangled. Neither of them mentions my nakedness, so I do not notice it either. We are silent.

Instead of taking my customary post in the car—jammed against the passenger door—I sit between Cass and Dru. Cass presses her soft flesh against my left side; Dru imprints her mass against my right side and firmly clutches my thigh. Their touch clothes me.

The porch light reveals greenish-brown alluvial deposits on our skin. Embedded in Cass's red hair and paleness and freckles they look iridescent. They give Dru's skin a scaly texture but soft, inviting exploration.

We survey one another, then they strip away their wet clothes, leaving them in oozing piles. They race.

By the time I get to the bathroom, Cass and Dru are already in the shower. I hesitate. I want a cigarette. I feel naked.

"Get in!" Dru demands.

They meticulously soap and scrub every part of my body. Without a word and with very little movement, I direct my bath, indicating my pleasure with subtle expressions and shifts of my limbs. I make no attempt to wash either of them, but observe the sediment sliding off their bodies and down the drain. When I am spotless, Dru turns off the water, we step out of the shower and just as carefully they dry me.

Cass takes my hand and leads me toward their bedroom. We have turned on no lights, and the house is fuzzy with shadows and heat. Even in the dark, I recognize the unique combination of odors that signals my roommates: Dru's clean-edged, freshly laundered–bedding scent, and Cass' fertile, incense-and-strawberry smell. When Cass lays me down on their bed, the odor envelops me. The raspberry-colored walls and dark purple comforter turn moist and womblike in the heat and the light from the setting moon.

Cass crawls over me and sits cross-legged against the wall. She leans forward and begins to stroke me. "Hard," she remarks. "Strong!" Dru stands at the foot of the bed, watching, nodding her approval. I lie still, lacking will.

Cass's hands begin to linger in their path. My breasts get extra attention. Each time she passes from belly to thigh, her path veers more centerward.

Dru walks around to kneel beside the bed. After examining me for seconds, she slips her long arm under my legs, pushes one thigh upward and pulls her longest fingers through the thickest wetness between my legs.

Cass unfolds, hoists herself over my belly and, with her tongue, begins to stroke and suckle my breast.

The bedding under my ass is already soaked. I cannot exhale without moaning.

The shape's heat is rising in the room, and the light seems brighter, more reddish silver, than the fat, setting moon could reflect. These are my friends; I can see that in their bodies and their faces, smell it in their room. But the ritual is ancient.

My skin, my breath, my cunt did not relinquish what began at the lake, I realize; they merely took it in, transmuted it.

Dru's mouth and tongue are at my cunt now, Cass is everywhere else. I have my hand in Cass's cunt, and Dru is riding her own hand. Our voices are once again joined, more in tumult now than harmony, but just as powerful, just as sacred. I can feel Dru in me; she carries me off. I arch and arch, she pushes against me and comes into my cum again and again. My hand clutches and stiffens in Cass; she thrusts her ass against me and warbles into my breast.

We are tireless, almost ruthless. We go on and on and on, until all of us are so swollen and exhausted that we can no longer either come or move. We finally fall wetly asleep, Dru curled with her cheek still resting on my drenched pubic hair, my hand still inside Cass, Cass and Dru touching across my sweaty belly.

We wake up sticky and smug, comfortable with tired laughter but not very talkative. Dru makes a pot of coffee. Cass brings in the newspaper and we share it, sipping coffee, on their bed. I smoke, knocking ashes neatly into the ashtray that Dru has brought in; neither of them complains. We shower and dress groggily.

Before we float off to our respective jobs, I ask, "Did you dream?" They look at each other, then at me. Everybody has a secret smile. "Yes," Cass says, "didn't you?" I just widen my smile into a foolish grin.

In my dream, the shape girlishly tried on a number of familiar and unfamiliar faces and I was the shape, the girl, the faces, and my cunt was not worn out in the dream and pursed its lips against Dru's sleeping cheek.

As the bus rolls downtown, I wonder. What did Cass and Dru make of the shape in those few hours we lay asleep, linked? I wonder whose face it wore.

None of us ever speaks of the dream. When Catherine Deneuve visits, she mentions the meteor shower and we are silent. Except for the smile, of course. We share it, the three of us, and she scowls. I pretend not to notice.

Susan St. Aubin

This Isn't About Love

Ilka on the road in her yellow Volkswagen, traveling from job to job: I can see her as clearly now as I could then. Monday nights she's at City College teaching English as a Second Language; Tuesday and Thursday afternoons she teaches two sections of remedial composition at Cabrillo College thirty miles south; Wednesday nights she's thirty miles north at the College of San Mateo teaching self-defense; and Thursday nights it's self-defense again at the Women's Center, which doesn't pay much but she doesn't have to drive so far.

"I'm exhausted," she says when she walks into the university gym where the Women's Center holds its self-defense class.

We sit on the floor dressed in leotards or sweat pants. Lynne, who's gay and wears men's jeans, removes her heavy hiking boots reluctantly because street shoes aren't allowed in the gym. Patty, a sophomore math major with long red hair who says she's sick of male logic, whispers to Louise and Janice from the Women's Studies program, whose breasts float loosely beneath their cotton T-shirts, one aqua, one bright yellow.

I sit against the wall in my black leotard, my long braid of brown hair over one shoulder. We're the regulars; others come for a few lessons then leave.

Ilka dumps a green shoulder bag bursting with books and papers on the floor and pulls from it a rumpled white cotton karate suit.

"This material is so sick," she says, shaking the knee pants and jacket. "It'll last forever."

She means "thick," not "sick"; she's Swiss-German, and though she's taught English for years, her consonants sometimes slip.

A dozen years later I can shut my eyes and watch as she bends to unlace her knee-high boots, then pulls on the heavy cotton trousers before sliding off her denim midi skirt and vest. After she unbuttons her blouse, there's an instant when she stands in her pink camisole before it's covered by the cotton jacket she ties around her waist with a brown cloth belt. She wraps a silk scarf around her head to contain her long blond hair, except for the bangs that cover her eyebrows. She has our rapt attention when she's ready to begin the class. I'm not gay but my breath comes quicker, then and now.

Her green eyes, which she rarely blinks, stare intently as she leads us through our warm-up exercises.

"It's best to be a generalist," she tells us while we stretch. She's taught for years, first in Japan where she tutored businessmen in German and English, and then in California, where she specializes in English as a second language, a subject in which she has personal experience as well as a Master's degree from our university. The self-defense course is her own invention, loosely based on the karate, judo, and aikido she picked up in Japan.

"Use your opponent's energy against him," she tells us as we glide together across the floor of the gym, moving our feet and arms as she's taught us.

"These are the vital spots of the human body," she recites, jabbing her right arm with fingers stretched straight. "Eyes. Base of the skull. Solar plexus. Groin. Knee cap. Christine!" She calls to me across the gym. "Your movements are far too weak. Put some muscle in your arm, push against the air, like so." Her arm swings forward in a controlled punch. "Imagine your attacker."

After class we go to a coffeehouse called Sacred Grounds in the basement of a church where we drink espresso and listen to Ilka talk about her life on the road.

"The freeways are full of boys in delivery trucks," she tells us, her green eyes round and staring. She says she's bisexual and once told us about a woman in Japan named Mika whose body was so smooth and hairless that making love with her was like being caressed by a silk scarf. But only when she speaks of men are her eyes this big. Patty leans forward, while Lynn sits back in her chair, arms folded across her breasts.

These aren't long-distance truckers high up in the cabs of their semis with their eyes fixed on the road, these are boys driving local routes in vans and pickup trucks with signs painted on the side: Doug's Pharmacy, Race Street Fish Market, Global Paint. They honk when they pass her yellow Volkswagen, and she honks back.

"That's stupid," says Lynne. "No matter how good your judo skills are, you're defenseless in a car. What if one of those guys forces you off the road? What if he has a gun? I still say it's better to carry a gun, because if your attacker's got one pointed at you, you can't very well throw him over your shoulder."

Lynne and Ilka have a variation of this conversation nearly every week.

"If you're in control of your own healthy body, you'll never need a gun to defend yourself," says Ilka. This time she smiles, leaning her elbows on the sticky table, and adds, "Besides, you're assuming I'd be unwilling. How can I be defenseless against what I want?"

Lynne's mouth opens, then closes tight.

Still smiling, Ilka tells us about Denny, who has lips like Mick Jagger's and delivers stereo components to a chain of stores up and down Highway 101. He's a drama student at City College whose ex-girlfriend took Ilka's self-defense class at the College of San Mateo. The first time they met, he motioned her off the freeway in Belmont and bought her a drink in a bar, then took her in his company's van into the dry October hills where they made love on the floor among boxes of speakers, turntables, and tape recorders. The van's back doors hung open so they could watch the planes take off from San Francisco Airport to the north. Ilka tells us that except for his shaved face, his whole body is covered with black silky hair that's as smooth as Mika's skin.

Once every couple of weeks she runs into him—the literalness of this expression when applied to their freeway meetings makes us laugh. They always drive somewhere in his van: up to Crystal Springs Reservoir where they make love in the moonlight on the concrete steps of the Pulgas Water Temple or over the mountains to the beach where they lie in the back of the truck and watch the afternoon fog roll in.

It's 1975 and nobody's heard of AIDS. Ilka's on the pill, so all she has to worry about is that Denny might turn out to be a crazed killer who'll pull an ax from behind a stack of stereo speakers and chop her into little pieces which he'll scatter between San Jose and San Francisco. She knows if she wants to she can kick the ax from his hands and paralyze him with a chop to his Adam's apple, but still it excites her to imagine cowering before him, especially when they lie wrapped in each other's arms in the back of the truck on a deserted road in the hills at sunset.

"If there's a part of me that wants direction, I can't be defenseless," she tells us in Sacred Grounds. "The trouble is, I can defend myself too well. I feel so safe with men it's a bore."

"I wouldn't mind being bored like that," says Lynne.

When Ilka stops seeing Denny on the road, she's not too disappointed. Perhaps he quit his job or was fired. Did his boss find the red silk underpants Mika sent her from Japan in an empty turntable box? Did Denny get back together with his old girlfriend? Does he swerve off the road whenever he sees a yellow Volkswagen in the distance?

"He was very immature," she says, sipping coffee. We're all kids, nineteen and twenty years old; she's twenty-nine and we're flattered to be included in her maturity.

One night while pulling out of the parking lot at City College, she sees a quick flash of headlights in her rearview mirror. For a second she thinks the van is Denny's but this one is light blue; and when it passes, she sees no writing on the side. Inside, a man leans back casually as he drives. She catches a glimpse of him, hair unfashionably short, seat tilted back, a cigarette dangling from his lips and then he's gone.

The next week she sees him again at one of the other colleges.

Once more it's late; her night class has just let out, or she's spent
the evening tutoring students from her afternoon English class.
She watches his eyes in her rearview mirror all the way home.
When she changes lanes, so does he: they dance together across
the nearly empty highway. When she exits he's close behind, but
three blocks from her apartment he pulls ahead and disappears
around the corner. His license plate reads "ZIP," but she keeps
forgetting what the three numbers are.

When she sees him on a Tuesday afternoon, she gets a better
look. "He has a very long nose," she tells us in a whisper. "Of
course, you know about men with long noses."

We look at each other for clues.

"They have long penises, too," she says.

Late one warm night in May, he stays on her tail, changing
lanes when she does, getting on and off the freeway when she
does. When she stops for gas, so does he, but instead of getting
out of his van she sees him wave a thick, stubby hand to the
attendant sitting behind the flickering light in the window of
the gas station. The attendant gets up and strolls out to lean on
the open window of the van before filling the tank and washing the windshield.

Ilka rolls her eyes to the side to watch without seeming to as
she cleans her own windshield, and so she doesn't see much. His
fingers do look short, though, which she thinks contradicts the
mythology of the nose. After paying the cashier in her booth
beside the gas pumps, where she sits with candy bars and cigarette packages stacked up to her ears, Ilka drives away with the
mysterious van close behind.

When he passes, blinking his lights, she follows. He signals
right without moving out of his lane and she signals too but stays
behind him. When he actually does exit at a sign that says "Rest
Stop," Ilka is close behind. The moon is so full and bright that
she sees every bush, every rock, almost every blade of grass. She
follows him up a winding road that ends at the top of a hill in
a circle of picnic tables beside a lighted building nearly as big as
a house, with two entrances, one for women and one for men.
Two men come out of the men's entrance, one behind the other,
and stroll into the bushes behind the building.

She passes the restrooms and parks beside the light blue van, where her pursuer sits staring straight ahead, one arm resting on his steering wheel. The arm looks heavier than his neck and shoulders, but she can't see it clearly because it's hidden by his loose jacket.

She gets out and walks around her car to the open window of the van. At first she thinks he has no legs. Then she realizes his bare feet with their clean, stubby toes *are* his hands, his heavy muscular legs are his arms. He sits in a padded, velvet-covered seat, with one of his legs resting on the open window, the knee crooked like an elbow, while his neatly manicured toes drum the steering wheel.

He laughs as she gasps. He wears bell-bottomed denim pants and a dark blue shirt whose short sleeves flap loosely. With his free foot he pulls a lever on the dashboard, which looks like an airline cockpit with lights and buttons everywhere, and his seat tilts back. He raises his legs straight up above his head, lacing the toes together like fingers as he watches her, then stretches with a thrust of his pelvis and puts his feet back down on the floor where they belong. She backs away one step.

"Why have you been following me?" she asks. With one kick she could knock him out of his van. She can't imagine an attack he might win.

He smiles at her and shrugs; without arms, the shrug seems to originate in his groin. "I could ask you why you followed me up here. What's your name, anyway?"

"Ilka," she says.

His eyes are dark in the moonlight. "Where're you from?" he asks. "Isn't that a German accent?"

"Originally Berne. In Switzerland," she answers before she can stop herself. This is more information than she usually gives the guys she picks up on the road. Her heart beats faster.

"Come for a ride with me, Ilka." The door on the other side of the van pops open when he pulls a lever.

She feels like she's been hypnotized, and knows that even if she needs to, she won't be able to make herself throw him. Obediently she walks around the front of the van and gets in, landing on a padded velvet seat identical to his. He pushes a lever with his big toe and the door shuts. She feels disarmed, and finds this intoxicating, as though she's just smoked a joint. She listens to herself breathe as she rubs her arms across the armrests. He puts one foot on the seat of his chair and moves it rapidly back and forth, brushing the velvet. The moon hangs frozen in the van's windshield.

"We don't have to go anywhere," he says, turning on a light that dimly illuminates the windowless interior of the van. There are two bunks built into each side and covered with velvet spreads to match the front seats. On one of the bunks is a fur rug. The ceiling is glued with squares of mirror; a reflection of the light glows in each one. When he swivels his seat around to face the bunks, so does she.

"Do you live here?" she asks.

"No, but I could if I had to."

He stands up and moves, half stooped in the low van, to the bunk with the fur rug, where he lies down. She kneels on the carpeted floor beside him.

In Sacred Grounds we look at each other, at her, at our cups.

She laughs at us. "You don't believe me! But his legs were so much like arms it seemed like there was nothing missing."

She tells us how he wraps a leg around her waist with a grip so firm she feels she can't escape, and pulls her down on top of him. Her hands slide across the thick fur rug. With his foot he strokes her back, then with one deft motion pulls off her long skirt, which has elastic at the waist, and her underpants. His foot slides up her legs and those toes, she tells us, her mouth slightly open, those toes know just what to do. As they lie side by side, one of the toes—the big toe, she thinks, but she's not quite sure—penetrates her while two or three of the others move around faster than anything she's ever felt before, faster than her own fingers. This can't be a human foot, she thinks, and listens for the hum of a vibrator or maybe some sort of electric arm or mechanical hand, but hears nothing. One leg holds her while the other plays until she comes with a rushing sensation she's never felt before.

"I wet the fur," she whispers to us. "I came like a man. Can you imagine?"

We stare at her, and then I start to giggle.

"I've heard of that happening," says Lynne.

The others shake their heads.

"No," says Janice, who's organizing a library of feminist writing for the Women's Center. "That's not possible."

Lynne glares at us until we're quiet.

Ilka shrugs and says, "It happened."

He rubs the wet spot with his foot and kisses her again. She's still embarrassed, but he finds nothing odd about this wetness; if anything, it seems to arouse him further.

"I don't meet many women like you," he whispers in her ear. "Take your blouse off."

While she sits up to unbutton her blouse, he lifts a toe to his crotch and pulls his fly apart with a rip to expose his erect penis. Where a zipper should be she sees strips of blue Velcro. He slides out of his pants like a snake shedding its skin, but leaves his shirt on. She's fascinated by his short, military haircut.

His leg is around her waist. He pulls her down to his penis, which she takes in her mouth and sucks until she feels he's about to come, then she pushes his leg down and seats herself on top, riding while he writhes beneath.

After he comes, she comes again, but she can't tell if the wetness is hers or his. She rolls onto her back beside him and feels with her hand, then sniffs and licks her fingers, but it all tastes and smells the same.

She sits up. "I've got to leave," she says, and is disappointed when he slithers back into his pants without comment, passing a toe over the Velcro closure. She wants those legs to grip her again so tight she can't move.

Ilka puts on her blouse, fumbling with the buttons. She imagines him reaching under a bunk with his foot and pulling out a gun, but she knows she can unbalance him easily with a kick. She feels let down.

He sits on the bunk smiling at her while she binds her hair in her brown silk scarf then crawls to the front of the van and opens the door. In her mind he jumps on her, pulling her to the floor with his powerful legs while she struggles to break free, but when she looks back, he just sits, smiling.

She jumps out of the van and runs to her car, wanting him behind her, then roars out of the parking lot in a sputter of gravel. She keeps checking the rearview mirror all the way home but he's not there.

Yet he's caught her. Ilka begins driving even when she doesn't have to—Saturday nights, Sunday afternoons, early in the morning she cruises up and down the freeway from San Jose to San Francisco, looking for an unmarked light blue van. She wants his legs wrapped around her waist again while his toes massage her spine. She imagines holding him where his arms should be and shaking him until his heavy legs pull her down. She imagines him with arms wrestling on the floor of his van, his fingers—real fingers—so tight around her neck that the light turns gray.

Did he come into the world unarmed, more helpless than most of us? Or was there some sort of accident—arms ripped from their sockets in a car wreck, arms burned to the shoulder in a fire? Did he lose them in Vietnam to a Viet Cong soldier with a knife or one of his buddies gone mad? She does research in the library on the babies born in Germany in the early sixties without arms because of a drug their mothers took for nerves and nausea, but he's too old for that; he's at least thirty. She hadn't felt his shoulders where the arms should be, so she wonders if he has some sort of residual flipper attached to each one like the thalidomide babies she sees in medical textbooks, reaching for rubber balls with sprouts of tiny hands. She closes her eyes and sees wrists and arms emerging from his shoulder stubs like plants growing in slow motion. His body is outlined in a glimmer of light that remains even when she opens her eyes again, making everything she sees look faded.

That summer Ilka teaches more than ever: Remedial Reading, English as a Second Language, and Freshman Composition at four different colleges. Twice a week she drives across the bay to teach in Hayward, where she tells us there's the possibility of a permanent job. Though her territory has expanded, she doesn't see the blue van for two months.

Then one night she says she's started seeing him on the road again, but always so far behind she has had to drive slowly to let him catch up. She sees him in her rearview mirror, the short hair, the dark eyes staring, even a glimpse of the smile, but when he gets close to her, he speeds ahead and vanishes into the traffic. She ignores the other boys in their vans, who honk and wave as she dodges in and out of traffic after the one van she can never catch.

"It's like I'm hypnotized," she says. "I can't stop." She's not smiling now; her face looks thinner and her wide eyes are swollen.

One day when his van passes she's able to follow him up the freeway, changing lanes when he does, and flashing her signal right, right, right until she herds him up to the rest stop where they met before. His license plate reads "ZIP," and she thinks the three numbers are the same. It's noon and the sun glints off the chrome of parked cars whose license plates are a map of the United States, from Maryland to Oregon, Alabama to Minnesota. Families with small children sit at the picnic tables. A man in his fifties peers at her from the light blue van. He has the short hair, the long nose, but he leans his arms on the open window of his car and says, "Lady, what the hell do you want, anyway?"

"I'm sorry," she says. "I thought you were someone else. A friend of mine has a van just like this."

"Yeah? Well, you've got a hell of a nerve trying to run me off the road like that." Turning abruptly, he climbs back into his van and drives off, wheels spinning in the dusty gravel of the parking lot.

She sits alone in her yellow Volkswagen for nearly an hour before driving down the hill to the freeway.

Though Ilka laughs with the rest of us, I think I can feel her sadness, and I curl my hands into fists under the table when I picture the unarmed man chasing Ilka, catching her, then throwing her back out on the road again so he can play with her without letting her defend herself. What good is her karate if she can never touch him again? Lynne's right, I say to myself, Ilka should carry a gun and shoot him through the windshield the next time his teasing blue van speeds by.

"Maybe you dreamed him. Dreams can often be more true

than reality," says Patty, who plans to change her major to psychology.

"No, he exists, I can assure you." Ilka takes off her silk scarf and shakes out her long blond hair, fluffing it away from her head with one hand while the other plays with the scarf. "But I did dream about him the night after that guy told me off at the rest stop."

We lean forward.

In her dream, the armless man drives up and parks beside her as she sits in her car halfway up a hill. It's not the rest stop, just a green meadow with poppies in the grass. There isn't even any road. She smiles at him; he smiles at her.

"You never told me your name," she calls to him in German.

He answers in English, "I'm one of the unnamed."

When he jumps out of his van, she sees that he's armed with a pistol held in his right foot. His Velcro fly bursts apart so that his penis, too, points straight at her, just below the gun. She's out of her car now, running up the hill. When she looks back she sees him hopping behind her, gun and penis aimed, clearing bushes in one bound. She's panting; she can't quite reach the top because the hill grows as she runs. He dances after her, faster on one leg than she is on two, and she wakes up just as she hears the gun explode.

She breathless as she reaches the end of her story. "I was having an orgasm when I woke up," she says. "It was as though the gun that woke me started the orgasm. He finally gave me what I wanted."

"Death?" I ask. My fingers are clenched under the table. "How can you think you're in love with someone who shoots you?"

"But it was like being shot to life." Ilka looks at me and sighs. "He shot his power into me. I can't explain it, there are no words in any language I know. I'm not talking about love, Chris."

Lynne rolls her eyes to the ceiling and chuckles. "Well, Ilka, that's one way of looking at it. If you won't carry a gun, suck power from his. It's not a bad dream when you think about it."

Ilka smiles into her empty coffee cup, turning it around in her hands as though trying to see the future, while Patty nods like the therapist she wants to become.

I can't find words in any language for what I want to say, either, so my mouth stays closed while I watch Ilka bind her hair up into her scarf again. Though I long to stroke the smooth light hairs on the back of her neck, there's no language in my hands for this desire. I tell myself I'm not gay and never have been, yet I know I could love her better than any man without arms, no matter what she thinks she wants. Sitting across the table from her that night in Sacred Grounds I think I can have her just by putting my arms around her, but I can't move them; it's as though all their muscles have been pulled out.

We didn't see each other much after that. Ilka had so much work in the fall she had no time for self-defense. When the job possibility in Hayward fell through, she wasn't disappointed. "One job would be as boring as one lover," she said.

She began teaching farther north at College of Marin, and moved to San Francisco to be in the center of her work. I heard she had her hair cut short, bought a black Honda sedan, and started wearing suits and carrying her students' papers in a brief-case. In this costume, she began to meet a higher class of men who drove Jaguars or BMWs instead of delivery vans. But by then I'd lost touch with her. I heard that she met the unarmed man again, but he didn't recognize her; I heard that when she saw him again he had arms, and smiled slyly at her confusion. Patty still claims the whole thing was Ilka's fantasy.

The truth is I don't know how Ilka's story ended, though I often think about the possibilities. Does she still expect to see him whenever a light blue van comes up behind her, close on her tail as she heads down the freeway to San Jose? These days, self-defense has a different definition. Is she a cautious woman who carries condoms wrapped in pink cellophane in her briefcase instead of a karate suit? Does he keep a box of them in the glove compartment below the dashboard of his van? Does he pull this box out with his toes, take off the lid, rip open a plastic packet with his teeth and, with his skillful big toe, glide the glistening pink sheath onto himself? Or does he reach his foot into the glove compartment and pull out a pistol, swirling it around on his big toe before he shoots her, just the way she likes it?

Daphne Slade

The Shape of the Feeling

When alone, I prepare for my orgasms just as I would prepare to bake bread. First, I wipe off the counter. Then I carefully lay out all the utensils I will be using. My body is the dough. I knead it in my hands like putty. I toss it up in the air and wait for it to fall into my arms like a lover.

Often, I want an orgasm so bad I feel it before it comes which prevents it from coming. For years that's what I thought pre-orgasmic meant: feeling prematurely.

Sometimes I have to take my orgasms. Like a horse extending her neck down to the trough for a drink of water.

Each time, I know exactly how far down I have to go. As if I am digging for them in the garden and can see the level clearly, like liquid in a measuring cup. They are always there, concealed in the soil, but I sometimes can't decide if it is worth the dredging. I sense I will have to dig deeply this time. To the point where there will be dirt under my nails and perhaps my hands will start to bleed. It is an important decision. Because after a certain point, there is no turning back, no matter how hard the struggle.

What does an orgasm look like? Like fish shooting out in all different directions from a pebble dropped in their pond.

The most wonderful orgasm is like popcorn popping all over.

The orgasm sometimes comes as easily as pop sucked through a straw.

I keep going back to the fireworks analogy to describe my orgasms, because each one is different and once I set it off, I can never predict the outcome. Some start out with a bang but fizzle. And some start as misfires but suddenly, way high up in the sky, just when you thought they were gone, spread out into the most brilliant umbrella.

At times I think of the orgasm spreading through my body like news spreads through a neighborhood.

The only time I can concentrate anymore is when I am having an orgasm.

My orgasms generally don't come easily.

Orgasms often play hide-and-seek like the keys I can hear, but can't find, at the bottom of my purse.

I have "slight orgasms" like I have "slight headaches." I wish two aspirins could cure both.

It takes me so long to reach orgasm I feel like I am on a freeway caught in a major traffic jam.

I always feel hungry after an orgasm, perhaps because I never feel licked clean.

Sometimes I become frustrated about orgasms in the same way I become frustrated when I am hungry for something I can't quite put my finger on. Was it salty or sweet or . . . ? Oftentimes, I won't eat or masturbate, which makes me even more frustrated. Or worse, I eat the wrong thing or have a worthless orgasm.

The orgasm was dead on arrival, a tired bubble meandering to the top of an old bottle of Calistoga water gone flat.

The orgasm teases like the fish I can feel down below, nibbling on the bait but never grabbing the hook.

It is senseless to pursue certain orgasms. I am like a kitten licking and licking the white bowl after the cream is long gone.

The orgasm looks like the sad, dark face of the sunflower.

I can't understand why my orgasms embarrass me. I don't want anyone to see me having them. When I was a little girl, I ran around Kiddieland joyfully getting on every ride while my parents stood watching me with delight. I loved them looking on as much as I loved the rides. So why am I so self-conscious now?

Upon reaching middle-age, I take an aesthetic interest in orgasms. Some nights, I even have "working orgasms" so I can write about them. Orgasms for the sake of art. Or, sometimes, I schedule my orgasms as if they were some sort of athletic event. Still others, it is as though I am shopping for the right one.

I dream that when I am applying for a job, one of the questions on the job application is: how many times per week do you masturbate? Come? Give up? I am told that corporations have discovered, through their human resources departments, that they can tell how productive an employee will be based on her/his response to the preceding question.

At times, my orgasms seem to have little to do with me, just like various summer odd-jobs I have taken. So why pursue them?

I've concluded that orgasms are just like people; some are more likable than others.

My final orgasm always feels like an afterthought because I never know when to quit. I think the phrase "you should know when to quit" was started by someone who knew exactly which orgasm to stop on. . . .

. . . Yet I somehow enjoy the final orgasms of the evening in a different way, even though I have to search harder for them. Like looking for a memory hidden in the body. The first orgasms come to me; the final ones I have to hunt for. It is like a game of tag: I get tagged, and then I'm it.

To "achieve" orgasms I have to play both sides at once. I have to hold on and give up at exactly the same moment.

Somewhere in the world I believe there must be a dark room with a sign on the door saying "Lost Orgasms" where all the orgasms I almost had are. If I ever find that room, I knew exactly the number of orgasms I will try to claim and wonder if everyone else knows their number, too.

I have orgasms that feel like they are happening somewhere else, perhaps in a foreign country.

It is one of those orgasms, that, if someone asked me, I'd have to say, "Yeah, it's mine," though I am not sure. Like the way I feel upon leaving a party when the host approaches me with a generic black umbrella and asks, "Is this umbrella yours?" Though I know that I came with one like it and take it to be polite, I am not quite sure it is mine.

I offer my orgasms up on a bare table covered with an immaculate white sheet, higher and higher out of my body to reach the birds that peck at the invisible crumbs. I must sacrifice my orgasms in order to have them, constantly letting them go, letting go.

Serena Moloch

❦ ❦

I Visit the Doctor:
A Tale

In this country where I live it rains in the summer and snows in the winter and I bleed every month; I have been bleeding every month for two years. When I bleed the world caves in at my stomach, I scream and keen, pain drives through me like spikes with poisoned tips. In this country where I live there are many rules: no one can touch me or check me in my pain. The rules of the family cell are very strict: no touching of the daughter's body permitted until the touch of her husband at marriage. All girls must be virgins at marriage, the certificate from the doctor must attest to that. When the cramps overtake me my mother and older sisters look at me in pity. They would like to touch me and help me, gently take up my limbs and massage them as they could when I was a baby—I do not remember this, they have whispered of it to me—but they are not allowed. No touching of the daughter's body once she is able to walk; the rules state it very clearly and the consequences of disobedience are dire.

Finally one day I stopped screaming from the pain and began instead to rip my clothes and shred my lips. Finally, it was conceded, I must be sent to a doctor, and an appointment was made for me the next day.

Only women can be doctors for women in this country and I

243

had imagined that this doctor would be stern and forbidding. She was not: she was beautiful. When I walked into her office I saw one woman seated at a desk with another woman leaning over her, pointing at something on a paper. The woman who had been pointing straightened up and looked deep into my eyes. She was tall when she stood, very tall; she wore a green blouse and gray skirt and her eyes were very black. Her hair was pulled back tight; her mouth was loose and full. Her might and sweetness momentarily stunned me. I had never seen a woman who looked quite like this. My sisters, my mother, and my teachers always looked subdued and pressed dry: this woman looked like no amount of wringing could ever quite sap her of her juices. I stood rooted to my spot as she walked toward me and put her hand out to shake. I took it. "Melissa Parker?" she asked. I nodded, squeezing her hand. She didn't let mine go. "I'm Dr. Simone Blackstone." We squeezed hands again. "Come this way."

We moved into a dark and woody office. All over the walls hung diagrams of pink, exposed flesh with stringy extensions and gaping, pulpy cuts. We sat down and she smiled at me.

"Before we begin, I have to ask you several questions. This is called 'taking a history.' Have you been to a doctor before?"

"No," I said. "Since the rules don't permit girls to go to a doctor except in case of emergency, I suppose that this is my first emergency."

"Yes. Well, I will take care to explain things to you as I do them. Next, the law says I must ask you if you are married or unmarried?"

"Unmarried," I replied.

"And virginal or not?" she asked. Smiling wryly, she said, "The official terms, I am required to state, are pure or tainted."

"Virginal," I responded blandly, but she had caught my interest even further. Was she a renegade?

"And what is the problem for which you are here today, Miss Parker?"

"I have unbearable pains when I bleed every month," I answered.

"Those can be difficult to endure. I see many young women like you who have the same problem. It seems to have an in-

creased incidence under this new regime. How long have you
been getting your period?"

"Almost two years."

"When do you experience the most pain?"

"The day before I bleed," I said, looking wistfully into her
face which seemed so kind, so caring, and so competent to save
me. "You can't know how much it hurts. I want to die, I think
I am dying, but then it's never over; I have to go through it over
and over again."

Her hand moved, almost twitched toward me, then rested
where it was, on top of her pen. "I think I can help you. There
are a variety of tests we can run and treatments I can prescribe."
She hesitated a moment and sounded my eyes with her own. I
gazed at her studiously. "Some of my recommendations are a bit
unorthodox," she said, "and you will have to carry them out
privately and secretly. You are, of course, not obliged to follow
my directions, and I can always refer you to another doctor if
you object to any of my practices. One final question: when was
your last period? The last time you were bleeding?"

"I'm bleeding now," I replied.

"Are you in pain?" she asked sympathetically.

"I am," I answered.

"I'll do my best to help you," she said.

Her voice was mellow, deep, and melodious. I had watched
her hands intently as she wrote down my spoken words; they
were big, well-formed, and strong. Her neck curved away from
her tied-back hair and I could see the slope of her shoulders
beneath her shirt. I had never been this close to a grown woman
before. My mother and sisters had to keep a distance from me,
as the law commands. But the law also designates those who can
exercise a "sanctioned touch," and doctors are among these chosen. Soon those hands would be on me.

She told me to go into the next room, undress, and drape myself with the white cloths on the table. I moved into a very clean
and cold white room. There were counters that dipped into sinks
at each end, long burnished surfaces adorned with gleaming
metal objects stacked with tiny bottles and piles of small, rectan-
gular, greenish glass plates. In the center of the room stood a

narrow raised gray bed with two footrests swerving upward at one end. I took off my clothes, folded them, and neatly arranged them in a corner. I wrapped the drape around myself, and not knowing what to do about my blood, I held my hand between my legs to catch it. The doctor knocked on the door. "May I come in?" Her smooth voice nibbled warmly at the cold goose-flesh creeping up my arms and legs. I shivered and called out, "Yes, I'm ready."

She opened the door and saw me standing in the center of the room, trembling, with my hand cupped between my legs. I felt hot blood trickle onto my fingers and more blood rush to my cheeks. "Leave your underpants on for now," she said. "Here," She knelt down by my pile and rummaged through it until she reached my underwear—the sanitary pad was already sodden and she lifted it off saying, "Wait—let me give you a fresh napkin." She fished one out of a drawer and adhered it skillfully to my white underwear. She handed me a tissue and said, "Here—would you like to wipe your hands?" I accepted her offering and blotted my reddened hands on it, then stood bewildered, not knowing what to with the damp red tissue. I couldn't see a trash can anywhere. "Here," she said, opening a cabinet that magically produced one for me, "drop it in." She flipped the lid open with an authoritative slam of her foot, and we both let our bloody cloths drop from our hands into the can. She handed me my underwear and turned around so that I could put it on without her seeing me. Cramps twisted my insides and I grimaced with the pain. I climbed into my underpants and gently touched her back; she didn't start. "Okay," I said.

'First I have to weigh you," she said, "come this way." She pointed to a scale. I padded over to it and clambered up on to its rubber platform. She moved iron pieces back and forth knowledgeably; as she did so, her arm passed over my shoulder and her hand flashed back and forth in front of my chest. I could hear her breathe. "All right," she said, "now please sit on the table over there." By table she seemed to mean the bed. I mounted it and crossed my arms in front of my draped breasts to stay warm.

"Are you cold?" she asked me.

"A little," I said.

"I'm sorry. You should warm up soon. Please extend one arm so I can take your blood pressure." I gave her my right. She wrapped it in a prickly cuff and began to squeeze an oval ball in her hand. My whole arm felt constricted, my blood stopped, I felt panicked. I looked at the plastic boa she had laced around my arm. She seemed to be counting to herself. She released the ball and freed my arm from the cuff. Stooping a little to look in my face she said, "I'm sorry. That tightening feeling is frightening, I know." She lifted a sinuous instrument from her neck and placed two tubes in her ears, holding the silvery disk at the lower end with two fingers.

"The next part is easy," she said, "I'm going to listen to your heart and lungs. Please lower your drape."

I dropped it. She placed the shiny, round pendant against my breast and listened. She moved around me and placed it on my back. "Breathe out." My breasts lifted up and down, swelled and sank. "Breathe in," she said. "Breathe out."

My midriff contorted as a series of cramps momentarily distracted me from the novel sensation of a voice so close to my ears and hands so firm on my skin. Then the pain receded and I concentrated on the pinpoints of feeling her cool fingers left on my flesh. No one had ever touched me before. I had never been this close to another woman's body. Hers was a doctor's body, a sanctioned body, and a doctor's touch, a sanctioned touch. Yet in the wake of her fingers and through the supple cloth of her shirt I felt the honeyed musky heat of a woman's body, one that I recognized from my own, from having sniffed myself out, under my arms and between my breasts, as I tossed and turned on sleepless nights. My back seemed to crackle with this heat even as her calm fingers examined me methodically.

I felt uncertain, wobbly, yet on the brink of an enormous clarification. She snapped the instrument out of her ears so that it lay draped around her neck, a snaky talisman. I was still cold but I didn't raise the drape. She looked not at my breasts but into my eyes.

"Since you've never had an exam before, I'm not going to try to complete one today. Today, in fact, I will not touch you at all. I'm going to show you in a mirror what you look like and I'm going to teach you a way to treat yourself for your pains."

I felt strange. Her manner, her words, were very distant and poised. But will you think that I'm crazy if I tell you that it was love that I felt flowing between us? Love in her concern for me, in the attentive searching and probing of her questions, her eyes, her hands. Love in the crazy way that my heart beat so hard I almost expected her snaky necklace to be charmed up toward it, to lift its head up to my breasts so that I could hear it crashing in spasms against my bones. . . . But crazy, I thought, I must be crazy, because her voice just moved steadily on and on, "If at any time you feel pain or discomfort, tell me and I'll stop what I'm doing. Okay?" I nodded; what I had just assented to, I didn't know. I lifted my eyelids all the way up to try and slow my heart down. She raised the back of the bed so that I was sitting and asked me to remove my underwear. She helped me get it off my ankles and bent down again to place it with my other clothes. Her skirt pulled tight against her as she did this and I looked. I did look.

She brought a large purple mirror over to me and said silkily, "If you hold this by your knee you'll be able to see your genitalia. I'll point out the structures to you." I placed the mirror and looked—I saw only the dark, downy skin of my thighs. "Let me help you," she said, and placed her hand on mine to angle the mirror. The shock of her flesh on my flesh met the shock of black hair, masses of it swirling around purple, swollen skin, skin I'd never seen, skin that made no sense, except for the muddy red sap that fled from it. I was terrified.

She sat on a stool and moved between my legs to open a drawer from which she pulled out beige, powdery gloves, matte and sanitary counterparts to the lurid nest between my legs she had revealed to me. She put her fist against my thigh: "You're going to feel me touch you now." She put a finger on each side of the purple skin and then spread it: I saw now that this eggplant-colored, engorged flesh arranged itself into layers and folds, pyramids nested within one another. She began to point but not touch with her finger.

"These," she said, gesturing toward the hairy billows closest to my thighs, "are the labia majora, the outer lips. They have hair on them, and that's normal." She moved in toward the deep-eyed skin, which, as I looked more closely, seemed to resemble gathered, ruffled cloth, or the whorls and swirls of fingerprints, or the windings and turnings inside exotic puff-pastries. Curiosity began to edge out my dismay and I craned my head forward to peer closer into the mirror. "These lips," she said, "which are somewhat darker and don't have hair on them, are the labia minora, the inner lips." She gestured toward the space between them and told me, "This is the vagina, the internal opening. Your hymen, or virginity, is a thin membrane partly covering the entrance to this opening. Your blood passes through it during your periods." No mention of my husband, my babies, which I had been told often enough would also pass through there one day if I was good.

My gaze drifted up from the vagina and I saw that a tiny rounded cone crowned all the other structures. Its shape exactly matched that of a ring that had been mine as a very young girl. Here it was again, between my legs, only no longer sapphire but red like the red of angry skin, skin that's been cut or burned. I watched the doctor's elegant fingers ripple along the two inner lips without touching them.

"The labia minora meet up top," she said, "to form the hood of the clitoris." She moved her hands off me—I almost clawed at her with regret—then laid them on me again, on the hair swarming on my lower belly. She pulled the skin beneath my hair up, stretching back the paler covering of the clitoris and exposing the ruddy cone more perfectly. "You see?"

"I see," I replied.

She stood up. "That's all I'm going to do today by way of a physical exam. But I would like to teach you a way to relieve your pain. By touching the clitoris you can produce sensations which may feel strange or may feel pleasurable to you, perhaps both. If you continue to touch yourself patiently and carefully, you will begin to feel a tension building up, the feelings increasing until it feels like somehow they must stop. Try touching the clitoris directly, or in a sidelong fashion; you can hold it between your fingers, rub it, roll it—there are an infinity of approaches.

You must continue to touch yourself until you feel what is some-times called a climax. It is difficult to describe but impossible not to recognize. Afterward your heart will beat rapidly, your breath will come quickly, and you will experience a feeling of peace and well-being. Your body releases chemicals upon climax which will temporarily relieve your pain." She looked at me somewhat archly, I thought, considering how businesslike her recommen-dations had been. "The prescription," she said, "is to repeat as often as necessary."

All this, I knew, had to be among the things that were "strictly forbidden." For the only transgressions more serious than allow-ing someone else to touch you was to touch yourself. Was this a test? I kept my silence.

"I know that strictly speaking this is not permitted," she said soothingly, her voice seeping with as much assurance as reassur-ance. She seemed taller than ever and suddenly I forgot my pain in my hunger to let her hair down loose around her face. "But I am prescribing it to you as a medical treatment and I sanction it as such. I will leave the room so that you can practice this technique in complete privacy. Just permit me to place this cloth beneath you, to catch any liquids. Your touch may stimulate the flow of blood and other fluids from your vagina." She picked a cloth up from the side table and without being asked, I raised my hips so that she could place it beneath me. "Call me in when you have successfully completed the course of treatment," she said, "and don't be afraid to take all the time you need."

She left and closed the door behind her and I pondered my situation. Was it a trap? I could always plead ignorance, if it were, for I would have been disobeying one order only to follow another. Another screeching pain coiled within me and I decided to try. I watched in the mirror as my left hand crept down and gently prodded the clitoris she had revealed to me. I rubbed two fingers back and forth across it and felt the stirrings of—irritation? Wriggling? Tautness? Melting? Blood did begin to ebb hotly out of me and hit the cloth. I tried pinching the clitoris between my thumb and forefinger and moving it back and forth, which pushed all the feelings out along my thighs and backside and somehow made my hipbones ache. Perhaps this would paralyze me—perhaps the transgression would be its own punishment. Perhaps I should stop, but I was a bit beyond stopping already. I dared to wet my finger in my own blood and use the moisture to help glide over the clitoris more quickly. The skin between my legs began to feel hot and demanding all over and very naked, flesh with its nerves exposed instead of buried beneath the clothes and skin and laws. My whole body began to writhe and it became difficult to steady the mirror, but I held onto it rather than put it down because the scene reflected in its purple frame interested me, the blood smearing my thighs a bit now, my fingers jerking back and forth rhythmically, my inner lips puffing up even more and moving toward the mirror, then away from it, then in, then back, then in again. . . . I needed more, even more, though I also feared that I would hurt myself if I pressed harder—but the damage didn't matter anymore, no possible harm could stand between me and my rushing blood. Dark spots blotted my vision, my arm began to tire but that pain didn't matter either; I pushed harder and harder on the clitoris, which had gotten hard and rearing. I dug my fingers into it and pushed, pushed until I felt something coming, roaring through me, bursting, gushing, then dropping away and leaving me almost dead on that bed that was called a table. When I finally caught my breath and stopped hearing my heart, the rats gnawing at my entrails and stomach had begun to dissolve.

I had slid forward on the table so I shifted into a more composed position, bracing my feet against the metal supports and gliding back up. I cleared my throat and called out, "I'm finished."

The doctor pushed the door open and stood before me, her dark eyes looking closely into mine. "Well?" she asked. "Did it work?"

"I think it did," I said to her, examining her as I spoke. My rapturous and drowsy state brushed all that my eyes could see with a hazy aura. The instrument around her neck gleamed more brightly and more softly. Her captured hair looked even more inviting, her neck smoother and her mouth more lush. I tried to read her eyes to see what she might be feeling. Did she know pleasures like the ones she had just taught me to give myself?

She must, and more. Did the same country of damp russet marshes and wild reeds grow between her legs? Could I ever see it? I thought wildly of all the forbidden things I had ever heard about, the many laws and transgressions: there were words that meant things that I knew were wrong, bad, dirty, filthy, forbidden, but I only knew the words, I could hardly picture the deeds. "Kiss" was forbidden, I knew, and "fondle" and "deflower," if it wasn't your husband—all these prohibitions I had heard proclaimed in official gatherings and teachings. Then there were the whispers at school, "Put something inside you," the other, older girls sniggered, "feel you up," "do you," "fuck you" were hidden, scorching words that came back to me now. I wanted to learn more and to make this woman teach it to me. She had laid her hands on me once and I had felt my body rise, leaving its pain behind. She would lay them on me again if I had my way. Surely I could trust her not to punish me even if she did refuse my demand.

Her dark eyes caved into mine and I risked all. "Kiss me," I said imperiously, raising my arms, reaching up for her. And then a miracle came to pass. She bent her head toward mine and placed her lips against my lips, snaked her arms around my tilted neck, and nuzzled my face with hers. I pulled her shoulders toward me and stroked them through her shirt as her tongue touched my lips, my teeth, my tongue, moving deeper into my mouth and licking it inside. I did the same and felt the rough wetness of our mouths together, licking each other, sucking each other, gliding back and forth. I reached up to remove her hairband and moved my face away from hers to enjoy the cascade of dark curls. I sighed with pleasure and then asked coyly, remembering the insinuations of the girls' hallway, "Will you fondle me? Will you take me?"

She lifted her head from mine and gripped my shoulders while her eyes interrogated me. Perhaps she too feared a trap. "You know it is forbidden?" she asked.

"I know," I said earnestly, but I returned her look steadily with what I hoped was persuasive forthrightness. I twirled her ringlets about my fingers. I thought again, of how they said, "put something inside you," and "deflower," and all the trouble that could follow. But I also knew that it was doctors who provided the certificates of virginity for marriage, and doctors who could attest that they had deflowered you for reasons of medical necessity. She could do this for me: show me what was forbidden and guarantee my safety. "You could give me a certificate of medical cause," I said as respectfully as I could with my hand delving into her hair and my breast heaving. "I would never breathe a word," I said shyly, trying to bury my head in her shoulder as I murmured, "you have opened one door for me; I know there are many more. Please." I gently pressed the nape of her neck and moved to kiss her again. "Please." I heard her breathing begin to deepen hoarsely and felt her fingers grab for the drape that lay bunched around my stomach. She flung it to the floor. "Wait here," she said.

She left for a moment and returned with a candle. She locked the door behind her, turned off the light, placed the candle on the counter, and kindled it. The room's bright sharp glare eddied into mysterious half-tones; deep huge shadows hurled themselves onto the walls. She moved stealthily toward me and raised her finger to her lips: hush, she indicated, nodding, and I nodded back. As she neared me she steadily unbuttoned her blouse and then took one of her breasts out, lifting it from its corset so that it spilled forth, smooth and swollen, the soft brown nipple at its center. Her breast was no bigger than my own but as she brought its rounded expanse and sheen closer into my field of vision, it looked enormous, a polished globe approaching my hungering mouth.

She bent over me and opened my mouth with her fingers and said softly, "Suck. Lick me with your tongue and suck." I felt smothered in steamy softness and did as she said. She took my hands and placed them around her breast. "Squeeze it," she said. "And stroke it." I obeyed, gently pressing her breast as I felt the flesh in my mouth crinkle beneath my tongue and become hard and pointed. I sucked on the knob that had formed, harder and harder, and even dared to bite it delicately. Her breath rasped and her hands pressed mine harder and deeper into her breast. She leaned into me and then backed away slightly, almost tugging her breast away from my clamped teeth and suckling lips, then covering my face with it again. Where she went, I went; my mouth followed her breast and our flesh formed one fevered mass. I sucked and stroked fervently, hopefully: could this, too, produce a climax? She chuckled me under my chin and with her fingers again opened my mouth. "Let me go now," she whispered. "Let me do this to you."

The excitement had set my stomach churning and the cramps had begun to creep back through my legs. Her mouth found mine again and she grasped my lips firmly between hers as she lay her hands on me, one on each breast. She teased my nipples with a feathery touch, circling them so softly I had to strain to identify her fingers on me, teasing the ends of my breasts which began to tingle with the same naked irritation I had felt before in my clitoris. She fluted the tip of her tongue into all my mouth's moist parts and began to pinch the tips of my breasts which, like hers, had gotten wrinkled and firm. She pinched them as I had pinched my clitoris, then moved her mouth down toward them, bending over me as she stood so that she could lick at the bits of tight, tender flesh that protruded from between her fingers.

Hot blood bathed my thighs. She moved both hands to one of my breasts and gathered its plumpness up like a feast between her fingers, molding my breast beneath her hands as she kissed its tip and grazed it with her tongue, then sucking all she could into her greedy velvet mouth. Her hair draped me, deliciously, temptingly soft. Shocks came in and out of my body from all directions and I almost groaned, but remembered our vow of silence just as one of her hands left my breast to cover my mouth. I licked her fingers and stroked them with my hands, twisting and turning on the narrow bed she called a table. I took her hand and moved it down on my body.

"The cramps have begun again," I said. "Do me," I almost chanted in a low voice in the fiery, dim room. "Put something inside me, take me," I sang to her. She caressed my stomach forcefully, catching the rhythm of my pulse and meeting it with her own hands. She moved around the table so that she stood between my legs which she massaged. My hands fluttered gratefully toward her, for my legs were sore from the position imposed by the supports, but I could not please her in return; she was out of reach. She sat again on the stool and rolled it in closer between my legs. I ached to touch her. She looked up at my imploring figure and said, "Put your hands up and hold onto the table behind you. Do not let go until I say so." I followed her order and grasped the corners of the table; my raised arms anchored me securely and lifted my still damp, still pointed breasts, made my stomach stretch so that I almost thought I could see the blood coursing underneath it, not merely feel it pass out of me, drenching the white patch beneath me.

She moved closer in and spread my legs even further apart as she bent her head toward my ravenous purple mouth framed with hair as black and wiry as her own. She flicked out her tongue and ran it between my inner lips, drawing a trail of blood up into her mouth as she went. My hands clasped the table spasmodically as she reached my clitoris with her tongue, drawing it to a point with her tongue's tip, then broadly licking it. She sank her chin in to the dripping, bloody space between my inner lips; it fit there perfectly. She turned her head from side to side and I began to feel sensation where her chin rocked back and forth, sensations that met the sharper ones above, there where her tongue pummeled my clitoris. She moved her hands from my thighs and slipped them under my behind which I was desperately raising as I tried to push myself deeper into her lapping, stroking mouth, her jutting chin. She grabbed my behind as she buried her face in me, now sucking my clitoris which she had trapped between slightly open teeth, a sugar cube for her to suck her tea through. The blood was gurgling out of me now and the cramps tightened their hold as if to protest their imminent silencing.

"Please," I said. "Please take me now." She stopped and moved back; the candlelight flickered and caught the blood glowing on her chin, dyeing her teeth ruby red and flecking her cheeks in spots. "Please end this pain," I implored her quietly. "Please take me." She kissed my stomach, my breasts, my lips, leaving a trail of O-shaped red marks on my skin. She stood to the side of me and said, "Where do you feel the pain?" "Here," I said, placing her hand on my stomach. She laid her hand flat and rotated it back and forth, pressing my pain with the heel of her hand, then her fingertips. "Where do you feel the pleasure?" she asked. "Here," I said, placing her free hand on my breast. "And here," moving the other and shoving it down between my legs.

"Where pain was," she sang to me, "there pleasure will be." The cramps leapt up toward the surface of my skin and vied with the joys her palpitating hands created in my breasts and clitoris. Her fingers slid into the bleeding cleft between my purple lips and slowly prodded my opening, toyed around it, then deepened their hold in me with a tiny thrust forward, circling around, then entering, while her thumb pressed my clitoris to and fro. The cramps began to overtake everything, their pain blinding me to anything I might ever have known, forcing my feet to dig into the supports, ramming my hands into the spongy table, arching my back so that I met her fingers which had moved even deeper. I felt a pain inside me, within me, her fingers pulled back and forth within me, dragged back in by my bloody ring of desire. Her thumb on my clitoris raced to match her insistent in-and-out inside me and I knew again the force which said that nothing could hurt me in my violent wish to feel that explosion once again. I hurled myself back and forth on her hand, wrenching my shoulders as I forced myself onto her fingers.

Again I felt the climax, the pain dissolved, subdued, the sleepy blindness as the candle seemed to fire up, then snuff itself out. I shuddered and relaxed my body more fully onto the table. Soon, she called out softly to me, "I'm going to remove my fingers now."

She drew them out gradually and lifted the cloth from beneath me. "Your blood is here," she said softly. "They call it virgin and deem it holy, but it is mixed with blood even more holy, the blood of your pain, the blood of your pleasure, the blood that comes, the blood that goes." She crumpled the cloth up and clasped it in her hand. Her face loomed above mine, illuminated by the candle soaring behind her. I sat up and turned my face toward her and the words I had heard so often lilted off my tongue though I had forgotten what they meant: "blood of my blood and flesh of my flesh." I licked the blood from her fingers and her chin, then pressed my cheek to her breast as my arms circled her hips. I tasted metal, salt, and savored her heartbeat.

Angela Fairweather

The Trojan Woman

Margo is staring at the telephone and feeling foolishly adolescent. Her only reasonable option is to make the call. And she can't. Nervously, she twists the copy of *Penthouse* into a roll and releases it. She does this twice more, then sets the magazine down in a gesture of determination and picks up the phone receiver.

"Bill Meyers, please. This is Margo Winstead calling. Hi, Bill? Margo. I've got a problem and I need your help." She winces as she says this. "Well, no, I don't want to talk about it right now. I was wondering if you're free tonight and if you are, I could treat you to dinner. . . . Okay, well, how about tomorrow night? Great, think about where you'd like to go. . . . Oh yes, of course it can wait. . . . No, I'm not upset, it's really kind of funny, but I just don't want to talk about it right now. You'll understand when I tell you. . . . Yes, I'll be home tomorrow afternoon. Why don't you come over around five . . . sure, we can go somewhere intimate and romantic." Margo stifles a giggle. "No, that doesn't freak me out. So I'll see you tomorrow at five."

The next dilemma is how to broach the subject. Bill is, after all, the best male friend she's ever had, like a member of the family—like a brother. No, that doesn't feel right; you don't have sex with your brother. But it isn't exactly sex. *What the hell is it, then?* Well it's an experiment. No, it's research. Margo wrestles with this complex issue for a while then decides it's too much to think about until she must.

But it keeps creeping back into her consciousness. She's not sure she can do it. Why not? Because he's got a great body and he's my friend? Because he might not want to. Oh. Would he want to? He tried to talk me into it a few times. Yeah, but that was six months ago. Margo feels a hot rush of insecurity surge through her body. Maybe she should wear something slightly provocative to set the scene. Oh for God's sake, this is research, not a seduction! Yeah, but maybe he won't be in the mood. Is a man ever *not* in the mood? Sometimes John wasn't in the mood. Yeah, but you were married to him; that's different. Maybe.

At 4:30 the following afternoon she's still not sure what to wear. This is ridiculous—just put something on. Like your purple print dress. It's kind to your figure and the color's good. No, a dress would be too obvious. Wear pants. Pants? Yes, wear the black silk pants and your teal-colored sweater. You can wear that pretty scarf with it. But what if . . . ?

The doorbell rings. Margo throws on a robe and lets Bill in. He's dressed casually—almost Ivy League—in a button-down shirt, slacks, and a sports jacket.

Margo's not uncomfortable in her robe. After all, she's practically camped out at Bill's some weekends. But they haven't been lovers. Not that Bill would mind. The collapse of her marriage has made her hesitant. Bill is a patient man.

Margo apologizes, says she's running late. "I'll be ready in a sec," she says as she goes back into the closet and puts on the purple dress.

"You look especially pretty tonight," Bill says after their wine is served. "Problems seem to agree with you these days. What's up?"

Margo takes a sip of Beaujolais. "Oh, nothing really," she replies, trying very hard to sound offhand. "I've just been puzzling over something at work and thought you might have some insights I hadn't considered."

The waiter arrives at this moment with a steaming pot of mussels. This is helpful as they can't shell mussels and stare meaningfully at each other at the same time. It's a few minutes before Bill returns to the problem.

"So what kinds of insights could I possibly provide a medical anthropologist?"

"Well." Margo hesitates. "Well, I'm real concerned about the HIV virus spreading so quickly through the local drug community. We're seeing a dramatic increase in infected women—the women in my clinic group, for instance. They don't have much resistance—once they're infected it's only a matter of months, even weeks, before they're sick. Since most of the women have husbands or lovers who are junkies, and since some of them are also prostitutes, it's a real serious issue." Margo pauses to eat a mussel which she has carefully placed on a piece of French bread and dipped in the broth.

"At any rate, last Thursday at the clinic outreach group I asked the women if they used condoms during sex. Most of them said they didn't because their men refuse to wear them." She pauses. "Have you used a condom?" There. The ice is broken. Margo is blushing slightly.

"Sure," answers Bill. He doesn't seem the least bit put off.

"Well, what's your opinion?"

"Sex feels better without them, but if my partner felt they were necessary, I'd use them." He continues, "I don't know how guys looking for prostitutes feel, but if I was buying sex, which I don't, I'd definitely use a rubber."

"Can you tell if you have one on?" Margo doesn't feel quite so awkward now that she's broached the subject.

"Yeah. Sure you can."

"So, supposing a woman were to put one on you, you'd know you had it on?"

"Well, of course I would."

"But say she did it with her mouth. Like if she went down on you." As the talk gets more specific, the going gets tougher.

"To tell you the truth, I've never had oral sex performed on me with a condom on, so I don't know." They could be discussing suntan lotions as far as Bill's concerned. He doesn't fluster easily. All of a sudden, he laughs. "Margo, are you asking about this because of the article on the Puerto Rican bordello? You know, the one in the *Penthouse* you snuck out of my house last weekend?"

This catches Margo off-guard. "No," she answers too quickly. Then, "Well, in part, yes, I guess." She sets her fork down and looks at Bill. "Originally I borrowed it thinking the article might have insights about certain men resisting condom use, but I hadn't gotten around to reading it before group last Thursday. One of the women mentioned she heard of someone who put condoms on her tricks while having oral sex—actually, to be specific, she said, 'I heard 'bout a whore from Texas puts the rubbers on their dicks with her mouth.' "

They both chuckle. It amuses Bill to hear Margo use slang.

"So then when I read the article in *Penthouse* and the American woman talked about doing it too, I just wondered if this was fairly commonplace or not—or if it was the same woman."

Bill laughs. "Well, it hasn't happened to me yet, honey, but I wouldn't resist if I had the opportunity to try it! But how does this tie in with your problem?"

Margo giggles self-consciously. "Oh, shit. You're probably going to think I've gone over the edge, but the other night I did something really crazy."

"You tried it on someone." He gives her a wicked grin.

"Bill! Now be serious, this is embarrassing." Margo looks stern, then breaks down again. "No. After I read the article I decided I wanted to see if it was even possible, so I walked down to the all-night drugstore and bought some condoms. And, geez Louise, I had no idea there were so many kinds! You need a consumer's guide to figure out what to buy. I mean they come in different sizes and colors and flavors and there were 'pet condoms' in a special box . . . it was pretty remarkable!"

"So what did you get?" Bill asks, fascinated by his dinner companion.

"Well, it was so overwhelming I just bought some Trojans because I recognized the name." This isn't quite accurate, actually, as Margo also purchased a couple of boxes of the more exotic varieties on impulse. She isn't ready to disclose this yet, however.

"And then I went to the market and bought some bananas." She pauses, suddenly amused at herself. Bill chuckles. "And I brought them home, and I set the bananas on the table and started experimenting."

"How did you do?"

"They taste terrible!" She grimaces. "I guess it's the spermicide. I don't know, I never used condoms, but at any rate, I ate a Lifesaver and that helped."

"What flavor?" asks Bill, thoroughly enjoying her agony.

"What does it matter? Peppermint, if you must know. Anyway, I practiced for an hour or so and I finally got pretty good at it, but a banana's a stationary object, so I still don't know if it really works."

"How are you going to find out?" Bill looks Margo directly in the eyes.

She blushes again and looks down at her plate. "I thought about asking one of the girls to try it with her partner, but that isn't very professional."

"So you want to try with me." Bill's voice turns gentle.

"Actually, yes I do." Her voice is barely audible. "I mean, you're the only person I could possibly ask, and it is research, after all. That is, if it's okay with you . . ."

"I'd be happy to assist with your research, Margo." Bill smiles and reaches over and squeezes her hand, then tactfully maneuvers the conversations to easier subjects while they finish their meal. He also insists on picking up the check.

Bill's house is in a hilly, wooden area of Marin. It's masculine, artistic, and subtle. Besides that, he keeps his house orderly and clean, a trait found occasionally in men who have lived alone for more than a year or two. Bill builds up the fire in the stove, puts on Coltrane, and opens a bottle of good wine. He's quite aware that Margo feels awkward and he's doing his best to ease things. Actually, he feels a little awkward himself. He's wanted her for a long time, but the fantasy hadn't included being a research subject.

Margo's doing her best to appear relaxed as well. It's been quite a while since she's had sex; it's been a whole lot longer since she's had sex with someone new. But Bill's not really new and this isn't really sex. It's research, remember?

Bill lights candles next to the bed, places the wine and glasses on the bedside table, then gently takes Margo's hand. This isn't the first time she's been in Bill's bed. They've literally slept together a few times when it was too late for her to go back to the city. But that was different.

Margo takes off her jacket and shoes. Bill does the same. He sits down on the bed and leans back against the pillows. Margo is still standing in the middle of the room, her purse on the floor by her feet. She feels uncertain. Should she casually take the condoms out of her purse or should she toss the purse on the bed as if purses are always taken to bed? Bill stretches his hands out to her and beckons her to him. Margo picks up her purse, walks over, and places it on the bed. She sits down, feet on the floor, next to him.

"Well, dear scientist, how do we proceed?" he queries.

"I guess we have another drink," she replies. Then she laughs, sounding exasperated. "I don't know, I guess you take off your pants."

"That's romantic. Are you going to stay clothed?"

"Actually I hadn't really thought about it. Yes, I guess I am."

"How am I supposed to get 'stimulated,' as they say?"

"Close your eyes and fantasize?" Margo offers weakly.

"I'd rather keep them open and look at you," Bill replies. "I'll tell you what," he continues, "I'll take off my pants if you'll take off your dress."

"Okay," she responds after a moment's pause. She stands up and removes her belt, fumbling with the buttons of her dress. The dress slips from her shoulders, leaving her in a black demi-bra and a half-slip. The candlelight highlights her dark hair and her fair skin is luminescent under the black silk. Bill removes his shirt, all the while watching her. He pulls off his socks, then rises to his feet, unfastening his belt and fly and slipping off his slacks. Margo looks at him from the waist up, her admiration immediately followed by a rush of anxiety. She sees her ex-husband's face and remembers his disgust at her enthusiasm for lovemaking. She remembers how he only enjoyed sex when he was in control. She tries to push away these feelings. But she knows she isn't ready for more than research with Bill. Or so she thinks. . . .

Bill removes his shorts. Naked, he returns to the bed. Margo struggles with her feelings. She reaches for her glass of wine and then sits next to him.

She opens her purse and takes out one of the "extra-sensitive" latex condoms. "You aren't going to laugh at me, are you? It's been a long time since I've done anything even remotely like this." Her voice is tentative.

"I might laugh with you but I won't laugh at you," he answers playfully, not responding to the edge of fear in her voice.

Finally Margo looks down. His penis is waiting limply. It doesn't look nearly as willing as the banana or bratwurst (which she hadn't mentioned), both of which were naturally ready. She wonders what to do. Finally she puts her hand on his penis and gives it a little stroke. It responds by moving slightly. She looks up at Bill and gives him a helpless look. He grins at her. His eyes imply that she's got the lead in this game. She looks back down at his penis and lifts it up. It stiffens only slightly, certainly not enough to slide a condom on with her hand, let alone her mouth. For a brief moment she thinks about placing his penis in her mouth. She quickly rejects that thought—after all, isn't the point to put it in when it's time to roll the condom on it?

Bill reaches into the bedside drawer and brings out some lubricant, and helps out by putting a drop on the tip of his penis. Margo removes the condom from the foil packet and prepares to place it on him. That distracts Bill enough that his penis loses what stiffness it had gained. They both laugh, albeit, nervously: she's almost enjoying herself.

Bill hands Margo her wineglass, then has a healthy drink from his. "Come here," he says reaching for her. Margo looks up at him, uncertainty clouding her face. Bill smiles and shakes his head, saying without words that there is no need for fear. He takes her into his arms and kisses her gently on the forehead. Then he traces down her face, kissing each eyelid, her cheeks, her slightly upturned nose, and her mouth. Much to her surprise, she responds willingly, and her mouth opens slightly. And then a little more.

Bill pulls her on top of him and they kiss. Without breaking the embrace, he rolls her over. Margo feels long suppressed-sensations return to her body in a great surge. She doesn't fight it. She presses her body against his and they kiss as if they have just made an amazing new discovery. Bill slides his hands down to her breasts. She doesn't object. Deftly he unfastens her bra and cups them in his hands, first one, then the other. He kisses each nipple with his tongue, then his mouth. Her nipples grow erect. Margo closes her eyes and gives in. She isn't even aware that he is ready for her research.

Instinctively she reaches down to him and strokes him, only half-aware of his erection. He responds appreciatively, then carefully removes her slip and panties. He places his hand between her legs, which part immediately, and slips his fingers into her moist vagina. An intense charge of electricity runs through her body, causing her to tense, not in fear but excitement. This brings her to her senses, however, and she slides down the bed—just like the woman in the *Penthouse* article. She starts stroking him with one hand as she reaches for the condom with the other. Cleverly, she has put a mint next to the condom and now she slips it into her mouth. Then she places the condom in her mouth, and with all the skill of the best sporting lady in the finest bordello, slides the thin latex over the shaft of his waiting penis. She runs her mouth up and down the shaft again and again, as he sighs with pleasure. She's so absorbed in the moment that it doesn't even cross her mind that he might be a candidate for the extra-long size next time.

Bill draws her back up to him, pulls her on top of his body, and slides his leg between hers. Her body willingly complies.

He massages her back and hips; long, strong, sensual strokes. Margo resonds by pressing tightly against him, arching the small of her back as his hands slide up her spine, causing her breasts to rub along his chest. She then slides her other leg over his so that she straddles him and raises her body so that he can enter her. He deftly guides his penis to her now moist vagina, teasing her by rubbing it against the entryway. Her breath catches and holds in anticipation. He purposefully enters her a little at a time, holding back, and finally he thrusts into her fully. Margo's breath is knocked from her in a sharp cry, though she is hardly in pain. For a moment they remain as they are, Margo fully straddling Bill's perfect erection, allowing herself to resonate in sensation, giving each nerve ending its erotic due. Then she drops back down onto Bill's chest and holds on to him tightly, submitting to the delight of being filled with his love.

The bottle of wine is more than half gone. Bill and Margo lie next to each other, the bed sheets and blankets in a tangled heap partially covering them. They both look happy and slightly dazed.

"You were very good at it," Bill tells her.

"At what?" she responds dreamily.

"At putting on the condom. This was really your first time?"

"Yeah, if you don't count a banana and a bratwurst."

"You tried it on a bratwurst too?"

"Um-hmmm," she says, only a little embarrassed.

Bill slaps her playfully on the bottom. "You are truly crazy and that's part of why I've waited so long for you. I knew you'd be worth every day of waiting."

"Really?" she says, her voice incredulous.

"Really," he responds. They start all over again.

The nicest part about the next morning is that they already know what they want to fix for breakfast and that they actually have things to say to each other. They've had over a year of practice together with details such as these. Bill brews the coffee while Margo tears open the English muffins and places them in the oven. She already knows that the jam is on the second shelf in the back. They separate the Sunday paper. He takes the comics and she takes the "Punch" section; later they trade.

"Did you put a mint in your mouth last night?" Bill asks suddenly.

"I certainly did. Have you ever tasted spermicide?"

"Is it terrible?"

"It isn't chocolate syrup. And I figure that if I can't handle it, my clients certainly aren't going to either."

"Are you going to teach them what you've learned?"

"Yes, but I'm not quite sure how to go about it."

"You could use the banana tricks—I don't think I'm up to performing in front of a group of hookers."

Margo looks at him wryly. "Don't worry. Now that I know it works, I don't have to continue my research. Well, at least not in front of anyone," she adds quickly.

"So how are you going to bring it up?" he asks.

"I'm going to go into group on Thursday with several boxes of condoms and some Lifesavers and I'm going to tell them you can put a condom on a man with your mouth and that the man probably won't mind. Did you mind?"

"Not in the least."

"But did you feel it?"

"Some. It felt so good to have your mouth on me that I didn't care."

"Okay, so I guess if I need to I'll demonstrate on the banana and then I'll suggest they use the technique on their men."

"What kind of rubbers are you going to use?"

"Well, I don't know. I'm thinking about approaching Trojan on Monday to ask for a donation of some better-quality condoms."

"And what flavor mints are you going to use?"

"Oh come on, Bill, what kind of question is that?"

"No, really, I mean it. Did you know that if you bite wintergreen in the dark it makes sparks?"

"Really?"

"Really."

"I don't believe you."

"Well, I just happen to have some in my desk. Let's go into the bedroom where it's dark and I'll show you how to make sparks fly."

Jane Handel

The Devil Made Me Do It

Dear X,

It may seem strange that I am writing a letter to you instead of phoning, but I know of no other way to clarify my rather confused thoughts at the moment. Somehow the process of writing helps to put things in order.

As you know, a current obsession of mine is with the concept of sin. I have been trying to analyze to what extent my knowledge of sin affects my enjoyment of sex. "But love is simple," you've said, "don't think so much." And yet I continue to ramble on about my assorted transgressions, and you listen patiently—understanding that as a refugee from the constraints of Catholicism, I am caught in the crossfire between taboo and a conscious desire to violate it. I am convinced that my awareness of sin contributes greatly to the enjoyment I derive from flouting it—the old pleasure/pain principle is pretty intoxicating stuff for some of us.

I often wonder how you were able to emerge unscathed from the repeated lashings meted out to almost everyone in this culture by the Judeo-Christian patriarchal whip. How is it that, for you, fucking is as easy as quenching your thirst in a mountain stream; plunging your face deep into the crystal clear melted snow, oblivious to the hidden microbes of anguish it may contain? Why are you so able to dispense and receive pleasure without the embellishment of guilt, and enjoy it no less than one who thrives on the illicit and forbidden? I can see you shrug and smile inscrutably as you read this . . . but please indulge me as I play the role of kneeling sinner while you listen to yet another confession. With face upturned in penitent supplication, I imagine that you are licking the burning tears of remorse from my cheeks.

Nothing is ever quite as it seems on the surface, but I can assure you that the following sequence of events occurred in an environment of prosaic innocence—my studio, behind what I thought was a tightly closed door.

I had been hard at work on my painting of St. Sebastian (perhaps this scenario is not so innocent after all), and began to feel chilly and irritable. As I was contemplating the blood dripping from the saint's pierced armpit, the fog lifted and warm sunlight flooded the room, forming a golden rectangle in the middle of the floor. Drawn like a cat, I took off my clothes, lay facedown on the bare wood, stretched, and almost purred. The tension in my neck and shoulders began to dissipate as the sun's rays penetrated my aching muscles. I reveled in the sensual warmth, soporific to my brain but arousing to my body.

As the sun's aphrodisiac sent palpitations through my groin, I felt a deep longing to taste and smell you but was too relaxed and sleepy to do anything more than daydream. Perhaps I even dozed off for a while, I don't know. Admittedly, I was in a trancelike state, but whatever happened next was neither dream nor fantasy.

At first, I attributed the vague sounds to wind rustling the branches of a tree outside the window. But then I heard the floor creak and felt warm breath on my cheek as a low, soothing voice murmured, "Don't move and don't open your eyes." The voice was genderless and totally unidentifiable. It was firm, although nonthreatening, yet my heart skipped a few beats. Still, I obeyed.

Suddenly I remembered an incident that had occurred just two days before. While walking to the bank, I had stopped briefly to look in a store window, when a similar voice whispered huskily into my ear, "Hello, sweetheart, why don't you come up and see me sometime?" I turned and looked directly into the mesmerizing gaze of a young Gypsy woman. Her eyes were like pools, drawing me into their chasmal depths. With a half-smile that revealed a gold-capped canine, she handed me an orchid-colored business card. "Readings by Katrina," it said, in dark purple letters. In the time it took me to glance down at the card, she vanished. And now, with this voice in my ear, I wondered, even hoped, that perhaps Katrina had tracked me down, picked my lock, and found her way into my inner sanctum of sunlight. Gypsies, you know, have powers a mere mortal such as I cannot hope to comprehend, though a voodoo queen like you would probably accept such enigmatic behavior as a matter of course.

In any case, my thoughts of Katrina and Gypsy magic notwithstanding, I was filled with an intense desire to question authority and open my eyes. You know how I hate being told what to do! But I continued to keep them tightly shut as my mind raced with a multitude of questions. Who was it really? How did he or she get in? Was it you? A stranger? The latter prospect was especially intriguing. As you learned during the course of a earlier confession of mine, I used to enjoy consummating my then considerable lust with strangers whose anonymity remained forever intact. Of course, this is no longer a viable form of expression, so whereas I had never felt endangered in the past, I now felt a strong twinge of panic and began to hope fervently that you were my mystery companion. But hadn't you returned my key after house-sitting that last time? Unless, knowing my secret, you'd made a duplicate for just such a purpose as this . . . you're a trickster and capable of anything.

I lay with pounding heart for what seemed like an eternity—awaiting either the stab of a knife or a caress. And of course this netherworld of anticipation was visited by my old nemesis—guilt. Because, quite frankly, the sexual arousal I felt at that moment was far greater than either my fear of an assault or my righteous indignation over having been told what to do. It's quite possible that this conflict of emotions even contributed to my state of excitation. So, despite the fact that long ago I rescinded my bid for sainthood, this new dilemma seemed to jeopardize any viable case for redemption.

Now I know you find this psychic can of worms to be absurd, and I, too, make these comments with tongue in cheek, but on a primal level, in spite of myself, I still worry about burning in hell. Subsequently, when nothing happened I didn't know whether to laugh or cry, and simply felt foolish. I then began to think that if tricks were being played, my own imagination was culpable—not you, and certainly not Katrina!

The wet tongue that slowly began to draw intricate patterns behind my ear and down my neck was not the product of an overactive imagination. It traversed the area between my shoulder blades, down my spine, and plunged into the crevice at its base. Lips nibbled at my flesh and teeth gently bit as my pulse raced out of control. Hands pushed apart my thighs, fingers spread my labia, then probed deeply inside as if to test the response. By this time, I had resumed breathing—rapidly. I moaned involuntarily, and pungent, sticky fingers were thrust into my mouth. "Shut up!" the still unrecognizable voice commanded. The fingers were removed from my mouth and shoved back into my vagina, while I stifled any further moans by biting my bottom lip.

It suddenly dawned on me that there was a remote possibility that my uninvited guest might be my teenage neighbor, Jamal. I had given him a key about six months before when I went away with you for the weekend and needed someone to feed my cat. He never returned it, a fact I'd totally forgotten until this very moment. I had been lusting after his beautiful young body for ages, and by the disarray in which I'd discovered my underwear drawer upon returning from that weekend, I imagined the feeling was mutual. But he was definitely still jailbait, and besides, I just couldn't imagine Jamal, the friendly kid next door, having the nerve to actually sneak into my apartment and fondle my naked body, much less having the wherewithal to order me to "shut up" while doing it. No, he was a titillating fantasy object, but it just didn't seem possible that he was capable of the sophisticated dexterity now bringing me to the point of frenzy. And, the idea of not being able to lick him in return was simply too excruciating. All around, it seemed wise to relinquish my desire for Jamal.

You can see my dilemma. There I was, being expertly transported to the brink of orgasm, unable to thrash or moan (a very difficult requirement for me as you well know), and totally in the dark as to the identity of my seducer. In some ways, I dreaded the inevitable dénouement, especially since my fate was not in my hands (no pun intended). So I really did have to rely on the kindness of a stranger. Fortunately, my guest compassionately brought me very quickly to one of the most intense climaxes I've ever had. At that point I couldn't restrain my voice any longer and let out a long, low howl as my body convulsed repeatedly.

I uncurled from a fetal position and opened my eyes. No one was there. The door of my studio was wide open, as was the front door of the apartment. Leaves had blown in off the street and were doing a crazy little dance in the hallway. The last rays of the setting sun created a sharp angle of yellow light on the wall.

I crawled on hands and knees to the front door, closed it and turned the lock. I picked up one of the leaves, admired its beautiful shape and color for a moment, and then crushed it against my breast.

Is a moment's bliss worth an eternity of flames? Let's get together again soon and find out. . . .

Fondly,

O

Moxie Light

❦❦

The Company Man

My dispatcher, Mickey, used to weigh three hundred pounds until he was diagnosed as diabetic. He'd lost most of the weight, but he still ate enough for a family of four. All night long I heard him order lemon-filled donuts, Italian subs, and raspberry lime rickeys. The other drivers brought him whatever he wanted because then he would give his chosen few the best calls. In the taxi business it's known as payola. Mickey could chew while calling out addresses in a carefully modulated voice, keep one eye on a portable television, and rank out those poor drivers who could barely speak English. "Why don't you get a job as an elevator operator," he would tell them. "You can't get lost if you're only going in two directions."

Mickey oozed scorn for anyone who didn't know the city as well as he did. Before he became a dispatcher he was a radio announcer. I never met anyone who knew as many people as Mickey did: nurses and television personalities and arthritic women who depended upon him to get them to their appointments on time. Dispatchers wield a lot of power, and Mickey, for all his good points, was a megalomaniac. Once I picked up a young girl, a poet, bent out of shape that Mickey had called her "dear."

"Who is that dispatcher?" she asked. "He's got a lot of nerve. I'm not his 'dear.' He doesn't even know me."

"When he calls me 'dear,' I don't mind," I said. "Mickey is a gentleman. It probably never crossed his mind that anyone would be insulted."

"Well, I don't know him and I don't like it," she said.

"Wait until the first time a saleslady calls you 'madame,' " I said. "It's a real comedown from 'dear.' "

Another passenger told me that he'd gone to high school with Mickey. "He used to be so nice. President of our class. All sports and what a comedian!"

"He should have been a politician," I said. "He knows how to manipulate people with his voice. It really turns me on."

Indeed, Mickey's voice did not sound like Mickey looked, which was about eight months pregnant. His voice purred as if filtered through a throat of velvet, causing little flip-flops of lust in my stomach. It was a wonder I wasn't cut in half by a street-car, much as it distracted me. I picked up bits and pieces about him from my passengers who either loved him or hated him and the other taxi drivers who grumbled but never quite revolted against his favoritism.

A woman customer I had once told me: "I was mugged once, beaten up real bad. To get over it, I drank a lot. For a while. Mickey used to call me up just to see how I was doing. Every week. What a sexy voice!"

"You mean you never met him?"

"Just when I called for a cab. What does he look like?"

"Well, he's got a nice face. Really, very ordinary. His hair is brown and he's shorter than me. Did he ever ask you out?"

"No. All we ever did was flirt. You say he's short. How disappointing! His voice makes him sound six feet tall."

I never had the chance to talk to him much. Most of the time I was too tired to do more than make out my waybill. Mickey would help me with the figuring. Once, I remember dragging myself out of the cab, dirty, bladder screaming, and seat of my pants rainbow-hued with stains from blueberries and M&M's and a spilled Coke on the front seat. I ate continuously so that if anyone ever decided to splash my brains all over the inside of my windshield they wouldn't be tempted to rape me first. It's a hard, boring job, taxi-driving. When I first started, I thought it was romantic.

"If you keep that up, you're going to start looking like me, you poor little chicken," he said. I liked it when Mickey worried about me. In the beginning, he guided me as if I were flying a 747, so considerate and solicitous. When he sent me into the most dangerous neighborhoods, I never complained, never considered that a white woman in Roxbury had less of a chance than someone who could pose a bigger threat than I, even on my meanest night.

"Keep your doors locked and always keep your mike between your knees. That way you can signal me if you get in trouble, and you'll get more business by radio than by picking up off the streets. Believe me."

Mickey knew the taxi business inside out. He denied taking kickbacks but I'd seen him palming the long green in the corner of the garage when he thought no one was looking. That's when I got the idea that if I had sex with him I could make more money. I quickly put aside the thought. I was too proud, too moral. I could have slipped him a few bucks to get on his good side, if I'd wanted to, but I was never that hungry. A lot of girls I knew had sex just for fun. Not me. I wanted no involvements, no complications, no waiting by the telephone. My friends were all slaves to sex it seemed to me; dropping their personal interests when a new lover came along, wasting precious time suffering the pain of broken love affairs. I had resolved not to let it happen to me.

But I couldn't have spent as much time chasing nickels if I hadn't been half in love with Mickey. That Christmas I had given him twenty dollars. Harry, the garage manager, had given us each a canned ham. And a few of us had gathered in the dispatch room to smoke a joint to celebrate the holidays. But it was New Year's Eve we'd been waiting for. Mickey had said he would double us up with people going to house parties, affluent people who knew enough not to drink and drive, who tipped well, and were grateful for the transportation. After work I planned to stop at my boyfriend's to split a magnum of champagne. None of that domestic stuff, either. My boyfriend was no slouch even though the medication he took for hypertension made him a dud in the kip.

I didn't mind working New Year's Eve until a quarter to midnight when I broke down. I had just dropped off a young executive who'd been working late for her boss. She tipped me an extra dollar. The crowds from the waterfront were just beginning to flood through the streets. My cab sputtered and bucked until it came to a stop, hoses steaming as if it were on fire. I got out of the cab and banged on the door of the closest bar. There was a sign on it that said: PRIVATE PARTY. Nothing was going to stop me from using their phone. I banged on the door until the bartender took pity.

"I'm only three blocks away," I told my boyfriend. "I'm stuck till the tow truck comes. The driver has to stay with the cab. Isn't that awful?"

"I don't want to hear it," he said, with subtle loathing. He was sick of worrying, and didn't understand that if I got a 9 to 5 job, it would kill me faster than the traffic fumes and the constant fear of death. "I'm tired of listening to myself. You always do what you want, anyway. What's the use?"

Everyone in the lounge seemed to be having a good time, except for a few losers at the bar. At the dimly-lit tables, it was a regular bacchanal. Girls were sitting in guys' laps, shamelessly nuzzling and kissing. Lots of tongue and heavy breathing. The bartender looked at me in my grubbies and without smiling, ushered me to the door and locked it behind me. I don't think I've ever been more miserable. I felt my face tie into hard knots and felt a sudden longing for red satin underwear and feathers in my hair.

Midnight in Boston. Pandemonium reigned: kazoos, church bells, cow bells, bleating car horns. Couples carrying balloons walked arm in arm, dragging half-asleep kids behind. The revelers streamed past my cab. Teenagers with crazy hats on their heads began to bang on my fender. "Happy New Year," they called. I turned the key in the ignition and picked up the mike.

"Happy New Year, Mickey," I said. I turned the radio up for "Auld Lang Syne." A couple of kids began to shake my cab, jumping up and down on the fenders. I clicked shut the door locks and shot the kids a look of disdain. I heard the grand finale of fireworks, explosive sounds ricocheting against the buildings overhead, and thought sadly of Arthur Fiedler. Then, I reached under my seat for an old copy of *The Watchtower* which I'd found earlier in one of my pit stops, the bathroom of St. Elizabeth's Hospital.

Gloom and doom. The story of my life. New Year's had turned out to be a big nothing. I'd been out on the road all night and I had seventy-eight whole dollars, most of that earmarked for the company. Where were the big tips Mickey had promised? That liar. He'd stoop to anything. Like Thanksgiving when he'd said business would be good after the football games and it wasn't. Mickey was a company man.

It was starting to get cold. I stuck my hands in my pockets to warm them. I spent a lot of time feeling sorry for myself. My friends said I needed a team of lawyers following me to pick up the pieces. I felt sorry for the rest of the world too, the poor, the hungry. Weren't we all about to be blown to bits in a nuclear war?

I turned the radio off to save the battery and scrunched down in my seat, sitting on my hands. I was bored. The light wasn't strong enough to read by. One stretch limousine after another passed with pretty girls popping out of sun roofs. Would the masses never end? How would the tow truck be able to get through? I picked up the mike and listened to Mickey until I could cut in. "Have you forgotten me? Is someone coming? I'm freezing, in case you're interested."

"I'll give you something to warm you up when you get here," Mickey said, laughing. "The tow truck's on its way."

"Don't talk to me like that over the air. It gives me hot flashes." It was harmless banter that Mickey didn't know I really meant. Just because I was past forty didn't mean I was dead. All that raw sex back at the bar had triggered an overwhelming yearning to be touched. What was I saving it for, anyway?

Finally, with the crowd beginning to thin, I saw the tow truck slinking its way up the street. Bruce, my good buddy, who'd taken a whole night after drunken-driving school to teach me a few tricks, and driver-cum-mechanic, Joe, hooked my cab to the towline. As I climbed into the truck, a warm feeling came into my heart. Bruce and Joe could have left me sitting for hours if they'd wanted to. It was almost like being part of a family. "How sweet of both of you to give up your tips for me," I said, gratefully, in a rush of emotion.

"We couldn't leave you all alone on a night like this," Bruce said, passing me a bottle. "Take a sip."

"I'm frozen through to my bones," I said. "Thanks." Joe honked his horn and cursed out the window at the pedestrians as we slowly made our way. He passed me a joint, then the bottle, partying all the way to the garage, so that by the time we arrived, my depression had faded and something like euphoria had taken its place. I was feeling warm and lovable; kind of cute, in fact. High. My cheeks were hot and I could feel the blood careening crazily through my veins.

"Aren't you going back out?" asked Mickey, when I came in and threw my waybill down in front of him. "You need the money." A space heater in the corner blasted out heat.

"My stride is broken." Thanks to the pot and the whiskey my alter ego took charge. I could hardly believe it was me who continued: "What do you say we go to my apartment and get to know each other?"

"What do you want to know?" Mickey asked.

Mickey's T-shirt read HARVARD. I ran my finger along the edge of his collar. It was very unlike me to be so bold and I did it with full knowledge that I would never hear the end of it if the other drivers found out. The edges of his ears became bright red. I could tell I was embarrassing him, but I was too overwhelmed by lust to stop. I wanted to make love to Mickey. I wanted to watch the expression in his eyes when he came, and see him naked, beer-belly and all. I wanted to fuck him like he'd never had it before, so that every time he dispatched to me, he'd have to remember, so that if the bomb did come, we could both die with a smile. I'd been repressing my sexuality too long and too much of anything, as everyone knows, is unhealthy. We would have a last tango, a lost weekend, a brief but beautiful love affair. Once I'd made up my mind, Mickey didn't stand a chance.

"I'll go home and wait for you," I said. "You know where I live. I have a bottle left over from Christmas."

I ran around my apartment shoving kitchen clutter into the oven, swishing out the toilet bowl and shutting all the closet doors. When Mickey got there, I was bathed and perfumed, with all systems go. After a few more drinks, we undressed. As Mickey folded his clothes into a neat pile by his side, I strategically placed an unopened Christmas gift in my lap so that all he could see were my shoulders. The war against my puritanical upbringing was not yet won for all my loose talk.

"You don't have to worry about me," he said. "I have this condition . . ."

"What condition?" I asked, though I half knew what was coming. I was jinxed. Premature ejaculators gravitated to me. Some of them, I scared. Some just wanted to get me under their control. Some, I was quick to sense, were merely interested in a conquest. Most of them wanted to be mothered. What irked me the most were the men who got me all hot and bothered and left me hanging. It gives a girl a complex.

The only man I'd ever dated who knew how to please me was my boyfriend. That was the reason I stayed, but the irony of it was no sex and no money. With little in common, every day was a new challenge. Thinking of him made me feel guilty and I began to put my clothes back on.

"No, don't," said Mickey, taking my sweater out of my hands. He leaned to kiss my breast. "It's the medicine I take for my diabetes. Maybe if you're patient with me, it will work. Please?" He whispered love talk into my ear, bringing goose bumps to my skin.

"I love it when you talk dirty," I said. "But since we work together, it's probably better if we just stay friends."

"We'll always be friends," said Mickey, breathing hard, and then kissing me, hungrily. "I'll always be there for you."

"Will you start giving me some good calls instead of all the blood runs?" The medical laboratory, one of our company's biggest accounts, gave us fifty-cent tips. The specimens came in plastic bags, but we never knew if we were carrying a lethal virus or if someone would attack us in some lonely stretch of

hospital parking lot. Mickey would give the plum jobs, the ones
that came into the airport or the bus terminals, to the drivers
who gave him a kickback.

"How can you think of money at a time like this?"

"What was all that about giving me something to warm me
up?" I said. "You are a bastard. Just like the cabs this summer
you said had air-conditioning. Sometimes I hate you."

"Shut up," Mickey mumbled. His face was in my crotch, hands
fluttering all over my body like falling rose petals. And as much
as I had all kinds of reservations, I was dizzy with desire, answering his probing tongue with the rhythm of my hips. I felt
glued to his finger. The energy charged into me like Michelan-
gelo's Adam on the ceiling of the Sistine Chapel.

"My God," I moaned, gasping. "I never wanted anyone as
much in my whole life." It was true. The loneliness of the holidays had erased all my defenses, all my Bostonian reservations.
My whole body began to tremble. "Don't stop!"

Mickey clambered onto me, unceremoniously, one hand still
working in me, fondling his penis with his thumb. I could feel
his testicles, soft and warm, knocking on my thighs. I was in a
state of perpetual orgasm. Small animal sounds came from my
throat. I heard them as if they belonged to someone else. I panted
until I couldn't catch my breath, the sides of my throat like Velcro.

"The neighbors . . ." I managed to break away from his
grasp. "I've got to get a drink of water," I said. But he was
quicker, dragging me into the bedroom, the connection between
us broken momentarily. He pulled back the covers and threw me
onto the mattress. Shoving a pillow onto my face, he kneaded
my breast with a sure hand. I could feel my thighs slick with his
spit, smell the sex rising from my body, earthy and warm like
peat. There wasn't a square inch on my body not begging for
relief.

Mickey was indefatigable. Impotent, but indefatigable. I felt
as if I were having an out-of-body experience, lost in the universe
somewhere, or maybe underwater, a stranger to myself.

For a day and a half we hardly came up for air or knew the
time of day. I vaguely remember the phone ringing unanswered

◆

and scrambled eggs, but for most of that time, I was in a sexual coma. Mickey's tongue rode me like a surfer, crest after crest. I was powerless to speak, think, or leave, until the pain began to leak through my miasma. I was unable to pee without a terrible burning nor look at Mickey for shame.

"You've got to leave," I said, at last, when my rationality reappeared. "My boyfriend has a key. What if he comes?"

"I'll hide in a closet."

"He also has a gun," I said. He really didn't, but I couldn't bear the thought of another lick. A razorlike pain bisected me where the skin was chafed. Mickey looked as if he'd been on a bender. He needed a shave and his eyes were bloodshot. I hated it when men gave me those puppy dog eyes.

"I've got to go home and get my insulin," he said. "But I could come back. I know you're too good for me. I'd ask you to marry me, but you could never be happy with an ordinary guy like me."

"I'll never have sex with anyone else after this," I promised, "not for a long, long time, anyway. But I feel terrible about your condition." Words. What I really felt terrible about was not sharing this part of love with my boyfriend. Maybe it wasn't too late. Maybe I could strip myself of all the manners and be a real woman. Yeah.

"Hey," said Mickey, matter-of-factly, "it's my own fault for not taking care of the diabetes when I had the chance. The important thing is, did I satisfy you? Did I enjoy it?"

I walked him to the door, my arm around his waist, leaning on him, I was so weak. "What do you think?" I rasped. What a dumb question! My boyfriend would never have been so stupid to ask. I didn't want to appear ungrateful. God forbid I should lose all of my feminine virtues and become as crass as anyone who took what they wanted, as unfeeling as if it were a shower.

"It was an experience I'll never forget. Thank you." It was as if my body had been saving itself, as if orgasms could be stored like memories. Why had I been so helpless to fight it? Why did I have this feeling that it had been meant to be? My head went into a transcendental swirl as I contemplated the universe and my tiny part in it. What rot! I was as basic as your gum-chewing

East Boston person. It took someone like Mickey to help me realize it.

"What will you tell your boyfriend about why you didn't answer the phone?" Mickey asked, concerned as always for my well-being.

"When he sees how much weight I've lost, he'll believe me when I tell him I've been sick." My boyfriend loved me. Of that I was sure. As I would not deny him, he would not deny me. We were both too conventional to verbalize this, but I suppose, at the very bottom, it was why we had never married. Call it an understanding. I smiled at Mickey, toyed with the doorknob, and blew him a kiss. "Sex is a sickness, you know. I really believe it."

As Mickey shrugged his shoulders, his eyes gleamed. He was back to his normal jaunty self. "I wouldn't have missed it for the world. But don't think I'm going to start giving you better calls. Some of these drivers have been with me for years. They have to come first."

"I always knew you were a company man," I said. I couldn't wait to get rid of him now. "Someone has to carry those little old ladies who make a big deal about giving a dime tip. I just hope you don't go shooting your mouth off at the garage."

"My lips are sealed."

But, of course, either someone had seen his car outside my apartment or Mickey's friendship with the other men included using his big mouth in other ways. I had to put up with a million smirks. Even Joe, the tow-truck driver, who'd always treated me with respect, asked me to pose in some fancy underwear for his Polaroid. When Mickey pestered me for a repeat performance, I always said no.

After a while, he began to treat me like everyone else.

Pat Williams

Ellen, From Chicago

On the dresser was a small photograph of a woman. It was in an old gilded frame, the kind that tarnishes with age, but this one was kept polished to a warm gleam.

The woman was an aviator. I think I would have guessed that even if it hadn't been for her helmet and the upraised goggles. Her eyes seemed to be looking at a vision or at some great expanse, her smile soft but self-assured. A luster seemed to permeate her brown skin. Heroic? Adventurous? I had to smile at those impressions yet I couldn't take my eyes from her picture.

"That's Trina there," Rose's soft voice said.

I jerked my hand back, though I had barely been touching the photograph. Rose Owens smiled.

"She was one of the first colored flyers," Rose said. "Aviatrices they called them. She was the only one from around these parts."

Rose glanced at the picture a time or two while she put the extra blankets on our beds and I could see the fondness in her gaze. "We came up together," she went on. "We were both in the choir at Reverend Clark's church."

She looked about the room to see that all was in order.

Rose didn't look worn with age and there were only a few

strands of gray in her hair, but she did look tired. Sixty-one years of living in the South does that to a black woman.

"Everything's fine, Miss Rose," I said.

She nodded but looked around as if there was still something she thought could be done to make her visitors feel more at home.

We heard a footstep in the hallway and Ellen stepped into the room. At the same time a fragrance of honeysuckle came through the screened window on the night wind.

Rose smiled a greeting at Ellen but she came over to the dresser where I stood. "That's the picture they put in the colored paper down at Cane City," Rose said. "I'll have to show you the pictures in the album I keeps."

"Does she still live here?" Ellen asked.

"She was killed in a crash. A car crash. In France," Rose said. The smile had faded from her lips, but it remained in her eyes. "She had the . . . prettiest hands."

She looked at Ellen and me. "Well, I'll let you girls get your rest." She asked us if there was anything else we needed and when we said, "No thank you," she left.

When I had come upon the photograph, I had been looking at the things on the dresser.

It was something I'd taken to doing at the houses we stayed in. Looking at, examining, touching the keepsakes—old perfume bottles, saucer ashtrays, jars filled with marbles and trinkets, photographs. I continued my exploration of this dresser though I was very aware of Ellen rummaging in her travel case, of her footsteps around the bed.

I didn't turn around then because I didn't know what to say to her.

I am not normally tongue-tied with strangers. Every year I face a new bunch of them from the front of a classroom. Things had gone along all right with Ellen, too, at first. I remembered the moment I'd been brought up short.

We were on the drive from Mobile to Lewiston. Kenneth, Diego, Albert, Ellen, and I. Kenneth and Diego were joking with Ellen. She sat against the window and the wind lifted the collar of her loose white blouse. She was answering some comment of Kenneth's and she said to him, "Well, you know the finest black women on the planet came from Chicago, ain't that right?" And her voice was serious but she smiled and gave a halfway wink to me.

Something, some little cue in that, caught me off guard so that I couldn't speak just then. Fortunately Diego dove in with his own comment.

When I looked into the dresser mirror I saw that Ellen had put on her light-green kimono. It looked cool and soft.

There was a slight frown on her face, not much more than a deep thoughtfulness, that accentuated her easy-curving brows and her wide, full mouth. She ran her hand once across her Afro cut that in sunlight looked for all the world like jewels shimmered in it.

When she'd got her washcloth and a little bottle of something and left for the bathroom down the hall, I finally turned away from the dresser.

I came back from my turn in the bath to find her lying in bed with the sheet tucked about her and her arms folded behind her head. She watched me as I got ready for bed.

"Ka-ma-li," she enunciated my name softly. I looked at her and she raised an eyebrow in question. "What does it mean?" she said.

"It's the name of a protecting spirit," I said.

"What nation does it come from?" she asked.

"It's Mashona. From Zimbabwe," I said. She smiled slightly, watching me.

"I like the sound," she said quietly and closed her eyes for a moment. Her long lashes shadowed her cheeks. The smile still on her face. Then she opened her eyes and caught me looking at her.

I walked around to the other twin bed and let my short robe fall—I had only my panties under it—and slid between the sheets.

"Are you tired?" Ellen asked.

"It's been a long day," I said.

"Good night, Kamali," she said and there was a subtle amusement in her voice. The lamp was on her side of the bed and she pulled the cord on it.

I didn't go to sleep, I was too aware of her there.

I thought of the talk she'd given in Mobile two days past.

Ellen, Diego, Kenneth, Albert, and I were following the path of the sixties' civil rights workers through the South. We were on a more modern-day crusade; instead of fighting segregation we were lecturing on African history. Kenneth, Albert, and I all taught at the same college. We had scraped together what funding we could and set off at the end of the school year. We were speaking at churches, summer classrooms, lodges, sometimes in private homes. We stayed in folks' homes because we couldn't afford hotels. In Mobile, we spoke at a lodge hall.

Something drives Ellen when it comes to her beliefs. I would sit next to her as she stood and talked about ancient African civilizations in Zimbabwe and Egypt. I would be very aware of her then, aware of the very faint orange fragrance she wears. When she spoke I could watch her as closely as I wanted.

The light in her dark eyes burned when she made a point that she wanted her audience not just to know but to believe. Moisture formed on her neck and her brow, and when she became excited a little hoarseness came out in her voice.

I heard her breathing in the bed next to mine, and finally I slept too.

In the morning I woke to find her sitting on the side of her bed. I didn't think that she noticed me watching her right away. She leaned forward, examining her hands. All of the passion that could fill her face seemed to be gone; only a faint smile played on her lips.

"Good morning," she said, without looking up, then a moment later she did, and smiled. Caught again. I smiled back at her.

"What were you thinking about?" I said.

"How quick the time passes," she said. "How few people we'll reach this summer after all. But," she said, shrugging, "I'm thankful for even small favors."

"I don't see how anyone could listen to you and not believe every word you say," I said.

There was a mischievous spark in her eye. "Thank you."

We held each other's gaze for a long time. Morning sounds came from the window and downstairs—some farm machinery droning across the fields, jaybirds hijinking out in the woods, voices in the kitchen. I think it was just then that something was decided between us. "What are you thinking about?" she said.

"You."

I lay on my stomach and the pressure against my mons felt good. My fingers pushed into the pillow. There was no mischief in her eyes now, no amusement on her face. It was open.

"Miss Rose's friend," I said, "was not from Chicago. But she sure was fine."

Ellen smiled. Uh oh, now who was shy? She bit her bottom lip just a little.

I got out of bed and put on my robe—for some reason—and I fastened it loosely. The beds were right beside each other so all I needed to do was reach out to stroke her cheek. For a moment I allowed my hand to lie on the soft, soft skin of her shoulder beneath her kimono. I imagined how her breast would feel, imagined the taste of her plum brown nipple. I was aware of her close, fresh, morning smell.

"Lady," one of us said.

I sat down beside her. "This is a long trip," I said. "And I find you very attractive."

She placed a hand on my thigh where my robe fell open and rubbed me gently. We kissed as softly as her touch.

We held each other breast to breast and played just a moment with the tips of our tongues on our lips, inside our mouths. She moaned and just then there was a sudden sound from the dresser. A loud click. We both jumped.

No one was there, but the picture of Trina had fallen over. Ellen chuckled.

"Yes ma'am, Miss Trina."

A moment later we heard footsteps in the hallway.

Miss Rose set a cup of strawberries and two glasses of cold milk in a place she cleared on the dresser. She inquired as to how we had slept and I wondered if she noticed the odor that our touching had brought.

Rose carefully set Trina's picture upright again. "Once Trina took me up in that airplane." Rose carefully raised her hand from the picture. "I was so scared. But I wasn't worried. Ain't that funny? I wouldn'a gone up with nobody else but Trina."

She looked at us and I saw, for the first time, how sharp and young her eyes were.

"This was her second home too. She was always over here. Little place where she grew up, they turned into a colored library. I have to show you my picture album before you go."

Ellen still sat on the bed but I gathered my things to go to the bathroom. I wanted to be alone for just a little time. I wanted a quiet place for my thoughts of what was happening.

Once there, I stood in front of the mirror and pushed my long dreadlocks back so that they lay across my shoulders. Kenneth called them my lion locks. I touched my face, taking account of the golden-brown skin, the cheekbones and brown eyes and assuring myself that Ellen liked them.

The fellows were downstairs. They commented on how refreshed we looked that morning. Kenneth looked at us closely— he knew something, I'm sure—and he said, "You two complement each other."

We sat next to one another, and all through breakfast my leg lay next to, barely touching, hers.

Toward the end of breakfast Rose held court. She told us the history of her house, built for the white Owens by her great-grandparents when they were still slaves. Now the black Owens lived in it.

Rachel, who ran the beauty parlor in the basement, came up to join us. She was light-skinned with gray eyes and a blond streak in her hair. She grinned as she sat back, crossed her legs, and said, "Miss Rose don't know it, but she's the state historian."

The morning lingered full of sounds and smells that I recalled from growing up in that part of the country. The morning radio gospel show from Memphis, the smell of dry grass and dust. It was already hot, and there were beads of sweat on the back of Ellen's hand.

The day grew warmer; the wind died, and touching the bright chrome on a car sitting in the sun could burn you.

We would give another talk that night, so we were staying the day. I lay across the bed in our room that afternoon, attempting to keep cool. The curtains were drawn against the heat so the light was dim. The door opened and Ellen came in.

She thought that I was sleeping because she moved quietly across the room to her satchel. I watched her take out a small book and pick up her straw sun hat from the chair. "Ellen," I said.

She looked toward my bed and then walked over. "Baby, I din't mean to wake you," she said.

When she sat down I reached up and touched her hair, warm from the sun. My fingers ran easily down her back. She shivered a little. "You're not going to let up are you?" she said.

"No."

She chuckled. "All right."

Then she whispered, "Nobody's objecting to the way this is going anyway."

I touched my finger to her lips and she kissed it. And my hand rubbed across her breast when I lowered it. It rested on her thigh. And caressed her hip.

"Kamali, Kamali," she whispered, leaning over me. I pulled her body to me. My hand on her hip stroked firmer, moving up the fabric of her skirt. When I am about to touch another woman, when I'm just beginning to, I can already taste her, her sweat and her juices and I can already feel my fingers in her wet places. Ellen had filled my mouth already and I swallowed. "Baby," she said and she kissed me.

My hand smoothed around to the damp inside of her thigh. "Come with me," she said, and I nodded. She laughed and pulled back a bit more. "No, come with me to the library. It's closed today. But Miss Rose gave me the key. She said I could spend the afternoon there. I'm going to give them my copy of *Stolen Legacy*."

We walked to the library, wide sun hats on our heads, holding hands because I didn't want to lose contact with her flesh. I listened to the sound of her voice as much as to her words when she spoke of her passion, the ancients. There were ancient black civilizations, people had to know that. Philosophies we had founded at the beginnings of time were still around today.

Lies had covered all of that but we were going to uncover the truths. People had to know. *Had to.* I nodded my agreement. Her passion had drawn me to her long before I knew her body.

It was cool—almost—inside the tiny one-room library.

The Trina Brown Library. We could hear the waters of a stream that passed a few feet away, shaded by the same gigantic oaks that covered the tiny building. We walked about, fingers linked, and looked at the precious old volumes.

"Miss Rose takes care of this place," Ellen said. "She brings flowers once a week. In the winter she gets them from the florist in town."

Petunias and bachelor's buttons sat in a blue vase by a window. There was a couch there, worn and old and soft. Ellen pulled me to her. I wrapped my arms around her, her breasts pressed against mine; her whole body against mine thrilled me.

We kissed long and slowly, tasting and sucking each other. I pressed into Ellen and she moaned.

I smoothed her body with my hands and she caressed me, kneading me all the way down my back, my behind. I opened the front of her dress, slowly. When we were both naked we lay down on the couch. I was wet, my clit was hard, and when her hand brushed between my legs it sent tremors through me.

She pulled me down onto her. "Is it going to be good?" she whispered and kissed me again before I could answer.

Her nipples hardened between my fingers as I pulled and squeezed them. I moved slowly between her legs. Kissing her neck and down to her shoulders. Such a fine, pretty woman, such a sweet, sweet good-tasting thing.

I remembered the sweat on her neck, I remembered her wink and the first time her leg touched mine in the backseat of the car. Fine, pretty Chicago woman. She found my mouth again, kissed me hard.

I bit softly at her nipples, slowly licked the sweat salt on her stomach, then found the juices between her legs and drank them. I licked the little bud there and heard the breath rushing in her and her moaning. I felt her hands all in my locks and when she pulled me up and kissed me roughly, clawing at my back, I loved it.

She rode me, her mons pushing deeper into mine, pressing

harder as it built up in me and I wanted to pee and I wanted to come. I shook and held her close enough to be a part of me.

I held her as her trembling eased and as I caught my breath. Her hands were already exploring my body again. She moved into me, feeling my wetness as she sucked my breasts, ran her tongue into my navel. . . .

I opened again, wide.

We went down to the stream sometime afterward and climbed in naked. The water was the coolest and sweetest.

Then we walked across the soft grass back to the library.

Ellen ran her finger down the spine of the slim little book—her favorite—that she was leaving behind; she took my hand again and we left. We joked that we should have exchanged dresses and seen if anyone would notice.

"You girls have a nice afternoon?" Rose said. She did not look up from the cake that she was decorating with berries and peach slices.

Ellen pressed her lips into a smile, her dimple showing.

I put on some raspberry tea—hot things in hot weather cool you down, so they say—and called down to Rachel and her customer to come up and join us.

Rose did show us her picture album.

Late that night after our talk, Rachel called us into her beauty shop where she had Rose on the recliner chair giving her a foot rub.

Rose had the album on her lap. "Come over here and see this," she said to us.

There was a picture of Trina in the plane that she flew down from Cincinnati. There was Trina and Rose in their choir robes in front of the church. Here was Trina and Rose caught by somebody's camera while they lay sleeping under a shade tree. Here was Trina Brown in her fine fur coat and her scarf and her genuine Spanish leather boots getting ready to leave for overseas.

"Kind of fond of that flyer, wasn't you, Rose?" Rachel smiled.

Rose looked down into her photograph album. "She's my hist'ry."

Cindy Walters

❦❦

Window Shopping

I've never been to Copenhagen but I understand the whores sit in storefront windows marketing themselves.

I fantasize that I am in a window wearing a pair of leopard-skin boots that I saw once in Paris. The heels are high, spiked, with all-spandex uppers in leopard skin that reach to my thighs. I like to sit in the window on a large chair with my back to the street. Between clients I lie back, legs around the chair, and masturbate.

To stay legal, I can't show my pussy directly to the passersby or expose a nipple to the street. So I wear a matching leopard-skin teddy, panties, and a little mask that covers my eyes with pointed ears and cat whiskers.

I lie with legs around the old chair and my back arched; head hanging so my pussy is hidden near the chairback but anyone can see my mound bulge as I jack myself off. Did I say that in this wild city I'm not allowed to expose a nipple either? It has to do with street zoning, I believe. My Danish isn't too good. Anyway, I keep ice water by my chair in the spotlit window and wet down the front of my teddy when I get hot. The ice excites my nipples till they show through the thin silky top, 3mm, 4mm, 6mm. . . .

I use my right hand on my clit, the other on my nipples. I've always been right-handed in this way. It takes only a minute or so to get my clit hard—I'm used to my own touch. My clit gets hard just as my right nipple does. I can feel it: 3mm, 4mm, 6mm. . . . I rub it side to side or rotate it and glance at the people watching me from the street. They point at me and I point to my breast, apply more ice water, and push it toward my audience.

I arch naturally, just keeping in mind not to expose my pubic hair so I don't lose my license. My pussy-water begins to trickle down my perineum. A drop of it tickles my anus. I almost indulge myself with a finger but it's risky; I lose track of what is exposed when I have my index finger up my ass, and the cops are on the street tonight. So I think about it instead and continue the little circles on my nipples and on my clit, harder now; it's so slippery I almost lose the sensation in there. My head rocks back and forth, for the clients outside who expect more movement from my excitement.

Diane and I have been window-buddies for almost a year now, and we know each other's masturbation styles. She must have seen my panties turn dark and wet because she has discreetly slipped a finger into my anus. I arch, and she nibbles my tit so it sticks out like a leopard-skin gumdrop.

I feel the luxury of three-way excitement on my clit, my iced nipple and my asshole. I come, squirting into my panties, wetness trickling down to my boot top. Diane brushes her hand through my hair.

A young man leaves the window and walks into the house. I hear him discuss the price. He asks for Diane.

Karen Marie Christa Minns

Amazon: A Story of the Forest

Because she had so recently come out of the desert I did not expect it; she carried the forest in her eyes, the greening golds and olives, the emeralds breaking apart the shattered light. I noticed when she first glanced up from the podium. The auditorium was packed, the slide show over as I dropped my Walkman with a resounding clunk. She stopped speaking for a moment, glancing up at the tiered assemblage, glancing up and finding me.

My breath caught like a stone in my throat. She said nothing, no cruel joke, no offhand remark, skipped only a beat and continued about the female deities of ancient Egypt. She kept watching me. I felt the heat rise like a touch on my face, knew my friends were stifling giggles, poking me in the ribs, nudging my feet, but I didn't care. I had entered the forest, I was already lost.

"I want to, um, to apply as a researcher with you, um, you said tonight that you were looking for someone who could make a six-month commitment. . . ." I took her hand and shook it, feeling the strength drain from my fingers as they connected with those long, cool hands she used so carefully. Both of them closed around my one, pressing back in a way that marked a possibility I'd only dreamed of since first seeing the video of her early excavations. But no, it was only a student's unabashed crush for

293

the brilliant doctor. I fumbled against the set-up bar, knocking over a bottle of cheap chablis. The undergraduate bartender scowled as he wiped up the mess. I turned to apologize but she'd already been led off by the head of the Humanities Division. I could only watch in soggy misery as her tall, dark head was blotted out by the taller, graying heads of the men of academia. I could still feel the press of her hands, could almost smell the scent of the forest.

"She's tired of the desert . . . no, really, that's a terrible thing to say . . . a poor Egyptologist joke . . . forget it. Look, I think it's exciting she's made the Amazon connection . . . if she gets MacKenzie as her guide she'll be fine . . . don't mention it. However, there is one favor . . . one of my graduate students . . . she wants to volunteer for the internship. Yes, the entire six months. Yes, of course she's good, she's mine, isn't she . . . ? Stop, that's tacky . . . seriously, now, I think she'll do well by the good Dr. Livingston. So, can I tell her it's a go or do you have to wait and confirm . . . excellent. Always said you were a fine man, Muldoon . . . best to Barb . . . will I see you in Florence . . . ? Yes, we've got the same place; what can I say? Clout . . . pure and simple . . . right, then good-bye." My adviser hung up, his grin stretching his usual hangdog face into an almost happy expression. He thumped his Mont Blanc against the blotter . . . two points . . . oh, how these guys like to rack them up with each other!

Still, I had to grin back. Dr. Campbell Livingston . . . the Amazon . . . and I was going, I was going.

The air was almost fluorescent, hyper-oxygenated, alive. It was like drinking a long glass of cool spring water from an emerald cup; this was more than air. I stood over my L.L. Bean rucksack, squinting through the glare, looking for the woman of the forest. She was nowhere to be found and the edge of the runway was not exactly packed with tourists. Then, a quick shadow, a tap on the shoulder. I spun around, all toothy grin and immediate blush, "Dr. Livingston, I . . ."

"Sorry, she's downriver. I'm supposed to bring you back with me. You must be Langley, I'm Mac, officially 'the guide' . . . though the bloody Doc won't let me 'guide' so much as her bloody canoe. Sorry, five weeks in the bush with that woman will make anyone a bit cranked. Are you hungry? Last chance for some decent food. There's only the canned crap at camp and what we can trap or get from the river. Do you know how to shoot?" The big man scratched a red stubbled chin. He knew how to dress the part anyway.

"Shoot? What . . . ?" I thought Nikon, I thought Fuji.

"Shit, just as I thought, a college kid. I told Livingston to have them at least send her a boy. Shoot, shoot, like bang-bang. It's bloody wild out there, you know, and she doesn't have a little fridge at the cabin. You want fresh meat you have to go and . . . forget it . . . just forget it. We're all going to wind up fresh meat before this thing's through. C'mon, the jeep will take us to the river." Mac didn't so much as offer to pick up the pack. He blew his nose using a finger against one nostril, the other open and spewing disgustedly.

It was a bad movie with a good set. What the hell was I doing?

The river was not the roaring Amazon I'd imagined. We traveled through vine- and brush-tangled inlets, the canoe paddled by Indians wearing Nike shirts and bark loincloths. They talked some kind of presumed derelict mission dialect. Mac got along fine. They passed a long wooden pipe back and forth, but didn't offer him so much as a whiff. I was not even worth a second glance. My Banana Republic outfit was already going mildewed, my hair in tight curls, plastered to my sweating head. I trailed my burning feet in the river over the long boat's edge.

"Hey, Langley, that's how the last 'researcher' left—toeless. If the piranha aren't hungry, the giant catfish might be. Keep all appendages in the craft, now, will you? This isn't some damned Disney ride!" Mac spit into the water. Something rose from below, investigating, then, before it would show itself on the surface, blew a cloud of bubbles, all iridescent greens, and disappeared. The Indians laughed, relighting the pipe, pushing us on.

The dark was fast, a giant hand scooping the screaming orb of sun clear from the sky. Palm inward, the dark turned and fell over us. How they found the makeshift dock, I'll never know. I was barely keeping back the shakes. The night seemed to drop thousands of insects onto our heads. Every exposed inch of my skin began to itch and burn. We were, as Mac had predicted, fresh meat. My swatting and swearing was, at first, cause for instant delight, the Indians laughing and making bird whistles each time I smashed a crawly off of a leg or arm. Then, my choreography began to sway the boat. A growl from Mac and two answering glares from the men made me barely keep the creeps under control. I prayed a silent thanks as the bow of the canoe bumped the wooden dock. Somewhere, back behind the curtain of vines and overhang, somewhere was the woman that I'd come to find . . . maybe. Mac stepped out and offered a gallant hand, which I accepted out of fear and exhaustion. One of the Indians tossed my gear up with a quiet laugh. Mac shoved them off with a push of his boot. Their gentle whistles were engulfed by the night as the river turned away from us. And now it was Mac and I alone in the dark, nowhere else to go.

"You know, it's a real waste . . ." Mac moved ahead of me on the unseen path.

"What is?" I whispered, hushed as the night around us, aware that all the screaming birds and other hunting animals were silent at our approach.

"You wasting a chunk out of your best years to be in this bloody cesspool with a madwoman. I've seen her type before. You better watch yourself, missy." I could feel his leering wink even in the black.

"What do you mean by that? Seems to me that's my business. Anyway, do you realize how important this woman is, how remarkable her work . . ."

Mac stopped dead on the trail and caught me by my shoulders. "Langley, out here, it doesn't mean spit. I've been guiding hunters, researchers, Peace Corps volunteers, priests, and nuns all my life. I know how to read people. Campbell Livingston fell full-blown, complete with field gear, right out of her mum's snatch. Whatever she's got to teach I think you should consider twice about learning. Christ, the Indians don't even think she's really a human. Lost tribes . . . endangered artifacts . . . the fucking forest is going up in smoke all around her and she doesn't even notice. What she really needs she doesn't want and believe me, I've already offered. Mark my words, little girl, you be careful around this one. She's half-devil, even if she looks like an angel. You be careful." His voice dropped.

"Careful of what?" The question was all velvet hush.

I almost peed in my outback shorts! Jesus! Where had she come from? No flashlight, no lantern, blackness like the inside of a glove all around us. Yet there was no mistaking that husky voice. Dr. Campbell Livingston was directly in front of us!

"Welcome to base camp, Langley. I'm pleased you could make it, you come with strong recommendations," she said.

I could feel the sparks. Could swear little emerald stars sparkled and cracked where I knew she stood. Jesus, my legs trembled. No crush, this; just full-blown terror. I knew nothing about field research, less about jungle survival or proper technique. This was like a dream where you arrive for an exam in a class you never took. But I couldn't say any of this. Not to him, never to her. I mumbled some idiocy and followed them both, best I could, up the mucky path, toward the misty cabin light. I was home.

I was given the screened-in porch to sleep on. Campbell's room was the only one with a door. Mac had constructed his own sheltered camp out back, a few hundred yards from the tin-and-board cabin that made up the research facility. Things had obviously been a bit more than tense for them these past few weeks. And now, I was a new factor.

"Up with the sun . . . lots to do . . . downriver, about twenty miles . . . an easy paddle . . . a village with the same icons I found along the Nile . . . a kind of sea-animal, dolphinlike, only once before . . . never mind. Tomorrow . . ." Her voice trailed off. I couldn't keep my head up. Outside, only the screen between me and the night-hunting things, the forest watched. Mac watched and I fell deep asleep.

The river was almost sapphire as we paddled. The current was swift. Huge shapes moved below us, following, and then, off the starboard bow, a quick whistle and flash of pinkish white.

"It's the dolphins!" Mac hollered, his canoe following ours.

"Dolphins?" I turned to look at Dr. Livingston. In a freshwater river so far from the ocean? Come on . . . a myth . . . *pink* dolphins?

"You didn't know?" Livingston's eyes snapped olive and khaki, muddied with anger at my obvious ignorance.

"I'm an anthropology major . . . I knew you were studying the art but—" I blurted out, not wanting her to know I was there because of a favor, because my adviser wanted to prove his power and pull some strings. I was making him look mighty good by being out here.

"Good God, they told me you'd had some background in biology. Never mind, just let the river carry us. They'll follow if we're quiet." She turned from me, shielding her eyes from the morning's glare, watching the flying underwater figures as they streaked under and past.

Pink dolphins, pink dolphins in an emerald stream . . .

Once Dr. Livingston found the huge holes in my education, she relegated me to writing letters and filing papers. The smell of mildew and fungus filled my every waking hour. Occasionally I'd catch her watching me as I sat at the lone table, hunched over the ancient typewriter, pounding and cursing. Gone were my romantic fantasies, the moaning dreams at midnight. In their place came blisters, a constant case of dampness, boredom bordering on manic depression, and an increasing awareness of my own lack of genuine researcher worth. Mac would pass by, tip his khaki cap, laugh out loud, then disappear until dinner. That task also fell to me. I never realized I'd actually invent twenty-three ways to cook catfish and canned hash. This was not the lavender paradise I'd constructed. Whole days would go by without human contact. I'd type, file, sweep the cabin, try to wring out my clothes, gather cooking wood, make a smoky fire in the little fireplace, then watch the parade of animals and insects both inside and outside of the house.

Finally—it must have been the third week there—Campbell Livingston decided that Mac was intolerable. Their fight lasted until dawn, ending in two of the big cooking pots being bashed against a rubber tree and a machete thrown at the door. When the toucans began to reclaim the trees next to the cabin, I realized Mac was gone. The pit of my stomach froze. Hellion or not, Livingston wasn't big enough to protect us from God-knew-what-lurked-in-that-river. Even if Mac was a pig, he was an honest pig, he could talk to the Indian guides, he could find his way to the airstrip, he could shoot. I didn't even know for sure whether Livingston could shoot.

"Look, Langley, you have a choice, but if you decide to stay, I promise no more filing. You can come back on the river with me. All right, I'll admit it, with Mac gone, I *need* you on the river. Please?" She couldn't look at me when she asked. The hiss of the pressure lamps and the thrum of the night insects were the only sounds. I stared at her, then, standing so damned tall and straight above my sleeping bag, her smoky hair curling around her face in long tendrils, her fiery eyes low, and those glorious "David" hands stuck into her jeans' pockets. Campbell Livingston was actually asking me for something.

I pulled the bag closer around me. "Okay." My whisper was hoarse, heavier than I'd wanted it to be.

"Okay," she said, and reached out gently, one long finger brushing my cheek. "Okay."

I lay there until the moon rose, spilling liquid silver over me, ambushing me in the middle of my haunting, burning ache.

"They're almost gone, just a few dozen left." Campbell stretched her long, muscled legs in front of her, not so much as making the canoe lean to either side. "It's what made me change direction. The tomb of the Goddess, the last one . . . dolphinlike beings . . . and then, letters telling of a tribe out here with similar artifacts. I hunted a long time, never really believing I'd find more than the myth. But here they are, and the only direction is to protect them, keep them safe, here, as long as we can."

I watched the mammals surface, splashing us playfully. They knew us now, would often come close enough to nuzzle her hand, sometimes shoving each other out of the way for her attention, her touch.

"I wonder what it would be like to make love to a dolphin . . . ," she whispered as we came back.

We heard the motors before we saw the boats. All around us the dolphins were screaming.

"No!" Campbell almost bent in two as she struck the paddle deep into the seething water.

"Ahoy, ahoy! Who are you?" The Adventure Tour Guide's voice boomed over the river.

"Dr. Livingston, Campbell Livingston, and this is restricted water!" She hollered above the roar of their engines and the cries of the panicked animals.

"What? Come in closer, we can't hear you!" The guide was wearing an outfit tailored after Bogart in *The African Queen*. The huge inflatable carried twenty people, all in neon or khaki, many sporting zinc oxide on their faces; all with cameras aimed and clicking. And I was worried about piranhas. . . .

"Goddammit, Langley, paddle! I've got to get these idiots off this river!" Campbell's face was almost maroon with fury. We finally came abreast of the guide.

"Dr. uh, Livingston? C'mon, you're kidding, right? Hey, folks, believe it or not, we didn't set this up! Outrageous! What are you doing way out here in a canoe, Doc?" The snapping of shutters almost drowned out the mosquitoes.

"What are *you* doing here? I have a government permit to be on this branch of the river. I am a scientist doing fieldwork. You have no right . . ." She was almost stammering, her face contorted, witchlike. I thought she was going to climb aboard the raft and hit the guy over the head with her paddle.

"You're way wrong, lady. Look, maybe we took a wrong turn or something, but this ain't exactly posted property. Don't have a coronary! I've got a permit. Let me just get us turned around and we'll be out of here, okay? No need to spoil the day for all of these good people . . . Jesus!" The guide smiled through gritted teeth.

"Aren't you that lady scientist that was on 'Geographic' a few months ago? But I thought you studied pyramids." A large woman wearing a babushka leaned forward, her life vest reflecting orange into her face. A man wearing nothing but hair on his chest and a seedy Speedo grabbed the woman by the elbow and shouted into her face, "Maude, they've got pyramids down here too—remember 'Chariots of the Gods'?"

"Let's get out of here." Campbell pulled hard and spun our canoe around.

"Nice meeting you too, lady. Bitch!" The guide soaked us in his wake.

We fought the river all the way back.

I turned off all of the lamps. Outside, a soft, warm rain bathed the jungle. I listened to the syncopated storm as it played across the face of the river. The forest was coming closer to me, no longer the creeping green terror, no longer the monster waters. I lay there, drifting off to sleep, wondering if the dolphins listened to the rain.

I woke with a start, aware the cloudburst had passed. Outside, the sounds of the night prowlers, in the cabin something more. Then I saw her, sitting, a few feet away, watching, almost keeping guard over me on the porch.

"Campbell? Are you okay?" I rubbed the dreams from my eyes.

Her smile was sad, slow; the ache of it went straight through my navel. God, did she know her effect on me yet? The heavy, wet pull, the throb, almost like the first time I'd seen her in the lecture hall. The sleeping bag fell away from my shoulders. The cooled air stroked my flesh. My nipples went hard with the shock of air and fire of seeing her there, so close, only the mosquito netting between us.

"I didn't mean to frighten you." The hush of her voice had a ragged edge, as if she'd been crying.

I thought about wiggling down into the synthetic depths of the bag, protecting myself from her vision, sure she could see through the net, sure it was another power play, she clothed, awake, watching. But I only moved out of the fiber-filled cocoon, the rising fever washing over me so suddenly I had to gasp. She heard my breath and moved in closer.

"Thank you, for today, on the river. You didn't run, you tried to help. It meant, it means a lot to me, to the dolphins." She pulled back the edge of the mosquito net, moving inside the lacy cave.

I could not move, could not answer. Kneeling now, not in prayer but in the midst of something equally powerful, my body was clenched, poised, wired.

How many weeks had we shared this tiny cabin, barely brushing shoulders? Even in the canoes, we were careful not even to graze toes. Now she was kneeling in front of me, taller by a head, dark, a warrior come from the forest, fully dressed, touching my face with her powerful hands, and her touch burned.

My heart hammered a new language against the pillars of my ribs. I was sure if I died and they performed an autopsy, they would find her name carved in ideograms there.

She moved her palms from my face and let them drift down my neck, stopping only briefly to rest her fingertips at the bend of the great artery as if she were reading the pulse of a jungle drum, reading my desire, reading the fever and staccato yammer she caused in my heart.

All the blood in my body was focused, listening, waiting for the movement of those finely veined hands. She moved over the sensitive skin of my shoulders, rode my flesh like the river dolphins ride the water, trailing over collarbone and then, almost as if she were clasping her palms together in prayer, she moved her hands between my breasts, only the dry, smooth edges barely brushing against my skin. I closed my eyes, not needing to watch—I'd memorized her handsome, sunburned face, those emerald eyes, the fine, high forehead and chiseled cheeks months ago. No, I needed my other senses, needed to allow the sound of my heart, the sound of her breathing, the scent of rainwash and our rising sweat, the minute sensitivity of each pore, every hair as it rose in greeting to her touch. I needed the taste of her, please Jesus, I needed her inside of me.

She lowered her hands, the palms held flat as they brushed across my breasts, making the nipples rise, hard, tight, aching, and I could do nothing, nothing but feel the long, heavy wetness between my thighs, feel the tightness in my throat, the screaming ache of cunt that was going to explode, so swollen, so swollen, oh how many nights had I tried to sleep, the netting a shroud over me, witness to my wide-eyed fantasy, this exact scene played out, played out to the final cut before it could climax. Too dangerous, even for a daydream. How many nights in this same place, trembling, my skin moist in that heated dark, the edges of what I'd imagined keeping me awake for hours. Now, now her hands pulled gently on my nipples, rolling them between her fingers like two fine berries, checking their ripeness, about to pick them to eat. She drew me in closer, close enough to feel the heat rise from her own fever but still not against me. Still kneeling we were, but not touching except where her hands traced new trails over my chest. I could feel her hot, moist, sweet breath over me, a steaming cloud, it made my lips bruise like overripe fruit. I exhaled deeply, almost swooning.

She stopped, her hands dropping from my full breasts, then, in one startling sweep, her hands caressed my lower belly, wrenching such a moan that for moments I didn't realize it had come from me. Pure electric shock at this intimate touch, a full, gentle press, her fingers memorizing my curves and cups of bone and muscle, the flesh stretched tight, and she tracing each outline, the tips of her fingers barely connecting with the moist, curly hair at the top of my mons. I moaned again, afraid I would die with the tickle and wet burn. So much, so much feeling. Never like this before, she was killing me slowly, scalding me with her probe and press.

Her hands tangled in my thatch of hair, pulling and teasing, the moisture now covering her fingers as she played only on the mound, never dipping in, not having to find the eruption. Wet, so wet, wetter even than the rain-soaked jungle only a few feet away, her fingers traced moist circles again and again there, and then, with only the warning of a quick, light, almost feathery brush against my throbbing lips, she plunged one hand deep, deep, opening me wide, splitting me even as this entire ghost dance had split open the night. At the same instant she fell, hard, full body pressed against me, rough denim sudden against my prickling skin, my nipples scraped almost raw by the press of her heavier breast, my belly smashed and yearning against her own tighter one. Her hand moved hard inside of me, against me, and her mouth finally found mine, her hard tongue filling me even as those "David" hands filled me, her teeth biting at my tender-fleshed lips, her tongue all probe and power, sucking me back, sweet fruit, splitting me like a ripened fig, lapping me inside, drinking me like rain, taking my breath into her own body. Her hands pounded against the walls of my cunt, beating a rhythm like the earlier rain outside, playing me like a new jungle drum, forcing another huge storm cloud to build, freeing the lightning

that was running through every vein. I couldn't hold back,
couldn't think, could only let the feelings envelop and explode.
Too much, too much, oh Jesus, what I prayed for but too
much. I was in liquid meltdown, the burn one vast cloudburst of
surrender. No words, no words in a jungle of sense and sound, no
words, only the pelvic thrust and thunder, only the sparking fire
from her fingertips, the buck and grind as she forced me down,
sinking and sobbing and sucking her in, on top of me, this glorious wild beastwoman, and my hands came alive and began to
shuck the clothes from her. I needed the taste of her, needed to
suckle there. So much was being wrenched free, I needed some
back, and she took her mouth from mine, the loud, pulling suck
filling the room, our breathing ragged, hard, bestial, her eyes
flashing gold and ruby and emerald, filling the dark like spark-
lers, filling the dark even as the stars crashed and burned and
filled the night canopy over the cabin, her grinding hips beating
into me, her hands still working, hard and fast and baby slick.
How did she fit, how did she reach so deeply inside and bring
back this joy? She pulled one hand from the cuntcave and
propped it behind my head, then, rising, a behemoth, a goddess,
she lowered her breasts over my face, dragging their heavy lobes
across my burning lips, letting me nip and suck, then pressing
my face to their soft centers, suckling there like some hungry
child, but more, more, the taste maddening me, making me fam-
ished for her salty center. She felt my need, felt me move and
cry and thrash against her, my own coming caught in stop action, my clit between her fingers now, held at that one point.
Heaving back the final release, I broke loose, moved out from
under, gasping, unsure of where exactly I was, only positive I
must have her in my mouth, must have my face pressed deep in
her own jungle, must feel the soft tangle of her there. In the
midst of my own fire, the volcano in check, she, shocked at the
sudden switch, but laughing, wild, willing, allowing anything
in this night, let me strip off her sodden jeans, fling them from
the swamp of bed. I swam down, down her soaking flesh, my
face grazing at her navel, her mons, nipping, tasting, lapping
the wet from her thighs. She held my head, her hands pulling
hard through my hair, sobbing now, in surprise and shock at her

own happy surrender, watching me dive in the dark, like a dolphin, her beloved pet, but no pet, untamed, fierce. Fiercely I took her, the good, clean womanscent and marsh taste, the weighty salt and sweet-tickled burn; her lower lips almost purple in their desire, swollen, swollen, the moisture pearly in the moonlight, and I fell there, my face close and smooth, my teeth tickling the hood of her clit, my tongue another animal, swooping, flat and pressing, around and around, then dipping in, molten, making her scream, her purpled coming like a waterfall, filling me with the sacrament I'd come these thousands of miles to find. She screamed my name, fighting her own legs to stay open, and still I pressed and pushed and wanted all of it, all of her, this burning Amazon, this icon, this renowned scientist now split wide and moaning, needing me as much as I did her.

My hand found my own center, my hips thrust in time to her calls, the sleeping bag a soaking ball between my legs. I pressed against my palm, against its soft embrace. I thrust my tongue and teeth and lips into her cunt and she pressed back, her hands moving over my hair, then up to her own breasts, pinching the ache from each ripened nipple, each sucked nut, until there was no more than could be held in check. The night was ablaze, the stars beating on the roof, calling our names, calling to be let inside, and she was coming, crashing in my mouth, she was coming and bucking and taking me out over the edge with her and the storm burst inside of me, a long, slow, screaming explosion . . . the trembling deep, so damned damned deep, it seemed the hours of ache had built to this final release. The waves not over, not over, she held the edges of this makeshift bed, gasping my name as I echoed hers, my own thunder and rain as yet unstopped. We were so wet and limp and weak in this miracle.

Finally, the hush of the jungle outside a silent witness to our acts, I moved up the long path that is her body, moved over, and through and up, finally meeting her lips again as old friends. And we lay there, arms wrapped tight, legs atangle, cunt to cunt, heartpound to heartflesh, her hair a smoking halo around our heads. We lay there in helpless release. If anyone could see they would see that now, I, too, carry the deep forest in my eyes. . . .

Marcy Sheiner

A Biker Is Born

When I was a teenager, I hung out with a crowd considered by the more clean-cut kids to be "hoods." Like the other girls in our crowd, I wore black elastic pants, gobs of black eye makeup, and a fake ponytail that reached down to my ass. A lot of guys had motorcycles, and the biggest thrill for us girls was to be taken for a ride—and with some of those guys you could be taken for a ride with or without wheels, believe me.

What I love most about bikes is the exhilarating feel of the wind whipping around me and the vibrations of the machine between my legs. There's no foreplay that gets me hotter than a ride on a Harley.

I always wanted to drive a bike myself, to be the one up front, the person in control of all that energy and power. The one time I sat in the driver's seat, though, the bike immediately tipped over. Being a typical female raised in the fifties, I figured it was hopeless, and never made the attempt again.

Before I was twenty I had settled into marriage and babies with a nonbiker, leaving my "trampy" ways, as he called them, behind. As might have been foreseen, the marriage didn't last very long, and in the late sixties I became another statistic—a single mother.

Even though I now had two kids, my wild ways resurfaced after my divorce. I went out with a lot of different men, but I was mostly attracted to the type of guys I'd grown up with—leather-jacketed Brandos with heavy metal machines throbbing between their legs. I even looked up an old boyfriend who took me riding back and forth over the George Washington Bridge while I sang our old love songs in his ear.

One weekend when the kids were with their father, I took the train upstate to visit my friends Ron and Janet. Our old friend Louie arrived unexpectedly on a brand-new Harley-Davidson. Louie and I had at one time been lovers, but it was an affair doomed before it began. We're too much alike—willful and headstrong—to be compatible. In the few months we were together, we tore each other's guts out, until finally we settled on a platonic relationship.

Louie had been talking about getting a bike for years; I couldn't believe he'd finally done it. Ron, Janet, and I all went outside to admire the machine and congratulate Louie on having made it all the way from New Jersey on his first trip. He was struttin' proud in his new leather jacket and boots, high as a kite over his accomplishment. The four of us hung out, listening to music, eating and drinking, playing cards, and generally cracking each other up. There's no laughter as easy or natural as that shared by old friends.

On Sunday Louie took us each out for a spin, he asked me if I wanted to ride back with him to the city. I was thrilled—two solid hours on a bike! Never mind that it was starting to drizzle and that the driver was a novice. I felt like hot shit putting on a helmet and straddling the Harley behind Louie. I just wished I had on black elastic pants and a fake ponytail.

It was nearly summer; the air warm though damp. We set off with a roar. I held my arms tightly around Louie, taking pleasure in the feel and smell of his leather jacket, my body tingling from the machine's vibrations as we sped down the thruway.

After twenty minutes or so, the light drizzle became more substantial and I noticed that Louie had slowed down and was driving with far less confidence than before. I could feel and see the tension in his back, and every so often I sensed a slight wobble in the bike. I looked at his face in the mirror—it was tense and drawn as he concentrated on the road ahead.

I didn't know if I should talk to him or not. Given our history, a word from me could easily spark a battle, especially with Louie in his present condition. As we continued sliding down the slick road, I stared with terror at the huge boulders in the "fallen rock zone," imagining us crashing into them, our blood spattering across the highway. I envisioned Ron and Janet attending our double funeral; I was lost in a reverie of tears and flowers when Louie pulled over near an exit and stopped.

"Are you okay?" I asked.

"Don't start acting like a mother!" he snapped. As I'd suspected, he was in a volatile state. "It's just a little slippery, and I'm not that used to the bike yet."

"I thought you were doing great," I said, trying to reassure him. "In fact, I felt so secure I drifted into a daydream." I didn't tell him what kind of daydream.

Louie calmed down a little. "Yeah? Well, that makes me feel better. But I think maybe we should get off the thruway before the rain gets worse."

"That sounds like a good idea."

We set off again, exiting the thruway and getting onto a slower-paced route. For a while Louie seemed to be more in control, but soon I saw and felt him tense up again. This time he started yelling at me.

"Don't hold onto me so tight, ferchrissakes, I can hardly breathe!"

"Will ya stop leaning on my back, dammit!"

"When are you gonna learn how to lean with me on the turns?"

"Your goddam hair is blowing across my mirror!"

It was the nightmare of our relationship all over again. In the past I'd have yelled right back, but now my life was on the line.

I may not know how to drive a motorcycle, but I know that when you're tense about anything—whether it's threading a needle, having a baby, or riding a bike—you're bound to fuck up, whereas when you do something in a relaxed, easy manner, the moves come smoothly. I had to find a way to cool Louie out before we both became history.

I remembered that the surefire method of calming Louie down was to jerk him off. Of course, he became relaxed after any orgasm, but for some reason, being jerked off cooled him out more than any other sexual activity.

I'd handled plenty of hard cocks inside moving vehicles, but never out in the open air. This would require some preparation.

"Louie," I shouted.

"Whaddya want?" he growled.

"Can we turn down a side street?"

"What the fuck for?"

"Just turn, okay?"

"Ya gotta piss, right? Jeez, you are one pain in the ass!" Despite his complaints, he turned onto a deserted road. I slid my hand down to feel the bulge I'd known would be there, not from lust, but from tension. In the mirror I saw Louie crack a smile.

As we slowly drove along the rutted, narrow road I unzipped his fly, released his hard prick, and began a steady movement. Louie kept right on driving; I wondered how it felt to him to have his cock waving in the wind.

It only took a minute. He said nothing, made no sounds. Afterward, he zipped up his pants, picked up speed, and returned to the main road. All the tension had vanished from his body. In the mirror I saw his face, relaxed and confident as he easily guided the bike down the still slippery road. He reached back and briefly touched my arm; I knew it was his way of apologizing for yelling at me earlier.

Now the only problem was me—after all that, I was turned on. I pressed down hard into the leather seat with my upper torso firmly against Louie's back; with the bike tearing smoothly and effortlessly through space, all thoughts of funerals left my head. I began to fantasize myself as the one in the driver's seat; I leaned my cheek against Louie's leather jacket, shut my eyes, and envisioned myself dressed from head to toe in black leather, expertly steering the Harley through the streets of my hometown. I imagined my old boyfriends lounging against the candy store as I roared up, gave them the once-over, and selected one from the pack. I imagined driving my pick to a deserted spot outside of town. I was just about to fuck his brains out when the bike slowed to a halt. I opened my eyes and saw that we'd arrived in front of my apartment building. Inwardly I cursed; I was inches away from orgasm.

"Well, we made it," Louie said proudly as he parked in front of my apartment.

"Of course we made it. I had total confidence in you."

I got off the bike, removed my helmet and kissed him on the cheek. He lit a cigarette, leaning back on his seat with an air of pride. He looked like he'd been riding the thing forever.

He grinned suggestively. "Aren't you gonna invite me in for a drink or something?"

I looked at him uncertainly, remembering what a disaster our relationship had been. But my cunt was twitching, and Louie's air of self-confidence was an aphrodisiac. I shrugged, and Louie followed me upstairs.

The minute we were inside, his hands and tongue were all over me.

"You really turned me on out there," he whispered, scratching his rough beard against my cheek and sliding his hands under my blouse. I inhaled his strong masculine scent, intensified by the tension of our journey, mingled with the smell of leather. He slid his jacket off.

"No, wait," I said suddenly. I took the jacket with me into the bedroom where I quickly stripped off my clothes, threw on the jacket, and called for Louie to come in.

"You're gonna wear my jacket while we fuck?" he asked, incredulous.

"I wanna see what it feels like."

Louie laughed and shook his head, thinking this was another of my crazy quirks. I helped him undress, then gently pushed him to his knees and pressed my pussy against his mouth. He wrapped his arms around my ass and began to lick around my clit, prying open my wet labia with his fingers. I glanced into the mirror and feasted my eyes on myself, with my long red hair, damp and windblown, flowing down my back, the open jacket grazing my taut nipples, and Louie on his knees lapping at my pussy. Overcome by the vision, I fell back onto the bed. Louie held on, his tongue fastened to my clit. After all the stimulation

I'd gotten on the bike, it took only a few minutes before I was groaning in the throes of orgasm, gripping his head with my legs and grinding my cunt against his mouth.

He climbed on top of me and slid his rigid cock into my palpitating cunt. Slowly and deliberately he fucked me, his hands roaming under the leather jacket to fondle my breasts, his eyes locked on mine. With slow sure strokes he thrust his cock into the recesses of my pussy, and I watched his face crumble in ecstasy as he shot his cum deep inside me.

We fell asleep almost instantly. In the morning, we examined each other warily over coffee. Did this mean we were lovers again? I was terrified of the consequences.

"Still friends?" Louie asked, apparently as nervous as I was.

"Always," I answered. "But—"

"Hey," he said, "this was an unusual situation, right? Let's just say it was for old times' sake. Or better yet, one for the road."

He put on his jacket, and smiled when he caught me gazing at it longingly.

"You know," he said thoughtfully, "you could learn to drive a bike. I could teach you."

"Would you?"

"You bet. Tell you what—I'll come by next Saturday for your first lesson."

Happy as a clam, I walked him outside and watched as he climbed onto the Harley. Slowly he revved up the engine and stubbed out his cigarette. He leaned over, cuffed me playfully on the chin. "You're gonna make a first-rate biker, kid."

Jane Longaway

❦❦

My Pussy Is Dead

Dido's vagina was dead. Her pussy was dead. No manner of book or finger stimulation of any sort seemed to get it going again. She went along as she had, looking the same on the outside with her body functioning much the same as it had before, except for the fact that her pussy was dead.

A young man spent over an hour licking it with his greedy insistent tongue, but she had no feeling down there at all. Her clit expanded balloonlike but she didn't even approach orgasm.

It was, all in all, an annoyance. The young man went on to fuck her, which she tried to imagine was exciting. She tried all the old fantasies; she looked at her lover who was handsome and exotic with long black Japanese hair in a ponytail. He was hep. He had expertise. He desired her. There was nothing wrong with him at all. As a man he was about as near perfection as she had gotten. But her cunt was dead.

She looked at the ceiling of the little square room and then at the mirror that ran alongside the wall next to the bed, a low sort of thing. She could see herself, flattered in the afternoon light, big-thighed, big-breasted with a pretty face like a Persian, only blond-haired. The man on top of her was the color copper with strong, flat muscles which complimented her softness. He was extraordinarily active. It was a pity not to moan.

She thought as she blinked his sweat from her eyes that her cunt was directly connected to her brain and, as yet her brain was still functioning. Those lobes concerned with imagination had run through so many erotic scenes, flipped through old lovers both male and female. Her brain was working. She thought her cunt should be connected not only to her brain (which still functioned admirably) but also to her heart and there was the actual problem. Her heart was no longer connected to sex. Her heart had gone shrinking through the years until it was almost beanlike, hard, not even decorative. A thing you could perhaps trot out at Christmas and funerals. When she realized this she rose up with a shudder which sent her lover into ecstasy. He gave a little yell and came all over her belly, which was round and white like the belly of a pure white cat.

Afterward, they kissed and promised to meet again. Perhaps for drinks some boring Saturday afternoon when it was too rainy or too overcast for anything else. He left with a subdued smile on his face. She, however, was greatly troubled. She lay in her bath, scrubbing away all traces of him, and thought about the state of her heart.

Dido worked behind the perfume counter at Macy's. Mostly she leaned against the glass behind the displays of crystal and precious bottles that smelled of sweet flowers and wicked nights and stared at the people who walked, dazed, through the store. Some of the women were beautiful. More beautiful than the women behind the counters who were for the most part chosen for their beauty. Some of the women who passed her counter were ugly or funny-looking and the rest were plain and wore ordinary pathetic-looking clothing. Dido imagined them all suddenly becoming naked. The lady with the slick handbag and the carmine lips suddenly appeared without her leather coat and black silk suit, without her pumps or expensive pearls. Would her pussy hair be as flaxen as her head hair or as well-groomed? Dido had heard of such things.

It was rare to see a truly beautiful man in the perfume section. Perhaps beautiful men had no reason to buy perfume, but Dido thought that even the middle-aged doctor who had bought a large bottle of *Obsession* and a smaller, more expensive bottle of *Que-sais-je?*, would look much more interesting if his expensive Italian suit, his shirt, his Jockeys, all disappeared and he was leaning with a hairy, pale arm against the counter, his small, pale penis dangling between his legs like a fish.

Of course this sort of thing was no more than idleness at work. Dido loved her job and she loved idleness. She loved the women who made faces at the different scents and rubbed samples studiously over their wrists. The sight of a woman smelling herself gave Dido a tiny jolt of pleasure. But none of these people sparked desire in her, even though she did rub her thighs together vigorously when a handsome, voluptuous dark woman who smelled already of sex, death, and money, charged her purchase of a large bottle of *Opium*.

Still, she had no desire to touch this woman or be touched by her. The woman held the pretty lacquered sack close to her foularded bosom and it sank between the huge breasts like a stone. Dido truly appreciated the gesture, but it did not arouse her.

No, she figured she was lost. She had lost the connection. She twisted a fat strand of yellow hair between her fingers and studied the split ends. There had been a time when some spark might have passed between the *Opium* woman and herself, even a heated glance, but not now. Her pussy was dead.

That evening she went to dinner with her best friend Max, who loved to watch her eat. Since he paid, she obliged him. She ordered grilled salmon and asparagus tips from a waiter who made much more money than she did and who had huge diamonds on his fingers. Max always dieted, so he spent most of the time watching forkfuls of food disappear into her greedy mouth. He leaned forward as she sucked on a spear of asparagus and sighed as it slid into her pink mouth. Usually his desire and excitement charged Dido up, until she felt a thrill every time her small teeth bit into substance. Tonight, however, she merely rolled her eyes when she saw him move forward and she sighed.

"Max," she said, putting the asparagus down gently next to its brothers, "something is terribly wrong with me."

His face registered dismay when she stopped chewing and

started talking, but since she was his friend he drew himself up and folded his hands studiously in front of his plate and asked her what was up.

"It's here," Dido said, being very theatrical and clutching her left tit with such force that she almost brought it out of her dress.

"Do touch up your lipstick, Dido. It's smeared," Max said. He watched her take out a little gray plastic compact and a tube of red with which she regreased her lips.

"That's much better," he said with some relief. "Now about your heart . . . are you in love again?"

"No, that's just it. I'm impotent!"

"Shhh!" Max whispered in despair, glancing wildly around the room at the other diners. "Dear," he said with an avuncular smile, "it's impossible for you to be impotent. You might be frigid although I think in your case that's impossible, too. Perhaps you have burnt out." He closed his eyes and thought for a while, making his forehead wrinkle up. "Well," he said after a pause and then he coughed and said, "well," again.

"It's fucking horrible!" Dido moaned, smashing a forkful of salmon into some thick white sauce. "I don't know what to do about it. What if it lasts forever? When I think about how full of sex I was . . . I want to scream." She threatened him with an open mouth and then continued. "Now, even thinking of Louis, Pat, Marie Francis, or Cenzi doesn't do a damn thing for me. You could stick your fingers up me right now and I'd be dry as a bone."

Max winced at the thought of sticking his fingers anywhere in such a public place. Just then the waiter placed a dish of ice cream in front of Dido and she daintily prodded it with her spoon before she lifted some to her mouth, licking it like a cat with her little pink tongue. Max leaned back and shut his eyes in pleasure. When he opened them she was still lapping at the ice cream with her heavy yellow hair hanging around her face.

"There is always the Fabulous Tony Lee," Max said.

"Nah, it wouldn't work. It's not a matter of size. If it were a matter of size I could use an eggplant."

Max raised an eyebrow and considered the problem. "It's a

love problem, isn't it? I mean it's a love-thing. You need to feel something."

"No way, I hate being in love." She waved the spoon three times in the air in front of her. "Every time I fall in love I suffer. Every time I fall in love it's the absolute shits. I swore I would never fall in love again. Nix on that. No, it has to be something else. Perhaps I should bag it up."

"But it doesn't have to be a person. I mean think about it," Max countered, trying to think of what he meant.

"If it isn't a person . . . what could it be?" Dido asked between licking the spoon.

Dido had skin like a hot apricot and so much of it! Max had dreamed of fucking her for years but subliminated this risk into a pleasure at watching her eat. The girl could put it away. He tried to answer her question honestly, but her big brown eyes looked blank.

"My friend Jeff has one of those New Age places up in Sonoma that has workshops, mineral baths, massage, nature, lots of naked people. I think they give workshops in sensuality. Maybe you need something like that to boot you up. A few days away from the counter at Macy's, running around naked might be the thing."

"Would you go with me?"

"Are you crazy? Hell, no. But I'll pay for it and I'll loan you the Jeep if you take Bosco up with you. He's been so neurotic lately, making poop on the hard pavement. And Jeff adores Bosco."

Dido scraped the bottom of the little silver dish. Of course she would take him up on it but she didn't want to appear too eager. Bosco was not her favorite dog; he took on a high smell in close quarters because of his age. But the thought of leaving town thrilled her.

"Okay," she said.

The trip had been good, Bosco's smell notwithstanding. The minute they hit the tree-lined drive leading to Angel Springs, Bosco set up a howl and scratched with black claws against the window. Jeff Angel was waiting for them both where the road opened out into parking. He was leaning against a signpost that read ANGEL SPRINGS—NO CARS BEYOND THIS POINT.

Dido opened her window and Bosco tried to cram his body through the small space while doing a wild dance on her lap with his hind legs. She flung the dog out of the car with disgust and Jeff was soon down on the ground with him being licked to death.

He looked up and saw Dido's large, shapely bare legs in front of him, then moved his gaze up her thighs to her tiny white shorts and her sweet little belly button, hidden like a secret. When he got to her face, he was wearing a sappy grin.

"I could do him," Dido thought, "but so what?" She smiled at him anyway and he got to his feet, brushing the dog away with his hands. It wasn't that Jeff turned her off but he didn't interest her. She felt glad that she had her Ray-Bans on because it was easier to be polite that way. Jeff carried her small suitcase down to a cabin and waited for her to put her things down so that he could show her the place. Apparently there were not only the sulphur baths and sauna, swimming pool and nature trails but also classes in yoga, t'ai chi and various forms of meditation and movement. The list in her hand was so long and involved that she sat down on the bed and wished that the place had a bar instead of a Vegi-rite juice concession.

She took off her shirt which was sweaty from the trip and wiped her breasts with it. Jeff hovered in the doorway like a bee. He had one of those cute California ponytails, a thin, fierce face and a bulge in his pants like a fist.

"Well, let's go," she said.

"Ah, you can go totally nude if you like," he said, and something in his voice led her to believe that *he* would like it very much. Anyway, she wanted to keep her shorts on because it had been a struggle to get them on in the first place and for her money they could stay there the rest of the trip. She put on a straw hat and a pair of zoris and they went off side by side to explore the resort. It wasn't crowded, being the middle of the week, but the people there seemed happy and languid. A number of them were playing volleyball; another group sat in a circle talking while others lay out in the sun getting brown as toast.

"Max told me you were having some sort of problem," Jeff said.

"Ah, Max!" Dido kicked at Bosco who was running between their legs trying to tackle either. The dog was in heaven.

"The baths are down over here and that big brown building is where the classes and massage are; over here, if you follow this path, is the swimming pool." He took her by the elbow and walked her over to a small clearing surrounded by bushes. "Over here, that cavelike thing where the towels are hanging is the sauna. Max said something about you having sexual problems and I want to tell you that we have a sexuality program you're welcome to join. It's on the handout I gave you. I think you might like it."

Dido looked at him and lowered her sunglasses. "I am impotent," she said, and seeing him about to protest her use of the word, she put one hand over his mouth lightly. "I am. My pussy is dead. I can only have mechanical orgasms. Men don't interest me, women don't interest me and I don't interest me. That is my problem." Saying this she removed her hand and wiped it on her shorts.

"Well, maybe you just haven't had the right lover," Jeff offered.

Dido let out a laugh that sounded like a bark and put her sunglasses on; she walked toward the sulphur baths with Bosco at her heels and Jeff had to trot to catch up with her.

"You don't have a towel," Jeff yelled and she shrugged her bare shoulders in reply. He watched her ass strain the white cloth that bound it and let out another feeble protest. "Dogs aren't allowed near the baths."

"Take him back then," Dido said, turning toward him momentarily. He looked like someone whose ship had left the harbor leaving him behind as she turned again and strode away, big fat white butterflies circling her head.

There was a group of young men sitting on a low rock fence. They looked like computer programmers or young executives although they were as naked as savages. One stood up in a mock bow. Dido stared at his pale prick, half-swollen in greeting. She knew herself to be an object of desire and stood there for a moment with her big-nippled tits pointed right at him. Three of the men looked away but the one she was aiming at boldly came up to her and introduced himself as Eric Maybear. He was young and eager with a sort of doggy look to him and his dick kept hitting her on the hip. She pushed it aside with her hand but it kept bobbing back. Eric didn't seem to notice since he was busy talking about himself. He followed her right up to the disrobing room and watched while she took off the tight little shorts and folded them up into a white little square. He lunged for her then and there, grabbing one soft breast in each hand and holding on for dear life while she swatted at him with her hands.

"We could do it right here," he said a bit breathless. "It would only take a minute."

"I'm sure it would." Dido swished past and left him in the dark damp room by himself.

The tub was huge and smelled slightly sulfuric. Six eyes fastened on Dido as she carefully put one foot then the other into the hot churning water. It was delicious to slip into the slick warmth which covered her to her neck. As soon as she finished sighing she noticed the three people who were watching her through the steam. One was a black woman who smiled lazily at her. The other two were a couple who immediately started kissing each other. Dido simply relaxed and shut her eyes, opened her legs to the pulsing jets, let her heavy breasts bob up weightless in the water, and felt the tension of the trip leave her body bit by bit. The heat made her body feel like a flower opening out and out, hugely pink and soft. Just as she was sinking into the luxury of her sensations another person entered the tub, setting up a wake of water. Dido opened her eyes and right beside her was a large man with the sharp features of an American Indian, eyes like live coals and black hair tied back in a ponytail.

He edged a little away from her, then sank down in the water so that only his eyes were revealed. They were dark eyes and they didn't look at Dido but seemed to be focused on some distant point. When he surfaced, his profile was handsome, strong and imperial, the nose fine and noble. Dido was looking at this face when she felt a hand (and it could only be his since it was not her own) move gently up her thigh and right between her legs. It seemed extraordinary at first. The fingers moved into her cunt like a hermit crab looking for a new place to live. Dido opened her legs wider.

The man didn't change his facial expression one bit but continued to stare straight in front of him with his eyes half closed and a rather stoic look to his mouth. Dido was pleased when the fingers rubbed her clit, and shifted her body so that he could hit the right spot. It was bizarre but it actually excited her.

His hand seemed quite sure of itself.

The other people were unaware. The black woman continued to smile at Dido and the couple stayed wrapped in each other's arms, the woman occasionally nibbling on her lover's ear.

When Dido tried to touch the man's cock with her hand, gliding between his smooth thighs, he stopped her abruptly. He put her hand back on her own turf, so to speak, and then and only then continued his rubbing and searching of her hidey-hole. She abandoned herself to his attentions, all the while keeping her eyes wide open, staring first at the black lady who smiled lazily back and then at the couple who, for the most part, ignored her. The finger moved against her clit-button until she was ready to explode; she bit down on her underlip and moved against the digit. It rubbed and stopped, rubbed and stopped, and then just stopped. Before her impending orgasm the finger left and for a while her legs scissored the water in desperation. It felt like her cunt was on fire with no firehouse in sight. A quick rub with her own hand brought almost instant relief, although she moaned so loud that the couple were clearly startled. The Indian, however, did not respond at all to her dirty looks but stared straight ahead at nothing.

Dido put a little distance between them. Her pussy still smarted as it had been a violent orgasm—comparable to an umbrella opening up inside her and catching fire. Well then, she thought to herself, it is happening anyway. I started to get all loose and shivery, open and wet before the bastard pulled his finger from my pot. Maybe it's nature or the hot water that's making me feel more relaxed, or maybe it's because this man is still staring at nothing at all and so, in effect, I had sex with a finger and not a person. Dido pondered this for a while until the warmth of the water submerged her into a long laziness where she thought of nothing at all.

The couple left the tub and two men entered it, talking rapidly and intensely of draperies. Dido felt she had spent enough time in the water so she got out and showered. The woman from the tubs followed her into the shower area and once again smiled at her. It was a rather provocative smile. The woman began rubbing her own body vigorously with a loofah sponge so that her skin began to take on a coffee-colored sheen. Her nipples were large and she rubbed those tender things with the loofah as well, causing Dido to widen her eyes. The woman turned and offered to rub Dido's back for her, which felt very nice indeed, but when the woman began to swack Dido's meaty bottom with the loofah and rubbed it almost raw, Dido pulled away. The woman pulled her back by her blond pussy hair, laughing a low sort of "ha ha" real far back in her throat, and whacked away until Dido's ass felt inflamed.

Drawing Dido toward her with her incredibly strong arms the woman fell to squeezing and massaging Dido's titties, rubbing her own full warm body against her. Dido figured she had landed in a strange place indeed. Although her ass cheeks stung from the loofah, she felt wild heat grow inside her and once again she longed to play with her partner. But the minute she reached out to touch the woman's large soft breasts the woman removed her hand. Dido allowed herself to be alternately fondled and spanked for some time until the woman gave her a final love bite on the neck and left to dry off with a large turkish towel.

"Wait a second," Dido called out, but the woman only smiled and disappeared with the towel slung low over her hips.

"Damn," Dido said aloud, finishing up her shower. She walked back to the little room where her shorts and sandals were and bent over to pull the tight shorts over her aching cheeks. In that moment, and it was so sudden that she gasped, an arm was around her waist and a large, smooth cock was working in and out of her pussy. She was shocked at first and began to protest but the cock felt so right going in and out that soon she was moving herself to accommodate. Feelings were opening up inside of her that were extremely dangerous. Her pussy was flooding with moisture, and the urge to let go completely presented itself to her like a flaming imperative. Just as she started to moan and respond to the thrusts of her unseen partner, he withdrew, leaving her trembling on the little cot. She turned to catch sight of him, but all she could see was one sandaled foot leaving the door.

At this point she was pissed. She lay down on the cot and played with her cunt which was engorged and frustrated. Her fingers were wet with the juice and dipped in and out of her sex; she felt insatiable. Still she couldn't come. She wanted to suck and lick something so she put a finger into her mouth and tasted herself.

Although she tasted quite good, big tears were running down her cheeks because she wanted someone. Her pussy was on fire for someone and even with masturbation the orgasms didn't satisfy. She calmed herself with her fingers, then pulled on the little white shorts, put on her sandals and sunglasses and went out into the sunlight. There was no one in sight so she walked on in the silence of nature until she came to a creek where she sat down and stared at the water.

The sun was very hot so she stretched out on the ground. It was an idyllic spot with a tiny white stream, low-hanging trees, wild grasses and the smell of hot sulphuric springs and warm earth. Barely into a nod she felt someone nuzzle at her crotch. She leaped up screaming, "No, you don't . . . not this time, you bastard," only to find it was Bosco. Jeff was right behind the dog, standing on a rock and looking fondly at her. He had a bottle of juice which he offered her. She sipped at the drink while venting her anger at the manners of the clientele he had at Angel Springs.

Jeff scratched his smooth face while Bosco played with two tiny orange peels. "Well," he said after some thought, "you did get turned on. You did get heated up."

"But not satisfied!" Dido protested.

"Then come with me to the quiet room," Jeff said lowering his voice.

"I don't want you!" Dido said rather unkindly. But Jeff was undaunted. He insisted she come with him and told her that he would do nothing that would in any way upset her. Reluctantly, she followed him to a small low building with shuttered windows. They left Bosco outside.

Inside it was dark. Thick tatami mats and several futons were on the floor and pots of incense filled the air with dark fragrance. Bodies were in supine positions, and in the dim light Dido could see that they were either sleeping or meditating. The couple from the hot tub clung together in a corner.

"I don't need a nap!" Dido hissed but Jeff gently pushed her down on a futon and told her to take her shorts off, which she did. Then he told her to close her eyes, which she also did. She heard him get up and leave. In a while she relaxed and started to enjoy the quiet; then she felt someone rubbing her feet softly and gently. This felt wonderful so she kept her eyes closed and enjoyed the nonintrusive massage. Another pair of hands began to work on her breasts, touching as lightly as insect wings brushing against her nipples. Hands were now working up her thighs, opening her legs. Her nipples were covered with lips and were sucked on until they were stiff. She could make out the profiles of the people who surrounded her but she couldn't see their faces clearly, nor did she want to. A tongue was in her cunt, licking her wet. A big thick cock was placed between her lips and rubbed over her teeth. She sucked like a baby on it. It excited her to be handled by so many at once, so many fingers, mouths, tongues, lips, cocks and pussies, hands, hands all over her body. Her pussy was flooded, hot and honey-thick with juice.

A cock went into her pussy while fingers played with her clit and pink asshole. Her mouth was engaged with a warm cunt all buttery sweet and Brillo-pad wild with hair. She felt herself lifted up, turned over and penetrated from behind. No longer was she bound by her ego or her skin but expanded into pure sensation, every cell trembling and on edge until the orgasms started rolling through her, making her fling her arms around the hips of the dark woman who straddled her face and burying her face between those strong thighs; moaning and cursing into that dark sweet hole.

The fucking went on long after her orgasms came to a stop. She was flung from one level to another, not closing up but opening more and more until she reached the absolute limit of her pleasure. Wet and exhausted, she struggled from the embraces of her lovers, which she now realized numbered four. Her body idled like an overheated car and she fell into a soft dreamlike state and thought about why the anonymity of her lovers excited her so much. Somehow it had made her regain her sense of wholeness. Perhaps it was because there was no shred of relationship, no need to be anything but alive in her own body and complete in that.

She dozed in the darkness, listening to the sounds of the couple making love in the corner. She gave herself up to the darkness.

Margo Woods

Wheelchair Romance

It still hurts to talk about my affair with Richard. I met him at a birthday party for a mutual friend. All I noticed at the time was that he was quite good-looking, gray-haired, and that he lived in a wheelchair.

Several months later our mutual friend approached me, saying that Richard was accustomed to paying for sex, and that he had noticed me at the party. The friend knew I was desperately broke, had exchanged money for sex in the past, and probably would not be freaked out by a guy in a wheelchair. He asked me if I would agree to see Richard.

Hey, no problem. After I saw Jane Fonda do it with Jon Voight in *Coming Home*, I realized that functional legs were not necessary for sex.

We met in a bar. I wore an orange silk blouse that made my reddish hair look redder and showed off my small, round tits. I wore blue jeans to show off my little ass and long legs, boots to make me look even more sexy, and several necklaces fell between my breasts. I towered over his wheelchair until he invited me to sit down. Then we were equals. He remarked about my braless tits right away, and after a couple of drinks asked me to come home with him. He offered me $100.

He drove a yellow Cadillac equipped with controls. He opened the door for me, wheeled himself around to the driver's side, heaved himself into the front seat, and leaned back over to his chair to fold, lift, and slide it behind his seat.

His apartment was small with an entry directly off the street. I was learning what it is like to live in a wheelchair: no stairs, no rugs, lots of space between furniture. He had exquisite taste, however, and the apartment was beautifully decorated, filled with plants, and blessed with a sound system that made any music a mystical experience.

So we drank a little more, listened to music, and I smoked some grass. He said his favorite drug was coke, but he was out at the moment, and he refused my grass because he said it made him sick. When it came time to go to bed, I watched him heave his body from the wheelchair to the bed, then grab his legs and haul them over. His torso and hands were well-developed from all the lifting they had had to do, and they were as handsome and attractive as his legs and pelvis were strange and withered. Attached to his left leg was a heavy plastic bag connected by a tube to his lower belly, apparently emptying urine.

I jumped into bed beside him, curled up in his arms, and began to kiss him.

I'll always remember Richard's mouth. In addition to having a remarkable sculptured shape, it was also the most pliable, sexy, delicious mouth I have ever encountered. We must have kissed for hours; long, deep kisses in which I easily became lost. I love the feeling of drowning in a kiss, of disappearing into a sea of sensuous feeling. It's a magical experience for me, in which I stop thinking of myself as a person or my partner as a person and am conscious only of the rushing, rolling, and trembling of sexy feeling in my body caused by the connection of two pairs of lips.

And I remember his arms, which held me and caressed me and kept holding me like the everlasting arms of God the Father. I loved the way he held me.

"Play with my tits," he said after a while. "I haven't used the lower half of my body for so long that all my sexual energy has moved to my tits." And it was true. Not only were his pectoral muscles well-developed, but his nipples were as big as my own. And very sensitive. He liked to have them sucked, of course, but also twisted, rubbed, and pinched. He went into ecstatic states when I teased and played with them.

But he kept steering me away from his cock. "It doesn't work," he said. "My back is broken in the lumbar area." So we concentrated on my body and the top of his, and I forgot about his crotch for a while.

He was extremely good at sucking my tits. He was so sensitive to my reactions and able to tell whether and when to do what. When my hand slid down between his legs again, it was greeted by a very long, hard cock, with a slight bend on the end. I was startled and confused, because he had told me it didn't work, but I really wanted that cock in my mouth or in my pussy. Reluctantly I let him guide my hand away from it and back to his tits and his mouth and his godlike arms. Why wouldn't he let me have it? His cock wasn't necessary for orgasm, because I could come with him eating me or sucking my tits while I played with myself, but I wanted his cock too, and I hoped I would get another chance at it.

The next day I was still in a glow from being so well-loved. I was deeply satisfied with this man, and I was waiting for the next phone call. The $100 wasn't bad either.

In the following weeks and months we got together many times, almost always at his place, occasionally at a bar. He refused all my invitations to movies, drives in the country, or any other sort of entertainment, and he never took me out to eat except breakfast after we had spent the night together. It was just too much trouble for him to get around. He had his world arranged around him—his stereo set, his magnificent record collection, his multiple cable channels, and his VCR. I didn't mind sitting for hours with him, appreciating the sights and sounds that came out of this equipment. But what really endeared him to me was his lovemaking.

Recently a new lover asked me what I liked in a lover. I replied, "Tenderness and enthusiasm." Richard had been both tender and passionate, making me feel like I was the most desirable and sexy woman on earth.

I'm quite sure that I take sex more seriously than most people. An affair without sex, or without good sex, is disappointing compared to one which is garnished with sexual energy. I am always confused and chagrined when a lover makes sex unimportant. And I am very likely to cross him off my list if he doesn't have lots of other interesting characteristics to recommend him. So Richard was high on my list at that time.

He really did love coke. He sent me running all over the county to get little piles of white powder with which we laced our lovemaking. Of course it meant we were into all-night stands, and of course it meant that I didn't see his cock get hard again after the white powder appeared. Once in a while in the morning, before he did his first lines, he would get semi-hard, about half of what I had seen before. But he always dragged my hand away when I tried to do something with it.

One time I turned him on to mushrooms. I have always experienced them as a positive drug and I hoped to wean him away from coke so that he could have more erections. However, far from being a positive experience, the mushrooms made his legs twitch violently—a natural condition for a person with his problems, which he corrected by continual use of Valium. Something about the mushrooms overrode the Valium, and instead of enjoying the trip, he twitched uncontrollably for hours. He was very angry at me and turned his back on me for the entire night, making me feel abandoned and paranoid. Luckily the next morning the symptoms were gone, along with the anger.

Toward Christmastime he started getting very romantic with me, saying I was his lover, and telling all his friends he had a lover. I took the bait, and waited for his phone calls. Christmas night, after the festivities were over, I went to visit him. We drank champagne and watched the Playboy Channel. He confessed he had no money and asked if I would let him pay me with his love. Of course by this time I wanted him so much that the money was just a little frosting on the cake, and of course I hopped into bed.

I was going to New York the next morning to visit a friend and get away for a while. The trip had been planned for a long time. Over breakfast Richard moaned, "How am I going to get along without you?" I assured him that I would return.

One of the things I do when I travel is look back at my home and think about what's going on there. I think about my work, my writing, my kids, and my friends and lovers. In New York I thought a lot about Richard. It was clear that he was no longer a client, this was a love relationship. I missed him terribly and called several times to tell him so. We were both very gooey over the phone.

I thought a lot about his cock. I wanted another chance at that tall member with the curved end. I had been a consulting therapist in a sexuality clinic a few years before, and I knew that men with spinal cord injuries sometimes get erections when their cocks are played with, even though they have no sensation in their genitals. Then the doctors give all sorts of drugs to regulate the body and its processes, many of which inhibit erections. They often don't tell the patient about the side effects, or give him any choice as to whether to take the drugs. With large quantities of alcohol, cocaine, and Valium laid on top of an already weakened sexual response, Richard's sword didn't have a chance, except in the mornings when some of the drugs had worn off, and on that first occasion, when there was no coke, and we had the added excitement of the first time. I wrote him a gentle letter, explaining these things, and also asking him for money to help me rent an apartment.

When I got back from New York, I called to say that I had returned. He was friendly, but he didn't ask me over. Nor did he call me in the next few days and weeks. I was crazed. "What is happening? What have I done? Was it something about the letter? I shouldn't have asked him for money? I shouldn't have talked about his cock?" I resisted calling him for three weeks, and then finally dialed his number to timidly ask if anything was wrong. He said no. "Then why haven't you called me?" I shrieked. "I don't know," he said. "No special reason." What could I do with a response like that? "All right then," I said. "I'll leave it to you to call me."

He did call once, several weeks later, and asked me over. I was nervous and confused, and my heart wasn't in it. We did everything we used to do, deep kissing, holding and hugging, lots of tit play for both of us, oral sex for me. My body reacted as usual, proving that it does have a life of its own, but my heart was in pain. I was surprised that I could make love to him with my body and not my heart, and I wondered if he could tell. In some ways our lovemaking was the best it had ever been. If he had been able to explain what was going on with him in the last few weeks perhaps we could have bridged the gap and been open to each other emotionally. As it was, he paid me and I left. He never called again.

For weeks I tried to sort it all out and recover from the shock of being dumped. Was it the money? Was it my references to his sexuality? What was with this guy and his cock? The very last time we made love, up to our eyeballs in coke, he grabbed his soft cock and whipped it furiously for a long time. It was the first time I'd seen him touch his cock. I found it very erotic and told him so. Most men like to hear such things.

But Richard gave me only the barest notion of what was going on in his head during our affair. Still, he couldn't hide the reactions of his body, and I know his heart participated for a while.

But that was the last time I saw him. I imagine that by now he has found another woman who hasn't fallen into a personal relationship with him, and he is paying her $100 each time they get together.

Tea Sahne

There's More of You

We were getting ready to go to bed. As always, Alex, who slept naked, was quicker than I and was already under the covers when I was still getting into my nightgown and robe and brushing out my long hair. " 'He had unusually short forearms,' " I said; "that's my first line."

"What do I care?" Alex said. "I'm cold, and I want to make love. Can't you come to bed?"

"Nope, not quite yet," I said, putting my brush and hairpins down on the mantel, checking that the fire screen was tight around the last glowing embers of the fire and picking up the sheaf of paper from the table beside my side of the bed. I settled into the wingback chair in the ring of light from my bedside lamp. "Not until you listen to what I wrote tonight," and I read. . . .

He had unusually short forearms. Though he was a very big man, nearly six-and-a-half feet tall and burly, his hands could barely reach down around the cheeks of her buttocks when they made love. More than a foot shorter than he and less than half his weight, she perched on him, arms and legs furled around his barrel chest and round belly like a small fragile spider tackling

331

a great furry bumblebee. His raised thighs pressed hers higher against his sides and wider apart, pulling open her vulva, vagina, anus.

As he strained to reach lower, into her wet, open cunt with his thick fingers, his shoulders were drawn down hard against hers, compressing her breasts against his. If she hunched her back then—hollowing her chest—and squirmed sideways, she could make their erect nipples—hers cold, hard, almost damp—brush. Sometimes she came then, shivering, before he had let his penis even touch her.

But she preferred to wait, moving her hips up a little and forward, willingly offering her genitals to his probing fingers. His short arms would press harder, crossing back past her waist and under her hips, as his fingers reached from behind for her labia, pulling them aside to insert first his right forefinger, then his left as well, into her vagina, feeling his way into the ridges and folds, at the same time filling her with his hands and pulling her wider and wider open, exposing her clitoris too, to contact, until she felt a channel being opened up through her fully exposed self into the pit of her belly—even higher, up through her abdomen and past her navel, hands opening and making her open, beyond mere sexual parts, even up into her gut.

His fingers worked in and out of her bursting vagina until her breath came in gasps, drawn faster and faster.

"What do you want?" he would ask hoarsely. "Tell me what you want now."

"I don't know, I don't know," she would moan. "Put your cock in, too—don't take your hands away!"

And he'd say, "No, not yet. Come for me first. This way."

"No," she would wail hopelessly.

"Yes, yes, like this," he would hiss and he wouldn't stop. Arms straining across her buttocks, he'd put his full hands over her then, one thumb first slowly, carefully worming its way into her anus, and then the rest of his fingers into every spreading fold of her vulva, working his hands forward and back rhythmically between her legs, higher and higher forward, harder against her pubic bones, and deeper, too, under them, more insistently, stroking, kneading, pressing out, stretching out her clitoris into its blazing, screaming, naked miniature erection.

"Come," he'd whisper; demand. "Come, come now!"

And when she couldn't stand the pain ballooning from her agonized clitoris up through her belly any longer, she always would, whether she wanted to or not, pulled wide open yet encapsulated in his hands—crying out—sometimes laughing wildly—bucking upward from his torso, then collapsing into it . . . coming, coming, fully into his hands.

I was still sitting in the armchair beside the bed, but Alex was out of bed now, too; half kneeling before me, half into my lap, not at all caring, as I had teasingly hoped and intended, about whom I had been writing. We had done this before—reading aloud what I had written or (it turned us on just as much) what someone else had. For both of us, words made what we were doing more intensely real, doubly lived through whoever's experience mirrored ours in the prose. Subsumed into that undifferentiating world of passion, body pressed against mine, not caring by whom or how I might have imagined being turned on as I wrote, Alex cared only about being with me here and now, part of the acts themselves.

I looked down at the wisps of Alex's black hair against the pink of my robe, the tan-peach glow of my flesh where my nightgown was raised aside. Darker, glowing rosier than my skin, darker even than the purplish-rose of my engorged cunt, Alex's blunt fingers pried into me. Even in that detail Alex's hard, athletic definition was a vibrant contrast to my pliable softness.

"Wait," I said, my voice muffled in the growing confusion of sex, of Alex's mouth now devouring me, "and listen."

Sometimes he came then, too, before entering her, and without her ever having touched his penis. He loved feeling her come into his hands that much. But it didn't matter. He was amazingly virile. After she had recovered her breath and giggled, she delightedly snuggled herself around his torso and under his chin while he lay with one protective arm around her, peacefully sniffing and licking the fingers of his cunt-gored other hand. If she so much as licked his neck or eyes or the corner of his mouth, his penis began to harden again. It would bulge upward suddenly if she slid down along his side and licked and nibbled one of his nipples. She could turn her head sideways and watch, or put a hand down and feel it happening—she could do that until his penis was fully, enormously erect again, listening to him suck in his breath if she closed her teeth on a nipple, flicking her tongue quickly against its trapped, sensitive end-pores. He would press his hands harder against the sides of her waist or the small of her back then, pressing her into himself; but she would make him wait, as he had her, swelling in gradually less controllable spasms of increased pain and ecstasy.

Then, in one quick move, she would shift her weight over him and bring her vagina down unerringly around his engorged penis. Or she would draw out his pleasure and pain longer, moving her body away from contact with his, kneeling beside him, then slowly, without touching him with her hands, take first the tip, then more and more of his penis into her mouth, mimicking his hands as she rhythmically worked it further and further, teasingly, inch-by-inch down her throat until its tip touched her epiglottis. She could not feel what happened when that contact was made, but knew that this gag-reflex bit of her flesh must do something when his penis touched it, because it always made him sigh and moan and clutch for her hair and breasts or face. If she withdrew very far then, his hands always sought her cheeks and chin and lips, touching his penis, too, urging her to take it back deeper into her mouth. She would, bit by bit, wrapping her tongue around it from one side, then the other; and she would touch him then with her hands, too, one cupping and rolling his testicles, the other sweeping over his belly and chest, tweaking a nipple and swiftly moving on flat-palmed, inserting a finger, then two, then three into his mouth.

Always, as more parts of her body became engaged with his, she would feel herself swelling and moistening again, no matter how completely she thought she had already come. She would want then to make him say, "Please, now!" as she sometimes begged him when she felt she could not bear not to come, but could not bear either to come unless his penis was inside her. But he never did then—or she did not give him time to. She would hear his breaths coming faster, and drunk with the craving to have his semen inside her, with one strong, last, base-to-tip-long suck, she would release his penis and swing herself over and down onto him. Their genitals were like magnets to each other. Without the need for groping hands, his penis always slid firmly, solidly, completely into her vagina, and, as their arms gathered their bodies into one another, he—crying out in half-groans, half-grunts (and often she again, too, crooning, whining)—would come.

He liked to talk to her afterward; nonsensical, half-enunciated, affectionate clichés as likely as not. Lying with his eyes closed, his arms around her loosely, they felt the gradually diminishing, warm, after-shock pulses in their still-joined bodies. Their couplings always reached climax so quickly that neither of them lost arousal immediately, and sometimes they began to move again against each other almost without meaning to, as if in an initial rather than last stage of intercourse. A few times, they did indeed within a short time resume, slowly, serenely, for the sheer pleasure of the motion in and out of each other, without at all expecting to come again; though once, to their delighted astonishment, they both did. More often, one or both of them fell asleep while they were still joined. But usually they waited drowsily for his erection to subside and his penis to slide out of her. Her small "Ohs" of dismay as it did might have seemed a mere ritual if both of them had not known it was a shared loss and regret she expressed.

And then they slept. Often for the first hour or so, she was still at least partly on top of him. If her body was in an especially awkward position, she would waken and move to his side, and in his sleep he would automatically draw her back against him. If they slept then all night, still they would waken in the morning touching. If she stirred first, it was to lift her head and look at his face; and he, without opening his eyes, would draw her head down against his chest. She would wrap her small self against him so hungrily that she wakened breathless. And then, however it happened, it would all begin again.

* * *

I shuffled my sheets of paper together and lay them aside. Rammed into the chair on top of me, nakedly beautiful and small, her knees dug in on each side of me between my thighs and the chair's arms, cunt to cunt and all the rest of her body pressed to mine, Alex seemed to be asleep, exhausted with the simultaneous experience of what I had read and what had happened between us. Her arms were around my shoulders, her forehead against my neck. Her curly hair bristled against my cheek. I put my arm around her and kissed that rough tousle.

"I love you," I whispered. "Nothing I write is as wonderful as you are—none of it's more than a hairsbreadth or forefinger joint to you. It can't be . . . Alex?"

"I know, I know," she answered groggily. "How could I care if it were? Love you—*have* you. Come to bed now."

Catherine Tavel

Claudia's Cheeks

Claudia had a problem. Some women might not have considered it a problem, but Claudia certainly did. You see, Claudia had a beautiful ass. A big, bouncy, beautiful ass. And everywhere she went, people wanted to fuck Claudia in her big, bouncy, beautiful ass. Truck drivers said lascivious things to her rear end as it innocently crossed the street. Gray-haired dykes had an overwhelming desire to spank her bottom. Whenever Claudia met people for the first time, that was the first thing they noticed—her plump and pretty posterior.

There were drawbacks to having such a juicy, jangly behind. Claudia hated wearing panties, but whenever she didn't wear them, she would cause a commotion. There was never a doubt in anyone's mind that she was panty-less under even the loosest of skirts. Her ass enjoyed the freedom and insisted upon jumping out in all directions. Strange men would smile, follow her, and tell her to have a nice day. Even the constriction of control-top pantyhose did no good in quelling the allure of her sweet cheeks. And a garter belt? It greatly enhanced Claudia's already-dangerous curves. Tight stretch pants, the current fashion rage which other women seemed to wear with no problem, resulted in minor traffic disturbances when Claudia wore them outdoors.

Claudia didn't know exactly how to take the praise which was lavishly bestowed upon her rump. She liked it when men looked at her, even when the spittle collected in the corner of their mouths. She thought random erections were the greatest compliment a man could give a woman. But to be labeled and lusted after solely for her pear-shaped ass? There was so much more to Claudia than that.

For instance, she had an adorable face, expressive brown eyes not unlike a sad cocker spaniel's and soft ruby lips that more than one gentleman had referred to as a "cocksucker's mouth." True, Claudia's breasts were minuscule, a handful at most, but they were unique nonetheless. They were topped with dusky dun nipples that poked out more than a half-inch when she was hot. And she was hot very often.

Claudia was slim with long shapely legs that seemed to go on forever. They looked especially nice locked around someone's neck in missionary position when her cocksucker's lips were open and panting, and her sad eyes were heavy and dark with passion. That's when Claudia looked her best, when she was being fucked. Her lovely feet were topped with toenails that were always painted bright red and her left ankle always sported a thin chain of white gold. When Claudia watched her legs propped up upon a fellow's heaving shoulders, she felt especially naughty and slutty. And she liked that.

Then there was the matter of Claudia's cunt. It was an exceptional cunt, decorated with pudgy outer lips and fudge-shaped folds within. Like an exotic flower of some variety, if you pushed the outer petals apart with your fingers, you would see that Claudia's cuntlips graduated to a rich shade of pink. A two-toned cunt, a lover had noted. And Claudia's slit was so, so tight. Sometimes too tight. If you slid even one finger inside, the resilient walls of her pussy would cling and suck on that thin digit.

Claudia had a tiny clit at the top of her pussy. You really had to work to make it come out and play, because it was hidden under small flaps of flesh. But Claudia's clit loved to be kissed. If you nursed on it just right, then it would get stiff and stand out like a delicate corn niblet. Sometimes it took a great effort to make Claudia come, but when she did, it was well worth it.

To see her writhe and moan and spasm was quite a magnificent thing. You could feel her demure pussy throbbing against your face, as if gulping and gasping for air. Claudia's pussy would throb for a long time after she came. Men thought it particularly wonderful to stick their prick inside while it was still pulsing, wet and gushy.

But alas, many men didn't take the time to get acquainted with the intricacies of Claudia's pussy. A few licks, a few pokes, a few fondles and they wanted to dig their fingers into her butt-hole, flip her over like a one-hundred-and-fifteen-pound pancake, and dive into her derriere. Or else they wanted to fuck her doggy-style so they could at least gaze at her glorious orbs jiggling with each stroke. Then they could play with her cheeks, knead them like warm bread dough and grapple with them to their heart's content. Sometimes they would even pretend to fall out of her cunt and then try to put it back into her ass, thinking she wouldn't notice. But Claudia knew all of their tricks.

Claudia had a few tricks of her own. She was skilled at deep-throating cocks way down to the hairy balls. Her favorite fellatio posture was on her knees. She especially liked to lick a man's testicles while her throat engulfed his boner. Men liked this too, but usually in combination with squeezing her firm hindquarters in both hands. If a guy stuck a finger up her tush, Claudia would stick her finger up his. He usually got the message—dry digits weren't much fun.

Claudia was also very good at being on top, but rarely did she get the opportunity. Although the man could occupy himself with twisting and tweaking her sensitive nipples and cupping her bouncing ass cheeks in his hands, he generally wasn't thrilled because he couldn't actually *see* Claudia's ass bouncing. Thus, her enthusiastic performance would be trashed. Sometimes the fellow would ask her to turn around so that she was still on top but with her back facing him. Claudia didn't like this position because the man couldn't see her eyes smoky with desire. Not only that, but he could easily pretend that he was with someone else. Claudia felt very unconnected, and it seemed almost an impolite posture. Plus, it was both uncomfortable and unnatural. The walls of her vagina went one way, the curve of his

erection went the other. Claudia could feel the rock-hard cock
pushing the wrong way inside her. It grated upon her nerves,
almost like fingernails on a blackboard. Perhaps it was a good
position for women with wide cunts because it might make them
feel smaller. But for Claudia, it seemed to go against nature.
Like ass-fucking.

Few men knew the significance of Claudia's rump-humping
aversion. Whenever she tried to relate what a terrible experience
the first time had been, instead of feeling sorry for her, guys
would get incredibly turned on.

When Claudia was eighteen, she had dated Mike McCall, who
was twenty-eight. There was an edge of nastiness to him, but
they always seemed to have hot, rough sex. Maybe it aroused
him that she was so innocent and that he was only her second
lover. Perhaps this is why he fucked Claudia so hard. Perhaps
he just had a mean streak, but Claudia, who liked to give people
the benefit of the doubt, thought he acted like that because he
was afraid of falling in love. The rougher he fucked, the less it
felt like love.

In any case, Mike could munch on Claudia's almost-virgin
pussy for hours. He enjoyed making her talk dirty, too. Their
faces just inches apart, he would pound her like a sledgehammer
with his short, fat prick. Claudia would let loose with a litany
of filthy phrases, which Mike liked a great deal. She would bite
his neck and he would bite hers. It was a purely physical relationship. That was evident, but Claudia kept trying to make
Mike fall in love with her. She had been raised to believe that
making love was far superior to fucking. Actually, both were
pretty good, but thanks to people in her past like Sister Elizabeth
and Sister Mary Colleen, Claudia couldn't appreciate sex for sex's
sake. Not yet, anyway. The truth of the matter was that Mike
saw Claudia as just another chippy. Mike McCall couldn't see
women any other way, but Claudia, for one, was much, much
more. She just had to realize it herself.

Claudia and Mike worked at the same newspaper, him driving a truck and her behind a typewriter. On occasion, he'd dry-
hump her against a nearby mailbox. One time, he even lured
her into the back of his panel truck and had her suck his cock.

It was wintertime and it was freezing. Claudia took a while to find the shriveled little sausage buried in his long johns. Eventually, she did and she slurped at it until he came in her mouth.

One day, when they were at his place, Mike McCall said to Claudia, "I'm going to fuck you in the ass." Claudia didn't feel strongly about this one way or the other. She had never given much thought to her anus. It was an erogenous zone which she pretty much ignored. But that night, she told Mike okay because she figured it was about time to give her asshole a test drive. Maybe it would even make him fall in love with her.

What happened next was somewhat foggy in Claudia's mind, especially since her back was turned during most of it. She seemed to recall a jar of Vaseline on the floor. Whether it was ever uncapped or actually used remained a mystery. Perhaps it was only there as a prop. There was little in the way of anal foreplay. Claudia didn't even recall Mike sticking a finger up her behind. The next thing she knew, his stumpy, chubby penis was wedged up her rear end. Or at least it was trying its best to get up there.

Another thing Claudia remembered—it hurt like hell. Mike hadn't been the least bit considerate. Both of them were on their knees on the floor. He pressed her face against the daybed's mattress so that she could hardly breathe. This upset Claudia to some extent. Breathing was an extremely important function to her, especially during sex. As she struggled to get out from under his iron grip, she was almost crying. Mike's penis tore at her virgin orifice. Yet somewhere behind the pain, somewhere behind his lack of respect for her, it felt almost good. Then came the sensation that she had to go to the bathroom. Very intensely.

"I have to go to the bathroom," Claudia told Mike.

"No, you don't," he said. "That's the way it's supposed to feel."

Claudia wanted to ask him how he knew this tidbit. Had he ever been fucked in the ass? But whether it was supposed to feel that way or not, one thing was for certain: Claudia had to shit. "No, you don't," Mike insisted, pumping into her posterior without missing a beat.

Claudia started to cry. "If you don't let me go, I'll shit all over you." But Mike wouldn't listen. The more Claudia begged and struggled, the harder and faster he thrust into her tushie. "I swear . . . ," poor Claudia sobbed. But Mike didn't seem to hear. He was lost in a tight, dark, ribbed tunnel otherwise known as Claudia's asshole.

Claudia dug her elbow into Mike's chest. She cursed and cried some more, but nothing seemed to work. Mike only stopped reaming to pull out and shoot his cum all over her bare bottom. Then he collapsed on top of Claudia and sighed, "Oh baby," in a soft voice.

Claudia couldn't shit for three days.

Most men had the same reaction when Claudia finished telling this sad tale concerning the ravaging of her rosebud. Instead of it acting as a deterrent, they wanted to bang Claudia in the butt even more. It wasn't that the men were cruel or heartless (which all humans often are), but that Claudia was so unintentionally titillating in her guiltless candor. It was the *way* she told the story that got them so aroused. The sorrowful saga describing how Mike McCall squeezed into Claudia's cheeks always gave listeners blistering erections, which they tried to mask with their fists. Instead of the story illustrating how carefully one must approach an anal encounter, it made guys want to tear at Claudia's heinie, and then some.

Claudia's friend Jerry had a slightly different reaction, however. Jerry was a porno actor and had performed unsafe sex with the best of them. Although Jerry wouldn't have minded bopping Claudia in the buttocks either, at least he could be a bit more objective. He burst out laughing at her anal sex story. "That'll teach you to let a guy named Mike McColon near your asshole."

The episode with Mr. McCall left Claudia with a memorable souvenir—hemorrhoids. Once upon a time, her bunghole was a cute, puckered, winking thing, but now it was swollen and quite deformed. Even when she told her many admirers about his misfortune, they still didn't care. They still wanted to boink Claudia in the behind.

Since anal sex seemed to have such a fan-club following, Claudia decided to try it again this time with a gentler man, Charlie. Charlie didn't particularly like assholes. "It's dirty up there," he told Claudia with a grimace.

"I know," she said, "but so many people like to fuck them, they must have some sort of charm."

Reluctantly, Charlie lay on his back while Claudia positioned herself above him. She lowered her ass cheeks onto his stiff pole. It went in fairly easily and it hurt less than it had with Mike McCall, but it still couldn't be called a pleasant sensation. And just when Claudia was getting the hang of it, she looked at Charlie's face. It was all scrunched up, as though someone were forcing him to eat raw liver. Claudia stopped pumping. She felt like an anal rapist. After she wiped Charlie's dick with Ivory soap and a blue washcloth, she gave him a blow job. He seemed much happier then.

Claudia hadn't had anal sex since that time, but she was constantly on a quest to broaden her hinder horizons. She read about women who masturbated with broomsticks and chair legs up their rectums and couldn't understand why. A liberated kind of nineties gal, Claudia tried getting off a new way. With the middle finger and forefinger of her right hand, she made a fleshy V and invaded both her pussy and her posterior at the same time. It felt . . . interesting. She was especially intrigued with being able to feel both digits moving through the thin membrane of skin between. Very adventurous, she also got her thumb into the act and employed it by rubbing her clit. A confusing configuration, to say the least. Claudia felt like a circus juggler but did manage to have an explosive orgasm. Her clit was wiggling. Her pussy was spasming. Her asshole was twitching. It was a well-coordinated effort, but not something she could enjoy as a steady diet.

More than anything, Claudia wanted one special boyfriend, but there was no one. It was a never-ending odyssey. Claudia was becoming tired of guys only wanting to fuck her in the ass. She continued to meet new men who wanted the same old thing. She was tired of having to tell the Mike McCall story over and over again. She was tired of being recognized by former boyfriends from the rear. Although she had the perky kind of behind which women sought to achieve through ruthless repetitions of Jane Fonda workout tapes, Claudia didn't see herself as fortunate or blessed. Beneath her bouncy dream butt, there was a warm, loving lady. But no one could ever see past that protrusion. There were other things about Claudia which were pretty wonderful, but men often ignored these numerous niceties. She was tired of being judged solely by one beautiful body part.

In a perverse way, she saw the AIDS epidemic as an escape. No one in their right mind would want to butt-fuck, no matter how tempting, no matter how perfectly pear-shaped the behind. She was right, in part; still, far too many men were willing to use a condom to get into a cute behind like Claudia's. But she found even this repulsive.

So Claudia spent many nights at home alone. She sat in front of the TV and watched reruns of *Dallas* and *L.A. Law*. She made buckets of microwave popcorn and topped them with gobs of butter. She munched on Chocolate Babies and Doritos while flipping the remote control. And when she was horny, Claudia masturbated with a cute guy in an X-rated video who alternately lifted weights and jerked off. He didn't see Claudia as a body part. In fact, he didn't see Claudia at all.

Pretty soon, Claudia's thighs started rubbing together when she walked. She had to buy queen-sized L'eggs pantyhose. She favored skirts and pants with elastic waistbands. In a few months' time, the smallest actions—even shaking Jiffy Pop popcorn over the stove—exhausted her. Soon, she couldn't even bend to paint her toenails a bright, slutty red. The polish eventually chipped off. The white-gold ankle chain didn't fit around her ankle anymore.

There was no doubt about it. Claudia was on the road to becoming humongous. She didn't care about much except stuffing her face. Food became almost like sex to her. It was practically orgasmic to stick a fluffy Twinkie between her lips, to lick the melted puddle of Häagen-Dazs from the bottom of her dish. It gave Claudia great pleasure to spoon sour cream straight from the container into her mouth, just as it did to devour crunchy peanut butter, marshmallow creme, and all the rest. Men finally stopped calling Claudia on the telephone. They finally stopped seeing her as a body part, because now she was a blob. Claudia was one huge body part.

Before long, Claudia realized that the person she was hurting most was herself. Her cholesterol level skyrocketed and so did her blood pressure. Sure, the guys had liked Claudia's stream-lined frame, but more important, she had liked it, too. And she missed it. Claudia didn't hate men. In fact, she craved them, but she just hated the way they treated her sometimes. She also hated the slaughtering of seal pups and the destruction of the rain forests, but she wasn't about to leave the planet.

So Claudia went on a sensible diet. The sight of a Twinkie soon made her gag, as did soggy Oreos in milk. Claudia bought a membership at Jack LaLanne's. Gradually, she was able to bend and paint her toenails once again. Claudia worked her way up to three sets of a hundred sit-ups and mastered the Universal machine. Many months down the road, as she pedaled the ex-ercise bike, she noticed the eyes of the male patrons at Jack LaLanne's intently studying the curves of her ass as she rode. But it didn't bother Claudia as much this time around. Claudia had already decided that she wasn't going to be the victim of her own ass any longer. But then, throughout her life, she had al-ways seemed to be a victim of one thing or another.

One evening after work, Claudia went to a neighborhood pub to enjoy a white wine spritzer and to relax. The bar stool framed her once-again gorgeous butt alluringly. An entire softball team seated at the table behind her gasped in adoration every time she moved. This didn't upset Claudia. It did just the opposite. Claudia squirmed in her seat as often as she could just to torment them. She now realized the power she possessed in her cheeks. She had something that other people wanted.

Before she was halfway through her spritzer, a handsome man walked into the establishment and sat a few stools away from Claudia. From where he sat he couldn't even see her buns nestled snugly on the vinyl seat. All he could see were her long, delicate fingertips toying with a straw and her serious, abandoned puppy eyes. Very politely, he introduced himself as Al. Very soon, Al and Claudia were engaged in friendly conversation which touched upon everything from Hemingway to dolphins to Billie Holiday to the names of the Teenage Mutant Ninja Turtles. Claudia refused a second drink, but couldn't decline the invita-tion to an impromptu dinner next door at East China. Slithering from the bar stool, she took note of the expression on Al's face when he saw her ass for the first time. It was a look of surprise and delight. But instead of feeling angry or hurt, Claudia felt proud.

After pungent mu shu pork and curried shrimp that tickled her tongue, Claudia took Al home with her. His kisses tasted faintly of jasmine from the tea. It had been a very lovely evening and a very long time since Claudia had been with a man. She lured Al into bed. When she peeled off her sensible businesswoman's skirt to reveal black lace G-string panties, Al sighed loudly. Then he said, "Wow."

"Wow is right," Claudia told him. They kissed and groped hungrily. Al palmed Claudia's nether cheeks as though they were fabulously fleshy basketballs. "Mmmmm," said Al.

"Do you like my ass?" Claudia asked. And before Al could answer, Claudia was stroking it. He watched her with a thin smile on his lips. She rested on one side, like a pensive Cleopatra, taunting him with her motions, with her words. "Touch it some more," she cooed. He did. "Spank it." He didn't.

"I don't like hitting people," Al explained.

"But I'm asking you," Claudia emphasized. "*Telling* you."

Al still didn't move, so Claudia spanked herself. It didn't hurt, but sort of tickled. Red blotches stained the meaty surface. Soon, you could decipher her palm prints. "Don't you like to watch it jiggle?" she asked. And Al nodded.

"Kiss my ass," Claudia whispered to him. "It's beautiful."

"It is," Al agreed. "But I've never been a 'butt boy.' "

"You will be," Claudia said. "Starting tonight." She drew herself onto her knees like a lace-clad kitten. She cupped one warm, firm globe in her hand and traced a feathery circle onto the skin. It felt very, very nice indeed. "Come on, kiss it," Claudia told Al.

The commanding, yet gentle tone of Claudia's voice surprised even her. Al's eyes were glazed with lust as he listened. He seemed almost hypnotized, and did just as she said. There was a little thread of spittle in the corner of his mouth. Al took each of Claudia's hips in his hands and drew her ass toward his face. His kisses were feather-light, yet they penetrated her to the core. She felt a sea of goose bumps rising on her flesh. Al softly spread her cheeks apart and soon, Claudia's chocolaty sphincter muscle was winking around his tongue.

A few moments of this made Claudia's pussy hairs very damp. "Don't you want to fuck me?" she asked. It was a rhetorical question, but Al answered anyway. With a grunt into her rosebud. From the nightstand drawer, Claudia pulled a string of condoms and ripped off one with her teeth. (She was horny, but she wasn't stupid.) Al's dick was rock hard with anticipation. Claudia rolled the lime green rubber onto his long, slim rod, careful not to snag his pubes. With her legs spread wide apart, Claudia offered Al her milky, white globes. Instead, he slid into her pussy. "No. Up here," she said, gesturing to her tongue-moistened crack.

Al bit her neck. "I've never done that before."

"Do you want to?" Claudia wondered. He was tugging on her nipples now.

"Yes," he answered, but it was more like a gasp.

"Then I'll show you how." Claudia carefully backed onto Al's sheathed prick. For a moment, she almost laughed, feeling like a truck backing into a tight parking space, but the wave of pleasure, intensity, and almost-pain stopped her. It tingled and tickled and twitched. Al didn't move. He just groaned and made small gurgling noises, his hands still at his sides. Claudia moved her rump up and down on his cock. Slowly. Deliberately. For the first time in her life, she felt that *she* was doing the fucking and not getting fucked. And Claudia liked it. She liked it a lot.

Every so often, a droplet of Al's sweat plunked onto her back. He reached around and stroked her clit, taking it between two fingers, almost jerking it off like a tiny cock. And then a strange thing happened: Claudia came. While gasping and sobbing and collapsing onto her belly, Claudia somehow managed to wiggle a finger into her pussy. She felt it throb and contract. She also felt Al's friendly dick through the membrane of her perineum. And do you know what it felt like? It felt like power.

You see, Claudia had finally learned how to get on top using her bottom.

Molly Brewster

Double Date

"Look at those bedroom eyes," Nadine whispered, taking a long swallow of her drink.

"Where?" I asked, gazing around the bar, trying to be unobtrusive. Though exceedingly nearsighted, I never wore my glasses when Nadine and I went out on a Friday night. The idea was to be devastating and maybe meet the love of my life, so glasses were left in the car. "I don't see him."

"Jill, I can't point him out, you know," Nadine spoke, barely moving her lips, ostensibly staring off into space. "He's at the end of the bar. The one with the sandy curls. A mustache. I can't believe you don't see those blue bedroom eyes. You are truly blind. And now he's looking right this way." Nadine spun around on her bar stool, facing now into the room and away from the bar.

"Oh, yeah, I see," I replied a little too loudly. He wasn't only looking this way; he was looking at me. I felt myself flush under his inspection. Not my type at all, I thought. Attractive, well-muscled, but too macho. I liked more softness in a man. Besides, I never liked mustaches.

"Stop staring," Nadine hissed. "Turn around. You're missing some other nice sights. Look at the tall one in the green sweater.

348

Looks like a lawyer. I bet he's rich. I'm so sick of men who can't afford to buy me a drink, much less dinner."

"I'd rather they were nice than rich," I replied.

"You are so naive. Don't you think a rich guy can be nice? Besides, if he were rich enough, I might not care how nice he was." She lit a cigarette and took in the whole bar in one sweeping glance. "Oh, here comes Bedroom Eyes. But he's practically a dwarf. He sure is cute."

He was making his way through the crowd, heading in our direction. Nadine, having dismissed him as too short, was now in animated conversation with a thin man with a beard. The man with the sandy hair and compelling blue eyes got closer, two bar stools away now, and was looking right at me. Into me was more like it. I was helpless to turn away. I stared wide-eyed, with my heart pounding and a flush creeping up my neck. He was nearly a head shorter than me, but that didn't seem to matter.

Just as he reached Nadine, she hopped off the bar stool, and grabbed the arm of the thin, bearded man. "Let's dance. I love this song." The two of them moved toward the dozen squares of parquet that passed for a dance floor, and Bedroom Eyes slid into the seat Nadine had vacated. I pretended to be unaware of him, but that was the biggest lie. My eyes ached to look at him.

"You are the most beautiful woman in this place," he declared in honey tones.

Oh God, what a line, I thought, but his voice was even more compelling than his appearance. I glanced nervously at him, scarcely able to breathe, and found the deep blue eyes looking steadily into mine.

"You are, you know. All these women"—he gestured, dismissing the crowd around us—"they'd kill to have what you have."

"What's that?" I asked, trying to modulate my voice in what I hoped was an aloof-sounding way.

"Sex appeal. You are the sexiest woman I've ever seen. Those long legs. The way you move. And your mouth when you smile. I can hardly stand it. You're gorgeous."

As he talked, my mind kept saying, What a line. No subtlety at all. How come no one else has ever noticed how gorgeous I am? But my entire body melted as he talked, his voice hypnotizing me and his blue eyes caressing my limbs. I glanced at his hands and noticed the small blond hairs above the knuckles. He didn't push a pencil with those strong hands. I couldn't help imagining what it would be like to have his hands on my body.

"You sure like to exaggerate," I said with a smile and a flip of my long hair. I drained the last of my glass of wine.

"Oh, darlin'. The way you toss that hair around is really turning me on. What's your name? Here, I'll buy you a drink," he said, gesturing toward the bartender with my empty wineglass.

After he paid for the drinks, he moved his bar stool closer to mine. I felt his warm breath on me and my head spun with intoxication at his nearness. His name was Lee.

I don't think I ever drank that glass of wine, because the next thing I knew I was standing in the parking lot with Lee's hands sliding up under my sweater. His head was buried in my breasts and I pressed up against him. He ran his hand down my thigh, making low sounds in the back of his throat. "Oh, I want to wrap those long legs of yours around my neck."

"You don't mind that I'm taller than you are?" I panted.

"Mind? Oh, darlin', I've dreamed of legs like yours. I love your legs, your whole luscious body." He grabbed me tighter and pressed his mouth to mine. Was he swallowing me or was I swallowing him? His tongue moved about my mouth exploring and caressing. When we broke apart gasping, his mustache was covered with our saliva. I reached over and touched it, deciding I liked the mustache after all. He pulled my finger into his mouth and thrills raced up and down my body.

"We need a bed," he purred. "Let's go find one." With hardly a moment's hesitation, I climbed into his pickup truck and moved close to him. As he drove out of the parking lot, I slipped my hand onto his thigh, and he groaned with longing.

As soon as the door closed behind us in the motel, he began undressing me. "Oh, what breasts you have," he hummed as he held them in his hands, his tongue tracing circles around my erect nipples. I unbuttoned his shirt and pressed my bare breasts against his hairy chest. He unzipped my skirt and it fell to the floor. He began working my pantyhose down, kneading the flesh

on my thighs and buttocks. I pressed against him and felt his
hard cock straining against his pants. As I pulled the zipper
down, he moaned with anticipation. His pants down, his cock
was released and moving against me. For a short guy, he sure
had a large penis.

Pushing me onto the bed, he separated my legs and caressed
the inside of my thighs. He moved his mouth toward my moist,
willing lips. His tongue moved around the outer lips, toyed with
the clitoris, and then thrust deep into me. I was panting and
giving out little cries of pleasure. What a tongue. Raising my
head, I looked down my body to see his curly head between my
thighs, his sandy mustache, now covered with vaginal juices,
sweeping the dark curls of my pubic hair.

"Oh, I want to feel your whole naked body against me," I
cried, my fingers in his hair. He rose up and lowered his body
to mine, and every pore of my flesh opened to receive him. His
fingers now reached deep into my vagina, his erect cock pressed
urgently against my belly. Then he raised himself, lifting my legs
into the air, and plunged his swollen penis into me. I cried out
with a sound that brought tears to my eyes. He moved fast and
hard, thrusting deep, then pulling almost all the way out, then
plunging all the way in again. His muscular arms encircled me,
pressing us together. I grasped at his back and moved in rhythm
with him. Flesh against sweaty flesh, cock into cunt, climbing
to the peak, both of us crying out as he came, pulsating, filling
me with his cum.

We lay in a sweaty heap, panting and gently moaning. After
a few minutes, he propped himself on one elbow and ran his
other hand up and down my body. "Oh, Jill, you are somethin'
special. I could make love to you all night."

"You're something special yourself." I smiled at him, thrilled
that he wasn't the kind that fell asleep and snored in the afterglow. I fingered the soft, curly hair on his chest, and watched
his hand moving on my skin.

We talked and cuddled, and after a while his cock swelled
again in my hand. I sat up and bent my head toward this wonderful cock, first gently licking, tasting, exploring the soft skin,
then opening wide and taking him deep into my mouth as he

writhed and moaned on the bed. Soon, he leaped up, pushed me back on the bed, and entered me again, with such force that it was as if we had not made love only a short time before.

In all we made love, I think, five times that night, snuggling, giggling, and talking in-between. It was incredible every time.

As we reluctantly got dressed, I remembered Nadine back at the bar, and that we'd gone there in my car. I looked at my watch; it was long past closing time. Oh, well, Nadine was resourceful. Besides, she liked going in my car, so she wouldn't be encumbered with me if she found someone she liked. I usually drove home alone, being less bold than Nadine.

Lee, now dressed, looked at me deeply and stroked my face. "Jill, I know this sounds like a stupid question, but did you come?"

"You mustn't worry about that," I said.

"I want you to have every possible pleasure. Pure ecstasy is what you deserve."

"You've given me that in spades, love," I replied.

"But did you come?"

I shook my head. This man could see right into me and wouldn't be fooled by the usual evasive answers. I had to look away to think. "I don't come with fucking, so don't worry about it."

"How do you come? I'll do anything for you."

"So far just with a vibrator," I replied. Why was I telling him all my secrets?

"Well, next time I see you, we're going to try that vibrator out, and after a while, you're gonna come lots of ways. I think you just need more attention."

"Whether that's true or not, I love your kind of attention." I wondered if Lee was right.

"What's your phone number?" he asked, tearing the corner off a piece of motel stationery. I gave it to him, but I thought that this had been too good to be more than a one-night stand. I'd probably never hear from him again.

But it was only a few days later that he called. "Oh, darlin', I've got to see you. I can't stop thinking of your long legs and your sweet honey pot. Do you think your friend Nadine might want to meet my friend Tom?"

Saturday night Nadine and I sat waiting in my living room. Both of my children were with their father for the weekend. "Did he say how tall his friend was?" Nadine asked.

"Six feet plus. They must make a funny pair." I smiled, wondering if I'd still like Lee as much.

"Well, I hope Tom's good-looking, and not some kind of weirdo."

I heard their steps on the stairs and felt my panties grow moist. I opened the door and there they stood. Tom was a regular Tall, Dark, and Handsome, but I saw only Lee, and had all I could do to keep from ripping off his clothes.

After introductions, we settled down for some awkward conversation. Nadine and Tom sat at opposite ends of the couch. I poured wine into four glasses, then sat on the floor. Lee sat down next to me with his arm around me. He was obviously as hot as I was. Why had he insisted on bringing Tom to meet Nadine? She was being outlandishly rude, as only she can be when she doesn't like someone. Why she didn't like Tom, I couldn't tell. He was certainly attractive and seemed like a nice guy, too. Not rich though. Both Lee and Tom were truck drivers. After argumentative attorneys who made love in the dark, and boring intellectuals who thought sex was a five-minute sport, I liked making love with a truck driver who really loved sex and could do it all night. Both Lee and Tom were pretty macho, definitely not Nadine's type. For the first time, that didn't sound bad to me.

Tom tried to make conversation with Nadine but she put him down at every turn. Meanwhile, Lee's hands became more and more aggressive. Nadine turned her back on us, which meant she had to face Tom, who appeared to take no notice of our heavy breathing and moving hands. Lee, his breath hot in my ear, whispered, "I want to see your bedroom." I protested, gesturing toward the duo on the couch, but he pulled me to my feet. "Just for a few minutes."

Once in the bedroom, we tore off our clothes and were on each other, in each other, fucking like maniacs. I was hungry for him, insatiable. There could be no "few minutes" for us. At one point, I thought I heard Nadine leaving. On and on we went, touching, sucking, licking, tasting every inch of skin. After we exploded with cries and moans and his hot cum gushed into me, I remembered Tom in the living room. I didn't think he'd left with Nadine, so what was he doing? I became self-conscious thinking about him sitting out there listening to us, but Lee showed no sign of leaving my side. He was holding my breasts in his hands, alternately tasting the nipples and nuzzling my neck.

"What about Tom?" I asked.

"Oh, he'll be okay. I'm not done with you, not by a long shot. Maybe he and Nadine are getting it on."

"She left. Didn't you hear her slam the door?"

"Jill, when I'm making love to you, the only thing I hear is your sweet moans." He was moving his hand up and down my thighs, barely brushing my moist outer lips. Involuntarily I moved toward his hand and he obligingly slid two fingers inside. "Oh, what a beautiful cunt you have."

"What a beautiful cock you have."

"The better to fuck you with, my dear." With that his cock grew hard and he moved on top of me again.

I heard a footstep in the hall. Tom was definitely still in the apartment. "Lee, I think you should go see about Tom. I feel bad about leaving him out there, while we're in here . . ."

"Okay, okay." He sat up and thought a minute. "Jill, I have a favor to ask you." He paused and took my hand. "Would you . . . go to bed with Tom? It would mean so much to me if you would. You are sooo fantastic. You'd do so much for him. Would you, please?"

I sat bolt upright. Entranced as I was with Lee, the idea of having sex with Tom didn't interest me very much. But what the proposal said about Lee really excited me. I took a deep breath and began hesitantly, "Well, there's only one way I could do that." He didn't say anything, but he turned his blue eyes on me eagerly. I couldn't look him in the eye. "Have you ever been three in a bed?"

"Oh, darlin', wait right here." Depositing a kiss on my mouth, he grabbed his pants. "Back in a flash."

When Lee returned to the bedroom with Tom, I felt too exposed. I pulled the sheet up around me and let my hair fall across my bare breasts. "Oh, no, Jill, I've been telling Tom how beautiful you are, so don't go hiding under a sheet." Lee slipped out of his pants and climbed back into bed. Tom sat down on the other side of the bed, at the very edge. I looked at him and smiled. Slowly he took off his shoes and set his glasses on the nightstand.

"Are you blind now?" He nodded. "That makes two of us. I guess we'll just have to feel our way along," I said, smiling and reaching for his hand. He moved a little closer and I worked at the buttons on his shirt. Tom was more than good-looking. He was an extremely sexy man. Dark, dark eyes and shiny black hair. Long, thin, but muscular limbs. I felt myself becoming aroused as I touched his smooth, nearly hairless chest. Or was I just so turned on to Lee that I was hot for any man who happened along? I leaned forward and touched his face. He kissed me, at first tentatively, but when I slipped my tongue between his lips, he opened wide and thrust his tongue deep into my mouth. I savored the new sweetness of his mouth, a different flavor from Lee.

As Tom struggled out of the rest of his clothes, Lee drew me to him, "Oh, Jill, you're fantastic. Look at the hard-on I got, just watching you kiss Tom." Lying on my side, I wrapped my arms around him and lost myself to kissing him. I felt Tom slip into bed behind me and move up against my buttocks, pressing a very hard cock against the backs of my thighs. Lee's equally hard penis pushed against the front of my thighs. Surely this was heaven.

As I continued kissing Lee, I arched my back and lifted my buttocks to allow Tom to enter me from behind. His large hands moved up and down my legs and buttocks, and he moved his penis in and out, slowly and deliciously, making me writhe and pant, which seemed to excite Lee as much as if it were his own organ sliding in and out of me. Our three sets of legs became more and more entangled, and hands were touching and caressing and loving every which way. So much skin, all moist and sensual, like a dream, only this was really happening.

Afterward, we sat up in bed and smoked cigarettes, talking of our pleasures. How rare it was to find a man who wanted to talk about sex at all, and I had two who wanted to do it and talk about it and then do it some more. We giggled and told tales of our sexual adventures. They told me about the time Tom left some woman's house so rapidly that he left his shorts behind. Lee insisted that I was so fantastic he couldn't remember any other women. I told them about another time I'd been three in a bed, but that time with a man and another woman. They went wild, wanting to hear all the details. "I like this better. Two men all for me. I can't think of anything nicer. Have the two of you ever been in bed together like this before?"

"Not quite," Tom replied. "Almost, though, one time. Remember that redhead, Lee?"

"Oh, yeah! Too bad she chickened out. Me and Tom have been buddies a lot of years so being in bed together—with you that is—seems natural in a weird kind of way." Lee was busy caressing my inner thighs as he talked.

"Yeah, it is," Tom agreed. "When I first walked into the bedroom, I thought: I can't get into bed with Lee, but somehow once I got my clothes off, it felt fine, even when sometimes I wasn't sure whose leg was whose."

As the cigarettes died in the ashtray, Lee and Tom began caressing me, and before long I was aroused again. "Where's your vibrator?" Lee asked matter-of-factly. "I want this time to be just for you."

No man had ever done this with me. I was nervous but eager. Reaching under the bed I pulled out the already plugged-in vibrator. Before I could explain anything to Lee, he had taken it from me and was applying it gently to just the right spot. Tears welled in my eyes as he brought me quickly to the edge of coming. Tom was pressed against me, his cock once again hard and eager. Lee just looked at me with those incredible blue eyes and kept the vibrator humming. Like inching to the edge of a waterfall I moved toward orgasm, building, swelling, breathing hard, opening, and then up and over the edge and into thin air with a cry. "Oh, Lee . . ." I breathed as he tossed the vibrator aside and climbed on top of me while Tom caressed and kissed me. After having made love with Tom and then come with the vibrator, my vagina was juicy and hungry for Lee's tireless cock. We grinned at each other as if we'd invented sex.

"Too bad Nadine missed all the fun," I said.

"Well, I don't miss her," mumbled Tom.

"Nadine who?" quipped Lee, still moving in and out, kneading my buttocks with his hands.

Then there was no more talking, as Lee moved toward his climax as my body opened wide to receive him. Tom's cock in my hand was hard and excited, and the three of us moved together on the bed, higher and higher, electricity shooting through us, then gasping and crying out with bliss.

We lay quietly, three happy people, now tired as the sky started to lighten. I drifted off to sleep, curled up against Lee and with Tom wrapped around me from behind.

Martha Miller

Seductions

We watched sun dogs in the winter sky all the way down I-55. Every now and then the wind blew up dark clouds, and then they passed. I looked at Elli. She was smiling, swaying gently, sometimes humming with the music from the tape player: "Diamonds and Rust."

I had talked to my friend Judy that morning. I'd told her about my ex's new Mustang, my shattered self-esteem. She said her first husband took a European vacation when they broke up.

I said, "I feel like I've been abandoned. Even though I threw her out."

"K.C. *made* you throw her out. You didn't want to."

"After she started the new job she was angry all the time," I said. "She treated me awful. It felt like she was my worst enemy and I never did anything but try to love her."

"It sounds like she wanted out and didn't know how to do it."

That hurt. Judy was right. But why? What did I do? K.C. had always told me I was special. Was that just another lie?

I rubbed the ring imprint on my finger. It had taken four years to get there. I wondered how long it would take to go away.

Stubble fields sped by. They were dotted with snow. It was mid-January.

Cahokia had been Elli's idea. I think.

I had said I wanted to see the new museum on one of her visits. She suggested we leave my kids with their father and go today. She'd driven two hours north to pick me up and now we were headed south again. We would see the museum, have dinner, and drive home. Six hours on the road. Was she that interested in the mound builders? It seemed extravagant. But, in the past weeks I'd come to think of Elli as just that.

I looked across the car at her. She was small.

My ex and I were both large women. K.C. was shaped like the Venus of Willendorf. I'd found beauty in that. Never thought of wanting anything else. Elli was shaped different: round hips, slim shoulders, small hands. I was three inches taller and probably outweighed her by fifty pounds.

I'm going to sleep with her, I thought. If I can figure out how to bring up the subject. How had I done it with K.C.? I tried to remember. A voice in my head said, "Stop it. She's just being friendly. You haven't had sex for a month. Your thinking's distorted."

Okay, I thought. I won't sleep with her. I don't want to mess up a good friendship by hitting on her. I need all the friends I can get right now. Besides, she always had much younger lovers. I'm not her type.

"Look, there's another one." Elli pointed at the sky.

On either side of the sun were spots of rainbow colors.

I looked at her round thigh, faded jeans, western boots. Maybe if I said, "You just broke up with your lover. I just broke up with mine. We could help each other out."

"Do you have any Carole King?" I asked, shuffling through her tapes.

What if she were horrified? Put me out beside the road? I decided to wait until we were home before I brought it up.

I remembered our conversation a week ago in a restaurant. We talked a lot about sex. She kept bringing me back to it. What did I like? How often? Did I think it was too soon? "She wants you," said a voice in my head. No, I thought, you're reading sex into everything. Chill out.

It was late afternoon when we pulled off the interstate. A

strong gust of wind blew an empty paper bag. It turned end on end in front of us, then fell behind the car. .

"I'm going to sleep with Elli," I had told Judy during one of our daily conversations.

"That's nice."

"Do you know anything about seduction?" I asked.

"Sure."

"How does it go?"

She laughed.

"I'm serious. I want a flow chart."

"You mean if 'yes' then . . . , and if 'no' then go to . . . ?"

"Exactly."

"How soon do you need it?" She was still laughing.

"Tomorrow. Cahokia."

"You think the mounds will get her in the mood?"

"They'll remind her of cunts," I said. "Everything reminds her of cunts."

"You don't need to seduce *that* woman."

I watched Elli walk ahead of me toward the museum. Her round hips bounced with her quick dykey stride. Her body went in where K.C.'s went out. It was distracting. I tried to imagine her naked. Tripped over a curb.

"Okay," Judy had said. "First you give her long looks. Lots of eye contact. Then you find things to laugh about. Do lots of laughing together."

I listened, thought about Elli's visits, the things we'd done and said, the things we'd found to laugh about in spite of the pain.

"Then," Judy went on. "You have long talks. Not about sex. Anything but sex."

I remembered the conversations about our children, our break-ups, our ex's.

"This doesn't sound like seduction," I said. "This sounds like the story of my life."

"Trust me," Judy said. "Next you get her alone. And have a long conversation about sex."

I thought about dinner the week before. Could Elli be seducing me?

"Go on," I said.

"Then you get her in a vulnerable position and *don't* take advantage of her."

I remembered the night after the restaurant conversation. I thought she was going to sleep with me and was a little scared. At bedtime she'd made up the couch just like on every other visit. And I lay alone in my room, hurting, wanting.

"Don't?" I asked.

"Right. Then, when she feels pretty sure you're not interested—move in. Start by changing the way you touch her. Make it suggestive. Usually by then she'll be so off balance that she'll be trying to figure out how to seduce *you*."

"You've tried this?"

"Works every time."

We sat next to a family with at least three children under the age of four in the museum theater. K.C. would have said, "See what happens when straight people fuck?" Elli simply smiled and scooted closer to me to make room for them. The lights went low.

I'll just say, "Look, we're both without lovers. Neither of us wants to get involved with someone right now. But people need sex."

Her thigh pressed against mine.

A little girl behind me leaned forward to see the village campfires as a tape played night sounds. I could feel the child's moist breath in my ear. It felt nice.

The night before I'd been on my way home from work as the sun was setting. I'd been thinking about Elli. Things didn't feel the way they had with K.C.

The sky in front of me was turquoise and coral. The clouds were gold. It occurred to me that I would never love the same way again. For the rest of my life, K.C. would be the most in love, the most invested I would ever be. And it was over.

Maybe it was a good thing, I'd thought. I would always hold a piece of myself back. I would never hurt this bad again.

Tears turned the sunset into a kaleidoscope. I had to pull the car over.

The worst had been the day she had come for her bookcase and albums. I set them outside the door and watched her load them in the truck, K.C. and her new roommate, heads close to-

gether over Janis Joplin. I watched them through the window, the
pain exploding inside me. I couldn't imagine my life without her.

We wandered through the exhibit. In front of the flint knap-
ping Elli stood close to me. I could feel her body heat.

The voice in my head was going on about how she was a good
friend, and if we did have sex where would that leave us? Suppose it didn't work out. How could we be friends then? "Lover"
was certainly a more vulnerable status then "friend."

Look, I said to the voice. I'm going to forget this and go to
the bar. Maybe I could pay somebody.

We found a Mexican restaurant for dinner. The food was too
hot and the prices too high. Elli seemed in a hurry to head home.
It was dark by the time we pulled back on I-55.

The trip home was quiet. There was a knot of fear in my gut.
What if she says no? Is insulted? Leaves and doesn't spend the
night?

At home I made a pot of coffee and put on some music. We
sat in the living room and talked. I had trouble paying attention.
There were awkward silences. The voice in my head tried. "Say
something nice to her. Tell her she's attractive, that you like her
boots." I looked at her boots. They were nice but not—

"You want to go somewhere?" She interrupted my thought.
"Do something?"

"Not really."

Silence.

"Get the conversation back to sex," the voice said. "Remember
the restaurant. Ask her what she likes? How often? Does she
think it's too soon? I looked at the clock. Time seemed to crawl.
She picked up a magazine and thumbed through it.

What if she's insulted? What if she just walks out?

"Don't be silly," chided the voice in my head. "She's two hours
from home. She's been on the road all day."

"Are you hungry?" she asked.

"No."

The ticking clock drummed in my ear. An hour had passed.

"You must be tired," I said.

"Yes, a little."

"That's it," went the voice. "You waited too long. Even if she wanted to, she's too tired now."

I stood to get a blanket. I tried to accept that we would be sleeping in separate rooms again.

She stood. Walked toward me.

I looked at her.

"You know," she said, "I've been fond of you for a long time. I was wondering if you would be willing to share some pleasure with me?"

I let out a sigh. "I've been trying to figure out how to bring that up." I reached for her, and pulled her toward me, never really saying yes.

She pressed her lips to mine. Her tongue darted into my mouth. I returned the kiss, holding her.

K.C. and I had been monogamous. Before K.C., my lovers were mostly men. Elli was the first other anybody for years. The pain of wanting washed over me.

"It's been a long day," I said. "I want to take a shower."

"Don't," she said.

I looked at her. I'd just learned something else about her. Or had I? Maybe she didn't understand. I was suddenly afraid. I didn't want to screw up.

"*I* would feel more comfortable," I asserted.

"Quickly then," she said.

I lit candles in the bedroom. I looked at the bed K.C. and I had bought together, made promises in, had our final fight in. The knot of pain tightened.

"Get on with it," the voice in my head said. "It will be good for you."

I turned and saw Elli silhouetted in the bedroom door.

"Lovely," she said.

I looked down at myself. My body was still damp and warm from the shower, wrapped in a black towel. I blushed. Shit, I thought. This feels like high school!

"Please take your clothes off," I said.

She stepped into the room and started to unbutton her shirt.

"Don't just stand there," said the voice. "Help her." I stepped toward her.

"I need to know," she said as the shirt fell off her shoulders, "if you usually come one time or several?"

"Once," I said, thinking that probably on the first night with her even once would be a miracle.

"I'm multiply orgasmic," she said evenly.

My knees felt weak. I sat on the edge of the bed.

She unzipped her jeans and stepped out of them. Her body was beautiful, ivory and glowing in the candlelight. I took a deep breath. I'd never seen anything quite like it. Her breasts were smooth, nipples erect. Her waist was small, hips round. The black hairs of her cunt glistened, inviting me to touch them.

Oh God, I thought. Then she ripped the towel away.

Our bodies pressed together. Our breasts. Our cunts. I ran my hands down her back as we kissed. I was fascinated with her ass. I wanted to touch it, knead it, bury my face in it.

We rolled all over the bed. Each time I made a move she made another. She was clearly in charge. My cunt was throbbing as I twisted away from her.

"I want to go down on you," I said.

"You do?"

"Yes, that would please me."

Who would do what, and when, had always been a power thing with K.C., so when Elli rolled off me, threw her arms over her head easily and said, "Then do it," I was surprised. It upset my sense of routine. My timing. There would be no struggle about it. What would I do with the energy I'd always put into that?

Go down on her, that's what.

I planted tiny kisses on her mound. I washed my tongue slowly over her swollen labia. She moaned. My tongue found her clitoris, firm, waiting. I worked slowly, applying what felt like perfect pressure. My tongue felt like an extension of her fragrant cunt and we both received pleasure. My lips were covered with the faint taste of the sea. My hands massaged her ass.

She moaned again and again. Louder. I was glad the kids were at their father's, remotely wondered about the neighbors. She cried out and pushed my head away, holding it in place, inches from her throbbing cunt.

"Well, how many do you think multiple means?" The voice inside was breathless.

Good question, I thought.

"We know it means more than one," the voice said.

Right. As she relaxed I started the tiny kisses again. She spread her legs. Gently, I ran my tongue over her wet vulva and found her spot. The second time was quicker. Her moans were louder. My face was wet. My tongue and lips were hot and tingling.

She pulled me alongside her. Her hand found my cunt. Then three fingers were inside me, writhing like the hairs of Medusa, her thumb pressing my clitoris. Each place she touched felt on fire. She thrust her fingers slowly. I arched my back. Met her thrusts. She kissed my shoulders, found a nipple, and began sucking. Then in one swift motion, her fingers still thrusting inside me, her lips were covering my clit and she was sucking with the same sweet pressure. It pushed me over the edge so quickly that I was stunned.

When I found my voice, I said, "How did you know I like penetration?"

"The restaurant," she said, and started moving her fingers again.

"I only . . ." I couldn't think straight. The words were lost.

"Am I hurting you?"

"No."

"Do you want me to stop?" Her thumb moved across my clit.

"No. Don't stop."

She went down on me in earnest then. Her fingers moving harder. I rocked, meeting her thrusts. At first I was sure I couldn't come. Then the sensation rushed through my veins right to my fingertips.

"Oh God!" I cried as I pushed her away.

She moved up and lay on top of me. I held her, trying to catch my breath. My heart was pounding.

"How did you know I could come again?" I asked at last.

"Lucky guess," she said.

We lay there kissing and holding each other.

"Twice." The voice inside me was excited. "You came twice!"

Well, it's been a long time, I told the voice.

"What's she doing now?" the voice said.

She had straddled one of my legs and was moving slowly.

"What are you doing?" I asked.

"Do you have any lubricant?" she answered.

"Ah . . ."

"That will do." She had spotted a bottle of hand cream on the nightstand. She reached for it and spread it on top of my leg, cold and slippery. She pressed her cunt against me and started moving.

"What . . . ," I murmured.

"It feels so good." Her voice was soft. "You want to try it?"

"Die!" It was the voice inside me. "You're going to die right here in this bed!"

"Sure," I said.

She put hand cream on her leg, then my cunt. I held her. Face-to-face and we moved. It felt pleasant. Intense. I could touch her. Kiss her. Hold her.

It was late. Elli lay in my arms. I watched two candles flicker on the dresser. Remembered the sun dogs. Cahokia. The day.

"I wonder why they're called sun dogs?" I asked lazily.

"Sun dogs?" She raised her head and looked at me. "I don't know."

"Where did you first hear them called that?"

She thought for a moment. "I think it was my second husband. It must mean something, otherwise they'd just be called spots in the sky."

One day, I thought, I'll say to a lover about something, "It must have been K.C. who told me that." And K.C. will be just someone who used to be part of my life and isn't anymore. Someday.

"What are you thinking?" Elli asked.

"Oh," I sighed, "I was just trying to figure it out."

I looked at her then. Her face was aglow in the candlelight. Her eyes met mine.

We looked at each other for a long time.

At last she sighed, "The thing is, kiddo, some things you never do figure out."

ABOUT THE AUTHORS

CASSANDRA BRENT has always had a thing about locomotives. She is an avid calligrapher, and her favorite place to spend an afternoon is in the Tactile Dome at the Exploratorium in San Francisco. She is working on a collection of her short stories, some of which have been previously published in *Open Wide* and *Aché*.

MOLLY BREWSTER is the pen name of a Northern Calfornia woman who lives in the woods. She is an accountant for small businesses, as well as a writer of both fiction and nonfiction.

*ANGELA FAIRWEATHER has been writing for the past two decades, primarily about education, health, and food.

WINN GILMORE grew up in the South, was schooled in New England, and lives in Calfornia. Her writing has appeared in *Aché, On Our Backs,* and *Sinister Wisdom,* and the anthologies *Unholy Alliances* and *Riding Desire*. She has a short-story collection entitled *Trip to Nawlins*.

*This author has stories that appear in *Herotica* (Down There Press, 1988).

JANE HANDEL is a writer, visual artist, and most recently, publisher. In early 1990, she founded SpiderWoman Press, whose first release was *Swimming on Dry Land: The Memories of an Ascetic Libertine*, written and designed by Handel. She lives in San Francisco with her husband and daughter.

AURORA LIGHT has contributed stories, nonfiction articles, and poetry to a variety of publications, including *Woman's World*, *Country Woman*, and *Broomstick*. She is a contributing editor for an international Meniere's Disease newsletter and publishes a haiku magazine.

*MOXIE LIGHT is the author of many journal articles and has recently received her MFA degree. She has also been involved in establishing a women's shelter in New England.

*JANE LONGAWAY is a writer, printer, and longtime San Franciscan who believes imaginary excess is the answer to safe sex.

MAGENTA MICHAELS lives on the coast south of San Francisco with her husband and parrot. These are her first published short stories, coming from a writing class and her personal journal.

MARTHA MILLER gets up at 5:30 A.M. and writes; then goes to her bank job where she is frequently late. She's a lesbian who's allergic to cats, a writer who can't spell, and a perfect example that nobody's perfect.

KAREN MARIE CHRISTA MINNS has been published in such diverse places as Britain's *Sex Maniac's Diary*, *Sinister Wisdom*, and *On Our Backs*. One of her two published novels, *Virago*, was nominated for a 1991 Lambda Literary Award.

SERENA MOLOCH maintains active ties to the women's health movement. She dedicates her story to Princess Snatch.

*This author has stories that appear in *Herotica* (Down There Press, 1988).

*LISA PALAC lives in San Francisco, where she also works as a freelance sex journalist and leads sex writing workshops. She performs carnal and comical monologues under the name Lisa LaBia.

CAROL A. QUEEN is a San Francisco writer, sex educator, activist, and adventurer. Her work has appeared in *On Our Backs*, *Taste of Latex*, *Frighten the Horses*, and other publications. She is committed to and inspired by exploring nonnormative sexualities, kissing and telling.

KATE ROBINSON is a thirty-nine-year-old lesbian separatist bisexual who harbors fantasies of roaring through the halls on a Harley at her Yuppie job. She writes and edits for business, technical, and community publications.

TEA SAHNE is a coffee addict, gardener, freelance writer, teacher, and widowed mother of two sons. In her forties she earned an advanced degree in medieval literature.

*SUSAN ST. AUBIN is working more and writing less these days, writing an occasional erotic story as a way of relaxing and preserving her sanity.

*MARCY SHEINER is fiction editor of *On Our Backs* and is still riding on the backseat of motorcycles.

DAPHNE SLADE didn't even realize what she was writing at first—this is her first venture into writing erotica. She has been a member of a political satire troupe and several improv groups, performed stand-up comedy, and written prose. Her day (and night) jobs have included waitressing, stockbrokering, and currently, technical writing.

ROBERTA STONE is a fifteen-year lesbian activist living in Boston. When not going to meetings she likes to relax with a notepad, pencil, and her own dirty thoughts. Her stories have appeared in *Bad Attitude*.

*This author has stories that appear in *Herotica* (Down There Press, 1988).

CATHERINE TAVEL is an erotic scribe of fiction, nonfiction, poetry, and adult video reviews. Although she usually writes under a number of *noms de porn*, this happily married former Catholic schoolgirl from Brooklyn, New York, gained notoriety after joining forces with Robert Rimmer to assist sex industry stars in writing their autobiographies.

MAGGIE TOP is a poet, essayist, and performance artist. This is her first erotic short story.

CINDY WALTERS enjoys Eros in reality and in fantasy, alone and with partners, or any combination of the above. This is her first published story; her earlier writings were for her college storytelling class.

PAT WILLIAMS, born and raised in the countryside of west Tennessee, now lives in Berkeley, California. She reads a lot of science fiction, fantasy, and ancient history, practices yoga and writes science fiction.

MARGO WOODS, a writer, student, and lover, has two adult children and one published book, *Masturbation, Tantra, and Self-Love*.

JOANI BLANK is the author of several sexual-awareness books for children and adults, and the founder/owner of Good Vibrations, San Francisco's unique vibrator store. She is also the publisher of Down There Press, which brought the first *Herotica* collection into the world.

SUSIE BRIGHT is the author of *Susie Sexpert's Lesbian Sex World*, editor of the first *Herotica* collection, and former editor of *On Our Backs*. She is the mother of Aretha Elizabeth. In addition to her writing projects, she is a connoisseuse of X-rated video.

HEROTICA 3

*This collection is dedicated to
the memory of Jane Longaway*

Contents

Contents

Introduction

I collect sexy stories: erotic fiction, dirty books, porno, sensuous reading, you name it. I started acquiring these stories when I didn't have any name for them, except *Don't Let Anyone Find Out About This*. I collected them underneath my bed, in the back of my underwear drawer, in the knothole of a tree on my way to school.

I accumulated my stories in secret—finding them in other people's underwear drawers, or at garage sales where I could lift them without anyone noticing, or in the back of baby-sitters' cars, where I sat while they went out for cigarettes. After puberty, I started writing my own stories to arouse myself. I'd enter elaborate fantasies in my diaries in code, or rip out the pages the next day.

My collection matured over time. These days I buy erotic fiction without hesitation in any bookstore in town. Moreover, I publish many of the sexiest stories I can find. I have been editing erotica for ten years now. I get interviewed by journalists, grad students, and fellow travelers regarding my sex fiction collection and expertise. Inevitably, the conversation turns to politics. The reporter leans into me and states the question as if drawing a line in the sand: "Are you a feminist?"

Each time I'm asked, I pause for a moment, because if it's a one word answer they're looking for, it should be as plain as the nose on my face. Isn't it obvious?

Tragically, feminism is perceived as "down on sex" and against pornography. "Feminist pornography" is considered a contradiction in terms; "feminist erotica" only marginally less so. Women's liberation is always being counterpoised to erotic freedom, despite the fact that sexual liberation has always been a cornerstone of modern feminism. One of the oldest feminist challenges is to eliminate the double standard, to move from barefoot and pregnant to orgasmic and decisive.

So why isn't the sex field treated by feminists as just another Old Boys Club that needs to be shaken up and infused with a woman's point of view? Feminists have zapped other male-only institutions from construction sites to the halls of Congress.

Sex is different. It's different because our culture is so puritanical that we can't even discuss sex publicly without our worst fears and fantasies rendering us mute, embarrassed, inarticulate. It's not about Equal Pay for Equal Work, it's about Different Strokes for Different Folks. Those differences are unpalatable to some, unspeakable to others. We haven't been honest about sexuality— we've denied it. Our prudery turns us into liars, yet despite all these factors, sex is compelling. Women's desire does not change through fear of condemnation.

The women claiming the erotic frontier are woman-centric, no-compromises, read-my-lips Amazons. They're the women writing sexual fiction, the women publishing it, the scholars teaching it, the entrepreneurs selling it, the politicos on a soapbox debating it. If they have one thing in common, it's that one day they picked up a sexual story and said out loud to themselves, "I like this." Then they said the same thing to their lovers, their families, over dinner, to audiences. They are risk takers, women who say yes to sex as forcefully as they've been raised to say no. Any woman who confesses enthusiasm for erotic writing or visual materials is on the erotic frontier. Why is the existence of these women so hard to believe? Because we're a minority? It's true there aren't a lot of politically active feminists who go public with their erotic adventures, but we've been vocal and inspiring enough to make an impressive dent.

Sexual liberation for women is certainly not all jolly and climaxing with happy faces. In many years of teaching and talking sex, I have never had a man come up and say, "I don't know where my penis is and I've never had an orgasm." It never will happen either. It's feminists who have put the clitoris on the map; now we're concentrating above the neck.

Why do the anti-porn feminists still dominate the public perception of feminist views on sexuality?

I've often participated in debates where some woman "against pornography" tells me that a woman is being raped every ten seconds, and that my work is at the core of this devastation. An entire women's studies class picketed my lecture on lesbian erotica in history, passing out a leaflet that said, "First slavery in the Roman Empire . . . then the Holocaust . . . Now, Susie Bright comes to the University of Minnesota campus."

This last example may have pushed the argument to its surreal limits, but the U of M protesters' sentiment reflects the more comprehensive statements by anti-porn leaders like Andrea Dworkin, Catherine MacKinnon, or Robin Morgan. Their position articulates the anti-erotic lock on feminist ideology. On the one side they incite the visceral female reaction to male violence; on the other, they play to traditional middle class Anglo-Saxon prejudices within the women's movement. And all this controversy exists within a national climate of sexual ignorance defined by religion and superstition, so that even with the best intentions, we know so very little. Eros is a universe, and we haven't even gotten off the launch pad.

The feminist "sex wars" have been going on since the early 1980s, from the first bloom of the women's erotic renaissance. It has always been exasperating for me to articulate my anger with the feminist status quo. It now seems that a lot of my pro-porn arguments of the past have been as superficial as the prejudices of the anti-porn feminists and even more defensive. It may sound reassuring to say, "Fantasies shall set you free, nothing you imagine in your mind can hurt you," but these are only feel-good sentiments, Dale Carnegie with a vibrator in his hand. There's often

a long and unpredictable road between our fantasy and consciousness.

Feminists worry about the effects of written and visual
expressions of sexuality in the same way that parents worry about
violent TV programming, or that consumers worry about sensa-
tional advertising. How much effect does it have on us? How easily can we be swayed? Why is it that I can stay up all night with
insomnia, watch a four-hour infomercial about molecular hair
curlers, and race on down to the mall to buy a set the next day
even though I have never set my hair in my entire life, yet when
asked if men get the idea that all women become whores by reading *Playboy*, I reply, "Don't be ridiculous."

It's not a ridiculous notion that we get ideas and inspiration
from the media or the arts. It's not news that you can be suckered
by anything. But we also find ourselves skeptical of these same
images or inventing our own interpretations that may be quite the
opposite of the producers' intentions. Certainly I learned to look
for lesbian associations and sympathies in Hollywood movies
when I knew in reality that they never meant to speak to me.
Most women's entire experience with pornography is taking material that was made for men's tastes and manipulating it to our own
purposes.

There is one thing for certain about the effect of pictures and
words on our minds: Sexuality has been preposterously singled
out as the most vile influence around. I am hardly the first person
to point out how we are inundated with violent images from our
earliest fairy tales and cartoons. Nearly everyone sees Hollywood
movies and network news shows and the violence they contain.
Relatively few people see hardcore pornography, yet this is where
all of our law enforcement, legislation, and political condemnation
is focused for attack. How can we think we are assessing sexual
expression fairly when clearly we have a knee-jerk reaction to it?
Our attitude toward sexually explicit materials is riddled with hy-
pocrisy and second guessing, and feminist attitudes towards it are
no exception.

The first time I heard Andrea Dworkin, the most charismatic
anti-porn orator of all, speak about what men do to women, it

turned my stomach. I was one of many young women in the audience, most of us either crying, pale with anger, or shocked. Her descriptions jarred memories of events I'd love to forget. My thoughts turned to my teenage years and the soldier who came back from basic training and raped me. My nails raked bloody scratches down his back, but they didn't stop his cock from moving in and out of me like a piston. I have fractured recollections of a drunk who followed my mother home and broke into our house. I hid in the closet with my roller skates clutched in my hand to bean him with if she couldn't succeed in talking him out of the room. I remembered, not so long ago, the young kid who held a knife to my breast and stuck his dirty hand in my pants before he fled with my purse.

Every woman around me at the lecture must have recalled her own catalog of male cruelty, sadism, and indifference. Inside each one of us who loves a husband, father, or son is a wound of resentment that can be opened every time she is reminded of the bullies, the pigs.

Feminists are accused of man-hating, the implication, of course, being that they are infantile, as stubborn and undiscriminating as two-year-olds who hate their bedtime. But hating one's oppressor, hating the bullies, is entirely natural. What's unnatural is for women to deny that we feel so strongly. Any minority that has successfully stood up for itself has had to address hating whoever has hurt its members. You can't just "hate" sexism and racism without contemplating the individuals who enforce that ideology.

But my memories weren't the only thing upsetting me the night I saw Dworkin speak. She took the anger of her audience, an audience charged up with humiliation, guilt, and titillation at her explicit descriptions, and she turned them all against a culprit that most of those young women had very little first-hand experience with—pornography.

I could not find my release down that path. I know my friend who joined the Air Force was not acting out what he saw in a magazine when he raped me. He was a virgin when I met him, tender and open; after nine months in the service, he became hardened and mean. I don't think that drunk who harassed my mother had been looking at anything but the bottom of a bottle for a long time. And the babyface with the switchblade in his dirty hand—I don't know who his role models were, but I think they were closer to him in flesh than celluloid.

Dworkin's explanation of pornography as a rapist's tool is unbelievable to me. The idea that dirty pictures mixed with testosterone equal a time bomb doesn't add up. It's as though she pulled only one worm out of the whole squirming can.

My dread of male violence is only a single thread in my need to know why human cruelty exists in the first place, why some people lose control, and how unexpected and vicious those manifestations are. My questions are given little reassurance by the limitlessness of erotic imagination—but I'm not looking for a pat on the head.

It's not that sexual fantasy is so incompatible with feminism; it's that politics—any political philosophy—does not adequately address sexual psychology.

Close your eyes for a moment, and remember the last time you had an orgasm. At the moment of climax, how many of you were thinking about a lovely walk on the beach, or a bouquet of balloons? Be honest. Beach walking is a really nice romantic fantasy, and so are sunsets, dinners for two, and a bearskin rug in front of a blazing fireplace. But as erotic fantasies that get us off, they don't often come up. The highest levels of arousal are often reached with thoughts that frighten us, anger us, overwhelm us. What is awful, what is forbidden, what is taboo, what is dreaded, is *exactly* what is erotic—up to a point. In fantasy, nothing can actually harm you. And the point at which a particular thought or image goes past that point and becomes *anti*-erotic is as individual as your fingerprint.

Look at one example of a common fantasy—the anticipation of getting caught having sex. The titillation might be the small chance of being seen or heard. The bedsprings squeak too loudly. You can't stop, you're with the lover of your dreams. The phone rings. Someone bursts in. Your mother. No, your ex. With a gun. With an accomplice. And an alibi. Does the bed still groan under your sweating bodies? At what point in this scenario does the heat turn to fear, the hard-on go limp, the wet pussy turn to dry mouth? This is what different strokes are all about.

Scientists, sex researchers, psychotherapists—none of them knows why we have the fantasies we do. That's right, they *don't know*, and most of them admit that in public.

Of course, sexual fantasies can be interpreted, but not easily or reductively. A sexual fantasy of a homosexual experience does not mean one is queer. A lesbian who fantasizes a tryst with a man is not living a lie. A rape in fantasy is certainly the antithesis of a rape in reality, where nothing is under the subject's guidance, limits, or control.

From the time we are small, we develop a very strong sense of what is make-believe and what is reality. I learn from watching how my own toddler has grown; sometimes she defers to others' boundaries and at other times she gets to act as if she were omnipotent.

My kid's idea of ecstasy is being tickled—very popular at her age. I call it the original S/M activity. She loves to run around saying, "Catch me, catch me!" and playing hide and seek. When I find her and get my fingers under her arms she laughs and shrieks, "Stop! Stop!" as in the original *Perils of Pauline*. But the moment I stop tickling her, she is absolutely certain to take a big breath and cry out, "Again!"

On the other hand, when I really lose my temper at my daughter, there's no mistaking the pain. She cries, I swear and steam, and there's nothing consensual about it. My daughter, like every other child, is learning about boundaries and trust, long before the media gets to her.

When we are face to face with a grown-up who doesn't see limits, for whom there is no line between pretend and real, we are not dealing with someone who just has naughty sex fantasies or who reads too many *Hustlers*, or who takes Madonna's latest pop tune the wrong way. We are dealing with a pathological lack of compassion and empathy that overrides fundamental adult Dos and Don'ts.

Historically, men as a group have been chauvinistic, egocentric, accustomed to gaining entrance. But if every man who had an aggressive rape fantasy acted it out, we would be living in a state of absolute barbarism. The sexual sociopath our society dreads is not just a villain of feminism or women's rights; his beliefs and preferences are superseded by a lack of conscience, a drop from reality, a failure to feel guilt or accountability that goes beyond conceit.

The Unstoppable Testosterone Rampage is a very popular mythical stereotype, and it's ironic that there's also an opposite stereotype with a ring of truth to it. It is that men specialize in keeping their feelings under tight control. The successful man is always putting his sexuality aside in consideration of other ambitions, saying, "No, I can't do this now, I don't have time for my family, I don't have time for my sex life, I don't have time for my body, I don't have time for desire." Men struggle to express themselves sexually with any kind of sensuality, or gladness.

If men are capable of exercising tremendous control in every part of their lives, and routinely stifle their sexual desires, then why should we believe the sulking Casanova who insists, "She looked at me like she wanted it, *and I couldn't stop myself*"? Is this the one moment when a man becomes a wild animal, not able to use his masculine discipline to respect another's limits? This is in itself a sexist prejudice. Men's sex is supposedly out of bounds without a leash, while women are deemed incapable of impulsiveness, passion, or just plain horniness.

We hear the same clichés over and over again: men are turned on by porn, women are not; men look at a sex act, then run out and start imitating exactly what they saw. Women, on the other hand, supposedly find satisfaction with soap operas and a big box of chocolates.

Men and women will be separated by artificial notions of sex and romance as long as we cling to traditional gender roles. Fears of violence and chaos will haunt us as long as we struggle with the notion of civilization. Beyond both of these debates is one constant that defines the most important differences in erotic appreciation. It is the element that absolutely dominates the feminist anti-porn position. It is something that Americans in particular are loathe to talk about—our class values and how they define our rules of sexual propriety. The feminist sex wars have not been routinely defined as class wars—and it's time that they were.

What are middle-class values regarding sex? They are based solely on this question: Am I doing the right thing? The right thing is very important because of the middle-class investment in a secure future, which depends on deferred gratification. If we deny immediate gratification, and suppress spontaneous feeling, the future may seem more promising, i.e., secure.

These values are not only perpetuated by the upper class but are also the values everyone else is encouraged to adopt. That's why a lot of people who don't have any money or social standing whatsoever think this way.

Of course sex is often a matter of immediate passion, impulsive actions. If it *feels* right, then it is right; this is the motto of the body. Sexual fantasies are led by our unconscious, not by our superego. Our erotic impulses don't follow a schedule, they don't care what anybody thinks.

Since everyone has sexual feelings, the degree to which one controls those feelings will often be reflected in one's economic or cultural background. The expression "going native," or slumming, is the juicy evidence of the Dr. Jekyll and Mr. Hyde dual life that many middle- and upper-class people assume in order to handle their sexual (and other) desires, which they believe are inappropriate to their milieu. Occasionally these people are exposed, and it is truly grotesque to see the contrast between what they practice and what they preach. J. Edgar Hoover and Jimmy Swaggart are some of our most recent outrageous examples. No one has yet unearthed the pervert masquerading in a feminist anti-porn crusader's clothing, but it's only a matter of time.

Women of every class are brought up to circumscribe their sexuality on a different threshold than men. Some manage to suppress their sexual yearning to such a degree that they don't allow themselves to fantasize, masturbate, or make love with another person. Our society is so puritanical and materialistic that this self-control is actually lauded. Women will brag about being celibate as a "choice," but not about being fertile or lusty.

In such a sexually repressive society, state power stays centralized at the top. It should not come as a surprise to anyone that the most powerful religious and right-wing demagogues use "feminist" anti-porn rhetoric to defend their anti-erotic, sex-negative campaigns. The feminist status quo has defined itself by these same upper class values since its origins. There are endless historical examples of the women's movement excluding and alienating others who deviated from upper class, white, and heterosexual (or discreetly closeted) values.

Sojourner Truth electrified a nineteenth-century women's rights convention when she criticized the white suffragettes:

I think dat 'twixt de Niggers of the South and de women of de North all a talkin' 'bout rights, de white men will be in a fix pretty soon. But what's all dis here talkin' about? Dat man over there say that women needs to be helped into carriages, and lifted over ditches, and to have the best place everywhere. Nobody ever helped *me* into carriages, or over mud puddles, or gives me any best places ... and ar'nt I a woman? Look at me! Look at my arm! I have plow and planted and gathered into barns, and no man could head me—ar'nt I a woman? I could work as much as a man (when I could get it) and bear the lash as well—and ar'nt I a woman? I have borne 5 children and I seen 'em most all sold off into slavery, and when I cried out with a mother's grief, none but Jesus heard—and ar'nt I a woman?*

The more privileged, wealthy, and discreet elements of the women's movement have prevailed in public policy. The same is true of gay liberation: Angry Puerto Rican drag queens may have been the street fighters of the Stonewall rebellion, but they are not the ones advising the President on gay rights.

Erotic language is the language of the streets, the one-on-one revolution that happens every time one lover speaks plainly to another. Sexual fiction, especially, is often an autobiographic statement—it tells a private story, a story of the body, surrounded

*Robin Morgan, ed., *Sisterhood is Powerful: An Anthology of Writings from the Women's Liberation Movement* (New York: Random House, 1970).

by the most important aspects of the lover's life. The stories that evoke the most controversy over political correctness are those that raise fears of violence (sadomasochistic material like *The Story of O*, for example) or stories that evoke an atmosphere that is "sleazy," "tawdry," "coarse," or "animalistic." Henry Miller's work was a perfect example of class-conscious censorship in his time, and Erica Jong's in hers. The *Herotica* series has received the same type of criticism. All those belittling adjectives are euphemisms for saying that such stories are not in the upper-middle-class comfort zone. While they may titillate many who live there, those same people will do their best to keep these revelations from public view.

In recent years, the comfort zone has been seriously shaken up into an "Every Woman for Herself" zone. Feminists who pursue erotic inquiry are not only lifting a veil, they are among the instigators of a new wave which can only be described as the democratization of kinkiness.

I won't turn my back on sexual exploration even when I sense darkness there. That's exactly what keeps me pushing. I am making a different kind of "investment" in the future, one with such intimate riches that it cannot be deferred ultimately; one that we cannot hold back, disguise, or deny.

Susie Bright
San Francisco, August 1993

Serena Moloch

My Date with Marcie

Queens, New York City

So get this. This guy David, David Josephs, who is in my AP Bio and English classes, who I've sort of been seeing for a while, he calls me up and says, "Oh, do you mind if we make tonight a double date?" "No, I don't mind," I tell him. "Who with?" "Keith Welz and Marcie Loewenstein," he tells me. "Oh God," I say, because I *hate* Marcie Loewenstein too much to even begin to describe it in this paragraph, and I'm not too eager to fritter away my swiftly passing youth in the company of Keith Welz either. "Do we have to?" I moan. "Lighten up, Barbara," he says. "Don't be so neurotic." "Oh fine," I say, "well, fine. So what time are you picking me up?" So here I am, about to go out on a double date with Marcie Loewenstein, which is absolutely positively totally unbelievable.

Let me explain, even though I can't, because it is just beyond belief. How can I begin to tell you how much I despise, detest, loathe, *excoriate* Marcie Loewenstein? (My SAT teacher made me learn all those words. I hate my SAT teacher, but not as much as I hate Marcie Loewenstein.) Marcie Loewenstein is a muskrat. She has bleached blond hair and wears a ton of makeup and spends all her time in classes freshening up her lipstick; she has a big fat mouth that takes up most of her face. The only part of her I can tolerate looking at is the part of her

389

hair where the roots show all black. They contrast so well with her nasty pale skin. She's short and not that developed, really, but she wears extremely tight clothes—you can count the change in her pockets. And it's pretty obvious to anyone who looks that nothing comes between her and her Calvins. *Or* her Jou-jous *or* her Sassoons.

Marcie does not mix with the likes of me and I do not mix with the likes of Marcie Loewenstein. We are the Cold War of our high school. I'm considered a brain. This offends me, but I'm not going to start failing classes so that people will realize I have a body just like everyone else. Marcie Loewenstein is willing and eager to play dumb to make boys like her. And they do. But behind her back they call her a slut. I call her one of the Purple People—purple eyeshadow, purple suede fringe boots, purple Cacharel jeans, purple underwear if she ever bothers to put any on, which as I've mentioned I'm pretty sure she doesn't. I think we would have noticed a panty line by now.

Marcie smokes in the bathroom, where she shows off her inhaling skills and blows smoke rings in everyone's face. Mainly mine. Which is what she did the time she cornered me in the girl's bathroom and started up with me. I mean maybe a little bit of it was my fault. I was smoking with some friends (other nerds like me, we get the urge to be bad sometimes too, just like the Purple People; a woman has needs) and we lit some toilet paper on fire by mistake, but we were putting it out, and laughing and screaming, and Marcie Loewenstein and her purple cronies came barging into the stall where we were, like they were the fucking security guards or something, yelling "Okay, who's starting a fire?" And Marcie Loewenstein came up to me really close and stuck her face in mine so that I could see her beige foundation and the layer of blush caked up on top of it and I could smell her second-hand smoke and the grape bubble gum she chews incessantly and the Love's Baby Soft she slathers all over herself. She snarled, "You're trying to get us in trouble, aren't you? You know they'll just blame us if anything happens here." I mean, she had a point, not that she gave me a chance to apologize or clean up the mess or anything like that.

Also, she completely ignored my two friends who were doing their best to fade into the toilet bowl.

So then she goes, "You want to smoke, huh? Well, if you want to smoke, let's see you smoke." She took out a cigarette and lit it, and then drew in this huge breath and sucked smoke down for at least five minutes. Much as I despised her, I was impressed. Then she exhaled through her nostrils, just like Bette Davis (not that she would know who Bette Davis is) and said, "Okay babe. You wanted to smoke. Go ahead. Smoke." She handed me a Marlboro and I was at this point pretty scared and the way out of the stall was blocked by Marcie's purple sweater and purple pants and all I could do was try to stare down her purple-rimmed green eyes— snake eyes—while I lit the cigarette with my hands shaking. And of course I lit it at the wrong end which just amused everyone *immensely,* including my supposed friends, and when I finally did light it properly of course I couldn't inhale without choking and she made an utter fool out of me, which you think would have satisfied her. But no, next thing I know it's a week later and she's starting up with me in the hallway. "You stepped on my foot. Don't you say excuse me? You're so rude." That whole routine. And I hadn't stepped on her foot; I don't know why she's so obsessed with me. The whole thing ended up with me talking into the air going, "She's having delusions, she's insane, she's mentally impaired," and with her hissing at me, "You are so rude," until finally a teacher stepped in.

So then she has to tell me she's going to get me after school. These people are obsessed with "after school"; it's like it's their special imaginary friend, Mr. After School. So there she was, true to her word, after school, following me down the street and sort of poking at me with a whole crew of spectators trailing behind her.

I'm not very good at fighting so I just ignored her until she started announcing, "I'm going to slap her face." So I turned around and said, "Marcie, give it up. I didn't do anything to you. Why are you bugging me? I'm flattered that I'm so important to you, but you mean *nothing* to me. Why don't you just ignore me?" Not very effective really, but I was trying the gentle art of verbal self-defense.

So she goes, "I don't want to leave you alone. I want to bother you."

So I say, "Well, I'm too busy to be bothered by you. You bore me."

I started to walk away but she grabbed my arm. I happen to have very strong arms, even if I can't do the number of push-ups required to pass the Presidential Fitness test (but then I bet the President can't do them either), so I shook her off really hard and kind of twisted her hand in the process. She changed her tune then. "I know boys who wouldn't mind beating a girl up for me, you know."

For some reason I found this statement really pathetic, so I just snorted and said, "That's great. I'm really happy for you, Marcie. Tell them to call me so we can make an appointment for them to beat me up," and walked off and that was the end of that and we haven't spoken since, except that when people make fun of her in class I laugh really hard and when people make fun of me in class she laughs even harder. This is why I hate Marcie Loewenstein. This is the girl I am going on a double date with tonight. I can barely contain my joy.

Well, this is even more unbelievable, I mean even more unbelievable than the concept of my going on a double date with Marcie Loewenstein was what actually happened on this double date. I mean, you're not going to believe it, and the only reason I believe it is because never in this world could I have imagined it. I mean, it didn't start out unbelievable, it started out like a perfectly normal horrible double date with Marcie Loewenstein. Marcie was dressed, or should I say undressed to the nines, in royal purple of course: purple halter top, purple short shorts, and purple Candies which made her about two feet taller than me. You could totally see her nipples through this top. I felt pretty boring in my jeans and chenille top; I knew I'd look good in the clothes Marcie had on, but my mother wouldn't have let me out of the house in them.

I sat in the front of the car with David, and Marcie sat in the back of the car with Keith, and I didn't say a word and neither did Marcie, though her wad of gum was speaking volumes: *snap,*

snap, snap about every ten seconds. I looked at her in the rear view mirror and got some genuine insight into her eye-makeup technique but absolutely none into how to start a conversation. The boys were wrapped up in talk about sports teams I had never heard of so Marcie seemed like my only option, but she wasn't biting.

Somehow we ended up at a Chinese restaurant. Marcie was still refusing to communicate with me directly. "I wouldn't mind Indian food," I said to David, who said to Keith, "How do you guys feel about Indian?" So Keith goes, "Yeah, I don't know, you like Indian, Marcie?" "No, I hate that shit," said Marcie. Back reports to front: "Marcie doesn't want to eat Indian." Front confers. "How about Italian?" You can see how it all took some time.

They don't card at this restaurant so we all had drinks, the kind with pink plastic ferns in them and names like Zombie and Killer and Sloe Comfortable Screw. I'm not allowed to drink—who is— but my parents are always asleep by the time I get home. I was well into my third Sloe Comfortable Screw and feeling pretty sorry for myself for being on this miserable double date when Marcie said to me, "Come with me to the bathroom."

"What?" I said. I would have liked to have a snappy reply but I was too soaked in self-pity to be anything but shocked that she'd spoken to me.

"I hate going to the bathroom alone. Come with me."

I trailed behind her purple butt like a puppy, following her into the bathroom. It was all ornate with a dressing room when you first come in, and the stalls and sinks in a separate room. We stood in the dressing room and I felt my head spinning.

"What are you afraid of the bathroom for?"

"I just hate going alone. Just wait out here, okay?"

"Yeah." When she went in to pee, I looked in the mirror. It was smoky gray and had light bulbs all around it. I looked at my face in gloom. I kind of got lost in contemplation and took out my hairbrush and started to work on my hair when all of a sudden Marcie was saying, "Can I use your hairbrush?"

My English teacher always says everyone has several hygienic principles that they break constantly and one or two to which they are excruciatingly attached. I sit on toilet seats without covering them with toilet paper, I don't wash my hands after I go to the bathroom, I even share tissues—but no one touches my hairbrush.

So I said to Marcie, "Sorry, I never lend my brush out."

"I guess I'm not good enough for you," she snapped. "You think I'm dirty, right?"

She seemed genuinely insulted, which surprised me, but all I said was, "No, I just never lend it out." I started to walk to the door, but she grabbed my arm from behind.

"Why are you so snooty to me? You think you're better than me?"

"No, Marcie, I don't," I said wearily.

"Yeah? Well, then prove it."

"What do you want me to do? Lick your feet?"

"Maybe," she said, moving closer to me. "Maybe I want you to suck my face. Come on. Kiss me. Kiss me right here on the mouth." She moved even closer. "Come on, you let David do it. Don't you think I'm good enough for you?"

"That's sick," I said, "I'm getting out of here." And I ran back to our table where my fourth drink was waiting for me. I dove right into it. She followed and sat down like nothing had happened, but we kept sneaking looks at each other, staring when we didn't think the other was looking. I felt edgy about what was going to happen when we got back in the car and started making out, which is always how these double dates end. I didn't want her to watch David kiss me.

But we didn't end up in a car. We ended up in a motel near the expressway because David had his father's credit card, and I guess his father's permission to use it to take girls to motels and try to fuck them. You know how fathers are with their sons—go ahead, son, enjoy yourself, wink wink, you take after your old man. It had been a while since I'd had sex—the last time was four months ago, right before I broke up with Jed—so I figured, what the hell, I'll live it up tonight. I didn't have to be home until two.

We found ourselves in a tiny room in the Kew Motor Lodge, Marcie and Keith on one of the beds and David and I on the other. I was still pretty drunk and I was really enjoying what David was doing to me. Okay, this is what he was doing (I feel like such a pervert for writing this down): He had my pants off and my top pushed up to my neck and he was rubbing his chest, which has lots of really nice hair, against my breasts and grinding his . . . his I don't know what, his *loins* into me; it felt good and I kind of moaned.

Most of the time my eyes were closed but when I opened them I couldn't help but see Keith and Marcie. They were a lot further along than we were; she had all her clothes off and so did he; she was lying on top of him with her legs apart and her head thrown back, and she was sticking her fingers in his mouth and watching him suck on them. Once in a while she took her fingers out of his mouth and played with her breasts, circling around her nipples, getting them really big and red. It all looked very bold and I got even more excited looking at her, but I was afraid to be caught staring, especially after our scene in the bathroom. So I concentrated on David again, who'd started stroking my thighs, moving his hands up and down and kind of pushing my legs apart as he did it. I felt my underwear get hot and wet from me, and I reached down to his crotch and rubbed my hand over his penis, which felt all fat and hard and was leaking, I bet, just a little bit at the tip. They explained that to us in health class—the pre-ejaculate. That's why I kept my underwear on, because of the pre-ejaculate. He slipped a finger into my underwear and rubbed it around in my wet, then he got a thumb in and started stroking my clit. It felt really good. I got my hand into his shorts and wrapped it around his penis, which I started jerking off, real slow—I've done that a lot and I think I'm getting good at it. My last boyfriend said I had nimble fingers.

I looked over again at the other bed where Marcie was still on her stomach on top of Keith, but reversed this time, so that her head was between his legs. I could see her shiny pale butt moving up and down, like she was humping him, and then she started rooting around in Keith's crotch with her mouth. She'd pulled out his penis and was licking it up and down, and then sucking just the first inch or so in and out of her mouth while her hands bunched up around the bottom of his thing to hold it steady.

When her mouth got free for a second she'd go "Umm, good" in a really sexy voice. Keith was writhing around but Marcie kept pushing his hips down. I threw my legs around David and twisted around his fingers, almost forgetting to jerk him off I felt so close to coming. I made little noises in my throat even though I really wanted to scream. I had my spare hand around David's neck holding him tight against me, and from what I could hear Keith was about to come all over Marcie too. David had three fingers up me and was working them in and out hard and slow, his other hand was under my butt, squeezing my cheeks, when all of a sudden Marcie pulled away from Keith, flicked on a light, sat up, tossed her hair and said, "Let's watch porn flicks."

Keith groaned and tried to pull her back on him but she swatted his hand away; David and I had both broken stride and had taken our hands off each other. I pulled my shirt down and hiked my underpants firmly back up. "Come on, Marcie," Keith said, pointing to his penis, "come back here and finish what you started." He's always been kind of a pig, ever since elementary school.

"Oh, I will," she said, "but first I want to watch some porn movies. Come on. They're really cheap, and there's a big selection. What do you want? 'Wet Nurses'? 'Pretty Pink Pussies'? 'Hot Rods'? 'Lesbo Lust'? Or 'Tittie City'?" She looked straight at me. "Come on, what's your vote?" I looked down at my fingernails. It's one thing to all be in a room naked when the lights are down and you're just paying attention to the person you're with. Of course the turn-on is knowing the other couple is there, but no one really cops to that. It was different to have Marcie staring at me when all I had on was a shirt and soaking wet panties, and she was totally naked with the biggest nipples I had ever seen staring me right in the face. I noticed that her pubic hair was a lot darker than the hair on her head. I remembered how she'd looked when she wanted to suck my face, but I couldn't tell if she'd already forgotten about that.

Keith and David answered before I had a chance to, and their vote was unanimous: "Lesbo Lust." I didn't feel like exercising veto power, so we switched the TV on to cable and got the channel. We all crowded onto the bed right opposite the TV and watched.

"Lesbo Lust" was a real revelation. In it these three women were making a porn movie but the man who was supposed to be in it was late, so one of them started playing the man. She was a petite blonde and she put on this cute deep voice and started telling the others, "Come over here and fuck me, babe," which they did. One of them had a huge silver vibrator which she slid in and out of the other and they were all licking each other's breasts and going down on each other and moaning and whispering a lot too, a constant stream of whispers: "Suck my cunt," "Come on, lick my hole," "That's right, yes, yes, fuck me." I think it was the whispering that got to me; I felt it all under my skin and in my ears and I got so excited. I had never been so excited before in my life without being touched at all. The same went for everyone else in the room and pretty soon David and Keith developed the bright idea of having Marcie and me put on some kind of show. "Come on," David said, prodding my butt with his hand, "you two show us. Do what they're doing in the movie."

"No," I said.

"Be nice," Keith said. "Do it for us to be nice. You're never nice. Don't you want to do it, Marcie?"

"Yeah," David said, "you want to do it, don't you, Marcie? Marcie will do anything," he laughed. "I heard about Marcie in the back of that car with Steve and Alan and Paul."

What a mistake. Marcie's face got really mean and really smart. I thought she was almost baring her teeth, she looked so ferocious. "Oh yeah," she said, "really? I'll do anything, huh? You guys think you're so smart, maybe you should put on a little entertainment for me." She leaned over the edge of the bed, grabbed a belt, lashed David's hands behind him and looped the belt around the bed frame before he could do anything about it in his drunken state. Hey, I thought, hands off, that's my date; but I kept quiet.

"What are you going to do to me?" he chortled. "Make me lick your pussy or something? Yeah," he snorted, "that would be a big punishment. P-U," he sneered, "you smell."

It was getting ugly now. I mentally berated myself for not having brought enough money to take a cab home.

"No," she said, "you're going to put on a show. You and Keith. 'Hot, Homo and Horny.' You're going to sit there while he sucks your cock. Because there's nowhere for you to go, is there?" She flicked her nails at his penis and he inched away as far as he could, but she'd immobilized him pretty well. She turned to Keith. "Well," she said, "let the show begin."

"Very funny, Marcie."

"I'm not kidding," she said. "Get on with it. Do you need instructions? You were pretty sure about what I should do. Just do unto others, asshole. Love thy neighbor. You'll be fine."

"We're not going to do this," he said.

"Yeah," David echoed. "We're not going to do this. Get me out of this thing, man."

"You wanted us to," I said. "Why shouldn't you?" Marcie looked surprised but nodded in appreciation. I was beginning to think we girls had to stick together. And I was curious to see what they would do.

"Yeah," Marcie said, and threw in the refrain from her theme song for the evening, "aren't we good enough for you?"

"We won't do it," said Keith.

"Yeah," David said, "we won't do it."

"Okay," Marcie announced, "fine. But if you don't do it, I'll spread it all over school that you did do it. I'll tell everyone that you're a pair of faggots, and you'll be lucky if you make it out of homeroom alive. And just think," she said, "what would your parents say?"

It was a pretty weak threat, if you ask me, and maybe they secretly really wanted to do it, because they didn't call her bluff. So the next thing we knew, they were both swigging tequila to get their courage up—Keith had to hold the bottle for David because David was still tied up—and then Keith was down on his knees, his hands pulling David towards him, then holding David's penis while he kind of tentatively cupped his mouth around it. David jerked wildly when Keith touched him.

"Come on," Marcie said, "use your tongue, lick him, take it in your mouth and suck it, really get in there."

Keith was turning red but he dipped his head down and David's penis disappeared all the way into his mouth, and he sucked on it hard, moving his mouth up and down over it. Then his hands slid down to David's balls and stroked those—pretty inventive, I thought. David strained at his bonds and thrust his hips up so that he could push his penis further and further in. Eventually they worked out a rhythm where David pushed up and Keith drove down, then David pulled back while Keith sucked up. David strained and twisted when Keith's hands roamed and grabbed David's ass and then Keith's head was deep in David's crotch and he was pulling David's ass toward him. From the side, I could see David's penis bulging in Keith's mouth as he sucked furiously. In the meantime, Marcie got behind Keith and started jerking him off while he sucked, and in two seconds David came all in Keith's mouth and Keith spat it out all over David's legs and then Keith came all over Marcie's hands and the pink patterned carpet. But as far as I could tell, Marcie hadn't come, and neither had I, though I was very, very close. I was almost tempted to take advantage of David by sitting on his face and making him eat me, but what with the tequila and all, he and Keith basically passed out seconds after coming.

Which left Marcie with come all over her hands and me on the bed squeezing my thighs together under a sheet, wishing she'd go away so I could masturbate fast and then just go home. Not knowing what else to say—it was definitely an awkward situation—I decided to be helpful.

"You should be careful about that sperm," I told her. "You can get pregnant, you know, even without having intercourse."

She stared at me in disbelief. "You are such a nerd, I can't take it," she said. She came over to me and yanked my sheet off and started wiping her hands all over me. I tried to struggle away from her and all of a sudden we were wrestling and she pinned me down fast and rubbed her hands on my stomach. "It dies within three minutes," she informed me.

"I didn't know that," I said politely, always happy to add a new fact to my arsenal of contraceptive information. She kept rubbing my stomach, in almost a sexy way. Part of me felt good. Part of me wanted to start talking about the weather so we could get back to normal again.

"You're such a nerd that you're kind of cute," she said, grinning. "Maybe we *should* put on a show together. Look—we can see ourselves in the mirror." She pointed at the huge mirror over the dresser. "But you could see us better if you took off your top." She was like a hypnotist, talking slowly in a husky voice, moving her hands up me very steadily, taking my top off, pressing her cheek against mine to turn my head towards the mirror. I couldn't look. I slipped my face away and said, "No way, Marcie, no mirrors." She looked pissed and moved her hands away; they'd felt good and she'd felt good and it almost felt like we were getting to be friends so I said,

"Anything else, but no mirrors. They freak me out."

"Anything? You wouldn't have the guts."

I may be a nerd but I can't resist a dare.

"Is that a dare?"

"It isn't even a dare. It's a half-dare, a quarter-dare, a—"

"—mere infinitesimal fraction of a dare!" we both yelled at the same time. We were in the same math class and our teacher was always using that expression.

"No, look, dare me," I said. "I'll even bet you."

"What?" she laughed. "The savings from your piggy bank? Okay, I dare you. I dare you to lie on top of me and put your tits on top of mine."

Tits, I thought to myself; she sounds like the women in the movie. I pushed her onto her back and got up on top of her and carefully laid my breasts on top of hers. Mine were bigger. I held my face up away from hers.

"Not like that," she snorted. "Act sexy. Like this."

And she arched her back and started rubbing her nipples against mine. I could feel them hot and crazy and a huge flush started going all over my body. She grabbed my face and started kissing me, and before you could say Roseanne Roseanna Danna our tongues were all over each other. Her body was amazingly hot everywhere, even her tongue felt hot and my mouth went all warm sucking on it. She circled my ear with one finger and her other hand stroked my hair.

"You feel good," she whispered to me. "Bite me."

"Bite you?" I whispered back.

"Yeah, give me a hickey."

I pressed my teeth against her neck and started sucking. She was so soft, I'd never felt anyone like her before. So much soft hot skin and her hand grabbed the back of my neck as I nipped her. She put one of her legs between mine and we started rocking and rubbing against each other. I could feel her wetness against my thigh and all of a sudden I really wanted to put my fingers inside her; I'd never thought of doing that with another girl, ever. I started moving my hand down. We moaned as loud as we wanted because there wasn't anyone awake to hear. But she pushed me up so we were sitting, her back to me, and now we were in the mirror. There she was, all blonde, with her raspberry nipples jutting forward, and she grabbed my hands and put them on her breasts. I didn't exactly know what to do, but I remembered her circling around her own nipples before, so I did that. "Harder, harder," she moaned, and so I pinched them more and more and watched her face in the mirror, all ecstatic. I stopped for a second to give her a break—her nipples were so hard I was afraid they were going to explode.

"You're so pretty," I told her. "I'm excited."

"I know," she said. "I'm going to go down on you. Just touch me a little more first."

"I'd like that," I said, my index fingers teasing her nipples. "But I want to go down on you too."

"Okay, let's sixty-nine."

"What's that?"

"God, I can't believe I know something you don't. Sixty-nine is when two people go down on each other at the same time. The numbers look like what you're doing because the nine is like, flipped over, sucking the six."

"Well, don't be so conceited about it."

"I'll be even more excited after I make you come all in my mouth." We were grinning. From enemies to X-rated Bogart and Bacall all in one night.

"You or me on top?"

"Whatever—it doesn't matter."

"Here goes," I said. I pushed her down, put a pillow under her to support her neck, and turned myself around on top of her. I started kissing her thighs, she opened her legs and I saw her vagina. I don't look at mine very much, so the sight was kind of unfamiliar, but I started getting acquainted real fast, working my way down to kiss her there. I wanted to taste her. She was pulling me down over her, and with no work-up at all I felt her tongue flick against my clitoris—just that little touch was more incredible than anything I'd ever felt before. I hoped my legs wouldn't start shaking uncontrollably. She smelled really musky and good and I started licking her, hoping I was in the right place, trying to concentrate on her while she was driving me crazy on her end. I loved how her hairs felt, all swirly and wiry. I put one finger, then two inside her, she was real soft and tight inside, pulling on my fingers, moving up and down them while I clamped my mouth to her clitoris and sucked and licked it. I was pushing myself all over her face, and things got wilder and wilder, and then she came—I actually made her come and I could feel it all around my fingers. I took my mouth away and I just stayed over her on all fours. My arms were tired but I stayed like that while she kept licking me and fucking me with her fingers and then I came too, and then we both collapsed on each other, holding each other and trying to get our breath back.

Things got a little awkward then, the way they always do after you've had sex with someone for the first time, even when it's normal sex. (Maybe especially when it's normal sex, boys can be so weird.) We got dressed and stuff but we didn't act really romantic. I mean, we both date guys. I don't know.

We concentrated on unbuckling David and trying to dress him and Keith. I kind of wanted to ask her if she thought they'd remember what happened, but I wasn't sure we wanted to remember what we'd just done, so I didn't bring it up. We shared a cab home; it turns out she doesn't live that far from me and she'd been smart enough to bring some money with her—but of course we couldn't talk about anything in the cab.

So I don't know what's going to happen, but today is Sunday and I thought maybe I'd give her a call and we could go shopping or to the movies, but what if she's really obnoxious to me on the phone?

If this were a book report I'd have to state the main idea. Maybe I'd say the main idea is to stay away from double dates; they seem innocent but they can really get out of hand, like a journey where you've lost the map and forgotten your destination. My English teacher would like that. She's really into analogies.

Lenora Clare

The Boy on the Bike

The black straps of her garter snapped against the back of her thighs in a slight off-rhythm with her stride. She was angry—the set of her jaw and the pace of her walk made that clear. The man beside her kept talking. A bead of sweat rolled down her back and the lace of her panties rubbed against her.

"You know it's the best thing for the firm." The man was wearing a gray suit, nearly identical in fabric to hers. They were continuing the argument they'd had at lunch. The Florida sun hit the metal of his wire-rimmed glasses as he turned to her, still speaking. "We've got the votes. It's just a matter of whether you're with us or not."

"You don't have the votes. If you did, you wouldn't have taken me to an early lunch and been your most persuasive, charming self." Looking at him now she had the uncanny feeling that he was her male clone. Same age, same glasses, malcontents, lawyers, new partners in the same firm. Until now, the same goals and philosophies. Same hometown. That still meant something to both of them.

"Depends on whether it's straight majority or voting shares of partnership stock," he said.

"Either way. I did the math, okay? I know you've got to have my vote and my stock to win this battle."

At a basic level, she knew his way was the best for the firm. But she also knew his motive was his own ambition, and that made her stubborn, unwilling to give in. Pausing to stare at Hank, she caught a quick reflection in the glass window behind him and turned suddenly back to the street.

The boy on the bike was pedaling by. She saw him almost every morning on her way to work as she drove her expensive, gold, Japanese sedan down the causeway. She would see him riding his bike: shirtless, cut-off jeans, heavy construction boots, with a tool belt and box tied to the back of the bike. Every time she saw him she watched until he was out of sight. A teenager, he was tan and muscular in the way slightly built young men could be despite their thinness. "God," she thought, "I'm lusting after a boy I could have given birth to."

When Hank laughed, she realized he had followed her stare. "So, Janis, that's what you like. Young construction workers. All this time I've been wasting my efforts." His quick perceptiveness made her uneasy.

"You've never made any effort," she snapped at him. He was married to a thin, beautiful woman, probably not much older than the boy on the bike. "Don't give me grief when you've got the same thing waiting for you at home."

The boy was gone. She glanced back at Hank, and, looking past him into the glass storefront, saw her reflection. Dress-for-success suit, silk blouse, pageboy hair with a touch of gray, strong jaw: a face still handsome but showing its age, showing the first pattern of lines and slackness to come. It scared her sometimes to see how serious, how tough she could look.

She was not the sort of woman the boy on the bike would ever want, and knowing this felt like a physical blow to her stomach.

"If you want my vote, earn it. Make me feel like I'm eighteen, beautiful and desirable. Make me feel like that boy could make me feel."

Hank, she saw, was plainly startled, and he laughed nervously. "Janis, you *are* beautiful and desirable."

"Then make me feel it, by God, make me feel it."

* * *

They walked back to the office without speaking; intense, fast paced. Once inside, they found the office was nearly deserted. Hank had deliberately taken her to lunch well before the regular noon hour, so they could sit without interruption or worry about who was at the next table eavesdropping. Her secretary was gone from her desk.

Janis went resolutely into her office, Hank trailing. When Janis turned briefly toward him, she thought he looked unsure. He shut the door and stood looking at her.

"Don't look so scared, it's not flattering," she said. Without waiting for a response, she went behind her desk, pulled out a small purse, cupped something in her hand and returned to the front of her desk. Hank had not moved from his perch by the door. "Lock it," she said. He did.

She took off her jacket and threw it on the couch with an uncharacteristic lack of concern. Janis unbuttoned her blouse and left it draped open, revealing a lacy camisole with pearl buttons that strained just a bit across the top of her bra. Leaning backwards until the desk supported her at her hips, she opened her arms to him.

The kiss startled them both. Janis pulled back with a gasp, as if she had been shocked by a small electric current.

"Take off your shirt and tie," she commanded, "and hurry." As Hank obeyed, she slipped off the blouse, unhooked the bra, and pulled it off from under the camisole, which she left on.

Under the sheer material of the camisole, she finally exposed her breasts to him. All the years he had sat next to her at meetings just to peek down her blouse, he had never caught a glimpse of anything more than a lace border. She was not the sort of woman to let cleavage show at the office. Now, as she let him, he looked at her breasts, perfect, round, firm, neither too large nor too small. She wondered why she had never used such an asset before. Hank's obvious admiration made her appreciate her own breasts, the perky way they stood up to his touch, the almost adolescent pinkness of the tips. Just a peek now and then, a careless bend over a file with a round-necked dress, and she could have won over the men in the firm a lot sooner, she thought.

"Don't just look," she said. Hank, as if waiting for permission, dove into her, licking her breasts through the silky camisole, tasting the faint salt and smelling the clean scent of perfumed soap still clinging to her skin. He sucked each nipple in turn. The lacy fabric that covered them became wet from his tongue; it became only the thinnest damp touch of silk against her breasts. When he pulled his tongue away, the silk still clung to her, mimicking the sensation of his mouth on her skin.

While his lips were on one breast, his hands were on the other. He reached under the silk to touch the bare skin of her pink nipple. Pinching too hard, he made her gasp and pull back suddenly. He backed up and looked at her, at the red imprint he had made on her skin. While he stood back, Janis slipped out of her skirt and stood facing him in only the camisole, her lace panties, her black garter and stockings. She didn't flinch at his study of her body, his obvious appraisal.

"My God, you really are still beautiful," Hank said. Janis knew she had a certain appealing roundness, a softness that would seem very womanly to Hank, although he bragged about liking skinny women. When Hank moved toward her lushness, Janis knew he had momentarily forgotten the taut, weight-lifting body of his wife.

Janis pushed his head down to her panties. "Take them off with your mouth," she said. Hank caught the top edge of the panties in his teeth and pulled them down. He could only get them as far as the hooks on the garter straps that held her stockings. When he reached up with his hands to unhook the garters, she pushed his hands away. "Use your mouth, your teeth," she said.

After a brief struggle, he managed to unhook the garters using his tongue and teeth. This freed him to pull her panties down to her ankles so she could step out of them. The stockings, still clinging to her slightly damp skin, stayed in place with the garter belt cinching her waist.

Hank was hard. Janis laughed, tauntingly, as he struggled out of his gray woollen pants as if he were about to explode. He rose from Janis just long enough to undress. When he approached her again, she held a condom she'd gotten from the purse in her desk. Without speaking, she tore open the package with her teeth and pulled it out with her mouth.

Cupping his buttocks with her hands, using only her mouth and her tongue, she put the condom on the tip of Hank's penis. With the soft, wet skin of her lips, she slowly began to unroll the condom down the length of Hank's erection. Halfway on, she stopped and used her tongue to tickle the uncovered part, to dart and tease and forage into his hair and about his balls. Then she sucked and pulled on the covered part. All the while her hands were moving, probing, touching, exposing.

Slowly, she began again to roll the condom on the rest of the way, backing up now and then to tease and suck upon the tip of him. When she finally had the condom all the way on, Hank was flushed and breathing hard. For a moment she had the full length of him in her mouth; she gave him a smooth, tight suck at the back of her throat before he pulled out.

He pushed her against the desk and entered her, pushing too hard and too fast. Janis had intended to make him explore her, taste her, make her come first with his tongue, but when she took him deep into her mouth, she had felt his urgency. She'd have him make it up to her later if she required it, she thought, as he pushed deeper into her.

Like the sudden disconcerting kiss, this too caught them off guard with a power they had not expected. Janis was moaning without control, without regard for the possibility other people might be returning from lunch. She realized vaguely, somewhere in the back of her mind, that someone might hear them. For once, she did not care.

Janis lifted her feet off the floor and wrapped her legs around Hank's back. She was balanced on her buttocks on top of the desk, with Hank holding her waist. The stronger and more urgent his pushing, the further back on the desk she was forced. Finally, with a grace that amazed her in later reflection, Hank used a chair for a boost up and, without ever uncoupling, was up on the desk, his knees on the hard rosewood, scattering loose papers.

Janis felt the imprint of a small dictation tape in her back. Under Hank's pressure, she heard the plastic covering crack under the movement. It was a small pain, vaguely recognized. Nothing was going to break them apart now.

She moved her stocking-covered feet up and down his legs.

Under his hands, the skin on her hips, stomach and buttocks felt like silk. As Hank stroked her bottom she was seized with a new idea. Pushing him out of her with an odd roughness, to his protest, she shoved him off the desk and jumped off too. She turned her back to him and bent at the waist over the desk, the black line of her garter belt over the pale cream of her ass, her thighs, faced up at him. Bent as she was, her buttocks were thrust out toward him like an invitation.

"Do it," she said.

He pulled open her buttocks, and using a finger, then two, explored the narrower entrance. With the fingers still in, still moving in rhythm to Janis's movement, he entered the now familiar, wet entrance he had just left. Within minutes, Janis came with a definite convulsion of inner muscles she knew he could feel both with his fingers and his penis. Her coming was the permission he needed; he came in her with a quick, sure violence that left him panting. Her legs were quivering.

On the way home that night, Janis saw the boy on the bike along the side of the road. He was dirty. A red handkerchief was rolled and tied around his head to keep sweat and his hair out of his eyes. There was a flush of sun on his face and shoulders. She slowed the car as she drove next to him. The wetness between her legs returned. Keeping her car slow enough to pace herself with his pedaling, Janis studied his young face. If he noticed, he gave no indication.

Janis thought of Hank and their noontime scene at the office. All the irritation and anger had left her when he took her on the desk. Firm politics didn't matter. This boy didn't matter. Suddenly she laughed. Youth wasn't everything. She hit the gas pedal and drove off, still laughing at Hank and the fun they'd had. A bargain is a bargain, she thought. Tomorrow she'd give him her proxy, and he could vote it anyway he wanted to. But tomorrow and for days, months afterward, he would pay her back, reward her. That was his promise, her desire, when he had left her office that day.

Pat Williams

Tennessee

I loved Rohn because she was neither a woman nor a man.

She wasn't black, but she wasn't white either. She wasn't crazy, and she was not sane. She was pretty and she liked to fuck. I was fifteen and that was ideal.

I first met Rohn in the summer down South. The weather was hot and the air was close and heavy with dry grass and small dead rotting animals. Snakes slid out of their skins.

Before I met her I had seen her up at Bell Eagle Esso, the little grocery and filling station that our landlord owned. Sometimes she was with her mother, a thin, pale woman who wore big hats to keep the sun off her face, and who, whenever she spoke, mumbled. I did hear her speak once, and she sounded funny. My grandfather said that she was a foreigner. She usually had Rohn by the arm. Or Rohn was with her older brother, the one most like the mother. People always looked at them funny.

The day I met her, she was astride a big roan mare.

She had a black cowboy hat on, pulled low so that it shadowed her eyes. Her thick red hair fell down onto her shoulders.

We were in the middle of a pasture. Over by a pond some cows

Previously published in *On Our Backs*. Reprinted with permission of the author.

stood still as if they'd been painted there. I was walking home
from a neighbor's house, where I'd gone after school.

I kind of stepped backwards because the horse was so big.

She grinned, flashing her dark face under the hat's shadow.

"How you t'day?" Her drawl was soft and gentle. It wasn't
high-pitched and evil like a peckerwood's, so it didn't scare me.
I said, "I'm all right."

She pushed her hat back and I saw that her eyes were green
in gray. Her brows arched with the grace of a bow. I think my
heart did something.

"You wanna ride home?" She told me later I had a kind of half
smile on my lips to make her wonder.

I climbed up and she pulled me the rest of the way onto the
horse. From up there I could see the tin roof of my folks' house.
Smoke was coming from the chimney, going straight up. Grandma
was starting supper.

I wedged into the saddle between her thighs. Her arms encircled me and she rested her hand holding the bridle on the horn
between my legs. Her breasts were small and firm and pressed
against my back. I was too shy to move.

She asked me what grade I was in, and did I like going to
school in town, and she bet I didn't like arithmetic. I thought, at
the time, that she was a senior in high school or maybe already
in college. We rocked in time to the horse's movements. I felt her
arms tightening about me and the horse walking slower.

"You got a boyfriend?" she asked me, and I said no.

"You want to go for a ride?" she asked, and I said yes.

I knew I would get scolded, but I could no more have refused
than turn down strawberries and ice cream. We turned away from
the sight of my house. The cows came back into view. A big orange and black butterfly hung in the air. The sky was clear.

"Hold on," she said. When the horse sailed over the fence, I
thought my heart would shoot out of my mouth. My terror evap-
orated in her laughter, and then her low chuckle brought another
feeling altogether. She was holding me so tight still.

Rohn loosened the rein some more. She put her face down next
to my cheek. I heard her breathing and felt her long fingers moving on my body, as if they were gently searching for something

just under my clothes. I stopped breathing for a minute. She smelled of Ivory soap and the heat of the day. Once, her hat brim brushed my face; it felt soft as cotton.

"Can I touch your breast?" she whispered.

I managed to say yes.

With just two fingers and a thumb she rubbed softly in circles. Around and around through my blouse, from the fullness of my breast to its tip. She did it softly and once she squeezed the nipple a little. Her hand held the reins on my bare thigh where my skirt had come up.

She put her whole hand over my breast and kneaded it. I noticed the wetness between my legs. I tried to open them wider and they pressed against her. She kissed my cheek. The dampness her lips left there cooled in the air.

She kept squeezing and playing with my tit, and I think I moaned or gasped or something because she kissed me again. I turned my face toward her. She took off her hat and gave it to me to hold.

She unbuttoned one button of my blouse and slipped her hand inside. It was warm, dry and smooth. Her hair fell against my face, and it felt like the silk scarf my aunt had sent my grandma from New York.

She held my tit hard and then she pinched the nipple a little. The small pain heated my whole front. Her mouth was on mine and I thought I would die. It was warm and wet and I thought I would starve before I moved away. I opened my mouth and she pushed her tongue in. She licked the inside of my mouth, inside my jaws, the roof of my mouth. I took her tongue and sucked it.

Her hand, pressing my breast, pinched the nipple more, and each burst of pain filled me enough to almost lift me. And she was kissing me harder and spit was all down on my chin.

She pulled away suddenly, breathing hard, and I came awake. Her gray-green eyes were soft and heavy, but they started to clear until they had the depth and transparency of a cat's eyes. I tried to smile, but she had looked away. One of the cows lowed, a long, deep chest sound. I heard birds which had been there all along. She took her hat and put it back on, pushed up this time.

"I'ma take you home. All right?"

I didn't say anything. It was hot. My blouse was damp from sweat and there was moisture on the back of my hands. If I tasted them, they would be salty. Rohn read my mind, the first of many times. "It's all right," she said, "you didn't do anything wrong." She kind of smiled as if there were something on her mind. I smiled back.

Southern nights are full of stars and crickets and mosquitos.

The stars hang down beside your head. The crickets are inside your head. The mosquitos bite. They are there for the purpose of reality, I imagine. If they don't often find their way into romantic stories, it is not their fault.

I used to sit out in the front in my rocking chair after watching "Amos and Andy" or "Ozzie and Harriet," until it was well after dark. I used to look up at the stars and try to fathom how far away they were. It was hard to comprehend that the light I was seeing from a certain star had started from there eight years ago. I thought of furnaces bigger than the earth. I thought of people who'd been alive eight years ago and weren't anymore. I heard somebody quietly call my name, or thought I did.

I listened and I heard it again. "Pa-tri-ciaaa." I walked around to the side of the house.

She was standing not more than six feet away, as quiet as a haunt. I grinned in the dark and I think she smiled. She didn't have her hat on, and her hair was all tousled. She had on jeans and a man's big plaid shirt.

I stood close to her, and we whispered, because the house was right there.

"Can you go for a ride? In my car? It's right down the road."

"Naw, I don't think so."

"How about a walk?"

I shrugged. "It's late. Grandma won't let me."

"Just inside the pasture. Over that fence. Just over there."

I waited a minute. I wanted to so badly.

"Okay," I whispered.

Then she was touching me, lightly, her arm around my shoulder. We were about the same height because I was tall for my age. She smelled of some odd perfume; I learned that it was her mother's.

We walked through the garden, stepping across the rows of turnip greens and the tomato vines. It was a new moon, and everything was dark blue. She held the barbed wire apart while I climbed through, and I did the same for her. She slipped through without touching it anywhere, like she'd done it a lot.

We sat on the ground, close enough to feel the warmth of each other. I pulled out blades of grass and waited. There was nothing to hear but the crickets. She lay back, her hands folded behind her head.

"I bet I know what you were doing. Looking at the stars, huh?"

I nodded. I felt her smile.

"Bet you were sitting out there, trying to think how they could be so far away?"

I giggled.

She reached down and gently tugged me down beside her. She could read my mind. It felt good, like somebody else in there with me. I have never waited for anything as hard as I waited for that first kiss.

She pulled me onto her so that my breasts touched hers for the first time. Then she pulled my chin down with two fingers and gave me a lingering taste-kiss right on the lips. It was better than the kisses two days before on the horse and I might not have had one like it since.

She ran her tongue across my lips. I opened my mouth and she started kissing me harder. Soon it was like the other day with her tongue halfway down my throat. We rolled over slowly until she was above me. She was on me with her legs straddled, when I felt something I shouldn't have. It woke me.

"Rohn . . .?"

She laughed low and deep in her chest. "I told you I wasn't like other women. Didn't I tell you that?"

But she was soft. And her voice was a woman's. And her breath was a woman's. And her breasts. She kept kissing me and pushing down on my body and grinding her hips into me until I responded.

I had on jeans that night. My blouse was already open and now she started to undo my pants. I helped her and we got them off.

Then she was up on her knees, still straddling me and doing something with the zipper on her pants. She took her penis out. It was warm and hard and at first she rubbed it back and forth against my clitoris. It made me lose my breath. I pulled her toward me and she told me to open my legs wider and I did.

At this time I was still a virgin. She was big for me and it hurt going in. I squirmed and she covered my mouth with her own.

It hurt but I kept pushing up to her and trying to open my legs wider. So we lay there, twisting and rutting on the ground. I came. I'd never come before with something inside me. And my bud between my legs filled up until I felt ready to burst. I was panting and she seemed to suck the air right from the center of my body. Taking my breath.

I came again and then she did. We were wet and sticky and a mess. My grandmother could call any time. Rohn held me.

I wanted to ask her, "How can you be?"

I could not comprehend.

Later that night in bed, I kept waking just at the edge of sleep, warmed by the soreness between my legs.

Carson McCullers wrote about "freaks" and "misfits." Faulkner wrote about freakish habits, and then there was Huck and Jim. There is a strange kind of tolerance down South when it comes to personal habits. Just don't involve politics. Just keep it behind closed doors so that it can be gossiped about. Fantasized about. Keep it under cover of night so that tales can grow.

I was your basic black adolescent tomboy with pigtails everywhere and a pointed chin. I looked from beneath long-lashed eyes without raising my head and gave tight-lipped secret smiles and rakish grins. I shrugged off the impossible.

What was nasty was funny to me and I smelled of sweat and my jeans had grass stains. I masturbated to movie magazines and let boys feel me up because it felt good. My experiences had, in some twisted way, prepared me for Rohn.

I was told that I would burn in Hell if I did practically anything. I was inevitably going to Hell, but I was too terrified of that fact to give it much thought. So I ran wild like the heathen I was, amid flowers with odors sweet and heavy enough to drug you; ran with dogs and other beasts that copulated when the spirit struck through the tall grass on hot summer nights. This was as real to me as Bible verses. So Rohn was real to me.

Rohn was the bill for some long ago charge that her mother—or her ancestors—had run up. Her mother accepted her as such.

She had not been made to go to school. Legally they got her declared an idiot or something. She was taught at home, better than the schools around here could teach her, most likely, because her mother was educated.

Her mother and her elder brother were the only ones who had anything to do with her. The others despised her. She told me that her younger sister had twice tried to kill her with rat poison. Her father beat her whenever he came home and found her there without the mother or the brother.

She told me later, after I was allowed to go riding in her car, that she was always afraid somebody would tell my grandparents some wild tale about her.

But she also told me that when she was in her teens, her mother took a turn to her. The same bed that she had nursed her in. Her mother, convinced that Rohn would never find a lover, took her in. This time, instead of opening her blouse to nurse Rohn, she opened her legs to her. Anytime she wanted it, she said.

I was in love with Rohn by then. I figured that she had to like me more than most, else she would never have told me those things. On the other hand, they could all have been lies.

One Sunday she came by in her '56 Chevy; it was green and white and shiny.

I ran out to the car and leaned on the window. "Hi."

She smiled. "I just came by to tell you how pretty you are." Which she knew would make me grin.

"Can you go for a ride?" she asked.

I shook my head. "I don't think so."

"Ask."

So I ran back in and asked, and was told no, I couldn't go for a ride in anybody's car, and what was I wanting to go for a ride with Miss Rohn for anyhow?

I ran back out and told her. Her smile changed to somewhere between sad and disgusted, and she nodded. "Oh, well." Then she looked at me and winked. "Maybe some other time, okay?"

"Yeah maybe."

"You take care y'hear?"

"All right."

Never occurred to me to say ma'am to her, ever.

I was up at the store to get some things for Grandma. It was getting near to evening. Rohn's car was there.

I'd never felt this way about a real person before. I felt about her like I only felt about fantasy movie stars.

She watched me approach the car. She was sitting with her back to the door, one leg up and her arm stretched across the back of the seat. She half smiled.

"Hi."

"Hi."

I explained about my errand; I'm not sure what there was to explain. She looked at me quietly. I think that she knew what she was doing. Driving me insane. So I took my leave and went inside.

When I came out, she offered me a ride home. Her eyes darted toward the store and then she opened the car door. She set my groceries in the back.

We pulled out of the station. Dark was falling and the bright Esso sign came on. We sped past my turn-off road. I sighed in relief.

She cut the radio to the black station from Memphis, WDIA. It had already been set on the signal dial. At home I could listen to WDIA only three times a day, when the gospel programs came on. Now some sister was singing about not having enough meat in her kitchen.

We drove across the railroad tracks and pulled off a dirt road near a stand of trees. We didn't have much time. Already I was wet.

We walked into the woods and she pulled me to her and kissed me. We kissed a long time. I began moving a little bit, and I felt her growing big. I wanted her inside me and I kissed her harder.

But she had other plans.

She undid her zipper and told me to get on my knees. Halfway down I realized what she wanted.

I'd never done it before, I'd never even read about it, but it seemed a natural thing to do.

She took my face between her hands; her hands were smooth and they felt hot. The sky was still light though the wood was dark. One dead tree without any leaves stood in front of the others. There was an old sack or something caught in its high branches. "Don't use your teeth none, hear?"

I opened my mouth. It was like a fat sausage, tasteless except for a little salt. I slid my mouth over it, like she told me, against the plump vein underneath. And I let her shove it against the back of my mouth. I squeezed her hips firm in my hands and she massaged my cheeks and my throat with her thumbs, and ran her fingers all in my hair and on the back of my neck. She rotated her hips slowly. And then faster and harder I sucked until my tongue felt like lead, but it had begun to taste so good. She twisted real slow, and I grabbed and sucked. Time was passing. Grandma was waiting. Time was, I think, standing still. For us. A sheriff on a horse with a posse could have come out of the trees and we wouldn't have known. Or two boys could have been watching us.

She came. I jerked my mouth away and spat, but some of it got on my shirt. Rather, my grandfather's shirt.

I was hot, too, and between my legs was very sticky, so we lay on the ground and dry fucked with our pants up until I came. She was hard again, I think. But she said that she would go home to her mother.

We sped away in the car. The wind felt good. The slide guitar from the radio drowned out the crickets.

I had a playroom. It was just a curtained-off place between the kitchen stove and the wall where I kept all of my magazines, and where I went to read them and to fantasize.

One day I was sitting in there when I heard Rohn's voice. My grandfather said something back to her and then called my name.

I went to the door. She was wearing a white shirt and old jeans and loafers. Rohn didn't look like a boy and she didn't look like a girl. I was afraid that my grandparents would see what I saw. If they did, they'd take it away from me. But Grandma kept on working in the tomatoes and Grandpa went back to help her. Only the dog followed Rohn over, sniffing her.

"Hi."

I asked her into my playhouse. The curtains could be pinned closed and I could hear footsteps on the wooden steps if need be.

Her shirt smelled of starch; it was a white so new and clean that it had a bluish tinge. I kissed it. I kissed her. Her teeth touched my tongue. She sucked it. She had such a fine mouth. We hardly ever talked. I knew what she wanted from me, and she could have all she wanted. That particular day she was going to take much more than I'd ever imagined she could.

We pressed against each other, all our clothes on, and I felt her soft breasts pressing mine. I breathed in, and pressed against them more. It's the feeling I still like best when I'm with a woman. Those round soft tits pushing.

We lay on the floor tight and moving just a little. She kissed, with her lips parted slightly and soft and moist, first my mouth, then my cheeks and my nose and my throat.

I started to pull down my shorts. She grinned; sometimes she just did that, out of the blue, like a Cheshire cat. I wonder what went on in her mind.

I kneeled in front of her and she cupped my buttocks in her hands and squeezed them. She put her mouth on my shoulder, right at the stem of my neck and sucked a bit until I had more of a welt than a hickey. She bit me, and I drew in the pain like a scorching breath.

I had my hands all in her hair. In the silk and the curls. I loved that hair. I felt it on my hands when I awoke in the night. Outside the kitchen door I heard the dog give a loud yawn and then, I think, he turned around and lay down.

We kissed. She worked her hand around in front and slid it right between my vulva lips. She wriggled her finger a little and I groaned and squeezed her to me. Her other hand was still squeezing and rubbing my behind. She kissed my neck, rubbed her mouth up to my ear and stuck her tongue in. I laughed and pulled my head away.

Then she moved her finger from around the front and stuck it up my asshole. It was hard and sticky, and I jumped. She pushed it and it hurt just a little, so I sucked my breath in. I'd never tell her to stop when she was hurting me because I liked the deep kisses that she gave me when she did. She always kissed me like that when she was hurting me somewhere.

We kissed deep and slow and she kept working her finger deeper up my asshole. Every once in a while I would whimper. We stopped kissing and she buried her face in my neck and pressed me to her, moving herself into my pussy and rotating her hips. I creamed. She was hard. We twisted and rubbed; I got the lips of my cunt over her dick and stroked up and down, and rubbed up and down, streaming across my bud and covering her joint with cream. Her finger was still there, I don't know how far in it was. She groaned.

She eased her finger out and chuckled; I felt the laugh in her throat. "Do you have any Vas'line?" she asked.

We had just a little, so I brought back the jar of bacon grease that was sitting on the stove to go with it.

She eased me around so that my back was to her. I felt her lips and tongue on the back of my neck. For a moment her hands cupped my breasts.

She told me to bend over and spread my legs as far apart as I could. I said she couldn't, that it was too small. She said we'd manage. She wiped the grease on me.

So I did what I was told and I told her to be careful. She dipped her finger a few times in my cunt and I shuddered.

I was spread so wide I could already feel the pain. I held my breath. She told me to relax.

I did, except for biting my lip when I felt the tip of her joint probing around where it shouldn't. I told her again to be careful. I was scared, but the fear was part of what was making me sweat and tremble. She pushed and immediately I felt the impossibility of the whole thing. But it didn't change anything.

She rubbed my clitoris again with her finger, just barely skimming it. I was already on the brink of coming. I opened wider and she pressed in more. It hurt.

A fraction of an inch by a fraction of an inch. She pushed and I gasped. "Relax. Relax, baby." I felt her voice.

"Come on," she whispered right in my ear, her voice more like wind or dry leaves.

"I love you. I love you. I love you." I said it every time I gasped.

She gathered me in her arms, crisscrossed like a straitjacket, and buried her face in my hair. I could hear her carefully placed breaths like somebody measuring something just so. My ass began to burn.

She pushed, she held me so tight I could hardly breathe. Something started to fill up my ass; it felt good, and at the same time I felt I was going to rip. My clit was swollen; my clit wanted to swell up big and long as my tongue. She started a regular pump now and I think I whined. The burning was a red-hot rod sliding into moist pink flesh. Mixed in with her gasps loud in my ear were groans as if she were in a little bit of agony. She touched my clit and I jumped. She pushed a finger up my vagina. Two fingers. I covered her hand with mine to make her take it out, but she didn't. My hand lay on hers, softly, as if it were helpless.

The pain was so intense I was almost dizzy; I moaned a little, like I was getting the shit fucked out of me. I'm sure that the dog, psychic as he was, raised his head. With one finger she stroked my bud and the pleasure made me call her name.

I started to squirm, we moved like wrestlers; she was inside me and all over me. I loved it and I couldn't bear it. She might have had it all the way inside my body. We wrestled and knocked over a stack of movie magazines. We tore and twisted their pages, and they carpeted the hard linoleum beneath us.

I felt saliva covering all of my chin and strings of it wet my nose when I lowered my head. There was something wet and warm moving on the back of my neck. She came.

I felt as if I was going to explode, as if steam was building up in my bowels. She held me tight, still and silent for a minute as we both trembled. We relaxed and she pulled it out through my raw flesh. Right after, a brownish egg-white liquid streamed out of my asshole like the runs, and covered the movie stars' eyes and mouths. I expected it to smell but it didn't.

Her face was covered with sweat and around her temple a few curls lay flat and darkened with moisture. My shirt, which I'd left on and open, was wet and my breasts glistened. The playhouse seemed close, steamed. Then sounds came back. A truck passing on the road; from far away, my grandfather's voice. That was all.

She took me in her arms and kissed me gently on the mouth and face. There was blood on my bottom lip; she licked some off. I held her weakly. I kissed her back softly. We kissed for a long, long while.

We laughed a little and I noticed something warm still running down my neck and I patted it with my fingers. It was blood. I twisted around and it was all over the collar of my shirt. Then I realized that my breasts hurt; I touched them and they were tender and bruised. I felt like I had been in an accident. I felt like ...

"I love you," she said.

She knew just what to say after putting me through a meatgrinder. I was so thankful.

The next night at church was the Lord's Supper.

It was a night full of stars that I didn't want to leave to go inside. But I filed back into the building with the other girls. A sweetish yellow light filled the church.

The preacher got up and, in a conversational tone as if he were down among us, said what he always did about eating the flesh of the Lord with sins on our conscience. We would burn in Hell if we did. I broke out in a sweat. If I had died since the last Lord's Supper, I knew that I would be in Hell.

But then something happened worse than Hell. Rohn left me. She was just gone.

I didn't see her at all the week following the Lord's Supper. I thought that maybe she had gone somewhere with her mother. But she didn't come back the next week either.

The Saturday night following the second week I knew that something was wrong. I cried a whole night so silently that my grandmother, sleeping in the same bed, didn't hear me.

I learned, mostly by listening, that she had indeed disappeared. Rohn had disappeared and so had Fauna Dipman.

Fauna Dipman was a light-skinned girl with freckles. She went to the Baptist church. She had just gotten married that past spring. I'd never paid her much attention and Rohn had never mentioned her. I heard somebody saying that Rohn was crazy and Fauna was probably dead. Fauna's young husband walked around like somebody had hit him on the head.

One day I went to a small hollow down past our garden at the edge of the woods. It was another of my secret places and I had taken Rohn there. While I was there, something made the hair on the back of my neck stand up. It was just a feeling.

She had already started haunting me. I ran out of that hollow so fast I had a stitch in my side. I still run from that place in my dreams. I wake up sweating and feeling the hollow, not as empty as it should be, at my back.

I didn't see Rohn again for twenty-eight years.

I lived up North then, and one spring I went to visit a long-distance lover who lived in New Orleans. On the morning of the day I was to leave we drove to a shopping area where there were a lot of small craft shops just opening. It was early and there weren't many people about. My friend, Emily, had run back to the post office for something and I waited near the car, under a huge oak tree. I hardly paid attention to a car that drove up and parked just a few yards away.

Rohn got out of that car.

I had no doubt it was her. Her dark red hair was shorter and slicked back. She'd put on a little weight. She wore men's trousers. Her face was quiet and mature.

She walked into a little candle shop. I could not move. Burst after burst of light was going off inside me. Rohn.

I looked at her car. It was a long, blue, shiny Oldsmobile. A car for adults. And I looked at the woman in the passenger seat. It was Fauna. Fauna, as the young wife would look almost thirty years later. With her lipstick and her powdered cheeks and her hair pulled back. Her contented smile as if she were happy. Or at least was that morning.

I tried to think of all the things that I would say to them. I imagined the scene. I thought of dinner that night. When Rohn appeared at the door of the candle shop I didn't move.

I stood there concealed by the large tree and I did not move. I stared at Rohn. I stared as hard as I could.

She was handsome. She had long, dark curving eyebrows. A one-sided trace of a smile on her face. Sideburns. And she seemed to walk with just a bit of a limp. What happened, baby?

I let her get back into the big Oldsmobile. It tilted slightly at her weight on the seat. Closed the door. Backed out of the little drive. I saw Fauna laugh at something Rohn had said. And drive away.

I watched the car go further and further until it disappeared.

When Emily came back we got into the car. Emily is beautiful. She is a dark, honey-skinned New Orleans woman with amber eyes. She is all woman.

I was still seeing Rohn and Fauna. I still saw the point at which their car had disappeared. Emily threw her arm across the back of the seat and playfully tugged at my hair. She was just turning back to start the car when I said, "I love you."

She raised her eyebrows and smiled. She thought it was meant for her.

I leaned closer to her and she reached toward me and took my hand in both of hers. We kissed. She brushed my upper lip with her tongue and then she brushed my lower lip. She kissed both sides of my mouth just a taste and my mouth opened just slightly and she licked the insides. I took her tongue and sucked and sucked and we kissed and kissed . . . but my mind was on Rohn. God, she must have done something powerful to me. If Emily had been like Rohn, there is no way I would live nine hundred miles from her.

There's a certain kind of woman I can never resist, no matter what she does. A certain hair color that makes me want to touch it, a certain slow swagger that I'll turn around on the street to look at, a certain accent; that combined with a tone of voice I remember, can make the hairs stand up on my neck.

Rohn was on my mind and I let Emily touch me where she wanted to. But it was Rohn making me feel so weak, nearly thirty years later, sucking all my breath away.

Mary Maxwell

Trust

She lies curled on her side, facing away from him. The window is open, and he hears the sounds of the city outside: a bus, sighing to a stop at the curb, rap music blaring from a car, two drunks arguing on the street corner. He can't make out the words, but the tone is unmistakable. Summer in the city.

"Did you come?" he asks her.

She doesn't move. "I'm okay." Her voice is flat.

"But you didn't come."

She turns onto her back. Light from the streetlight shines through the thin curtains and he can barely see her face. "Why does that question always sound like an accusation? Like it's some affront to your manhood that I didn't come."

"I just wanted to know. If there's something I could do better . . ."

She shrugs, the slightest movement of her shoulders.

"I'm willing to try if you give me a chance. What can I do? What do you like?"

She is silent, staring at the ceiling.

"Look, just trust me a little. Tell me what I can do."

"Do you trust me?" she asks him.

"Sure I do. If I wanted something, I'd tell you."

"Yeah." Her voice has an edge of doubt. "You trust me."

"Why shouldn't I?"

"No reason. I was just asking." She turns her head to look at him, and her face is in shadow. He can see the glitter of her eyes. "I just wanted to know."

"Why?"

"I had an idea . . ." Her voice trails off.

"What idea?"

"You wouldn't be into it." Her tone dismisses him.

He leans forward, wishing he could see her expression. "Try me."

"I like knives," she says. She casts off the sheet and sits up suddenly, turning so that she faces him. She is naked, sitting cross-legged on the rumpled sheets. "That's all. I like knives."

"What about knives?" he says hesitantly. "You want me to hold a knife or—"

"Oh, no." Her tone is amused—how could he have misunderstood her so? "I hold the knife."

"You hold the knife?"

"Sure." She reaches into a drawer in the bedside table, turning momentarily into the light. Her face is flushed, excited; her mouth a little open, her eyes bright. From the drawer, she takes a knife. The blade is as long as his hand, curved slightly, like an erect cock. "This knife," she says.

He doesn't move, watching her. "You're serious."

"Yes."

"What do you do with the knife?"

"Just hold it. I've never hurt anyone. Here—feel it."

He holds out his hand for the knife. She doesn't hand it to him; instead, she grasps his wrist with her other hand, warm skin against his, and rests the blade lightly against his wrist.

"It's cold against your skin, isn't it? It takes your warmth away. It takes your breath away." She strokes his wrist with the flat of the blade. "Go ahead and breathe. There's nothing to be afraid of." She stops stroking his wrist and slowly turns the blade so that the edge rests against his skin. "Even now, as long as you don't move, it won't hurt you."

After a moment, she lifts the blade away and releases his wrist. The skin where the blade had rested tingles from the chill of the metal. His wrist is a study in heat and cold: hot where her hand had held him; cold where the blade had touched.

She watches him, the hand with the knife held loosely in her lap. She lifts the knife and touches one of her bare nipples with the flat of the blade. "I can feel the warmth of your skin in the blade. I like that."

With her free hand, she reaches out to touch his leg, running her fingers up from knee to inner thigh. A delicate touch, so soft and tender. He shivers.

"You're cold," she says. "I can warm you up." Her fingers move on his inner thigh, the back of her hand gently tickling his balls. "You know I can." She brings her legs together and shifts to a kneeling position beside him. Her hand cups his balls, and the tips of her fingers caress the sensitive spot just behind them.

He can still see the knife in her right hand. The blade glitters in the streetlight.

"Why knives?" he asks.

She laughs quietly. "You might as well ask why tigers have teeth, why scorpions sting. It just is." Still on her knees, she moves her leg to straddle his thigh. She leans in and kisses him, her tongue soft against his lips, darting into his mouth. Her hand squeezes his balls gently, then fondles his cock. Her fingers are warm and persuasive. He feels his cock grow hard.

He keeps his eyes on the knife. While she kisses him, the blade traces patterns in the air, catching the light and reflecting it onto the ceiling, the walls.

She sits up and glances at his face. "It's beautiful, isn't it?" she says. "Don't you think so?"

Not waiting for an answer, she kisses his chest, sucking lightly on his nipple while her hand strokes his cock, moving up and down the shaft with increasing urgency. She moves against his leg, and he feels the wetness of her cunt. He closes his eyes. A moment later he feels the flat of the knife blade against his nipple. The warmth of her breath; the chill of the knife. He feels the chill all the way down to his groin. He opens his eyes, looking up at her. Light shines full on her face, her bare breasts. Her nipples are hard.

He reaches up, meaning to lift the knife away from his body, but her hand strokes his stiff cock, and he reaches for her breasts instead, caressing the warm flesh.

She smiles at him, shaking her head. "No," she says. "I told you: Don't move." With the flat of the blade, she pushes his hand away. "I'll move." She leans closer, bringing her breast to his lips, and he sucks on her nipple. She brings the blade back to his chest, and he feels the cold metal, but it no longer seems important.

"That's right," she says. "Yeah, that's it."

She lifts the knife away from him and kisses the spot where the blade had rested, warming his skin. Her body slides down beside his until he feels her breath on his thigh. She kisses his balls, then runs her tongue up the hard shaft of his cock, taking the tip into her mouth.

"Oh, yeah," he moans.

Her tongue swirls around the tip of his cock, each circle bringing a new level of sensation. He feels the chill of metal against the shaft of his cock, and the breath catches in his throat. But her tongue circles again, warm and urgent, pressing against the head of his cock. He tenses his thigh muscles, resisting the urge to lift his hips and push himself deeper into her mouth. He feels the cold touch of steel on his belly. For a moment, she lifts her mouth away from him. "Don't move," she says.

"Please," he says. "Please."

She laughs and once again takes his cock into her mouth, moving so that he is deep inside her, pressing against the warm wetness of her tongue, her throat. She positions his leg between her thighs, and he feels her wet cunt rubbing against him.

He cannot move, he knows that. He aches to grab her head and push his cock deeper into her throat. He feels the chill of the knife as she moves it to touch his ass, his thigh, his chest. He is afraid of the touch of the knife against his balls. Does he trust her? Why not? Does it matter? What matters is the heat of her lips on his cock, her hand on his balls. The chill of the knife on his chest, his side. Her mouth moving faster, sucking him harder, again and again, with hot-lipped urgency. He moans, trying to form a word. "Please . . . ," but he doesn't know what he is asking for. He knows nothing but the heat of her lips and the touch of her hand and the chill of the blade. "Please . . ."

She takes his cock deep and he feels the chill of the knife against his balls as he comes, frozen into stillness by the touch of the blade, his hands in fists at his side, moaning as she swallows his hot cum.

He lies very still, feeling the sweat drying on his chest. She lifts the knife away. "You can move now," she says.

Marcy Sheiner

⤳

Two Guys and a Girl

When I moved across the country for a prestigious new job, I was forced to leave behind one of the best, and certainly the most avid, lovers I'd ever had. I begged Jack to come with me, but he had his own career, his own life—and besides, we'd never even been monogamous. We saw each other an average of every other weekend—not much, but with Jack, that's all I needed. That entire weekend was spent in bed, fucking and sucking, sometimes all through the night; we'd try to sleep, but one or the other would invariably wake up and claw at the other.

Now, in sunny California, I was seeing Brian, a younger, adventurous guy who was willing to play out just about any sexual fantasy, at least verbally. One of my favorites was to be with two men at once, something I had never managed to pull off. I'd been with women, by myself or in threesomes with men, but I had never been able to find two men at the same time with whom I felt comfortable enough to engage in a threesome. What's more, half of my girlfriends, all of them far less sexually adventurous than I, had managed it, and reported that it was exquisite.

Brian indulged my fantasy; that is, we talked about it during sex, pretending another man was with us. Sometimes he used a dildo on me while I sucked his cock, and was pretty good at creating the illusion of another man being there. What Brian didn't

431

know, however, was that not only did I want two cocks at once, but I also wanted to see them get it on together.

Years ago I had discovered a fascination for male-male love through gay men's magazines. I'll never forget the rush I got the first time I opened one of them and saw two extremely large dicks rubbing up against each other. For days I couldn't get the image out of my mind. I began reading and watching gay men's porn regularly; it turned me on because men turn me on, but also because it's the raunchiest, most aggressive, down-and-dirty form of pornography around. These reading materials, needless to say, were kept hidden from Brian, who expressed no interest in being with men at all.

One day Jack called to say he was coming to California on a business trip. My pussy juices began flowing immediately; there was no way I wasn't going to sleep with him. But I worried about Brian—we hadn't really decided whether we were monogamous, and an old lover is always a threat. Then suddenly it hit me: maybe I could finally fulfill my fantasy.

It would be tricky: neither man had ever been with a guy, and both had more than a touch of machismo in their personalities. One night, I waited until Brian was pumping his cock into my pussy, on the brink of orgasm, then whispered, "Wouldn't you love to see me get fucked by another guy?"

Brian, of course, thought this was just our usual fantasy play. "Oh, yeah, baby, I'd like to see you with six or seven cocks jackin' off on your face, on your tits . . ."

He didn't get much further—we both came.

Later on I casually mentioned Jack's upcoming visit, gradually sharing the information that I'd like to try a threesome. Brian was understandably hesitant, but over the next few days I worked on him, describing visions of a cock in my pussy and one in my mouth, while gently stroking his organ, coaxing him into cooperation. I didn't reveal any hopes that he and Jack might suck and fuck each other; I figured I'd cross that bridge when and if we got to it.

Brian valiantly agreed to let me see Jack alone the night of his arrival, so I could feel him out on the subject. After a year apart, we immediately fell all over each other—clawing clothing, biting flesh, sinking into old familiar rhythms. When we were finally sated, I asked Jack if he remembered how I had always wanted to be with two men. He did. Then I told him about Brian, and asked if he was up for it.

He agreed. The next night found me on my knees in front of a full-length mirror, sucking Brian's cock while Jack fucked me from behind. The sensation was indescribable—like being totally filled, totally satisfied.

After a while I took Brian's dick out of my mouth and said innocently, "Honey, I'd really love it if you'd lick my pussy while Jack's fucking me."

Both men did a double take, but shrugged agreeably. We moved onto the bed and I lay down on my back. Jack climbed on top and resumed fucking me, while Brian knelt and put his mouth near my mons. He slowly licked my clit and my outer lips while Jack's cock slid in and out of my hole.

"Down lower," I murmured, gently pushing Brian's head down between my legs.

He moved down hesitantly, to where he could no longer avoid the cock furiously pumping in and out of me. He tried, but just as I had hoped, excitement finally overtook him, and soon he was licking Jack's prick as it made its journey in and out. I watched Jack's face and saw he was excited, and with one neat movement slid myself up and out of the way.

For a moment that seemed like hours, we were suspended in time. The men realized what was happening, and I wondered if they'd let it go further. Then the moment passed, and Brian took the whole of Jack's cock down his throat, sucking eagerly, his fingers kneading Jack's large balls. Jack pumped in and out of Brian's mouth just the same as if it were mine.

Brian sidled his way around so his cock faced Jack's mouth, and Jack stroked and squeezed the head, finally taking the pulsing meat into his mouth. I lay back and began stroking my pussy, feasting on the sumptuous vision before me.

Feelings of lust coursed through me, along with a little bit of jealousy. The men became so involved in sucking each other, they forgot I even existed. I reached into my bedside drawer, grabbed my trusty dildo, and began fucking myself. How ironic, I thought.

Here I've got two flesh-and-blood men in bed with me, and I'm using an artificial organ.

I fucked myself with my dildo while I watched them sixty-nine, and my orgasm coincided with both men shooting hot cum into each other's throats. As their hard-ons withered and they returned to reality, both men looked at me with a mixture of embarrassment and apology. They broke apart to lie on either side of me.

"That was so hot," I finally said.

They both let out a sigh of relief. After a while I reached down and took a cock in each hand, stroking and kneading them until they were again erect. Eventually I sat up and pushed their cocks closer together, rubbing the head of one up and down the other's shaft. I knelt and licked each of them, then took both inside my mouth, though I could only fit an inch or two. We were all breathing heavily. Interestingly, while I had always expected I'd be a passive partner in this kind of triangle, I was orchestrating all the action. The men wanted to get it on with each other but were too inhibited to do so without my encouragement.

And encourage them I did. I told Brian to lie on his belly, then directed Jack's cock to his asshole. I lubricated the head and Brian's hole, then gently guided the cock inside. Brian moaned, spreading his ass cheeks as Jack sank it in inch by yielding inch. He began to fuck Brian, slowly at first, then faster, until Brian was on all fours, pushing against Jack's dick, silently begging for more. I slid beneath Brian and spread my legs. He entered me easily as Jack thrust in and out of his asshole without missing a beat.

I thought I'd die of pleasure right then and there. I have always loved the sensation of having a man's weight on me, pounding me into the bed, dissolving all my tension; now I had the weight of two men on top of me. It felt as if Jack's cock reached right through Brian, and both men were fucking me. Jack was grunting, making animal sounds I'd never heard from him before, and Brian was sighing in ecstasy, having totally surrendered. I felt his cock stiffen and I gripped it hard with my pussy muscles. As he shot his load into me, spasms rocked my cunt. At the same time, Jack let out a loud grunt that was almost a lion's roar, and the three of us shook together as one organism, holding onto each other for dear life. I felt as if we'd just experienced a minor earthquake.

We collapsed in a sweaty, exhausted heap. After a while I got up and made us something to eat. I chattered on about the experience, talking about everything I had felt and learned. But boys will be boys: though they had managed to break through some heavy cultural barriers, Brian and Jack remained locked in masculine silence when it came to talking about their feelings.

Jack returned to the East Coast but left a lasting legacy: Brian and I have added a new dimension to our sex life—we watch gay men's porn together. Though he isn't cruising gay bars, the memory of our threesome infuses our lovemaking, and I expect it to be with me for a long time to come.

Magenta Michaels

Sileni: A Moonlit Tale

"A tail?" she grinned up at him, repeating his words, delighted at the outrageousness of the notion. "You have a tail?"

They were packed in against the crowded bar; flame-haired Samantha in her witchiest, clingingest, this-is-the-night-that-we're-going-to-do-It black dress, and this starkly beautiful dark-haired man, their shoulders jammed together beneath the arcing green of potted palms and the low jeweled light of Tiffany lamps that made up Henry Africa's: The Watering Hole.

"Is it soft and fluffy like a bunny's," she teased him, "or does it have a little pom-pom on the tip, like a poodle's? Can you hold things with it? Does it wag furiously when you're happy? Did it give you complexes as a child?" She ran out of breath and stood beaming as she waited for his response. He had remained silent during the whole barrage of questions, smiling down into the amber lights of his drink as he drew circles with the base of his glass through the wet spot on the bar.

"You must be serious about this," he chided her through soft Italian syllables. He reached out to smooth a stray lock back from her face. "I'm trying to tell you something."

Samantha flipped her wild red crinkles from one side of her face to the other. She eyed him as she considered. It was true that she had wondered at the oddness of his halting gait, and she had

436

puzzled over the full, almost old-fashioned cut of his obviously expensive suits. But she had finally dismissed these things as Italian "style" and Continental eccentricity. A tail had not been one of her considerations.

"Can I see it?" she demanded, smiling over the rim of her glass, enjoying what her question implied.

"Yes," he responded, after a time.

They readied themselves to go.

It took them twenty minutes to pay the check and find a cab, and another twenty to get to his ritzy, uptown address; during the whole of the ride, the subject of his tail didn't cross her mind again. She was busy congratulating herself on her great good luck at having found such a treasure. He was polished, he was European, he seemed to have money, he was sexy and he was beautiful. She turned to his profile. His beauty was impossible, immaculate; not the virile, masculine good looks assigned to western cowboys, but rather the finely chiseled, almost inbred aristocratic beauty that a mother might wish for her only daughter. He turned to find her studying him, and he captured her hand, bringing her fingers to his lips. So it was only when they stood before the wide door of his apartment, her stomach leaping in anticipation of what lay ahead, that the floating remembrance of his talk of a tail bubbled to the surface of her mind. But then he was pushing open the door, and she was following him inside, slowing her step in the wake of his peculiar walk, her feet sinking down into the thickly padded carpet.

He asked her to wait in the entrance hall as he went ahead flipping on the lights, and she stood in the echoing semi-dark, listening to him move around the apartment.

"Come," he said finally, holding out his hand to her, now the perfect host, "let me see to your comfort." And he took her arm, leading her blinking into the light.

It was not the vastness of the room nor the richness of its architecture that made her draw in her breath. She had seen high vaulted ceilings and mahogany-paneled doors and floor-to-ceiling French windows that banked an entire wall before. No, it was that the grandeur of the room in which she stood had been turned into a wooded grove, an enchanted forest brought indoors.

No ordinary man lived here. It was as though the most sump-tuous furnishings, the most beautiful objects had been collected onto the face of a brilliantly patterned Persian kilim and set down carefully in the midst of a perfect forest glen. Trees of different leaf and size grew clustered, sometimes three or four deep, their limbs and leaves overlapping, their containers hidden by small granite boulders and lengths of dried branches scattered among their bases. White garden roses, voluptuous in their antique vases, covered every surface, filling in the spaces between the piles of handbound books and the collections of whimsical arti-facts from every century, every corner of the world. A domed sil-ver bird cage perched atop a freestanding stone column, the column itself spiraled with small dark ivy, the burnished floor of the silver cage littered with rose potpourri and crushed gold leaf. Soft deep sofas covered in white-on-white silk vied with the graceful curves of upholstered chairs that offered tapestry seats. A tall, beveled mirror in an ornate gilded frame nestled among the foliage of a cluster of trees so that in passing, it seemed that one saw oneself reflected in the Garden of Eden. The room stood poised, alive in its vibrancy.

He took her coat and then busied himself mixing drinks while she wandered around the room, examining the masks and sculp-ture and fingering the spines of ancient books. She came to stand before a muraled wall, its haunting scene done in trompe l'oeil so that it spilled over onto the curved ceiling and surrounding walls, creating the illusion for the viewer of being part of the artfully done painting. The scene was a depiction of a wild and thunder-ous falls, its ocean of falling water beginning a half-mile in the air. And at the crest of the cliff where the waters began their descent perched a lone medieval castle, its dark stone towers and landward-facing battlements rising up from the very edges of a massive granite shelf that jutted out from the living rock over the turbulent water's fall.

"What is this place?" She spoke in a whisper, awestruck that such a scene could exist, even in an artist's mind.

He came to stand beside her, pressing a drink into her hand.

"It is beautiful, is it not? I was born in the great forests behind the fortress that you see. The castle is my family's. Over the centuries we were pushed to the edge of this terrible water by those who were not like us. I am of the Sileni. We are not as ordinary men."

"Ahh ... ," she said as she smiled at him over the rim of her glass. "Of course ... the tail."

She took a sip from her drink. It was frothy, smelling of roses, but had a slightly bitter bite.

"A potion," he answered her before she could ask, "so that my tail does not deter you." He led her away from the mural to a low sofa, bending to kiss her after she had settled herself among the cushions. His breath was wonderful, strange, bringing up odd, swirling images behind her closed eyelids. She arched up to his kiss, parting her lips, but he slid his mouth away, pressing it instead to the ridge of her throat and the base of her ears, drawing the lobes into his mouth and then softly letting them go. He sniffed at her skin as though delighting in the scent beneath her cosmetics and perfume.

After a while he knelt before her, biting softly through her dress at the surface of her thighs moving upward, his teeth finally finding her risen nipples through the thin fabric of her dress. His arms rested on the sofa at either side of her hips and he burrowed his face into her lap, kissing her fingers out of his way as he gathered her skirts up and up until they lay in a soft heap around her hips. Then he pulled her hips to him, pausing a moment before he pressed his face to her crotch. It was as though he could not get enough of her smell, pulling her essence into his nostrils with slow deep breaths. He rubbed his nose up and down on either side of her clitoris as it pushed outward, swollen, against the silk of her panties. Then he opened his lips to her, dragging his tongue in wide, slow strokes over the lace-covered lips of her vagina, soaking the fabric with the wet of his tongue and making her hips push upward toward his mouth; aching for the lace to be pushed away, aching for the softness of his tongue to curl bare around her dark-hooded kernel of flesh.

"Let me see you ... let me see how beautiful you are," and he stood up to help her with her dress.

In a moment she was naked, except for her panties, but she

stepped away from his hands when he moved to slide them from her hips.

"Let me see your tail first," reminding him even now of the words that had gotten her here in the first place. "I want to see your tail."

"You are certain?" He searched her face, and when she nodded yes, he rose without speaking, crossing the room to the far wall where he slowly lowered the lights until there was nothing left but a rectangle of moonlight, spilling its many-paned shadow across the carpet floor.

He approached her now from across the darkened room, stopping just outside the puddle of moonlight, his eyes on her face as he stood before her, removing his shoes, unbuttoning his shirt in the dark. She lay her head back against the sofa, listening to him unbuckle his belt, unzip his trousers. And when she finally heard him step from the cloth, dropping the garment to the floor, she raised her head to look.

Even in the dimness she knew that the deep coloring of his lower body had nothing to do with suntan. It was as though his torso and arms floated bottomless, white and reflective in the dark.

And then came the movement behind him. It was more of a sound coupled with something, something she felt with her skin rather than a thing that her eye had identified in the dim light. There was a short cracking noise, and a whooshing sound, as though the air behind him had been moved and cooled by the fierce hard snap of cloth or hair.

A low vibration began in the muscles of her forearms and the fronts of her thighs as she stared at him, her eyes searching the velvet space around the dark half of his body.

He stepped toward her, directly into the puddle of moonlight, pausing in mid-stride to give complete illumination to what the pale light revealed. His lower body was that of a horse. Not a deformed man, not some pitiable creature of twisted limbs and crusted skin, but a clear and exquisite creation unto himself, the bones of the horse half enabling a gait that nearly mimicked that of a man. He stood before her in all his magnificence, the thick muscles of his rump and thighs knotted and rippling beneath the glistening dark brown of his coat.

He turned for her slightly, just so she could see the tail. It developed out of the base of his spine, lying tight against the top of his buttocks. Full and wild, it was not a romantic version of human hair, but made up of hard black strands, as coarse and strong as those that made up the tail of any barnyard animal. It dropped headlong past the v-shaped backs of his veined legs to stop just before his hooves.

He took a step toward her, this time out of the moonlit box. The wonder of the tail was now shadowed by the mystery of his unsheathed sex. It hung heavy before him, a pink speckled shaft as thick as her wrist, its weight not allowing an upward curve. She could not take her eyes from its dark tip. It rose as a lure, baiting her eye, its color as deep as the dark brown of his coat. He took another step toward her, knelt before her, tugging gently at her panties, easing them over her hips, his eyes never leaving her face. He placed one of her legs and then the other over his shoulders, and finally, dropping his eyes from her face, he bent once more to the triangle between her thighs.

It seemed to her that she floated from her body, that she watched their coupling from a high corner of the room; she found the scene breathtaking and beautiful. She saw moonlight streaming through the tall French windows, over the paleness of the low couches and her own naked shoulders, over his head moving ever so slightly as he bent to his work, and finally over the dark glory of his tail as it spread behind him like an open, finely etched fan. She watched how her hips lifted to his kiss and how he eased her knees down from his shoulders to wrap her legs around his waist, her heels crossed and propped at the base of his tail. He was pulling at her now, gathering her to him as he slid her thighs onto the tops of his own. The backs of her legs were prickled by his ruffled coat as she slid forward against the natural grain of his hair. Their faces were inches apart now, his nose and mouth glistening from his labors. He lifted his cock from between his legs and lay it between them, against her belly. It poked dry and immense, nothing like any man could ever be. He took her hand and closed it around the girth of him. When she did not shrink from its weight and size but opened and closed her fingers along its length, he fitted the dark head of it to her opening.

"Do you find me a monster?" he whispered against her lips, his breath smelling of her pussy. She found herself responding, her self now back in her body, as she wound her arms around his neck in answer. He gathered her onto him, a little at a time, allowing her wetness to ease his way. And when finally they sat belly to belly, his cock curved hard within her, he rose with her, his hands filled with her buttocks, and walked to the tall gilded mirror among the trees so that she could see herself impaled upon his animal sex.

"Let me down," she murmured, and she slid from his hard flesh to a pile of sheepskins spread before the mirror. She arranged herself on her knees, offering him her backside. He curved his torso over her back, parting her cheeks with the head of his member.

She stiffened, thinking he would enter her there, but he did not, instead rubbing his tip slowly up and down against the slick puckered mouth of her anus. Then he slid it under and into her, stretching her sides as he began to rock, a small thrusting, as he waited for her to respond. Finally, she matched his movements with her own, and he climbed to the rounded hooves that were his heels to begin his animal thrust.

He rode her, he rode her, his hips scooping under and up, then shuddering into her; a cadenced rhythm marked by the loud squishing sound of his dick as he stroked. Her naked sides were stinging from the wicked slap of his tail, which whipped furiously behind him. His balls slapped against her as the weight of his flesh pulled her inner lips downward, yanking the hood over her bursting clitoris.

She was wild with her need, grunting with her need, her legs lifting from the floor as time and again she rammed herself backward onto the impossible girth of him, her hips whipping ovals in the air.

Then came her release; the creeping wave of it rising up from her calves and spreading quickly over her like gooseflesh, as her body ignited and she bucked against him unchecked. Whimpering, she sought only to satisfy herself, her face pressed hard into the sheepskins, her hands now claws that kneaded the rugs. Her back arched itself and her toes cramped as every part of her body coiled, impelling her toward her finish.

When it was over, it was she who lay exhausted, and he rose to tend to her, rubbing her back, kissing her buttocks and covering her with a silken afghan drawn down from a chair. Unable to keep her eyes open, she snuggled down into the lushness of the musky rugs, nearly asleep with floating dreams of being mistress of the castle above the waterfall. She heard, as she drifted off to sleep, the clip-clop of rounded hooves stepping from the padded carpet to the marble tile of the bathroom floor.

Catherine Tavel

∽

About Penetration

It was simple. Thomas just couldn't penetrate Diane. Or more specifically, he wouldn't. But Thomas had his reasons, his own personal rationalizations. In a way, they made perfect sense to Diane's mind, but not to her body. And definitely not to her heart. They were married, only not to each other. But really now, what difference did it make whether or not he stuck his tongue into her mouth or his cock into her pussy? Adultery was adultery, whether you technically penetrated someone or not. Right? Of course it was.

How did they meet? If Diane had told anyone about his existence (which she hadn't), she wouldn't have had the nerve to be honest. But the truth was that she and Thomas met on a lonely Saturday night in May. Only they didn't actually meet. Their voices met. You see, he phoned her that night, dialed seven anonymous numbers because he was feeling empty and alone. He wasn't seeking sex, even though the first thing he said to Diane was, "I want to eat your pussy."

Why hadn't Diane hung up the telephone then and there? She frequently received phone calls of this nature and, as a rule, would hang up. But there was something in Thomas' voice, something that sounded just as sad as he felt inside. Something in his voice seeped into her skin. And that was that.

Diane had been in a bad frame of mind that night. Her husband was out and she was transferring documents from disk to disk on her word processor. She simply wasn't in the mood for cunnilingus. In fact, when she finished her chores, she was seriously contemplating settling down for a nice long cry. That's when the telephone rang.

Diane was by no means an easy lay, even over the phone. She was bitchy. She was smart-assed. She was abrasive. But still, Thomas wouldn't give up. He kept talking smut; she kept trying to change the subject to decipher what kind of person he was beneath the raunch.

"Come on, touch your cunt for me," Thomas said.

And Diane wondered aloud, "Are you married?"

"Yes," was his answer.

"For how long?" she prodded.

"Three years."

"Where is she now?" Diane pressed.

"In New Jersey visiting her sister with our daughter."

"How old is she?"

"Three weeks old," Thomas admitted. Diane was surprised that a woman would venture away from home with such a young infant, but this said a lot about Thomas' wife. She was always leaving—if not physically, then mentally. That's probably why Thomas was on the phone with Diane after all, now, wasn't it?

There was a long pause, then Diane asked, "Why did you marry her?"

After an even longer pause, Thomas responded, "Because we were compatible."

Diane burst out laughing. "Computers are compatible. There has to be much more between people."

That's how Diane and Thomas began speaking of other topics—their lives, their childhoods, their beliefs, their unfulfilling marriages. The parallels were uncanny—their mothers had the same first name, each of their spouses were Jewish while Diane and Thomas were raised Catholic, Diane was five days younger than Thomas' wife, and Thomas was now living in the neighborhood where Diane had grown up. And they were both unhappy. Then Thomas and Diane started to talk dirty again, and both of them faked orgasms. Maybe they wanted to get back to plain talking.

When it happened again, the sex part came naturally. Thomas told Diane to get her vibrator and she fucked herself with it. Diane told Thomas how much she loved to suck cock, that to her, semen tasted fresh and clean, like the ocean. Thomas chuckled even though his dick was hard. He called her many names. He called her a whore, a slut, a cunt. No one had ever called Diane those names before, but for some reason, she liked it. She liked it a great deal. And Thomas liked calling her those names, even though he respected her and sensed she was actually a good person. She called him a bastard and a motherfucker even though he sounded like a very sweet man when he wasn't cursing. Thomas and Diane uttered the kind of words they couldn't say to their spouses, no matter how intense it got. Besides, Thomas needed something, something for himself. Only he wasn't exactly sure what it was. He thought he found it in Diane's voice.

When Diane and Thomas climaxed, it was for real and it was together. They called out each other's name. Now, the same old names sounded different, special. Diane almost cried, which was what she did when she came hard and strong. The crying was almost involuntary, like sneezing, only it frightened some men. It frightened Diane, but she had learned to accept it, to embrace it, simply because it was hers.

After the orgasm, Thomas and Diane talked more. He waited patiently on the line while she ran off to pee. Diane didn't think Thomas would be there when she returned—and she didn't want to lose him, not so soon anyway—but he was there, waiting patiently. Thomas admitted that he didn't remember what number he had dialed at random. It was 332-something. Diane told him the last four digits, 9610, because she wanted him to phone again.

Next they described themselves to each other. Diane told him how small her breasts were, even about the gray flecks in her black hair. Thomas told her his height, weight, and how big his dick was. Later he confessed that he'd lied—he was only five foot eight. She thought this fabrication odd because most men would have lied about the size of their genitals, but Thomas was more sensitive about his height. Since Diane was only five foot five, it didn't matter. But it wouldn't have mattered anyway.

So Thomas and Diane talked. And talked. They talked until she heard her husband unlock the front door. And after she softly clicked down the telephone, Diane noticed that she and Thomas had been speaking for more than two hours.

Diane existed in a sort of euphoria for the next few days. She couldn't sleep that night, but she smiled restlessly in the blackness, still giddy from her orgasm. The thought of two strangers reaching out to each other in the middle of the night was such a romantic notion. Was it fate? Was it destiny? Perhaps it was the luck of the dial. Would Thomas ever phone her again? Something about that prospect scared her, but something else about it made her long for him. An empty hole of emotion had somehow been filled by the sound of his voice. What would she do if he never called again? How could she live with a cavern inside her chest?

Two days passed. And two nights. Diane's mood peaked and ebbed constantly. Her heart rose each time the telephone rang and it plummeted whenever it was anyone else but Thomas. Her husband noticed nothing different in Diane's behavior because he was so tangled up in his own ghosts. Plus, her odd attitude shifts were not unusual for Diane. When she had sex with her husband (which had always been frequent and calmly satisfactory), she imagined what it might be like to make love with Thomas. His words rang out in her head as she had orgasms with her husband, and it was good.

But then he called. Thomas actually called! Her heart dropped, and then floated upward at the sound of his voice. They made plans to meet a few days later. In the morning. At a nearby park.

Thomas was not what Diane had pictured, although she hadn't really pictured anything. Thomas, on the contrary, said that Diane was exactly what he had imagined. But how could anyone have imagined eyes so chestnut brown, so knowing, yet so starkly innocent? Diane was afraid to look into Thomas' eyes, which were green and as piercing as broken glass. It almost hurt when he studied her. It was as though he were cutting through her, digging for something that she was desperately trying to hide. Diane had to turn away at first.

They stood in the middle of the playground, between the swings and slides. It was too early for anyone else to be there yet. (Diane had told her husband that she was going out for a jog, and Thomas had told his wife he had to be at work early that day.) They just stared at each other, and then held each other. Thomas felt odd in Diane's arms. She gazed into his eyes, like a child about to ask a question, and then he said, "Don't."

She didn't.

At first, Diane was afraid to get into Thomas' car. She asked him to show her some identification. Right there on the sidewalk, he opened his wallet. Besides his driver's license, Diane saw Thomas' wedding picture. She certainly didn't need to see that. It gave her a chill in her stomach, but she got into the white Toyota anyway. Thomas tossed the car keys into her lap, in case she still didn't trust him. She tossed them back because she did.

Thomas and Diane sat there getting used to each other. She didn't know what to say. They said it all on the telephone, but in person, face to face, they were strangers. She knew things about him that few people did. For example, she knew what he sounded like when he was coming. But then, she didn't know things that everyone else did. And she wanted to know everything.

Thomas had a scar that sliced through his right nostril. Diane thought it was curiously sexy. She reached out and touched it. "How did you get this?" she asked.

"In a car accident," Thomas said, quite matter-of-factly. "I went through the windshield."

"Oh."

So, Thomas and Diane did what they did best. They talked. And talked and talked. Then, for some reason, Diane said, "I'm so wet," and blushed. She didn't know why, she just had to say it. She wanted him to know.

All Thomas did was smile. Then he moved as close as he could in his bucket seat to Diane. "Touch yourself," he whispered. "Touch yourself for me." It was broad daylight. People were passing the car, walking their poodles. But Diane did as Thomas said. She touched her pussy through her black, lace-trimmed Spandex shorts.

Thomas wouldn't touch her, though. Diane didn't think too

much of this at first. Perhaps he didn't want to bring home her pungent scent to his wife, or else he was playing an erotic game. In any event, Diane tried to satisfy herself with his voice. It drifted to her ears from the other side of the Toyota. It tickled her eardrums, then oozed down to her crotch, where it tickled the tip of her clitoris. Diane's panties were soaked. She could feel it through her clothing. The seam of her shorts dug into her slit. Her fingers pressed the seam into the crack of her cunt even deeper.

"No," Diane kept saying over and over again. Even though she meant "yes." She didn't want Thomas to see her face turned inside out, her limbs trembling, her lower lip crumbling, her eyelids fluttering, yet in another way, she did. In her mind, Thomas *had* to see everything. Even the ugly things.

But to Thomas, nothing about Diane was ugly. Not the tiny cobweb of cranberry-colored veins on her left thigh. Not the nose that was far too large for her delicate features. Not the callus on the middle digit of her right hand, which was now shoved into her cunt. Nothing about Diane was ugly, because it was real.

Thomas reached over and caressed her thigh. He would later tell Diane that her skin was as soft as his newborn daughter's cheeks. And in the future, that would make Diane smile many, many times. Thomas' hand felt very big and warm and strong as it stroked Diane's smoothness. His hand traveled up past the lace leg band of her shorts and stopped at the outside of her panties. But he would not go any further.

Thomas leaned forward and opened the glove compartment. He took out a plastic cigar case. Printed on it were the words IT's A GIRL in fancy script. Thomas slid the cigar holder up along Diane's leg and under the elastic of her panties. It slipped easily into her pussy. Diane gasped. Thomas looked into her dark eyes. He wiggled his finger inside the plastic casing which wiggled inside Diane's cunt. She felt as though she would climax immediately, but she didn't want to. Then he would see. He would see everything.

Thomas took a second cigar case and fit it onto another finger. There were now two plastic tubes wedged in Diane's pussy. It was perverse. It was almost funny. It was intense. It was silly. But whatever it was, Diane was going to come. She turned her face toward the car door and bit into her lip and came.

Afterward, Thomas smiled again. Diane was near tears. She needed more of him and she wanted to make him come. Only he wouldn't let her touch him. He wouldn't even kiss her. Yet, when he grasped her nipples, he knew how she liked to be touched. She liked to have them squeezed. Hard. Very hard. And no one, except herself, did it right. Up until Thomas.

It was getting late and Thomas really had to get to work. He left Diane on the curb, not unlike an abandoned puppy. Well, she did have those abandoned puppy eyes. She felt full and empty at the same time. Would Thomas ever call again? Would she ever see him again? Probably not, Diane told herself.

But Thomas called the next day. And a few days after that. And so on. They shared stories and secrets and laughed and came together. He told her things that he told no one else, things so private they can't even be mentioned here.

Another time, Thomas disappeared for six weeks. She counted the days, the weeks. He didn't meet Diane in their place by the park. He didn't even phone her. Diane thought it was over, but then, she always thought it was over. "Why is it," she once asked Thomas, "that whenever I see you, it feels like the last time?" Thomas wasn't sure what to answer.

Those six weeks had been almost unbearable for Diane. Thomas wouldn't give her his telephone number and it was unlisted anyway, so she couldn't look it up. She started checking the obituaries, even though she didn't know his last name. During that period, Diane asked herself many times whether it had been worth it, meeting Thomas. Worth all the pain. Worth all the rejection when he wouldn't touch her. And many times, her silent response was the same: "Yes."

Thomas resurfaced, safe, with no real explanation. It was ridiculous. It was pathetic. It was love. It was hate. It was anger. It was acceptance. It was all of the above and more. Diane convinced herself that she was psychotic, obsessed, immature, insane. Then she realized that she was only human and she was probably just in love.

Diane and Thomas continued to meet in secret places. Sometimes they would talk. Others, they would sit there and sigh. Diane would always try to touch him and he would constantly push her away. Why did Thomas do this? And more important, why did Diane accept it? First, it was a challenge. Second, she harbored the hope that her sensuality would triumph over his will. It was an erotic power struggle of sorts. Sometimes Diane did win, but only partly.

"Not in the car," Thomas would say. Then the next time they were in the car, he would jerk off and splatter semen all over her pussy while she fingered herself into a frenzy. "Never again in the car," he would swear, but then he would stroke his prick and she would struggle to lick the jism as it shot onto her face and neck. He stroked with one hand and held her face away with the other, not even permitting her tongue to make contact with the head of his cock. Diane was confused. But perhaps Thomas was even more confused than she was.

One night, they sat in the car in the parking lot of Seaman's Furniture store. They studied the stars. "What's your favorite ice cream flavor?" Diane asked.

"I hate ice cream," Thomas said.

"But what if someone put a gun to your head and made you choose?" Diane wondered.

"Then I'd have to say vanilla," Thomas admitted.

After a few moments, Diane wondered, "And your favorite color?"

"Yellow," Thomas said.

"Yellow like the sun or yellow like gold?" Diane prodded.

"Like the sun. And yours?" he asked.

"Blue," Diane stated most emphatically. "Blue like the sky."

Thomas nodded. "The sun and the sky."

Diane couldn't decide what her favorite song was. There were so many. His was "Turn the Page." Magically, it came onto the radio. She lay her head in his lap and listened to the words and tried to figure out why he liked it so much. There were chills moving up her spine during the saxophone solo. Somehow, she understood. She understood perfectly.

Thomas looked into Diane's eyes. Then, he held her head in his hands and rubbed it against his cock. He began getting hard.

Diane moved her head of her own accord. Suddenly, Thomas said, "No," and made her sit up. The magic was broken because Diane had tried to take control of the situation. Thomas liked to believe that their silent lust was actually under control and he was only an innocent bystander, swept away in the undertow. There was less guilt that way.

Sometimes Thomas and Diane talked on the telephone and watched television together, each in their own apartment, miles away. This was very nice. Diane cuddled herself beneath a blanket and pretended that they were in bed together. Sometimes they would flip channels. Other times, they would switch to comedians or movie classics and comment on how beautiful Elizabeth Taylor was in *The Last Time I Saw Paris*. Diane rented Thomas' favorite movie, *Cinema Paradiso*. She saw it alone one night, hoping her telepathy would make him phone her. But it didn't. When the movie was over, the ending touched Diane so deeply that she cried for half an hour. And cried bitterly. She cried because she understood why Thomas loved that movie so much.

Finally, one day, Thomas explained why he couldn't penetrate Diane with his finger, his tongue or his penis. Even though his wife had always been ambivalent about sex, he had never been unfaithful to her. And he couldn't be, because his own father had abandoned his family when Thomas was only three years old. And Thomas didn't want to be like his father.

Diane tried to accept Thomas' explanation, but no matter how she tried, she couldn't swallow the whole thing. She couldn't help but think that Thomas really liked the power of refusal. It strongly resembled the passive might his wife held over him. It occurred to Diane that all four of them were like sexual dominoes. Thomas slept with a woman who rejected him, and rejected a woman who ached to take him inside of her body. Diane's husband craved her body, yet ignored the rest of her. And Diane, she lusted after Thomas. Go figure.

Thomas couldn't understand that Diane didn't want to take him away from anyone. She merely wanted to make love to him. To cling to him like a life preserver when life began to hurt too much. They could cling to each other to help stay afloat in this crazy world and then return to their respective families afterward, slightly more sane. Only Thomas wouldn't hear of it.

So, upon his suggestion, Thomas and Diane tried to be just friends. But it didn't work out too well. It had started out as a purely sexual relationship and only being friends was like back-pedaling. Diane told herself that she would rather have Thomas in her life, if only as a buddy, than not at all. He had opened Diane up to herself, awakened parts that she never knew existed. And she didn't want to lose that. Plus, Diane harbored a teeny-tiny, teensy-weensy hope that maybe, just maybe, Thomas would weaken and finger-fuck her with a cigar holder again.

But Thomas refused her even that. Whenever they were alone, or even in a crowd, their eyes would bore holes through each other. There was passion. There was fire. They would have to turn away or else try to ignore the electricity that sizzled between them. Thomas would start to talk facts and figures whenever his cock grew erect when he was with Diane. But even that did no good. Should they stop seeing each other? That would be too painful. But then seeing each other was painful in a different way.

Diane tried to accept Thomas' decision, but she wound up feeling remorseful, and worst of all, foolish. She couldn't help but remember all of the promises, about how they'd sneak off for a weekend in the Caribbean, how they'd make love for hours, how he'd make her climax again and again. Had they really been lies? In the curls of her cerebrum, Diane knew that Thomas longed to give Diane all of those things, but he simply couldn't. Thomas always told Diane the truth. And sometimes the truth hurt.

Did Thomas try to hurt her on purpose or did it just seem to happen that way? It hurt when he spoke of Monique, his former lover. It hurt when he spoke of how, in a rare display of passion, he convinced his wife to drip mother's milk all over his face and then lick it off. It hurt because these women had something Diane would never have—him. Diane wanted to hurt Thomas like she'd been hurt, but she couldn't. Then she realized that he was probably hurting too. She saw it in his eyes.

In her more fragile moments, Diane wondered if Thomas was using her to feel like a man because his wife had emasculated him. And it was pretty wonderful to make another woman wet, to make her squirm for you, to make her desire you, even in her sleep, wasn't it? All that, without technically committing adultery. But then again, Diane knew that Thomas was probably in love with her. Only it frightened him. And when men are frightened, they usually pull away. When women are frightened, they usually open up even more, throwing reason to the wind, like delicate flowers of flesh, poising themselves for the pain. After all, pain was better than denial. Wasn't it?

Then the holidays came around. Diane's husband was so wound up in his own sad, little world that he still didn't notice anything. Not her mood swings. Not her tears. He had hardened himself to other people's feelings a long time ago. The only thing that existed and mattered was his own irrational sorrow. That could be why Diane clung so tightly to the idea of Thomas; at least he didn't ignore her. Although Diane's husband often entered her body, he rarely ventured into her mind like Thomas did.

For Christmas, Diane bought Thomas an earring. She had had a pair of white gold crosses made up especially for them. The only two of their kind in the entire universe. She put hers through a hole she'd pierced in the cartilage of her left ear the day after Thomas' birthday. The piercing was intensely painful, yet seemed significant. Thomas wouldn't accept his earring, however. He told her to hold it for him until he was ready. That's exactly what Diane did. She waited. She had become very adept at waiting.

Then, one fateful day in February, Thomas agreed to meet Diane at a local diner. But only if his friend Kenny could come along. "That way I know nothing will happen," Thomas explained. But when Kenny went to make a phone call, Diane's foot found its way to Thomas' crotch. He held it there.

Out of the blue, Thomas asked for his earring. How did he know Diane had decided to take it with her that night? Thomas knew all sorts of things. He slipped the post through the hole in his ear. It was almost a religious experience. The two of them felt it, but Kenny had no idea. He ate his souvlaki, then finished half of Diane's grilled cheese and tomato.

It was early, and none of them wanted to go home to their respective apartments alone. Thomas' wife and baby were visiting her parents in Florida, so perhaps he felt brave. Or maybe just lonely. In any case, they headed back to Kenny's apartment. Kenny's wife was out playing cards and wouldn't be back for hours. "She's a creature of habit," Kenny began as he drove. Thomas and Diane intertwined hands while Kenny spoke. "Linguini on Monday . . . ," Diane's fingers traced Thomas' fingertips. "Chicken cutlets on Tuesday . . . ," Thomas drew a tiny circle on Diane's palm. "On Wednesday, it's . . ." Kenny went through the entire week while Diane and Thomas practically made love, barely even touching. By the time they reached Kenny's apartment, it was clear.

Yes, Thomas was especially brave that night. "Maybe, just maybe, Thomas will make love to me tonight," Diane told herself. The safety of Kenny might quell his fears of falling in too deep. Only Thomas was in too deep already. Very openly, Thomas touched Diane's perfectly up-turned ass and made certain Kenny admired it too. He had Diane show Kenny how stiff her nipples got. Sure enough, when she took off her bra, they jutted out like little pinkies. At that point, Diane would have done anything, anything for Thomas. Anything for the hope that he might make love to her. And she did anything and everything that night.

Kenny's son was away playing basketball at college. The two men led Diane into the boy's unused bedroom and laid her down on the forest green sheets. Thomas sat down on the tattered weight-lifting bench and watched while Kenny ate Diane's pussy. Kenny was in ecstasy and compared its essence to lobster. Diane was in ecstasy too. She looked at the blue-eyed man with his head nestled between her legs. Then, she looked at Thomas. The sight of Diane's pussy splayed open like a moist butterfly might compel him to make love to her. But Thomas didn't move; he sat there studying her.

Diane rubbed her swollen clit against Kenny's lips. He held back the hood that shrouded her button with his thumbs. "Look at this, Tommy," Kenny gasped. And Thomas studied the glistening nib of pleasure. Diane's clitoris stood out irreverently and boldly, throbbing with each pulse beat. Kenny pursed his lips around it and sucked. Diane looked at Thomas while she was coming, his face a blur behind her flickering eyelids. Thomas licked his lips, as if he could taste Diane from across the room.

Her orgasm empowered her. Diane felt like a comic book superheroine or a mystical oracle of sensuality. That was the moment Diane realized her own strength. She would penetrate Thomas without even touching him. She would penetrate him with her eyes and with other things. She would take him inside that way. She would use the power generated by her orgasm to pierce him.

Diane's eyes snared Thomas while she sucked Kenny's dick through a condom. Her tongue traced its way up the sheathed shaft, then her lips encircled the head. Thomas swallowed hard when Diane did this, as though he were fully aware of what she was trying to accomplish. Still, Diane continued. She kneeled and eased Kenny's prick inside her, as far as it would go. Her juices coated his balls, drenched his pubic hairs.

"How does that feel?" Thomas asked Kenny.

"So tight . . . so wet," Kenny moaned. "But why don't you fuck her?" Thomas didn't answer, but Diane already knew the reason.

That night, Diane rode Kenny like the wind as she studied Thomas' expression. He tried to avoid her gaze, but a few times he became lost in it. Diane looked directly into Thomas' eyes when his friend took her from behind. Thomas talked dirty to her. Through Kenny, Thomas gave Diane pleasure in an indirect way. Plus, he got to watch. In a sense, it was even better than *Cinema Paradiso* because it was his orchestration.

"I'm fucking you," Thomas whispered into Diane's ear while Kenny pounded against her buttocks. "That's me fucking you." But still, it wasn't the same as if he really were.

Thomas even pinched Diane's nipples and helped her climax a second time. Didn't he realize that he was contributing to her strength? This was an even stronger orgasm than the first one, it shook Diane at the very root. She trembled and screamed. Tears streamed down her cheeks as her face pressed against the cool bedsheets. "Thomas . . . ," she cried in barely a whisper. Yes, Diane uttered Thomas' name, even though Kenny was fucking her. She hoped he didn't get insulted. Kenny was a nice guy, but he surely wasn't Thomas.

In a way, it was pathetic. In another way, it was sad. But no matter how much Diane pleaded, Thomas *still* wouldn't penetrate her. She even fell down to her knees and begged. But then she remembered. She remembered about her power. Diane stood up and began to dress, thinking of that power.

Kenny and Thomas drove Diane home. They sat in the front seat and she in the back, like a child or puppy. The earring Diane had given Thomas dangled from his lobe. It caught the brightness from a passing car's headlights and shone like a star for a moment. But just for a moment. Diane touched the cross with her finger. She felt strangely courageous, even though her legs were shaking. Then she began to speak. And when she spoke, it was like a writer writing a story. It was like a story she was writing in the air instead of on paper. "He was afraid to penetrate her," Diane began. "But what he didn't realize was that she had already penetrated him. She had penetrated him with her heart and with her mind."

Thomas smiled vaguely in the darkness. "And with her eyes," he said. "Don't forget her eyes."

Cecilia Tan

❧

A True Story

You know what I love about masturbation and a creative imagination? There's always something new to try. Don't ask me what it is about my parents' house that makes me tremendously horny. Perhaps it's the lingering memory of my teen years, spent poring over teen magazines, being frustrated, spending hours on the phone with cute but unapproachable boys, more frustration, and masturbation.

I went back for a visit when I was in the area for a business trip, and one night I found myself wandering around the house alone after everyone else had gone to sleep. I was tired of the jill-off-and-zonk-out five-minute orgasm routine. It was time to work up the willpower to dominate myself again. Self-bondage has been a part of masturbation for me as far back as I can remember, and that's pretty far (age five, if you must know).

Heading back to my bedroom, I knelt on my bed, pulled my panties down to my ankles and wrapped one foot around twice, binding them tightly together. Pulling my T-shirt over my head without removing it, I exposed my breasts, shivering. Twisting my shirt between my wrists, I bound my arms behind my back, with just enough room between my hands for me to reach the interesting parts of my body if I tried hard enough. Then the Top in me

458

ordered me to shut off the lights—it's much more effective than a blindfold. You can't peek. I nudged the wall switch with my shoulder and the room went black.

I sat that way for a few minutes, resting my buttocks on my heels and my head on my knees, letting my mind go blank. I don't know how long I sat like that, but at some point I was surprised to feel that one of my heels was wet. I was dripping with anticipation.

"You little bitch," I thought to myself. "You can't wait for it, can you? Well, you're going to get it." I had the sudden inspiration to try on a belt I had brought with me. It was made with three large metal rings, attached by two thin strips of leather; I wondered if there was a more creative way it could be worn than just around the waist.

Of course, I had to find it in my suitcase in the dark. I hobbled over on my knees, reaching backward into the bag to feel for it. Not very hard to find, though I mistook my leather-studded dog collar for it—that gave me another idea to try later.

I kicked the panties off my ankles and threaded one leg through each set of leather straps, putting the center ring right over my vagina and clitoris. I didn't have anything else to attach the two end rings to, so I hooked them together behind my back. I praised my Topself's cleverness—she let me turn on the light for a moment to see how it looked. Delicious.

I danced around the room in the dark a little, feeling the leather squeeze my thighs and the hard pressure of the ring drawing more and more blood to my vulva. I threw myself down on the bed and slapped myself with the dog collar. But no matter how hard I tried, I just couldn't hit myself hard enough. Perhaps it's like tickling yourself—can't be done. I gave up on that when another idea for the collar came into my head.

I stood up and threaded it under the ring, so it was pressed into the crack from my anus to my clitoris. I pranced around some more, feeling the leather rub against my skin as I moved my feet. I looked around the room for something the right size and shape. Hmmm ... I rolled a condom onto a sample bottle of shampoo and tied a knot in the end. I took the collar out of the ring, slid the bottle into my vagina, and put the collar back. It held the bottle in place perfectly. I moaned, then mentally gagged myself with one thought—my parents were asleep in the next room. I wasn't about to try to explain anything, so I kept quiet (oh, it was hard to do, especially near the end!).

My Top decided I was going to wait some more, though. The number of minutes past the hour would be how many times I was going to pull that collar through, from one end to the other, as slowly as possible, before I could come. It was twenty-five minutes after. That meant twenty-five long, slow, agonizing strokes— each cold, round, smooth stud on the collar grinding slowly over my clit. After about twenty strokes, though, I lost count. What was I going to do? I couldn't get away with cheating.

"You're so sensitive down there, aren't you? You couldn't count because you're thinking with your clit," I told myself. "So, count with it." I decided to count the number of studs on the collar as I pulled it through. Every time I was wrong, I would get five more very slow strokes. In that instant I became a prized slave, on display, to be sold. I would fetch a higher price for more stamina.

I counted fourteen studs on the collar, gritting my teeth and whispering the numbers to myself as each nub of metal tweaked my clit. Then I pulled the collar free and counted again with my tongue, licking the juices from it. Sixteen studs. I counted again with my fingers. Damn. That meant ten more strokes! I lay still for a full minute as punishment for my impatience. As the numbers flipped on the clock radio, I started the collar moving. I thought I would never get to ten, my clit throbbing, but I imagined veiled masters watching me from behind diaphanous curtains, bidding on my price, betting on my abilities. I finished the tenth stroke—which I made extra long and slow—and then struggled up from my back to a kneeling position.

Putting one leg through the shirt between my wrists, I got one hand in back, and one in front. Holding on to each end of the collar, I started moving it back and forth in a sawing motion across my clit. As I pumped my hips, the shampoo bottle fucked me, and I couldn't have stopped myself from coming even if I had wanted to. I collapsed forward in a wet heap (and almost fell off the bed in the dark). I never get this sweaty when someone else works me over, I thought. I slept soundly next to a small pile of damp leather and clothing, and waited until my parents had left for work to wash the shampoo bottle.

Jane Longaway

❧

Erotoplasmic Orgasmic

Dottie leaned against the window and breathed, creating a patch of uneven fog in which she wrote the initials of her lover, SB, and her own, DM. Around both of these initials she drew a lopsided heart. She had been in love with S for over four months and being apart from him was painful. She studied the initials with mild satisfaction, then resumed her study of the paper she was to present the next evening at the Institute of Parapsychology in San Francisco.

She took the train because she found it less anxiety-provoking than flying. And it gave her nine full hours to work in relative peace with just the click-clack of the wheels to lull her into a receptive frame of mind. Her paper dealt with mediumship, or what has come to be known as trance channeling. She had been involved in a study of this phenomenon and had spent considerable time with the famous Sister George, who trance-channeled sex partners from different planes, much to the delight of her many followers in the greater Los Angeles area. There was simply no safer sex to be found, since all bodily contact was on an astral plane and participants used only their astral bodies. Apparently, even in this ectoplasmic state, people of both sexes and all persuasions had extraordinarily vital orgasmic experiences. Dottie never personally participated since she had to keep her scientific

462

objectivity (plus she had more than her hands full with SB). However, she had witnessed participants awakening from induced trance states flushed and trembling, with dampness between their legs and languid eyes.

Now, facing a week without S, she found herself wishing Sister George was with her on this trip. Perhaps a fling with some entity from another plane would help relieve the ache she felt in both her heart and her cunt. She shifted her legs around. Her nylons rubbed together, and her suit felt just a little too tight. She unbuttoned the jacket and two blouse buttons, and kicked off her high heels. There was no one in the compartment with her, so she put the armrests up and stretched out full-length on the seat to watch the scenery whip by. It was mildly hypnotic. She rested her brilliant red hair on a tiny paper-covered pillow and attempted to read her paper from start to finish. If S had come with her, this would have been a wonderful trip. After reading two pages of graphs and statistics, she took her glasses off and laid them on the floor, then closed her eyes and allowed her mind to drift.

Sister George appeared in all her 200-plus-pound glory, with her crinkly dyed-blond hair and tiny green eyes, her red rosebud mouth pursed and ready to speak. Dottie opened her eyes and Sister George disappeared. She saw a small town whiz by the window, then closed her eyes again, trying to think about S, who was tall and slender with a blond ponytail. But the minute she closed her eyes, Sister George was there; Dottie could even smell her Opium perfume, which she used a bit too liberally. After opening and closing her eyes a few times, she gave in to the vision: Sister George, wearing a pink and yellow tent dress, opened her small cherry lips and began to speak.

"So," she said, "you're ready to try. It's about time. What good is all that research without experience? Keep your eyes closed, darling, and something fabulous will happen."

Sister George took her into a trance state by counting down, using colors, and Dottie felt herself floating. She tried to fight it at first, but Sister George was good and kept it up until the image of the large woman faded completely, and Dottie found herself floating in a silver haze. Looking around her she saw land just below, and as if by magic, the second she saw it she was on it. She stood on a flat blue rock surrounded by giant ferns and thistleberries. A stream gurgled in the background; she could hear the water dash against the rocks and smell the freshness of the air. She looked down and noticed that she was naked, but it was warm enough that the goosebumps on her flesh were more from fright than from being chilled.

There was a sound of plants being pushed aside, the flat clip-clop of horse hooves, and then suddenly she saw the black muscle of a stallion. Seated on the horse was a man dressed in red leather with a black feathered hat on his head. He was large, about six foot eight from the look of him, and his face was shaded by the huge feather that hung over it. Around his waist was a silver chain, and his thick fingers were covered with glittering jewels. Dottie was astonished to find that people on the astral plane smelled rather strongly of horse and sweat.

Not quite believing in this apparition, she didn't flee when he dismounted and tied his horse to a palmetto tree. He walked toward her slowly, as if he weren't too sure if she was real either. When he got close enough to cover one entire breast with his hand, she let out a shrill scream, and he made a noise in the base of his throat and spat on the ground. Quick as a wink, he grabbed her waist with both hands, picked her up, and shook her, trying to see what she was made of. Her hair whipped back and forth. She saw that under the hat he was a strong-featured gentleman with black eyes and white teeth.

He set Dottie back on the rock and took off his hat with a flourish. Blue-black curls tumbled around his head. He let the hat fall to the ground and quickly unfastened his garments, which were held together by intricate strings. Naked, he stood before Dottie with so much to look at that she almost fainted, like one of those old-fashioned heroines; but faint she didn't. His neck, arms and chest were huge and well-muscled, the skin fair. Hair tufted from both armpits and from his groin and spread in an eagle-shaped design across his chest. His thighs were enormous, knotted with muscle; his cock, which rose out of a mass of wiry black hair, was the size of a baby's arm.

"My, my, my," Dottie said. The man made more strange noises deep in his throat, and made a speech in a language that made no sense to her whatsoever; however, she was sure it was a language. He moved up slowly, once again took her by the waist, and gently pulled her close. She was getting used to his odor; in fact, she found it sportive and stimulating. He ran his fingers over the red hair tumbled around her shoulders and smoothed his hands over her curly pubic hair, which was as blatantly red as the hair on her head. He stuck his fat finger into her honeypot, as she grasped his dick with her hand to find out what the ectoplasm felt like.

"Well," she thought, "it feels like a big, fat, engorged cock." His finger, which was prodding her sex with great success, also seemed to find that she was no mere apparition. The man withdrew his finger and smelled it. A smile appeared on his face, and Dottie found herself smiling back. She idly continued to stroke his member as the big hairy balls swung back and forth.

The man started to moan a little. He shifted from foot to foot and tenderly held on to both her breasts, giving smart little tweaks to her nipples from time to time. Then the surprisingly smooth hands ran down her belly to her pussy, and his thumbs went to work on her clit. She began moaning with him and pulled him closer, all the while keeping a tight grip on his prick. He picked her up and carried her off the rock while her hands fluttered aimlessly, then set her down in a field where the grass was thick and dew-soft. She lay down spread-eagle and waited for him while he hovered over her.

Shaded by his huge body, she took a fleeting look at the sky, which was violet in color and lit by a silvery orb. Dottie blinked and the man went down on her. He pulled her legs over his massive shoulders and, with a tongue that felt as wide as a washcloth, he licked and teased her. She wondered where the fuck she was.

He sucked on her toes, manicured only a few days before, and licked her instep. Then, pulling her by the hips, he took her buttocks in his hands and lifted her up to drive his penis right into her. She let out a huge moan. He was so large that for a moment she thought she would pass out, and she wiggled and struggled to get comfortable. Finally it started to feel good, then damn good, then goddamn good. She wrapped her legs around his waist and caressed him with both hands. He continued to mumble and moan in his strange language. A lizard appeared and came quite close to her face, darted its tongue twice, and disappeared again. The lizard had been completely transparent; she had seen its organs, the small heart opening and closing like a tiny fist.

Then, with a quick violent thrusting, he pulled her toward him as she clawed frantically at his back. An explosion was coming, an explosion that would send both of them in a million jillion pieces into the universe, flung up like a handful of sand. He came with great heaving cries and she came seconds later, her womb and pussy fluttering and convulsing. Rivers of sticky, hot spunk ran down her legs and she fell to the ground, hitting her head softly.

She opened one eye. She had hit her head against the compartment wall. The train was rocking back and forth, going into curves. Through the window she could see the brown and green farmland repeating itself over and over. Dottie caught her breath and sat up painfully. It felt as if she had bruised her back; it felt, in fact, as if she had *fucked a giant*. She got out her purse and found her silver-plated compact. The tiny mirror showed that her make-up was rubbed off and her hair disheveled. She quickly fixed herself up and rubbed her hand over the small of her back. There were traces of scratches on her skin. She found all of this very bizarre. Still, the dream had been satisfying; the big man was so different from S. The sex had been a little rough and smelly, and so completely nonverbal. S talked all the time, like an English professor. He loved to name parts, both his and hers, and he smelled like cologne, not horseshit. Dottie found a cigarette and lit it, then curled up in a corner with her thoughts. What a very nice dream, she thought, and what an extraordinary cock the big man had; it had made her feel like her insides were all hot, pink expansiveness.

She started to nod, the cigarette dipping between her fingers. Soon the heavy lids closed over her baby blues and she saw Sister George again.

"Well, aren't we the slut!" Sister George boomed. Dottie blinked up at her, speechless. "Now I'll take you even further," Sister George said, her voice becoming softer and very persuasive as she began the countdown. Swirls of sea-green color began to flow around Dottie.

"No, no," Dottie cried out, "stop this, I don't want . . ."

She was falling, had been falling for a long time. Her body passed through colors and patterns of light, tones of music, and even different smells. Her mother's smell, the smell of baked apples, the smell of lavender, the smell of forty-weight oil, the smell of wet asphalt and the smell of chocolate mints. She fell until she thought she could fall no more, yet she kept falling. And all the while she clenched and unclenched her now transparent hands. She found that she could pass through solid rock and ice; she had no weight, and more important, no clothes. She put her hand to her breast, and it swelled to meet her grasp. Her hair fanned out around her head like an Ondine's, and like an Ondine she was falling through emerald-green water. Falling alongside her were strange creatures: a penisfish propelling itself by deflating its two huge balls; a winged creature of both sexes, with four round and pert breasts, and a smallish cock under a wide-open vagina; mermen and mermaids fucking in daisychain style; a huge mouth that seemed on second glance to be a sexual organ, the dreaded *Vagina dentata*. She drifted in this strange place until she came to rest on a plant whose silver-green protuberances embraced her and caressed her body. Two thick stamens emerged, covered with a sticky substance that worked as a lubricant as they entered her pussy and anus. She was being fucked by a *plant*, and quite nicely too. She started to moan and wiggle, helping the plant along. Amorphous figures circled her and the energetic plant, and began to flow into each other at a frantic rate. She watched them, but the plant creature was beginning to overwhelm her. Its leaves and stamens were covered with fine hairs that tickled and stimulated her to distraction. Against her better judgment she found herself responding to the plant, calling it "sweet cabbage" and "my dear little honeysuckle." It held tight to her, tentacles holding her legs slightly apart so that her clit was exposed to the delicate fronds delighting her. She wondered about getting this thing back into her world, as it would have made the perfect house plant. But then the ectoplasm, which had been dancing and merging in front of her eyes, coalesced into a huge, flower-shaped vagina and an equally huge towerlike penis. It began fucking, the flower vagina quivering like a jellyfish as the penis thrust in and out. This went on with increasing vigor until the penis-shaped ectoplasm pulled out and ejected a spray of matter which covered both her and the plant.

While the plant examined itself, she managed to free herself from its wild embrace, and ran as fast as she could in the first direction she found herself facing. Seeing something to her left, she headed for it and found herself in a forest of mirrors of all shapes. Even the ground beneath her was reflective, so she saw her image everywhere she turned her gaze. It was cut up, distorted, fractured, whole here and fragmented there. She was surrounded by images of herself from every possible angle and in every possible light. She saw her face with twenty blue eyes at once, ten lips opening and closing. For a moment she was so astonished that she just twirled around and reveled in the different views of her own naked flesh. The swell of her buttocks, her sharp little knees, her fiery red hair all captivated her. She twirled and danced until she felt unmistakably that someone or something else was watching her.

At first she shyly covered her breasts and pubis with her hands and called out, "Who's there?" No one answered, but she could feel someone just the same. The presence was unmistakable; it was as if she were inside some huge consciousness. The mirrors reflected her distress and bewilderment. Now a thousand blue eyes looked piteously back at her, and then she saw one brown pair. It was a pair of honey-brown eyes with big pupils. The eyes were languid and appraised her frankly, while she turned around in vain to find who was behind them. Then, as she grew quiet and waited, a face appeared bit by bit: the eyebrows, the nose, the lips, the chin, and so on until a stranger's beautiful face was visible. She realized with a jolt that it was the perfect face she had been looking for all her life. Whoever it was had taken on the mask of her ideal of male beauty. He continued to evolve body part by body part, slowly, as if pulling the ideal dimensions from her own imagination. There he was, but in the mirror.

She ran her hands over the cool reflection. The image was tall, well-muscled, with strong thighs, narrow waist and broad chest and shoulders. His head was molded from all her dreams: high cheekbones and patrician nose, sensuous lips and perfect teeth just a little crooked in front; his jaw was strong, and he had the hint of a black beard. She was so enchanted by this image that she pressed up close to one full-length mirror and undulated against the glass. Her movement gave her no release, although in other mirrors, if the angle was right, they appeared to be joined at the hip. Dottie was desperate to touch the man in the glass, and he seemed to be sharing her desire. His cock, which now reached his belly button, was pumped up with lust. As she kissed and licked its reflection, the illusion in another mirror was of their touching hands.

He made no noise, but his face was superbly eloquent. His bushy black eyebrows knitted together as his eyes shut in plea-sure. She caressed the mirror with her backside and imagined what he could do in the flesh. If only they were on the same side of the mirror! Thinking of this, she had an inspiration, and looked around for something that would smash the glass. He was hers if only she could get him out. The image of the perfect man gri-maced as she moved away from the glass, and he banged his fists in frustration. She looked around her, but everything was mirrors; it seemed impossible to move any of them. Each one reflected her lover, pleading with her to come back. She walked from the forest trying to find some rock to smash the glass, but she only saw mirrors and more mirrors. The beautiful man beckoned to her repeatedly, until she screamed and ran headlong into the nearest mirror, shattering it into a million pieces. Suddenly the man, the forest, everything disappeared and she was in a room with one open window but no doors.

The room had a huge platform bed heaped with pillows of yel-low silk and draped with netting. Dottie ignored the bed and ran to the window, still aching for the mirror man with the Calvin Klein fashion body. The window looked out on a landscape that seemed tiny; she was very high up and the drop was sheer. She enjoyed the cool breeze for a moment, then sighed a little and sat on the down-filled bed. She thought she might just take a little nap, since nothing made any sense. For some reason the glass had not cut her, but she felt devastated by the loss of the perfect man. Soon she was curled up in the delicious bed with her hair spread out on the yellow silk.

She sank down into the softness of the bed, and had almost

drifted off when she heard something. It was the pad of feet. Wrapping some yellow silk around her naked body, she sat up. To her joy, it was the mirror man looking at her with nine types of desire burning in his caramel eyes.

"Oh, it's you!" she said breathlessly, touching him. Yes, she could touch him, and his skin was quite warm and real. He lifted her hair with his hands and ran his fingers through it. Dottie let the silk slip down. Her nipples were soft, rose-colored lips ready to pucker at the slightest touch. He bent down, his curly hair tickling her throat, and sucked on them.

"How did you get here?" Dottie asked.

"I didn't, you got into the mirror," he said, in a voice that sounded like he had breathed helium seconds before.

"Shhh, darling, don't speak," Dottie counseled her dream date. She put a finger over his mouth and licked his nose, then, on second thought she raised herself, rolled him over and sat on his face. This ruled out listening to him sounding like Truman Capote. They occupied themselves with licking each other until they were both drenched in juice. Then, with his prick as hard as hunger, he mounted her and they had the most profound fuck she had ever experienced. It felt like his cock was swimming in the ocean of her being, as if he was redesigning her interior. She felt the buildup of all the cum in his balls, bursting to shoot, and she felt herself building up to a similar extravaganza.

They both began to shudder and groan; the tension was more than the usual tickle, it felt dangerous. His cock seemed to penetrate not only her womb but her stomach, her lungs, even her brain. Every atom in her body was bracing itself; and then it happened. It started at her toes and worked its way quickly up. She gushed and undulated as he exploded his load deep and hot inside, a shower of stars. She screamed, she clawed his most perfect back with her fingernails. She came to the tenth power; dripping with his sweat and her juices, she was blasted right back into the train headed north.

Dottie groaned on the seat and opened her eyes to find her legs wide apart and her blouse open to the waist. She felt exhausted and tingly all over. She sat up, buttoned her blouse, tucked it into her skirt and ran her fingers through her hair—all the while feeling like she had run a marathon and placed first. Her notes were scattered on the floor. She quickly picked them up, straightened them, and snapped them into her briefcase where they could damn well stay until she gave her presentation. She no longer gave two figs about it; it was all statistics and rhetoric as far as she was concerned. The real meat was in the experiences themselves.

S also seemed like a pale runner-up in her book; although she thought kindly of him, he was so vulgarly alive and constrained by the laws of this plane. Still, she would send him a postcard from San Francisco as soon as she got settled—and after, she thought, *after* she called Sister George.

Stacy Reed

∾

Tips

Andrea stood before the mirror, arms raised. The rows of dirty incandescent bulbs lit her like a shrine. She thought herself a sort of sarcastic virgin. A fisher of men.

She sat down on a metal folding chair. It was still slightly warm. She could never get comfortable in these; if she leaned back, she couldn't see her face, and if she leaned forward on her elbows, she couldn't do her makeup. She got up again and shifted her legs. Stilettos didn't suit women who stood still for long.

Andrea took out her eye shadows, blew softly on the applicator, and wondered whether Sunlit Burgundy or Sassy Periwinkle went better with dark green.

She put down the eye shadow. Fuck it. She walked over to the full-length mirror, turned, and bent over. She slid her hands beneath her T-back. She just couldn't stand it when those things got twisted. She'd heard it could give you hemorrhoids.

She walked slowly through the club. It was too cold, but less smoky than it had been a couple of years ago. The pulsating lights and noise merged into the drinks. They overwhelmed the senses to an almost desperate level. But she always smiled, made eye contact. At the vaguest sign of interest, she'd stop. All it took was a raised eyebrow or a pause in conversation.

"Hi. Are you guys having fun tonight?" She hated this part. It was too boring even for money.

"Yeah—what's your name?"

"Andrea." She extended her gloved hand. She always wore long black gloves. She didn't like the men to be able to really touch her.

"No, no. Your real name." She turned her head briefly. They all thought they were smart if they showed her they knew it was a stage name.

"Madame Extravaganza. May I join you?"

"Sure."

The redhead seemed the most lively. Andrea sat down very close to him in one of the club's overstuffed chairs.

"So what do you do?"

"I work for Walmart. I'm one of the regional managers."

In the three years she had been working, she still couldn't figure out how to feign interest in Walmart managers. She propped her elbows up on the table, flung her leg over his thigh, and did her best to look fascinated.

"Oh, really?" He was studying her fishnets. Good. Maybe she could skirt the intricacies of Walmart management altogether tonight.

They sat like that for a song or two. He didn't seem to want to talk; she was grateful. His hand on her thigh felt comforting. The music was too loud, a handy excuse to avoid the banter. Perhaps she was going to get away without even knowing his name. She'd forget it anyway.

"Hotel California" came on. She turned to him. He was watching Jackie on center stage and she could see his crow's feet, too harsh in the soft light. Some stray white hairs edged in around his temple. This was about his speed.

"Do you like this song?"

"Yeah."

"Would you like me to dance for you?" It was illegal to ask that—solicitation. But some guys took too long.

She stood up. She turned and rolled her short, sheer skirt down over her undulating hips. When she had it around her thighs, she bent over and slid it down her legs. She held the pose a moment.

This would give her time to stretch. He looked at her tight hamstrings and thought about her pussy being right there, right beneath that sequined black panty thing, right in his face. He shifted in his chair.

She could see from between her legs that he was hard. Perfect. Still bent over, she reached up and let her fingers slowly slide down her ass to the backs of her knees. They loved that.

She turned at the song's line about pretty boys and dipped down. She unclasped her bra from behind with one hand and held her breasts in its cups with the other. It was a lacy emerald under-wire that created a little cleavage. The thin satin straps hung down over her shoulders and beneath her arms. All she had to do was take her hand away. Now her breasts were at his eye level. She swayed there for a bit. She had small breasts and was never sure if they liked looking at them or not. A waitress asked her to move so she could get by. The place was filling up.

She threw her leg up on a table. Her spike-heeled shoe was right beside his beer. It made him nervous and hot. Should he watch the naked woman in front of him, or the drink?

Andrea went down on her knees. She raised her head up at him. He smiled. She whipped her head around and let her hair swing across his crotch. He couldn't feel anything, of course, and that was the point.

She stood and turned away from him. She let herself drop onto his chest and belly, her back arched above his lap. He liked her breasts from this angle; they fell slightly to her sides and up. His hand wandered up her waist. It tickled. Deftly, she crossed her arms beneath her breasts and turned her hands up prettily at their sides. He'd been foiled, but couldn't help admiring the new cleavage she'd created. Tact had its rewards.

When the song ended, he folded a pristine twenty in half and slid it under her T-back at her hip. She sat down and let him order her a drink. She looked across the club. It was going to be a good night.

She had already made sixty-four dollars before it was time for her to get ready for the stage. She stood in front of the full-length mirror, admiring her efforts, searching for flaws.

She thought she looked stately. She had put her hair up; this was a breach of strip bar norms, but she couldn't resist exposing her throat. Her eyes had hovered tenderly over its contours more often than any man's had.

She was a real dancer, and she resembled the ballerinas she had trained under; her dark hair offset her fine features, and her breasts were small and round. They were the breasts of thirteen-year-old virgins or Parisian women. They didn't quite belong on a stripper; they were best suited to young tomboys or gymnasts.

Her stomach was soft and flat. It wasn't the hard sort of flat that some of the older dancers had acquired through endless sit-ups; it was the gentle flatness only youth insured. You could look at her stomach and admire it, but it didn't demand the same respect as chiseled muscularity.

Men told her that from behind she looked like a mare; her ass and upper thighs were sturdy and dense, and when she walked, you could see the muscles shifting beneath her skin. When you looked at her, you could almost feel her bones and blood and salt. Her body was a hymn to human form. If he could bring himself to it, a religious apologist could point to her body: she wouldn't be possible if not for the intention of some Being.

But to Andrea, her body was a simple asset. Although she appreciated it, it remained a commodity and a tool. She allowed herself no sentimental indulgences.

She was young, only twenty-one, but Andrea was more honest with herself than other strippers who had been in the scene longer. She had perspective. It was plain: all workers had a supply that filled a demand. Strippers peddled arousal to the lustful.

Why not exploit her body while she could? Her college degree would last longer.

She was turning over these long-familiar reflections as though they were cherished heirlooms when the DJ introduced Chloe. Andrea was next on stage.

"How's the crowd, Steve?"

"Pretty lively for a Tuesday." He pressed his middle and index fingers firmly against the top of Andrea's neck as he put in her CD. Steve was a friend, and Andrea let him touch her casually. She allowed no other male employee such license.

She closed her eyes and felt the pressure of his fingers against her muscles. He circled them slowly and purposefully to the persistent bass in Chloe's second song. One wayward glove was slouching beneath Andrea's elbow. He watched her arms; he felt disappointed unless he raised their sparse black hairs. Andrea was just beginning to fall in step with his goals when Chloe's song began to fade. Andrea smiled at her DJ, checked her teeth for lipstick, and strutted onto the stage.

Her pulse and breathing caught up with her legs in seconds. She surveyed her audience and hit the floor like oil. Her knees bent and her back arched into the long line of her outstretched arms. She drew her torso back and lifted her eyes. She had them, all right. She raised up, threw one leg out at ninety degrees, and thrust her hips forward so that her pelvis twitched provocatively.

Then she was on her feet and hopping over to a tip. The man held out the bill a little too brazenly for her sensibilities. She'd show him. She fell back onto one hand and perched the other one effortlessly onto one raised knee. Her legs were spread wide as she offered the surprised client an uncensored view up her loose silk skirt. The filmy green fabric fell further back to her waist with each contraction of her ass. She stood and then knelt down to his level. He raised his eyebrows and slipped in his dollar respectfully.

That first tip was always the toughest, but once she had demonstrated her talents to one unsuspecting voyeur, business skyrocketed. Now they were surrounding the stage.

She executed five flawless chaîné turns toward her second patron. She stood still before him a moment, making him wait. Then she knelt and rested her wrists across his shoulders. She thrust her breasts toward his face several times. Just as he began to beg her to lose the bra, she spun around on one knee, lowering her torso so that her breasts hugged the polished parquet stage, and popped her pelvis for him. His jaw slackened slightly while he peered at the curve of her pussy straining against her T-back. He wondered if the tight-fitting garment pressed against her little clit, and got an immediate hard-on. When she turned for her tip, he looked stupidly at her for a moment before remembering to slip it in.

When her second song eased out over the club, Andrea was kneeling on the stage. Her head was thrown back and her eyes closed. The pose looked beautiful and gave her a moment to collect herself.

She raised her right arm above her head, looked out sleepily at the men, and dragged her left index finger down the length of her arm before letting it skirt the curve of her right breast. Nothing legally classified as lewd conduct, but unmistakably suggestive.

In any city, just find out what you can't do, and then do everything else. If you can't touch your own damn breasts, drag your gloves over them. If you can't handle the men, then blow in their ears.

With this in mind, she let her atrociously long string of pearls dangle down between her legs. She swayed very slightly and got them to move back and forth across her upturned cunt. Guys dug that; they imagined that the little plastic baubles were dragging across her clit.

Andrea turned on one foot to find her patrons waiting. She got down to business. Her pelvis rotated, her hips swiveled, every gesture an exaggeration. She crawled around like some depraved slave girl.

She looked leisurely up at the last one. His nose was almost touching hers. He watched her. The way she breathed through her mouth, the way her eyes darted from his eyes to his lips and back, like he had just kissed her. Oh, his cock was getting very hard. So real, so real.

He flashed a fifty and whispered, "Please touch yourself a little. Rub your clit for just five seconds."

Fifty dollars. She let her fingers edge around the elastic of her T-back.

The song ended. Andrea felt relieved and a little disappointed. She accepted a ten and wondered how much she could make if she went to that man's table.

Steve was wiping off the dressing-room counters when she walked off the stage and Gabrielle took her place in the spotlight. He was a good DJ; the others tended to whine about their less glamorous duties, but Steve accepted his chores graciously. It was crazy, but he genuinely enjoyed tidying up after his dancers or getting them sodas from the bar as they preened.

He offered her a fresh towel. Andrea always worked up a good sheen.

"Were they biting?" Steve asked.

"Sure. But you know me. I lose out on a lot of money 'cause I take too long on each client. I only got a few dollars."

"You may not take in much on the stages, Andrea, but every man who tips you is floored. You do your songs and you stay busy. Don't bitch about those little tips to me. I know how much you put out. Man, you probably aren't even giving me ten percent."

Steve had her. If she made three hundred and fifty dollars, she'd give him twenty-five. Most nights she topped three hundred, but he had never seen more than thirty from her, and only that much on the night she had made four hundred and sixty-seven dollars. All the dancers were supposed to tip the DJs at least a tithe. Few did.

She changed the subject. "Steve. Are you gonna finish rubbing me, or what?" She felt a twinge of guilt at exploiting this nice young man's weakness, but, God, his fingers were strong.

"Uh-huh. You just meet me in Staten's office after your sets on the runway."

Andrea walked back to the dressing room after her final set. She wiped off again, touched up her makeup, and straightened her stockings. She chucked her bills into her locker and slammed it. She didn't bother putting her skirt and bra back on.

Steve was waiting for her in the manager's office just as he had promised. "Who's taking care of Eden's music?" she asked.

"I had Staten replace me for a little while. I told him that one of my dancers had gotten a nasty cramp and I was obligated." He grinned and cut his eyes sideways. Yes, yes. Get rid of the manager. Very good.

Andrea draped herself all over Staten's old soft couch. Its familiar contours whispered of all the bodies it had held; Staten upheld one inviolable policy in his club: tired dancers were always welcome to come and snooze on his sofa. He even kept a worn down comforter and a little pillow handy for them. Best of all, he really let them sleep.

Steve knelt on the floor behind her and resumed his massage. Andrea closed her eyes and concentrated on his nimble fingers. He manipulated her trapezius muscles persistently, waiting for them to soften and spread under his touch.

"You're so tight," he whispered. Oh my, she had a live one on her hands tonight. He had placed his mouth very close to her ear on purpose. When she realized that Steve wasn't going to politely draw back, she closed her eyes. He continued to breathe nonchalantly onto her neck, and she creamed right through her T-back.

He knew he had gotten to her. Dancers weren't a simple matter; they tended to develop callouses. Money wouldn't work, and God knew compliments were a waste. You had to shock them just a little. Jar them.

He stood up and knelt down on the sofa in front of her, between her legs. She reluctantly opened her eyes and looked over her catch. He was an object of beauty. A bit roughened. Steve had to be charming because he was a devious little thing at heart. He had a slightly malicious streak and she saw it.

"What do you want, Andrea? Hmm?" he mocked cautiously. He thought she might be the sort who bit back. God, he hoped so. But she wasn't going to answer him. He bit his lower lip. He looked down and saw that she had wet herself. "Andrea," he drawled in feigned surprise. "You're making a mess."

What a bastard. He took her breasts in his hands and twisted her nipples softly. It humiliated her a little, to be handled like this by a co-worker, but he was relentless. She moaned.

"Andrea, Andrea. You like having your nipples pinched, don't you? Don't you?" He was merely stating the obvious, but this senseless reiteration of her pleasure intensified it. She had a verbal fixation. She'd read so many dirty books when she was little. Words got to her and few men knew how to use them.

"Where would you like for me to touch you? Do you want me to rub your neck?"

He slipped his hand under her T-back. "Is your neck still bothering you, Andrea? You know, I can massage it for you some more if you like."

He had her clit captured lightly between his thumb and his index finger. He looked at her with exaggerated doubt. "Your neck feels better now, doesn't it?"

This one wasn't going to stop until she played. Her clit was engorged and trembling. His touch was very light. Andrea drew in a breath. "My neck is fine, Steve. Thank you. You are terribly considerate."

He increased the pressure of his fingers and she shuddered.

"Good. I want you to feel relaxed when you go back into the club. Staten would be angry with me if I had taken time off for nothing. You are beginning to feel a little better, aren't you?"

"Yes. Steve. I feel . . . You're really turning me on."

"I am?" His fingers were dripping as he withdrew them from the T-back. "Oh, look at this," he said, holding up his hand. He licked off his fingers. "Yum."

Andrea snatched the opportunity. "How hard am I getting your cock, Steve? Let me see," she sneered sweetly. She pressed her hand between his legs and retaliated.

He grabbed her wrists hard. "No."

"Why not, Steve? Are you about to come in your jeans? Can't take what you give?"

He glared at her. "Think I ought to get back to work, Andrea? The work you dancers are paying me for?"

She briefly considered her options. "No."

His venom rushed out as soon as she answered. "No? You mean you want me to stay here a bit longer?"

Before she could respond, he was slipping her T-back down over her hips. He smiled at her and looped it around his long mousy hair, making a haphazard ponytail. He was getting too confident. Cocky even. Arrogant men were Andrea's favorite vice.

Steve peered studiously at her trimmed pussy. He didn't take his eyes off it as he meticulously explored its every fold and crevice. She was soaking and open. Her clit had swollen. She felt self-conscious, being examined so impersonally. Completely absorbed in his probing, he ignored her.

He looked back up at her face after a few excruciating minutes. "You're blushing, Andrea. You shouldn't. Your cunt is absolutely exquisite. It is just as beautiful as your face or your ass. I just love it. You don't mind if I pay it a little bit of attention, do you?"

"No." She was almost panting now. He worked three fingers of his left hand up her and had his pinky wriggling in her ass. He could feel the muscles in her pussy envelop his prying hand, clenching and relaxing and clenching again. She was very strong. He felt grateful that his cock wasn't in her; with a cunt this wet and demanding, he would have come long ago.

His right hand kept on playing with her clit persistently. He would tease, circling her clit mercilessly without really touching it, then flicking over it gingerly until he had her whimpering out loud. Now he got her clit between his second and middle fingers and massaged steadily. She couldn't stop him.

"You're gonna make me come, Steve." This time he offered no reply.

He leaned forward and traced his tongue over her lips. He looked at her face. He loved seeing a woman aroused, half out of her mind. He played with her lips and tongue cautiously. It was about time he kissed her.

She came so violently it startled him. She went over the edge suddenly and viciously. Her body absolutely writhed against his hands. He stood his ground, though. He had her screaming for nearly two minutes before she had finished with him. When he withdrew his hand she virtually flooded the sofa.

"Thanks."

"Oh, you're more than welcome, Andrea. It was my pleasure."

Andrea didn't get back out onto the floor until 11:45 and most of the men who had tipped her had gone home. She made only a hundred ninety-eight dollars that night, but when she left, she tipped Steve forty.

China Parmalee

Local Foods

Oh my darling, I see you so rarely now, my dearest love. These lonely letters from my room are really not enough. Why tonight, I don't know, but I have been thinking of you and missing you. Do you remember the last time we were together? It was here, five feet from where I sit. You, your smell and your skin and your warmth filled the room so suddenly. Have I ever told you how much I love the way you just appear with no warning, how when I leave you in the morning I never know if you will be there when I come home? I never know how long you'll stay. You remind me so much of a cat. Not just your eyes and your little mouth and the slow way you move, but other things, harder to describe. Your transiency, I think. You come and go and I have no control; I can only pet you and make you purr and hope you will stay with me a little longer. And yet I know you love me too and that you'll always come back, if I just hold out my hand and sit still long enough. Lately I have seen you much less than is usual even for us, but when I do I remember why I love you so much.

Yes, I think I came home and you were just here. There are times when I cannot sit next to you and breathe the perfume you put on without wanting to hold you, stroke you, scratch your white, white neck. And this time we were doing homework and it got late and we turned out the light and we talked like always.

And then too soon of course, goodnight, goodnight. It starts as always. You tickling my back gently with your nails and sometimes harder and I squirm and writhe a little, not too much yet. There is the delicious feeling of waiting, knowing that we have all the time in the world, that we can take it slow. And then you move around to my front, take off my shirt which is, I suppose, a joke to begin with. And you are so good, my dear, and not always gentle like one would fear, no, you know how to bite and scratch and fight too. You are as strong as I am, then stronger and you push me down and I breathe harder, a little hoarse now and you whisper to me, "You're so beautiful, I love you, I love you, so beautiful," and I believe you. I will believe anything you say and do anything you ask and you kiss me, your sweetest mouth so soft, mine feels large, bruising, but you move down my neck and shoulders. The funny buzzing begins, it feels a little serious; your lovely, tiny, pink mouth finds my breast and sucks and nibbles. You've made perfect soft bites from my belly, my sides, a hand tracing down and resting on the inner thighs. Now is the time to moan a little, please sweet, yes, please, you are so close but not there. I remember quite suddenly, awake from the daze, that I have my period and reluctantly I tell you, but you are not afraid and you reach down and tickle and tease, and what is there to be scared of anyway? Your hand locks on my womb, my clitoris, the games are over. I buck and sweat and move with your hand back and forth so fast, little hummingbird speaking now, don't know what I am saying, little sighs, louder ones, warmth is building your heavy breasts against me, I'm feverish, I'm floating, I'm buzzing all over the final movements. You don't stop and yes, now, yes, throw my arm around you, hold you against my heart and you hold me and wait for me to stop shuddering and you kiss me and tell me you love me, how much you love me, and I can only whisper a small assent.

We laugh and we pet and we sigh while I recover, we tangle our legs up and giggle and then I want to kiss you again, feel you under me, and the same dance begins again and you move so much, you moan so loudly. But I am not embarrassed, I am proud, of you and of myself and of the terrible racket we are making with no thought of the radio to drown out our own music. I love the way you arch when I touch you lightly, I love the large creaminess of your breasts, I love the way their nipples feel tiny and firm in my mouth, how they roll between my lips. I love the way your back marks so easily and your body flushes so readily; I love your body more than my own, its every softness and wetness, I feel beautiful to be with you, to create this glowing in you.

Now it is my turn to taste at your stomach, and yes, your thighs and the pudgy backs of your knees and your soft feet and back; a bite at the tendon of the thigh, a long sigh from you, a question perhaps. I ate a fresh tomato earlier today and this is what it was like. You lift your hips, an offering, and I stick a shy tongue into the dampness that marks you. Your own sweet smell is magnified all around me and I lick around trying to find the core. I slip a finger in and you are waiting, you gasp. More in earnest now I find the center, the pit, the hard little seed caught in such softness and I suck on it, circle it, play with it, try to nibble it and you are moving wildly and breathing loudly. I press another finger into you. I love the feeling of you encasing my fingers with pure heat. I know that despite soap your smell will remain on them all day, and I work my mouth, kissing and fondling you. I continue as long as I can, as long as you can stand it, and it becomes difficult to keep up with your movements, and finally you say stop, "I can't take anymore," and I rise and I kiss you and your juice, dear tomato, is spread on our mouths as we lie together panting.

Ruby Ray Leonard

Story for a Man Who Will Never Write a Story for Me: An Unfolding

There is domestic violence under our very noses. Every night, I listen to her screams. He is no cultural event. I see him in the incinerator room, removing yesterday's papers. She's the magistrate: fur-robed, bedecked in high ideals. One night, I hear the unmistakable sound of a beating behind their locked door. The muffled whimperings of a man as a larger woman methodically punches him. Were it a woman's sobs, I would immediately notify the authorities. I do not report this spousal abuse. I mock myself: Afraid of being laughed at by a policeman?

Not likely. I am only choosing to live vicariously.

You and I meet for soda and argue philosophies of evil. Discuss the past briefly, ungraphically. I am married now, so things can go no further. At home, later, I am without reason. I masturbate next to a sleeping husband, imagining you blindfolded. Better still, blind. I squat nearby and feed you wet fingers. I cannot decide whether I've already tied your hands or if you've voluntarily complied with their passivity. I squat closer to your face, examining your teeth and gums. Every child molester in my past wears your face. You know, the ones that get you when you're too young to scream. Through terror and disgust, they make your body betray you. Forever after, the repellent act leaps to mind just as you come. It's not so different with you, my friend. Here, next to a dreaming husband, the body betrays better judgment. It's only a fantasy, I tell myself. Breathe into the fear.

Last night, I reread the book of poems you penned at twenty. Such an addiction to women, even then, and such contempt! Stuck in the flyleaf is a poem you wrote when your daughter was born. In blue ink you've written: "Never published—or submitted (anagrams don't do well these days)." By then you were thirty, a cynic's eye deeply embedded in your skull. I spent the next eight years waiting to meet you.

I fly to Miami with my husband. I imagine you in every waking moment: lapping the cunts of adolescent coeds, paying boys from dysfunctional families to bend over. I see you diddling old ladies in wheelchairs and laughing as fat men with small penises grovel at some harridan's feet. I picture you, me, and the buxom, black stewardess in a room in Paris. You are milking her teats. You spy me, hair short as a boy, and order me to fuck her. I strap on a dildo and do it until she passes out. We dine on rabbit stew and later dump her body in the closest river. You have a moment of conscience, but I whisper: No one will miss her. Let's go dancing tonight.

The second night, I have a dream. We couple, and I tell you my husband will kill us if he finds out. When we leave the bedroom, he is waiting with his henchmen. "I am going to kill you both," he states unequivocally. He does. My murder wakes me up.

The next morning, I wait for women to vacate the hotel steamroom, so that I can relieve myself. Never enough privacy. Finally, I do it in the spa shower. Not pretty, no pornographic ballet. I lie down in the stall, sprawled on wet tiles, rubbing furiously. I imagine us, spooned on the bed—you between my legs, my nipples pressed against your back. I close my hand over yours and guide these hands to your cock. Lap at your ear like a dog and whisper: show me how you do it. Our biceps grow strong with movement as I pour stories into your head. During a job interview, an old man made me tie a scarf around my crotch and rub the fabric in to test it for stain resistance. I was thirteen and he claimed to be a bathing suit designer. Even then, I wasn't so naive. I was just anxious to test my tolerance for fear. Parading in high heels, silk against pubescent down. Eyes searing me like a brand. Oh baby, he said, sit on my face, let me put my tongue up your ass. And I did.

But the story doesn't end here, I whisper, my skin against your back becoming wet plaster. Some months later the old man arranged a meeting between myself and another thirteen-year-old girl. Maria was Mediterranean, sloe-eyed. I sat stiffly behind a desk in the old man's office. She sat on the desk, her dark legs bare and dangling. She was the kind of girl destined to star in a Times Square flick opposite a German shepherd: this is all I can say. The man directed us toward a back room with a makeshift cot. Her tongue flicked the very back of my soft palate; this was the nicest part, her broad tongue in my mouth. I felt I'd seen the cot before. An epic film with scores of Civil War soldiers laid end to end; a sea of dead and dying. Her saliva was thin and sweet. The ceiling had exposed water pipes. A good place to swing a noose. She moved down between my legs. It was a quiet room. Her small, soft hands were deceptively strong as she pushed my upper thighs apart and fixed them there, like splayed butterfly wings on an entomologist's glass slide. Her tongue wiped me back and forth; she placed two fingers at the very rim of my cunt, holding me open like a speculum. I didn't want to come. I fought my body. She insisted, pushing her entire brown face into me, humming against my clitoris. I was terrified of having to reciprocate. But I'd always been polite. I don't remember if I came, or only pretended. I moved between her legs in a blur. Roused not by pleasure, but by the need to please. Mommy, am I doing it right? Am I a good girl? Will you love me? Between her legs the air was heavy and sour. Her fingers grabbed my hair; she humped my face like a small, furry mammal. She came much more quickly than I. Or pretended to. Her labia glistened—a dark, red ruby in the fluorescent lights. I felt the old man's eyes on my back, but I never heard him breathe.

I am finally sated. Head near the drain, just like the shower scene in *Psycho*. At night, I watch every seedy street whore and picture your billfold on her bedside table. Perhaps I give you too much credit, painting you a lover of all women. In truth, the only other women that I ever saw you with were perfect, thin blondes, younger than you by a decade or two. They always seemed rather cranky and worn out. I wondered if they had been that way when you met them, or if you had just sucked the hospitality right out of them. A rapist with a rapier mind can exhaust even the most vital of girls.

I am astounded that you recall our first meeting. I am, in fact, consumed with guilt. I remember nearly nothing said at any time during our meetings, just these three conversational fragments:

1. You told me that you once came close to smashing a woman's skull with a lamp.

2. At a party, I mustered all my haughtiness and said to you (after you'd again used a word or reference unfamiliar to me): "You speak beautifully, but you know, the point of language is to *communicate* with other people, so what good is all your beautiful speech?" So many words that the harangue lost its sharpness.

3. In bed, when I bemoaned my subservient proclivities, you told me that to be a good masochist, one must know a great deal about sadism. Insinuating that you held the power to reverse all trends.

The things you've forced me to do! Now I'm being driven to poetry. I'm not even a writer, much less a poet. But I do write a poem, attempting to elevate lust to intellect. What I am really trying is an exorcism: if I expel these thoughts, they will cease to exist. I write the poem. For the next two weeks, I repeat its lines over and over in my head, as if I can turn sexual heat into something rote and unpleasant. If I can hear my own pathetic voice droning, I might tire and be done with it. Folly. Finally I decide to show the poem to someone else. Wisdom whispers that a secret shared abdicates its power. I show the poem to an English professor who believes that I have stories to tell. How about that: I show a crunchy poem about an English professor who writes poetry to an English professor who writes poetry. Sitting in his office discussing it, I suddenly don't know where to put my legs and arms. I am wearing daisy-patterned socks and a serious expression, but my extremities are twisting in an imitation palsy. My mouth opens wide around my sentences. I am ungainly; my feet and hands are too far from my trunk. I fight that old in-utero need to collapse on myself and suck a finger or toe. I am not a nail biter, but now that my locks are shorn, I'm a hair player. Not pulling it, never that. I splay my fingers wide and drag them backwards on my head from the temporal lobe to the nape, screeching to a halt by my adam's apple. Then I start over again. This poem about a poet is based on a true experience, I assure the poet. Things feel horribly incestuous. Are there secret meetings where all English professors meet to discuss the birth of the sonnet? Will my name come up? Will I end up a phone number on the English Department john wall? "Hello, so-and-so, who wrote 'A Cold Wind Blows and Other Poems,' gave me your number and I thought . . ." "I'm sorry, I've read that collection and it really sucked. Anyway, I've moved on to nonfiction now." My tricks have worked. I am so thoroughly disgusted with myself that I plan, suddenly, to discard the poem. I'll just bury it, like bones.

You're the superior poet, anyway. You've never written a poem about me. Over lunch you offered that your next book (a treatise on beauty) would be about me, although I wouldn't be mentioned by name. A master stroke and a good idea; after all, if my husband ever finds the poem I've written about you, I will say that it's about him. Luckily, the best writing is open to interpretation.

I tell the professor that I've run into an old lover (I am using you, I snarl in my head. Can't you see that you are party to the exorcism?). The *best* lover, I say, lest he think that I turn squishy and moist without provocation. Here's the conflict, I outline, switching to the third person. A married women has lunch with an old, best lover and is terrified because she is still attracted to him. She's got this husband, of course, so she absolutely cannot sleep with the old lover. The professor points out that if she can't sleep with him, it's not scary at all. Only if she entertains the notion that she *can* sleep with him does the thought assume nightmarish proportions. The poem is full of dread when she realizes not just how far she might go, but how far she *will* go! My head is full of wind chimes and my knees open and close like a bellows. I see how terribly right he is. Smugly unveiling his sticky little facts. Testing. I parry, telling him that I'm writing a story about you also, a very pornographic story. I mean to sound self-possessed, but I am just a high-heeled adolescent in a scarf, dying of exposure. (The scene is not without its small amusements, however. At work, I unravel rapists, killers, thieves and thugs. In real life, English professors apparently unravel me. They are so right, on two counts. The pen *is* mightier than the sword. Paper cuts hurt the most.)

On the way to work, I remember the first time that I masturbated. Seven years old? Eight? Older maybe—I was reading *Fanny Hill*. I hadn't gone to the bathroom in a long time. My bladder was full, belly distended. I became increasingly aroused as I read. When I could not stand the pressure between my legs any longer, I went to the toilet and urinated. I thought I'd had an orgasm. I arrive at work and during the long elevator ride, I sneeze. Bladder full of morning coffee, the tiniest trickle of urine escapes when I sneeze. All day long, my wet panties will remind me that I still cannot control my body.

I go to lunch at noon. Wishing you were here, watching me eat. Shoving greasy chicken into my mouth, lipstick smears like a lashmark across my cheek. "Fix your lipstick," you'd insist, a directive more intimate than an invitation to undress. My husband hates the way I eat. Says I'm not "dainty," I look like an animal. You and I know that is when I look the best. But it's no joke in everyday affairs. My mouth is too big and gapes too wide. The dentist is amazed, says he can practically see my larynx. When I'm with you, I think of the mouth only as a repository. A broad bin for whatever you wish to store.

Reflectionless, intransigent, you thought yourself a vampire. You loved the taste of blood. But you were not the one to teach me that. Had I ever told you that the first lover who kissed me between the legs did so when I was menstruating? Or did you guess it? I bled the way that only young girls do, my body a geyser in endless hemorrhage. The blood was everywhere, slippery and warm. We looked as if we had sacrificed animals or feasted on children. Every time I read of a sex slaying, I saw my bloodied palm print on that bedroom wall. I spied the boy twenty years later, pushing a rack of dresses in the garment district, wearing one of those jumpsuits with the company logo emblazoned on the breast pocket. I thought: life is so unfair to the precocious child. He was brave and sophisticated at the age of fifteen. Now, at thirty-five, he is someone's servant. Life itself is bloodsport.

I study myself sideways, poised like a question mark in the full-length mirror. Opalescent skin, blood-red hair, swelling hip, meaty thigh. The doubling hides more than it reveals. A slight, ribbed torso craning forward. My nipples still rosy and upturned. A stiff reminder: I just can't seem to make babies. The glass reflects one half, an unscarred back. I am as ugly as a gull. I let saliva dribble from the sides of my mouth. You know, I always drool when I come; my husband's neck gets slick with spit. He says I belong in a barnyard, or a home for the developmentally disabled. I turn my back to him, facing you. You, of course, feel that drool adds the proper note to my debasement. At work, I examine the backs of incarcerated felons for signs of childhood abuse. Their backs all scream a story. Burns and whipmarks and slashes from electrical wire. When I discuss my work with you, you interrupt, say, "I think a beating is the best form of discipline. Don't you agree?"

I am again confounded, tongue-tied. I might as well be twelve, or nine. Or four, three, two or one. (That's how much I lose my mental faculties in your presence.) I will wear plastic pants and diapers and lie on the changing table, face down. Fingers snake inside the band of tight elastic. The smell of cross-stitched, quilted vinyl; pushing cotton cloth aside. Duck print wallpaper and gold belt buckle in the corners of my eyes. You rub hard with the washcloth, for my own good. Terrycloth scours skin. When I cry, you stroke my back, beneath the undershirt. My tiny vulva is clean, as it should be. Your shoulder is wet with my spit.

My husband watches, poised above us like a guillotine blade. Over these winding years, I've loved him more than I can say. I was thirteen years old when I came under his spell. Much younger than when I first drew your breath into my throat. They say the genius of the rapist-murderer is in choosing the appropriate victim. The girl-woman who moves toward, rather than away; the prey who is unaware of the hunter's motives and thus accommodates his lust for power and control. She is a mere gosling imprinted on the largest moving object, following the daddy-thing to her death. But *I* am the conniving architect of my own martyrdom. I stalk: jaw slack, body loose. I drew him upstairs to the roof and offered a tasting. I was heroin, sure of my addictive powers. Years later, I wedged an insistent thigh between yours on a dance floor. You were older than he, more cunning and quick-witted. You knew these games. He acquiesced quickly and quietly. I had the swift movement of the cat snapping the mouse's neckbone. You were older, more clever. Your voice, like an ooze down my spine, spoke of bad girls and spankings. I smelled you both. I ferreted you out. He fell in love, a function of youth. You fell only a few short inches onto a bed. During your respective falls, I performed a deft transfer of power. An insidious Dr. Frankenstein, switching the brains of anesthetized charges. I let my own self ebb away, leaving dank, hollow pits. I became nothing beyond breath. I waited to be rewritten. The line between hunter and hunted blurred in a quick spiral dance of tongues.

A few weeks later, a draft of this story is stolen from the English professor's mailbox. I am awed and mortified to imagine a strange, thieving creep running his hands over my private thoughts. The professor says: Why are you so distraught over someone reading this, I mean, except for the content. Huh? (Why were *you* so upset when mom discovered you masturbating?) Caught. Again. Like the time that my husband discovered the hundred-dollar phone bill from the phone sex line. The prerecorded kind, offering a menu of sexual perversions (if you were lucky enough to have touch-tone service; those with rotary dial heard, "Hang on and we'll choose for you"). I was one of the lucky ones. I always requested "Annie (she likes it in the back door)" or "Candy (and her little friend Susie)." The messages were so short that I'd have to call back ten or fifteen times. My husband, cold as ice, dropped the bill in my lap and said, "Take care of this." He has grown into manhood, become a collector of old debts, a settler of scores. I called the telephone company and pretended to be the mother of an errant teenage boy. The (male) operator said, "Don't be too hard on him, ma'am, he's just a kid." My husband received full refund in the next month's mail.

Magazines will tell you that women fancy men outside the marital bed because their husbands do not tell them that they are beautiful or buy them enough flowers. Ho-hum, and such a lie. Clearly, I need something darker. Every nasty part spread-eagle on the operator's table: each fold examined, opened back upon itself. A close inspection, humiliating exposure as someone probes and describes. Not just this—I wish to be both voyeur and viewed. To have someone to ask, finally, what the others are like. How does this one smell and that one taste? How silky is the fair one's hair and did the dark one moan into your mouth? Which virgin's bravado was eclipsed by your bulk? Whose ass invited a reckoning? Do you like it hairy or smooth, red or pink, yielding and pliant or requiring forced entry? But more than this, I need to see what I could not see in the mirror. If I bend over, grasping my ankles, what will be your view? How far can I be opened? How does it look with your whole hand inside and what is the sound when I whimper? Dilating me until I know that I exist. Whispering stories that confirm my invisibility.

And what have you become? Across the table, clutching restaurant coupons. Telling me of books that you will translate from the original German. Fifty-three now. Unsettled. But still.... Your hand runs over the old pictures I've brought, almost a caress. You say: "I remember this girl." Letting the width of both palms cover my mouth in the glossy photo. "I remember the night we met. You danced like a whore."

You know, I lied before. I didn't wait to get home before masturbating. No, I didn't do it in the diner restroom as you might have hoped. I am, after all, a sensible girl. Dressing to meet you, I was unconcerned with my appearance. I only wanted to feel open, vulnerable and sticky. I fingered myself until I was wet, but didn't come. Sat opposite you in the restaurant. Parting my knees beneath the table, as you discussed a strumpet's dance. I wore no panties. If I were free, I thought, I would telephone. I'm coming over. No, you'd say, I have a plan for the weekend. Well, think of me while you're fucking her. I hang up. You call back, your plans canceled. I come over. (I'd never been to your apartment in the old days. I was afraid that it might smell like menstruating women in there.) I wear a tight, white structured thing. (My husband hates me in white panties, a sanitary napkin pressed between my legs. Says I look like Baby Huey.) Lie on the bed, I tell you, face down. You are tentative, momentarily unmasked. Hey, this isn't what . . . Shut up. A growl. Just *do* it. (My father was omnipresent with his camera.) I pull down your pants. Spread your cheeks. (The old man put his whole tongue in my ass.) *SMILE.* Introduce my finger to your sphincter. You grip my finger like a newborn. Now, tell me what you want. (I nursed at Maria's clit.) Tell me. Pushing deeper, even as your muscle clenches. I want . . . *TELL ME.* I push my finger deep into your ass, knuckle by knuckle. (When I was seven, I had my tonsils out. They used a pre-op anesthetic which was administered rectally. A rubber finger coated with a gel-like tranquilizer.) Ask me, ask me nicely. Now, my whole finger rotates inside you. *THIS WON'T HURT.* (I was only seven; I think I wet the bed.) Tell me. I lean closer, whisper: Can you take two? Sarcastic. *ASK ME.* (Did I only imagine us with that small Arab boy? He was handcuffed. I cradled his head in my lap while you fucked him.) Yes, you say, but only *sotto voce. YES, WHAT?* I make you beg to be fucked, until you are hoarse.

(Someone is screaming.) Now you know what it feels like. (I have that recurring dream about the stabbing. As I plunge a hatchet into the body, I feel its blade wedge between my own shoulders.) To be a good sadist, one must know a great deal about masochism.

I suppose that I will never cheat on my husband. Some things get harder as you get older. Learning to drive, dumping bodies in lakes, being a traitor to those you love. When the story is finished, I'll stop thinking about you. I'll go shopping, for books on feminism or collections of holocaust cartoons. When I buy clothes, I will occasionally imagine you in the dressing room. Watching me change, saying nothing. Your eye contact methodical, deliberate. I'll have to turn away before I become transfixed by my own reflection. If I should beat you to death, who could blame me?

I'll see that couple from down the hall, looking slightly sheepish. Not to worry, I'll tell them, everyone's secrets are safe with me.

Lydia Swartz

Laundromat

Sun slanted through the east windows of the laundromat and scorched Syl's back. Wiping her neck, she wished she had something clean besides the torn tank top that was stuck to her nipples and the too-tight cutoffs riding up her butt. July was not Syl's favorite month. She shoved her two bulging baskets toward the washers and began to load.

Besides Syl, there were only men in the laundromat. A stocky, bearded guy wearing a T-shirt with a faded zebra advertising a zoo. A wiry kid who had a sparse ponytail, baggy shorts and heavy boots. One emaciated old man slowly pulling smelly socks out of a blue box decorated with silver stars. And a hairy-legged guy wearing a bicycle helmet.

The Jehovah's Witnesses came in while Syl was overloading the second washer. The man spoke: "My wife and I want [squealing noises from a malfunctioning dryer] for the world. My wife and I would like to give you [sound of dropping coins at the change machine]." Silent and neatly coiffed, the woman stood just the right distance from the man's shoulder. Syl slammed coins into all her machines as they leafleted everybody else. As they approached, she glared at them and fingered the pentagram tattooed on her shoulder. She was ready for them and they knew it.

The woman glanced toward Syl, then took her husband's arm,

quickening his pace toward the door. Syl smiled triumphantly and dropped herself into the least broken chair on the south wall. Coffee does this to me, Syl thought. Heat does this to me. It's easier than hurting.

The bearded guy sat down right next to Syl and smiled shyly. Syl looked directly at him for a minute from behind her sunglasses. Then she turned and gave the old man a slow, lascivious grin. He dropped a sock. The bearded guy cleared his throat and fumbled in his pocket for a cigarette.

All of the men in the laundromat were pointedly not looking at Syl now. This left her free to examine them.

Maybe this would be a good time for an affair with some guy, Syl thought. Maybe fucking wouldn't hurt now that my herpes is better. Maybe somebody who doesn't know me so well would treat me like a lover. Maybe if somebody else did, Elsa wouldn't have to. Maybe she'll have an affair first if I don't.

Syl remembered how little boys had seemed when she was a little girl: loud, sweaty, full of fruitless locomotion. She recalled the possessive energy siphons they'd turned into when she was a young straight girl in estrus. And she thought about how the sons of her friends seemed now: fragile, tender, fearful. How did those appealingly vulnerable little guys turn into the men she saw now—pitiful as individuals and dangerous in packs?

Maybe this would be a good time to become celibate. Live on organic fruits and vegetables. Roots and berries. Drink quarts of pure artesian water. Exercise. Light candles and do rituals. God, I'm full of shit.

Well then, maybe this would be a good time to try to have casual sex with girls. The other dykes I know can do it. The dyke sex magazines are filled with stories about it. I certainly can imagine it when I'm checking out the girls at the Wildrose. Maybe there's something wrong with me. Maybe I'm not completely out yet. Maybe I'm not really lesbian. Or bisexual. Or whatever I am.

Syl considered the possibilities. Jan's lover was in Holland and Jan hadn't had sex for at least six months; what harm could a friendly roll in the hay do? Or how about Dena—Dena'd done just about everybody else, why not Syl? And of course, there was always that nineteen-year-old who'd been hanging out at the women's center for two months, hinting less and less subtly that Syl should be her first.

Or why not just invite them all over for a naked solstice party! Right, Syl. Get a grip. Remember the last time you were going to have a brief, passionate fling with a girl? That was two years ago. Elsa came to play for the weekend and she's still there. Only now she doesn't play, of course. Now she's got other uses for that wicked, hard flame in her gut.

Everybody in the laundromat was now staring at Syl. Oh shit, Syl thought. I've been rubbing my fingers up and down the inside of my thigh all this time. Great. Now everybody here has a hard-on.

There's the ticket! Exactly why she'd fucked so many men before she came out. It was pre-holocaust, and they'd known their way around casual sex. No respect, no repercussions. Just whip it out, do the thing, light a cigarette. If only Syl could get hard, get laid, get the hell out. How simple. All Syl needed, she realized, was a dick and a time machine.

With a clunk and a groan, one of Syl's washers went into imbalance and stopped. Syl sighed noisily and hauled herself over to look inside. One pair of jeans had wrapped its legs around the agitator and was hanging on so tight the agitator couldn't move. Syl pulled and poked and pushed and stirred until everything looked okay, then dropped the lid. She leaped onto the lid and crossed her legs, waiting to see whether the load would tangle again.

With a vintage 1973 dick, Syl thought, I could get what I want without risking my heart. Just in and out, gone before things get sloppy. Any hole will do. That guy over there, for instance. The one with the little ponytail. I bet he'd bend over and I wouldn't have to ask him twice.

The guy had a heart-shaped face, stubble over pale, soft-skinned cheeks. Young and innocent-looking, but also away from home and looking for some notches on his belt.

Syl could see it. She'd walk over to him and ask him to come outside to look at her shirt. *Still see a stain on this?* He'd lean over to get a closer look and she'd put her hand on his crotch. He'd wiggle. She'd tell him, a little roughly, to pull his pants

down. He'd look a little scared, a little pleased, and do it. He'd
turn away from her and incline forward.

She'd pull out a condom and roll it on, then rub lube rudely in
the guy's asshole. And she'd stick the dick up him. When she
went in, he'd start slamming his butt against her pelvis as she
banged into him. In a couple of minutes, she'd come, then pull
her deflating cock out. After she threw the condom in the planter,
she'd tell him to take off his shirt and use it to wipe the cum off
her dick. He'd do it. She'd zip up, they'd go back inside and finish their laundry. Never ask each other's names, probably never
see each other again. Even if they did, just smile and nod slightly.
No hello.

Yes! That was it. If Syl had a dick, she could just fuck Jan. And
since she was a boy, it wouldn't count. Well, maybe not Jan. But
definitely Dena. Dena would be up for it. Dena would be hot for
it, as a matter of fact. Syl would call up Dena and say, "Dena,
guess what? I've got a 1973 dick." And Dena'd be waiting for her.

She'd get to Dena's and find the door ajar. Inside, it would be
all dark except for a trail of little candles leading to Dena's bed.
Dena would be wearing a merry widow and crotchless panties (a
typical Dena outfit). Her pussy would already be rosy and feverish (Dena'd started without her). Dena would be lying back on
satin pillows (typical Dena decor) with her legs apart. "Where is
it?" Dena would rasp (Dena was a heavy smoker). "Let me see it."

And Syl would. Syl would slowly open the buttons on her 501s
and let the dick flop out, all long and hard and ready. "Come
here," Syl would say, and Dena would scoot down on the bed.
(Neither of them would make gynecologist jokes.) Syl would stick
it in a little at a time, moving it in small strokes at first. Dena
would demand more. Syl would be stern. She'd give it to her little by little, make Dena squirm. Syl would finally be fucking
Dena hard, leaning her whole weight against Dena's upthrust
thighs, Dena gripping the bedposts and pushing back. Syl would
feel Dena coming, gripping her dick as it shot cum.

Syl would collapse against Dena. They'd both sleep for a few
minutes. Then Syl would pull her softened dick out of Dena's
wetness, wipe it on the bedspread a little and stuff it back into
her jeans. She'd lick Dena's buttocks and thighs, then stand and

walk out of the apartment, closing the door softly behind her. Dena and Syl would never mention it.

The washer had stopped, Syl realized. Another imbalance? She hopped down and looked. But no, the washers were done. Time to load everything into the dryers.

She threw wet jeans viciously into the chapped lips of the dryer. Three of Elsa's impossibly tiny panties and one of Syl's tank tops flew in, clumped together. Their shared "Dykes to Watch Out For" T-shirt. Two pairs of boot socks. A hot pink bath towel. Well, at least Syl didn't have to carefully pick out her black bustier so the underwire wouldn't get twisted. Syl hadn't worn that in a while.

She mused. Wonder what it would do to that nineteen-year-old—what's her name? Debbie or Susie or something?—if I shut her in the library at the center and stripped off denim and leather until I was down to black lace, garters, and silk. See if she knew what to do. See if she'd follow my directions.

"Wonder if she'd be squeamish?" Syl thought. "Wonder if she's really a virgin?" Bet she'd go for my tits first, just brush them with her hands to start, then go after 'em with her lips and tongue. Easy, easy. Then I'd guide her hand to my wet pubes, let her get the feel of that. She'd be breathing pretty hard, scared of what was going to come next, scared she wouldn't be able to do it, scared she would. All the time sliding her fingers up and down, circling my clit. Feeling how it's different, feeling how it's the same as hers. *That's good,* I'd tell her. *A little harder. On top. Now around . . . like . . . thaaaaaaaaattt . . .*

Before I came, I'd pull her hand away. She'd look hurt, confused. Was she doing it wrong? Hurting me? Then I'd lift her hand up to her own mouth and stick her fingers between her own lips. *Like that taste?* Her eyes would be all round and dark. Before she could answer, I'd lean back on that couch, the one that smells like it's been used for the same thing a thousand times before. *Taste me,* I'd tell her. *Lick it, come on.* I wouldn't smile. I'd make myself sound harsh. She'd look pale. I know what she's been thinking all these weeks; I've seen her watching me. She's been checking out all the sex books at the center, one by one. And here it would be. Her first wet cunt, her first pair of hungry thighs.

She'd get on her knees awkwardly, put her hands on my ass too gently. Put her tongue on me tentatively. Goddess yes. That little shy thing, just thinking about her . . . she wouldn't know what it's doing to me, she'd be too nervous and afraid of making a mistake. She'd lick me slowly, tasting, trying to swallow, until I got her face and chin so wet she knew it didn't matter. I'd push myself against her until she got the idea to push back. She'd find my clit with her tongue and fumble with the hood until I was about to fly off that couch. *Yes yes yes*, I'd yell at her. *Yes right there, like that, yes!* And she'd have her first woman climaxing all around her. She'd let go of me when I bounced.

Syl would make sure she landed in the neighborhood of that sweet little mouth. *Do you know what you did to me?* She'd flush with victory. She'd go for it again, an eager student.

Syl continued her fantasy. I'd tell her to put her fingers inside me. I'd be open and wet and soft by now. I'd move and make it easy for her to find the right hole, no matter how excited she'd become. She'd go slow, just careful, not knowing that it drives me crazy. Well, I guess she'd figure that out pretty soon. And then I'd be begging her to go faster, harder, to fuck me. She'd be confused at first. I mean, we're lesbians, aren't we? We don't fuck, do we? But I bet when she felt the way my cunt grabbed her hand, she'd catch on. She'd fuck me and lick me until that couch was a soggy mess.

And then, I'd push her hand, her face away; I'd roll her over and strip her. I'd move my hot, wet body above her. Gently suck her hard little nipples. Tease her wet cunt until she was moaning and pressing against me. Get a scream out of her with my fingers first, then go down on her. Grab her soft young hips and smash her sweet virgin bush into my face. And eat it slowly, eat it fast, eat it with my fingers in her, stick my tongue in her while my fingers gently tortured her clit.

By the time I got done with her, she'd be soaked, I'd be soaked, we'd both be too exhausted to move and the room would reek in the best way any room can reek . . .

"You finished with this washer?" It was the hairy-legged guy.

"Oh, er, yeah. I'll just get the rest of this out of the way. Sorry."

Syl threw the rest of the wet laundry indiscriminately into the last two free dryers. With that much in them, it'll take an hour for it all to get dry, Syl thought. But the alternative was standing around like a playground monitor, ready to jump on the next open machine.

Hell and damn, Syl thought. I hate laundromats. I hate heat. I hate July. I hate goddamn Elsa. Lets me wash her goddamn clothes but never lets me help her get them goddamn dirty.

The cigarette smoke in the laundromat's stagnant air was making Syl a little bit sick, and a little bit sorry she didn't smoke any more. She scowled at the rotating wash. Five minutes went by. She stared sourly at the back of the old man, who was ever so slowly loading a dryer. One sock. Pause. One shirt. Pause. Another sock.

With a decisiveness startling even to Syl, she turned and strode to the bearded guy's chair. She stopped and looked down at him. He looked alarmed.

"Can you spare a cigarette?" Syl growled, finally.

"S-sure," he stuttered, scrabbling desperately in his pocket. With shaking fingers, he lit the slightly sweaty cigarette for her.

"Thanks," Syl spat at him. She walked out to smoke in the parking lot. The guy smoked menthols, wouldn't you know. Ugh. Syl took small puffs and blew them out quickly.

Goddamn menthols heat laundry July bearded guys Elsa old men tight sweaty goddamn clothes to hell. *Maybe if I had some ice cream . . .*

The cigarette was burning close to the filter when a familiar car turned into the parking lot. There are lots of rusty blue Datsuns on the road, but Syl knew of only one with a silver "E" nailed onto the door.

Elsa pulled up the Datsun right in front of Syl. It squeaked loudly when it stopped. Elsa had her hair slicked back in a ponytail or something. Syl couldn't see the usual brown flood flowing over her face and shoulders. In fact, Syl couldn't see anything on Elsa at all.

Elsa got out of the car, all five feet and one inch of her, pale and lean and determined Elsa, looking greedy and feral in a black bandeau top, doeskin short-shorts, and a pair of stiletto-heeled sandals.

Syl could smell the filter starting to burn in her fingers but discovered she couldn't move to stub it out. Elsa slunk toward her, almost smiling. She took the smoldering filter from Syl's fingers and crushed it beneath her heel.

"I thought you were painting this morning," Syl gurgled. Something had happened to her voice. With a sudden panicky feeling, she wondered if this were really Elsa—Elsa the distracted, Elsa the absent, Elsa the frantic or stone-tired.

This Elsa had brushed her hair shiny; it spilled down her back, lighter brown strands shattering sunlight. She cocked one hip toward Syl in a way Syl dimly remembered from their first days together, two years ago. This Elsa was pouring power out of her tiny body.

"What are you doing here?" Syl asked in a small voice. "I didn't realize you'd heard me leave."

"I was waiting for you to leave," Elsa said in her deep voice. "I wanted to surprise you." She spoke softly enough so Syl had to lean forward to hear her. And then Elsa darted one hand around Syl's head and forced it forward. She engaged Syl's lips, then her tongue, then all of her mouth, before Syl could get a word out. Syl would have said something about the boys just inside the windows who would be watching, but after ten seconds it didn't matter.

After ten seconds, Syl had her hand inside Elsa's shorts, cupped around a buttock. And Elsa had her hand inside Syl's tank top, squeezing a nipple. Then Elsa found the wet seam on Syl's jeans. Syl whimpered. Elsa laughed into Syl's tongue.

Syl had half-leaned, half-collapsed into the laundromat's window, and now it creaked in its frame. Syl got a millimeter of air between her and Elsa and whispered, "Not here, for godsake."

Elsa grabbed Syl's wrists roughly and dragged her larger, limp body toward the Datsun. Elsa yanked open the back door and shoved Syl backward onto the seat. While Syl was trying to get her balance, Elsa nimbly unzipped the cutoffs. Syl lurched forward to stop Elsa, bringing her ass off the seat just long enough for Elsa to yank the cutoffs down to her knees. From there, Elsa planted her feet and tugged until, with a little backward stumble, Elsa peeled them off onto the ground outside the car, underpants coiled inside.

Elsa didn't bother to pull her shorts off, but climbed on top of Syl and began riding Syl's thigh while rubbing Syl's crotch with her hip. Syl could hear another car pull up nearby; she reached up to push Elsa away. She missed, and found her hands full of Elsa's breasts.

Elsa's wetness was coating Syl's leg, even through the shorts.

Syl dimly heard a child's voice through the ringing in her ears and the waves threatening to crash outward from her groin. "Mommy," a high-pitched voice lisped outside the car, "you dropped my shirt." There were more words, but Syl couldn't identify them.

Veins were standing out on Elsa's neck and she was making the soft yelps that Syl knew preceded full-force howls. She was slamming herself up and down on Syl, rocking the car, which was squeaking louder than a cheap motel bed. Brown-gold hair thrashed around Elsa's face; Elsa's deep brown eyes held Syl's hazel eyes, daring her to look away, to break the bond . . .

Syl knew she was going to lose it. She was losing it. Those yelps, those intense brown eyes always made her cunt flutter and her vulva turn inside out. Elsa began to keen, and let her whole weight down on Syl, and rocked. Rocked hard.

Syl lost it. She still had her hands full of Elsa's tits; her fingers sprang out straight and sounds she didn't recognize as her own scraped her throat. She was vaguely aware that somebody might be standing at her feet, watching, but that just made her come harder. There were voices.

Syl's waves and Elsa's were bouncing off one another and building the momentum of both. It went on. It went on some more. The car's squeaks were quick and anxious now. Finally, it was too much—for Elsa, for Syl, for the rusty Datsun. With one huge groan, they all lifted up for a long throbbing minute, then settled in, sated and sweaty.

Syl and Elsa, busy kissing and licking sweat off one another, did not notice anything else for a while. Then Elsa rolled to Syl's side a little, and Syl could see out the car door.

The old man was crumpled against the cab of the pickup parked beside them. His red, shriveled dick was just visible inside his open fly, and there was a wet cum stain on his pants. The man was breathing with his mouth open, his head back. He was pale and damp. His hand, still resting near his organ, was trembling slightly.

Elsa turned around to see what Syl was staring at. She waited until the old man moved his head forward a little bit.

"Would you mind handing us those cutoffs and that pair of panties?" Elsa asked politely.

The old man looked at her, at them. He moved his mouth for a while before he managed to produce any sounds. When he did, they were garbled. Mumbling, he bent down and groped for the cutoffs without taking his eyes off the two women.

Elsa took the proffered clothing from him and said, "Thank you." He replied, "You're welcome," in an almost normal tone of voice. He just stood for a moment, looking sweet and grandfatherly, then tottered away, zipping his fly with still-trembling hands.

Syl tenderly pulled strands of gold hair off Elsa's sweaty forehead and smiled. "Well," she cooed, "are you going to help me fold the laundry?"

Elsa smiled in a familiar way, a diabolical way. "Of course I am," she drawled. "What do you think I came here for?"

Emily Alward

❦

Nicolodeon

When I walked back into my office he was leaning against my desk, unhurriedly waiting for someone. A tingle of pleasure warmed my cheeks. He was a real hunk, and nobody else used this office, so he *must* be seeking me. Then territoriality and caution took over. My office was not public space but was snuggled cozily within the walls of my lakeside house. I froze in place. I took a deep breath and tried to sound both friendly and firm.

"Oh, sir. Excuse me, but are you sure you're in the right house?"

"Nemel," he said.

"What?" I asked. The man was making no sense at all.

"Nemel. Isn't that the proper form of address for a gentleman? In the world you're writing about," he added, as he saw my frown of confusion.

"Uh . . ." My thoughts floundered. He could have read some of my stories, I guessed. Was he one of those obsessed fans who harass celebrities? Not that I was much of a celebrity; those stories had only been published in a few obscure magazines. Unlikely but possible, I concluded regretfully. I couldn't think of any other explanation. If I could just unobtrusively open the top left-hand drawer and find the letter opener I'd have a weapon. I fumbled in the clutter. At the same time I fixed him with my prized truth-raking stare. He stared back. Instead of flinching, a trace of annoyance clouded the good humor in his storm-gray eyes.

"Nemel," he repeated. "Nemel Ryenn, to be exact. First name's Nicol." He held out a hand.

Alarms clanged all over my head. He'd given the name of a character in one of my stories. *A story that hadn't been published yet.* The greeting was being proffered at a slightly different angle from a normal American handshake, too. Very much like the Cionese gesture of homage, *and I'd never described that gesture in print.* Things were definitely getting strange.

I reached out and clasped his hand. It felt nice and strong and competent, just as my story's heroine had found when she first met him. *STOP IT,* my sense of logic screamed at me. *CHARACTERS DON'T WALK OUT OF YOUR WRITING AND INTO YOUR LIFE.*

Oh don't they? I screamed back silently. *Then how do you explain this?*

My logic-monitor had no answer.

"Well, Nemel Ryenn, what can I help you with?" I sighed.

"We need to negotiate about my life. You didn't give me much of one in that last story." The merest hint of amusement edged his voice: almost the exact same tone he'd used on my heroine the last time she'd spoken to him.

"Oh, uh, I'm sorry about that. You see, the story is really about Lirriane and that baby she adopts, and finding time for her writing . . ." I floundered.

"Yes, I know. You didn't even bother to let me start in my new job. How did you suppose I was going to support myself?"

"Now wait a minute! That's unfair. I *did* say that you'd started work, and were doing wonders organizing the House's accounts. Except the editor asked me to cut that part out."

"Literary women! They're all the same," he said disgustedly. He dropped his hold on my hand. I jumped back, with the strangest flutter of regret at losing physical contact with him. "On any world. You're only interested in getting one thing from me."

"And what is that?" I asked coolly.

He didn't answer. He just stood there, watching me, appraisal and little-boy vulnerability mixed together on his marvelous face.

Hmm, I thought, *he's right. I never even sensed this clash of emotions in him. I just used him as a foil for Lirriane's mid-life restlessness.* My cheeks tingled again, this time with shame. It was a very uncomfortable feeling. I wondered fleetingly how he had traveled here, and if I could find a time-space gate to send him back, so I wouldn't have to deal with these complaints.

"The part you can't bring yourself to write about," he said finally.

The last of my composure skittered away. How had he managed to see into my mind so clearly? For while I was deploring his complaints I had also been admiring his physique, and wondering if it would be possible to further enjoy his body without promising to give him his own story or novel. I gulped, took a deep breath, and reminded myself that he was, after all, only a fictional creation. It calmed me, slightly.

"Look, I can see why you might feel that way. But try to see it from my point of view," I implored. "If I wrote at length about all your management innovations, nobody'd want to read it. Then we'd *both* be out of a job. . . . You're a very attractive man, you know." I smiled shakily at him.

He smiled back, but his eyes were fixed on my left hand. "Do you suppose you might put that weapon down? Makes it hard to concentrate on what you are saying."

Suddenly, I realized I'd been clutching the letter opener the entire time we'd talked. If he was truly who he claimed to be, no wonder he was edgy. The Cionese had legends of empresses who dispatched their favorites to the Nextworld before the men could trade on the lady's pleasure for power. The usual instrument was a ceremonial dagger.

"Oh." I dropped the letter opener. "Sorry. I didn't mean to threaten you, Nicol . . ." I watched for his reaction to the shift to familiar usage, but he didn't flinch. "It's true; we do need to talk. If you can tell me more about what you want out of life, possibly we can give you a terrific future. Are you here on a tight time schedule, or can you get back whenever you want to?"

"No. The only time I can go back is when Koii and Clarit are both full and riding on the hundred-and-tenth demarker, which brings them into alignment with your moon. It should happen halfway through your night, this evening."

COME ON NOW! The internal skeptic screamed at me again. *SURELY YOU DON'T BELIEVE YOUR LITTLE INVENTED SATELLITES, PRETTY AS THEY ARE, CAN REACH OUT AND TRANSPORT PEOPLE ACROSS THE GALAXY? THE CIONESE DON'T EVEN HAVE A VERY ADVANCED ASTRONOMY.*

I said as much.

Nicol Ryenn gave me a hurt look.

"You're letting Lirriane's nephew develop a whole system of biology. What makes you so sure we couldn't do the same with astronomy?"

Logic-monitor subsided, muttering incoherently. This whole happening was impossible anyhow; why worry about a few more inconsistencies? I checked my watch. The afternoon was almost over. There was an obligatory party scheduled at my cousin's house tonight. I looked at Nicol Ryenn appreciatively, and inspiration hit. It would be nice to show up with a handsome escort, and let people speculate how he'd come into my life. My cousin Sheila always serves a sumptuous buffet—surely even a man from a far-off world could find something there to eat. We could talk about his personalized life plan during any awkward lapses in the conversation.

And, I told myself, it would also provide a valuable reality check. If nobody else at the party could see or hear my visitor, I'd turn myself in to the local psychiatric clinic.

That didn't happen. Nicol was a big hit at the party. Nobody had trouble seeing or hearing him. Some of the women perceived him far too intensely for my liking, in fact. I had to pull him away from three bright-eyed flirts and one New Age touchy-feely type. Women in his world are extremely possessive of "their" men so fortunately he didn't mind these proprietary actions. Somehow he managed to pick up enough of our culture—maybe gleaned from mind-reading me—not to make a fool of himself in conversation. When computer glitches or Elvis-sightings came up he just listened; he was perfectly able to join in the "big issues" discussions on war and peace and conservatives versus liberals.

Sheila pulled me aside at one point and said, "Jeannie, he's charming! And so knowledgeable. What's he do for a living?"

"Uh, he's sort of an accountant, I think."

"He sure doesn't *look* like an accountant." She eyed him appraisingly. "He's European, isn't he?"

"He's Cionese."

"Huh? Is that how he identifies himself? I know the Soviets and the Yugoslavs are breaking apart because of ethnic differences, but the *Italians?*"

I shrugged. If Sheila thought Nicol the heir of a proud Italian family, it would avoid a lot of unanswerable questions.

Actually, from his appearance, the European identity was a good guess. His soft suede boots and subtly tailored wool pants fit right into the image. The open-collared white shirt looked eclectic—and great—against his tan, but was pure American, salvaged from some clothes left by my ex-husband, because his intricately embroidered Cionese tunic would have caused too many comments. He'd needed help with the unfamiliar shirt buttons, so that had given me an excuse to touch him again, which was very pleasant.

Watching him now from across the room, I clutched the warm memory close. A clock chimed eleven times. I fiddled with the cat's-eye pendant I was wearing, and worried about carrying out my part of the bargain. Everyone seemed to be having a grand time at the party, Nicol included. Maybe he'd forget that he had come here to hassle me about neglecting his life. Should I feel guilty if he did?

Nah! the answer came quickly. *Just enjoy him, the way a Cionese woman would.*

Somebody turned on the TV. A crowd clustered around it, and Nicol joined them.

The next thing I knew, he had turned away from the set, color draining from his face, looking like he was going to throw up. He staggered toward me. Sheila and I eased him toward the bathroom, but he shook his head, so we found a secluded corner out of the line-of-sight of the TV and the group.

Could electromagnetic pulses affect him so strongly? It was entirely possible; an author doesn't always realize everything she's put into her world. There was much I didn't know about his people's physiology, despite the fact that they look just like us. His next words interrupted my chain of thought.

"I'll be all right. Sorry to alarm you. Those flickering lines gave me a headache, that's all. Can't imagine why you people want to torture yourselves with them."

"Yes. Well ..." There was no way to bridge *this* culture gap. The Cionese representations of human figures were always three dimensional: statues, amulets, drama, even visions of the holy women resemble holographic projections. Having never seen television before, he truly could not sort the two dimensional signals into a coherent pattern.

I reached out to touch his cheek in reassurance. He put his hand over mine as we stood there silently, exchanging the empathy we dared not talk about.

Meanwhile, Sheila had disappeared, sparing me the problem of explaining why a sophisticated Italian businessman couldn't comprehend TV. Nicol and I found a window seat with a nice view into Sheila's moonlit garden. He put his arm around me. I nuzzled close to him. He began to talk about his hopes and dreams.

He had grown up on a back-country farm but always knew his future lay elsewhere. Ambition and curiosity led him to the capital city in his youth. After a stint of studying at a respectable collegium, he knocked around the world a while, working and lodging wherever the enthusiasm of the season led him. He'd even spent a year chasing pirates around the Sea of Themeny.

"Ahh!" I murmured. "Wonderful! We can get some good adventure tales out of *that* year."

He groaned. "Just put them in a flashback, will you? I don't want so much excitement anymore."

"Very well," I conceded reluctantly. "What *do* you want?"

He wanted to try some new techniques for staff and inventory management, he said, without the constant built-in hassles that plagued him in his previous jobs in the mercantile cooperatives. The chance to do so was one reason he took up Lirriane's offer. He added, almost embarrassed: "I need some security. A place where I belong. I want some time to raise flowers and read poems and figure out why we're here at all."

I longed to enfold him in my arms and heart. What he wanted was so reasonable, so in accord with his own world's values of civility and self-fulfillment. It was no usual event, either, to find a man who'd admit to such an inner agenda, although of course Cionese men are more aware of their emotional needs than most American men are.

But Lirriane had a different agenda for him. Kind and honorable she might be, but she shared the Cionese female attitude that men basically exist to make women happy. I had my own agenda too. Writing low-key stories about mid-life crises was not going to further my career in the action-oriented field of science fiction.

Nevertheless, I had a certain responsibility toward this Nicol Ryenn, didn't I? I sighed—the darned man was evoking an inordinate number of sighs from me—and reached out for his hand.

"I think I can give you what you want. But I'll have to make you suffer, too."

A wash of moonlight spilled down on the shore path we followed home, putting me in a romantic mood. Nicol seemed equally mellow; he ambled along like a man who had just set down a heavy burden. We didn't need to talk much. When a frog jumped onto the path, or a duck swam alongside, he stopped and watched delightedly. I was glad he felt free to enjoy these small glimpses of an alien world.

The first awkward moments back in my house were broken when he fumbled with his cuff buttons. I rushed to help. After we'd unfastened them, the shirt came off. I leaned against his bare chest. His hand cupped my head. The other hand turned my face toward his. He traced my profile tenderly with a finger.

It was all so tentative, so different from the precipitate sexuality I'd written into his world, that I had no idea how to make matters proceed. And how I wanted them to! Any doubt that Nicol was a real flesh-and-blood man had vanished. I could feel the slight nubs of beard when my hand touched his cheek, and breathe in the faint smoky essence of male from his skin. He was altogether one of the most desirable men I'd ever met.

Nicol himself didn't help or move things along at all. He just stood there, radiating virility, and gazing at me like a connoisseur admiring a work of art. *Why doesn't he kiss me?* I raged, baffled. The next moment I realized why. In concentrating on the consummation of various romances, I had always skipped past the kissing stage in those stories. I would have to show him how.

My lips found his. Going slowly, sampling the delicious texture and taste of him, parting in delight as he responded with a gentle abrasion that ended in the welcome invasion of his tongue. Anticipation burst into a flame of seeking. Our mouths and hands and neurons reached out to bridge the barriers of self. The rest of our clothes began to slip off.

We spiraled slowly into passion. It was a slow, deliberate slide with the promise of ecstasy to come. The dynamics of our coming together seemed foreordained. I unbuckled his belt and reached to stroke him; he was caressing my hips. All at once he turned away and said, "I can't." His voice shook.

My senses shrieked from the sudden jolt. My ego shrieked too. I floundered for the balm of some reasonable explanation. "I know I don't shimmer in heat like the women of your world do. Maybe I'm not attractive to you?" I ventured fearfully.

"That's not a problem."

From the usual signs I hadn't thought it was, but what other explanation could there be?

"Is it Lirriane?" I asked.

"No," he whispered.

A mauve streak of light fell on him. I could see warring emotions reflected on his face.

"Believe me, I want to," he told me.

I stayed silent, churning with hopes and fears.

"You're—you're my creator," he said finally. "It would be sacrilege."

Oh gods! What a tangled web I'd woven with my words! Neither of us deserved these torments. I still quivered with desire, achingly aware of all the places I wanted him to fill.

"Don't you know each ruling House of Cion started when someone made love with a deity?"

"My ambitions don't go as high as progeniting a new House," he said, but he was smiling.

I did not mention the unlikelihood of fertility in transspecies union.

He held out his arms and I went into them, noticing happily that his erection had not faded. It teased me with small seeking pulses as I pressed tight against him. My clit replied with flutters of desire. My hands struggled frantically with the unfamiliar clasps of his trousers. I felt his fingertips caressing the line below my buttocks, and then a glissade of pleasure at the delicate queries he traced between my legs. My wraparound skirt had dropped easily at the first of these gentle explorations, but not until his touches played me into a jangle of longing did I manage to unwrap *him.*

He was worth the wait. In our mental meetings I had always seen Nicol clothed, the taut curve of muscle and glint of little golden hairs on his skin mere hints of the man beneath the clothing. Now my arms held, and my cells reached out to, a male who met all my fantasies, and more. I pulled back, slightly out of his embrace. Seeing him in the duskiness of night shadow, I absorbed the lines and angles and swirls of his body; felt the beat of his blood and the crest of its surging in his cock.

Very tentatively I knelt and licked the little drop of moisture off the tip. It tasted like semen should taste, but it was also like heather and life and the sun-mist of a faraway planet. I lifted my face up to look at his and caught the expression of bliss as my tongue wrote tickle-phrases around the shaft.

"I'm glad there's something you want from me too," he said.

"Um," I agreed, thinking of how women in his world focus more directly on their own needs.

Then I did too, as he lifted me up and we fell in a joyous tangle on the bed. Caresses by hands and lips and nose and phallus covered me. My nipples, tingling, rubbed against his chest. Our bodies pressed against each other with raw delight. Dizzy with the flickering anticipation in my cunt, I wriggled to demand him just as he pushed in.

"Welcome to my world," I whispered.

Thrusting slowly but tentatively at first, then faster, then surprising me with exquisite circular motions, he blurred my world with bliss. I matched him as our rhythms and perceptions meshed. We careened and plunged along a brink of rapture, sometimes dipping in. Finally, almost ready for a break, I tried to simply lie there and let him do what he was so expert at doing.

But then he eased me around, so that his hands cupped my breasts and his thrusts caressed my magic spot. I stayed very quiet, waiting for the pleasure to surge back.

Instead of building up in small increments mixed with tension, I exploded. I fell through stars . . .

. . . and stars . . .

. . . and more stars. Half a galaxy must have whirled through my dazzled consciousness.

When I could talk again, I murmured, "We must do this again sometime."

"Of course," he said, and held me closer.

In a little while he fell asleep. I stirred in my cocoon of contentment and raised my head. A streak of light still poured across the floor. I eased out of Nicol's arms and walked over to look out the window.

There were two moons.

Even when I fled back and pulled the covers over my head, mauve Koii and pearly Clarit still burned behind my eyelids.

The last thought I had before falling into a restless sleep was of Spinrad's novel where jumps through hyperspace are propelled by the female orgasm. Somehow, even when you write science fiction, you don't expect somebody else's wild idea to reach out and slam you across the universe.

The next thing I knew, morning noises were battering my ears. Carts creaked along the street. Shuttlegulls squawked on the windowsill. Someone was pounding on the door.

"DON'T YOU WANT TO GET UP AND SEE THE WORLD YOU BUILT?"

"No!" I moaned, burrowing deeper into the pillows. Across a zillion miles of space, that damned logic-monitor had still managed to follow me!

Nicol got up to answer the door. I could hear his voice, husky but calm, countering a woman's excited questions.

Then firm steps clipped across the floor. I pulled a quilt around me and looked up into hazel eyes darkened with fury.

"Hai, at least you have good taste, Nicol Ryenn. She looks a lot like me, even. Is there any other possible extenuating factor?"

Several excuses flashed briefly through my mind. *He hasn't signed his contract yet?* Or, *He's my dream man; I have special rights?* Nicol looked really uneasy, as distressed at my embarrassment as at her anger. I hoped he wasn't going to explain that I was a goddess. It would be easier to deal with his outraged lady than with one more twist in the reality continuum.

Clutching the quilt tighter, I held up my hand, stalling for time. What could I ever say to make things right? I liked Lirriane. At least I did before this unfortunate clash of property rights occurred. I liked her so well I'd sent Nicol into her life, to give her sexual delights and honest management practices and loyalty and love. She too was looking for the flowers and poems that make responsibilities bearable. But Lirriane was a proud woman. She might well send her new companion away because of what I'd done.

I looked at her again. There was as much hurt as anger in her eyes.

I made the only possible excuse.

"My deepest apologies, Nemelyya. He didn't do anything to dishonor your trust. It was entirely my fault. I seduced Nicol Ryenn. He couldn't help himself." True, or at least universally believed in her world. "Here, I will gladly pay the fine for unauthorized access to this man of yours." This brought me up short; I suddenly remembered I had no money with me. And even if I had, American money wouldn't work here, where they used semiprecious jewels for currency.

The cat's eye pendant still dangled between my breasts. I'd put it on for the party last night because it was striking and festive, and I had been in a mood for adventure. I pulled it off and held it out to Lirriane.

She nodded formally. She took it, and started to turn away. Then she asked, "Was he as good as he looks?"

I smiled at her. "Better."

Nicol walked with her into the other room. Amid their mur-

mured conversation I heard her tell him to be in her office by
suncrossing.

"Do what she says," I told him when he returned to me. "You
need each other. I won't make you suffer any more than absolutely necessary."

"And you?" he asked. I think by now he had forgotten I was a
deity at all.

"I'll be all right," I said, and meant it. Not that I was trying to
be noble or anything. But I'd had a lovemaking that would keep
me glowing for a month, and I wanted Nicol to get on with his
life. Besides, I had to figure out how to get home before I com-
plicated any more story lines.

Michelle Handelman

Blood Past

The blood passed slowly through his lips like fire on a lake, simultaneously caressing and drowning the fever of excitement that passed through the audience. He was Juris, the great glass-chewer of Haiti who devoured shards of glass like a lover sucking the sweet juice of his woman's vagina. Slowly, he rolled the glass between his teeth and tongue and a great spray of saliva shot forth, covering the audience in a moist shroud of love. This was the art he was most practiced in, having been trained in his youth to carry on the tradition of his father. Though he was wise he was still not a master, as sometimes the blood would escape from his heart. But the audience did not care. They were there to be entertained, not enlightened, and when the blood came, they would rise to the occasion, human torture being the greatest entertainment of all.

I stood in the back of the crowd. There was a circle around him on this sweltering Spanish night and bodies pressed hot together, simultaneously arching forward to gain a better view of the show. When Juris took an old bottle of perfumed water and broke it beneath his foot, I felt a shiver run through my body like the slight release just before orgasm. The audience moved closer, I felt the breath of one hundred steamy bodies down my neck. The scent of roses and lust filled the air. He picked up a piece of the bottle and placed it on his tongue, and as his teeth met the glass I felt another orgasmic surge. The combination of the movement of his lips and the sweltering bodies being pushed against me made me dizzy; the sound of Spanish guitars played the strings of my sex. I wanted to be that bottle. Yet, as he chewed I realized that it was not only the intoxication of this magical act that was touching me, but the actual presence of a hand from the crowd which was gently searching beneath my skirt. I didn't dare turn around. The introduction was already made.

I felt this foreign hand rub itself tenderly along my thighs. The fingers were warm and smooth. At once I recognized the hand to be that of a masseuse or one who often wore gloves. I could not tell whether it belonged to a man or a woman and I did not care. My nerve endings were tingling, and as Juris put another piece of glass between his lips, my body shook as two fingers separated the lips of my vagina. They pushed in and out of my cunt, slowly at first, gradually building up speed until I couldn't hold back. Heat poured forth from my swollen cunt and I coated the hand in a large spray of juice. Outwardly, I had to control my body so no one would catch on to this public display, yet the fingers pushed deeper every time I stood more rigid. I arched my buttocks to allow deeper penetration and offer the tip of my clitoris. His hand . . . her hand . . . that mysterious hand that belonged to the entire audience grabbed my clit just as Juris was at the climax of his act. In perfect synchronicity, Juris chewed the glass, the audience gasped and I orgasmed. The hand moved faster and slid in and out of my vagina several times before it came around to grab my clit again. The two fingers left my gasping pussy. Throbbing. Pulsating. They pinched my clitoris and remained there for several moments as the pressure built in my cunt for the pleasure of several orgasms. The blood appeared on the lips of Juris and my cunt shot forth a river of ecstasy. The performance was over, the crowd was satisfied and my stranger disappeared.

I walked back to my hotel room languorous and fulfilled. It was the act of glass-chewing that amazed me more than the act of sex. I had seen it with African fire walkers and snakesitters—the ability to leave your body and mind at will for a higher state of spiritual existence. The body was left to work as a finely tuned machine trained to avoid all points of pain while concentrating on that space between emotion and thought. The blood pressure was lowered, the breathing deep, and the heightened nerve endings . . . numb. One could endure death without fear. Pleasure through pain. I planned to return the following day.

The next evening, as I turned down the road heading into town, I was taken by a surge of the scent of magnolias and salty sea air. My nose lifted like a child to her mother's nipple—I wanted to consume the flavors of life until I was full and plump. A wind flirted with my skirt and I felt the pale hairs on my labia ruffled gently by the gods. Upon entering the center of town I noticed the crowd was larger this evening and there were several more children chasing each other through the adults' legs. My attention was directed toward Juris as he introduced another performer: a beautiful woman with golden hair piled high atop her head; she was dressed in a corset of polished steel. Strapped to her hip were three exquisitely carved daggers. This was Alia, a sword swallower and Amazon whose mere presence pushed the audience to the precipice of enchantment. She swallowed swords like liquid, and the men in the audience couldn't help but feel a great bulge rise between their legs as Alia opened her larynx and consumed twenty-two inches of cold steel. She was a true feat of nature. I felt so small watching this remarkable example of human concentration—a woman able to chase her ghosts away with the flick of a tongue and capable of satisfying any man.

After Alia's act, Juris took the stage while she softly sang octaves to soothe her throat. Juris pulled from his robe a shimmering crystal phallus, about five inches high; it had a vein of blue running through the center. When light struck the crystal, rays of color pierced the whole audience, and as he held up the hypnotic phallus, Juris told a story of the Haitian voodoo priest and his queens.

"In every kingdom, the head priest chose his favorite concubine for sacrifice on the holiest of days. She was prepared in the finest silks and bathed for hours in olive oil and coconut milk. At dusk, the voodoo priest would meet her for a long walk by the river, then they would retire to the royal chambers to make love until sunset. As night fell, the priest would recite a spell while still inside the sacrificial whore, and pass a poisoned capsule from his lips to hers—she would bite down and die instantly. A bit of blood was extracted from her body and placed inside a crystal phallus, which the priest then used to satisfy his other whores. You see, the blood is blue," Juris said as he held the phallus higher, "because it has never had a taste of oxygen. The more blue crystals the priest attained, the higher his status within the sect. This is where we get the term 'blue blood.' "

The audience didn't know where his talk was leading. It didn't matter. Juris had such a seductive way of speaking and gesturing to the audience that no one could move in his presence.

Juris continued: "And so there was a great priest from an unknown town who I met in the market one day. He told me he could no longer live in his land because he had sacrificed a sacred goat to feed the townspeople after a severe drought. The people refused to eat the goat and banished him from the land. He was on his way west with one last possession to release.

"He gave me the crystal you see before us. This was the blood of his last concubine during his final days as the high voodoo priest. Yesterday, when Alia came to meet me here, she spoke to me of this great holy man's death. His town received his body with flowers and feasts because after the death of that goat all their crops began to grow. Tonight I shall consume the blood of his life force. But I need a woman from the audience to assist me. Is there anyone here strong enough to join me?"

It was a moment when I could choose to take the leap onto the other side or remain forever an observer left to watch someone else fulfill my dreams. It was the magic of Spain. It was hot, and as the sweat poured down my thighs, I stood, a stranger surrounded by the magic awaiting me. I stepped forward and Juris took my hand to help me out of the crowd. His power electrified me. I felt the heat pass through my fingers, up my arm to the crook of my shoulders, through my breasts and straight down my belly to nestle hot in my sex box. A truly virile man. He placed the phallus in my hand, and as he bent his head back he told me to slide the crystal in and out of his mouth. My juices were already flowing. In front of all these people, Juris and I were performing the act of fellatio with a holy relic of his motherland. A relic containing the blood of a whore and the scent of a thousand lovers.

I slid the strong rock into his mouth. His lips enveloped the instrument until there was no space between the phallus and his mouth. I pulled it out and pushed it in. I pulled it out and pushed it in again; each time it shimmered in the evening light, covered with the saliva of Juris and getting wetter and juicier every time it entered his mouth. And it was all too much for me to take. My legs were trembling and I could feel an orgasm coming on. My nipples hardened beneath my blouse and my breasts heaved with each stroke of Juris's tongue. I caught a glimpse of Alia on the side of the ring, completely immersed in the sharpening of her blade, and then my attention returned to Juris and the ever-moving phallus. I pushed it into his mouth deeper than before, and my pussy quivered with the power of seduction in a public arena. All eyes were upon me, a hundred or so tourists, locals and lovers; their gaze made the event all the more eroticized. I slid it in one more time. Then, under the power of the setting sun reflecting in the eyes of the audience, Juris bit down on the crystal phallus and the blue blood poured forth ... down his chin, mixing with oxygen for the very first time and turning bright red as it reached his neck. Then Juris did what he was trained to do: he chewed the glass for the women, men and children as he did every night, bringing magic and illusion to the curious travelers and hospitable locals in the south of Spain.

Like new initiates into a secret service, the crowd broke off into little groups, huddling and whispering. The essence of the evening, the sharing of this holy experience, created a bond among the members of the audience which would forever connect them. And when they crossed paths again, their mutual nods would acknowledge this bond. As the crowd slowly disbanded, Juris asked me where I was from.

"I come from Chicago, but I'm on my way to Africa to teach English. I'll be there in two weeks. I came here last night and admired your show very much, which is why I returned tonight. I have always been fascinated with sword swallowers, and I would like it very much if you would introduce me to Alia."

Juris told me to wait a moment. He walked over to the van

where Alia was packing their belongings. After a brief exchange, Alia came toward me and Juris continued the loading. She extended her hand, which was just as strong as Juris's, introduced herself, and spoke English with some difficulty.

"I have been swallowing swords for thirteen years now," she said. "It is a beautiful tradition and I am proud to continue its life force. I trained with the bravest man in all of Cuba. He watched his mother die by the sword of a soldier, and felt driven to defeat the strength of the sword himself. If you like, come with us to have a glass of wine and I will tell you of my training."

I followed her to the van and the three of us drove south. We drove to a cove on the beach where Alia and Juris had set up camp. Their dog was there, along with a stove and two hammocks slung in the trees. Juris went to greet the dog and give him a run on the beach as Alia and I brought out the wine and a few glasses. We made ourselves comfortable on a large, smooth rock. Now she was more candid with me, and with a throaty laugh she began talking of her early years: "The first time I performed in public, I was so nervous that I gagged on the sword. I had to concentrate, I had to imagine that I was sucking on my lover's cock, which grew larger and larger with the depth of our love. And my throat loosened only with that idea—that I could consume all the love being given to me by the man I loved most."

"So sword swallowing is an act of love?" I asked, upon which Juris jumped into the conversation.

"Don't let her fool you. It's all about sex, completely about sex."

Alia jumped on him and the two of them wrestled around in the sand, poking each other and throwing teasing remarks. We drank and laughed for hours, and Juris began caressing my neck. Before I knew it, we had our tongues in each others' mouths. Alia whispered something to the two of us and then whistled to the dog; the two of them walked down the beach. Juris's tongue probed every inch of my mouth. The tip of it ran back and forth across my gums. He flicked the inside of my upper lip while sucking my bottom one—it felt like being sucked by the tides of the sea. With long smooth strokes, his tongue searched and retreated. Each time I was dizzier with passion. He moved down to my breasts and began rolling each nipple in his mouth like the glass between his teeth. All the attention and skill he used with his glass chewing were brought to his lovemaking. He sucked harder on my nipples, surrounding them with soft little bites; the harder he sucked the deeper my cunt swelled. His hands lightly brushed over my throbbing vagina and he grabbed hold of my knees with all the power of Haiti. He spread my legs open and just looked at my dripping cunt, glistening and palpitating like a moist creature from the sea. He just sat there and looked. The power of his gaze sent my muscles into a frenzy. To have my cunt fully exposed to the sea and the air . . . his breath on my breath . . . his eyes on my sex . . . I couldn't stand it.

I begged Juris to have me right there. The tension was building, and already my cunt started shivering in orgasm. Juris took a vial of blue glass from his pocket and slid it right up my cunt while I moaned in relief. The glass was cold and smooth, and as he pushed it in and out of my pussy the difference in temperature created a fine vapor that mingled with the sea air. Then he placed the glass back in his pants, removed his trousers, and deeply thrust his cock all the way up my pussy to what felt like the bottom of my belly. He fucked me and fucked me and each time he entered I felt my insides tremble, and the tip of his penis seemed to fill my body until there was nowhere left to go.

When I regained some composure and looked up, I saw Alia behind Juris's back, fingering herself. When our eyes met she took one of the daggers from her hip and began touching the tip of her clit with it, all the while keeping eye contact with me. The blade just barely touched the clitoris and every time it brushed her swollen cunt her eyes rolled back in her head and her knees collapsed a little. She was driving me crazy and there was no stopping her. Then, when I could actually see the juice pouring from her pussy, she slid the blade of the dagger about four inches into her cunt and remained very still. The juice flowed over the blade and her hand, leaving a small puddle of this dangerous love in the sand beneath her.

Juris turned around, sweetly laid her down in the sand and began lapping up all the juice of her cunt like a cat cleaning his sister. He slowly licked her clit over and over, until she was screaming with orgasm for the second time around. Then, as I watched Alia dig her hands into the sand, Juris pulled the blue vial from his pocket, placed it in his mouth, and bit down, shattering the whole thing into tiny pieces. He chewed. The great Juris chewed the glass more vigorously than he ever did in public. He no longer possessed his mind or his body, only his mouth. And then, with a mouth full of glistening shards of blue glass, Juris started licking Alia, sucking and spitting the glass into her vagina . . . ecstatic and sublime. Alia was now in an orgiastic trance, their magic being transferred from orifice to orifice. I watched with honor, and was reminded of all mortality. For as Juris chewed, small drops of blood fell from his mouth like flaming rose petals to the sand and the sea . . . burning the sand with the blood of these modern mystics.

Blake C. Aarens

Table for One

Damn! Three hours before I'm supposed to meet her for dinner and then be her dessert, Joanne calls to cancel. Again. I know she said she likes to build up anticipation, but this is ridiculous! That woman's been stringing me along for three months now.

I refuse to believe that my being in this wheelchair has anything to do with her canceling. She asked me to dance at Keisha's birthday party, and sat on my lap while we watched the video of Sweet Honey in the Rock. But you know me, I still had to check out that possibility.

I don't know whether to laugh, cry, or roll around my apartment cussing and moaning. I went out and bought a new bottle of musk oil, spent forty-five minutes trying to iron my clothes; I even trimmed my pubic hair! And I can tell you it was hell getting those little curlicues out of the bottom of my seat. I did all that just to hear her tell me, "Something came up." I was polite to her on the phone, but right now, I'm angry. And so horny.

I go into my office to check my book and see when we'll be able to reschedule. Next weekend is out; I have plans every night from Thursday to Sunday. Then I notice that tonight is the full moon. I smile, finally understanding why I am so tense and aroused.

I go into the kitchen and open my back door. Sure enough,

there she is, glowing full and round up in the sky. I check to make sure Mrs. Lopez isn't outside singing to her birds. I can't smell cigarette smoke from Nona upstairs, so I slyly open my robe and let Her light shine on my body. The cold night air makes my nipples stiffen and I close my eyes and arch into the breeze. I slide my hands down my neck and over my breasts. I draw circles on my belly. And though I can't really feel the pressure, I stroke my thighs and delight in the sight of my hands on my skin. I feel as if I'm rubbing the moon's very glow into me.

"Uhnnnh, girl. You sitting out here turning yourself on." I laugh out loud and go back inside, shutting the door.

"What I need," I say to my tortoiseshell cat Sonja, perched on the back of the couch, "is to meditate, do some kind of ritual to mark the moon's changes and the ones Joanne Taylor is putting me through." In response, she throws me a cat kiss—a long, slow blink—and then settles her head on top of her tucked-in paws. I take that to be a sign of approval.

I want to be undisturbed for at least the next hour, so I put Sonja's dinner out, turn the ringer off on the phone and the volume down on the answering machine, and put out all the lights. I sit in the dark for a while, listening intently to my own breathing and the rhythmic sound of Sonja's purr. Then I begin to prepare my bedroom for the ritual.

I light four candles on my altar: a black one for identity, a white one for purity, a purple one for gaiety, and a dark cherry-red one for, well, you know, lust. The room is glowing, but not brightly enough. I grab my yard stick from behind the door and open the top curtains on my bedroom window. That way the only being who can peer in is the moon Herself. And She does, her cool, strong glow falling down the center of my bed. She knows what I have in mind. My attendant helped me put fresh sheets on the bed this morning, and I can't wait to slide under the warm cotton flannel.

I light one stick of patchouli and one of sandalwood incense. The room smells like a temple and is ablaze like one too. I inhale deeply and am dizzy with the heady scent. I bend over the smoke, letting it pour over my nipples and seep between my fingers. I even hold my dreads over the incense burner until my entire body smells like a church. With my bracelet of bells wrapped around both wrists, I clasp my hands as if in prayer and shake them, cleansing the air with the high, clear sound of the bells.

I touch my chakras with the heart-shaped amethyst crystal that my ex-lover gave me for Valentine's Day two years ago. After sticking my finger in the glass of wine on my altar, I suck it dry, filling my mouth with the bittersweet taste.

"Mawu," I say, bowing my head, "Goddess of the Earth, the One who gave me birth and continues to sustain me. Be with me. Mawu is here." I tilt my head to look up at the moon.

"Yemaya, Goddess of the moon, who changes monthly in Her circled orb. Show me by your example how to likewise flow through my changes. Be with me. Yemaya is here." I pivot in my chair to call forth the Goddesses of the remaining four directions.

"Maat, Goddess of the west, where the sun sets, the teacher, the feeling self. Be with me. Maat is here. Aphrodite, Goddess of the south, where the light comes from, the healer, the emotional self. Be with me. Aphrodite is here. Amaterasu, Goddess of the east, where the sun rises, the visionary and the child, the spiritual and intuitive self. Be with me. Amaterasu is here. Skaadi, Goddess of the north, where the cold comes from, the warrior, the communicating self. Be with me. Skaadi is here. The circle is cast and I am between the worlds. What is between the worlds is of no concern of the worlds and affects the worlds. Aché."

After a silent three minute meditation, I open the top drawer of my bedside table and survey the contents. I take out my bottle of Probe, a jar of jasmine massage cream, a handful of silk scarves, and my bright red, five-and-one-half-inch battery-operated vibrator. I've never turned the thing on, but with the batteries inside it, it's nice and heavy. My lap, too, is heavy with the implements of my ritual.

I put on a CD of African drumming, and wheel myself over to my bed. After turning down the covers, I slip my arms out of my robe and sit for a moment with my eyes closed. I cup my hands over my mound and rock to the drumbeats. I take the things out of my lap and put them onto the pillow. Then, I lock the back brakes on my wheelchair, grab the chin-up bar rigged overhead, and hoist myself up into bed.

The sheets are warm and my body still retains the heat from my bath. I drape the scarves over the bar above me, so that whenever I move they graze my skin. The sensuous caress of silk sends an impulse throughout me: the tops of my ears grow hot, my throat constricts, my nipples stick out from my body, and the lips of my sex begin to swell and moisten.

With the jasmine-scented cream I give a loving massage to every inch of my body that I can reach, paying extra attention to those parts I don't much care for. My belly's not flat, but then again, the Earth herself has hills and valleys.

The aroma of jasmine mingles with that of the burning incense. I close my eyes and imagine myself in a dense forest, the sound of running water close at hand. Seeking out pleasure in unexpected places, I cup the rough skin of my elbows, knead the hollow of my throat, and probe into my belly button. The massage completed, I lie on my bed with my hands at my sides, my breathing slow and concentrated, coming from deep in my belly. My body resonates with the vibrations of the drums and the pleasure of my own tender touch.

With delicate strokes from the tips of my fingers, and the brief slips of silk against my chest, I turn myself on in stages. My fingers feel like feathers on my naked skin. I feel the flow of blood through my veins, the throbbing of my pulse in my throat, the sensation of tingling in my fingers, and the expectant clenching of the muscles of my cunt.

I am ready. I slide my hands under my hips and lift my legs one at a time until I have spread them wide open. My fingers move through the coarse bush of my pubic hair, my thumbs and forefingers outlining the V of my mound. I tap my clit lightly and feel it draw away from the sharp contact. I press and pull on my oily inner lips, enjoying their softness, their fullness, opening them up like the petals of a flower. And then I am within the moist temple of me, pressing at the walls and gripping around the fingers I wedge deep inside.

Exploring different strokes, touches, and pressures, I run my finger around the outside of my mouth and then suck it inside. I drag my wrists across my swollen nipples, gently pull my pubic hair, make increasingly smaller circles around my clitoris, slowly plunge four fingers into the luscious wet of me and then yank them out, stimulating myself to just before the point of no return.

I stop touching myself then and inhale deeply, holding the pleasure in. My left hand is at my side and with my right hand I trace a path from my cunt to the center of my chest, drawing the fire of arousal into my heart. The pounding of my heart is strong and sure, and I am shaken by the power within me. With relief I exhale and let the energy I have built up spread to the rest of my body.

I repeat this process eight times. For that is the number of the Infinite. At first it is exquisite torture, but by the eighth time, my ritual has transformed genital arousal into whole-body ecstasy.

I am lightness. Floating. My energy expands beyond the boundaries of my body. I could swear I feel the weight of my thighs on the bed, a slight bend in my knees, tingling in my toes. And when I spread myself open with the tip of the red vibrator, it is all that I can do to keep from coming. Then I realize that I no longer need to keep from coming.

Pinching my clit between my thumb and forefinger, I nudge myself toward orgasm. When it comes, I moan loudly, invoking all the names of the Goddess my mind can recall, including my own. I plant kisses of benediction on Her full, heavy breasts, lap at the holy water between Her thighs, writhe in ecstatic agony on my bed.

And then I am spent. My breathing slows to normal and my vision clears. The clenching of my cunt has expelled the vibrator from my body. I cup both hands over my mound and sigh.

It is then that I hear the clicking of the answering machine on my bedside table. On instinct, I reach over and turn up the volume to screen the call.

"Amani? Are you there?" Joanne's voice asks. She waits to see if I'll pick up and then continues on when I don't. "Sorry I had to cut you off earlier. Minor crisis with one of my clients; I think she'll be okay now. I guess you decided to go out on your own—"

I pick up the phone. "Hey girlfriend. Naw, I didn't go out, just decided to call it an early night. I'm already in bed."

"Oh, you are?" she says, her voice flirtatious. She clears her throat. "Do you think I could come join you?"

"I'm ready and waiting. You know the address."

"Ten minutes," she says.

I hang up the phone and await her arrival.

Genevieve Smith

Academic Assets

Dr. Catherine Andrews
Director of Graduate Studies
Department of Political Science
Plymouth University, VA

Dear Professor Andrews,

I am writing this recommendation on behalf of Kyle
William Harper, who is applying for a graduate fellowship to your political science program. I have had
the pleasure of knowing Kyle since his freshman year at
Kent, when he was enrolled in my Introduction to Western
Civilization course, and he was most recently a member of my senior honors seminar on The Politics of
the French Revolution. In both courses he distinguished
himself. His work is thorough, insightful and original, and
his aggressive yet respectful classroom personality indicates his strength of character and ability to both
assist and learn from his fellow students. He never hesitated,
as many less ambitious students do, to take advantage
of special departmental workshops, colloquia, or my
own office hours. We are quite sorry that Kyle has not

chosen to pursue his graduate degree here at Kent. Our loss in this case will certainly be your gain. I cannot recommend Kyle highly enough, and should you accept him he will surely be an asset to your program.

Yours sincerely,
Emily E. Jackson

She proofread the printout one final time and sighed. It was a good letter, and along with Kyle's record, it should do the job. She fished a clean sheet of department letterhead from the tray next to her office computer, then returned it restlessly to the stack.

She just wasn't satisfied.

Because it didn't say what she really wanted to say.

She checked the clock—another hour until her current "significant other" got out of his meeting in the Philosophy department. They had exchanged angry words before he left, and the scene had sent her straight to some work she had been putting off. Initially a chore, now Kyle's letter provided a needed distraction.

Pouring herself a fresh cup of coffee, she started a new document file.

Dr. Catherine Andrews
Director of Graduate Studies
Department of Political Science
Plymouth University, VA

Dear Professor Andrews,

You're only human, right? Well, so am I, so I hope you'll excuse me when I say that you really should give Kyle Harper a graduate fellowship to your department because he has the world's most perfect ass. Honestly. It's stunning. If you asked for pictures with student applications instead of GRE scores you'd know exactly what I mean. But maybe not—I think you have to see him in the (firm,

rippling) flesh to really appreciate him. My first sight
was four years ago when he was a freshman in a standard
Western Civ course. My first thought: "Promising. Very promising." He would have stood out even if he hadn't been
practically the only black student at a school nicknamed
"Wonder Bread U." But eighteen-year-olds always look pretty
green to me (do you find that too?), so I honestly didn't
much notice him. I gave him his grade (a respectable
A— or something like that) and he went the way of hundreds of other freshmen.

But then he reappeared in my senior honors seminar this
fall. At first I didn't realize that this was the young man
I'd seen almost four years ago. Suddenly (or it seemed
sudden to me) he was six feet tall, with a body that just
shouldn't be legal—perfect proportions, gorgeous brown
skin. And that ass. I wonder if the other students noticed
me watching him every day as he made his way to the
same spot: back seat, middle row (he knows he has a perfect
ass—he took that stroll every day on purpose just to torture
me). Maybe the men who weren't looking at him themselves noticed; anyway, most of the women were straining their peripheral vision to watch Kyle and his glorious
ass.

It was bad enough to watch him in my classroom and
not be able to touch. Then he started showing up during
my office hours. Orifice hours, I began to think of them,
because those were the most attentive parts of my body
when he sat down and scooted his chair up close to
mine. He was always the proper, respectful student, but
most of the time his questions were pretty lame; I really
think he just wanted attention, and like most beautiful people,
couldn't resist watching the impact he had on me. I
would try very hard to maintain my polite-but-firm pro-
fessorial classroom persona, but Christ! All I could think
about was lunging for the door, locking it behind us, and
dropping him to the carpet for an afternoon of sweaty
sex, starting with the best blowjob he'd ever had (which
reminds me—why don't we have a nice word for oral sex

that doesn't sound like work? Or pasta? If you can think
of one, let me know). I've since added a big overstuffed
chair to my office furniture, and if I had had it then,
the temptation to dive onto it with him might have been
too much. But I'm not completely amoral; I lusted after
Kyle, but I lusted, alas, in silence.

Is this getting too graphic? Sorry—I did warn you
that I'm only human.

Emily glanced at the clock. Ten more minutes until Nick
showed up. Better hurry. Nick was always so prompt. Especially
when he was cranky.

I suppose that I should say something about Kyle's academic
status. He is a good student; not spectacular, but very good.
And he is definitely serious about his career plans. His
best quality is his determination and ... but what am
I saying?! Sure he's smart, but his best quality is still his
ass. Bar none. Would that I could have gotten my hands
on it. If you do accept him into your program (and you
honestly should), be prepared to suffer pangs of lascivious torment. At least until he graduates in two or three
years.

Then he's fair game—for a game I suspect he's up to.

Very Truly Yours,
Emily E. Jackson

She leaned back on her swivel chair and surveyed the glowing
screen with satisfaction. "Now that," she thought, "is more like
it."

Her reverie was cut short by three quick taps on her office
door. Ordinarily he would have just walked in, but their heated
exchange had clearly left Nick uncertain about his welcome.

She stood up and stretched, taking her time to let him in.
When she did, he entered slowly and stood by her desk, shifting
from foot to foot. She remained silent while he gazed around her

office, searching for a neutral conversation opener. Finally he noticed the overstuffed chair.

"That's new, isn't it?" he said with a cautious smile.

"Yes, it is." She took him by the hand, led him in front of it, then pushed him down onto the cushions.

"Are you still angry with me? Because I'm really sorry that I—"

She put her finger over his lips, then began unbuckling his belt. Too shocked to move at first, he soon began to help her, and in no time his pants were around his ankles and she was savoring his warm flesh. She stroked his smooth shaft with her tongue, wetting him with her saliva, teasing the head of his penis with her closed, moistened lips. When he finally began to shift uncomfortably from the prolonged anticipation, she plunged his entire cock into her warm mouth. She was rewarded by his heavy groan, and the satisfying sensation of fullness that sucking him always gave her.

The unexpectedness of her assault and the novelty of sex in her office were too much for him. He came quickly, and hard. She swallowed his semen with pleasure, drawing on him until he moaned in half pleasure, half pain. From her seat on the carpet she rested her head on his lap, twining her arms back around his waist and up to his shoulders. He played with her hair gently.

"Does this mean you forgive me?" he asked quietly, after a comfortable silence had elapsed.

"Could be." She smiled as he began to knead her shoulders and neck. "Why don't we go to my apartment, where we don't have to worry about being caught by the custodians, and see if we can settle the rest of our differences? I've got some wine coolers and pop tarts." She stood and brushed off her knees, checked her hose for runs, then began gathering her things.

"Sounds good to me. But give me just a minute, will you? I'm feeling a little drained." Nick opened one eye just enough to gauge her reaction.

"Lame, very lame," she chuckled, turning off the computer.

"Then why are you laughing? Hey, wait!" He leaned forward, suddenly finding some energy. "You didn't save that file!"

This time she laughed outright. "Oh, don't worry about that," she reassured him. "It was a letter for a student. I'm not so sure I had the tone quite right anyway. Now hurry up and let's go, you big faker. You have a back rub to earn!"

Debbie Cohen

Look What the Cat Dragged In

It was a crisp and sun-dappled Sunday morning. As I stretched my leg and poked my toes out of the covers to test the air, Barnacle promptly pounced on them. Wiggling toes have been a weakness of his ever since he was a kitten. Tahiti was lounging on the pillow next to mine, quick to capitalize on the still-warm place my lover grudgingly left as he stumbled about, dressing for basketball. She casually placed her paw on my face and gently stretched her claws into my cheek. Though the day was mine to sleep away, my cats had an agenda of their own; they had decided it was time for me to get moving.

I lay in bed just long enough to prove to Barnacle and Tahiti that they had not won, then crawled out of bed and into my bathrobe. As I put on coffee, the cats chased each other around the apartment. Coffee meant Sunday and Sunday meant they would be adorned with collars and admitted to the outdoor world of scent and adventure. They sat on my newspaper, pounced on the drawstring of my robe, and stuck their noses in my juice until I opened the sliding glass door and let them roam free. Barnacle led the way and I watched as they disappeared around the bend of the deck, where they bounded down the steps onto the busy sidewalk and immediately sprang back up, their tails twitching caution and ears alerted to receive and translate every sound.

Such was our Sunday routine. With my lover gone for a few hours, I would spread out, scatter books and papers and lounge in my mess, treating myself to an occasional glance at the joyously romping cats.

I settled into the couch, swathed in my down comforter, and deposited three potentially interesting books in front of me. I had just tearfully parted with ten characters at the close of a World War II novel and was hesitant to re-engage in the realm of emotional devastation. So I selected my favorite, well-thumbed (and fingered) collection of erotic short stories written by women.

Slowly I read, pausing often to reach into my warm cocoon to cradle my breasts, circle my nipples, stroke at the firm wet muscles between my outspread legs. I invited the characters under the covers with me to play out their brief, potent scenes. I allowed curious tongues to travel my thighs, golden curved cocks to plunge into me as I cowered helplessly in a corner. I invited women's expert fingers to rummage through my insides and tickle me into convulsions. I saw myself, dildo in hand, bearing down on a trembling woman. I was tied to a bed and sucked raw. I was tenderly bathed and carried to bed. I groped and I pressed, I grappled and I lunged. I was swimming in a sea of honey and sinking sweetly.

As I came for the fifth time, a harsh background noise came sharply into focus. It was coming from the house next door, which was being reconstructed. I identified the noise as a jackhammer and wondered if the workmen had deliberately returned on Sunday just to aggravate me.

Time to collect the cats. Both of them are remarkably lacking in any survival skills; they stick their noses into flame, they crawl into the cavity of the sofa-bed as it's being folded up, they love running under heavy moving objects. I imagined Barnacle running up to the jackhammer to give it his ritual proprietary sniff. I'm not fond of this image, so when the workers come out, the cats come in.

I pulled on my robe and stepped onto the deck to start my search. I almost tripped over Tahiti, who was cowering behind a potted plant. Barnacle was nowhere to be found. I checked the stairs, a nook in the side of the house where he likes to nap, and then headed down to the street to peek under cars—another favorite hangout.

Finally, cold and cursing under my breath, I approached one workman who was taking a break. As I asked about Barnacle, I could just imagine the track playing in his brain: "Neurotic bitch over-concerned about her cats." He feigned sympathy and smilingly agreed to keep his eye out for Barnacle. Instead of slapping the smile off his face, I thanked him and returned to my book and quilt.

I was disappointed but not surprised to find that the stories which had me writhing minutes before could not penetrate my concern for Barnacle and the grating noise of construction. I abandoned the couch for the shower, where I hoped to at least drown out the noise. I let the water run over my face, my hair, my breasts, and then opened my legs and shuddered at the full, warm lick of water I received. Slowly I soaped my body, giving special attention to the tender cavities between my toes and the hollow where my neck and collar bones meet. I admired my long fingers as they stroked the soft flesh of my inner thighs. You are beautiful, whispered the steamy women circling me. You are just right.

There was a polite knock at the bathroom door—a knock my lover knows is expected of him before entering. This small gesture has eliminated a great deal of fright on my part, as it prevents me from being unexpectedly shaken from my steamy shower dream world.

"What happened, did the game end early?" I shouted above the water, as he is usually gone three hours at least. There was no reply.

"Honey, are you okay? Why are you back so soon?" Still no reply. I wiped the soap from my eyes and leaned out of the shower.

There stood the amused construction worker holding a sooty and confused Barnacle. As he lowered Barnacle to the floor, the cat took great interest in the man's jeans, and sniffed contentedly at a dark stain on his right leg. I, too, took interest in the man's jeans, as a bulge was steadily forming under my gaze. "Thank you," I managed to whisper, and stood riveted.

His look of amusement fell as his eyes traveled my body. I watched him appreciate my taut nipples, my round belly, my dripping hair. He reached out his hand as if to touch and then withdrew it. The shower rained confusion on me, pelting me with rage, fear and desire. I began to mumble something resembling "Get out of my house" when he spoke.

"Show me," he pleaded hoarsely.

"Show you what?" I replied, feeling very naked. What did he want to see that he wasn't already seeing?

"Show me. Show me what you were doing on the couch."

My jaw dropped. On the couch. When? Today? How could he have seen that? A flush began in my face and flowered throughout my body. He had watched.

"Okay, but I'll need some help" came out quicker than my intended demand that he leave the bathroom.

The jeans and T-shirt quickly came off. While he struggled with his boots, his eyes remained riveted on me as if I would be sucked down the drain any minute if he didn't keep a close watch. I turned the water off, but remained dripping in the tub. I showed him my ass, held up my breasts for his hungry examination and teased him with moans and thrusts until he was finally free of the boots. Then he came to me.

I was standing with my legs spread wide, and as he stepped into the tub he offered me his thigh: "You might be more comfortable resting on this." I was. Reaching for my hands, he took them from me. He gently kneaded my palms while telling my breasts what he intended to do with them. I began sliding myself up and down the thigh that held me. I pressed it tight between my legs, like a huge cock, and rode it until my clit was swollen solid.

He kept his promise to my breasts and cradled them as carefully as I had earlier. He teased them with the tip of his tongue until the nipples strained as if they would burst. Just as my yearning to have them surrounded became almost unbearable, he took one breast at a time into the warmth of his mouth while squeezing the other swollen nipple. As he lifted the second breast in consideration, a shooting fire ran from my asshole up my spine and I came in long, shuddering spasms against that rock hard thigh.

He sat me down on the edge of the tub, rubbed his erect cock gently against each of my flushed cheeks and said, "Now, show me." After pushing my knees open with his, he stood back and waited, holding his cock firmly and slowly rubbing up and down. He looked at me as if it were me he was stroking and I pretended he was. I mirrored his movements, parting my lips and stroking the soft inner flesh. I squeezed my bulging clit and spread my legs wide, wide open. Three fingers slid easily in, and they took up their familiar rhythm, pumping slowly and teasingly. I flicked my clit and my nipples alternately and waves of pained pleasure flowed over me. I withdrew my fingers when my ears started ringing, and a dam fell on the ripples rising to wash over me. Not yet.

As I writhed with the agony of postponed pleasure, he dove for my legs and pushed them open wider, spreading my lips back into a wide smile with his thumbs. With one generous sweep of his tongue against my clenched and straining clit, my body flew from me in powerful heaving convulsions. He held me against his chest until my body was mine again.

"Now I have something to show you," he said, producing his pulsing, hard cock for examination.

"Thank you, but we've already been acquainted," I responded, turning away, feigning disinterest.

He took the opportunity of a back view to spread the cheeks of my ass wide open. He whispered into my twitching hole, "How would you like to get reacquainted?" A rhetorical question, of course.

As the introductions were being made, I climbed out of the tub, got on my hands and knees and wiggled an imaginary tail. He sat there, interested, but did not move. Tail snapping the tile wall, I stalked him, nuzzled his shoulder and then took a fleshy bite which I rapidly followed with long, slow licks. His breathing thickened as he grasped my thigh and made a long scratch up my leg with his fingernails and followed the trail with his tongue. Taking me by the waist, he got up on his knees and entered my ass. He reached around and with three fingers fucked me from the front. "Just how you like it," he cooed in my ear; he got an incoherent gurgle as a response. With his other hand he tweaked at my clit and I spread wider and wider, surrounded, full. The rhythm of our bodies swelled up in me like music; I fragmented into sharp pieces of piercing pleasure.

As I lay entangled in his arms and legs on the bathroom floor, I became aware of the cold tile pressing into me. "Follow me," I told the nape of his neck, as I struggled to my feet and slowly made my way to the bedroom. He headed for the living room, where I assumed he would scoot out the front door. Instead, he returned with the comforter I had left on the couch and ballooned it over me as I lay curled in bed. He looked at me tenderly, and held my face in his hands for a moment. Again he briskly left me for the living room. This time he returned with Barnacle under one arm, Tahiti under the other. He gently deposited them against my belly, where they immediately took up grooming each other.

The last thing I remember was the low rumble in Barnacle's throat as Tahiti dug her mouth deep into the pelt of fur at his neck, and the sound of my front door softly closing.

Linda Niemann

Blue Letter

Your denials will do you no good, and your hands will be useless in keeping me from unfolding your secrets one by one, at my pleasure, once I have you in this place. Time will stand still, the hours growing fat and sluggish, the light reddening and swelling outside the dirty windows facing the street.

You will meet me here, even though you can't yet imagine you will, because you want to be spread under my hands, splayed out on the sofa, the sun from the window hot on your cunt. Sweat will form in the hollows of your thighs and the ropes will pull tight as your body reaches for my tongue or the whip, whichever I choose to caress you with next.

I have bound your breasts with rope so that they resemble cocks or obscene balloons, the nipples swelling with blood. They love the whip that merely stings and leaves faint traces like a cat's claw. I suck on them to bring your cunt forward into my hand.

You are so easy; the merest brush with my nail on the hood of your clitoris and my hands would fill with your come, but I won't allow you this yet. Instead I whip you for giving in to me so fast.

I force your belly down so that your ass straddles my knee. I can feel the heat, like putting my hand into a hot oven, a slick glove on the edge of a burn. I want to see your ass redden under my belt, feel it pull away from the ropes holding you open. I have a dildo in your cunt which I can slowly engorge with air as you take the strokes of my whip. When I am satisfied that it has stretched you enough, I turn my attention to that other opening you are trying to protect from me.

For that I think I will find some strangers, the ones with their hands on their cocks and their ears glued to the walls of their rooms. All I have to do is invite them in. I hear their footsteps outside my door now.

There are two of them, one young and slight, a worker fresh from the fields. The other is heavy and unshaven. I give the young one the pleasure of your ass, but only while his is being used in the same fashion. I tell them not to be too quick with you, because your mouth will be mine. I want to taste each penetration there, under my tongue, in your gasping cries.

When they have gone you will be untied and held in my arms, your body washed and rubbed with almond oil. With my long blonde hair I will kneel and dry your feet, and if you wish it, tell you stories until the moon falls off the edge of the world.

Susan St. Aubin

Hope

When my husband and I got married we agreed to share our fantasies and our lovers.

"Did you ever think of making it with two people at once? A man and a woman? Or two other women?" he sometimes asks just before he enters me.

He wants me to join him in his favorite fantasy, but I have a better one of my own, a memory of a girl named Linda Hope I met just once when I was five and she was twelve.

One Saturday, I went with my father to a farm where he often bought produce.

"Nothing like eggs warm from the hen," he said, his hands tapping the steering wheel while I bounced on the gray plush seat beside him.

"And corn and tomatoes off the vine—you can't get anything like that in the store." He turned off the highway onto a long gravel driveway that went uphill to a gray house. A woman in blue jeans and a big girl wearing shorts and a T-shirt sat on the front porch railing, watching the chickens that scratched and pecked at the gravel

"That's Irene and her daughter," my father told me as we got out of the car.

Irene smiled and waved as we crunched our way across the driveway.

"Linda Hope," she said to the girl, "why don't you show Patty the barn?"

"Linda Hope," I whispered. I could almost taste the sound of it, round like a chocolate egg.

My father and Irene went inside the house. "Any tomatoes yet?" I heard him ask.

Linda Hope tossed her long braid of brown hair over one shoulder and trotted across a field of dry grass. At the barn, she turned and said, "My name's Lin. That's L-I-N, if you can spell yet. Do you like horses? They're all out in the pasture today. We could go see them if you want."

"I don't know," I answered. I was afraid because I'd never seen one up close before.

Lin shrugged. "Well, there's some kittens up in the loft, if you want to see them."

Inside the dim, mud-smelling barn, I followed Lin to a ladder. Her bottom hung out of her white shorts in half-moons an inch from my eyes as I climbed behind her. In the loft above us were bundles of hay. Our climb seemed to go on forever, with Linda Hope's skin nearly touching my face and the sweet smell of her filling my nose. The palms of my hands were sweaty and I was breathing heavily.

This is what I think of when I make love with my husband, climbing and climbing. Whenever he tells me about one of his lovers, or one of his fantasies, I see the barn and Linda Hope bending over in her too-tight shorts calling, "Kitty, Kitty, Kitty," while scuffling the loose hay with her hands. I don't want to share her.

I could meet someone else to share, but it's a question of opportunity; he's a professor, so it's part of his job to talk to lots of attractive young people anxious to please him. I'm an administrative assistant in the registrar's office, where I stay eight hours a day and never see anyone unless they have a problem I'm supposed to solve.

My husband's lovers don't appeal to me. He displays them at

dinner parties like potential desserts, but they're usually too tall, too small, too stupid, or too phony. His women are thin and remind me of tropical birds with their green and purple eye shadow. His men aren't much more inspiring. One of them (too short) talks incessantly about his thesis on the bisexual nature of twentieth-century British literature.

"Consider Bloomsbury," he says. (Too stupid! Too phony!)

I remember Linda Hope's long braid and long full legs, and think I might prefer a woman as a lover, if I could find the right one.

In my office I write his lovers' names on scraps of paper and rip them into tiny pieces. It's a magic charm that sometimes works.

The short man's bisexuality thesis is rejected by his adviser. Another lover, a girl with long red hair who once wrote a paper on the comedies of "Shakesphere," but was forgiven because of that hair, drives her car off the road and into a tree. She only breaks an ankle (fate, too, can be forgiving), but heeds the warning and moves to New York.

My husband decides that older women (by older he means those in their early thirties, still five years younger than he is) make the most stable lovers. I write their names on scraps of paper and they disappear one by one.

I can't complain. If I want, he meets his lovers only when I'm at work, or out of town, and he tells me I'm the only one he enters without a condom. We're together every night. Sometimes I wear silk teddies and garter belts; I have a whip I made of braided strips of silk, and long peacock feathers I use to caress his shoulders and the back of his neck. We're just ordinary people, though. I don't wear spike heels or boots with spurs or anything like that. I have a silk slip the color of ripe peaches, slit up one thigh. It's too good to wear all day, so I only put it on at night, for him.

"I could eat you in peach," he says, and does.

Then he begins leaving me alone in my peach silk to spend his evenings at the library—not the university library but the public library downtown. This happens at first once, then two or three times a week. For an article he's writing, he says, involving city documents. One of the librarians is particularly helpful.

"I'd like to have her over for dinner," he says, as he always does when he finds a new lover. "Her name is Hope. You'll like her."

My heart catches in my ribs as an image of Linda Hope in the barn comes back to me.

"Want to see something?" she asked. She sat beside me on a bale of hay and slowly pulled off her T-shirt. Right in front of my nose were two bumps of flesh the size and color of small peaches. They even had a sweet peach smell to them. I pulled back.

She laughed. "They're breasts," she said, pronouncing the word so that each letter sounded distinct. "Breasts like our mothers have, only smaller. You can touch them if you want."

Carefully, I reached out my fingers. Her breasts were hard, like not quite ripe fruit, and covered with a light, invisible down that tickled my fingertips. I took my hand away and sat on it. My eyes filled with tears.

She pulled her shirt back over her head and smiled at me. "You don't have anything like that yet, do you?"

I stood up and said, "Of course not. Who'd want them, any-way?" I climbed down the loft ladder, then ran across the barn into the sun.

For the first time I'm curious about one of my husband's lovers, so one day after work I take the bus to the library downtown to have a look.

At a long counter by the front door are two librarians—or per-haps they're clerks—neither of them his type. The man's blond hair looks bleached, and is cut in bangs over his forehead. The woman has frizzy hair and wears heavy black eyeliner in a style popular twenty years back, though she can't be more than twenty herself.

The woman sitting at the reference desk has long blond hair and looks like she's barely out of high school. An older woman ap-proaches her, a woman of perhaps fifty with shoulder-length white hair curled under in a way that seems natural. She's not short or tall, not fat or thin, but has the kind of build my father used to call healthy. Her face is tanned and her long gold earrings have some kind of purple stone inlay that glints through her hair. Her skirt is purple too, and her lavender sweater scoops low enough to reveal the tanned skin of her full breasts, where a gold medallion, one of those Mexican ornaments like a primitive sun with rays stabbing in all directions, hangs from a gold chain around her neck.

"Hope?" asks the blond woman at the desk, her voice rising with her question, and they murmur together.

The name is a coincidence. Linda Hope was just seven years older than I, which would make her forty-two now. Still, this Hope is one of the most attractive women I've ever seen, and I stand transfixed as she puts one arm around the woman's shoulder and bends over the desk, revealing more of her breasts. They study a stack of yellow cards, and both look up as I approach.

Hope's eyes, a clear, dark brown, seem to tunnel straight through me. Close up, I can see her hair is only white on top; underneath, it's black as a shadow. For the first time I salute my husband's taste.

When I ask her for a book on Mexican art, Hope leads me to the card catalogue. She smells like lemon. I can't take my eyes from her breasts.

"That's a lovely pendant," I say. "Pre-Columbian, right?"

"Yes," she answers in her soft voice, "but just a copy. I bought it in Mexico last summer."

We talk of travel. She's been all over Mexico and plans a long trip to Peru next year. She finds me three books, one with color plates, and walks me to the door, still talking of boats and flights and donkey guides to Machu Picchu. I'm sure she has no idea who I am.

When I come out the library door, I see my husband parking our car down the street. I step behind the bushes and watch him stroll into the library, his full briefcase knocking against his leg, then I go to the car, unlock it, and leave my books on the front seat.

Back in the library, the clerks behind the circulation desk talk to three teenage boys who seem to be arguing about a book one of them holds behind his back. The blond woman's head is still bent over her stack of yellow cards. The nameplate on the desk where she works says Hope Caputo, but Hope isn't anywhere in sight, and neither is my husband.

I walk past the reference desk to the bookshelves, and past the bookshelves to a door that leads to a corridor with books lining both walls. I'm not sure this area is open to the public, but there's no one to stop me. I walk until I reach another corridor, and walk down that one to another. Here books aren't just on shelves, but are piled on the floor as well. I hear a man's voice, answered by a low pitched woman's laugh. I turn another corner and flatten myself behind a stack of books. I see my husband's back and, over his shoulder, Hope's face, eyes open, looking to see where the sound of my footsteps is coming from. He lifts her sweater and reaches his hands inside to feel her breasts; she strokes and kisses his face. His hands reach lower, to her skirt, which he lifts to her waist. Her thighs are heavier than he usually prefers, and her garter belt is stark white against her tanned skin; my breath catches when I see that she doesn't wear underpants. His hand slides back and forth between her legs, while her hand massages the bulge beneath the left thigh of his gray tweed pants.

I squat behind the books, reach inside my underpants, and slide my own fingers back and forth. At last I'm making love with my husband and one of his lovers, but he has no idea.

She's breathing faster, saying, "Oh, for once I'm glad we're understaffed," until she falls against him and they stagger, like a two-headed creature, knocking over a pile of books.

Startled by the noise, I take my hand away and scrunch lower behind the books, trying to hold my breath. My heart seems to wobble in my chest.

Hope's sweater and skirt drop to their proper positions and she begins to pick up the books. The blond woman comes pattering down the hall from the other direction.

"What happened?" she asks. "We heard a crash."

"Nothing, Julie," Hope calls, singing her words in three tones. "I'm just looking for a book I thought was back here."

My husband stands to one side while they restack the books.

"There." Hope dusts her hands against her skirt. "I'm sorry I couldn't find it for you, but if you check with the university library, I'm sure they'll have it."

"Thank you for everything," he says, and follows Julie down the hall.

In a minute, Hope goes after them, and I follow her on tip-toe down a short corridor that leads straight to the reference desk.

"Julie," Hope says, "tomorrow I'd like you to . . ."

The phone rings. Julie picks it up, while Hope turns to the shelves behind the reference desk and begins rearranging books. At the circulation desk, the clerks attend to a line of twelve people, all carrying piles of books. Hope turns around when an elderly man approaches her desk.

My husband isn't there. When I leave the library, the car and my books are gone, so I take a bus home, where I discover my books on the dining room table.

"Were you at the library downtown?" he asks. His eyebrows come together the way they do when he's anxious.

"I had some shopping to do," I say. "That's why I put my books in your car when I saw it."

He doesn't ask me why I have no packages.

At work I write Hope's name on a Post-it note, but I don't tear it up. I write my husband's name on another Post-it note and lay them side by side, then stick them together. I write my name on a third note, stick it to the other two, and fold all three into my purse.

One Friday night my husband invites Hope to dinner. Though I've thought of her constantly, I haven't seen her in the month since I went to the library. She shakes my hand with no sign of recognition when my husband introduces us.

"I'm glad to meet you, Pat," she says. She wears gray slacks and a gray cotton knit turtleneck, tight around her breasts. Her lips and cheeks are rouged deep pink, and her silver hair glistens in the candlelight. Behind her hair I glimpse the shine of her silver earrings.

At dinner, she drinks rosé from a glass that looks as silvery as her hair, and tells us she's had a lucky month: she found an antique rocking chair at a garage sale for twenty dollars; a lump she had removed from her breast turned out to be benign; and the city decided to allow a new librarian to be hired to replace one who'd left two years ago. I'm glad my power seems as great for the names I don't tear up as it does for those I do.

My husband looks at me with raised eyebrows. I smile and massage his foot under the table—at least I think it's his foot, though suddenly I'm unsure. I imagine corridors and stacks of books, and feel a warm glow that seems to travel upwards from the base of my spine to the top of my head.

I clear the table while Hope and my husband sit in the living room. I have simultaneous urges to join them, and to walk out the back door. I'm in the loft again, aroused and frightened all at once.

I'm wearing a black lace bra that shows the pink skin of my breasts. I could take off my blouse and join them, bringing coffee on a tray. My husband has never seen this bra, which I know he'll love. I look into the living room, where he's lit a fire.

Because I don't have the courage of my fantasies, I bring in the coffee with my rose silk blouse buttoned all the way up the neck.

"It's warm in here," says Hope, plucking at her shirt.

"Take it off," says my husband, raising his eyebrows at me again. "That's why I made this fire."

She looks at me. I sit beside them and pour coffee; I feel my cheeks flush as I unbutton the top button of my blouse.

My husband reaches over and unbuttons the rest of the blouse while Hope watches, catching her breath.

I let the blouse slither off.

"Oh," says Hope.

He touches my breast through its tracery of lace. Hope's cheeks and lips are a much darker pink than they were earlier; she watches my husband's hand on my breast. Then, in a sudden motion, she lifts her arms and pulls her turtleneck over her head, shaking out her hair, and flings the shirt onto the coffee table beside the tray holding our cups.

She's wearing the very same bra I have on, though her breasts are fuller and her skin darker. We look at each other and laugh.

My husband touches Hope's breast with his free hand and asks, "What's the joke?"

"It's not done," says Hope, "for two women to wear the same outfit to an affair."

We both laugh harder.

"One of us will have to volunteer to change." Hope fiddles with the clasp between her breasts and unfastens the black lace, which pulls apart, loosening her full breasts. I'm surprised by how little they need the support of a brassiere. There's a small red scar near her left nipple, which must be where she had the lump removed. She shrugs the black lace off her shoulders and throws it on top of her sweater.

I haven't looked so closely at another woman's breasts since I touched Linda Hope's hard peaches in the loft of the barn. I never saw her again after that day when I ran all the way to the horse pasture beyond the barn, where she caught up with me, her young breasts hidden behind her T-shirt. She told me the names of all the horses, then leaped onto the bare back of one of them and rode in widening circles, gradually moving farther away from me.

Now I reach out my fingers to Hope's soft fullness, feeling the same tingle in my fingertips that I remember from long ago. I move my hands slowly to her nipples, dark as miniature figs, and jump when I touch my husband's fingers. For a second I'd forgotten him.

Her hands reach for my breasts, unclasping the brassiere that holds them, and together we touch and look. I gently trace the red scar.

"They tell me it'll fade to nothing in a year," she says. "Careful. It's still a bit tender."

"Hey," says my husband, who doesn't want to be forgotten now that he's finally got his wife and a lover together. He strips off his jeans and shirt and stands before us, his penis erect at the level of our eyes as we sit on the couch fondling each other. With a united sigh we turn to him. Businesslike, Hope takes his cock in her mouth, neatly as she stacked the fallen books in the library, while I stand to kiss his mouth and stroke his ass.

What do three people do at the crucial moment; crucial, that is, for a man?

"I wish I had two penises," he pants.

Hope pulls her mouth away. "Sorry," she mocks. "No time to grow another one now."

We look at each other and manage not to laugh. I push him toward her like a gift. I see myself crouched behind that stack of books in the library, and remember how much I liked watching them.

Hope pulls him to the floor in front of the fire. He slides her out of her slacks, then lies on his back while she massages a condom onto his cock. She sits astride him while I hide behind a chair, pretending they don't know I'm there, until she falls forward and they're both still. Then I take my jeans off, too, and stretch out on the floor near them, feeling the warmth of the fire on my back.

His breathing is deep and regular with an occasional snore.

Hope smiles. "He's probably the only man in the world to fall asleep on *two* women," she says as she moves closer to me, then whispers, "You know, I saw you that night in the stacks," and kisses me on the lips. "I guessed who you were," she says, kissing my cheeks and my chin.

She kisses my forehead and the line where my hair begins and says, "I knew you were his wife the minute you walked into the library because he described you so perfectly, down to the last detail—the way you walk, the way you twist your hair around one finger when you get nervous. I could see you were nervous because you suspected who I was."

My husband moans in his sleep and mutters something like "move" or "more" as he rolls closer to Hope, who lies beside me, stroking my shoulders and kissing my breasts.

"I've wanted to meet you ever since I first heard about you," she says, "and knowing you were there that night, watching us, oh!"

Her kisses move down my stomach and across my light brown fur to my clit, which she licks and sucks until I glow and flash all over. We lie in each other's arms stroking and kissing and watching the fire while my husband's snores become slow and steady as rain.

I close my eyes to the feather strokes of her fingertips across my shoulders, and wake to rain tapping on the light gray of the windows. My husband still snores beside me. By the window, Hope pulls her gray sweater over her head and shakes her hair, running her fingers through it. The fire is out and the room is cold. I wrap an afghan around myself and throw a rug over my husband, who groans and rolls over on his side, pulling the cover around him.

"Ssssh," Hope whispers. "Don't wake him. I've got to go, it's nearly six and I've got to be at work by nine. It's my turn for Saturday."

At the door she puts her hands on my shoulders and kisses me, her tongue lingering in my mouth to caress the insides of my cheeks and lips.

"I'd like to see you again," she whispers.

"Both of us?"

She shakes her head. "You."

"What'll I tell him?"

She shrugs. "That you're working late. Let's make it Thursday. I'm off at five-thirty that night."

On Thursday I wait for her in Mario's Trattoria with a glass of red wine sitting before me on the black and white checked formica table. It's a new place with walls of glass and an open kitchen, where the cooks and waiters shout at each other in what sounds like Italian, though I entertain myself by thinking it could be Romanian or Bengali. This is not the setting for an intimate dinner, but Hope has told me the food is wonderful.

The library isn't far away, and at a quarter to six she strolls in, a large bag of books and papers hanging from her shoulder. Today she's in brown—brown and white striped shirt and brown wool skirt and sweater, with copper coins hanging from her ears.

We kiss quickly, like the old friends we're not, before she sits down and waves to the waiter, a thin, dark, balding man in a red apron, who brings her a glass of red wine and a menu for each of us. While the kitchen staff chatters, Hope smiles and says, "My family all spoke Italian when I was growing up. I was the youngest child, so I never learned to speak it properly myself, though I understand it. Half my sisters were born in Italy, and half here.

That's nine of us, all girls. I'm used to a lot of noise. I find it very restful, which must be why I love this place."

She recommends the tortellini, the eggplant parmesan, the baked lasagna. My head already spins from the wine. The steam rises from the kitchen, blurring the darkening windows. We decide on pasta pescatore, with shrimp and calamari and chunks of unidentifiable, salty fish in a sauce of garlic and tomatoes. Her foot feels for mine under the table; she has her shoe off and slides mine off too, and our nylon clad toes slip over each other. Coins clink into a juke box and Italian opera swallows the kitchen noise. We have more wine and, for dessert, a dense vanilla ice cream with small, light cookies that taste like they're made of ground hazelnuts.

"Biscotti," she says, crunching into one.

She tells me about her ex-husband, who also spoke Italian and was an accountant. She tells me about their son, now an artist living in New York. We don't mention my husband.

People leave the restaurant—it's eight o'clock, then eight-thirty, and I realize we're stalling. The kitchen is quiet and the glass walls are black. I feel like I did in the hayloft with Linda Hope: I can stay, or I can run. This time I stay. We have coffee and more biscotti. I tear the cover off a book of matches and tear half of it into tiny pieces, which I leave in the ashtray. When she asks, "Would you like to go back to my house?" I nod.

Only then does the waiter bring our check, which she pays.

"My treat," she says. "I invited you and we're only here because I'm too lazy to cook."

She excuses herself to go to the bathroom. The waiter returns the tray with her change and a receipt. I take out a pen and write my husband's name on the remaining half of the matchbook cover, then shred it, showering the pieces into the ashtray.

Hope comes back and picks up her receipt, leaving the change. We smile at our waiter as we walk to the door.

"*Buona notte,*" he murmurs, and we go through the double glass doors into the night.

Calla Conova

∽

Just the Garden and I

The white-noise whir of an electric fan covers the rattling of the neighbor's dishes. Cool from the shower, wearing a cotton kimono, I wind my way through the dark house and unbolt the door. My garden yawns a cricket song. Desert-dry air sweeps across my bare feet, billows up the undulating space between legs and foreign fabric. I cross the threshold and the garden unfolds like a secret lover. Kimono ties loosen as a cat rouses to prowl elsewhere.

Now I can begin to dance in rhythm with the murmur of patient moon-washed leaves. I am a cobra, cajoling my light garment to shed and slide its comfortable personality to the surprised lawn. The monotonous fan hums inside the house—it murmurs with the TV and says, "Cover up, come back in, don't leave me alone."

But I am free now, the floozy entertainer for a million rapt grass blades, who gaze up between my swaying legs. They transmit encouragement via alpha waves, sensitizing every inch of my pioneering body. I offer a dandelion a better view; my conspiring fingers unveil my night-blooming bud.

Bend, squat, lift leg—a dog in heat couldn't do better. Fingers, spit-wet, range to various erogenous zones, re-wet and stroke for the sake of the camellia bushes who spent themselves several moons ago in their own wild display. "Look! This is how it's done in July," I say.

Above, filtering the stars, the jacaranda tree with its swollen purple clusters notices my warm night openings. Unabashed pink four o'clocks drop a shiny seed or two in applause for my quivering thigh. I rival the perfumes of the night garden. The jasmine and I understand the satori of creating musk.

My song rises, breathy, sweet and raw. I press against the smooth sycamore tree. The back of my neck surrenders to its possessive love bite. The garden knows me. Knows how much is enough. Knows when to leave an ebbing echo in my ears. We swap sex stories. We laugh at age-old pollination jokes. I have shown this leafy audience the most private and shocking parts of me. They reply that they have always done so for me—and in broad daylight to boot!

I apologize for thinking that I was the first to make love alone, under the stars. But that doesn't diminish my sorority with the flowers. Lusty communion complete, I take back the kimono, forget to say thank you, and return, like an errant puppy, to the comfortable hum of the TV and fan.

Aurora Lighi

❧

Something Special

Jean called me on a Thursday night. "Will you please be an angel and come take care of Missy until Saturday? She won't eat if I put her in a kennel. I have to fly up to Seattle and get the Brent contracts signed." She had barely paused for breath.

We're identical twins, but she's a big-city businesswoman while I'm a desert-dwelling artist. Before she can go on I say, "Okay. Okay. Don't panic. I'll catch the seven a.m. flight out of Phoenix and I'll be there before noon." *There* being her tiny gem of a house on Russian Hill in San Francisco. "When's your flight?"

"Six-thirty. I'll leave the key in the usual place. I should be home Saturday afternoon. And I promise you something special to say thanks. I feel like my brain has turned to scrambled eggs. I hate these last-minute deals."

"Stop worrying. Calm down. Good luck. I'll see you Saturday. Bye."

The sky is a cloudless blue and the air soft as silk the next morning as I get out of the cab in front of Jean's house. The key is in a pot of geraniums on the small porch. As soon as I open the door, Jean's poodle, Missy, greets me with frenzied joy. Hunger sends me into the kitchen. While I eat I keep up a one-sided conversation with Missy. We spend the afternoon lazing in the back yard, and take a long, brisk walk before dinner. After eating we retire to the living room to watch television. By ten I am ready for a shower and bed; I let Missy out once more. When she comes back in, she curls up in her basket and promptly falls asleep.

As I am about to undress in Jean's bedroom, I notice a snapshot tucked in the corner of her dresser mirror. It is a middle-aged man with silvery hair and a nice smile. It must be Nathan; Jean has written me about him.

They are not yet lovers, and probably never will be. She'd said he was fifty-three, a widower and an engineer who apparently grew up on a cattle ranch in northeastern Wyoming. His father died recently and left him the ranch. Nathan was in San Francisco visiting his married daughter when he met Jean. They both happened to be at an exhibition of nineteenth-century western painters. That was less than a month ago, and I recall that Jean said Nathan was going back to Wyoming very soon. She couldn't understand why he wanted to give up a successful career in Casper and go back to being a cowboy. Loving the outdoors as much as I do, I understand completely.

Jean keeps her relationships lighthearted and brief. I've told her she's like a butterfly flitting from man to man, sampling their nectar then moving on. I imagine she is feeling mild regret that she has not sampled Nathan, but in a week or a month she'll have someone new.

Jean and I tend to like the same type of man—strong but gentle, intelligent, with a keen sense of humor and a very healthy appetite for sex. We have both been married and divorced. I am between relationships, and my hormones are raging.

I kick off my shoes, and slip out of my slacks, silk blouse and bra. Even at forty-four my breasts are still firm and full. I push my panties down, exposing the soft nest of my pubic hair. After hanging my slacks and shirt in the closet I go into the bathroom, turn on the shower and step in. No need for a shower cap, as I keep my honey-hued tresses cut short and softly curled. Jean wears hers shoulder length.

With eyes closed, I turn my face up to the gentle spray, feeling all the fatigue of the day drain away. When I open my eyes I almost have a heart attack. On the other side of the clear glass shower door is a man, wearing nothing but a big smile. Just as I draw breath to scream, I realize the man is Nathan. I had no idea he and Jean were on shower-sharing terms.

He opens the shower door and steps in. "I'm leaving tomorrow instead of next week, and I couldn't resist giving you one last chance to have your wicked way with me."

"How did you get in?" I gasp.

"I went 'round to the back when you didn't answer the bell. The window was open and here I am."

"Yes, here you are," I gulp, realizing there is an absurd humor in the situation.

"You've cut your hair! I like it." Our different hair styles are the only way most people can tell us apart. Is it possible that Jean hadn't told him she has a twin? A dozen other questions flash through my mind, but before I can voice them or simply say, "I'm not Jean, I'm Joan," he draws me into his strong arms and kisses me. My hands come up to push him away, then, as his insistent tongue slips between my suddenly yielding lips, my arms wind around his neck and I lose myself in the moment.

His hungry lips slide down my throat and close over one nipple, sucking it into a hard pink bud. My hand eagerly seeks and finds his erection. I am delighted to find him generously endowed. I gasp when his fingers deftly make their way between my pliant thighs and expertly tease my tingling clitoris. "Oh, God, that feels so good," I sigh.

"I can't wait to eat your hot pussy, then I'm going to fuck it," he murmurs huskily. It sounds good to me. Wrapped in towels, we move into the bedroom. I sit on the end of the bed, my legs slightly parted. He drops to his knees on the rug and kisses the inside of my thighs until I let myself fall backward onto the bed. Then he buries his head between my legs and pleasures me with his tongue. When I come he keeps licking and sucking until I come again and again, feeling as if I'm melting. Only then does he lie beside me.

"I love what you just did," I manage to gasp. He kisses me and I taste myself on his lips.

"I loved doing it," he says, his blue eyes glowing. "I'm really glad I came here tonight; I hope you are too. You might have kicked me out. I like a woman with a sense of adventure." I keep silent, afraid of giving myself away. And in any case, it's a time for action, not words. Impulsively, I roll over and straddle his thighs, all eagerness and heat as I lower myself onto his enticing, rigid cock. His warm hands clasp my waist to support me as his pulsing erection penetrates my moist, receptive pussy. Smiling down at him I sit on his rod, rocking gently.

His eyes glaze with passion as I clamp my cunt muscles tight around his shaft. Voluptuously I rise and fall, savoring the delicious sensations that bring soft sighs from my parted lips at each descent. I come with a convulsive shudder. He rolls me over and rests quietly inside me. When my breathing finally slows he begins to thrust, slowly, deeply, his cock submerged in the liquid core of my lust. Nathan gradually accelerates his movements until I'm on the edge again. Sensing it, Nathan pauses, tantalizing me by lightly licking my lips. My hands roam over his muscular shoulders and arms, coming to rest on his tight buttocks. My entire body begins to tremble as he moves resolutely within me. I feel the muscles in his ass tighten with each forceful stroke. Almost without warning, a blinding, breathtaking climax shoots through me. I hear my strangled cry as if from far, far away. Only then does he allow himself to come, his passion-contorted face glistening with sweat. Clasped in the circle of his arm, my cheek pressed against his chest, I listen to the muted drumming of his heart until sleep overtakes us.

It is past two when I wake. Nathan is sprawled in sleep, utterly relaxed. His face, below the mop of silvery hair, shows strength, in the strong jaw, and sensitivity, in the full sensual curve of his lips. His hands are shapely, with blunt cut nails. Stealthily I pull down the sheet. At the bottom of his taut belly his pale penis lies soft and small in a thatch of dark hair.

Just looking at him rekindles my passion. I take his penis entirely into my mouth, swirling my tongue around the velvety tip, sucking gently, thrilling as I feel it wake, thicken, grow long and stiff. His hands rest on my hair, and his gasps of pleasure make me want to fuck him again. Before he can come, I sit up.

"You can wake me up like that anytime," he laughs.

"Come down to the carpet with me," I order, getting off the bed. He raises an eyebrow but obeys. I get on all fours and tilt my ass up. "I want you to do it to me this way, cowboy." Just imagining him fucking me like that makes me wild and wet. When he puts his hands on my hips, I shiver.

He kisses and nibbles his way down my back to my ass. Then he presses against me and rubs his hard cock back and forth over my clit. I squirm and jerk, almost ready to come again.

When he mounts me, his hard cock slips easily into my creamed cunt. I see our reflection in the mirrored closet doors; the sight is wonderfully lascivious. Nathan's hands move to hold me by the shoulders as he humps into me. His penis, slippery with my juices, enters deep and slow, then pulls almost all the way out. Hearing our gasping moans makes me even hotter. Nathan's eyes meet and hold mine in the mirror. The cords in his strong neck stand out, his breathing sounds ragged. My cunt makes deliciously obscene sounds with each stroke of his cock. His body arches sharply over mine and his tempo quickens to short, hard thrusts. His sweat drips onto my back and ass. I see the room through a red haze; my heart pounds furiously, my muscles quiver, straining to hold me up. Weakly I let my head droop, oblivious to everything but the pleasure of my rapidly approaching orgasm. I have no sense of time; minutes or hours might have passed, but only our bodies matter.

At the very moment of our coming, split seconds apart, I can't tell where my body ends and Nathan's begins. Still connected, we collapse sideways onto the soft carpet, totally exhausted, breathless, drenched with sweat, his cock and my cunt slick with cum, and, at last, sated.

Eventually we find the strength to crawl into bed. We sleep, limbs languidly entwined. When I wake Nathan is gone. On the bedside table is a note scrawled in a masculine hand:

"Darling, You were incredible! Please come to Wyoming. I can promise you lots of good 'riding.' Yours, Nathan."

On Jean's return I tell her about Nathan's unexpected visit, my face blushing crimson. "He was just so adorable, and I was so hungry for sex I couldn't resist." I look at her anxiously. "You have every right to be mad as hell."

She smiles. "Don't be silly. Even though I didn't have Nathan in mind, indirectly I did give you something special."

Martha Miller

∽

Best Friends

I've known the day of Richard Nixon's birthday as long as I've known anything. Erin McCormick told me. She said Joan Baez and Richard Nixon were both born on January 9th. "How could anyone know that," she asked, "and still believe in astrology?"

We were fifteen years old and she was peeling onions for potato salad. I was spooning yellow stuff onto slick cooked whites of eggs. We were getting ready for the school band trip. Erin played the French horn. I was percussion.

"If you can't believe in astrology," she said, scratching an old mosquito bite on the back of her leg, "what's left? Events spin out of control, no plan or reason."

I stood there, crunched on a sweet pickle and thought for a minute. It had been a rough year for me. The rest of the girls were preoccupied with boys. Pressure to fit in was tremendous. I was afraid that I wasn't like anyone else on earth.

"What about God?" I started to say, then remembered a rainy day discussion on Nietzsche weeks before. Was everything in the universe random, then? Was there really no plan? Erin's back was to me. The cold water was running in the sink. She was waiting for an answer. I shrugged and said, "No control sounds exciting to me."

She turned and faced me. "Does it?" she said. Her green eyes were glazed from the onions, a spray of moist freckles glistened on her nose and cheeks.

Later I remembered that day. I see her standing in my mother's kitchen, her eyes watery, commenting on irony and the universe. I remember the way she sniffed and wiped her eyes on her madras shirt tail as I told her my theory that life was like a slot machine—you got what you got, and the only way to keep it from spinning was to not put your quarter in. I remember how beautiful she looked. The other girls were obsessed with boys. I was obsessed with Erin. I wanted her more than anything in the world. I told her all I knew about life. Tried to impress her. I was fifteen and I knew everything.

I broke my ankle doing a stupid stunt on my bicycle that evening after we made the food. I never got to go on the band trip. Later I heard the potato salad was thrown out. Hardly anyone in the band liked onions.

Then on the late-night trip home, in the bright yellow school bus, Erin was somehow impregnated by Vernon Pratt.

Vernon, sometimes a substitute triangle player, though usually on the pom-pom squad, didn't merit band trips, but was playing the bass drum in my absence.

Talk about ironies. Talk about the spinning wheels of fate. Okay, okay. It wasn't the first time they'd "done it." But Erin had said she'd quit.

For years, every time I heard Joan Baez I felt a twinge. Sometime later when Richard Nixon was in all the papers, I thought about Erin over my morning coffee and chocolate doughnut. Still wanting her, I couldn't figure how Vernon and the kids fit in.

Erin and I had grown up together. We had been best girlfriends since fourth grade when her father, who owned a fourteen-lane bowling alley, had let Erin have slumber parties there. A group of five or six girls would spend the night, then have milk shakes and hamburgers for breakfast. I learned to play a mean game of pool there when I was ten years old, a skill that served me in later years. When Erin's father had his first heart attack, she and Vernon took over the management of the bowling alley. The place became the young couple's life. They had three babies by the time I finished four years of college. Vernon's hairline had started to recede and his former flat stomach hung over his belt buckle. Erin had perpetual dark circles under her green eyes.

I had my coffee and doughnuts in the bowling alley on Saturday mornings one summer. I was getting ready to start grad school. Erin worked the early shift on weekends because of Vernon's part-time job at a filling station. When business was slow, she'd draw a cup of coffee, light a filtered cigarette and slide into the booth across from me. One morning in July she finally said it.

"I hear you like girls."

I looked at her over the rim of my coffee cup. I thought she'd known. I guess I figured everyone did. I sat the cup down slowly and nodded.

"Is there someone special?" she asked.

"Not right now," I answered. "In my junior year there was someone for a while. A pre-law student." I shrugged. "It didn't work out."

We were quiet for some time. Sun filtered through the Venetian blinds. Cigarette smoke swirled around her red hair like a halo. Striped shadows fell across her ruffled uniform, and her freckled face. She stubbed out a cigarette. "Were you always like that?" she asked.

"I suppose."

"Did you ever think about me?" It was almost a whisper.

Our eyes met. I nodded.

She fidgeted with her lighter.

I waited.

"Do you still?" she said at last.

I sighed, "Sometimes."

"Vernon and I do three-ways," she said quickly. "I really like the part with women."

The last bite of my doughnut slipped from my fingers and splashed into my lukewarm coffee. I watched it float then sink into the murky blackness. I looked at her again. My eyes were round. "You do three-ways," I said at last. It wasn't really a question.

She nodded. "Would you like to join us?"

"You and Vernon?"

"Sure."

It was too much. I mumbled "No thanks" and got the hell out of there.

I would like to say I never thought about it again.

I actually thought about it a lot. I wanted her. But every time the fantasy got to the part where Vernon unbuckled his belt, I stopped. Erin sent me a Christmas card at school that year with a chatty letter and a picture of the kids. In February, at my mother's funeral, she sat next to me and held my hand. Vernon sat in the back with a baby on each knee. When everyone went away and I was left to wander through the empty rooms of my mother's home, Erin tapped at the front door.

I looked at her standing in the yellow porch light, gentle snow flakes falling behind her, a bottle of rum clutched in a fuzzy red knitted mitten.

"I think we really need to get drunk," she said.

I opened the door wider and let her pass into the dim over-heated living room.

"Have you had supper?" she asked, throwing her coat across my mother's rocker.

"Ham," I said. "Everyone brought ham. I've been serving and eating it for days. I'm sick of the stuff." I was looking at her coat across the chair. "I'll probably never eat ham again."

"Here," she said from behind me.

I turned.

She was holding a glass up.

"Drink this. It'll make you feel better."

I took it obediently. "Doesn't Vern have to work tonight? Where are the kids?"

"I got a sitter."

"Just to come over here?" I picked up her coat and headed for the closet.

"How about we order a pizza?" she followed me. "Or I could cook a pot of chili?"

We ordered a large pizza with everything and got roaring drunk. Sometime around midnight, we ritualistically dumped twenty pounds of ham over the back fence to the neighbor's grateful dog. We rested our arms on the chest-high cyclone mesh that separated the back lots and watched the huge mutt eat.

The night was cold and clear. Patches of snow dotted the lawn. I could see her frosty breath. Erin touched my arm, her red mitten looked bright and warm against my navy pea coat. For the first time in days, I started to cry.

She pulled me into her arms and held me. I saw the nearly full moon over her shoulder. My tears caused the moonlight to waver and glow. There were just the sounds of the dog munching and growling and my icy sobs in the night air.

I woke late the next morning to the smells of bacon and coffee. My stomach lurched. I moved my head and felt a tremendous pain. I opened my eyes. Erin stood framed in my bedroom doorway. Her yellow sweater was rumpled. Her faded jeans were muddy around the belled bottoms. She held two glasses of tomato juice.

"You have a choice," she said. "Bacon and eggs or cold pizza."

I moaned and pulled the covers over my head.

I felt her sit on the edge of the bed and tug at the blanket. "Come on. If I can move this morning, so can you."

I lowered the blanket, "I'm going to puke."

"Drink this. It'll help." She stuck the tomato juice under my nose.

I pushed it away. "As I recall, those are the words that started this. Did we really feed the neighbor's dog twenty pounds of ham last night?"

She nodded. "He probably doesn't feel much better than we do this morning."

I sipped the tomato juice. "Coffee," I said. "I need coffee."

To this day I have trouble believing that I downed a half pound of bacon and four fried eggs swimming in grease that morning. I have more trouble believing that Erin asked me about sex again. And I turned her down again. But it happened.

"If you're not interested in a three-way," she had said refilling my coffee cup as we lingered at the kitchen table, "then what about just me?"

I looked at her. Her complexion was strikingly pale, due to the hangover. She'd pulled her hair back and held it with a green rubberband at her neck. Her eyes were puffy. And I wanted her. "I'm in a relationship," I said. "It's a committed relationship. I've promised not to sleep with others." I hesitated a second then added, "You're married. But if we're ever single at the same time, you've got a date."

She nodded, set the coffee pot down and said, "Okay."

Of course I was single a month later. I discovered that Letha slept with everyone while I kept my promise. The morning I was saying no to Erin, Letha was waking up under the flannel sheets of the woman who would be her next lover.

After the last fight with Letha, I called Erin in tears. It was Easter Sunday. I hadn't gone home because I didn't want to deal with the empty house or my extended family, who felt obligated to include me. It occurred to me much later that things came to a head because Letha had planned on my departure over the spring break. By staying at school I had messed up my lover's love life. We had a fight that started at breakfast and ended with Letha throwing her underwear and vibrator in a paper sack and slamming the trailer door so hard that she bent the lock.

I could hear Erin's children laughing in the background. I had my period and a bad case of cramps. I guess I'd taken too much Mydol because I couldn't stop crying and I knew that if I slept with Erin the pain would go away. Cramps and all.

"You don't sound good," Erin said. "Are you all right?"

"Letha and I broke up," I sniffed. "She's been fucking everybody."

"I'm sorry." Erin's voice softened. "I know infidelity is bad for a romance."

"What?" I blew my nose. Had I heard right?

"Well, Vernon and I have decided that monogamy is the best way."

I was sure she knew why I'd called. That this was the answer. "You're not doing three-ways anymore?"

"We only did a couple," she said. "Vern couldn't deal with it, even though it was his idea. He would mope around for days. Then he found out I saw someone else on my own and he suggested, after a two-day drinking and crying jag, that we close our open relationship. We both agreed to settle down. I think it's the best way. Don't you?"

"Yeah," I stammered. "Sure." I thought it was shit right at that moment. I heard one of the kids squeal in the background. Then Vernon's voice.

"Why don't you drive up for dinner?" Erin asked. "It will be just us. You'll feel better being with friends."

"It's two hours," I said. "Besides, I have plans." I was going to the bar. Shoot some pool. Find a woman.

"You sure?"

"Yeah. Thanks anyway."

"Look," she said firmly, "you're someone real special. You just haven't found the right one yet. You deserve the best there is."

"Sure. Right."

Then she said, "I love you."

"Huh?"

"You're the best friend a girl ever had," she said quickly. "And I love you."

"Erin . . ."

"Why don't you come to dinner?"

"No. I really can't."

When I hung up I stared out the window for a long time. Letha and I had shared a tiny trailer. I'd have to move or find another roommate. I couldn't afford the place alone.

I played *Diamonds and Rust* on the stereo all afternoon. I sat in my bathrobe and stared out the window. For Easter dinner I ate a one-pound solid milk chocolate chicken and several marsh-mallow eggs. I regretted not going to Erin's. I wondered if they were having ham.

I left school early that spring. I was so far behind in everything it was a nightmare. I couldn't live in my mother's home alone and, though I regretted it later, I sold the place and bought a condo. I got a counseling job at a battered women's shelter. The pay was low, but I found the work rewarding. The women's prob-lems made my pissy depression seem inane. If they could laugh and go on, I could too. No one cared that I was a philosophy ma-jor who had dropped out when real life got too hard. Once I was clowning around and mentioned Nietzsche in a staff meeting. The night shift counselor said, "Fuck him! He hated women too. He was just more eloquent about it than the bastards we have to deal with here."

I babysat for Erin's kids and helped her celebrate when Vernon was finally made manager of the filling station where he'd worked part time for years.

I met Elsbeth, a round, earth-mother type, who ran a print shop. Her fondness for tribadism and dildos enthralled me. We dated. She moved in. We gradually settled into a routine. There were always plants and sleeping cats in our windows, pans left from the night before soaking in the kitchen sink and smells of patchouli and baking bread in the air. It was a good life.

I was stunned when Vernon died suddenly. Everyone was. Oh, he was a prime candidate for a heart attack—a chain smoker, a heavy drinker and overweight. For the last several years he'd worked ten hours a day, six days a week at that filling station and helped Erin out at the bowling alley on weekends. One Sunday morning he simply slept in. It was the most graceful thing he'd done in his life.

I held Erin's hand during the funeral. Her children, three young adults, sat on either side of us. We all wept together. I have to say that even I was pretty broken up. I looked from the casket to Erin's profile. Not too bad for a substitute triangle player, I thought. He'd spent his life loving the most beautiful woman I knew. In a way, we both had.

A few days later I took a fifth of rum over to Erin's double-wide trailer. The kids were with their grandfather getting through the weekend at the bowling alley.

I poured her a strong drink and slid it across the kitchen table. "We need to get really drunk," I told her.

I watched her swallow the searing liquid. Her green eyes glazed with tears. I remembered when we were children—the band trip, the onions. I laid my hand across hers. "It'll be all right. You're going to be fine."

She sniffed. "My life is over. I'm forty years old. I haven't even finished high school!"

"Erin, don't . . ."

"I can't help it." Her shoulders shook with sobs. "I don't know how to be alone. I'm not a young girl anymore. I'm thirty pounds overweight, my hair is going gray and I'm scared."

"Erin, listen to me," I said. "You're someone real special. You deserve the best there is. You're going to be fine."

"Sure," she sniffed. "Right."

Then I said, "I love you."

She looked at me. A stream of clear snot trickled down her upper lip. "Would you hold me?" she said. "Would you make love to me?"

My head was spinning. What about Elsbeth? What about all the reasons I shouldn't do it that had nothing to do with my lover of ten years?

I pulled her close and hugged her. "Erin, I can't."

"I understand," she said into my shoulder.

I squeezed her hard and kissed her moist neck. There was a faint taste of salt from her tears. I felt swept along like a leaf on a swift current. I kissed her lips. They were soft. Warm. My hands trembled as I unbuttoned her sweater. It fell off her shoulders exposing a lacy bra. A faint spray of freckles marked the way from her neck to the valley between her round breasts. I unhooked the bra and pulled it off. She leaned against the corner of the horseshoe formica counter as I kissed and touched every inch of her exposed skin.

She pulled my shirt tail out of my jeans. Both of her thumbs worked at the buttons on my 501s. Then she pushed my jeans down over my hips and they fell around my ankles. I chuckled. "Right here in the kitchen?"

"Not in my bed," she shook her head slowly. "Please."

I stepped out of my jeans and took her hand. "How about the couch?"

She followed me obediently into the living room. Leaving her own Levi cords in a heap by the coffee table, she stretched out on the couch and raised her arms over her head.

I knelt beside her and ran my hands over her soft body. I kissed her nipples and stroked the fine moist hairs on her mound.

She opened her legs, like we'd done this a hundred times. The room was quiet. I could hear her breathing. Shallow. Quick. I could hear the first heavy drops of rain on the trailer roof. Flecks of ice gently striking the aluminum window frame. I stretched out on top of her and moved in a gentle fucking motion. From my own warm center I felt the most wonderful throbbing pain.

She rested one leg over my back and braced the other on the floor. I moved down her belly and ate her slowly, lingering over the most exquisite meal. She responded to my tongue, gently rocking and whispering, "Do it. Oh, do it."

She raised her head after a while and asked, "Is it taking too long?"

I stopped. I stroked her glistening vulva and pushed against the pink silken folds. She moaned as the warm flesh gave way and three fingers slid snugly inside her.

"I could do this forever," I said and returned to my dining.

When she came she cried out my name over and over.

I held her, rocking her like a baby, planting small kisses on her face.

At last she said, "Show me what to do for you."

"Erin, you don't have to do anything more," I said. "I'm very pleased as it is."

"Come on," she coaxed. "If we're going to do this, let's do it right."

I was aroused. "Put your leg like this." I straddled it and rubbed myself against her. My pubic bone pressed firmly against her thigh. I felt a feverish friction.

"Does that feel good?" she asked.

"Oh, yes. Yes."

She kissed my face. I felt the tension build inside me, then burst with tingling waves that seemed to electrify even my fingertips. We lay naked, pressed together.

At last she smiled, "This is better than getting drunk."

"It will feel better in the morning too."

She sighed. "Will it?"

"Hey," I said as love for her washed over me. "Nothing has changed here. We're still best friends. Right?"

She nodded in agreement, but I was worried by the time my heart rate slowed to normal. I've heard that once you cross a line you can never go back. Was I being naive thinking that things hadn't changed? What I knew was that I knew a hell of a lot less than I did when I was fifteen.

"Remember when we were kids?" I said tentatively. "And you told me about Joan Baez and Richard Nixon?"

"We've just made love and you're talking about Richard Nixon?" she frowned. "Boy, lesbian sex is sure different than I thought it would be."

It had grown dark. The furniture cast long, soft shadows. The sound of rain was slow and steady. The room was suddenly cold. I pulled an afghan from the back of the couch over us and moved to a sitting position. It occurred to me that what I did and said in the next few minutes could alter my life forever. Events spinning out of control no longer held an allure. I didn't want to make a mistake.

I pulled Erin close and told her. "If someone asked me what the most intimate, most meaningful relationship of my life was, I'd say it was with you."

"I know," she said softly. "Me too."

"Maybe random things happen. Maybe the fact that Richard Nixon and Joan Baez were born on the same day isn't as important as what they did next."

She pulled away and looked at me. "What the hell are you talking about?"

"Choices," I said. "I think we have choices."

She looked straight ahead. I guess she was letting it sink in. After a while she said, "You mean about this?" It was almost a whisper.

"Uh-huh," I nodded, wondering if I was being an asshole.

"You're still the philosophy major who thinks that how you look at things is all there is! That life can be summed up with fancy words." She sounded angry.

"You and I have never been about fancy words," I said. "Making love to you was very special for me."

She watched me, listening.

"You know," I said, "I always admired the way you took hold of life. You ran risks and took chances while the rest of us were making lists and weighing the odds." I rubbed her back. I could feel her muscles relaxing. "I know you're scared right now, but a little fear doesn't make you a coward. Making love to you was the most courageous act of my life. I think this was small potatoes for you."

"You're not small potatoes," she whispered. "You're my best friend."

I nodded. "And whatever happens I want that. I want it to last forever." I sighed. "I just couldn't go on without it."

"Can't best friends sleep together?" she asked, like she thought I had all the answers.

I started to say more, but her sobs cut me off. I held her. After a while I got up and made us both a stiff drink. Our naked bodies were warm under the afghan. The rum burned in my throat. The rest of the world was hard and cold. Around midnight I tucked her in bed, told her I loved her, that I had always and would always love her.

That night when I went home and crawled into bed next to Elsbeth, I lay on my side staring out the rain-speckled window. I watched the cold shadows from the neighbor's yard light reflected on the tree branches. They shone against the dark sky like a photo negative—like an image turned inside out. Elsbeth curled up behind me spoon-fashion and snored softly. I didn't sleep for a long time.

Carol Queen

Sweating Profusely in Mérida: A Memoir

The Boyfriend and I met at a sex party. No, really, this is a true story. I was in a back room trying to help facilitate an erection for a gentleman brought to the party by a woman who would have nothing to do with him once they got there. It turned out later she had charged him a pretty penny to get in. I actually felt that I should have gotten every cent, but I suppose it was my own fault that I was playing Mother Teresa and didn't know when to let go of his dick. Boyfriend-to-be was hiding behind a potted palm watching us. He crouched, eyeing me and this guy's unco-operative dick, which was uncut; it seemed Boyfriend had a thing for pretty girls and uncut men, especially the latter. So he decided to help me out, and replaced my hand with his mouth. That's when it got interesting. The uncut straight guy finally left and I stayed.

The thing about our relationship was that it only really worked when we were at a sex party. But it took us a few months to grasp that, and in the meantime we shared many straight men, most of them—Boyfriend's radar was incredible—uncircumcised and will-ing to do almost anything with a man as long as there was a woman in the room. I often acted as a hook to hang a guy's het-erosexuality on while Boyfriend sucked his dick or even fucked him. My favorite was the hitchhiker wearing pink lace panties

under his grungy jeans—but that's another story. Long before we
met the hitchhiker, Boyfriend had invited me to go to Mexico.

"Here's the plan. Almost all the guys in Mexico are uncut,
right? And lots will play with men, too," Boyfriend assured me,
"especially if there's a woman there." Besides, he thought it
would be a romantic vacation.

That's how we wound up in Room 201 of the Hotel Reforma in
sleepy Mérida, capital of the Yucatán. Why Mérida? Its popularity
as a tourist town had been eclipsed by the growth of Cancún, the
nearest Americanized resort. That meant the boys would be horn-
ier, Boyfriend reasoned. A fellow foreskin fancier who had stayed
there recommended the Hotel Reforma. Its chief advantages were
the price—about fourteen dollars a night—and the fact that the
management didn't charge more for extra occupants. I liked it because it was old, airy, and cool, with wrought-iron railings and
stairway tiles worn thin by past guests. Boyfriend liked it because
it had a pool (always a good place to cruise) and a disco across the
street. That's where we headed as soon as we got in from the airport and changed into skimpy clothes suitable for turning tropical
boys' heads.

There were hardly any tropical boys there, as it turned out. Apparently this was where the Ft. Lauderdale college students who
couldn't afford Cancún went to spend their meager spring break
allowances. And not only did it look like any Mexican restaurant-
with-disco you would find in Ft. Lauderdale, but the management
took care to keep out all but the most dapper Méridans lest the
coeds be frightened by the scruffy street boys. Scruffy street boys,
of course, were just what Boyfriend had his eye out for, and at
first the pickings looked slim. But we found one who had slipped
past security. He was out to hustle nothing more spicy than a gig
guiding tourists through the warren of narrow streets around the
town's central plaza. Instead he stumbled onto us. Ten minutes
later Boyfriend had his mouth wrapped around a meaty little
bundle—with foreskin. Luis stuck close to us for several days,
probably eating more regularly than usual and wondering out
loud whether we would take him back with us. Or at least send
him a Motley Crüe T-shirt?

One night Boyfriend stayed out for hours looking for gay men, who, he said, would run the other way if they saw me coming. He found one, a slender boy who had to pull down the pantyhose he wore under his jeans so Boyfriend could get to his cock. The boy expressed wonder because he had never seen someone with so many condoms. In fact, most people there never had condoms at all. Boyfriend gave him his night's supply and some little brochures about *el SIDA* he'd brought from the AIDS Foundation (*en español* so that even if our limited Spanish didn't get through to our tricks, a pamphlet might).

Boyfriend also learned that Mérida had a bathhouse. I had always wanted to go to a bathhouse, and of course there was not much chance of it happening back home. For one thing, they were all closed before I ever moved to San Francisco. For another, even if I was dressed enough like a boy to pass, I wouldn't look old enough to get in. But in Mérida, perhaps things were different.

It was away from the town's center but within walking distance of the Hotel Reforma. We strolled over one afternoon while the rest of the town was closed for siesta, and Boyfriend went inside. The place looked like a courtyard motel, an overgrown and haunted version of the kind I used to stay in with my parents when we traveled in the early sixties. Through the front door's one tiny window I saw a huge pâpier-maché figure of Pan, brightly painted and hung with jewelry. It looked like something the Radical Faeries would carry in the Gay Pride parade. Everything else about the lobby looked dingy, like the waiting room of a used-car dealership.

Los Baños de Vapor would open at eight o'clock that evening, Boyfriend told me when he returned. They had a central tub and rooms to rent; massage boys could be rented, too. And Mérida *was* different from San Francisco; I would be welcome.

The pâpier-maché Pan was at least seven feet tall and was indeed the only bright thing in the lobby. Passing through the courtyard, an overgrown jungle of vines pushing through cracked tile, we were shown up a flight of concrete stairs to our room. Our guide was Carlos, a solid, round-faced man in his midtwenties, wrapped in a frayed white towel. The room was small and completely tiled, its grout blackened from the wet tropical air. At one end was a shower and at the other a bench, a low, vinyl-covered bed, and a massage table. There was a switch that, when flipped, filled the room with steam. Boyfriend turned it on and we shucked our clothes. As the pipes hissed and clanked in their efforts to get the steam in, Carlos gestured at the massage table and then to me.

Boyfriend answered for me, in Spanish, that I'd love to. I got on the table and Carlos set to work. Boyfriend danced around the table gleefully, sometimes stroking me, sometimes Carlos' butt. "Hey, man, I'm working!" Carlos protested, but not very insistently. Boyfriend went for his cock, stroking it hard, then urged him up onto the table. Carlos' hands, still slick from massage oil and warm from the friction of my skin, covered my breasts as Boyfriend rolled a condom onto Carlos' cock. Carlos rubbed it up and down my labia a few times and finally let go, sinking his cock in. He rode me slow, then hard, while the table rocked dangerously and Boyfriend stood at my head letting me tongue his cock while he played with Carlos' tits. When he was sure we were having a good time, he put on a towel and slipped out the door. Carlos looked surprised and I had to try to figure out how to say "He's going hunting" in Spanish so that he'd go back to fucking me the way he had been. His solid body was slick from oil and steam, and if he kept it up I would come, clutching his slippery back with my legs in the air.

That was just happening when Boyfriend came back with David. He was pulling David in the door by his penis, which already seemed stiff; I suspected Boyfriend had wasted little time getting him by the dick. He had found David in the tub room, he announced, commenting on his beautiful, long, uncut cock. Boyfriend always enunciated clearly when he said "uncut." David did have a beautiful cock. He also spoke English and was long and slim with startling blue eyes. It turned out he was Chicano, second generation, a senior at Riverside High who spent school breaks with his grandmother in Mérida, and worked at Los Baños de Vapor as a secret summer job. We found out all this about him as I was showering off the sweat and oil from my fuck with Carlos. By the time I heard that he'd been working at the Baños

since he turned sixteen, I was ready to start fucking again. David
was the most quintessential eighteen-year-old fuck I'd ever had,
except that Boyfriend's presence made it unusual. He held David's cock and balls to control the speed of the thrusting—until
his mouth got preoccupied with Carlos' dick, which was ready to
go again. David kept his blue eyes open and told me I was beautiful. At that point I didn't care if I was beautiful or not, since I
was finally in a bathhouse doing what I had always wanted to do
and feeling more like a faggot than like a beautiful *gringa*. David
was saying he wished he had a beautiful girlfriend like me, even
though I was thirty, shockingly old. This was actually what most
of Boyfriend's conquests said to me. But I had a feeling most men
couldn't keep up with a girlfriend who was really a faggot, or a
boyfriend who was really a woman, or whatever kind of fabulous
anomaly I was.

Someone knocked at the door and we untangled for a minute
to answer it; there were José and Gaspar, laughing and saying
ours was the most popular room at the Baños at the moment.
Would we like some more company? At least that's how David
translated the torrent of Spanish, for they were both speaking at
once. Naturally, we invited them in, and lo and behold, Gaspar
was actually gay. So while I lay sideways on the massage table
with my head off the edge and my legs in the air, sucking David
while José fucked me, I watched Boyfriend finally getting his
cock sucked by Gaspar, whose glittering black Mayan eyes were
closed in concentration. I howled not simply with orgasm but
with excitement, the splendid excitement of being in a Mexican
bathhouse with four uncut men and a maniac—a place no woman
I knew had gone before. Steam swirled in the saturated air, bead-
ing like pearls high in the corner web of a huge Yucatán spider.
David's cock, or was it José's, or Carlos' again, I didn't even care,
pounded my fully open cunt rhythmically. I wished I had the spider's view.

If you have ever been to a bathhouse you know that time
stands still in the steamy, throbbing air. I had no idea how long
it went on, only that sometimes I was on my back and sometimes
on my knees and once for a minute I was standing facing the wall.
When Boyfriend wasn't sucking them or fucking me he was taking

snapshots of us, just like a tourist. Finally two of them were helping me into the shower and the floor of the room was completely
littered with condoms, which made us all laugh hysterically.
Gaspar and David held me up with Carlos and José flanking them
so Boyfriend could snap one last picture. Then he divided all of
the rest of the condoms among them—we had plenty more at the
hotel. He was trying to explain in Spanish the little condoms he
used for giving head—how great they were with uncut guys because they disappeared under the foreskin. And I was asking David what it was like to live a double life, Riverside High to Los
Baños, and who else came there. "Oh, everyone does," he said.
And did they ever want to fuck him? Of course they *wanted*
to. And did he ever fuck them? Well, sure. And how was that? He
shrugged and said, as if there were only one possible response to
my question so why was I even bothering to ask, "It's *fucking*."

The moon was high and the Baños were deserted when we left,
the warm night air almost cool after the steamy room. The Pan
figure glittered in the dim lobby light, and the man at the desk
charged us thirty-five dollars—seven for each massage boy, four
to get us in, and six for the room. He looked anxious, as though
he feared we'd think it was too much. We paid him, laughing. I
wondered if this was how Japanese businessmen in Thailand felt.
Was I contributing to the decline of the Third World? Boyfriend
didn't give a shit about things like that, so I didn't mention it. In
my hand was a crumpled note from David: "Can I come visit you
in your hotel room? No money."

About the Authors

*BLAKE C. AARENS is a lesbian of African descent. Her story, "Strangers on a Train," appeared in *Herotica 2* under the pseudonym Cassandra Brent. She is currently at work on a murder mystery, a screenplay, and a solo performance piece. Her feline companion Sonja approves all of her manuscripts.

*EMILY ALWARD is an academic librarian, the mother of two daughters, and the owner of three dogs. In her free hours she reads and writes science fiction, and her articles and book reviews have appeared in a variety of publications. She edits *Once Upon a World,* a magazine of stories set in other worlds.

LENORA CLARE is a pseudonym for a lawyer and former partner in a Florida law firm. She pursues other interests, including gardening and creative writing. She has been a regular contributor to a regional environmental newspaper.

DEBBIE COHEN lives with her two cats in San Francisco, where she is finding her voice like lint between her toes. She thanks Mary Rose for standing at the vista with her and sharing the view.

CALLA CONOVA, a poet, has spent many years learning the

*Author whose stories also appear in *Herotica* (Down There Press, 1988) and *Herotica 2* (Plume, 1992).

cycles and secrets of nature. She was inspired to write erotica when she discovered that ancient Asians veiled descriptions of anatomy and sexual acts with allusions to nature. This is her first published story.

MICHELLE HANDELMAN, a multimedia artist, resides in San Francisco, "making movies to get in your face, shooting pictures to get under your skin, and writing stories to get you horny."

RUBY RAY LEONARD is the pen name of a happily married doctoral student and researcher from New York City. Her scholarly work has been published in scientific journals. This is her first erotic short story.

*AURORA LIGHT has contributed stories, nonfiction articles, and poetry to a variety of publications, including *Woman's World, Country Woman,* and *Broomstick*. She is a contributing editor for an international Meniere's Disease newsletter and publishes a haiku magazine.

*JANE LONGAWAY was a San Francisco writer and printer.

MARY MAXWELL was raised by wolves. In subsequent years, she has adapted reasonably well to the strictures of civilization.

*MAGENTA MICHAELS is a poet and hand bookbinder. She lives on the California coast south of San Francisco.

*MARTHA MILLER is a Midwestern writer. Her short stories are widely published in lesbian and literary periodicals and anthologies. She writes a monthly book-review column for women and is currently working on her second play, to be produced by Mid-America Playwrights Theater.

SERENA MOLOCH was born in the Bronx and grew up in Queens. "My Date with Marcie" is for the Marcies of her youth, wherever they might now be.

LINDA NIEMANN is a brakeman/conductor for Southern Pacific Railroad, riding the rails on the West Coast. She is also the author of *Boomer: Railroad Memoirs* (Cleis Press) and has a Ph.D. in English.

CHINA PARMALEE wrote "Local Foods" as a member of a college writers group.

---

*Author whose stories also appear in *Herotica* (Down There Press, 1988) and *Herotica 2* (Plume, 1992).

*CAROL A. QUEEN is a San Francisco writer and sex educator whose aim is to create sexually explicit writing that is both hot and truthful about sex, especially underrepresented desires and behaviors. She is an activist in the bisexual, sex work, and anti-censorship communities.

STACY REED is an honors student at the University of Texas at Austin. For money she dances, but her real DJ's a goof. For kicks she writes for various dailies and magazines. Adult education remains her primary work. Stacy dedicates "Tips" to her best friend, Sheila.

*MARCY SHEINER is a journalist/ novelist/ pornographer/ poet whose work is widely published.

GENEVIEVE SMITH is the smut-minded alter-ego of a teacher and writer of scholarly stuff. She doesn't have any pets yet, but she does have lots of interesting friends and family members. She wants to live on the beach, ASAP.

*SUSAN ST. AUBIN is a fiction writer and occasional poet who likes to write erotica as a warm-up exercise. She recently bought a turn-of-the-century cottage from an elderly couple who left behind a riding crop and ten years worth of diaries, proving that stories can be found in the most unexpected places.

LYDIA SWARTZ is a dyke in the prime of her life who has published smut elsewhere, but would rather tell you about marrying the girl of her dreams and being the first queer to announce her marriage in the employee newsletter of the corporation that employs her.

CECILIA TAN, freelance writer, is the author of *Telepaths Don't Need Safewords* (Circlet Press) and the publisher of erotic science fiction and fantasy. She and her overactive imagination live in Boston, even though you can't ride a motorcycle year round there.

*CATHERINE TAVEL creates erotica under a variety of *noms de porn*. She is a freelance writer of fiction, nonfiction, poetry, and screenplays who hails from the concrete streets of Brooklyn, New York. She immensely enjoys exploring the complexities of

---

*Author whose stories also appear in *Herotica* (Down There Press, 1988) and *Herotica 2* (Plume, 1992).

our libidos in the printed word. Her written works have appeared in everything from *Seventeen* to *Hustler.* Her sexy scripts often surface on "adult" cable television channels. With Robert Rimmer, Tavel helped pen porn star Jerry Butler's biography *Raw Talent* and Mistress Jacqueline's *Whips and Kisses* (Prometheus Books).

*PAT WILLIAMS lives in Berkeley. She was born and raised in western Tennessee. At present she is working on her own Black Panther novel, partly as a way of exploring that group and getting past the lies told about it.

SUSIE BRIGHT is the editor of *Herotica* (Down There Press) and co-editor of *Herotica 2,* as well as of the annual *Best American Erotica* (Collier). She is the author of *Susie Bright's Sexual Reality: A Virtual Sex World Reader* (Cleis Press) and *Susie Sexpert's Lesbian Sex World* (Cleis Press), as well as numerous articles and reviews addressing the popular view of sexuality in culture. She is also a connoisseuse of X-rated film and video.

*Author whose stories also appear in *Herotica* (Down There Press, 1988) and *Herotica 2* (Plume, 1992).